It is difficult to sit down and write about one's self. Anyway, here goes and you will no doubt be able to find something of interest.

I went to a Public School where I received my OTC training. When I left College, I joined my Father in the family Men's Wear business and when my time came I volunteered for service in the RAF as a pilot, but my hopes were dashed when it was found that I was colour blind 'unsafe'.

I was persuaded by the interviewing board to volunteer for the Radio and Radar section of the RAF. I went to Technical College in London, living in private billets and then to RAF Cranwell.

During the latter part of my stay at Cornwell, my Father became very ill and I applied for a compassionate posting near to my home. I was lucky because there was a vacancy at RAF Exeter on the permanent Operation's staff for someone with my classifications.

From Exeter, I was able to keep the family business going, which I did when not on duty. Fate then put another spoke in my wheel and I met a beautiful WAF. We were married in 1946 and she still looks attractive, after having a son and daughter.

My Son now looks after the family business and I have been restoring Antique furniture.

I have a great interest in the countryside and Nature. When I was a small boy I spent most of my Summer holidays staying on a small farm. I used to help drive the cows down into the valley where they could drink from a stream, which is crossed by a Little Bridge.

I often visit this little bridge and have done so for many years. It brings back such happy memories and somehow it seems to recharge my batteries. This was also a favourite place for my son and daughter, and in time their children.

During my life I have been a member of Rotary and a District Councillor for thirteen years. I have been involved in the town's affairs as Mayor and chairman of other committees.

I have played a lot of Golf, used to sail and I was the President of the local Yacht Club for many years and I have been made a life member.

I hate having nothing to do and being the age I am, I started to write. Much to the amusement of my wife and family, I started to write my life story. At times the memories were sad but overall the good times have won the day. I enjoyed this task and when I had finished, my family, which now includes two granddaughters and one grandson, all enjoyed reading about their 'roots'. So I decided to write a novel.

I have enjoyed writing this book and I am very sorry that it is now finished. I have become part of it and there will be a sequel.

THE
LITTLE BRIDGE

Ronald Doel

The
Little Bridge

Vanguard Press

VANGUARD PAPERBACK

© Copyright 2002
Ronald Doel

A CIP catalogue record for this title is
available from the British Library
ISBN 1 903489 76 8

*Vanguard Press is an imprint of
Pegasus Elliot MacKenzie Publishers Ltd.*
www.pegasuspublishers.com

First Published in 2002

**Vanguard Press
Sheraton House Castle Park
Cambridge England**

Printed & Bound in Great Britain

Dedication

For my darling wife, Norma.

This is a story about a farmer's son, born in the year of Our Lord, 1920. Fate played such an important part in his early years and it was to have far-reaching effects in his future life.

The first chapters are perhaps too lengthy, but it is important to portray his early upbringing to see how fate played its part and how several events changed his life, which could have been so very ordinary.

The period being 1920-1939, and will recall preparations for war. Our main player has been groomed for service in a special Intelligence Service because of his gift of being able to speak French and German as a native. This takes him to Germany and Normandy where vital connections are made.

There are several love affairs, one of which gives an insight into the class structure of country life and how the preparations for war can break many barriers.

'THE VERY BEGINNING'

CHAPTER 1

It was morning once again, but this morning was going to be so very different. I was going to school for the first time. Mother had given me a good scrub the night before and had laid out my clothes all clean and pressed, not like the old bits and pieces that I wore about the farm.

As I dressed I looked out of my window and I could see the village on the other side of the valley, still shrouded in the early morning mist. That would be my place of torture for a long time to come. I could hear the cows fretting in their sheds eager to be let out to pasture. Dad always had his breakfast after milking so they would have to wait.

I felt a bit unsure and frightened at the thought of my new adventure, but I had to go and that was that.

I finished dressing and went downstairs for breakfast. Our kitchen was large with a large table in the centre. There were benches on the two sides and a chair at each end which were occupied by my mum and dad. John my older brother sat on one side and there was a place for my sister Jenny, but she was always learning to be a dressmaker or something like that. My place was next to Mum on the end where she could keep an eye on me. On the other side sat my aunt Betty, Mother's sister and next to her sat our hired hand who lived in a little room at the back of the house.

Dad started to give me a lecture, he said, "My boy, you must always be polite to the teacher and never answer her back. Do not do anything that will make me ashamed of you." He paused and added that I must not laugh at the strange accent the teacher had because that would be very rude. I asked what an accent was and he told me that the teacher, who was called Mrs Jenkins, was a German lady who was married to a very clever artist, and they lived in a cottage in the woods at the end of the valley.

Mother carried on where Dad had left of by saying, "Do try and learn what you can because who knows you might be able to win a scholarship to the large school in the town." Dad gave one of his snorts as if to say that's wishful thinking.

As I sat there I wished that I didn't have to leave the family nest. I know now how the small calves felt when they had to leave their mothers. They always make such sad cries. I have always hated it when

15

they are taken off to market. Anyway, I may feel sad but I won't be a sissy when I leave after breakfast.

My time had now come and Mother gave me my new lunch box which I put in my haversack and I was on my way. Betty had come out with my Mother to see me off. I was very fond of Betty, she was always so kind to me and I think that she liked me as well.

I was going to have to walk about two or three miles to school. If the weather was fine I could cut across the fields which would be the shortest way, but if it was wet I would have to go by the lanes.

As I walked down into the valley I wondered what the other boys would be like and of course, there would be girls. I didn't think much of girls if they would be like my cousins. They were horrible spoilt little brats, as Mother called them. Girls were best kept at arm's length unless they were an improvement on my cousins.

Perhaps I might find a friend at school. I would like a friend because our farm was out of the way and there were no children to play with, not that I minded too much because I liked to wander off on my own and watch the birds and wildlife, or I could daydream in the small wood near the farm.

It was a lovely morning and I wished that I could go on one of my favourite expeditions right over to the other side of the farm. There was a family of foxes living under a large elm tree. I had watched them several times. At first, when they were very young I had to wait for ages hidden behind a large bush and keeping very still until they came out to play. After so many visits they thought I was part of the landscape. I had watched them grow up over the last few months and soon they would be on their way to fend for themselves.

I have never told anyone about these foxes because the hunting season would soon be starting and I would hate for them to be killed. Anyway no visits today my lad, I have to go to school.

I walked through the village towards the school. There were other children of all sizes unwillingly being drawn as if by magnet to a place that they did not care to go to. We became a sort of herd being driven by an invisible force to a place of torture.

As we came nearer to school a boy about my age came up to me and said, "My name is Peter, what's yours?" I replied, "Henry Blake." As I answered I had a quick look at him and I liked what I saw. He was bigger than I was and he had a roundish, friendly face. Dad had told me many times that you should always look at the face and the eyes as they are a badge of character. I asked him what the school was like and he told me that Mrs Jenkins was very nice, but a part-time teacher called Mr Lloyd was very strict and he liked to use his cane. He grudgingly added that he was a good teacher of history and geography.

Peter led me into the school, at first to the cloakroom where we left our lunch boxes and coats. We then filed into the classroom. This was the start of a new school year and there were several new pupils. We all sat at one side of the large classroom and our names were on the different single desks and I found mine and sat down. By now I was feeling very shy and nervous and wished that I was miles away.

Sitting at the next desk was a girl and I could see by her face that she had been crying. The new pupils, all six of us, were looking very subdued. I could tell who they were because unlike the other children they had no books on their desks and nor were they fooling around and talking to each other.

Above the noise I could hear footsteps on the bare boards coming from the passage outside of the classroom. A tall handsome lady with very fair hair came in through the doorway. Immediately the talking and laughing stopped and everyone stood up. As if in one voice we said, "Good morning Mrs Jenkins." She returned our greeting and told us to sit down.

She stood behind her table and the large blackboard behind her seemed to act as a picture frame for this tall lady. She then told us to stand for prayers and she led us in saying The Lord's Prayer which Mother had taught me several years ago. I always say it before I get into bed every night so I was able to join in. After prayers we were told to sit down again.

She then told us that she was going to call the roll and for the benefit of the new pupils we were to stand up when our names were called so that we would all get to know each other.

The name Polly Brown was called out and the sad little girl stood up and said In a very quite voice, "Present Miss." When my name was called I also stood up feeling very nervous as all the pupils were looking at me. I said as boldly as I could the necessary phrase and quickly sat down.

Mrs Jenkins explained that tomorrow there would be another teacher joining the school to teach the new boys and girls the elementary beginnings to their education, whatever that meant. But today we were going to be tested to see what we knew, if anything. She added that she was going to write the alphabet and some very simple words on the blackboard and we were to write them down on a piece of paper that we would find in our desks.

During the winter evenings Mother had taught me to write and read children's books. In fact I could read the simple words in Dad's newspapers. Dad also had a go by making me count the eggs I collected every morning and made me write them down on a board that he had made.

Dad also taught me about money and would pretend to send me shopping with pennies for different things in our large barn. If I got it right he would reward me with a penny, so believe it or not, I soon got the hang of it.

Our time was up and Mrs Jenkins walked around to inspect our efforts. Some of the children had no idea what to do and it seemed that only the little girl called Polly and myself could read and write.

A bell rang for the lunch break and some of the children went home. The rest of us took our lunch boxes to the playground and I found a bench and started to eat my lunch only to be interrupted by a large boy who tried to snatch my box from me. He was standing in front of me and I was sitting down and without thinking I swung one of my feet back and gave him a hefty kick on the shin. He was about to hit me when Peter came up and gave him a hefty shove saying "Push off Joe before I get angry." The boy I now knew as Joe looked at me and said, "Look out you little bugger, I'll get you for this."

That was my first encounter with the school bully. Peter sat down beside me and we ate our lunch together. He didn't have much in his box so I gave him some of mine which he soon gobbled up. Peter told me that Joe was a nasty piece of work and I would have to look out for him in the future. I asked Peter where he lived and he told me that his Dad was a sort of odd-job man at the farm which was way past our farm. This was a fair old walk every day and he lived above the workshop where his father worked.

I had passed this farm many times on the way into the town. It was a very big farm and Dad told me that they employed many hands. Peter and I had a fair old chat. The bell rang and we returned to the classrooms. As Peter left he said, "Wait for me after school and I will walk home with you." I thought this was jolly nice of him.

The rest of the day was uneventful and it was soon time to go home. Peter joined me and we started to wend our way across the fields, Peter was easy to talk to. I had a good look at him as I walked along and I could see that he was very poorly dressed and the contents of his lunch box told me that his family were pretty poor. It was strange however that he only had a very faint Devonshire accent. I was to learn more about him and his parents as our friendship grew.

As we came to our farm he said, "Goodbye, see you tomorrow." and off he went to walk a further couple of miles to his home.

I walked through the yard and saw our other farm hand. He was called George. He was a young chap who lived in the tied cottage with his wife Olive, who helped Mother in the house.

I liked George, he took me on his cart during haymaking and in my small way I helped with some of the chores. He always called me Master Henry, which I thought a bit strange, but as he called my brother Master John no doubt this was how it should be.

As we were talking Dad and John joined us. George made a quick exit to get on with his work and Dad asked me how I had got on. I told him all about my first day at school including my brush with the school bully, Joe. John butted in, "Henry my boy, I will have to take you in hand. After tea I will take you to the barn and teach you how to put people like Joe in their place." Dad said that it was a good idea, but don't tell your Mother.

Sitting down to our evening meal I had to re-tell the day's events. I asked if I could ask Peter to join me on the farm next Saturday, if he wanted to. Mother asked who Peter was and where did he live. I explained all that I knew about him and Mother was quiet for a while before saying "Peter's father must be the man who makes all that lovely furniture for Langley Hall." Mother knew all about Langley Hall because she sold her famous butter and cream to the cook. I didn't know then that I would have to deliver some cream and butter to the Hall in the very near future.

After our meal John, in fun, took me by the ear and off we went to the barn for my first lesson in self-defence.

To my surprise John had filled a sack with straw and had hung it up in the barn. He started to teach me how to punch and protect my face with my other hand. We were there for quite some time and I was beginning to get the hang of it. When we were leaving he said, "We are only just beginning and I want you to come here by yourself and practise on this punch bag. We will have another go tomorrow." John was such a nice chap and I thought how lucky I was to have him as a brother.

That night as I lay in bed with the moon casting shadows through the curtains and the friendly calls of the owls living in the barn, I thought about my first day at school. It wasn't so bad after all, I had made a friend and an enemy. John had told me that bullies were usually cowards and that is why they pick on people smaller than themselves. Sometimes they were very unhappy people and had to make others feel as unhappy as they were.

Anyway, tomorrow is another day so I will have to wait and see what it has in store for me. I had to get up early so that I could do my morning chores before going to school. I was let off these on my first day at school.

I had to feed the hens and collect the eggs. When I first started this job the hens tried to peck my hands, but I had been doing this for some time now and the hens seemed to accept me every morning. I could see their point of view, here they were laying eggs expecting to hatch them only to have a horrible little boy pinch them every morning!

I decided that I would walk down the lanes over the little bridge. This was my favourite place of all. Who knows, I might even meet Peter on the way. I must have dropped back to sleep with these thoughts because the next thing I knew was Mum giving me a shake and telling me to get up.

I rose from my nice warm bed and went to collect the eggs. I fed the hens and threw a handful to the wild birds who were sitting hopefully on the wire fence. I always did this because I thought it would save them the labour of searching for food.

Before I set off for school I went into the barn and had a bash at the punch bag. Trying to put into practice what John had taught me, I made up my mind that no one was going to bully me.

When I got to school I met Peter and sat down at my desk. I started a shy conversation with Polly. She still looked unhappy and had very little to say. There was quite a noise with everyone talking until Mrs Jenkins entered the room with a young lady.

We all stood up and after prayers settled at our desks. Mrs Jenkins, with her strange accent, introduced the young lady as Mrs Howard who would be teaching us to read, write and learn arithmetic. When we had mastered these simple subjects we would learn other subjects. As she left she said in a strict voice, "If any of you are naughty Mrs Howard will send you to me for punishment." With this she strode out of the room like a soldier with her long fair hair flowing like a mane behind her.

There were about ten of us in my class, which was Class One for beginners, the slow ones were not yet able to master the elementary parts of their education.

Mrs Howard seemed a nice person but she was very strict and we soon found out that she would stand no nonsense. I found it all a bit boring because I was able to do the different tasks quite easily. With a crafty look at Polly's desk I could see that she was also doing very well.

At last it was lunch break and we were able to go outside as the weather was still fine and warm. I sat on the same seat and was very pleased when Peter came over to join me. I thought at first that Peter had his eye on my lunch box, but I was soon to learn that he just liked to have a good chat. Needless to say I gave him some of my food. I think that Mother thought that she was catering for a grown man when she prepared my lunch.

I asked Peter if he would like to come over to the farm on

Saturday morning to play. After a bit of thought he said that he would like to after he had completed the jobs he had to do.

The bell rang for afternoon lessons and as we went through the door Joe tried to barge past me. I side-stepped and he knocked over a very large boy who gave him a clip under the ear, much to the amusement of some of the other kids. I thought then that given time I would give him a good bashing!

The rest of the week passed by uneventfully and Polly and I now actually spoke to each other. I discovered that she was the daughter of the curate at the church in the village next to ours, Teigncoombe. She had to pass the little bridge on her way to school and one day we walked part of the way together. For a girl she was almost normal and like me she was interested in wildlife. I broke a golden rule by telling her about my family of foxes, making her promise not to tell anyone in case the hounds got them.

Every evening that week John coached me in the barn with the help of the punch bag. I now had to try and hit John and in turn he gave me some none too gentle punches. He told me to always keep moving my feet and to always look my opponent straight in the eye, I must never ever looked frightened.

John told me that if I was attacked by a boy taller than I was the best bet was to kick him in the shins. That would make him bend forward and his face would be low enough for me to hit it.

At last Saturday morning came and I had two whole days off from school. During breakfast I asked Dad if it would be alright for me to show Peter around the farm. He said this would be alright, but I was to keep away from the field where the bull was kept because he was very nasty at the moment.

When Peter arrived I showed him the barns and sheds. He had a go on the punch bag and then we went to my little workshop which was tucked away in a small shed which Dad did not use. I had very little in the way of tools but when I got the urge I went in there and made very crude models of ships. I was currently trying to make an aeroplane, but without much success.

Peter said, "You must come over and see my dad's workshop. He might give you some odd bits of wood which he calls 'off cuts'. When I get home I will ask him if he has any to spare."

We then went to see Mother's pride and joy and walked across the yard into the small field beyond the cow sheds. Here there were chickens of all age groups with ducks and geese all in separate very large pens. Most important of all the rest of the field seemed to be the turkeys.

The turkeys always looked magnificent. The cock birds had their fan-tails of black and white feathers on display. There were a few guinea fowl keeping together in one corner who looked dowdy compared to the turkeys. They had inherited the camouflaged feathers they needed in the distant land that their ancestors had come from.

When Peter saw the large number of birds he said, "My there are a lot of Christmas dinners there." I explained that this was my mother's domain and she would not let anyone else feed them. She took birds to the market in Newton Abbot every week and most of them will have been ordered by Christmas. We all helped to pluck them for the big event.

I then took Peter to one of my favourite places. We walked across some fields to a large wood. It always seemed strange to me that the wood was divided in two by a fence put up in a long narrow clearing. The wood on the other side of the fence was much larger than Dad's and I never ventured beyond the fence. I had decided that one day I would pluck up courage and explore this other wood.

I led Peter into the wood until I came to my tree. I had carried over odd planks of wood and with the help of some rope and nails, I had made a sort of hide where I could sit and watch the squirrels and other animals and birds that lived in the wood. I could see that Peter was enjoying himself. He had climbed much higher than I had ever ventured and I told him to be careful because if he was unable to get down we would be right in the soup.

We roamed all over the place but eventually we had to make our way back to the farm. Mother had asked Peter to stay for lunch but unfortunately he had to return home to do some jobs that afternoon. As he was about to leave he asked if he could come again as we had such good fun. I told him he would always be welcome and I would see him on Monday and with a wave he was off.

While we were having lunch I asked Dad about the other part of the wood. He told me that it belonged to a strange man who lived by himself in a small cottage in a clearing right in the middle of the wood. Dad had met him once or twice and he seemed to be a well-educated chap, but he kept himself to himself. It was said that he had plenty of money but had a very rough time in the war and now lived like a hermit. It was rumoured that he was a spy behind German lines living rough and surviving in awful conditions.

I asked Dad if it would be alright for me to have a look around the wood. He gave it some thought and said that I must stay near the fence.

After lunch I went to investigate this foreign land. I walked through my wood until I came to the fence. Looking at this dense and thickly wooded area I very nearly changed my mind, but at last I plucked up enough courage and stepped into the unknown.

I walked along part of the boundary fence until I saw what looked like a rough path, so I gingerly walked into the wood until I came to a small clearing. I sat down on a tree trunk to survey the scene. It really was a lovely spot and I started to daydream. I tried to imagine what lived in this magical place and what mysteries were hidden among the huge trees. When I was young Mother read a book about the little people and how they lived in places like this. These were fairy tales, or I thought they were, but sitting where I was I began to wonder if they did exist.

Suddenly I had the fright of my life! Behind me a very quiet whisper said, "Don't move or make any sound and you will see a sight worth seeing." I slowly looked over my shoulder and there stood a man in very old clothes. He was very tall with the brightest blue eyes I had ever seen. He had long fair hair and a beard. After I got over the initial shock I kept frozen to the spot waiting to see whatever it was that I was supposed to be seeing.

It seemed like a lifetime and I was getting scared. The man leaned forward and said, "Watch between those two trees over there." As he slowly pointed there was a rustle of leaves and out walked two large badgers followed by two very small offspring. The parents were moving the dead leaves around looking for food for their young.

I had never seen a badger before and to be able to watch then at fairly close quarters was in itself most unusual because they usually only came out at night, except when they know it is safe for them to do so.

Eventually they disappeared into the undergrowth and the stranger came and sat down beside me so that I could now have a good look at him. He had a nice but somewhat sad face, his eyes seemed to look right into me. He spoke in a very posh voice asking me who I was and where had I come from. I told him that I lived on the farm on the other side of the woods and before I knew it I was telling him all about myself and how I loved the wood beyond the fence.

It was so strange that in such a short time I felt so at ease with this complete stranger. He told me his name was Jake Spencer and he lived by himself in a cottage in the middle of the wood.

Eventually I got up to go and asked him if I could visit his wood again. After a pause he said that I would be very welcome and next time he would show me around. Before I could say thank you and goodbye he had got up and seemed to vanish into the undergrowth without a sound.

If or when I saw Mr Spencer again I must ask him how he can walk in the wood without making a sound. How I would love to be able to do the same. Who knows, he might even teach me.

As I walked home across the fields I thought what a smashing adventure I had experienced today and I was longing to tell Dad all about it. I do hope that he will let me go into the wood again.

John seemed to like teaching me how to box because he had me at it whenever he had the chance. Mind you he spent a lot of time chasing the girls according to Dad. As yet he had not brought anyone home but no doubt that was to come.

John loved farming and he was always talking to Dad about the farm. Mother sometimes got a bit fed up with talking about the farm all the time and would try and change the subject. If this failed she and Aunt Betty talked about women's things so at this stage I would push off and find something to do.

When I was at a loose end I went to the paddock where Dad kept his horses. There were three very large cart horses, two small ponies, which Dad and John sometimes rode and last but not least there was Daisy, a pony that was used with the trap before we had the old car.

Daisy was no youngster and I often pinched the odd sugar lump to give her a treat. When she saw me come into the paddock she galloped over and nuzzled a wet nose in my pocket. If she didn't see me I would call her name and over she would come. As I stood there playing with Daisy's mane I decided to ask Dad if Charlie could teach me how to ride. Charlie looked after the horses and as we were great friends I am sure that he would show me how to ride.

I had visions of riding to different parts of the farm and pretending to be a cowboy. Sometimes Mum and Dad had taken me to market and if they were going to visit my Aunt who had a shop in Newton Abbot, they would treat me to a visit to the pictures if there was a suitable film showing. I liked the films about cowboys and indians best and I had made a bow and some arrows with flights using some of the feathers that were always available.

Charlie was in the barn and I asked him if he would teach me to ride. He gave me one of his broad grins and said that he would be only too pleased. He said that there was an old saddle knocking around somewhere and he would try and find it, but only if my Dad said it would be alright. I must remember to ask Dad when he was in a good mood. I had found out a long time ago that grown-ups had good and bad moods so timing was of great importance when asking for anything!

It was now late November and winter had set in. Walking to school in the rain was no joke. The fields were too muddy to take the short cut and I had the added distance to cover walking through the lanes. The trees had shed their leaves making the branches look like skeletons in the half-light when I walked home after school.

I think Polly was a bit scared in the darker evenings and she waited for Peter and I so that she would have company for part of her journey. Sometimes we would jump out of the hedge and frighten her. She screamed but I think that she always knew who it was and really thought it was great fun.

I had started to really like Polly, that is of course as far as one could like a girl. We had a lot in common and could chat away so easily to each other. Together with Peter we had quite a bit of fun on our way home from school.

As I was getting on alright at school, Mrs Howard told me that I would be moving up to Class Two after Christmas and would be taught by Mrs Jenkins and Mr Lloyd. I told Polly and she was also moving up to Class Two. She seemed pleased that she would have company because a new class is bound to be strange.

There was only a week until Christmas and tomorrow we were having a school party. I had never been to a party before so I wondered what we would do. We had all been busy in class making paper chains. Mrs Howard had bought some coloured paper and made a paste out of flour and water. When the chains were assembled and dried they were slung across the classroom. This seemed to make this dull room come to life. We were all very excited at the thought of no school for two whole weeks and the prospect of Christmas presents. This made us unmanageable and Mrs Howard had to put her foot down.

At last the party day arrived, which was on the last day of school. Mother gave me a good scrub and I had to wear my second best suit. I met Peter on the way to school and even he looked all poshed up.

We didn't learn much that morning. The whole school helped to clear the big classroom of desks and we were crowded into the other two rooms. We were told to practise our reading under the eagle eye of Mr Lloyd. The older boys and girls were given other tasks more suitable for their age groups.

While I was sitting there and pretending to read I had a good look at Polly. She was wearing a very colourful dress and I thought how pretty she looked, that is, as girls go. I wondered what she would do during the holidays. I knew that I would be seeing Peter but for some reason I would miss seeing Polly every day, because, after all, she was only a girl.

After lunch we all trooped into the big classroom and at one end were tables covered over with white cloth, hiding our special tea which had been prepared by the ladies of the village.

We played games, some which I thought were very stupid indeed. We made a lot of noise and it was great fun. It was all organised very well by our teachers. At last the tea was uncovered and what a mad rush it was to get at it. The village ladies had done us really well and there was plenty for all of us. We all had a cracker each and all put on the stupid paper hats and laughed at each other.

It was now all over and some of the children were met by their parents. I saw a chap with a 'dog collar' on and Polly went up to him. He lifted her up and gave her a kiss. Polly saw that I was watching them and she waved me to come over. I walked over feeling very shy. Polly said to her father, "This is Henry who keeps me company on the way home in the evenings." So doing as Mother had taught me, I offered my hand to Polly's dad. I was a bit lost for words but he thanked me for looking after his daughter. We wished each other a Merry Christmas and I started to walk away. Polly called me back and pushed a very small parcel into my hand and said, "Happy Christmas Henry." I felt so guilty because I had nothing to give her so I unpinned a funny little brooch thing I had from my cracker and gave it to her. I felt so embarrassed that I ran off without even saying goodbye. I did however give her a wave as she left.

By the time I got home that evening it was quite dark. I was not in a hurry to get home because I quite liked the countryside when it was dark. I could hear some small animals moving in the hedges and I watched two owls flying between the trees. The moon had just come up and to see the light of the moon reflected on the owls wings was a lovely sight. They were all so busy looking for their supper. How sad it was for the small mice and voles to have their lives finished that fine evening, but then I suppose that is what life is all about, everything lives off something else.

When I got home I told Mum and Dad all about the party. They seemed in a good mood. Mother had sold all of her birds at the market and Dad had got a reasonable price for some bullocks. Dad would never say that he had done well, but then farmers never do.

Later that evening we were all sitting in the warm kitchen and Mother was in a bit of a state. She was trying to arrange for someone to take some cream and butter over to Langley Hall. Evidently the cook had sent one of the servants over asking for cream and butter to be sent over tomorrow morning and that there would be no one free to make the trip. Like a clot I said that I could take it.

Mother looked at Dad as if to say do you think that would be alright. Dad put his paper down and started to give me a lecture about being respectful and polite to anyone I might see because they were well above our station, whatever that meant. I wasn't quite sure what I had let myself in for but it had helped me get out of plucking some of the turkeys.

When I went to bed I opened Polly's present to find a small bar of chocolate. It must have got hot because it was very bent in places. I sat and looked at it for a while thinking that this was the first present I had ever received from anyone not in my family. I put it in my special box and went to bed.

When I woke up the next morning I thought of my trip to Langley Hall. I had seen Sir James and his wife in their posh car being driven by a chap in a smart uniform. I knew where the Hall was but I had never seen it at close quarters. Today I will be able to have a good look and perhaps the cook might ask me into the kitchen.

Mother had made me look respectable and loaded me up with the cream and butter, so off I went. It was a cold, frosty morning and the shaded sides of the hedges were covered in spiders webs all white with frost and looking like lace. The spiders will have to do without their breakfast today. The sun was getting up and I was enjoying my walk having the odd daydream here and there about this and that. Suddenly I heard a commotion coming from around the next bend in the lane.

As I turned the corner I saw Joe throwing a girl's hat into the air and being chased by a girl of about my age who was crying. Sitting on the floor was a smaller boy nursing one of his legs as if he had been hurt.

I put my basket down well out of the way and without thinking I charged into Joe knocking him off balance. He fell flat on the floor and as he got up I remembered John's advice and kicked him in the shin. His head came forward and I landed a punch right on his nose, followed by another one on his jaw. To my surprise he fell flat again. He started to get up again so with one of my muddy boots I pushed him back and told him to be off before I really hurt him. He got up with blood streaming from his nose and looking very sorry for himself. Off he ran down the lane.

I was feeling most strange. I had never lost my temper like this before and in a way I felt a bit sorry that I had been so rough with Joe. I had been training for this inevitable encounter and I hoped that this would be the last of it.

I now turned my attention to the boy and girl. The girl was helping the boy onto his feet and telling him not to be such a baby. She looked at me and in a very posh voice thanked me for rescuing them from that horrid boy and then asked me who I was. I told her my name was Henry Blake and that I lived on the farm over the way and I was on my way to deliver some cream and butter to Langley Hall. "Who are you?" I enquired. She told me that her name was Mary and this baby, her brother, was called Hugh and they lived at Langley Hall. Their father was Sir James Howes.

I collected my basket and the three of us started to walk along the lane. I was now able to have a good look at these two strangers. They were both dressed in very expensive looking clothes. Mary had dark hair and for a girl she was very pretty. Her brother Hugh was a very thin little boy with fair hair. He had such a kind looking little face which seemed sad to me. I knew that he had been hurt, but somehow his expression seemed to be permanently sad.

As we walked along the lanes we started to talk in a stilted way, but it was not long before we talked in a more natural way as children do. Mary asked me where I went to school so I told her all about the village school and the smashing party we all had yesterday. She looked a bit wistful and said that she and Hugh had a boring old governess to teach them at home. They would however be going away to school when they were older.

By now we had almost reached the Hall so I asked where the entrance was for the kitchen. Mother had told me not to go to the main entrance through the big gates, but Mary told me to go with her as she wanted to show me to her mama so that she could thank me for helping them.

All of a sudden I felt very self-conscious and the thought of actually going into the Hall made me want to run off. Before I knew where I was I was walking up the long drive flanked by trees I had never seen before. As we got closer to the very large house set in the middle of a beautiful park I had to stop and gaze in wonder at what I saw. There were gardens with neatly cut lawns stretching down to a small lake which was fed by a stream which meandered through the park.

There were a lot of strange large birds strutting around with colourful fan-tails and as we got closer to them they made the most awful noise. Mary told me not to be frightened because they always made a row when there were strangers about. They were called peacocks and gave warning of any intruders.

We climbed endless steps and stood in front of the largest door I had ever seen. The door was opened by a chap in a strange uniform, complete with breeches. I thought to myself what a clot he looked. He greeted Mary and Hugh with, "Good Morning Miss and good morning Master Hugh." He gave me a look as if to say what are you doing here my boy?

Mary took my basket away from me and gave it to the chap in fancy dress instructing him to take it to the cook. Much to my embarrassment she took my hand and led me through the large hallway into a very posh room. She called out, "Mama, Mama, where are you?" Her mother was hidden from view, sitting in a tall-backed chair.

Lady Howes stood up. She was a very handsome woman and she

walked over to where we were standing. I was now feeling quite sick with nerves. Mary told her mother that I was called Henry and that I had saved them from such a beastly boy. She then proceeded to recall the events of the morning with all the gory details which made me feel quite ashamed of myself.

Lady Howes walked over to me and instinctively I held out my rather grubby hand and said, "How do you do?" She took my hand and thanked me for looking after her children and how brave it was of me. I was very tongue-tied but I managed to blurt out why I was here and who I was. After a pause she told me to tell my mother that she should be very proud of me and that she made the best butter and cream in the district. She then told Mary to take me down to the kitchen and ask cook to give me some of her cakes to take home. As we were leaving the room she told Mary to ask Evans to come and see her.

What a relief it was to leave this sort of unreal room. I was led through passages and then down into a huge kitchen where I was greeted by a very rotund lady dressed in white. The smell was out of this world and there seemed to be food everywhere. Some food was cooked and some was in the process of being cooked. The cook, on Mary's instructions, filled my basket with all sorts of goodies.

By now I understood that Evans was a footman, whatever that was. Anyway he came down with a letter for my mother and told Mary that Wills would drive me back to the farm in the car. This was getting beyond me and I will be glad to get back down to earth!

In a bit of a daze I was once more led through the house and out of the huge front door. Here I was greeted by Hugh complete with a bandage on one leg. I asked him how his leg was and he said that it was still hurting a bit. In a shy sort of way he thanked me.

There stood the car and what a car it was. The whole car was polished like a mirror and a chap in uniform stood with the door open. He took my basket and put it into the car. To my surprise Mary and Hugh also got in. I had no idea that they were coming for the ride. The chauffeur was called Wills and in a very haughty voice Mary told him to take us to Long Meadow Farm. Off we went down the long drive through the park. I wondered what Mother would say when she saw this posh car drive up to the farm. I bet that there will be bags of rushing around to make herself presentable.

Hugh started to chat away asking me what I did with myself when I was not at school. I told him about my wood and explained my special tree. He was quiet for a while and then asked if he could see it one day. I said that of course he could, but I doubted that his mother would let him come over and play with me as our families were so different.

When we reached the farm out popped Wills to open the car door

29

for us. Mother came out of the house looking flustered. Seeing Hugh's leg bandaged she must have thought that I had an accident. The first thing she said was, "Are you alright Henry?" I replied, "Of course I am." Immediately Mary, full of confidence, told Mother what had happened and she went into great detail, which made me feel very embarrassed. After all, I had only given Joe a bashing for which I had been training under John's watchful eye.

We said goodbye and as Hugh got into the car he said, "I will ask Mother about your tree." With a wave they returned to the luxury of Langley Hall.

As the car drove away Dad came into view and he was soon asking us what was going on and I had to tell the story once more. Dad seemed pleased and gave me a pat on the head saying "Well done Henry."

We went into the kitchen and the first thing I did was to uncover the basket to see what was inside. There were mince pies, cakes and all sorts of fruit that I had never seen before. I remembered Mary telling the cook what to put in the basket, but I had no idea that the contents would be so smashing.

Suddenly I remembered the letter Lady Howes had sent to Mother. I had stuffed it into my pocket and it was looking the worse for wear. Handing it to my mother I wondered what the contents were.

Mother started to read the letter and I could see by her expression that the contents surprised her. Using one of her favourite expressions she said, "Well I never. We have been asked to the tenants' party after Christmas." Evidently this was quite an honour. Dad gave one of his snorts as if to say that he didn't like parties.

I asked Dad what a tenant was and he explained that Sir James was the owner of a lot of land in the district and most of the farms and cottages were let to farmers and other people and they paid a rent each year. Some of the farms had been in the same family for several generations. I immediately asked him if we were tenants and he told me that grandfather had bought the farm many years ago.

Over lunch I tried to explain all about the park and the inside of the Hall and what a nice person Lady Howes appeared to be. Dad looked up from his lunch and said that he had lived here all his life and had never been inside the Hall, except for the kitchen to see the cook. Here I was a young whippersnapper of only nine years of age and he had done what I have never been able to do. He then gave me one of his smiles and said, "Well done Henry."

Mum and Dad were in a very good mood and I thought that it might be a good time to ask about Daisy, so I asked if Charlie could

30

teach me to ride. Dad gave it some thought and said that if Charlie was agreeable to give up his spare time it might be a good idea. Oh boy! Was I pleased! Charlie gave me a wink as much as if to say well done.

After lunch I met John in the barn and I had to go into great detail about my fight with Joe and he seemed very pleased with what I told him. He told me that we would keep up the training for the future. What he meant by that I didn't know.

When I went off on my own I always told Mum where I was going. This had always been a golden rule. So I told her I was going to the wood and off I went to think about the morning's events.

I sat up in my tree and thought about Mary and Hugh. How lucky they were to live in the Hall with that smashing park. Although I was young I could sense that they were lonely and perhaps their life was not all that it seemed. Dad always said that, "Everyone's grass looks greener," and, "Money doesn't always bring happiness." To have just enough was the most important thing.

It was a nice afternoon and it wouldn't be dark for quite some time so I decided to venture into Jake's wood. I had met him several times and in my mind I called him Jake, but of course to his face it was Mr Spencer.

I got to the clearing where I had seen the badgers and I decided to follow the path further into the wood. As I walked I made note of different trees so that I would be able to find my way out again. After a while I came to a large clearing and there was a cottage with smoke coming out of the chimney. This must be Jake's home. How cosy it looked set among these great trees. If ever I had a choice I would like to live there.

I thought it best not to intrude uninvited so I made a hasty retreat. I managed to find my way back to my wood and headed home. As I walked I thought of Christmas morning and wondered excitedly what presents I would get. I would have to go into the village shop tomorrow to buy Mum, Dad, John and Jenny some small presents. Perhaps a cigar for Dad, a packet of Woodbines for John and sweets for Mum and Jenny. I had a few shillings pocket money saved and would have to see what I could do.

Jenny comes home on Christmas Eve and I am looking forward to seeing her again. She was such a nice sister to have and I loved her dearly. She had looked after me a lot when I was very young and I bet that I was a proper nuisance when I was small. I expect Dad or John will meet her from the station in Newton Abbot and if it is not too late I expect I may be able to go as well. If John collects her he will go early and have a few pints, which will count me out.

When I got home there was no one about but I heard voices

upstairs and I found Mother and Betty in a bedroom looking at dresses. I soon gathered that there was a bit of a panic because Mother's dresses were not posh enough to wear to the party. I heard her say to Betty, "It's not good, I will have to go into town tomorrow on the bus and buy a new dress. I dread to think what Sam will say."

It was now Christmas Eve and George had cut some ash from the hedge by the farmhouse. He had cut the ash into short lengths and it was my job to tie them up with binding cord into faggots. It was the custom to burn these in the grate during Christmas. Being green they made a series of bangs and made the sparks fly. They were supposed to ward off evil spirits. I must say I wished them further because it was quite a chore.

When I had finished my jobs I walked down to the village to do my Christmas shopping. I had worked out what I could buy and I was busy trying to find the best bargains when I heard a female voice say, "Hello Henry." I looked around and saw Polly. For some unknown reason I was glad to see her. When we had finished her shopping we walked home and when we came to the little bridge we sat on the old seat by the stream and watched the gurgling water of the stream passing under the bridge. I always loved the sound, it was so peaceful.

I told Polly about what had happened to me when I was taking the butter and cream to the Hall, and how the family had been invited to the party on the evening after Boxing Day. At this news her face lit up. She explained that her father was now the Vicar having been promoted from being the Curate at his church and they had also been invited. She said that she was glad that I would be there to keep her company.

As we sat there we could look down the valley with the stream curving to find its own level. Right at the end of the valley there was a small wood with a house on its perimeter. Polly could see where I was looking and she told me that Mrs Jenkins lived in the house. I thought to myself that one day I would explore this area as I had never been to that end of the valley.

We continued on our way and Polly ran off up the lane to her home. She turned around and shouted, "Happy Christmas Henry." I returned the greeting and with a wave she was off.

Slowly walking up the hill to the farm I thought what a nice morning it had been, but what could I do after lunch. It would be a good idea to keep out of the way otherwise I would be given a job or two, so I decided to have another look at Jake's cottage. I told Mother where I was going and she seemed glad to have me out of the way. She was so busy preparing for the feast tomorrow.

I walked through my wood and then through the fence and down the path I had found on my last visit. In the winter the countryside is so quiet and many of the birds have gone to warmer parts of the world. I must say that I like the Spring best of all. Life seemed to be starting again after being asleep for the winter.

There was no sign of Jake but he must have been around somewhere because there was a fire going in his cottage. All of a sudden I heard this voice behind me and there was Jake having a good laugh when he saw how he had made me jump. He told me that he had been following me because he thought I may get lost.

He was silent for a while and then said, "Would you like to come in and see my home?" So off we went through the glade and into his cottage. He led me into what he said was his living room and what an Aladdin's cave it was!

There were all sorts of guns and weapons on the walls together with numerous photographs of men in uniform. Over the fireplace there was a painting of a lovely looking lady. The furniture was very basic but comfortable looking. In one corner there was a desk covered in papers and a pile of well-worn books. There was a log fire in the hearth. It all looked so cosy and lived in. It seemed to be part of Jake. He asked me if I would like a cup of tea and went out of the room without waiting for an answer.

When he was out of the room I had a good look around and I saw a picture frame containing a lot of medals. They must have been what Jake had won during the war. I looked at some of the faded photos, some were of Jake as a young man looking very smart in Army officer's uniform. There were also others which looked like family groups and several of the lady in the picture over the fireplace.

Being nosy I had a quick look at the papers on the desk. I was surprised to see that some of the papers were in a foreign language. I continued walking around the room until I came back to the medals. I wondered what tales they could tell. Perhaps one day Jake will let me into their many secrets.

I looked around and there was Jake standing in the room. I do wish that he would not keep creeping up on me. As we sat down I plucked up enough courage to ask him if one day he would teach me how to walk without making any noise. He didn't answer for some time, but then he said that if he did I would have to practice and keep on practising because it is something you have to practice to be any good at it.

As I drank my tea and scoffed a plate of biscuits I told Jake about my encounter with Joe and my visit to Langley Hall and how friendly Lady Howes and the children had been.

Jake got up and walked over to the group of photos and pointed to a young officer and said that he had served with Sir James in the war.

So I got up to have a look at Sir James and I could see a slight resemblance to his son Hugh. I asked Jake if he was in the photograph and he pointed to a young man with a lot of ribbons on his chest. I thought how different he looked today. The war years must have taken their toll.

After a while I got up and said that I should be going. Jake told me to wait a minute as he had a small Christmas present for me. He opened one of the drawers in the desk and brought out a small knife in a fancy leather sheath. Handing it to me he said, "Be careful Henry, it is very sharp, but you will find it very useful. A young lad should always have a knife in the country." I was speechless for a moment because I could not believe that I could be so lucky. I thanked Jake most profusely and got ready to go. Jake put on his coat and said that he would walk with me to my wood as I might get lost.

It was very strange that I could talk to Jake so freely and in such a relaxed way and yet I had known him for a very short time. I was not to know then what a good friend he would be to me in the future. Anyway, we got to my wood and after wishing each other a Happy Christmas I was soon on my way home across the fields.

I stopped several times to look at my smashing present. Jake was right when he said that it was sharp. I had cut a stick so easily on my way through the wood. I will look after it because to me it is something special.

As I walked into the farmyard I could hear a lot of laughter coming from the kitchen so I went to see what was going on and there was Jenny. I ran up to her and we had a good hug.

How different she looked. When she left she was a country girl and now she was a smart young lady. To me she was always pretty but now she was a real beauty dressed in such nice clothes. Eventually she had managed to leave much earlier and she was home for a whole week.

I could not get a word in edgeways so I sat back and looked at my family. How lucky I was to have them all. I do hope that nothing happens to them, whatever would I do without them. I pray for them every night before I get into bed. In winter I cheat a bit by saying my prayers in bed because my bedroom is so cold.

Mother had put on a special supper for Christmas Eve. There was a huge piece of boiled ham and this was a real treat as we only had this at Christmas so I made the most of it.

I was dying to tell them all about my visit to Jake's house, but there was never a lull in the conversation. At last I told them about my present which was handed around. Mother looked a bit peculiar and said I was too young to have such a knife but Dad saved my bacon by saying that I was no longer a baby. I gave him one of my best smiles and he gave me a wink.

Mum and Dad were very interested to hear about Jake's house and questioned me quite a bit. Dad said that Jake had bought the wood and the cottage from Sir James several years ago and sometimes he would go to the Hall to see the Howes. John interrupted by telling us that he sometimes met Evans the footman in the pub and had heard that Jake often spent Christmas at the Hall. I thought it funny that he had not mentioned it to me when I told him that I was going there for a party. I had found that Jake was a man of few words and only seemed to speak when he had something of interest to say. Sometimes he would be silent for quite some time, not like me, I was always talking.

After supper we talked with the ash crackling in the fire. John pushed off probably to meet one of his girlfriends or go to the pub. Betty and Charlie said that they were going for a walk to get some fresh air.

As they left the kitchen, Mum and Dad exchanged winks. Thinking on this I noticed that Betty and Charlie were spending a lot of time together. Being innocent, I thought no more of it.

By now it was getting past my bedtime and Mother packed me off to bed. Jenny took me up to my room, holding the oil lamp to light our way. She had done this so many times before and it was so nice to have her back once more. Sometimes when I was very young she used to sit with me if I was unable to go to sleep. After a big kiss and hug she went downstairs.

I had lit my lamp and before getting undressed I went over to the window and looked out at the view I knew so well. It was something that I will never forget in the years to come.

I looked at the sky and there was a very bright star and I wondered if this was the same star that the three wise men followed to Bethlehem so long ago.

Mother had told me so many times about the Christmas story and I had been to the church in the village with Mother on Sunday evenings, so I knew a bit about it all. So, cold as I was, I knelt down by my bed and said some special prayers on that Christmas Eve.

As I lay in bed I wondered what presents I would receive tomorrow. I never got much, but whatever I received would be nice. I soon fell asleep and in no time it was Christmas morning.

Of all the mornings to oversleep! I looked at the end of the bed to find the familiar stocking. Reaching out I investigated its contents. There were nuts, an orange, a large bar of chocolate and two items which I couldn't understand. There was a toy lead horse and a dog, both with ribbons tied around their necks. I thought that was a poor do. If I was a very small boy I could understand it, but after all, I am 9 years old and past the toy animal stage.

I dressed and went down to the kitchen with my small gifts for my family. As I entered I saw that everyone was there and I was greeted by a chorus of, "Happy Christmas Henry." They were all very silent and then Dad asked me what I thought of my presents. Before I answered I handed my presents to one and all and then I said a very quiet thank you. To my surprise they all burst out laughing. Mother got up and gave me a kiss and cuddle and asked me if I would now like my real presents.

John got up and said he would go and get his present. Charlie also left the room. Dad said that he was unable to bring in what he and Mother were giving me. By now I was getting very excited. Dad then told me that I could have Daisy for my very own on the understanding that I looked after her in every way. I rushed over and gave Mum and Dad the biggest kiss I could muster. This was a present beyond my wildest dreams.

Then in came Charlie holding a saddle. He had found the old one and had polished it so that it looked like new. He put it down and said that by hook or by crook he would teach me how to ride and the first lesson would be after I had finished my breakfast.

By now I was beside myself and John came in leading a very young dog, not a puppy, but about one year old. He gave me the lead and said, "This is yours my lad." I knelt down immediately and the dog was all over me, licking my face and getting very excited. Mother told John to take him outside for the time being.

Jenny then gave me a square, flat parcel which I soon opened. To my delight I found a fret saw outfit, now I will be able to make that aeroplane. I wondered how Jenny knew that I wanted a fret saw.

My last present came from dear Betty. She had knitted me a smashing jersey in different colours. I had seen her unpicking several of her old jumpers so this must be the end result. How kind of her this was as I knew that she was very hard up. It was good of Dad to give her a home when her husband died.

I couldn't eat much breakfast because I was eager to see my new friend John had given me. When I went out into the yard he was tied to a pole in the fence. When he saw me he strained at the rope that was keeping him captive. I had no idea what sort he was, but he had such a lovely little face and was all mine. Now I had to decide what to call him. I thought for a while and for some unknown reason the name Micky came to me. So henceforth that would be his name. Perhaps it was because he had a black patch over one eye, like Mickey Mouse.

As I stood there John came over and I thanked him again. I asked him how he had managed to keep it so secret and he told me that George had been looking after him for several days. He had belonged to a friend who had to go away and John bought him for me.

John told me that I would have to train him to come to me when I called and the best way would be to take him into the field with tit bits in my pocket and reward him every time he came back to me when I called him. So I thought I would start tomorrow.

The first thing would be for me to take him for a walk. I thought that it would be a good idea to take him to George's cottage so that I could thank him for looking after Micky.

Walking to George's home I talked to my new friend and even in such a short time we got to know each other. I always had a very grubby sugar lump for Daisy so I let him off his lead. He went mad running all over the place and seemed happy to be free. As we got nearer to George's cottage I held up the sugar and called Micky. To my surprise he came rushing up to me and I gave him his reward and managed to put him back on his lead.

I called on George and Olive and after thanking them and wishing them a Happy Christmas I returned to the farm to find that Charlie had the saddle and a bridle on Daisy and it looked as if my first lesson was to begin.

I felt a bit scared about my first venture onto a horse's back, but here goes I must be brave. Charlie spent some time telling me what to do and what not to do and up I got for the first time. It seemed strange sitting up there so far from the ground. I do hope I don't fall off.

I picked up the reins keeping my legs close to Daisy's sides and Charlie led me around the field. I soon felt less nervous and thought this was smashing. After a while Charlie tied a rope to the bridle and I was now on a sort of lead. All the time Charlie was shouting instructions on how to direct Daisy by pulling first on one side of the reins and then on the other. Much to my surprise Daisy responded. I had always chatted to Daisy as I did now, perhaps this was why she did not object to having me on her back.

After quite a long time Charlie said, "That's enough for one day Henry," so I got off and that was the end of the first of many lessons that Charlie would be giving me. I gave Daisy a good hug around her neck and after Charlie took the saddle and bridle she was soon off to the other side of the field to join the other horses.

I went into the kitchen to be greeted by the most wonderful smell of a goose being cooked. Mother, Jenny and Betty were as busy as bees so they soon told me to buzz off.

I untied Micky from the fence and went to find Dad. I found him in the barn and told him all about my first horse riding lesson. He gave a laugh and told me that he had been watching and thought that I had done quite well for my first attempt. He told me to always let the horse know who is master, but to treat it as you would like to be treated yourself.

I was a bit worried as to where Micky would sleep and Dad said that Mother would not let him in the kitchen yet, but she might when he was older. In the meantime he could sleep in the spare pen in the next barn near my workshop.

We went to look at the pen and Dad fetched some hay to make a bed for him. I led Micky in and he sniffed around a bit before cocking his leg to leave his scent so that any stray dog would know that this was his territory.

Jake had told me about this on my first visit while we were watching the badgers. I had also noticed that the foxes did the same over a wide arc around their patch. I had often wondered why they had to wee so much.

Dad and I had a good chat. He was always giving me advice and telling me about things in general. I told him about Hugh wanting to see my wood and tree. He told me to forget it because Lady Howes would never allow her children to mix with people like us. I felt sorry to hear this because for some reason I felt sorry for the poor young chap. Anyway, I thought only time would tell.

Our Christmas dinner was out of this world. I ate so much that I could hardly move afterwards. As this was a special day we all moved into the large living room and while the females were washing up the menfolk sat in comfortable chairs and were soon having a snooze. I collected the leftovers for Micky's Christmas dinner and took it out to him. I found an old milking stool and joined him in his new home.

He seemed to have taken to me because as I sat there having one of my daydreams, he finished his feed and came to lay by my feet with his head resting on my boot. This made me think that we will indeed be good friends.

Laying in bed on that Christmas night I just couldn't go to sleep. I was still excited and full of the good food that Mother had provided. I thought to myself that this was the best Christmas Day I had ever had.

I kept thinking of Daisy and Micky. Fancy me having a pony and a dog all of my own. I still thought that it was all a dream. I began to make the most elaborate plans. I would be able to ride all over the farm and perhaps when I could ride properly I might venture down to the village or even over to Teigncoombe where I might see Polly. Tomorrow I will try out my fret saw set that Dolly had given me. At this stage I must have gone to sleep because the next thing I knew was that it was morning.

I got up early because I wanted to give Micky a run and give Daisy a sugar lump. I now had quite a stock because I pinched a handful when Mother was out of the way!

After a quick breakfast I went out into the yard and into the cow sheds where Dad and John were milking the cows. Christmas didn't exist for the cows, they had to be milked twice a day no matter what. I had a word with Dad and John and Charlie told me that I had to be ready to have another lesson later in the morning. Being Boxing Day he had most of the day off and it was good of him to give up his spare time.

I went to see Micky and gave him some fresh water and scraps I had found in the kitchen. He was really glad to see me and I now had a good look at him. He had short white hair with black patch over one eye. He also had black patches all over him. He had long legs so I thought that when he was fully grown he would be fairly big.

I put him on his crude lead and we went out to the paddock to see Daisy who was right at the other end with the other horses. I called her name as loud as I could and over she galloped. We went through the usual procedure of the sniffing at my pockets and of course she was rewarded with her bit of sugar.

Dogs and horses don't always go together and I was interested to watch Daisy and Micky sizing each other up and was glad to see that there was no visible animosity. This was a great relief to me because my plans would have fallen by the wayside.

I had my second lesson and I must say that I felt more confident. I had tied Micky to the fence and he sat down to watch events. As I was riding around the field I wondered if animals had thoughts like humans had and if so, what did they think about?

Wild animals probably spent most of their time thinking about their next meal. Daisy had plenty to eat so her thoughts must be elsewhere. Anyway, this is a question that will never be answered.

When I had finished my ride Charlie told me that we were now going into the barn and he would show me how to groom Daisy, because in future this will be my job. I would also have to clean out her stable every morning before I went to school. As the weather was getting colder the horses will be put inside every night.

I was soon to find out that grooming and looking after a horse was hard work, but it will be worth it. Looking at Daisy, she was in quite a state and I will have to spend quite some time to get her looking respectable. Perhaps Dad will get her coat cut in the spring.

I spent the rest of the day pottering around and trying to train Micky, but I went to bed feeling satisfied and thinking of the party I would be going to tomorrow.

I got up early the next morning to take Micky for a stroll and to see Daisy. She was already in the paddock looking much better after her grooming. I called her and over she came for her reward.

The rest of the day seemed to drag a bit, but at last I was given a good wash and sent up to my room to put on my best suit. It was getting a bit small but I managed to do up all the buttons. I don't look in the mirror very often, but as I stood in my finery I thought that I looked quite presentable and not my usual scruffy self.

Mother and Dad looked very smart and Jenny was indeed a picture with her city dress on. We all got into Dad's old car and were off. John decided that this sort of party wasn't his cup of tea.

As we drove down the lanes to the Hall I began to feel shy and nervous at the prospect of being with so many strangers and began to wish that I was back at the farm.

At last we were there and driving through the park to this magnificent house. Dad parked the car well away from the front door, probably because Mother was ashamed of its condition. I think that at heart Mother was a bit of a snob.

As we went in I was surprised to see that they had electric lights and the large entrance hall looked really magnificent. There were two footmen on duty but Evans came forward and took our coats. When he took mine he said, "Good evening Master Henry," and gave me a friendly smile. This seemed to impress Mum and Dad, why I really didn't know.

Further along the hall stood Lady Howes, Mary and Hugh. Next to them stood a tall handsome man in a very posh suit and I thought that this must be Sir James.

As we walked towards them someone shouted "Mr and Mrs Blake and family." We were greeted and our hands were shaken by the Howes family. I heard Sir James saying to Mum and Dad, "How proud you must be of your son Henry, I will have a chat with you later." Dad introduced Mum, Jenny and of course me.

Lady Howes was having quite a chat with Mother. Now came my turn and Sir James patted me on the head and said, "Thank you my boy for looking after Mary and Hugh. They have persuaded me to let them visit your special wood. We will have to fix this up one day." When I shook hands with Mary and Hugh there were broad grins as if to say what a bore this all is.

As we went into a very large room, by now full of all sorts of people, we were handed a glass. I had lemonade but my family had something which looked much stronger. The menfolk were looking at Jenny because she stood out in her smart clothes. Mum and Dad soon started to talk to the many people that they knew which left me out on a limb. Then I saw Polly come in with her parents. I recognised her father and looking at her mother, I could see the resemblance to Polly. She had the same fair hair and was not very tall. Come to think of it Polly was small for her age.

When Polly saw me she came over and we told each other what we had for Christmas. I must say that I went on a bit about my special presents. Polly had a new dress which she had on and it looked very nice, not that I knew much about girls' things. Mother came over and I introduced her to Polly, then she saw someone she knew and Mother was off. Polly stayed a while and then went off to join her parents. Once more I was on my own. By now I was feeling a bit fed up, until Hugh came over to join me.

Hugh said that his father would let him come over to my wood and he was going to arrange something with my Dad. There were a few other children in the room who were unknown to me so I was glad of Hugh's company. We both became a bit bored so Hugh told me to follow him. We left the room and started to climb the huge staircase.

As we went up the staircase I was amazed to see the many portraits hanging on the walls. There were paintings of men and women in very ancient clothing. Some were strange looking people and some of the pictures looked very old indeed. I asked Hugh who they all were and he told me that they were his funny old ancestors. One was supposed to haunt the Hall, but he had never seen him.

We reached the landing which had a lot of doors leading off both sides. I wondered how many bedrooms there were and who slept in them. We went into one of these rooms and at a glance I could see that it was Hugh's bedroom.

One wall was almost covered with drawings and simple watercolours. To me they looked very good indeed. Hugh said that this was what he did in his spare time because when he grew up he wanted to be an artist, which was not what his father had in mind. In one corner on the floor I saw a train set and what a smasher it was. Hugh got down and wound up the engine and started it on its journey around the track pulling several trucks.

Evidently this was Hugh's Christmas present from his parents. Looking at it I was green with envy and thought that it must have cost a great deal of cash.

We were enjoying ourselves when the door burst open and in came Mary. She told Hugh off for leaving the party and we were to come downstairs at once, so we had to join the boring party once more. As we went into the room we bumped into Polly who looked a bit lost so I introduced her to Mary and Hugh.

The two girls seemed to look each other up and down to see which looked the best dressed. I then noticed that Polly had on the funny little brooch that I had given her and this made me feel a bit embarrassed. Why on earth was she wearing that silly thing? We chatted for a while and then the food arrived so we separated to find our parents.

The food was handed around by servant girls in starched white aprons and funny white hats. I must say that I made quite a pig of myself.

I was with Mum and Dad and wondered where Jenny was, then I saw her talking to several young chaps. She seemed to be having a smashing time.

Mother asked me where I had been and I told her of my visit to Hugh's room upstairs. This seemed to surprise her somewhat. Then along came Sir James and his wife. Sir James said to me, "Well my lad are you enjoying yourself?" Before I had the chance to reply he told me to go and have a chat with Hugh and Mary because they are looking a bit fed up and he wanted to have a word with my parents. So off I went wondering what this was all about. I was not to know until much later.

I found Hugh and Mary talking to Polly and we stayed together for the rest of the party. I thought that it was so strange that Hugh and Mary didn't seem to have any friends, but on reflection I realised that this was of course a 'grown-ups' do. I expect that they will have a proper children's party at some other time.

I told my young friends about Daisy and Micky and how I was learning to ride. So far I had not fallen off. Mary said that she and Hugh had a pony. I thought to myself that I bet their pony was pretty posh.

By now people were beginning to leave and catching Mother's eye she beckoned me over, so saying goodbye I left my friends and joined my family. For some reason Mother gave me a bit of a hug.

We went into the hall and Evans gave us our coats. Sir James and Lady Howes were saying goodbye to their various guests and when it was our turn Sir James said to me, "I hope that you have enjoyed yourself and no doubt we will see you again." I had no idea what he meant by this remark and I thought no more of it.

We got into our old car and drove back to the farm. Mother and Jenny were nattering away, mostly about the other females that were there and I wondered why females always talked about each other.

During the drive back I thought about Hugh and Mary. In my mind I classified them as friends but I realised that this could never be because they lived in another world way out of my class. Of course Polly was different because we went to school together.

It had become very cold and I was glad to go into the warm sitting room which was still in use because it was still Christmas. I was glad because I could sit in the kitchen by myself and have one of my daydreams away from Mother telling Betty about our visit to the Hall.

I was soon interrupted by the arrival of Dad who settled himself in his chair. He said, "Henry I have something to talk to you about." I immediately wondered whatever had I done.

Dad continued by saying that Sir James had a chat with him and he wanted my help. I began to wonder whatever was coming next, Dad was a bit long winded when telling me things. Eventually he told me that Sir James was a bit worried that Hugh and Mary, having very little contact with young people, and as they would be going away to school in the future, it might come as a bit of a shock to them both. Would I have them over at the farm sometimes and also go over to the Hall to do whatever youngsters do.

This was quite a shock for me because I loved my wanderings by myself and to have a girl tagging along was not a pleasant thought. Dad could see my expression and asked me to try it as a favour to him. The crafty old chap knew that if he put it like that I would give it a try. Dad and I always got on so well together that I had to agree.

Dad then asked me if I had seen much of Mr Spencer so I told him all about Jake. Dad told me that he was an old friend of Sir James, which of course I already knew. Evidently Sir James had been talking to Jake and he had suggested that I may be able to help as he thought that I was a sensible young chap.

By now I was becoming more and more confused, but to hear that Jake thought highly of me made me feel good. For some reason I had taken to Jake and to have him as a friend would be great because somehow I knew that he could teach me so much.

Dad continued by saying that I must always remember that the Howes children were right out of our class and that I must treat them accordingly.

By now it was way past my bedtime and Jenny took me upstairs. In no time I was tucked up in bed. Tomorrow Charlie was going to let me ride Daisy without being on the lead. I am now able to get on her back without Charlie's helping hand, so I was making progress.

The next morning when I put my nose out from under the warm bedclothes, I knew that it was going to be a very cold day. When I got up the window was covered in frost and I soon got dressed and went down to the warm kitchen. Mother gave me some breakfast which included a slice of her bread covered with a thick layer of her famous cream. I thought that I would go and watch Dad and John milking. Mother made me wrap up well and off I went.

Standing by the door of the cowshed I looked at the large number of cows that were patiently being milked. It was so cold that their breath was coming out of their mouths like steam and their warm bodies were adding to the foggy atmosphere. There was a strong smell of their dung and wee, funny as it may seem it was a smell that I quite liked. I said hello to everyone and then went to see Micky.

He was very glad to see me, even more so when I gave him some food. Today I was going to let him off his lead and see if he behaved himself. He should do because after all he was no longer a puppy. When we got out into the yard I gave him his freedom. At first he went a bit mad but then he trotted by my side, just how a dog should walk beside his master.

After having a chat with Daisy I went back into the kitchen. As I came to the door and went in Micky slipped in and laid down in front of the fire. I thought that Mother would kick up a fuss, but she just looked at him and laughed. Perhaps the kitchen would no longer be off limits for the cold chap.

Putting on my wellington boots I asked Mother if I could go over to see Mr Spencer after I had done my jobs. She said that I could providing that I didn't make a nuisance of myself. She went to the dairy and came out with a jar of cream and told me to give it to Mr Spencer.

As I went out of the kitchen Micky roused himself and followed me. I decided to take him and if he misbehaved himself I would put him on his lead.

There had been a very heavy frost that night and the fields were white. The sun low in the clear blue sky and the light reflecting on the frozen grass gave the impression of a carpet of diamonds. The taller grass and weeds were laced with frozen cobwebs. It was noisy walking on the frozen earth but it was a sound that I always liked. It was so quiet except from the crunching of my boots and the harsh cries of some nearby rooks, which were always a noisy lot.

When I came to my wood I put Micky on his lead as I was not sure what he would get up to. He looked a bit fed up about being captive again, but I didn't want to lose him. As we got further into the wood I thought that I would test him. I let him off his lead and in no time at all he had disappeared into the undergrowth. I called his name and back he came. This happened several times, but each time he came back so I told him he had passed the test, not that he understood what on earth I was talking about!

When I came to Jake's cottage I felt a bit shy, but after all I was on an errand delivering some cream from Mother. Before I had a chance to knock on the door Jake had opened it. I thrust the jar of cream towards him telling him that it was from my Mother, which seemed to please him no end. He asked me in and I was about to tie up Micky when he told me to bring him indoors.

Micky greeted him like an old friend. It is strange that animals seem to know who their friends are. Micky made himself at home in front of the log fire.

I told Jake about my smashing presents and pointed at my knife which was on my belt. He told me that it was on the wrong side. If you are right handed it should be on the left side then you could always get it out of its sheath quickly.

I told him about having to play with the two children from the Hall. He was quiet for a while and then he said, "Henry, no doubt you are envious of what they have, but they are very lonely. Sometimes having worldly goods can be a bit of a hindrance to happiness and some people are jealous, which is very nasty. If you would be a friend to them you would be doing me a favour." I asked if I could bring them to see him and he said, "Of course you can, but not too often. Let them meet some of your friends."

After a cup of tea and a chat I said goodbye. Joined by Micky I made for the door and as I made my way across the glade Jake shouted after me "Don't forget Henry, you are always welcome here." Walking home I thought that perhaps Jake was lonely as well, or perhaps he was fed up with grown-ups after his experiences during the war.

I had to run back most of the way because I would be late for lunch. Micky thought that this was great fun running by my side.

After lunch Charlie asked Dad if he could give me a riding lesson and I was glad to hear Dad say yes. This was to be my first solo effort and I don't mind saying that I was a bit apprehensive.

As we walked to the paddock Charlie told me that he was going to let me try to put on the saddle and bridle. Daisy saw us coming and came over to meet us. After a bit of a struggle I managed to put on the saddle, making sure to pull the strap nice and tight. To get the bridle on was quite easy, so now I was ready to go.

After many instructions from Charlie I mounted Daisy and off I went. I found myself chatting away to Daisy as I experimented, at first turning to the right and then to the left and then stopping and starting.

After a while I plucked up enough courage to put her into a gentle trot which was a smashing feeling. While this was going on Micky was running alongside us.

I was concentrating so much on what I was doing that I had not noticed the audience that had gathered by the gate. The whole family were there plus Betty and Charlie. So feeling full of bravado I rode over to them.

It was lovely to see that Dad looked so pleased with a broad grin on his face and they all started to clap their hands. This startled Daisy but I managed to calm her down and dismounted. I thought that I would always remember this day as I felt so proud. Dad gave me a pat on the head and Mother gave me a big hug and I felt on top of the world.

I led Daisy into the barn and after taking off the saddle I gave her a good grooming and some oats.

I sat there a while thinking about the events of the day and day-dreaming about being able to ride Daisy all over the farm and perhaps in time I will be able to venture further afield. Who knows, I might even be able to go down to the village and to Teigncoombe to see Polly.

The next two days were very disappointing. It rained most of the time but in spite of this I had a couple of rides. I spent most of the time in my workshop trying out my new fretwork set that Jenny had given to me. The saw was difficult to use at first, but I soon got the hang of it. Perhaps at last I will be able to make a model aeroplane.

One morning Mother received a note from Lady Howes which was delivered by a groom on a large hunter. Mother invited this chap into the kitchen and gave him a cup of tea while she wrote a reply. Mother called me in and said that Mary and Hugh from the Hall wanted to come over to the farm tomorrow morning. I said that it would be alright by me, but would she ask them to wear old clothes, that is if they had any!

While the groom was having a natter to Mother I went up to the very large hunter. His ears went back which is a bad sign, but I started to talk to him and his ears came up and I was able to give his neck a friendly rub and give him one of Daisy's treats.

When the groom came out he seemed surprised to see me on such friendly terms with his horse. He told me that at times he was a very bad-tempered horse with some people. "Perhaps you have a way with horses young man," he said. I walked with him to the farm entrance and told him all about my riding lessons and pointed to Daisy in the paddock. He mounted his horse and was soon out of sight at a fast trot down the lane.

When I woke the next morning I lay in bed wondering what I could do to entertain these two children from the Hall. Here I was, a very ordinary young boy having to play with kids I hardly knew from a social world so very different from mine. Why had we been thrown together like this?

Dad was always telling me that our lives are planned out for us and what has to be will be. I was not to know then the parts they were to play in my future life.

I got out of bed early so that I could do my jobs before they arrived. I was feeling a bit on edge and would liked to have gone off on my own, but I had promised Dad that I would have a go for his sake.

Eventually a car came into the yard. It was a smaller car this time and I wondered how many cars they had. Wills the chauffeur got out and opened the door. I noted that he was not in his uniform this time. He greeted me by saying "Good morning Master Henry, I will be back to take the young Master and Mistress home at one thirty."

Mary and Hugh got out of the car. They were in fairly old clothes and were full of smiles. They looked as if they were being set free for an hour or two. Perhaps they didn't have the freedom that I had.

At first we were all a bit shy, but Micky came bounding over and made friends with them and the ice was broken. I quickly showed them around the farmyard and introduced them to Daisy. I told them that I could now ride and Mary said that I could ride over to the Hall one day and we could all go for a ride together. I said that their ponies would make poor old Daisy look very out of place. She seemed to get cross about this and told me not to be so silly.

We set off across the fields to my wood. When we came to my tree Mary was soon climbing up to the top platform. Hugh was more cautious. I shouted to Mary to be careful and once more she told me not to be silly. She was to tell me that many times in the future.

We had a smashing time and I enjoyed their company. Hugh asked if one day we could visit Uncle Jake's cottage. This surprised me as I didn't know that Jake was related. Hugh told me that they called him Uncle because he was a great friend of his Papa. Remembering what Jake had said I told Hugh that we will visit him one day.

The three of us were sitting on my favourite old tree trunk and I started to tell them about the wildlife that lived in my wood and how I sat here watching and learning all about them. I told them about the squirrels that lived in my tree and how tame they were. Mary immediately asked where they were today.

I looked at her in amazement. I thought that everyone knew that they went to sleep for the winter. I told her this and after a few simple questions I realised that she knew nothing about nature, so I made up my mind that I would try and teach them the wonders of this subject.

I saw that Hugh had a watch on his wrist so I asked him the time. He seemed surprised and asked me if I had a watch. I replied that I wasn't that lucky. With a smile on his face he said that he had several and next time they came over he would give me one. I told him to get his parent's permission first because there might be trouble as a watch was a valuable item.

After a while I told Hugh and Mary that we should start to walk back to the farm. They both looked a bit fed up about this, but at last I got them moving.

On the way back Mary asked me when could they come again. I said that they could come whenever they liked and to my surprise, without even asking Hugh, she said In her haughty way, "We will be over the day after tomorrow."

When we reached the farm the car was already waiting in the yard. There was no sign of Wills who we found chatting to Mother and Betty in the kitchen.

As they were getting into the car Hugh thanked me for having them and told me that he had enjoyed himself. I thought he had and he had more colour in his face than when he arrived. They waved goodbye and as they were driving out of the yard Mary poked her head out of the window and shouted "Don't forget Henry, I will see you the day after tomorrow."

Of course during lunch I had to tell the family what we had been doing and I told them that I really enjoyed having them over. I told them about the watch that Hugh had promised to give me and Mother told me not to take it. Dad told her not to be so daft, good old Dad!

After lunch Dad let me have a ride on Daisy. I was able to have a long ride by myself and I even put Daisy in top gear for a short spell. As we were taking Daisy to the barn I asked Dad when would I be able to ride around the farm. He told me that soon he would have a ride with me to see how I got on. This was smashing news. To go for a ride with Dad was something I thought would never happen.

When I was in bed that night I started to think about my two new friends and in some way I was pleased that I had made them happy. I liked Hugh and Mary was quite a tomboy. She was however, a bit on the bossy side and she will have to stop that nonsense when she was on my territory. Still, for a girl she was alright and she was indeed very pretty.

When I awoke the next morning I decided to ask Mother if I could go on one of my journeys. I wanted to visit the large forest where Mrs Jenkins lived. I would ask her to let me take some sandwiches as it was quite a long walk.

After a bit of a struggle she agreed and with food in my haversack and Micky by my side I set off. It was cold and frosty and there was quite a bit of ice about after the rain a few days ago. I decided to walk down the lanes because the fields were on a steep slope and it would be a bit tricky.

It was grand walking by myself, with my pal Micky of course. He was very well-behaved most of the time and stayed by my side. At times he would dart off in search of a rabbit, but he always returned.

In the winter there are very few birds about, but in frosty weather they were forever searching for food and unfrozen water to drink. I thought what a difficult life they had. Dad had told me that more birds die in the very cold weather, not from the cold but from starvation. I must remember to scrounge some scraps for them from Mother when I get back.

Mother never wastes any food. She has an old pot in which she puts potato peelings, old vegetables, bread and anything that is left over. She then puts it on the stove and cooks it for her chickens. Sometimes the smell is awful and Dad would complain. In fact we all do, but her poultry comes first.

It was so quiet except for the continuous sound of shotguns in the distance which came from Sir James' pheasant shoot. There would be beaters driving the birds towards the firing butts.

These poor birds are reared every year only to be shot at after such a short life. I have talked to Dad about this and his answer was very simple. He told me that if people didn't enjoy shooting in the winter they would never be brought into this world. I suppose that was one way of looking at it. They are well looked after for their short lives and it gives employment to so many people. They are a bit like turkeys and geese.

By now I had reached the little bridge and as the village was quite near I thought that I would spend the two pennies I had in my pocket on some sweets to fortify me on my adventure into the unknown.

As I came out of the village store I saw Polly and her mother. She ran up to me and greeted me like a long lost friend. I told her about the visit of the children from the Hall and that they were coming again tomorrow. When she heard this news she looked very wistful. Without thinking I asked her to come over as well, but she must wear old clothes. She rushed off to ask her mother and came back to say that she could. I must be daft to have to look after two girls, but somehow I was glad. She looked so pleased that I soon forgot my apprehension. I said goodbye and we went our different ways.

On that morning, with only a few days to go before it became 1930, I had no idea how the events of my venture into the unknown forest would play such a part in my life in so many different ways. Some of which I had no control over.

CHAPTER 2

I reached my starting point, which was the little bridge. I stood there for quite a while looking down the valley towards Mrs Jenkins' house. I was trying to work out how to have a good look around without being seen.

If I walked by the stream I would be visible all the time so I decided to make a detour down one side of the valley behind the several hedgerows until I came to the wood. I could then go into the wood and walk just inside of its edge. This way I would be invisible from the house.

Micky and I set off keeping under cover most of the way. After a long walk I eventually found myself opposite the house, but close enough to be able to have a good look at Mrs Jenkins' home.

It was a nice house with a very neat garden and smoke slowly drifting out of the two chimneys. I could not see anyone about. So far so good. Teachers should only be seen at school and not during the holidays.

We walked past the house and started to explore the main wood behind. The trees were very dense so I thought it best to keep to a rough path that I had found. There were many different sorts of trees looking undressed without their leaves. Some were very old and covered with moss on the sides sheltered from the wind. I wondered what tales they could tell during their long lives. I started to go into one of my daydreams letting my imagination run away with itself, so I did not hear the footsteps approaching behind me.

I nearly jumped out of my skin when I heard a voice say "Hello Henry, what are you doing here?" I knew at once who it was because of her accent. I turned around to see Mrs Jenkins, looking so different in her country clothes, in fact she even looked human!

For some reason I felt guilty for being where I was and I stuttered a bit as I explained that I was exploring this lovely wood, which I had never been to before. To my surprise she said how nice it was to see me and would I mind if she walked with me for a while. I had very little choice so we walked together. Micky returned from one of his trips into the undergrowth. He gave her a sniff and started to wag his tail so she bent down and gave him a good hug.

I told Mrs Jenkins about my Christmas presents and my visit to the Hall, leaving out the episode with Joe. I also told her that Mary and Hugh were now my friends. She asked me several questions about this as it seemed to surprise her somewhat. After a while she asked me what I had in my haversack so I told her that it was my lunch. She immediately said that I should come back to her home to have my lunch and she would make us a nice hot drink. Once more I had no choice so we made our way back along the path to her house.

Mrs Jenkins led the way through her garden, past a bird table covered with crumbs and bits of food. As we passed most of the birds were so tame that they carried on eating. I gave Mrs Jenkins full marks for feeding the birds and she went up in my estimation.

The house was so tidy and everything seemed to be shining and clean. I had to take off my boots before going in, not like in our kitchen. I was told to sit in front of the fire and Mrs Jenkins left the room to get our hot drinks.

When she was well out of the way I had a walk round the room and saw several books lying open on the table. Being nosy I had a look and I could see that they were in a foreign language, which I thought must be German. Without thinking I started to try to read aloud some of these strange words. I became so engrossed that I didn't hear Mrs Jenkins come in and I was not to know that she had been standing by the door for some time.

She made me jump when she called my name and feeling guilty I sat down by the fire. She handed me a cup of something I had never had before so I asked what it was. She told me it was coffee. It was smashing and I started to eat my lunch.

Mrs Jenkins sat down by the fire bringing one of the books with her. She sat looking into the fire drinking her coffee. She seemed to be deep in thought, but looking at me she said, "Henry, have you ever tried to read German before? Have you ever had the urge to learn a foreign language?" This question took me by surprise. I had heard of people learning to speak French, but never German. I was of course only nine, getting on for ten, but after knowing Jake I had thought how marvellous it would be to talk in another language.

I sat and thought for a while and then I told her all about my friendship with Jake and how he had said a few words to me in German. Then, for some unknown reason, I said that I would like to have a go. I would however have to ask my Dad.

Mrs Jenkins then went on to say that some people can learn another language quite easily, whereas others find it very difficult. She thought that I might be one of the lucky ones. "You can tell your parents that there will be no charge because I would like to see what I can do."

She started to natter on about when the evenings were lighter. I could come down on Daisy or she could fetch me in her little car that was parked outside. She then went out into the kitchen to get some more coffee.

This gave me a chance to look around the room. There were some lovely paintings around the walls which I presumed were the work of Mr Jenkins, where ever he may be. The house looked quite posh which made me think the Jenkins were well off. Dad had told me that Mr Jenkins was a well-known artist so I thought that he got a lot of cash for his work.

Mrs Jenkins came back with some more smashing coffee and said that just for fun she would teach me a few simple phrases such as good morning, good afternoon and goodbye. To my amazement I soon got the hang of it and I began to feel quite excited. Anyway, I thought that I ought to make a move so I raised Micky who was fast asleep in front of the fire. I put on my coat and boots and thanked Mrs Jenkins for the coffee. Without thinking I said goodbye in German. She had a good laugh as my pronunciation was not very good.

On the way back I said the three phrases over and over again until I thought that they were as near as I could get. It seemed a long way back but at last the farm was in view.

I began to wonder what Mum and Dad would say about my strange visit with Mrs Jenkins.

Dad had finished milking and he was having a cup of tea with Mother and Betty. John and Jenny were sitting at the table looking at a letter and some papers. They all looked in a good mood about something or other and I was greeted by a chorus of "Hello Henry."

Dad said that they had some good news for me and went on to tell me that at last he had received a letter from the electricity company to say that he would have electricity at the farm in six weeks time.

This was smashing as we had all been waiting for this news for a very long time and we thought it would never come.

Mother gave me a cup of tea and asked what I had been doing all day, so I told them all that had transpired. I told them that Polly was going to join the two children from the Hall when they came tomorrow. Then I told them about Mrs Jenkins and they all seemed to sit up and take notice.

Mother was the first to break the silence with her usual, "Oh my! Fancy learning to speak German." The others asked me questions about the Jenkins house which I tried to answer. Dad seemed to be in deep thought looking into the fire. He eventually said, "Well done Henry, I think that it would be a good idea, that is if you can do it. Who knows what the future holds for you, but it must not interfere with your other schooling."

Dad had spoken so the die was cast. John thought it was a great joke, but then he was only interested in farming. Mother said It was very kind of Mrs Jenkins. Dad snorted and said that Germans never did what they didn't want to do.

I went to the barn to feed Daisy and make her comfortable for the night. For once Micky remained fast asleep by the fire. He had well and truly worn himself out. I must admit, I felt tired after such a hectic day.

When I went to bed that night I had no time to daydream because I fell asleep as soon as my head hit the pillow.

When I woke up the next morning I was glad to see the sun was shining which would make it easier to entertain my three friends. I was hoping that Hugh had managed to find me a watch.

Polly came quite early and helped me to collect the eggs, which she thought was great fun. I took her into the kitchen. She seemed very shy but after a slice of bread and cream she chatted away to Mother and Jenny.

As we were in the kitchen a car drew up in the yard. It was the posh one today. I went to the kitchen door and to my surprise Lady Howes got out of the car followed by Hugh and Mary. When Mother saw what was happening she got in a bit of a panic and started to tidy herself and the kitchen all at once. In no time Lady Howes was at the kitchen door asking if she could come in.

Lady Howes said, "Hello Henry, perhaps you and your friend could go out and see Hugh and Mary as I would like to have a few words with your Mother." Polly and I made ourselves scarce. I was however wondering what was being said In the kitchen, perhaps I had done something wrong. Anyway, I would soon know.

Hugh and Mary were glad to see us and the two girls were soon having a good chat. Hugh dug into one of his pockets and brought out a wrist watch and in a shy sort of way gave it to me. It was a smashing watch and I stood looking at it for some time, hardly being able to believe my good luck. I thanked him and asked him if his mother knew all about it. He told me that she did and if I didn't believe him I must ask Mary, which I did and she confirmed what Hugh had said adding, "Don't be so silly Henry."

Lady Howes came out of the kitchen full of smiles, waved goodbye to Mother, told us to enjoy ourselves and then got into the car and she was off with Wills at the wheel.

We all trooped into the kitchen and of course the first thing I did was to show Mother my watch. Mother said that Lady Howes had mentioned it to her and what a lucky boy I was. I collected a bag of old bread so that I could give the birds a treat and then we were on the way to my wood.

The two girls were deep in conversation, talking about what ever girls talk about. Hugh and I walked behind them and I told him about my visit to Mrs Jenkins house and how exciting the large forest was. I had no intention of telling anyone about my future German lessons. I would keep that to myself for the time being. Hugh seemed more relaxed and was full of chat, telling me about his life at the Hall. He then told me that his mama had asked my Mother if I could come over for a whole day next week, that is if I would like to. I said that I would like to very much indeed.

When we reached my tree I scattered the contents of my bag on the floor of the clearing. I told Micky to push off for a bit and we climbed up into the tree. I told my friends to be very quiet and to keep very still and they will see many different sorts of birds.

It was not long before the birds started to arrive. I had done this before and always wondered how they got the message. There were pigeons, sparrows, robins, blackbirds and several other sorts. The big birds were forever trying to push the small ones out of the way. I could see that my friends were very interested in what they were seeing and they had managed to keep quiet and still.

Then, all of a sudden, there was a terrific commotion. The birds flew off in a panic as a hawk swooped down at great speed, catching an unfortunate sparrow in its wicked talons, for his mid-day meal. This upset the girls. Mary clutched my hand for comfort and this embarrassed me somewhat, but I must say that it gave me quite a nice feeling. I could see that she was close to shedding a tear or two. I explained to them that this was the way of nature and they all lived off each other. The birds ate the worms and insects and the birds of prey ate them.

After a while some of the birds returned to finish off the crumbs acting as if nothing had happened. They probably thought that the hawk had made its kill and they would be safe for the time being. Micky returned looking as if he had been dragged through a hedge backwards and this of course scared the birds away once again. We all got down from the tree to have a good look at him. He looked sorry for himself as if to say, the rabbit got away.

We played around for a bit and explored deeper into the wood. I pretended to be lost to frighten the girls which gave Hugh and I a good laugh, but the girls soon realised that it was only a game.

Looking at my new watch I decided that we should start to walk back to the farm. This decision was far from popular, time was time and after all I was in charge.

Mary told me that when I came over to the Hall I must wear old clothes because she was going to take me all over the place. I was so pleased that she had asked Polly to join us, which made me feel much more at ease. She also asked me if we could visit Uncle Jake's cottage when they came over again and I said that I would ask him when I saw him next. In any case, I had intended to go and see him tomorrow morning to get his views about the proposed German lessons.

Wills was waiting for them and as they got into the car they thanked me for having them. Mary gave my hand a squeeze and once more they were on their way home. I had enjoyed my friends' visit and was sorry to see them all go. They were such good fun.

Mother seemed pleased to see me. She had got over the shock of having Lady Howes in her kitchen and told me that the visit to the Hall was in two days time. Micky was not to go because there were several dogs there and they might fight. I showed her my watch again and she told me what a very lucky boy I was. She gave me a big hug and seemed pleased with me. I had no idea what for, but then I never did understand the moods of grown-ups.

Jenny was going away again tomorrow morning and I felt sad about this. I hung around the farm for the rest of the day talking to her whenever I got the chance. She was sad to be leaving, in fact we all were. She told me that she might have the chance of a very good job in London but she would not know for a few weeks, anyway, she was keeping her fingers crossed.

That night Jenny took me to bed like she always did when she was home. This made me feel very sad indeed. She told me that John was taking her to the station very early in the morning well before I got up, so she would say goodbye now. As she kissed me she pressed half a crown into my hand for being such a good lad. She blew out my lamp and went downstairs.

After saying my prayers and asking that Jenny would have a safe journey, I lay for a while thinking about my new friends and Polly. I wondered how Peter was getting on. I thought that I might see him during the holidays, still, I will see him next week when I go back to school. With the horrible thought of school I went to sleep.

When I woke next morning I no longer had to rely on how light it was to know when to get up. I now had a watch and to my horror it was eight o'clock and I had missed seeing Jenny off. I was sorry about this, but she had warned me.

I went down to breakfast and all of the family were fed up because of Jenny's departure. While we were having breakfast Dad asked me what I was doing today. I told him that I had thought of going to see Jake. Much to my surprise he said, "How would you like a ride around the farm with me after we have had lunch?" Like a shot I said that I would love to. This would be a real treat for me and I felt on top of the world.

As I went out of the kitchen Micky managed to move himself from his comfortable bed by the fire and followed me out. We started to walk across the fields and I started to say the German phrases that Mrs Jenkins had taught me.

I tried good morning first of all, "Guten Morgen Mrs Jenkins." It sounded similar to what she had said to me so I tried the other two phrases and repeated them time and time again until I came to the wood.

When at last I reached Jake's cottage I saw him sitting at his desk through one of the windows. I hoped that I would not be disturbing him, but he must have seen me because he opened the door before I had time to knock. He seemed please to see me so I went in. Micky darted in front of us and made himself comfortable in front of the fire. This made Jake laugh which was good, as Jake rarely laughed.

After Jake had got me a cup of tea and some biscuits and we were sitting by the fire, he asked me what I had been doing with myself so I told him about my visit to Mrs Jenkins' home. For some reason I wanted to get his views on her offer to teach me the German language. When he heard this his expression changed and he was silent for some time. I was used to this because he had a habit of not talking, sometimes for fairly long periods.

Then he started to tell me that he had a lot to do with the Germans during the war. Some were very pleasant, but others were very cruel and overall they were very different people from the English. "When you are older I will tell you more."

He went on to tell me that when he was a small boy he lived in a big house like the Hall and he had a German governess. She taught him how to speak German like a native of that country and on several occasions this had saved his life. He talked for some time and the gist of it all was that he thought that there would be another war with Germany in the future, because as a race the Germans hated to lose. There was a strange man gaining control called Hitler and there would be trouble.

Of course what he told me was well above my young mind but some of it sank in and I began to wonder what he was getting at. He told me that Mrs Jenkins was now a British subject and he had known her for some time.

He looked at me with those piercing eyes of his and he said, "Henry, see what you can do and I will help you all I can." To get this man's blessing meant a great deal to me.

I told him about Mary's request and he told me that I could bring the kids when they came over to the farm again. I asked if it would be alright to bring Polly as well which he also agreed to and with a smile he added that he would have to get some more biscuits.

Looking at my watch I saw that it was time to go. I put on my coat and Jake said that he would walk back with me. As we started to walk back he told me to watch his feet, and I could see that he stood on one foot and before putting down his other foot he used it to see if there were any twigs under the leaves and if there was he gently pushed them away. I started to copy him, step by step, It was a slow job, but it certainly worked.

After a while he told me that I should practise this whenever I could, but I should now hurry home otherwise I would be late for lunch. As I left him I said, "Aufwiedersehen Herr Spencer." This made him laugh and feeling a bit embarrassed I sped off with Micky at my heels. I turned around to wave and he shouted "Aufwiedersehen Henry."

I had to run the rest of the way home and I just made it in time for lunch. I was so excited about my ride with Dad that I couldn't eat all of my lunch. I made the eating of too many biscuits at Mr Spencer's my excuse.

After lunch Dad changed into a pair of breeches and a riding jacket. I must say that he looked quite the country gentleman. He was very good looking, being tall and very upright and I felt proud walking beside him. He made me saddle up Daisy, which he checked carefully before I could mount up. His horse was already saddled up. It was a large grey and it made Daisy look quite small, but then I was only a small chap.

Dad told me that we were going to ride around the perimeter of the farm as he would like me to see what land he owned. We rode side by side most of the time and he kept telling me to sit upright and to relax and told me other bits of riding information. We rode through a large herd of bullocks. I knew what bullocks were, the poor things had their balls cut off when they were very young. I bet that was painful. Dad told me that soon some of these animals would be going to market and he hoped that they would make a good price.

Dad was a very wise old bird and he was always telling me about this and that. He told me not to get too friendly with the kids from the Hall because children are by nature friendly with each other, but when they grow up they sometimes change. In this case when Mary and Hugh grow up they will be in such a different world and class to what I will be. Not that this makes them better people than anyone else.

We started to trot and then went into a fast trot. Then for the first time Daisy had good gallop. I found it difficult at first, this up and down effort in the saddle. The cowboys I had seen at the cinema didn't ride like this and I wondered why we were so different. When we were walking again I asked Dad about this and he told me that cowboys sometimes had to spend all day in the saddle and the saddles were designed to allow for this.

When we came to the field where the foxes were I told him all about my many visits and why I had kept it a secret. He gave me one of his smiles and told me that I was a crafty little brat. When we reached the hedge where they lived we got off to have a look, but of course they had gone.

I knew that we had a big farm but it was much larger than I realised. To be honest I had never given it much thought. I talked to Dad about this and he told me that he was thinking of employing another farm hand as he wanted to take life a bit easier.

As I rode beside my Dad on that Sunday afternoon I wished that it could go on for ever. We talked and talked and I looked at him and thought what a good chap he was.

I had no idea how many miles we had clocked up, but looking at Micky it must have been quite a few. He was now walking behind us looking worn out. When we got home to the farm Charlie kindly offered to groom Daisy, but Dad would have none of it. She was my horse so I had to look after her.

After supper Mother said that I had to have a bath because I would be very stiff tomorrow. I hated baths, but she knew best and tomorrow I would be going to the Hall for the day. I must say that I felt very tired and was off to bed early that night.

When I said goodnight to Dad I thanked him for the wonderful afternoon and he told me that I could now go out on my own on Daisy. This really made my day.

That night I fell asleep as soon as I got into bed and before I knew where I was it was another day.

Before I got up the next morning, Mother came in to tell me what to wear so that I would be reasonably presentable. I reminded her that I was told to wear old clothes, but she replied by telling me to do as I was told.

The car arrived just as I had finished doing my odd jobs. Wills was at the wheel of the small car and I could see that he had already fetched Polly. I had to squeeze in between Polly and Mary.

In no time at all we were on our way with a wave goodbye from Mother. It was quite nice sitting between the two girls and feeling the warmth of their bodies. We all seemed to be in high spirits and had a lot of fun.

After we had passed through the big gates into the park I was once more fascinated by the sheer beauty of the landscape and when the grand house came into view I thought what a lovely setting it was in. I turned to Hugh and told him that he ought to paint this view one day. In his quiet way he said that when he had more experience he would try.

Mary told Wills to take us around to the stable yard. We got out of the car when we reached a large yard surrounded by low buildings, some of which had stable doors. There were two young men in long dark aprons busy grooming some horses. Another older man came out to greet us. Mary introduced us to the head groom who was called Mr Jones. I had met him before when he had come to the farm. He looked at me and said, "Hello Master Henry, you are the young man that likes horses. How is your pony Daisy?" As we walked towards the stables I told him that I could now ride and was allowed to go out on my own. He told me that when I can ride as far as the Hall he would give Daisy a much needed trim and general clean up which I thought was jolly nice of him.

Mr Jones showed us all the many horses and then told Mary that he had something special to show her. He led the way to another building and there was a foal with her mother. Of course, the two girls went into raptures and started to smooth the foal's dear little face. The mare looked a bit put out and her ears went back, so I went over and started to smooth the side of her face. I found a grubby piece of sugar in my pocket which I gave to her. Her ears came up and she settled down. When I turned to look at the foal I felt a wet nose as the mare tried to find another sugar lump in my pocket.

We all had a good laugh and Mr Jones said that I had made a friend there. Mary asked him if the new foal had a name and he said that as yet no name had been suggested. Much to my surprise Mary said, "Let's call him Henry." I told her not to be so silly.

We spent the whole morning just looking around. We visited the blacksmith's shop and watched a horse being shod. We visited a smashing workshop where an oldish carpenter was making new shafts for an elegant small carriage and I marvelled at his skill. I thought to myself what a wonderful place this was.

By now it was lunch time and we went into the house. We were greeted by Lady Howes and she said that we would have lunch in the breakfast room, whatever that was. Nanny would look after us. I turned to Hugh and asked, "Who is Nanny?" He laughed and told me that she had looked after them since they were very small because Mama and Papa were away quite a lot. He added that she was a sort of second mother to them and they loved her dearly.

After we had washed our hands we were met by this nice looking lady. She had a very kind face and was full of smiles. The two kids ran up to her and she gave them a good hug. Mary introduced Polly and I and we went into a room off the main hall.

I had no idea why rich people had a special room to have breakfast. Anyway, I was more interested in having something to eat to bother about the habits of the rich.

We all sat around one end of a very long polished table and all had to get up while Nanny said grace. Then the door opened and in came a very smartly dressed man followed by two serving girls dressed in starched white uniforms. They were carrying trays loaded with food. On one tray there was a very nice looking pie and on the other there were vegetables.

I asked Hugh who the man was and he told me that he was Hooper the butler. He went on to tell me that he was in charge of all the servants and had been with the family for many years.

Hooper started to serve out portions of this smashing looking pie and when the plates were put in front of us the maids served the vegetables. The smell was out of this world and when everyone had been served Nanny said we could start. I was a bit embarrassed as I had no idea which knife and fork I should use, so I waited to see what Hugh did and then I started to tuck in. I tried not to eat too quickly because Mother had told me that it was rude to do so.

I could see that Polly was enjoying the pie but Hugh was picking at his, but after being scolded by Nanny he made an effort. The steak and kidney pie was followed by a fruit jelly. What a lovely lunch it was and how I enjoyed it. I must tell Mother about the fruit jelly and perhaps she might make one.

There had been very little talking during the meal, but as we sat there we all started to talk at once. The girls were giggling about something so I asked Hugh what were we going to do after lunch, he quietly said that we will try to lose the girls and play with his train set, which I thought was a good idea. Little did we know that Polly and Mary had a similar plan. Mary wanted to take Polly up to her room and talk about whatever girls talk about.

As we got up to leave the table, Lady Howes came in and asked us if we had enjoyed our lunch. Of course, we said yes. She told Polly and I that Wills would take us home at half past five.

When we came out into the large hall the girls ran off down a passage and this gave Hugh and I the chance to run upstairs to his bedroom. We had a smashing time with the train set.

Hugh told me about his two awful cousins and their ghastly mother who were coming tomorrow and staying the night. They were very spoilt by their mother and teased Hugh, sometimes even punching him.

When I heard this I came up with the idea of trying to teach Hugh how to box. I asked him if there was a barn that was not used and could he find a sack and a piece of rope. He said yes and I told him about John and his sack of straw and that I may be able to help him the same way.

Off we went and in no time at all I was able to give him a few simple lessons. I asked him not to tell his mother in case I got into trouble. It surprised me how quick he was to learn and we finished up by having a friendly sparing match. It was so good to hear him laugh so much, as he did not laugh a great deal. Of course the girls found us, but gave their word that it would be kept a secret.

Our next port of call was the kitchen. The idea was to get some old bread so that we could feed the ducks on the lake, but I think that Mary had an ulterior motive, because as soon as we got into the kitchen she asked the cook if she had any of her special little cakes.

The cook said she might be able to find one or two as a special treat, but we were not to tell anyone because it was bad to eat between meals. She went into another room and came back with a plate full of cakes with different sorts of icing on top. They were smashing and we soon cleared the lot.

We thanked the cook and left with a bag of bread and odds and ends for the ducks. It was a beautiful sight as we ran across the lawn down to the lake, even on this winter's day.

There were bullrushes and evergreen shrubs around part of the lake and on the far side were two large weeping willows. There was a slight breeze which formed small waves and the late winter afternoon sunshine was reflected on each small wave. As the ducks swam towards us their wake added to the turbulence causing the water to sparkle even more.

The ducks were quite tame and they even took the bread from our hands. The few wild geese were too timid so we threw them a few of the larger pieces of bread. There were fish in the lake and they gobbled up any food that sank below the surface. I would have liked to have spent a long time by the lake, daydreaming about what it would be like to live in such a lovely place.

My day in this fairyland was now to end and I said goodbye to Lady Howes and thanked her for a wonderful day. She took me to one side and told me how much Hugh enjoyed his visits to the farm and it was doing him the world of good as he was such a quiet boy and never seemed to be happy. I told her that soon I would be able to ride over on Daisy and that Mr Jones the groom had offered to tidy her up. Lady Howes said, "Henry, you will always be welcome here. Oh, by the way, Mary has persuaded my husband to call the new foal Henry, it was not difficult, she knows how to get round him!"

Polly got into the car and as I followed her Mary whispered in my ear, "Thank you for trying to teach Hugh how to deal with our awful cousins." I told her to make him practise on the bag of straw and to my great embarrassment she kissed me on the cheek. Out of the corner of my eye I saw that Polly looked most put out, I thought how strange girls are.

On the way back, at first to Teigncoombe to drop off Polly, we both seemed to be in deep thought, but soon Polly was back to her normal self. When we came to the vicarage she was about to get out of the car when she also, in a shy sort of way, kissed me on the cheek and said, "See you at school in two days time." Then she was gone.

When we reached the farm Wills opened the door for me, which I thought was unnecessary as I was only a farmer's son and not one of the gentry. I said, "goodbye Mr Wills, thank you."

"See you soon Master Henry." was his reply.

As I walked towards the kitchen Micky rushed out and greeted me as if I had been away for weeks. I felt pleased that he had missed me to that extent. When he was excited he had the habit of going round in small circles trying to catch his tail, this never failed to make me laugh.

Mother was full of questions of course so I told her all the events of the day, including the fruit jelly, hoping that she might take the hint. She looked most surprised when I told her that Lady Howes said that I would always be welcome. At last I managed to get away from the interrogation and made my way to the barn to bed Daisy down for the night.

I gave Daisy some fresh water and some food. After lighting my storm lantern I sat on a stool and thought about the smashing day I had with my friends. It was nice to be on my own once more, in my own surroundings with my two animal pals.

One thing is certain, I will have to stop the girls from kissing me as it embarrassed me too much, even if it did give me a nice strange feeling.

I wondered if Hugh would be able to stand up to his cousins. He is such a nice boy, but so shy and timid. Perhaps after all he may turn out like his tough looking ancestors that I had seen in the paintings hanging on the staircase walls.

Hugh's train set was missing a station and in one of my old comics I had seen plans how to make one. I didn't think that I had the skill, but I would try to make one for Hugh. I knew that I had plenty of plywood which I had salvaged from an old tea chest. I would spend the evening looking through my comics, not that I had many as they were a luxury to me. As I left Daisy I said, "Aufwiedersehen," which made her ears stand up.

When I looked out of my window early next morning I could see that it was raining cats and dogs. Of course, it would do on the last day of the school holidays. Still, I can have a go at making Hugh's station.

During breakfast I told Dad what I was trying to do and he said that he may be able to find some old tools he could let me have, so after breakfast I followed him to a shed that he did his odd jobs in and he found me a tenon saw and a chisel. He told me two golden rules – always let the saw do the work and when using a chisel use it away from your hand. He also gave me some strong glue.

It took me ages to understand the plan and the instructions, but eventually I made a start. I became so engrossed in my work that the time flew by and before I knew it Mother was calling me for lunch.

By tea time the station was beginning to take shape and it was so satisfying to stand back and look at my efforts. The wood was once an old tea chest and now it looked like a model station. I began to picture it in its finished state. Painting might be difficult, but there were lots of old pots of paint knocking about so I will have to see what I could do.

I didn't know it then, but this was the start of my love affair with wood and the making of furniture.

When I went to bed that night on the last day of my holiday I wondered what it would be like in the new class and what I would learn. I must try to sit next to Polly as I feel we could help each other. I also had to start the German lessons with Mrs Jenkins, or to be correct, Frau Jenkins. With these thoughts I must have nodded off because in no time at all it was morning.

I had to get up early, what with my odd jobs and mucking out Daisy's stable. I had to get a move on to finish in time. I was not exactly a willing schoolboy going to school on this cold winter's morning. I had enjoyed my holidays so much and so many things had happened to me over the last few weeks.

As the little bridge came into view I saw a forlorn little figure sitting on the seat, which of course was Polly. She said that she was just having a rest, but I think that she was waiting for me. We set off on the last leg of our walk to school when we heard the frantic ringing of a bicycle bell. We turned around to see Peter coming towards us on a bike.

It was a fairly old bike, but it had been painted and looked pretty smart. Peter was so proud of it. His mum and dad had given it to him for Christmas. He tried to ride it slowly beside us but soon fell off which made us all laugh.

Polly and I were now in the same class as Peter so we bagged three desks together. I felt a bit apprehensive being in this new class with Mr Lloyd as one of the teachers. We were all making a lot of noise when in came Mrs Jenkins. She always seemed to stride everywhere, perhaps all Germans walk like that. We became very quiet and stood up saying as if with one voice, "Good morning Mrs Jenkins." Under my breath I said, "Guten Morgen."

After we had said prayers the older children and the young and not so bright ones left for their classrooms leaving about ten of us behind for our first day of torture. It turned out to be not so bad after all.

As it was so cold outside the three of us got our lunch and ate it by our desks. In between mouthfuls we told each other what we had been doing during the holidays. Of course, I had to tell Peter about my adventures at the Hall and how I had punched Joe on the nose, which made him have a good laugh.

Peter told us that he spent most of his holidays helping his father in his workshop finishing off the jobs he had to complete by Christmas. He added that his father had quite a few odd pieces of wood I could have if I came over and collected them. This gave me food for thought and I wondered if I could somehow ride Daisy over and carry some wood at the same time. I would ask Dad if he had any bright ideas.

When the bell rang we settled ourselves down at our desks to await the arrival of Mr Lloyd. He was a small man, middle-aged with grey hair. He wore glasses which he seemed to always be looking over top of. He told us that he was going to try to teach us history, but he was not very hopeful at the outcome. I thought to myself that's not a very good start.

He started to tell us about the ancient Britons which I found very interesting. Two boys were talking to each other and like a shot he went over to them and hit them over the head with a book. This was a warning to us all. When he had finished talking about the Britons we had to write it all down in our books.

At last the bell rang and I just managed to finish. We handed in our books and he told us that he would correct them and give us his verdict tomorrow. Wow betide anyone that had made a mess of it.

As we left we saw Mrs Jenkins in the hall and she called me over and asked if I had spoken to my parents about the German lessons. I told her that they thought it was very kind of her and they had given their permission. She seemed very pleased about this and asked if I could visit her home on Sunday morning. I told her that I might be able to ride Daisy over, that is if Dad would let me. "Can I bring Micky please?" I asked, she laughed and said of course I could.

The three of us started our journey home and of course they asked what Mrs Jenkins wanted me for. I had to come up with a quick answer so I told them that I had a message from my Mother. I had no intention of telling them about the German lessons until I found out if I would be able to make a go of them.

It was so much lighter walking home from school and every day from now on it would be lighter still. It seemed no time at all since we had the shortest day, roll on the summer evenings.

Polly left us at the little bridge and Peter and I made our way up the hill to our farm. He had to push his bike, but told me that it was smashing riding down the hill. We parted company and I was on my own and looking forward to supper. I thought that I might be able to find an old book of Jenny's which was all about history so that I could see what happened after the early Britons.

When I arrived home Mother seemed in a good mood. Evidently Dad had received a letter from the electricity company to say that they had started to erect the poles and we would soon be having our house wired, which would be quite an upheaval. When Dad came in I asked him if I could have a light in my workshop so that I could work there in the evenings. He gave me one of his favourite answers, "We will see," which was an indication that I may be lucky.

The next day after lunch we waited for Mr Lloyd to give us his views on what we had written about the Britons. The marks were out of ten and some kids had very low marks. When he called out my name I held my breath expecting the worst, but to my surprise I had got seven out of ten. Polly had six and Peter only had four.

Mr Lloyd glowered at us and said that anyone with marks under four would have to stay behind after school and write it all again. This was to be the way he taught us history and geography. It certainly made us work and there was no time for daydreaming.

The first week was nearly over and on Saturday morning I was to go over to Peter's home. Dad told me that I could not ride a horse and carry back pieces of wood so I would have to walk.

I got up early on Saturday morning and after I had finished my jobs I set off to Peter's leaving a very sad Micky behind. It was a long walk, but interesting to see at close quarters the different countryside. I had only passed this way in Dad's car on the way to Newton Abbot.

When I reached the farm I asked a farmhand where I might find Mr Walker, who was of course Peter's father. I was directed to a large building with double doors on the ground floor and living quarters above. I knocked on the door and Peter came out. He told me to come in and meet his dad.

Mr Walker was much younger than I had expected. He looked a much older version of Peter and like Peter had a friendly face. He was making a large wheelbarrow. Looking around I saw a beautiful unfinished cabinet standing in one corner. We shook hands and talked as he worked. He made it look so easy. He asked me what I was making and I told him about the station for Hugh and I would also like to make a simple stool.

He put down his tools and found a stool which he had made for someone. It was a very simple design and he told me the easy way to make one. He said, "Always start with something very simple and easy until you know how to use your tools." While we were talking Peter was busy rubbing a piece of wood with some sandpaper. I asked if I could help and he gave me a wooden block with a piece of sandpaper wrapped around it and copied what he was doing. Here I was having only been in this workshop a few minutes and I had learned something already.

As I worked I watched Mr Walker out of the corner of my eye trying to absorb what he was doing. The three of us talked and the time seemed to fly. I looked at my watch and said that I should have to go home soon otherwise Mother would be cross. I was about to leave with a bundle of very useful pieces of wood under my arm, when the door opened and in came a huge man.

He said, "And who is this new assistant you have?" Mr Walker told him that I was a friend of Peter's, Mr Blake's son, Henry from Long Meadow Farm. The man gave a grunt and told me to give his regards to my father. He then left without saying another word. I asked Peter who that was and he replied that it was the owner of the farm called Mr Ware. He added that he was alright, but he sometimes drank too much of the special cider he made.

I said goodbye to Mr Walker and Peter and started my long walk home with my bundle of wood. The further I went, the heavier the wood seemed to get so I had several rests at gateways along the lane.

At one of my stops I looked over the distant fields which looked like a patchwork quilt. Some were green and others a reddish-brown, ploughed in readiness for the spring sowing of wheat and barley. In the far distance I could see Dartmoor with the tors breaking the skyline. Dartmoor always looked foreboding and full of mystery. Perhaps one day I will be lucky enough to visit that distant place.

I was nearly home when I came to a junction in the lane. Looking along this lane I could see workmen putting up poles. Our electricity was getting nearer. I would have liked to have watched them but I would be late for lunch.

I arrived home just in time and I was starving. I gave Dad Mr Ware's message and how huge I thought he was. Mother quickly said that it was due to all the cider he drank and Dad said that he was not a bad chap, but a bit on the rough side and would not like to fall out with him. He was a good farmer and not a bad neighbour. Mother said that she felt sorry for Mrs Ware.

After lunch I asked Dad if I could have a ride by myself. He said yes, but stay on the farm. I saddled up Daisy, which Charlie inspected, and I was off on my own for the first time with Micky acting as out rider.

I felt a bit nervous at first but soon felt more confident. What a grand experience this was! For quite some time I kept Daisy walking and then plucked up enough courage to go into a trot, which she seemed to like.

It was strange being able to see so much more sitting on Daisy. I could see over the hedges and I thought how nice it will be in the spring when the wild flowers are in full bloom and riding through a carpet of buttercups. Micky saw some rabbits in the distance, but he didn't have a chance. Perhaps one day he will catch one.

What a smashing afternoon I was having and how lucky I am to live on this farm and to have a horse of my very own. When I returned to the house I groomed and fed Daisy giving her an extra helping of oats for being such a good girl.

The next few days were uneventful. I managed to escape the wrath of Mr Lloyd and what I was learning at school seemed to be sinking in. I had met Joe on the way to school and after a few heated words we decided to bury the hatchet. I felt sorry for the poor chap because he didn't seem to have any friends. Perhaps he will grow out of his bellicose attitude.

When I got home one evening there was a letter for me. I had never received a letter through the post before. It was from Mary asking if she and Hugh could come over the farm on Saturday morning and could I take them to see Uncle Jake. If it was not convenient could I please let her know.

I had my leg pulled all through supper about receiving a letter from a girlfriend. I hated to be teased so as soon as I had finished my meal I got a lantern and went to see to Daisy's needs for the night. I fed her and gave her some fresh water. Sitting on my stool I got out Mary's letter.

She had very neat handwriting and the letter had a female smell about it. She must have been at her mother's scent bottle. I decided to put this, my first letter, away in my private box, to join Polly's battered bar of chocolate.

I had told the family about the electricity posts being put up and this news pleased them. However, it set Mother off. She was always on to poor old Dad about having this and that. Her latest nag was about us having a telephone. Evidently the demand for her poultry, butter and cream was on the increase and she argued that it would increase even more if she had a telephone by which she could receive orders.

She explained that when the poles were up they could be used to carry a wire for the telephone. To keep her quiet Dad said that he would look into it. Mother gave Betty a wink as much to say I'm halfway there.

I had asked Polly if she would like to come over and she arrived early, probably remembering Mother's bread and cream. In fact, after I had done my jobs, I went into the kitchen and there was Polly tucking into a large piece of bread and cream. I had to laugh because she had certainly made herself at home.

The kids soon arrived and in no time at all we were in the wood. I told them that Jake was trying to teach me how to walk without being heard. We all tried it but the girls soon became fed up. Hugh and I were getting quite good, but we also had to pack it in because it was very slow going.

I had not been able to warn Jake of our visit so I scouted around to see if I could find him to ask if it was convenient for all of us to see him. I couldn't find him anywhere and feeling disappointed I made my way back to my friends. There he was talking to them. He said he had been following us most of the way and I began to think that he was more like a redskin than a white man.

We all went into the cottage and as usual Micky settled himself in front of the fire. Polly was shy at first but she soon began to join in. We scoffed a large plate of biscuits after which Jake got up and said that he had something to show us.

I had never been to the back of the cottage before but Jake led the way and I saw several huts with wire netting runs in front of them. Jake got a tin of corn and other tit bits and after knocking on the tin several times, to our surprise, all sorts of animals and birds came out.

There was a young fox with its leg in a splint, a large owl with a damaged wing, two badgers with some of their fur missing and in a very crude aviary there was an assortment of small birds injured one way or another.

Jake explained that he had been running his animal hospital for some time. Many of his patients died, but he was able to save quite a few. This was a side of Jake's character that I hadn't seen before. I had always thought of him as a soldier and he certainly went up in my estimation.

The two girls went into raptures at seeing the animals at such close quarters and we watched the animals for some time. We continued our walk around Jake's domain. He had a very neat vegetable garden with two large apple trees and fruit bushes. He went into a shed and got us an apple each which we soon got rid of. Jake told us to save the cores for the birds in the aviary.

Jake seemed sorry when we had to leave, but we had to make our way back to meet Wills. We said goodbye and thank you to Jake and ran off into the wood, followed by Micky who came out of the cottage when I called him.

On the way back I asked Hugh how he had got on with his cousins. Mary burst out laughing and said how funny it was to see the cousin called Percy running off to his mother with blood coming out of his very sore nose.

Poor Hugh had been scolded by mama, but later papa had patted him on the head telling him that Percy needed that sort of treatment. He then asked Hugh who had taught him how to box. Hugh had to tell his father that I had made a punch bag and given him a rough idea what to do if the cousins started to tease him. This pleased Hugh's papa and he was told to keep up the good work.

We fooled about on our way back through the wood and had a lot of fun. I was so sorry when we had to hurry back to the farm. As we crossed the fields Hugh told me that their governess was back and they had to have lessons every day. There was also another lady who came twice a week to teach them French. She was in fact French and very nice, but it was all a bit of a bore. I was dying to tell him about my German lesson that I was going to tomorrow with Mrs Jenkins, but I thought better of it.

As usual Wills was waiting for his passengers. Mary had told Polly that she could have a lift back to Teigncoombe. Dad was talking to Wills when Mary, full of confidence went up to him and said, "Good morning Mr Blake, can Henry ride Daisy over to the Hall next Saturday?" This took Dad by surprise and he hesitated for a moment or two and then answered by saying "Yes, I think he can. If he gets lost we will have to send out a search party." He laughed and ruffled Mary's hair like he used to with Jenny when she was younger.

As Mary got into the car she gave my hand a squeeze and said, "That's the way to get what you want Henry, see you next week for the whole day." I asked her if her Mother knew about this and with a smile she said, "No, but she will when I get home!" Wills started the car and they drove off.

John had come into the yard and said what pretty girlfriends I had and asked which one did I like best. I blushed and told him to push off. He laughed and shouted after me "Is it Polly or Mary?" Dad joined in and I was teased off and on for the rest of the day.

I had not thought about John's question before but I must say that I liked them both. Strange, because they were so very different. Mary was a bit of a bossy boots and Polly was on the shy side. Anyway, they were just good friends.

As I would be going over to the Hall next Saturday I must try to finish Hugh's station so I spent the rest of the day in my workshop.

I had asked Dad if I could ride Daisy over to Mrs Jenkins for my German lesson and he said that I could providing I only let Daisy walk.

After loads of instructions from Dad and Charlie I set off on my ride to Mrs Jenkins cottage. I was not to know then that this would be a ride that Daisy got to know backwards and I would start a friendship which would last for many, many years.

This first time we travelled along the narrow lane to Mrs Jenkins' cottage. Now there was no need to keep under cover and consequently it was a shorter journey and the time taken would be far less. I was enjoying the ride, it was so peaceful with just the sounds of Daisy's hooves and the continuous calling of the wood pigeons in the forest across the valley. I wondered what I would do with Daisy when I got there. I suppose that I could tie her to a post like they do in the cowboy films after loosening the saddle.

Micky got there before we did so Mrs Jenkins was waiting at the door. Micky was nowhere to be seen so I expected that he would be stretched out in front of the fire. He was a great one for making himself at home wherever he went.

Mrs Jenkins called out "Guten Morgen Henry." So I gave a suitable reply. I took off my boots and coat and followed Mrs Jenkins into her living room. On the table I could see several books laid out for my first German lesson.

This was to be a sort of exploratory lesson. I was asked to copy a lot of German words to see if I had any idea how to get my tongue around this strange language. After about an hour Mrs Jenkins went into the kitchen to get some of that smashing coffee.

Mr Jenkins came in. I had expected a tall man to match the size of his wife, but he was short with a neat beard and longish hair. We talked for a while. He had the habit of talking very quickly and at times he seemed to be in another world. Perhaps he was thinking about his latest work of art.

I told him about my friend Hugh and what a smashing artist he was. Mr Jenkins said that he had been commissioned to paint a portrait of Sir James in the very near future and would ask to see some of Hugh's work.

When the coffee arrived Mr Jenkins said something in German to his wife, kissed her on the cheek and left. This made her laugh which I thought was rather nice.

While we were drinking our coffee Mrs Jenkins explained that she had written three columns of words in an exercise book. The first word would be in English, the second in German and the third would be spelt as if it was in English. She told me that the correct name for this last column was phonetic.

She read through most of these words which I had to repeat after her. She then told me to take the book and try to learn them off by heart and also try to write them. She added that later on she would teach me how to put these words together, which was very difficult.

Mrs Jenkins, which I had to call her in future, put her pen down and said, "That's enough for your first lesson Henry. Today was a sort of test to see if you could be taught another language successfully. So many children are taught French, but not how to speak it as a native. I think that you will be one of the lucky one that can be taught languages."

I put on my boots and coat, raised Micky from his slumbers and went outside to see poor patient Daisy. I tightened the saddle ready to mount. Apparently, it is the custom in Germany to shake hands when meeting and leaving people so I shook her hand and said, "Aufwiedersehen Mrs Jenkins." She laughed and said, "Goodbye Henry, I will let you know when we can have another lesson."

On the way home I thought of Mrs Jenkins and how her face lit up when she smiled. She was a different person when she was not at school. Anyway, to teach our lot must have been a bit of a nightmare!

I looked at my watch and saw that I would have to get a move on to be in time for Mother's delicious Sunday lunch. I disobeyed Dad and put Daisy into a gentle trot and just managed to get home in time. Of course I had to go through the whole rigmarole of how I had got on. I finished by saying a few words in German and for some unknown reason this pleased Dad no end.

During lunch I heard some bad news. We were to be invaded by some of my awful aunts. They were Mother's sisters but they bore no resemblance to her. I would hide in my workshop. On the other hand, there might be a bob or two to be gained. I thought that Uncle Will from Newton Abbot would be forthcoming, but the other's generosity would be anyone's guess. I thought that Dad looked a bit fed up because he would have to grin and bear it.

I had no grandparents, they had all died when I was very small. Dad had very few relations. He did have a very rich great uncle who farmed a very large farm near Bristol. I had only met him a couple of times, but what I saw I liked. Mum and Dad went to stay with him every year and I had been led to believe that Dad was one of his favourites. I had gone on one of their visits and had seen what a farm should really be like, but that's another story.

Mother roused me from my daydream by asking me if I would like another helping of roast chicken. As usual I replied "Yes please."

The next week was dry and I could walk across the fields to school which saved time and energy. I walked home with Peter and Polly and even tried to ride Peter's bike, but kept falling off much to the delight of Peter and Polly who thought it a great joke.

I was getting on quite well at school. It was strange seeing Mrs Jenkins in her role as head teacher after seeing her in her own home. She looked and acted in such a strict way compared to the relaxed and friendly person I had come to know.

I was cheating a bit at history by reading a history book in advance of Mr Lloyd's lessons. It paid dividends because he really was a bad-tempered little man and it kept him at bay. He was a deadly shot with his pieces of chalk which he threw at anyone nodding off.

If it was not too cold I practised the German words Mrs Jenkins had given me, in Daisy's stable. Of course only German horses and dogs would be able to react to commands in German. This was something that I had never thought of before. Perhaps Daisy and Micky will become bilingual, which is what I hoped to achieve with a little luck.

I was glad to be going over the Hall on Saturday morning because there would be great upheaval in the farmhouse. Dad had hired two men to wire the house in their spare time, thus saving a lot of money. This would put Mother in a fussy mood and I would be better off out of the way.

On Saturday morning I set off, after being inspected by Mother to make sure that I looked respectable and Dad checking that I had saddled up Daisy correctly. With his instructions still ringing in my ears I rode out of the yard.

Down the lane I passed the men putting up the poles. They were now very close to the farm and I asked one of them how long would it take before they reached the farm. He told me that it would be next week some time depending on the weather. This would be good news for Mum and Dad so I must remember to tell them when I got home.

I arrived at the Hall without any mishaps. I felt very strange and out of place riding along the grand drive up to the house. I loved Daisy and I would never be ashamed of her, but she did need a clean up. Perhaps Mr Jones will be able to have a go at her today.

As I got nearer to the house the peacocks started their warning cries. Daisy's ears pricked up and I thought that she was going to play up so I soothed her with a few words and she calmed down.

Mary and Hugh must have heard the peacocks and came running down the drive to meet me. Hugh told me to take Daisy straight to the stable yard as Mr Jones was going to get to work on her. Mary took hold of the bridle and led the way. When we entered the yard I dismounted and Mr Jones came out. He said, "Now Master Henry, I want you to go away and not come back until I have finished the job, don't worry, I'll look after her."

Mary said our first port of call would be the kitchen to have a hot drink and perhaps cook will be able to find some cakes for us. I loved to go into the kitchen with the shelves loaded with copper pots and pans of all shapes and sizes. The large table which was white from being scrubbed over the years, and of course the smells which made my mouth water.

The very large cook was such a friendly person who always seemed to have a smile on her face. She always asked after Mother and sent her regards. In no time we were sitting at the table with a hot drink and some of cook's special cakes. After we had thanked cook we made our way to the door and she told us we were going to have Hugh's favourite meal of Irish Stew for lunch. "I hope you'll like it Master Henry." I told her I could eat a horse. She laughed and said that there won't be any horse in it. She was still laughing as we left the kitchen.

We had a happy morning just wandering around the many out-buildings and after a while Mary told Hugh that they would show me where they swim in the summer. I had no idea what she was talking about, but after a long walk through a small wood we came to a narrow river which was wide in one spot forming a sort of pool.

Even in the middle of winter it was indeed a beautiful place. Coming out of the wood to find a patch of green grass leading to the river's edge. On the far bank a belt of trees were in leaf and today the sun was finding its way through the canopy of trees and the sunlight was dancing on the water.

I was spellbound standing there looking at the water rushing past eager to reach the sea. The level of the water was high with the winter rains and I thought that the water would be calmer and very peaceful in the summer.

I came back to earth when Mary dug me in the ribs. We started to walk along the river's edge towards a wooden platform and the three of us stood on it looking down into the clear water. Hugh shouted and pointed down to where there were several fish. He told me that they were trout and his father fished here in the spring and early summer. Sometimes he was lucky to catch salmon on their way upstream to lay their eggs. The small salmon would make their way down river to reach the sea. They would then swim many hundreds of miles to where no one knew where they would stay until they were older and then they returned to the same river to lay their eggs.

Mary was getting bored with Hugh's nature lesson and she changed the subject by asking me if I could swim. I told her that I could not, in fact I had only bathed two or three times in the sea when I had gone on a village outing to the seaside. In her bossy manner she said, "Hugh and I will teach you in the summer, it will be great fun." With that remark she was on her way back through the wood, so we had to follow.

On the way back I wondered how poor old Daisy was getting on, with her short back and sides haircut, anyway, I will soon know.

I told Hugh about my talk with Mr Jenkins and his face lit up at the thought of a real artist seeing his work. He thanked me and said, "Henry, you are a real friend."

As we climbed the steps to the Hall Mary warned me about their governess. She was called Miss Henshaw and was a bit of a dragon, but her bark was worse than her bite. She would be having lunch with us and she is always telling them about table manners. "If she starts on you Henry don't take any notice, just copy what Hugh and I do."

We went through the huge doors and Evans took our coats. As he did this he gave me a smile and asked how I was. As we came to the bottom of the staircase I saw Sir James and Mr Jenkins inspecting one of the many portraits. Sir James waved and Mr Jenkins shouted "Hello Henry." Then they seemed to get into deep conversation and both turned and looked at me. Sir James had a broad grin on his face and I wondered what that was all about.

After a cleanup we went into lunch. Mary took my hand which I found very comforting. Nanny was at the head of the table and sitting next to her was Miss Henshaw. She looked very severe, but using Dad's formula about people I decided she had a nice face. I was introduced to her and I had a very friendly greeting from Nanny. The cook had excelled herself once again because the Irish Stew was just the job. We were corrected several times about our manners by Miss Henshaw, but that didn't put me off my lunch.

Mr Hooper the butler gave me a second helping. I had only met him on two occasions but I had noticed that his face was without any expression. On giving me a second helping he gave me a friendly smile.

After lunch Hugh asked me if I would like to see papa's gun room. Not knowing what a gun room was I said yes. Mary thought that it would be boring but she still came along.

When we entered the gun room I got quite a shock because hanging on the walls were the heads of all sorts of animals. I could only recognise a few of them. There was a huge lion in one corner, a stag complete with antlers, a wild-looking dog, which Hugh told me was a wild dog from Africa, several stuffed birds in glass cases and other strange beasts. Mary told me that her father had shot them on his visits to Africa.

On another wall stood a long glass case containing guns of every description and above the case there was a display of native spears and wicked looking knives. I was intrigued by this display and wondered what tales they could tell.

As we were looking around Sir James came in and told us not to touch anything, not that we could because the animals were high up put of reach and the guns were all locked up. I asked him what some of the animals were called and he told me the names of the ones that I had been unable to identify.

Sir James then took me completely by surprise by saying "What is this I hear from Mr Jenkins Henry about you learning to speak German?" My secret was now out and I was lost for words. I managed to explain that I wanted to win a scholarship to a school in Newton Abbot and I was trying to learn all I could. Also, for some unknown reason, I would like to be able to speak another language. Then I proudly said that my friend Mr Spencer thought it was a good idea. As much as to say that if he thought it was a good idea, then it must be alright.

I told him that Mrs Jenkins had offered to teach me free of charge and Dad thought that I should have a go as he could not afford such an opportunity. Sir James looked fondly at his two children and said that his two lazy brats were going to learn French, that is if they were not too lazy!

Lady Howes came in to see how we were getting on and told me that Daisy was ready for inspection. Mary, Hugh and I made for the door and Sir James said, "Aufwiedersehen Henry," to which I replied "Aufwiedersehen Herr Howes." I had to say Herr because I had no idea what 'Sir' was in German. He burst out laughing and said, "Well done Henry."

On our way to the stables Mary said, "Whatever do you want to learn German for Henry? Most of them are horrid." I told her that I only knew one and she was very nice. This made her a bit huffy, but then girls can be like that.

When I saw Daisy I couldn't believe my eyes. She looked so different. All of the shaggy hair was gone, her mane had been trimmed and she looked like a different horse. Mr Jones told me that they had put on a new set of shoes to finish off the job properly. I thanked him over and over again which seemed to please him.

It would be some time before I set off on my journey home before it got dark so I asked Hugh if we could find his parents so that I could thank them for a lovely day and for letting Mr Jones groom Daisy.

To find them in such a big place was not easy and at last we found them. After thanking them I got my coat and Lady Howes came to the door with us. To my surprise when she said goodbye she kissed me on the cheek. Hugh and Mary came to the stables with me and as I was about to mount Daisy Mary also kissed me on the cheek and said, "We will see you soon Henry." With that farewell I was on my way.

Riding Daisy on the way home was very enjoyable. She seemed more lively and her hooves were making a much louder clatter as we trotted along. I began to go through my mind the events of the day and how nice my friends were. I had a lot to thank Joe for. If I had not come across Mary and Hugh being bullied I would never have got to know them.

When I reached the lane where the workmen were putting up the poles I was amazed how far they had gone in one day. I wondered how the electricians had got on at the farm. I hope that Mother won't be in too much of a state about the upheaval.

When I arrived home I went into the kitchen and asked the family to come out and see how Daisy looked. They couldn't believe it was the same horse. When Dad saw that she had been reshoed he said how kind it was of Sir James to allow his men to do so much work and when I told them that Lady Howes had kissed me goodbye all Mother could say was "Oh my, fancy that!"

The house was in a bit of a mess. There were wires sticking out of holes in the walls and in some places the floorboards were up. Later I was glad to see that the electricians had been working in the barn. Perhaps Dad will be kind hearted and give me a light in my workshop.

After my supper I went to see Daisy and bed her down for the night. I sat on my stool and practised speaking the German words Mrs Jenkins had given to me last Sunday. I had managed to learn how to spell some of them. I had no idea if I had got the pronunciation right or if they sounded like double Dutch. Anyway, I will know tomorrow when I go to see Mrs Jenkins. After all, it will only be my second lesson and I will have a long way to go. Now that my secret is out I will really have to try my hardest.

CHAPTER 3

At last winter had passed and spring had turned into early summer. The trees were covered in the glory of their foliage. The fields were carpeted with wild flowers and the birds were trying to satisfy their never-ending appetite. Most important of all, we now had electricity and Mother had got her way about the telephone. We also had a wireless set and I could hear what was going on in the outside world.

Over the past few months I had gone to the Hall many times and my friends had visited the farm frequently. Peter also managed to join us when he could and of course Polly was a regular visitor.

Sometimes, when I went to the Hall, Mary, Hugh and I went for a ride, but always in the company of one of the stable hands to make sure that we didn't do anything stupid. Henry the foal was growing and perhaps one day in the future I may get the chance to ride him.

I was getting on quite well at school and so far I had managed to keep out of trouble. Mrs Jenkins kept me busy with sometimes two evening lessons a week. She fetched me and brought me home in her car. On several occasions she came into the house and had long conversations with Mum and Dad. I was banished to the stable or my workshop, so I had no idea what they were hatching. I knew that Mrs Jenkins was pleased with my progress in my German lessons, perhaps that was what it was all about.

I was enjoying my woodwork and I had scrounged some empty boxes from the village shop. I made a stool as instructed by Peter's father and it turned out quite well. With my tongue in cheek I asked Mother if she could put it on her stall in the market. She told me not to be so silly, but Dad intervened and told her to give it a try for a couple of weeks. Much to my surprise it sold in the second week and I made another one and that sold as well. I was in business!

I took one of my stools down to show Peter's father and he advised me how to give it a better finish and said I should make two or three at a time which would be much easier. I had been a busy little chap, which I enjoyed, but most important of all was the fact that I now had some money which I kept in my private box in my bedroom.

The spring and early summer was a very busy time for farmers. Haymaking was now on the agenda. Dad and John were always listening to the weather forecast on the wireless. Hay when cut had to be turned and dried before it was collected, so the timing of the cutting had to be just right.

For me as a small boy, haymaking was great fun. I didn't have the worry that Dad and John had. I had told Hugh and Mary about haymaking and they asked if they could come over to the farm and help.

Dad told me that he was going to cut the grass during this week and he hoped to gather it on Saturday. I asked him if my friends could come and help. He said yes, providing that we kept out of the way.

I spoke to Mother about this and she said that she would telephone Lady Howes to see of the children could come over for the day on Saturday. Mother was very stingy about telephone calls, but she rang the Hall putting on her posh voice. Having fixed it all up, I asked her if Polly could come as well and she said that she could.

At school the next day I asked Polly if she would like to come haymaking and she seemed so pleased that I had asked her. She said she would ask her mother and let me know. She said she would also get round her father to let her telephone Mary to see if she could get a lift. It was no good asking Peter because he would be helping on the farm.

Dad was lucky, he had cut two fields and the weather was holding. There was always great excitement when a field of hay was being cut. Friends and neighbours came with their dogs and shot guns.

A field was cut, starting on the outside and working towards the centre. This drove the rabbits and hares into the centre. As the area of grass became smaller, these unfortunate animals tried to escape and were shot at, or chased by the dogs.

I arrived home from school just at the right time. Micky and I joined the party as the mower was getting near the centre. I had Micky on his lead and he was barking and pulling like mad, so I let him off and away he went like a shot out of a gun. Several rabbits were caught by the dogs and some were shot. The hares were very different, They had a terrific burst of speed and they ran from side to side. There wasn't a dog present that was fast enough to catch them. I felt sorry for the animals, but this was country life and I had to learn to accept it, also, I liked Mother's rabbit pie!

Much to my surprise Micky turned up with a rabbit in his mouth. He dropped it at my feet as if to say I too can catch rabbits. By now he had grown into a big dog and when he ran he loped along and if he felt like it, he could be very fast. When I get back to the farm I will have to give him a good brush otherwise Mother will create.

On Friday evening Mother and Betty were very busy making some of their smashing pasties. Evidently, we were going to have a picnic lunch in the hay field tomorrow, which will be great fun with my friends present.

I went to bed that night thinking of the haymaking. Perhaps George will let us help him load his cart.

I got up very early the next morning so that I could do all my jobs before the kids arrived. Mother now had a lot more hens so the egg collecting took some time and they had to be ready for the man to collect and deliver them to a packing place in Newton Abbot.

Mary, Hugh and Polly arrived and I was glad to see that they had old clothes on. The girls had sun hats as it was going to be a very hot day. We wandered around the field watching the men folk loading the hay on to the carts. The carts full of hay were taken to a corner of the field where Charlie was arranging it to form a rick. This was a very skilful job which he always did.

Dad came with his cart well loaded and he used a pitch fork to transfer huge quantities of hay in each go. It must be hard work and I bet he will be tired tonight. We collected what was dropped and gave it to Charlie.

When the cart was unloaded, Dad lifted the girls on to it and Hugh and I climbed up and we all had a ride to the other side of the field. I saw George about to go to the rick and I persuaded him to let us sit on the seat in the front of the cart. It was a tight squeeze and Polly sat on my lap. I had to put my arms around her waist which made her giggle, I must say it gave me a nice feeling. I gave her a couple of tight squeezes which made her laugh even more.

Mary started to tickle me in the ribs which set me off and by this time George was also laughing at our antics, but he soon became stern and told us to behave ourselves otherwise we might fall off.

This was my first childlike physical contact with girls and how innocent it was. Nature was beginning to take its course and it made me feel a bit peculiar in a way which is difficult to explain.

We all had a fine old time and when we saw Mother and Betty come through the gate loaded with large baskets, we realised how hungry we felt. Dad had set up an old folding table which Mother covered with a cloth and then set out the food she had prepared.

The table was placed in the shade of a grand old elm tree. I was glad to get out of the hot sun for a bit, but some of Mother's lemonade cooled us down. There was quite a spread – pasties, bread and cheese and a bowl of apples. There were several flagons of cider from Peter's farmer, Mr Ware. Dad had hired two extra men for the day because in the late afternoon the cows would have to be milked and the hay had to be brought in that day, even if they all had to work until it was dark.

This was the custom on all the farms. The farmer always supplied food and plenty of cider. Sometimes owners of large farms would send over some of their hands to help the small farmers with their harvests.

We all tucked in together with the farm hands and I wondered what Hugh and Mary thought of this. I had my doubts about whether they had ever had a meal with any of their many servants. Anyway, it will do them good to mix with other people. Somehow I think that this was what Sir James wanted for his children as it would broaden their outlook.

It was now late afternoon and looking at my watch I was sorry to see that my friends would soon be leaving. We had such good fun. Hugh and I had buried the girls in hay and we all covered with it. Mother was very cross about this but she managed to clean the girls up a bit just in time because who should come striding through the hay field but Sir James.

When Mary saw her father she gave a shriek and ran to meet him. He picked her up and gave her a kiss and continued to carry her to where we were all standing. Dad came over to greet his unexpected guest. Mother became very flummoxed and the farm hands looked surprised to see the big white chief in our hay field.

Sir James said that he had come to fetch his two brats and to see if they had been behaving themselves. Mother said, in her posh voice, that they had been as good as gold and they seemed to have had a very enjoyable time.

My friends and I started back to the farmhouse followed by Dad and Sir James, who seemed to be in deep conversation about something or other. I hope it was nothing to do with me. Mother had now joined them so we ran on.

When we reached the car, Mary told me that if it was as hot as it had been today, we could all have a swim in the river next time we visited the Hall. She went on to say that she and Hugh had tried it but it was very cold.

Before getting into the car my three friends thanked Mum and Dad for a smashing day. Polly gave my hand a squeeze and said that she would see me on Monday. With a lot of waving and shouts of goodbye, Sir James drove out of the yard.

During the next few weeks I had several swims in the river under the watchful eye of Miss Henderson. Hugh made quite an effort to teach me how to swim, and with the instructions given by Miss Henderson, I was making progress. We had great fun on those warm summer days.

My German lessons were becoming quite frequent and I could now say a few simple sentences. Jake had given me a German dictionary and with help I was able to enlarge my vocabulary. Jake provided this help when I went to see him on the many fine summer evenings.

Sometimes we played a sort of hide-and-seek and I did enjoy this.

The idea was for him to go into the wood, telling me roughly where he would be and then I had to find him and creep up to him as closely as I could without being seen or heard. This was very difficult because he seemed to have eyes in the back of his head. Learning how to do this was a very slow job, but it was great fun.

One evening Dad said that he was going to ride over to the far side of the farm with John, to look at a couple of fields and asked if I would like to come. Like a shot I said yes.

We set off, just the three of us, and I really felt great being with Dad and John. I had no idea what they wanted to look at. The swallows were flying high in the sky which was a sign of good weather. The fields of barley and wheat were beginning to turn colour giving them a golden look, with the sun getting lower in the sky. Micky was going mad chasing rabbits coming out of their burrows for their last meal of the day.

When we came to the two fields I understood from the conversation that Dad and John were not pleased with how they were being used. The problem being the fact that there were several very large rocks in various places. There was also plenty of weed about.

Lately I had been finding myself taking an interest in farming and I had wondered why so much beef was reared on the nearby farms. The price fluctuated so much that the farmers never knew how much they would fetch at market. I wondered why there were no sheep in this area. Was the ground too good for them, or were they not profitable?

I know that it was not my place to make any suggestions, as children of my age are meant to be seen and not heard. I took the bull by the horns and timidly I said to Dad "Why don't you rear sheep on these two rough fields? The hedges are tall and solid to keep them in." I waited for an outburst of mind your own business, but instead John burst out laughing and said to Dad, even Henry thinks that it would be a good idea. He went on to explain that he had been trying to persuade Dad to do just that.

Dad said that he knew nothing about sheep and John was no better. It would be quite a gamble. I also knew that Dad's rich uncle had died and when he and Mum returned from the funeral, I overheard Mother telling Betty that Sam had been left quite a nice legacy.

I put my spoke in again by saying that perhaps there was someone in the village that had reared sheep. John laughed again and said that he knew the very man for the job and he would work on a part-time basis. He was retired, but very fit and wanted something to do because he had been with sheep all his life and even had a very active sheep dog.

With a laugh Dad said that he had been out voted, so sheep it will be and if it didn't work out he would tan our hides!

On the way back I could not understand what made me think about sheep. Mr Lloyd had started to tell us a bit about the history of the West Country and how it thrived on the wool trade, but cheap and a better type of wool now came from Australia and New Zealand, which cut the demand for West of England wool.

We all galloped back to the farm, but Daisy and I were left well behind. What a wonderful evening I had with dear Dad and John.

When we eventually went into the kitchen Mother was in a bit of a state. She said that we would never guess who she had as a visitor. Of course we didn't try. She said that just after we had left Lady Howes arrived and dropped a bit of a bombshell. It gave her a shock to see this posh car drive into the yard and Mr Evans in his uniform. Mother started to natter on until Dad cut her short and asked what Lady Howes had wanted.

Mother calmed down and said, "Lady Howes would like our Henry to go to the seaside for two weeks holiday in August." She and Sir James were going to France and Nanny would be taking Hugh and Mary to Teignmouth. Hugh and Mary had kicked up quite a fuss and wanted Henry to go with them.

Evidently, the Howes had some friends who lived in a house on the seafront and they would be away themselves during August and their house would be complete with a cook and servants to look after us. Nanny would be there of course to keep us in order. If I wanted to go with them we were to let Lady Howes know.

I knew that this had given Mother a shock, but it had given me an even greater shock. I had only been away from home once before and that was with Mum and Dad to visit Dad's uncle in Somerset. That was on a farm and not a strange town. Mother asked me if I would like to go so I told her I would think about it.

With my mind in a whirl I led Daisy to her stable and started to groom her, thinking all the while about this holiday. I would be living in a strange house, sleeping in a strange room and in a strange place, without any of my family. Even at my age I thought it unusual for people like the Howes to ask a farmer's son to go on holiday with their children. I know that Hugh and Mary had changed since our friendship began and I had grown to like them very much. Hugh was no longer the shy boy I knew when we first go to know each other and Mary had become less of a 'Miss Madam'. Perhaps this was why I had been asked.

I was sitting on my stool when Dad came in and he asked me if I had made up my mind. As always I asked his advice and he told me not to miss such a treat and if I was unhappy I could always come home. He then went on to tell me that when Sir James had fetched his kids from the haymaking, he had said that his kids were very fond of me and they had become more 'normal'. He also said that he thought I was a grand young lad.

Dad started to walk to the door but stopped and turned around saying, "Henry, you go and learn how these people conduct themselves. Who knows, it might help you in the future. You have nothing to lose." At that moment Mother came in and said, "Your girlfriend is on the telephone and wants to speak to you Henry." I went red and ran up to the house leaving Mum and Dad having a good laugh.

I was not used to speaking on the telephone, not that I had much chance, because Mary never seemed to stop talking. She went into great detail about what the three of us would be able to do in Teignmouth. At last I got a word in and told her that I would love to join them. I heard her shout, "Hugh, Henry can come with us." So the die was cast once more and I had another adventure on the horizon.

When I joined Mum and Dad in the kitchen I was told by Mother that I would have to go into Newton Abbot to get some suitable clothes for my holiday as her son was not going to look out of place. I said that this will cost a lot of money and I looked at Dad. He gave me a wink and said that he could manage it.

When I went to bed that night I just couldn't go to sleep. I kept asking myself if I had made the right decision. I really had no choice because I didn't want to let my friends down. If I was homesick I would just have to grin and bear it. I had been to Teignmouth once before on a village outing and I thought that it was a smashing place. That was a long time ago and my memory was a bit hazy on the details. With these thoughts I at last fell asleep.

On the way to school the next morning I told Polly and Peter about my holiday. Polly seemed most put out and Peter said, "Fancy my friend Henry mixing with the nobs." Polly was very offhand for the rest of the day, which upset me because I liked this little friend of mine, she was back to normal after a day or two.

I went to see Jake that evening on Daisy. Of course Micky acted as out rider. Going through the woods was so different to the winter. Everything was growing like mad and it was slow going. As usual Jake was pleased to see me and we greeted each other in German. In fact, we could have a very stilted conversation in this strange language. When I told him about my holiday he said he already knew all about it. He always seemed to know everything that was going on. Perhaps he had a sort of bush telegraph. I then remembered that he was also on the telephone which for some unknown reason the Government had organised.

As usual I had a pleasant time with Jake. Dad had told me to say that he would always be welcome at the farm if he would care to come and to my surprise he said that he would like to very much indeed.

On my way back I took my time and enjoyed just being out and about on this summer's evening. There were rabbits, which Micky chased without success. In the distance I saw a dog fox looking for his supper. As I got nearer to the farmhouse the sun was one huge red ball sinking behind the distant hills. Looking around I began to think whatever am I doing, leaving all this for two weeks of my school holidays? I hope that it will be worth it.

Several weeks have passed and the school holidays have started. As the weather was not too good I had been to see Peter and his Dad on several days and I seemed to learn something new on each occasion. Mr Walker had sharpened my tools for me and this made the making of my stools much easier.

I had seen lots of Hugh and Mary and I could just about swim for a very short distance. I had got to know Nanny and she was very kind, but strict about how we behaved. She made it only too clear that when we went on holiday we were to be on our best behaviour.

Mother took me to Newton Abbot on the bus to get me some new clothes, which of course included swimming trunks. I hated shopping and I was glad when it was all over. I thought to myself that Dad will have a fit when he finds out how much Mother had spent. When we got home I had to go through the trouble of trying it all on. All the time I was being lectured on what to wear for different occasions, which I found very boring, so I switched off and had a bit of a daydream. I kept saying yes and no to Mother which at times were in the wrong places. At last Mother gave me a friendly smack on the bottom and told me to push off.

At last the time came for my holiday and I would soon be on my way to Teignmouth, my first holiday away from home without Mum and Dad. When I went to bed the night before my departure I looked out of the window at a view I was so used to. I wondered what I would be looking at for the next two weeks out of my bedroom window. Would I be able to adjust to a complete change of surroundings and a change of lifestyle?

Since I had known Mary and Hugh, like them I had changed. I was even speaking more like them and using words which I didn't know existed before. Was this a good thing or was I just aping my betters?

Somehow I couldn't talk to Dad about this so I mentioned it to my friend Jake. He was so much a man of the world and I felt that I could always ask him about things like this. As usual he went into one of his silent spells and then said to me "Henry, you don't know how lucky you are to have this opportunity to further your education, providing that you never forget who you really are and never try to be someone else."

I was not to know how right he was.

The next morning was bright and sunny. Charlie our weather expert said that we were in for a fine hot spell, which would be ideal for my holiday. He was pretty good at forecasting the weather. There were all sorts of signs he looked for, some of which were beyond me. Anyway, I hoped he was right.

I put on my posh new clothes which made me feel a bit of a cissy. My case was packed and much to my surprise Dad gave me two ten shilling notes. I had never had a whole pound in my pocket before. Dad told me that the Howes were going to pay for everything during my holiday, but it was only right that I should have some money of my own in case it was needed. He told me that I should only spend what I had to and if I could bring some back with me, all well and good.

At last the car came and I had to say goodbye to my family. Hugh and Mary were very excited and I could see Nanny was having a job to keep them in order. I got into the car and with a lot of goodbyes we were off.

I turned around to have a good look at dear Mum and Dad and a bit of a lump came into my throat. This feeling soon passed as we started to have some fun in the back of the car. Mary told me how smart I looked and they both pulled my leg about it.

It was a short journey and as we came down the hill into Teignmouth what I saw was indeed a lovely view. I could see the river flowing into the harbour where there were ships being loaded from the quays. On one side a large red cliff was guarding the entrance to the river. On that side there was a village and on the other side I could see Teignmouth with its pier and large buildings on the seafront. There was a long bridge across the river joining Teignmouth to the village, which I later found out was called Shaldon. With the blue sea acting as a sort of backdrop, what a smashing sight it was.

We drove into the town and then on to the seafront. There were a lot of people in holiday clothes and everywhere looked busy. The house that we were to stay in was at the river end of the seafront. It was a tall, grand looking place in a terrace. When the car stopped outside a lady came out to greet us. She was the housekeeper called Mrs Ryder and Nanny greeted her as an old friend, which was a good sign. Wills took the luggage in.

As Wills was about to leave Nanny told him that she would let him know when we needed him. I asked Hugh about this and he told me that Wills was staying with his sister who lived in the town. If the weather was not suitable for going to the beach, Wills would be able to take us to other places.

We were shown to our different rooms by one of the servant girls.

My room was on the same landing as Hugh's and Mary's and overlooked the river and harbour. I must say that it all looked very cosy. I was fascinated by the view of the busy harbour and I found it difficult to leave the window. I finally had to as Nanny had told us to unpack our clothes, put them away and meet her in half an hour in the hall. After we had all inspected each other's rooms we went downstairs.

Nanny was waiting for us and said we were going for a walk on the seafront to buy buckets and spades. If we behaved ourselves we might buy some ice cream as well. Just in front of the house there were tennis courts and then a green bank with a slope leading to the promenade. The first thing we did was to run over to look at the beach and sea. How inviting it looked. There were children and grown-ups swimming and paddling. There seemed to be a continuous sound of laughter and shouting. There were also boatmen shouting, "Trips in the bay." I asked Nanny if we might have a trip one day and she said, "Yes, but all in good time young man."

We all had an ice cream which was smashing. We then went into the town and Nanny bought us a bucket and spade each. We had a look around which took some time, especially in a large toy shop with a window full of model trains. Nanny managed to drag us away as it was nearly lunch time.

During lunch Nanny told us that we would be going to the beach after lunch and there would be a beach hut available for us. Mrs Ryder would take us down and get us fixed up. So after lunch we all trooped down to the beach complete with buckets and spades, swimming costumes and towels.

We reached our hut and on either side there were mothers with children of all ages. They looked us up and down and likewise we did the same, as if to say would we all join in and have some fun.

We changed into our swimming costumes and being children were talking to our neighbours in no time at all. Of course Mary was the first to break the ice, what confidence that girl had. Our new friends decided to have a swim and asked us to join them. Nanny told us to wait until she had put on her costume. When you are young there is a tendency to think that grown-ups are old, but seeing her in her swimsuit changed my mind.

Watching the other children I dived right in. The tide was only half in so the water was shallow and how much warmer it was than the river at the Hall. It was also much easier to swim in. I asked one of my new friends about this and he told me that salt water was more buoyant than fresh water.

Mary took some time to get under water so I started to splash her which was great fun hearing her shriek. Hugh was a good swimmer and

I felt envious. With Nanny's help I could swim reasonably well by the end of my holiday.

How I enjoyed that first afternoon on the beach and how friendly everyone was. There must have been a gang of about ten of us playing on the beach and at the end of the two weeks there were even more.

In my bedroom on the first night I felt a bit guilty at not feeling homesick for Mum and Dad, and of course Daisy and Micky. Posh people seem to have a rule of having a bath every night, which I thought was a bit daft after being in the sea several times during the afternoon, so I will be having fourteen baths over the next two weeks. They call supper dinner which is very strange. These small things made me realise what a different way of life I have got myself into.

The next morning I was awakened by Hugh and Mary jumping on the bed and Mary sitting on top of me. I got rid of Mary by tickling her in the ribs and after a lot of fooling around I chased them out of the room with the help of a pillow.

While we were having breakfast Nanny told us that it would be best to call her Mrs Lambert when we were on the beach because some of the children might tease us if we called her Nanny. I then made up my mind to always call her Mrs Lambert, after all she was not my nanny. She added that we could have a look around the town until eleven o'clock and then we would all have a swim.

She put on her stern expression and told us that there were a few places out of bounds to us. We must not go anywhere near the docks or streets leading to the docks. The pier was next on the list and also the sea wall by the railway line. She then told us to push off and to behave ourselves.

We decided to walk the whole length of the seafront until we came to the railway line. When we reached the end I could see the walking area on the top of the sea wall which protected the railway line from the sea.

The sea had become a bit rough and the tide was in. Looking along the sea wall we could see some of the waves coming up and over the pathway. No wonder this was out of bounds.

I saw a signal drop in the distance and heard the sound of a train coming down the line towards us. It was a grand sight seeing the smoke coming out of the funnel. The sun seemed to make the smoke change colour as it wended its way past the tall red and green cliffs on the far side. The engine looked so powerful with its parts of brass gleaming in the bright sunshine. The engine driver gave us a friendly wave and the noise was overwhelming as the train sped past us. I had never seen a train at close quarters before and for that matter I had never been on a train.

As we walked back to meet Nanny I went into one of my daydreams and I began to think about the train. I wondered where the train had come from and where it was going. I had been in the country all my young life and how different the outside world was to what I had been used to. It was like starting all over again.

Mary took my hand and asked if I was alright because I was so quiet. It was then that I realised that I was very fond of this complicated young girl who lived in another world to my simple existence. I explained my problem as best I could and I was told not to be so silly because she and Hugh would look after me.

The first week seemed to fly by. The weather was fine and very warm so we went on to the beach every day. We played cricket, which of course was new to me, but I soon got the idea. When the sea was rough it was great fun playing in the waves. Hugh was able to sort of float in on the breakers which looked great fun. Mary and I tried it but all we got was a mouthful of sea water, so in the end we gave up.

Mrs Lambert had organised a trip in the bay. This would again be something new for me. I had never before been in a boat and I do hope that I won't disgrace myself by being seasick or nervous.

There were very few passengers so we sat at the sharp end which I was to learn was called the bows. The other end was the stern. As we went out past the pier the sea became a bit rough and this felt like having a gallop on Daisy. Sometimes the boat would come down with a gentle bump sending spray into the boat. This caused shrieks of laughter from the females on board. Hugh loved it and stood up keeping his balance by moving his legs with the mood of the boat. I think that the name for this was 'getting his sea legs'.

I sat and looked at my friend Hugh and how very different he was to the shy, timid little chap I had met in the lane not so long ago. Perhaps he will be tough like his ancestors after all. Little did I know then how tough we will all have to be in the distant future.

The early morning visits to my bedroom by Mary and Hugh became a ritual. The three of us lay on the bed and talked about all sorts of things. I asked Hugh what he wanted to be when he grew up and without any hesitation he said that he wanted to be an artist. Mary butted in by saying that it would upset Papa. She turned to me, gave me a hug and said, "What would Henry like to be?" Apart from being embarrassed by the hug, I was silent for a time while I decided on my answer. I had often thought about this and I had come to the conclusion that it had to be a job to do with the country.

I knew that it was 'pie in the sky', but I would really like to learn about it all. I would like to go to the College of Agriculture which was on the way to Dartmoor. I told my friends all about my dreams and how they were only dreams because Dad could never afford it. I would like to manage a large farm or estate because I would never be able to own one.

I had never mentioned this to anyone before, but things tend to come out when I am talking to Mary and Hugh. Hugh said that this was what Papa wanted him to do, but he was not going to and that was that.

Mary said, in a sad sort of way, that she would have to marry some boring sort of chap in her own class. "Perhaps I may be lucky and marry you Henry, or someone like you." After that stupid remark I told them to shove off as we ought to be getting ready for breakfast.

Breakfast was quite a feast. There were heated containers on a sideboard containing bacon, eggs, mushrooms and all sorts of things that I didn't even try. I must say that I made a bit of a pig of myself. However, I was glad to see that Hugh was also eating well because I remembered our first meal together at the Hall and he only picked at his food. There was no need to worry about Mary, she ate like a horse and I sometimes wondered where she put it all!

During our second week the weather was not so good so Wills took us on several trips. We visited Torquay, which was a much larger resort than Teignmouth. There were a lot of large, posh hotels and some very big shops. We walked along the seafront but there was no long stretch of sand or beach huts as in Teignmouth. We all said that we were glad that we were not staying in Torquay.

One day we went to Dartmoor. Here I was at last seeing at close quarters what I had looked at from such a long way away. It was a beautiful, but barren, place and we drove for miles without seeing many trees. We went down a very steep hill to Dartmeet, this was a very lovely place with a river flowing between rocks. The water looked so fresh and pure. We climbed over the rocks with the water gushing past us. After we had played for a while we all had a Devonshire cream tea which went down a treat.

On another day we went across the river in a ferry to Shaldon and had a great time looking for crabs under the many rocks. We walked around the headland below the tall red cliff known as The Ness.

Hugh and I caught some small crabs which we tried to put down the back of Mary's dress. She screamed so much that we had to stop that prank. We enjoyed ourselves so much that we persuaded Mrs Lambert to take us there again.

Unfortunately, it was the last day of our holiday so we spent the whole day on the beach. To make the most of it we swam many times with Mrs Lambert watching us like a hawk. She had to keep shouting to us not to go out too far. I thought that the poor lady would have a sore throat by the time it was time for us to say our fond farewells to the many friends we had made. We felt so sad to think that we may never see them again. How wrong we were.

Going home the next morning and driving back up the hill, we looked back in envy at the view behind us. We were not the happy children of a fortnight ago. Mind you, we looked very different, all brown as berries and under our clothes our bodies were the same.

When we arrived at the farm there was Mother, who gave me a big kiss and a cuddle. She asked Mrs Lambert if I had been a good boy and before she had a chance to answer, Mary said, "Of course he has." The two grown-ups laughed. I watched the car drive off wishing that I was still in it.

Micky was going mad with pleasure and kept jumping up at me. He was now a big dog and at times he nearly knocked me down. Dad had now joined us and even he gave me a hug. We went into the kitchen and there was dear old Betty, so I had another kiss.

I had to sit down and tell them all about my holiday in great detail, which seemed to take ages. But they had to know everything, where I had stayed, what sort of food did I have, where had I been and so on. In fact the questions were endless. I dug into my pocket and handed Dad ten shillings saying that was all that was left out of the pound he had given me. He told me to save it for another time, because he thought that I would have spent it all.

When I managed to escape, Micky and I went to see Daisy. When I called her she galloped across the field and we greeted each other like long-lost friends. I told her that we would have a nice ride tomorrow.

That evening Mother made me sit down and with her help I wrote a letter to Sir James and Lady Howes thanking them for such a lovely holiday. I had strict instructions to go into the village and post it tomorrow. I didn't tell her that I would post it in Teigncoombe, because I intended to see if Polly was about.

I was in my own bed once more and I didn't have to have a bath! Although I must confess that I had enjoyed this ritual when I had got used to it. I looked out of the window expecting to see ships in a harbour and I was glad to see the countryside again, which I loved so much.

The next morning Mother let me off from doing my odd jobs and I asked her if she would mind me going off for the day on Daisy. She agreed and packed me a simple lunch and in no time at all Micky, Daisy and I were off.

First of all I went to see Polly. She told her mother that she was going for a walk with me. When we were out of the village she climbed up behind me on Daisy and as we went along I told her all about my holiday, leaving out my growing friendship with Mary. Polly was such a good friend and it was nice to feel her arms around my waist. We had a good chat and I took her back home. I had never been inside the vicarage and today was no exception.

My next port of call was to visit Mrs Jenkins. I found that she was at home and I had to go through the whole rigmarole about my holiday. I was allowed to tell her in English, but when the cross-examination was over we switched to German. When I was away I found myself trying to say in my mind what I was thinking about in German. For some unknown reason I knew that I had to be able to speak this difficult language. Of course, we had a cup of coffee and she told me that my lessons would start in a day or two and she would let me know when.

Then I went to see my friend Jake. When I got to his cottage I saw a strange car outside with a soldier sitting at the wheel. I knocked on the door and Jake asked me in. Sitting in a chair I saw an Army Officer with red tabs on his collar. Jake introduced me by saying "Peter, this is young Henry whom I was telling you about."

Then Jake took me by surprise by talking to me in simple German sentences which I managed to answer. Jake turned to his friend and said, "This lad will be useful to you in a few years time." Not knowing what was going on I left feeling quite confused. I made my way back to the farm and had the feeling that my young life was being taken over by unknown forces. As Dad says "What will be, will be." Only time will tell.

CHAPTER 4

It is now the spring of 1934 and I am once more sitting on the seat by the little bridge. I seem to be drawn to this quiet spot with my two friends Micky and Daisy. Daisy was now getting a bit long in the tooth and the best she could do was a fast trot. She will soon have to retire from active service. I try not to think about this because I will be lost without her as a means of transport and most important of all, her company.

Hugh and Mary were away at school most of the time and I only saw them during their school holidays. I was however a frequent visitor to the Hall. Sir James asked me to ride over and exercise the colt, Henry, who had grown into a handsome pony. He was temperamental and at times bad tempered, but when I rode him he was as good as gold. Horses are such strange creatures and some have a mind of their own.

On occasions Sir James joined me on these rides and I got to know the extent of the estate. There was a slump in the farming industry and he had two small farms unoccupied and liked to visit them now and then to see that the farmhouses were alright. He had a very gruff and autocratic manner, but his bark was worse than his bite. He was forever asking me questions about my family and what I was going to do with my life. He really was a nosy old so and so.

I am now fourteen years of age and no longer a young boy, although I am not yet a young man. What a difficult age to be. Strange things were happening in my lower quarters, which at times proved to be very embarrassing. I found myself looking at girls in a completely different light. My friendship with Polly was not quite the same. She has grown into such a pretty girl and I felt an attraction to her.

After a lot of swotting and good luck I had managed to win a full scholarship to St. John's College which was situated on the outskirts of Newton Abbot. Dad had managed to scrape together enough money for the uniform and books. I was a day boy and travelled to and from school by bus. I found this an awful fag. At least I had Polly's company on the journey, as she also went to school in the town.

The College was very strange at first, but I am enjoying it. That is to say, as much as anyone can enjoy school. I found myself in the Officers Training Corps, or OTC as it was called. We were in army uniform and were being taught how to shoot using old rifles with a small bore.

My German was by now pretty good and I listened to that idiot Hitler shouting his head off; that was when I could bag the wireless set from Mum and Dad. I could understand most of what he was shouting about and I didn't like what I heard.

As I sat there I had to laugh to myself. At our last OTC lesson a few of us were waiting for the retired Sergeant Major to turn up and I acted like the German officers I had seen at the cinema, shouting instructions to my friends in German. We were all having a good laugh, not knowing that the Headmaster was watching our carry on.

He was a very strict Head, but on this occasion he proved that he had a sense of humour. When he strode up to us we thought that we were in for a wigging and I thought that I was in for it. Instead he grinned, which was most unusual and started to give me military commands such as 'stand to attention', 'stand upright', 'slope arms' and so on, all in very good German.

I was taken completely by surprise but automatically did as I was told. I had not mentioned the fact that I was learning German when I was interviewed for entrance to the College because at the time I thought it unwise as anything German was not exactly popular. The Head told me to come and see him in his study after the parade.

Shaking in my boots after the parade, I knocked on the Head's door and went into his study. This place was only visited for punishments to be given to wrong-doers and so far, touch wood, I had not been sent to this torture chamber.

Much to my surprise he told me to sit down and said, "Blake, I want you to do me a favour." He then went on to tell me that he had a lifelong friend who was a German Jew. He and his family had managed to get out of Germany and were now living in London. He was something in the banking world, which was beyond me. Anyway, his son was coming to the College next week and would I help him settle in because he spoke very little English. He was to be in my class and he would appreciate it if I could help him.

Of course I said yes and anyway, I had no choice. On the other hand I thought that it would also help me to master this difficult language. The Head went on to say that he was a nice lad, about my age and as he was his good friend's son, he had to do what he could to help the family as much as possible. If he could make the boy feel at home in his new country, it would be one worry lifted from the family's shoulders.

I wondered what this German boy would be like. There were several Jews at the College and I found them quite nice chaps. Dad had always told me that he thought it unfair for people to dislike Jews just because they were Jews. Perhaps it was because they were able to make money easier than anyone else and they always kept together. He also thought that over the centuries they had been punished enough for crucifying Jesus.

I pondered all this as I sat by the little bridge but now it was getting dark so I made my way home. Daisy had made this journey so often that I just had to sit in the saddle and daydream. Micky was about somewhere. He kept coming in to view and when I looked again he was gone.

When I eventually went into the kitchen no one was there, but I could hear voices in the sitting room. I made myself look presentable and in I went to investigate what was going on.

There was Mother, Dad, Betty, Charlie and John's girlfriend, Gertrude. We all called her Gertie. She was a nice girl, very pretty and she must have been smart to snare 'Good time John!' Everyone had a drink in their hand and seemed in a very happy frame of mind. I asked what was going on and Dad got up and poured me a very small glass of beer. He then told me, "We are celebrating the news that John and Gertie are going to be married."

Gertie had been to the house several times and John had calmed down a bit. He only went to the pub at the weekends and no longer chased the girls, which used to be a full-time hobby! I went over and kissed Gertie and gave John a hug. I was so fond of him and I did hope that he would be as happy as Mum and Dad. John asked me who I was going to marry, Polly or Mary? This stupid question made me blush and they all laughed.

George and Olive had left the cottage several months ago to move to a town nearer to Olive's family. I had been sorry to see them leave because they had always been so kind to me when I was a small lad.

Evidently John and Gertie were going to live in the cottage after their wedding in a couple of months time. John was going to be busy decorating and making the place look nice and I thought that I would probably be roped in to help. Still, John had always helped me so I did not mind.

I sat there listening to the chit-chat and I thought about dear Aunt Betty and Charlie. These two seemed so fond of each other and somehow I thought that one day they would get married. Our farmhouse was large and there were several empty bedrooms. I thought, who knows, perhaps one day these two would marry and live in the house with us. Mum and Dad got on so well with these two kindly people and Mum would be lost without her sister. One day when I am out riding with Dad I will ask him about it. I was so lucky to be able to talk to Dad about anything. I have drawn the line about asking him the facts about boys and girls, living on a farm I knew the basics anyway, but one day I will have a chat with John, he must be a real expert by now.

We were late going to bed that night and as I lay there I thought about the farm. George had been replaced by a young man from the village. His name wasn't George, but for some unknown reason we all called him George. On the other hand he had been working with sheep so that was a great help, as our sheep rearing was a success.

The old chap from the village had advised Dad and John on how to go about this venture. He was called Jim and even trained a sheep dog for George to help him round up these stupid creatures.

I often laugh to myself about Micky's reaction to this newcomer. It took some time for him and the new dog, Skip, to get used to each other. Mother put her foot down and Skip was not allowed in the house.

At last I went to sleep still thinking about John's forthcoming marriage. It must be awful not to be free. I suppose one day I would have to get married, but thank goodness that was a long way off!

During the next week I had a message from the big white chief at school to visit his study. It was, as I had expected, to meet the German boy. I knocked on the door and went in. I was introduced to a very sad looking chap, about my age, but much smaller than I was. His name was Klaus Bernstein and I greeted him in his own language and made him laugh by telling him that from now on I will be calling him Bernie, because Bernstein was too much of a mouthful.

The Head gave me a note giving me permission to show Bernie around the College. He explained that this was in case a master or prefect asked what we were doing. He added that I could take the whole afternoon to do this.

Bernie could only speak a few words of English and it was a case of helping each other. I helped him with a few simple words and he corrected my pronunciation. While we were walking around I had a good chance to look at Bernie. He had dark hair, a thinish face and when he smiled his face seemed to light up. He was a bit upset when he knew that I was a day boy so I told him that I would find someone to show him the ropes.

There was a boarder nicknamed Podgy. He was very fat and always seemed to be eating. He was a nice lad and owed me a favour. It is a long story so I will not go into it, but I knew he would help me out. After classes had finished I found Podgy in the tuck shop and left Bernie in his care. As I was about to go home the Head caught me and I explained that Thompson (Podgy's name) would look after Bernstein.

The local bus now did a circular tour of our area, so luckily I no longer had to walk to the village every day. The bus stop was only about half a mile from the farm. This was a godsend, especially in bad weather. It also meant I was able to get my homework done at a reasonable hour.

When I finished my homework I saddled up Daisy and made my way to see if Jake was about. At last Jake had come out of his shell. He even came up to the farm, not always when I was there. He got on very well with Dad and they talked for ages about all sorts of things. In fact, he was now a very welcome visitor. He was also making regular trips to London and received visitors, always the cars were driven by an Army chap. I had no idea what was going on.

I did enjoy my rides through the woods. There always seemed to be something different to see as the seasons changed. The sounds were lovely in the spring. The cuckoos were very vocal, no doubt busy stealing other bird's nests and laying their eggs, leaving the foster parents the chore of feeding the young. What a strange way to carry on!

Jake was pottering around in his garden so I sat on his old seat and we had a good chinwag, of course in German. When I told him about Bernie his ears seemed to prick up and he started to ask me a lot of questions about him. I was unable to tell him much because after all, I had only met the poor lad a few hours ago. Jake was almost normal once more, but he still had these spells of silence. Perhaps he had always been like that, even before the war. When he came back into this world he said that if I ever asked Bernie to visit the farm would I bring him over to meet him.

Jake was always nattering on about Hitler, who had taken complete control of the country. As I was about to leave Jake went into his cottage and came out with a book which he told me was all about Germany. He said It was no good learning a language without knowing something about the country.

When I got back to the farm I told Dad about this book and asked him what Jake was up to, what with the visits from Army personnel and his visits to London. These questions took him by surprise. He had a good think before he answered. "Henry, I think that Jake has a lot of knowledge about Germany. He was in Germany during the last war as a sort of spy and it may come that one day we may have to fight the Germans again. If ever it comes, which I hope to God it doesn't, this country has to be prepared, not like last time."

This really made me think and the thought filled me with horror. I had seen war films and what a terrible thing it was for our poor chaps. This is something else I would have to add to my prayers each night – 'please do not let us have another war.'

When I went to College the next morning, of course sitting next to

Polly on the bus, I told her all about Bernie. She told me that her dad had asked his congregation to pray for the people being persecuted by Hitler. She suggested that I should ask Bernie to the farm and then bring him over to see her dad, because he had this sad problem on the brain.

After our morning service in the College Chapel, which did not included the Jewish and several chaps from Africa and the Far East who were not of the Christian faith, there was Bernie waiting for me. Hence forth he was my shadow. It was a bit of a fag to begin with, but it was something I had to do otherwise the old man would be on me like a ton of bricks.

Evidently Podgy had helped Bernie quite a bit, especially after being treated in the tuck shop.

This was the last day of the Easter term and tomorrow I would be free for three weeks. Bernie and I had become great friends and I told him all about my way of life. His English had improved no end and he told me that my German was now very good indeed. I was now being taught how to write in German by Mrs Jenkins.

Bernie came to visit the farm at the weekend, for the day on Sunday. He enjoyed Mother's lunch. Bernie had a ride on Daisy and I explained how old the poor girl was getting. I told him about Henry the horse that Sir James was trying to sell, but as luck would have it no one seemed to like him and I still had the job of exercising him, which I enjoyed so much.

We had a very enjoyable day and when he left to catch the bus he thanked Mum and Dad for having him. When Mum gave him a bag of cakes his face was sheer delight. I walked to the bus stop with him and saw him safely on his way.

I took my time walking home and began to think of what Bernie had told me about his life. His father was a banker and being crafty he had invested most of his money outside Germany and the family only just managed to get out in time. Many of their friends had been taken away to work in labour camps and some had just disappeared. They all had to wear armbands to let everyone know that they were Jewish. They were attacked by young Nazis and ridiculed where ever they went.

I got the impression that Bernie's old man was very well off and lived in a large house on the outskirts of London with servants like the Howes.

My last day at College was uneventful until the late afternoon. I was minding my own business and trying to keep out of trouble before I broke up for Easter. Matron entered the classroom and I was told to report to the Head's study. My heart sank into my stomach and I thought that this had to be bad news. I had seen this happen before, when a parent was ill or had died it was always Matron who came for the poor boy.

When I joined Matron she saw what a state I was in and quickly reassured me, laughing and saying that all was well and I had nothing to worry about. Even so, I felt very nervous when I knocked on the door and entered the room.

The first thing I saw was two people sitting on chairs together with the Head and his wife. At first I thought what on earth is going on? Then the penny dropped. Of course, it was Bernie's parents. The resemblance was uncanny. I was introduced by the Head who used my Christian name, which was more than unusual. Mr Bernstein came over and shook my hand and thanked me for looking after Bernie, whom he called Klaus.

The Head told me to sit down and I sat on the edge of the chair. Mr Bernstein started to talk to me in German and queried how I managed to speak such good German. I went through the whole story about Mrs Jenkins and Jake. Then he asked me about my friendship with the Howes family and why was a horse called after me. I began to think what a nosy chap he was, but even so, he and his wife seemed very pleasant.

Mrs Bernstein then joined in the interrogation by asking how Klaus was getting on and did he seem any happier. This was a difficult question because Germans were not very popular. There was no problem about him being a Jew and could he not say that he was in fact a Polish Jew living in Germany?

After I suggested this I thought that I had really put my foot in it. Bernie's parents thought it was a good idea so I breathed a sigh of relief. Anyway, with more handshakes and to my horror a kiss on the cheek from Bernie's mother, I made my escape. What made my day was that the Head said, "Thank you Henry." using my Christian name for the second time.

Because of this visit to the Head's study I had to catch a later bus home and therefore did not have Polly as my travelling companion. However, it gave me the chance to dwell on today's events. I knew every part of the journey home and every turning of the narrow lanes we had to travel through to reach the farm. The bus was almost empty and the only noise came from the engine. At times I wondered how the old bus managed to climb some of these steep hills. It seemed to snort and groan with the effort, but was coaxed on by the driver. It was always the same driver and I think that he had become part of the bus. When the relief driver was on duty the bus always somehow played up.

I began to drift in to one of my daydreams and reflected on what had taken place today. For that matter, what had happened to me over the past few years.

I had made some very strange friends, perhaps unusual friends would be a better description. I had a premonition that meeting Bernie's parents would have a part in my future life and I began to feel a little scared about what I have let myself in for.

I was very friendly with the children living at the Hall and I rode with Sir James. I could carry on a conversation in German, with a German and I am going to a College with pupils above my station (after all I was only a farm boy). Dad had always told me that our lives are mapped out for us, be it good or evil. Tomorrow I will see my friends Mary and Hugh and I wondered what being away at school has done to them.

The driver brought me back to earth by shouting "Henry, don't you want to go home?" We had reached my stop and I was miles away in my daydream.

When I went into the kitchen Mother told me that she had heard from Jenny who said that she was coming home for the Easter weekend. I was pleased to hear this good news, but not so pleased when she added that Jenny was bringing home a boyfriend. Somehow I didn't like the idea of Jenny getting married. I would be seeing even less of her than I already did. She would have a complete life of her own. Anyway, I hope that he will be a nice chap.

The next morning I was up bright and early and the prospect of freedom for the next three weeks filled me with joy. I did a few odd jobs and in no time at all I was riding through the lanes to the Hall.

Whenever I passed through the massive gates and started to ride up the drive flanked by the avenue of beautiful trees, my mind went back to my very first visit and I remembered how nervous I felt and wished that I was miles away. Now I am a welcome guest, how strange it all is.

Hugh must have seen me from the house and he came out to meet me. Full of smiles he seemed pleased to see me again. He had grown and filled out and was no longer the weedy chap I used to know several years ago. I asked him where Mary was, he laughed and told me that she was no doubt making herself pretty. She had started to spend quite some time in front of a mirror these days, but then girls are like that.

I put Daisy in one of the stables and we went along to see how Henry was. I gave him a sugar lump and smoothed the side of his handsome face. He put his head up as if to say hello chum, how about another piece of sugar.

As we stood there I heard a voice behind me saying "Hello Henry." I looked around and there was Mary. How she had changed in such a short time. She was indeed very pretty and had changed her hair style. She came up to me and putting her arms around my neck, kissed me and said how good it was to see me again. I was most embarrassed and blushed like mad which made Hugh laugh. We went into the kitchen where Cook had made some cakes which had just come out of the oven. Oh boy! didn't they go down well, together with her special lemonade. As we left Cook told me that I would be having some of her famous pie for lunch.

We decided to walk down to the river. We had a lot to talk about. I had to hear all about their schools and the friends they had made. Hugh said how glad he was that I had shown him how to bash the punch bag. This had enabled him to keep the bullies at bay. He told me that the lessons were difficult but he liked the art lessons and was allowed to spend some of his spare time by himself in the studio. He was also in the OTC which he found to be quite a bore.

I made them both laugh when I told them about the episode when I pretended to be a German officer, which of course led on to my tale about Bernie and how this had helped me perfect my German. I told them how the poor chap had to leave his home and friends just because he was a Jew. My two friends seemed to know nothing about what was going on in Germany. Of course they were both at boarding school and really in a world apart.

Now it was Mary's turn. She started by showing off about her posh friend at school and how wonderful it all was. But then the truth started to come out and she admitted that she had been very homesick and missed the freedom of being in the country. She had missed Hugh and me very much. She had now changed her act and was once again the Mary I used to know.

When we reached the river we could see a few salmon on their annual run up stream to breed. This was my favourite place on this large estate and when I came over to ride Henry I always made a point of stopping by the river so that Henry could have a drink. I could then sit a while in this peaceful place. Perhaps it was the sound of the water working so hard to reach the sea, but here and at the little bridge I always felt good inside, even when I felt fed up. My two friends were silent for a while, perhaps they also felt the magic of the place.

There was a flash of blue as a kingfisher dived from one of the trees and in no time he was gone with a small fish in his mouth. It came as quite a shock, breaking the tranquillity, but to see the graceful dive and then its strong wings making it airborne again so quickly, was indeed a wonderful sight.

We were still talking when we returned to the Hall for lunch. We washed our hands and went into the breakfast room to find Nanny and Lady Howes already sitting at the table. They both gave me a very friendly greeting and asked after my family. Talking was restricted by the speedy consumption of Cook's smashing pie, followed by baked apple and custard.

Lady Howes asked Hugh if he had told me about their invitation to stay with an aunt in Germany. Evidently this aunt was a sister of Sir James and she had married a German Count and they lived on a large estate near the coast of Northern Germany. They had no children of their own and they wanted to see Mary and Hugh. Mary butted in by saying that she wished that I could go with them, but this suggestion fell on stony ground. I quickly put my spoke in by saying that Dad could never afford such a costly trip and the subject was not mentioned again.

Sir James came in and said how sorry he was for being late. He had been attending to some business. He turned to me and told me that he had some bad news. I wondered what was coming. Sir James then said that a horse dealer had come to see Henry. It was a very strange visit because the dealer was only interested in Henry. He took ages examining the horse and said that he would report to his client and Sir James would let me know the result later.

This spoilt my day because I had grown so very fond of Henry and the thought of not seeing him again made me feel very sad. In his gruff way, Sir James was a kindly man and I sometimes thought that some of his ways were a bit of an act because of the position he held. He ran the estate with only a gamekeeper who was only interested in the pheasants and stopping people from pinching them. A Mrs Bloxham was his secretary and she lived in Teigncombe and came to the Hall only a few days each week. I often wondered why he didn't have an estate manager.

Sir James must have seen how upset I was about the possible loss of the use of Henry so he said, "Not to worry Henry, I will find you another horse to ride." I thanked him and we were excused from the table.

I asked my friends if they would mind if we went to see Henry as he might be gone the next time I came over. Mary took my hand, gave it a squeeze and said that they understood how I felt and of course they didn't mind.

Henry had been let out into the paddock and I gave him a loud shout and he trotted over to the gateway. As he came closer I was filled with envy at the thought of someone else being the owner of such a magnificent animal. The sunshine seemed to make his coat glisten, showing off his young rippling muscles as he moved. I went to meet him and put my arm around his neck, perhaps for the last time.

I felt a bit of a wet because I was near to tears, but then that was nothing to be ashamed of, after all I was about to lose a good friend.

We then wandered around the estate still telling each other all about what we had been doing for the past few months. Mary told me about her best friend at school called Martine. She was French and could speak very little English, whereas Mary could speak the language quite well having had two lessons a week with a French lady before she went away to school. Hugh had never been much good at it. This was similar to my experience with Bernie, only he could hardly speak a word of English.

It had been grand seeing my two friends again and I was sorry to leave them. We arranged for them to come over to the farm for the day, which Mother had suggested, providing they didn't mind a simple meal in the kitchen. Hugh laughed and said that they would eat in the barn if my Mother served up her delicious Cornish pasties. This really did make me laugh when I thought of all the posh food that they were used to. I told them that Polly would be there which didn't seem to please Mary. Well, anyway, she will be there and that's that.

I found Sir James and Lady Howes to say my goodbyes. As usual Lady Howes kissed me on the cheek and said that she hoped they would see me again soon and I was to tell my Mother that she would be over to see her in a week or two. I wondered what she meant by that remark.

My friends walked with me to the gateway and Mary gave me a hug and Hugh thanked me for coming. I thought that the boot should have been on the other foot because I did enjoy my visits into another world.

I mounted Daisy and was once more on my way home. I still felt a bit sad about Henry, but after all he never belonged to me. Mr Jones the head groom had told me of a short cut through some fields. It was grand riding through the grass which was by now quite long. In a few months time it would be cut for hay. I disturbed some pheasants and coves of partridge. I even saw a couple of hares acting in their peculiar way, which they always did during their mating season.

I had often wondered why the animal kingdom and the birds had such a carry on before they got together to produce their young. I had asked John all about the birds and the bees and humans were indeed more straightforward.

I came out into the lane and who should I see but Joe. Since our fight, which was now several years ago, we were not exactly friends, but we always passed the time of day whenever we met. I asked him how he was getting on and he told me that he was going to become a boy soldier and be taught how to drive and learn all about cars. This was at a place a long way from Devon. He had grown into a big chap and looked tough as nails. He had however lost that awful surly look he used to have. He was very pleased to be going away because his home life was pretty grim. His father was a real boozer and he bashed poor Joe about, which gave him that awful chip on his shoulder.

Eventually we went our different ways and I wished him luck and for some unknown reason I said, "Who knows Joe, I might run into you in the future." How right I was, but I didn't know then how our lives would cross.

I had this strange feeling again about the future and how it would all come together like a jigsaw. I felt sorry for Joe because I had heard of this school for boys who wanted to make a career in the Army. The discipline was very strict and their hair was almost shaved off. Once they had started at the school there was no chance of them changing their minds.

Before I went to bed that night I asked Charlie what the weather was going to be like tomorrow. He told me that it would rain in the morning but the afternoon should be fine, so I planned my second day of freedom on his advice.

If, as Charlie said, it was wet in the morning I would get on with my woodwork. I was still making stools which Mother was selling in the market. They were however a bit more of a sophisticated model than the early ones and I had started to make small tables as well with the guidance of Peter's father and the techniques I had been taught in the woodworking classes at College. All of this has enabled me to build up my savings at the Post Office.

In the afternoon I thought that I would go and have a chat with Jake. The book that he had given me was called Mein kamph by Hitler and I did not understand all that I had been reading.

As expected Charlie was correct. It was raining cats and dogs when I got up the next morning. I spent the morning in my workshop which I really did enjoy. Time seems to fly by when I am working at something I really love to do and it was soon time for lunch. It was smashing to have one of Mother's lunches instead of the rubbish served up at College.

I took my time riding to Jake's cottage. The grass was wet and as Daisy's hooves came down they sent up a fine spray of water which shone in the sunshine like so many minute jewels. I put Daisy into a fast trot and the spray became quite a sight.

When I reached the cottage there was no sign of Jake and the cottage was all closed up, so I sat on his old seat and surveyed the beautiful glade that Jake lived in. The foliage was young and so very green. Some of the youngest leaves were a lighter colour than those that had come to life earlier. They were still wet from the spring rain and the sun danced from leaf to leaf as the wind moved the boughs from side to side.

There were birds everywhere. Some were putting the finishing touches to their nests and others were frantically trying to find enough

103

food for their young, which were always hungry. Their mouths were continually open and they wanted their fair share.

I was just about to leave when I heard Jake's old car chugging up the narrow lane which was on the other side of the cottage. I left Daisy to munch the young grass and went to meet him. Micky must have heard the car and he came into view, looking like a drowned rat from the rain drenched bushes. He was off like a shot to greet Jake.

He gave me such a friendly greeting and I helped him to unload his old banger. Jake carried a suitcase and I loaded myself up with several parcels and odds and ends. We went inside leaving Micky outside because of his messy condition, he looked quite put out. I told Jake that I would call again later in the week as he would want to settle in and unpack. He wouldn't hear of it and insisted I stay, so we had a chat and I told him about Henry and my day at the Hall.

I told him that the kids were going to visit their aunt in Germany and that Mary wished that I could go with them. That of course was out of the question because Dad could never afford it. Jake then went into one of his silent spells, but I still prattled on. After a while I got up to go and as we walked to the door Jake asked me if I had ever used a camera. I said that I knew nothing about such things, at the time I had no idea why he would ask such a silly question.

Walking to where Daisy was having a good feed, Jake told me that the aunt in Germany was a great friend of his late wife, but unfortunately she was married to a member of the Nazi Party. This was none of my business and I had no idea why he even mentioned it. We said goodbye and I started to make my journey home. I never got the chance to ask Jake about Hitler's Book. Anyway, it was not important.

Riding home I thought about my friend Jake and how he had changed. He looked so smart in his posh suit and without his face covered with hair. He had been to London and I wondered what he did in this big city. Perhaps he had a girlfriend, but somehow I had a feeling that there was some other reason for his increasing visits. Who am I to pry into his private affairs?

My three friends came to the farm for the day. It was strange to see Hugh and Mary sitting around our old kitchen table with everyone in their old working clothes. Much to my surprise they were at ease and made themselves at home. I thought how they ate at home, being waited on by the maids in such posh surroundings. Polly was always relaxed when she was at our house. We all enjoyed Mother's pasties, I think that she had made a special effort for this occasion. There was a lot of leg pulling and we all had a very enjoyable lunch.

I took my friends to see the young lambs. Of course the girls went into raptures over these dear little animals. To see them run and give the odd jump for no reason at all always made me laugh.

We went into the barn to see the two orphaned lambs. Their mothers just left them and for no good reason they would have nothing to do with their offspring. Mother was there feeding them with the help of a baby's bottle and she let the two girls have a go, much to their delight. I think that this made their day. As usual Wills came to fetch them and we said that we would all meet again after the Easter weekend.

Just before they left I asked Hugh if Henry was still at the Hall. He told me that he had been sold but Papa had to keep him for a few weeks for some reason unknown to him. Evidently this was part of the deal with the horse trader. With a bit of luck I will be able to see him again once more.

CHAPTER 5

Easter came and went. Jenny and her boyfriend came for a very brief stay and it was grand to see her again. Her boyfriend seemed a nice chap, but a real city type who was out of his element in the country, but Jenny seemed to like him which was the main thing.

Hugh and Mary had unwillingly returned to school. I had seen a lot of them during the Easter holidays and they had kept grumbling about having to go to Germany in the summer holidays.

They kept saying that they wished I could go with them. At last I got it into their heads that it was out of the question.

At College we were well into the summer term. Bernie's English had improved no end and by now we were very good friends. It was no longer a bit of a bore having him tagging along where ever I went. We played cricket after lessons on several afternoons each week which I enjoyed, but I missed my rides home on the bus with Polly.

I was still having German lessons with Mrs Jenkins once a week and I enjoyed my visits. She was such nice person and I think that she was a bit lonely as her husband spent most of his time painting.

I also enjoyed the ride to her house in such picturesque surroundings. My lessons were now in the evenings and to sit by the little bridge and just watch what was going on around me gave me so much pleasure. Sometimes when I sat there I wished that time would stand still and I could stay there for ever. I was not to know then that I would remember these idyllic evenings in the future and yearn for the peace and tranquillity that they brought to me.

Bernie was now quite a regular visitor to the farm and sometimes Polly joined us. I explained our way of life and the way of nature. I took him to meet Jake and they talked for ages about the sad situation in Germany. In fact, Jake asked so many questions that I could see that it was getting Bernie down so I only took him on one occasion.

It was early July and when I came home Dad greeted me and told me that Sir James was coming over and wanted me to be here. He had a surprise for me. I could tell by Dad's face that he knew what was going on, but he wouldn't tell me. I had my supper and killed some time in my workshop.

It was not long before I heard Micky barking so I went into the yard and saw Sir James on his horse leading Henry. Sir James

106

dismounted and told me that I was a very lucky young man because Mr Bernstein had bought Henry for me.

I was speechless and thought that perhaps I was daydreaming. When I came to I went towards Henry and he gave his usual neigh, shaking his handsome head as he trotted towards me. With his wet nose he tried to find my pocket for his usual reward and when it was not forthcoming he gave me a push with his head as if to say 'where is it?' I gave him a sugar lump and to hear his teeth munching it made us all laugh.

I saw that Henry had a new saddle and bridle so I told Sir James that I would return these to the Hall in a day or two. He replied that the tack was included in the gift. By now the whole family were inspecting the new addition to the farm.

Charlie had a way with horses and he soon made friends with Henry. Dad and John were not so lucky, Henry started to play up a bit so I had to intervene and calm him down.

Dad asked Sir James if he would like to come into the house for a drink and they went off with Mother and John. I began to get a bit worried about how Daisy would get on with Henry, so Charlie said, "Let's go and find out."

We took off Henry's saddle and made our way to the paddock. I gave Daisy a shout and she came over to see who the stranger was. It was so funny to see these two horses. One was old and the other quite young. Henry had his balls cut off when he was a colt so he was now a gelding. They seemed to look each other up and down and then they trotted off together to the other side of the field to get acquainted.

Charlie left me and I leaned over the gate to watch my wonderful present. I will have to write to Mr Bernstein to thank him for his generosity. What ever made him do such a thing? After all, Bernie and I enjoyed each other's company so it had been no hardship for me to help him out in the early days. Anyway, I had no option, the big white chief had spoken and that was that.

I saw Sir James come out of the house so I ran over to say goodbye and to thank him for bringing Henry to the farm. I asked him to give my regards to Hugh and Mary when he was next in touch with them and he gave me a friendly wave and was soon out of sight.

Dad and I walked into the house and I asked him if we could still keep dear old Daisy. I thought of the cost involved and I was relieved to hear that Dad had no idea of getting rid of such an old friend. I think that he was just as fond of her as I was. After all, she used to be his only means of transport before he bought his old car and she deserved a peaceful retirement.

I found it very difficult to get to sleep that night, I was too excited. What a lucky chap I was to own such a beautiful horse. I would now be able to ride further afield. Daisy was really past any long journeys now, the poor old thing got so very tired and in the past few weeks I had dismounted when we came to a steep hill as it was too much for her.

When I met Bernie the next morning he started to laugh saying that he knew that his father had bought Henry for me but he had to keep it a secret. I asked him why his parents had done such a thing and Bernie told me that his parents had a difficult time persuading him to come to the College, but having me to help him settle in so quickly had made his mother happy and she had made Mr Bernstein reward me for my help. I asked him for his parent's address as I wanted to write and thank them for buying Henry for me.

I met Polly on the bus home that evening and asked her if she would like to learn how to ride. She was such a little thing that Daisy would be able to cope. I said that I could teach her and perhaps Charlie would help as well. She gave it great thought and said that she would ask her parents. A little later on during our journey home she sort of snuggled up to me and said what a dear I was to think of something like that. I then began to realise how fond I was of Polly and in my mind she became my girlfriend. I took her hand and gave it a squeeze.

It was now near the end of the summer term and I have had very little time to enjoy myself. I have been swotting up for the exams. Thank goodness they are now over. My results were far from brilliant but acceptable. I seemed to be good at some subjects, but not so good at others, so I will have to pull my socks up.

Polly has been having riding lessons on Daisy and to my surprise she took to it like a duck to water. To begin with Daisy became very obstinate and would not move, but in the end she got used to the stranger on her back.

I enjoyed helping Polly to mount, putting my arms around this sweet young girl was smashing. One day I was helping her on to Daisy when she turned around, put her arms around my neck and we had our first real kiss. That was quite an experience for me, which was now often repeated.

We both felt a bit guilty about it so we decided to keep it as our secret. I thought that it will be difficult when Hugh and Mary came home. I am sure that Mary had her eye on me.

It was the day before we broke up for the summer holidays and when I got home Mother told me that Jake had telephoned. Would I be sure to go over to see him that evening at seven o'clock. Mother said that it was important for some unknown reason.

In the course of conversation at supper, Dad mentioned that Sir

James had been in to have a chat that morning. He often came in to see Dad when he was in our area.

I saddled up Henry and together with Micky we set off to see what Jake wanted to see me about. I reached the cottage just before seven o'clock to find a car and driver sitting outside. I knocked on the door and Jake took me into his living room.

I was surprised to see Sir James sitting in a chair and another man sitting at the table with a briefcase in front of him. Jake said, "Of course, you know Sir James, Henry, but I would like to introduce you to Major Davis." Major Davis stood up and shook hands with me, saying in German, "So you are Henry. Mr Spencer has been telling me about you." Jake pulled up a chair and told me to sit down. By now I was becoming a bit nervous.

The Major started to talk again in German. "Henry, we know that your friends Mary and Hugh Howes are going to Germany on holiday in August. They will be staying at a place called Lubeck which is in the Baltic area. My Government Department would like you to do a small job for us." I sat there absolutely speechless, but I managed to ask, "What do I have to do?"

The Major spoke for ages, but what it boiled down to was quite simple. I would have to take dozens of photographs always with one of the children in them so that they looked like holiday snaps. At last I came to my senses and started to ask questions. I explained that I had never taken a photograph in my life and why didn't they get someone older and more experienced in photography. The Major said that someone would come down to Mr Spencer's home to teach me the basics. The answer to the second part of my question was very simple – no one would take any notice of a boy taking snaps with an old camera. It would look like an old camera, but would in fact have a special lens.

He paused for a while to let this sink in and then went on to say that there were special rules I must keep to. "First of all, you must not tell anyone about this." He went on to stress that Hugh and Mary must not know anything about this task. "Your father has given his permission, but your mother has not been told and you must not tell her." He continued "Secondly, when you are in Germany, try to speak very bad German and do not ask questions about Hitler and his Party. Most important of all – keep out of trouble."

It was my turn now. "Who is going to pay for this holiday? Dad is a bit hard up." They all laughed and the Major said that it was taken care of and I would be receiving some pocket money.

Finally the Major said, "If you do this job, Mr Spencer will give you full instructions."

Like someone in a dream I said that I would do the best I could. I was then told that I could leave but should remember that this meeting had never happened. I shook the Major's hand and left. I then realised that I had been talking in German all the time that I was there, perhaps I was bilingual after all.

As I left Sir James called after me to say that he would let Hugh and Mary know that they would have company for their holiday.

I kept thinking about what had happened in the last hour. The thought of going to Germany with Hugh and Mary was very exciting, but the reason for my going was something very different and I started to worry about the instructions I would receive from Jake. I must have a long chat with Dad as soon as I get home.

I put Henry in the paddock and went into the barn with the tack. Dad must have seen me arrive because he joined me. I sat on my stool and told him about my strange experience. Dad then told me what was behind it all.

He explained that Hitler had broken all of the disarmament treaties and he was building warships and fighter planes. He was also training a large army and airforce. Germany had left the League of Nations and the country was now under the rule of one man, making it a dictatorship. Some members of our Government were getting increasingly worried so they were playing safe by obtaining as much information about the lie of the land in several parts of Germany. Hence the need for as many up-to-date photographs as possible.

I asked him, "But why me? I have no idea how to take a photograph." Dad then told me that I had a friend who was a member of a special army unit who had a high regard for me and I would be staying with a member of the Nazi Party and would be under his wing so to speak. Also, being able to speak and read German was a great help. Dad made me swear on my honour not to tell anyone, even Mother or John.

Dad then told me how lucky I was to have this wonderful holiday and he was very proud that I had been chosen for this important task. He made me blush by saying that he did not know what my girlfriend Polly would say about me having a holiday with Mary. He gave me a friendly cuff on the ear and we went inside to tell the family about my holiday.

Mother went all quiet because of the thought of me going so far away to another country at my age. This really put the wind up her. Dad talked her round by saying what a wonderful experience it would be and how lucky I was. It would also help Lady Howes and the two children to have someone with them who was able to speak the language.

The next morning I met Polly on the bus and told her my news. She went into a bit of a mood, but I couldn't help that. I told her that I would miss her and this helped. I would have loved to have told her the whole story, but of course I could not.

When I told Bernie about the holiday he looked very worried and told me to watch my step as they were a funny lot now in control. He added that under no circumstances must I say anything good about Jews or try to help any in trouble. He added that it was an awful thing to say, but he was only thinking of my safety. I told him that I was going to an estate near Lubeck on the Baltic coast.

He told me that he had been to this part of Germany on holiday and it was a very nice area. He had a wistful look and said how sad he felt about having to leave the country he had been brought up in. I did feel sorry for the poor chap.

I said goodbye to Bernie and my friends and caught the bus home for the last time for nearly two months. Polly was on the bus and we were now back to normal. I said that I would ride over to see her in a day or two.

When I arrived home there was a message from Jake asking me to pop over to see him that evening. I guessed that this would be to receive my instructions.

It was a very warm summer evening and I found Jake sitting outside of his cottage with maps laid out on a table in front of him. He greeted me and told me to give Henry a drink and then to come and sit down.

He started by telling me what Dad had told me last night about the situation in Germany. He went on to explain what the countryside was like in the Lubeck part of the country. It was very flat with several canals and the River Elbe ran through it. Consequently there would be a number of bridges. In the north of the area was the Baltic Sea port of Kiel where the Baltic Fleet was stationed. Very large ships could reach the North Sea through a deep water canal from Kiel to the River Elbe.

Jake talked for ages and pointed out the different places on a map laid out in front of him. To cut a long story short, what he wanted me to do was to take as many photographs as possible of bridges, both large and small, but always in the background with Hugh and Mary as the main subjects, or anything else of interest. He said that he knew Hugh and I were interested in trains, so become a train spotter, because railway routes were also of interest.

"You must not go anywhere near the large canal, but if you do and you see war ships passing through, try to include them, but only as part of the photograph. As you would be pretending to be a train spotter there would be nothing to stop you just taking a snap of a train going over a bridge," Jake explained.

He then went indoors to fetch a cool drink and some biscuits. He told me that a friend of his would bring down a camera on Friday, two days time, and could I spend the day with him? "Tell your Mother that I will find you some lunch, but remember, do not tell anyone what you are doing."

As I was about to leave, Jake said how pleased he was that I would help and he knew that I would not let him down. With a laugh he said that he would make a spy of me yet.

On my way home, what Jake had said about being a spy, made me think. I had not thought that this job that I had to do really came into this category. However, on reflection, I suppose that it could.

When I arrived home Mum and Dad were having a drink with John and his girlfriend Gertie. It was so warm that they had gathered in the garden. Dad handed me a small glass of beer and lemonade which he called a shandy.

Mother told me that Hugh had telephoned and would I ring him back. She then told me to keep the conversation short because of the expense. Mother was so stingy about her telephone.

It was good to hear Hugh's voice again and to hear how pleased he was that I would be going to Germany with them. He then asked if I could come over for the day tomorrow and remember to bring my bathing shorts as we might all have a swim in the river. I told him that I would be over fairly early on Henry.

I went back to join the family and John started to pull my leg about going on holiday with Mary and what would Polly say? I got my own back by saying that I could go on holiday with whom ever I liked, not like him, because at last he had been well and truly caught and not before time. This shut him up and made Gertie laugh. She was such a nice girl and I do hope that they will be happy together.

It was grand sitting there with my family listening to the chit-chat with the background noises of the farm and the sounds of the countryside. It was now a sort of half-light and a few of the bat colony that lived in the barns had ventured out to feed on the insects that were in the air. I was always intrigued about how they flew without being able to see. They went at such speed weaving in between buildings and other obstacles only inches away from disaster. This was yet another of the mysteries of nature.

I got up early the next morning because now that I was on holiday, I had to help Mother with her ever-increasing chicken and turkey production. There seemed to be poultry all over the place. Some hens had the run of the whole farmyard. They were so tame that you had to push them out of the way. One day when we were having a meal in the kitchen, in walked a couple of hens who walked around the room and went out again, after making a mess on the floor. What Dad called those two birds was nobody's business!

When I reached the Hall there was no sign of Mary or Hugh so I rode into the stable yard and found Sir James and the two kids looking at two ponies. They both seemed very excited. Mary ran up to me and asked her to help her decide which of the two ponies she should have, because she had first choice. Hugh gave me a wink behind Mary's back and pointed to the handsome black.

I pretended to inspect them both and then told Mary that I thought the grey would be best for her. I felt a bit mean about it because without a doubt the black was a better-looking horse. But boys must stick together! I could see Sir James was having quite a chuckle to himself and he said, "Well done Henry, you have made the right choice."

One of the grooms took Henry to the stable and we made our way into the house via the kitchen to get some grub.

Eventually we made our way to the river complete with swimming costumes. We talked all the time. My two friends were so pleased that I was going to Germany with them because there were no young people in the house of their aunt, and their uncle was a grumpy old thing.

When we reached the river we were very hot, so we put on our swimming gear and dived in. It was smashing and we had a lot of fun. I had a good look at Mary in her costume and noticed how she had filled out. She had a lovely figure with her young breasts beginning to take shape. She had grown since I saw her last and was even prettier. The sun was shining on the small globules of water on her skin and she looked good enough to eat.

We lay in the sun to dry ourselves off and talked about our holiday. It would be a long journey, first by train to London and then to Harwich to catch a boat to Holland. We would then take a train to Lubeck. I knew all this of course, because I had looked it up in an atlas.

By now Hugh was getting a bit restless. He wandered off down along the river bank leaving Mary and I alone. I am not sure how it happened but we began to fool around. As we lay there Mary suddenly had her arms around me and we began kissing. It was a lovely feeling to have her warm body next to mine. The kisses were different to the innocent embraces I have had with Polly and the effect it had on me was most embarrassing.

Mary said how she had missed me and how much she liked me. I must say that I felt the same way. We stopped our escapade just in time as Hugh came into view, walking back along the river bank. We both looked at each other feeling a bit guilty, but happy. I took her hand and we dived into the cold river, which I hoped would quieten me down.

When we were in the water I told Mary that this was our secret as her Mother would be very cross. She laughed and used her favourite expression, "Don't be silly Henry."

We dried ourselves, dressed and made our way back for lunch. Lady Howes met us and said how glad she was that I was going to Germany with them. It will be such a help having someone to speak the language and most important of all, someone to keep the children company. I wondered if she would have said this if she had seen Mary and I down by the river.

We had a ride after lunch. Mary and Hugh got on fine with their new ponies and in no time at all it was time for me to go home. I thanked Lady Howes for having me and bade farewell to my friends. I told them that perhaps they would like to visit the farm in a day or two and we agreed to be in touch. As I left Mary gave me a cheeky smile and said that we would go for a swim again soon. She was quite a girl was Mary!

On the way home I thought of Mary and my reaction to our close encounter and how much I had enjoyed it. She really was a lovely girl, but so different to Polly. What a twit I am to get mixed up with females. I suppose that I will have to one day, so I might as well get used to it.

I went to bed early that night because I will have a busy day tomorrow. I have to meet the camera chap for the day and I was due for a German lesson with Mrs Jenkins after supper. I will be able to tell her about my holiday to Germany.

The next morning I rode over to Jake's and found him sitting on his seat talking to a fairly young chap. Jake introduced me and I was to call this chap David. Jake left us and my first lesson in photography began.

In very simple terms David explained how a camera worked. Light was let into the body of the camera through a lens by means of a shutter. The shutter opened for a very brief time and if the light was poor the shutter would be open for a longer period. If it was bright sunshine the shutter would be open for only a second or two. The picture would be recorded on the film inside, which would then be developed and printed in a room without any light.

The first golden rule was never open the camera until the film was used up, otherwise the film would be spoilt. The second rule was to try to have the sun behind you when taking the photograph.

David pulled out a very shabby box camera from a bag by his side. He explained that this sort of camera was used by hundreds of holiday makers, but this one was very different inside. This one had two shutter speeds which were changed by a small lever hidden under a wide strap at the top. To look at it no one would be able to tell the difference from the common box camera.

David taught me how to put in a new film, how to rewind it and take it out of the camera when finished. I had to do this lots of times until he was absolutely sure that I had the hang of it. By this time Jake told us that lunch was ready, but even while we were eating, David kept giving me information which I had to repeat to see if it had sunk in.

After lunch we wandered all over the place pretending to take photographs. I was taught how to hold the camera and focus and which speed to use. Jake joined us and I was shown how to take a picture of him while including something of more interest in the background.

By now I was getting a bit fed up with it all and I was glad when we got back to the cottage. David then tested me on what he had taught me, then turned to Jake and said, "This lad will do." That was a great relief.

Jake went inside and brought out a long envelope containing papers which Dad had to fill in. He was then to post them, with my birth certificate in the pre-paid envelope. This was of course for a passport. David took some photographs of me which would be needed for this. The camera was so different to the old box camera I had been using.

Jake said that he would keep the camera and have plenty of film ready for me to take with me. Jake then said, "By the way Henry, Major Davis will want to see you next week some time, I will let your dad know when. Please be sure to get the passport letter posted as soon as possible, because in three weeks time you will be on your way."

I put on Henry's saddle and together with Micky I was off with a friendly wave from Jake and David. What a day it had been. My mind was full of the information crammed into it in such a short time. Anyway, I had passed the test and what comes out of it remains to be seen.

When I got home I gave Dad the envelope from Jake and told Dad the instructions I had been told to pass on to him. I told him all about my day and what a chore it all was. He said, "Never mind, think of the holiday you will be having." With a laugh he added, "With your other girlfriend." After that remark I pushed off to have some grub, as I left Dad told me that I would have to go into Newton Abbot with Mother to get some new clothes. I asked if he could afford it and he said that it had all been taken care of, but I was not to tell Mother.

After supper I asked Mother if I could telephone Mrs Jenkins to cancel my lesson that evening. She said, "Of course you can't cancel your lesson, we don't want to upset her." So after my meal I was once more on my way. I stopped by the little bridge to let Henry have a drink and as I sat on the old bench I began to feel very worried about this holiday. It would be a big responsibility taking the snaps of the views

Jake would be telling me about.

David made it sound so easy. All I had to do would be to get the view in the view finder and then press the shutter lever. I know that I am unable to get out of it, but I now wished that I had refused the offer. Anyway, it is too late now, so I will have to make the best of it.

When I reached Mrs Jenkins house I knocked on the door and she called, "Come in." She had all the books all ready on the table and there was also a large map spread out. She greeted me by saying "Who's a lucky boy then." Evidently she had met Polly in the village who had told her about my visit to Lubeck with the Howes.

Mrs Jenkins had visited Lubeck several times and instead of my normal lesson we spent the time looking at the map and she explained the area to me in detail. Little did she know how useful this would be for me.

When it was time to go she said that there would not be any more lessons until after I return from Germany. She would however like to see me next week to explain some of the customs and manners, which would be very useful as the Germans were so different to us.

She had a wistful look on her face and said that she would like to visit Germany, but that was not to be. As I left I wondered what she had meant by that last remark. Perhaps she had Jewish blood in her veins, although she did not look Jewish.

When I got home Mother and Betty were making pasties for the haymaking which was to take place tomorrow. This was the last field so Dad and John would be pleased. As we were talking the telephone rang and Mother asked me to answer it as her hands were covered in flour.

I lifted the receiver and it was Mary asking if they could come over tomorrow. I told her that we would be haymaking and as I was older now I would have to help. She said that they would help as well, so I told her to hang on while I asked Mother if this would be alright. Mother said that she would like them to come.

We had quite a chat then and with a cheeky laugh she said, "What a pity we will be unable to have a swim Henry." Then she hung up.

I sat in the garden before going to bed. What Mary said, brought back only too clearly what had happened by the river. In fact I relived every moment. I then made up my mind to watch my step, because I must not get too fond of Mary. It could cause great problems in the future. On the other hand it will be damn difficult as she was such a lovely girl and I will be with her every day for two weeks.

We had a smashing day. Hugh and I worked really hard and I thought it so funny to see Mary helping Mother and Betty serve up the lunch. I bet that was the first time she had ever done anything like that. John was making her laugh about something. In fact she was getting on well with everyone.

When it was time for my friends to go, Mother made Mary and Hugh have a wash before they went home. She combed the hay out of Mary's hair only just in time because Lady Howes herself came to collect her offspring. This put Mother in quite a state. She took Lady Howes into our front room and they were there for quite some time.

When Lady Howes came out of the house I could see that she had some of Mother's cream and butter in a basket. They were about to leave, but not before Mary gave me a kiss when no one was looking. At least I thought no one was looking, but John saw us and I was teased for the rest of the evening.

I had to go into Newton Abbot the next day to buy some clothes. Lady Howes had advised Mother what would be needed. What a bore that was. When Mother told Dad what she had spent he paid up like a lamb, much to Mother's surprise.

The days passed by and tomorrow I would be off to Germany. I asked Mother if I could have some grub to take as I would like to have a wander around on my own. First of all I went to see Polly to say goodbye and she seemed upset that I was going away. I took her for a ride on Henry and we had a kiss or two. As I left I told her that I would send her a postcard.

I ate my lunch by the little bridge and began to think of the many instructions Jake had given me. We had spent a long time looking at a map of the area and he advised me to buy a town map if there was one available. He had given me a load of films and the camera. Major Davis gave me five pounds as pocket money, which to me was a fortune. He kept telling me that I was only a holiday maker and to act like one.

Mrs Jenkins told me a great deal about the way of life in the Germany she knew and told me how it was polite to always shake hands with whom ever you met, plus many other useful tips. She also told me not to mention anything about the Jews and if you see any trouble, walk away. It sounds very unkind not to help anyone in trouble, especially if it is a youngster.

"Would you do something for me Henry?" she asked. She named a street in Lubeck and said that if I was able to find it, look for number twenty and see if there is any sign of someone living there. Learn the name of the street and the house number and then destroy the piece of paper she had written it on.

She went on to explain that a dear friend lived there who was half-Jewish. "Do not and I repeat, do not ask anyone where the street is or why you are looking for it." As I left she gave me a hug and said, "God be with you Henry." This was most unlike her because she always seemed cool and on the haughty side.

117

I visited my favourite haunts during the rest of the afternoon and eventually made my way home to give Henry a good grooming.

Mum and Dad lectured me on how to behave and I was packed off to bed early. Tomorrow night I would be sleeping on board a ship bound for Holland. Jake had told me that it can sometimes be a rough crossing, I will have to wait and see.

Laying in my bed for the last time for fourteen nights, I must admit that was not over the moon. I was very apprehensive about what was in store for me.

CHAPTER 6

We were to catch the 1.50pm train from Newton Abbot so I had to hang around in anticipation. My bags were packed and I looked at myself in the mirror and thought that I looked quite posh. Dad and I had a long chat out of Mother's hearing and he gave me a five pound note and told me how proud he was and that I must do the best that I could.

I had just finished a very early lunch when the car arrived, driven by Wills in his uniform. I said goodbye to my family and climbed into the car between Mary and Hugh and set off on my great adventure. Lady Howes told me how smart I looked and Mary said that I looked smashing. It was nice sitting close to Mary. She had one of her legs close to mine and to feel the warmth of her body was indeed a joy.

My two friends were in very high spirits. We compared our passport photographs, which were pretty good. I then noticed that Mary and Hugh had the words 'The Honourable Mary Howes' and 'The Honourable Hugh Howes' on their passports and asked them what it meant. I was told that as Papa was a Viscount they also had a title. This shook me somewhat. What ever was I doing with these people who were so very above my social station? Mary whispered in my ear, "Now don't be silly Henry, it's a lot of rot anyway!"

When we reached the station Wills went to find a porter to help him with the heap of luggage we had. Mother had bought a useful haversack for me to carry my odds and ends in, including my camera. The train came in on time and the porter found us our compartment, which of course had been booked just for us. It was First Class and must have cost a bob or two. The seats were so very comfortable and had white cloths on which to rest one's head, with the words GWR printed on them.

We passed through Teignmouth which reminded us of the smashing holiday we had there several years ago. As we pulled out of the station we could see the beach crowded with holiday makers. This made me wish that we were on holiday there with the friends we had made. It all seemed such a long time ago.

I enjoyed the journey which I spent looking out of the window at the different sorts of country that we passed through. The fields were much larger than those in Devon. I must remember to ask Dad why this was so. Mary and Lady Howes were reading and Hugh was busy with his sketch pad, so I could enjoy some peace.

Lady Howes put down her book and told us that it was time for some tea. We trooped along the corridor to the refreshment coach and had toasted buns and cream cakes. I marvelled at the way the waiters walked up and down the space between the tables carrying tea and cakes. The train was swaying from side to side but they experienced no difficulty at all coping with this. I suppose practice makes perfect.

On the way back to our compartment we had a lot of laughs as we fell about, as the train was going a fair old speed. Perhaps it was a straight stretch of track and was making up time. It was quite a relief to sit down in our seats.

Lady Howes started to chat about our journey. A friend of Sir James would meet us at Paddington Station and take us to Liverpool Street Station where we would catch a train to Harwich. There we would board a ship for Holland. There would be porters to load our luggage. What she said next came as quite a shock. She told me that while we were away I should call her Aunt Pamela, after all we were on holiday together and she felt Lady Howes sounded too formal. She said It was very good of me to come with them to keep Mary and Hugh company.

Little did she know the real reason, but then as Dad would say ignorance is bliss. Mary gave me a nudge and one of her cheeky smiles. I wondered what my Mother would say about this turn of events, I expect she would exclaim, "oh my!"

We were due to arrive at Paddington Station at 6.50pm, so at 6 o'clock we once more went to the refreshment coach and had a smashing meal. We were all in good spirits and Lady Howes, or should I say Aunt Pamela, joined in the fun. In the past I had got to know Sir James quite well, but had little to do with her Ladyship. Time will tell what she is really like.

As we got closer to London I was fascinated by what I was able to see out of the window. No longer could I see countryside but large factories and houses. There was a sort of fog caused by the smoke belching out of the tall factory chimneys. When we passed over the streets and shops the people looked like ants scurrying about their business. How I would hate to live in a place like this.

We pulled into Paddington Station and collected ourselves together. Lady Howes called a porter and looked out for the friend who was to meet us. It came as quite a shock to see Major Davis coming towards us with one of his underlings. I quickly composed myself as I remembered that I was not meant to know him. We were all introduced to him by Lady Howes and he shook my hand and said, "How do you do?" That was all he said to me other than goodbye after he had seen us to our train.

I found it so interesting driving through London and seeing buildings that I had only read about. Hugh and Mary were also fascinated with everything we saw so there was very little chit-chat between us. Lady Howes and the Major talked as old friends, I gathered this from the bits of conversation I overheard.

Our train to Harwich left at 8 o'clock and once again we were in a First Class compartment. It was not a long journey and we arrived at Parkstone Quay at 9.40pm.

Henceforth Lady Howes became Aunt Pamela. She asked me for my passport and said that she would keep them all together.

When we left the train we made our way through customs. The officer looked at our photographs to check we were whom we said we were and we were then given our boarding passes. We walked up the wide gangway onto the ship.

An officer greeted us and asked a steward in a white uniform to show us to our cabins. Hugh and I were to sleep in one cabin and Mary and her Mother were in the cabin next door. The cabins were rather posh and no doubt First Class. There were two bunks one on top of the other so we tossed a coin to see who would sleep in the top one. I lost and put my overnight case on the top bunk.

Mary came in to say that we were all going on deck to watch the ship sail out of the harbour. The ship would cast off at 10.30pm so we went up to see England fade away in the distance.

There were lots of people on deck, some waving goodbye to people on the quayside. The ship sounded its hooter and the seamen cast off and we were on our way. We passed the harbour entrance and soon reached the open sea which looked pretty calm, thank goodness, though what the North Sea would be like remained to be seen.

We only stayed on deck for a short while. Aunt Pamela said that we ought to go to bed as tomorrow would be a long day and we had to rise early. We retired to our cabins and said our goodnights. It was strange listening to the steady throbbing of the engines in the bowels of the ship. I must have been very tired because in no time at all I fell asleep.

Hugh and I were wakened by the steward at a very early hour. He gave us a cup of tea and said that breakfast would be served in the restaurant at 7.30. It was now 6.30 so we had to get our skates on. We had just finished dressing when Mary burst in without any warning, luckily I had just put my trousers on!

She told us that when we were ready we could have some breakfast and then meet the agent from Thomas Cook, the travel agents who would see us on to the right train. Eventually we were ready and made our way through the long corridors which were flanked by highly polished wooden doors leading to the other cabins. We saw many other passengers all looking sleepy and bleary-eyed.

The restaurant was very large with waiters all over the place. We were shown to a table and I noticed a very long table at one end of the room which was laden with all sorts of food. However, it was not the sort of food I expected to see at breakfast, there was all sorts of cheeses, sliced sausage, cold meat, but not a fried egg in sight.

Aunt Pamela saw my expression and laughed. "Henry my dear, you will be having some strange food for the next two weeks. This is what is called a continental breakfast." A waiter came over carrying a large jug of hot coffee and some warm bread rolls. We then had to go up and help ourselves to the array of food on display.

We couldn't decide what to have so we tried a little bit of everything. I must say that this was a lot of fun as we had no idea what it would taste like. There was some cheese with very neat holes in it. Hugh decided to give that a miss because it looked as if the mice had been at it! We were so hungry and enjoyed it all.

As we ate the Thomas Cook agent came over to our table to introduce himself. He was a young man but had a look of efficiency about him. He was Dutch, but spoke fluent English. We were to find that many of the waiters and railway people were the same. Some of them could understand German as well, what a lazy nation the English are where foreign languages are concerned.

The agent gave us our itinerary and told us that he would put us on the train for Hamburg where there would be someone to organise our change of trains to Lubeck. We would cross the border near Enschede. The German customs officers would take some time over this as they had become very strict of late. They also carry out spot checks during the journey looking for people trying to leave the country. In Germany we must *always* carry our passports, that was most important.

He then said that he had some Dutch and German currency to cover our journey, as requested, and he told Aunt Pamela that she would be able to change her traveller's cheques at a bank in Lubeck.

We collected our overnight bags from the cabins and made our way off the ship. When I reached the quayside I took a photograph of the ship with Mary and Hugh standing in the foreground.

The agent found our compartment on the train and made sure that our luggage was put on the train. We were soon off on our first trip on foreign soil.

The compartment was very comfortable with nice wide seats and plenty of room to move about. I could not make up my mind about the nationality of the train until I looked at the notices and pictures on the walls, which were all in German.

Going out of the station gave us an insight into what Holland would be like. The houses were tall and close together with very sharp roof angles. Everything looked so clean and tidy as we continued into the countryside and the land was so flat that one could see for miles. It was criss-crossed by canals with lots of picturesque windmills. I had been taught about this by Mr Lloyd who told me that Holland was a very agricultural country and that they produced flowers and bulbs for the European market.

Mary sat next to me and chatted away. Aunt Pamela joined in and started to tell me all about our hosts for the next two weeks. Sir James' sister was called Countess Brecht and her husband was Count Brecht. They were very well off and had lots of servants. The Count, or as he is called in Germany, Graf and his wife Grafin, was at times a bit bad-tempered so I should keep out of his way as much as possible. To him children should be seen but not heard.

The Countess had arranged several trips out and of course there would be horses to ride. There was also a swimming pool of sorts. On hearing this news Mary gave me a nudge in the ribs. The conversation was then interrupted by a waiter telling us that lunch was now being served in the dining car.

As we walked along the swaying corridor I pulled Mary's leg about what we might have for lunch. When we settled at our table a waiter gave us a menu each. As I had expected it was in German. There was a choice of veal, pork or fish cooked in German style. Mary was sitting next to me as usual so I told her that she had the choice of boiled pigs toes in beer, calves ears baked in milk or some rather strange fish. Aunt Pamela burst out laughing which let the cat out of the bag so Mary gave me a hefty punch and told me not to be so silly.

The waiter's English was very bad so I gave the order, which made me feel very important. We had a smashing meal which seemed to put new life into us.

On the way back to the compartment Mary fell behind to tie her shoe lace. Like a clot I waited for her and by this time Hugh and his mother were out of view. Before I knew what was happening, Mary had her arms around my neck and we were kissing. It only lasted a second or two but it was a very dangerous thing to do with her Mother so close. We caught up with the others and Mary said she was so proud of the way I had spoken to the waiter in German. I thought that if this was the way she reacted every time I helped out with the language, I would soon be in the soup.

When we had been in our compartment for a short while the ticket collector came to inspect our tickets. He told us that we would soon be arriving at the customs point near Enschede where the German Police would board the train to see our papers and passports. After what I had heard from Jake I felt a bit nervous. This was so silly of course because we were only holiday makers. The train stopped and eventually a policeman walked in with a revolver in a holster on his belt. He was followed by a man in a very smart black uniform.

We were asked in German to produce our passports. I told my friends what was required and the officer took some time looking at our papers and then asked our destination and why we were going there. In poor German I explained that we were going to stay with my friends' Uncle Von Graf Brecht for a holiday. When he learnt the Count's name he turned on the charm and said in very bad English, "I hope that you all enjoy your stay in Germany." He clicked his heels together, bowed to Aunt Pamela, saluted and withdrew from the compartment. Aunt Pamela looked at me and asked what I had said to him to make him so polite.

I told her that Sir James had told me that the Count was an active member of the Nazi Party and had something to do with the SS Movement. He had told me that should we ever get into any trouble I was to mention who we were staying with because the SS had become very powerful and many people were scared of them, so I thought that this was a good opportunity to try it out.

Aunt Pamela looked a bit put out. People like her do tend to live in another world and many of the bad things in the world are kept from them. Perhaps it was just beginning to dawn on her what a strange place Germany had become in such a short space of time.

I felt that this was as good a time as any to talk about the conditions in Germany. I knew quite a lot because of what Bernie, Jake and Mrs Jenkins had all told me. Aunt Pamela looked shocked and said that it was not at all true. It was not my place to argue with her so I said that we will have to wait and see. But to be on the safe side we must not mention anything to do with Jews.

Our first stop was Osnabroek and I took a snap through the window of a line of engines in a siding. There was quite a wait as the engine took on fuel and water so Hugh, Mary and I stepped out onto the platform. I asked them to pose for a photograph in front of our compartment. The SS Officer strode towards us and I asked him if I could take his photograph with my two friends. He seemed very flattered and stood between the two of them. He told us to get back on the train as it would be leaving soon and with a friendly "aufwiedersehen" we got back on the train for Hamburg.

The countryside was very flat and the fields small. I could see farmhouses and enclosed areas full of pigs and I was to learn that pork and all sorts of sausage were great favourites for the bulk of the population. It was washed down with huge tankards of beer. We passed through stations and it seemed strange to see so many soldiers waiting to catch trains. At home it was quite an event to see men in uniform. The German soldiers looked so smart in their long leather boots and well cut uniforms, not like our chaps in their rough serge uniforms and army boots.

I called Hugh and Mary over to look out of the window to see the most amazing sight. As far as the eye could see, a road was being built. As the land was so flat the road was straight and very wide. There were hundreds of workmen looking like so many ants. There were also soldiers with rifles acting as guards.

Without thinking I said to Hugh that there were people from a nearby forced labour camp and may God help them. Aunt Pamela told me not to be so silly because they were probably criminals. I got out my camera and took a couple of photographs, which was not the most sensible thing to do because I had just put my camera away when in walked the SS Officer.

He asked us if we had noticed the road being built and went on to say that their leader, Herr Hitler, was building these roads, called autobahns, across Germany. They would give his country the best transport system in Europe. He asked us if we were having a pleasant journey and with a polite bow to Aunt Pamela he turned and left us.

We were by now getting closer to Hamburg which was a large town with factories on the outskirts. We pulled into a very busy station. As we were getting our baggage together the door opened and in came a man followed by a porter. Of course it was a chap from Thomas Cook. What an organisation they had, I bet it was an expensive service.

By now we were getting a bit tired and bored, but we were about to start the last leg of our journey. We had quite a time to wait for the train to Lubeck so we had some tea in the station restaurant. My friends and I were a bit greedy with the smashing cream cakes and so Aunt Pamela put her foot down and told us that we would make ourselves ill if we ate any more.

Eventually we boarded our train, which was not so good as the Hamburg Express, but by now we just wanted the journey to end. Mary curled up on the seat and with her head resting on my arm she fell asleep.

At last we came to Lubeck. The railway line skirted the main town and what we could see we liked. There seemed to be water everywhere in the form of canals. We were going to the north of the town so we had to stay on the train until we came to the nearest stop to Techau, where we would be met and taken to our home for the next twelve days or so.

Aunt Pamela told us that the Estate was near to a very large forest and not very far from a river. In fact she thought that the river ran through the Estate. One of the railway staff came into our compartment to tell us that the next stop would be the end of our journey and he put all our small pieces of luggage in the corridor in readiness.

When we finally stopped at the small station there was bags of panic. There was a large red-faced chap bossing everyone about, two uniformed footmen and a really lovely, elegant lady. This must be Sir James' sister.

I could see that our luggage was being taken out of a van at the other end of the train and taken by the two footmen and a porter to a car outside the station.

I was introduced to the Count and Countess as a great friend of Hugh and Mary. I greeted the Count in not very good German which seemed to surprise him somewhat. Hugh and Mary acted rather shyly towards their aunt and uncle. I was to learn later that they had not seen them for several years and were really like strangers. Adding to this, the Count was not a very pleasant-looking chap and he kept barking out orders to his underlings about the luggage.

We were led into the station yard and saw a smashing car with a long bonnet. It was light grey in colour and highly polished. The back doors opened to reveal the usual back seat, but in front of this there were other seats that folded away when not required. The Count sat in the front and the two women sat in the back seat. Mary, Hugh and I sat on the smaller seats. The luggage and staff followed in another car.

I sensed my two friends were not at ease. I must admit that I felt a bit apprehensive as we drove out of the station yard. I wished that I was home in Devonshire. I found Mary's hand and gave it a squeeze and she held on to it not letting it go. Luckily our hands were covered by our coats which were folded on our laps so no one could see. Perhaps we were all very tired, after all we had been travelling for the best part of two days.

I found the countryside very interesting. It was very flat with large areas of wood and very dense forest. There were a lot of what Dad would call 'smallholdings' mixed in with large estates or farms. There were some hills but overall it was a mainly flat scene and in its way quite lovely. It all looked so green and of course, the woods added to the charm.

The station was at a place called Timmendorf and not very far away from the Baltic Sea. The schloss, or Castle, where we were to stay was situated near Pansdorf and really quite a drive from the station. We drove through a very large forest, which I was to learn was called

Reinfeld Forest. We then crossed a river and at last we arrived at our destination in Germany.

This was quite a place. The entrance had very large gates with someone continually on duty. The gates opened and we drove through a very dark wooded area until we came to open country. There in front of us stood a fairy tale Castle, which was quite beautiful. On the other hand one could imagine a witch riding forth on her broomstick from one of the towers! The lawns and gardens were a sight for sore eyes and I could see the river in the distance winding its way through the parkland, which was part of the Estate.

I suppose that it is not unusual for two people to have minds that seem to think about the same thing at the same time. Mary turned to me and whispered that she thought the Castle looked very creepy and she hoped that there were no ghosts creeping around at night!

I told her not to be so silly, but I must say that the same thought had crossed my mind. Anyway we pulled up at the front door and the Count got out of the car and began giving orders left, right and centre to a host of lackeys waiting to be told what to do.

There was a line of servants, male and female lined up ready to greet us, which I found most embarrassing. However, this was the way things were done in this higher echelon of society which I have become caught up in. Fate had guided me on this path and all I could do is to go with the tide.

Unlike Sir James, Count Wilhelm Brecht treated his staff with very little respect. He was so different to the Countess, whom I was to call Aunt Geraldine. She was so charming and so very English.

I did not know at that point that I would get to know 'Uncle Wilhelm' quite well over our stay at Pansdorf. I had to act as interpreter as his English was awful.

We were taken into the Castle which seemed to be a huge place. The ceilings were very high and everything was indeed exaggerated by its size. We went up a very large staircase and shown to our rooms and I assumed that I would be sharing a room with Hugh, but that was not to be. I would have welcomed his company because he was such a nice chap. Our rooms were all on the same landing. Hugh and Mary were opposite and Aunt Pamela next door at the end of the corridor.

After a wash and brush-up we went down the vast staircase and entered the dining room for our evening meal. We were all very subdued and tired so soon after the meal my friends and I retired to bed. We had been travelling for almost two days and had every excuse for being worn out.

I fell asleep that night as soon as my head hit the pillow. In the morning I was awakened by a girlish laugh and a warm hand ruffling my hair. Before I knew what was happening, Mary was on top of me and we were kissing each other. She then tried to get into the bed but I came to my senses just in time to stop her and managed to push her away before Hugh came into the room.

Hugh and Mary sat on my bed and we wondered what we could do on our first day. Perhaps the grown-ups had plans for us so we decided to wait and see what might be forthcoming.

I managed to get rid of Hugh and Mary so that I could dress and as I chased Mary out of the room I gave her a hefty smack on her shapely little bottom.

After I had dressed I made my way down the stairs. I was now able to have a good look around. The place was dark and not very inviting. There was a suit of armour in one corner of the hall and animal trophies on the walls. There was a servant sitting bolt upright on a chair so I asked him where the breakfast room was. He seemed surprised to be spoken to in German and led me to a room with a long table in the centre. Sitting at the head of the table was the Count. We greeted each other in German and he told me to help myself to the food on the sideboard.

As I looked at the extensive display of cold meat and sausage, Hugh and Mary came in to join me. It was trial and error so we had a bit of almost everything. I was absolutely starving and it looked as if Mary and Hugh were as well. I enjoyed this first German breakfast and the sausages were smashing washed down with coffee.

The two aunts entered the room and after a while Mary asked her Mother what we were going to do today. Aunt Geraldine said that she would take us into the old town of Lubeck and we would be able to have a good look around and then meet up for lunch. This suited us fine and I had thoughts of buying a street map to try to find the house for Mrs Jenkins. I would also take my camera to carry out my other job.

The Count told me that he would look out three ponies for us to use so that we could explore the estate and nearby district. My friends and I had decided to call the Count Uncle Willie. So far he didn't seem a bad old stick. However, I did sense that he and Aunt Geraldine were not always the best of friends. They didn't talk to each other like Mum and Dad did, or for that matter like Sir James and Aunt Pamela. These were my first impressions of course so I may be wrong. Time will tell.

Soon after breakfast we were on our way in the large car to see Lubeck. To get everyone in the mood for having their photograph taken I took a couple of snaps of my friends and the two aunts standing by this magnificent car.

It was quite a drive into Lubeck. It seemed a very densely wooded area. We then came to the River Schwartu which was fairly close to the road. It was such a lovely sight and I asked Aunt Geraldine if we could stop so that I could take a photograph (I did not mention the two large bridges over the river).

We continued through the very flat countryside into the district called Bad Schwartu. In the distance I could see a lot of dust and building activity so I asked Aunt Geraldine what was going on. She explained that a new autobahn was being built by criminals from a nearby prison camp.

I didn't believe her and she knew it, in fact she began to look very sad and for a brief spell she let the mask of well-being slip from her face. She soon regained her composure and told us about the wonderful roads that Hitler was building right across Germany.

As we came closer to the road building I could see soldiers with rifles keeping an eye on the workers. The workers seemed to be doing everything in slow-motion. It is difficult to explain, but they were like robots just doing a specific task because they had to do it. There was no enthusiasm, or perhaps they were too weak.

Suddenly I felt very sad and to some extent, frightened about the future. I could see before my eyes an example of 'forced labour' which I had read about in the newspapers at home. The media had treated this sort of news as anti-German propaganda or rumour. I wondered who these poor people were, perhaps gypsies, Jews or others that did not agree with Hitler's policies. Of course I would never know.

I decided to break one of Major Davis' rules. I asked Mary to lean over me and pretend to look out of the window. She was only too pleased to do this, the sexy little so and so. Anyway, I managed to get my camera out and focused on the road building. I was lucky because the car was stopped by an army patrol and everyone's attention was on this activity.

I overheard one of the soldiers asking our driver if we had seen any escaped prisoners because some had managed to get away. Looking at the soldiers and the dogs they had with them, I thought that the poor devils would have very little chance of keeping their freedom.

What we had seen had quite an effect on us all. I think that the very fierce-looking dogs and the hunter look on the faces of the soldiers, made it all seem very inhuman. I didn't think that Mary had taken it all in as she was soon back to her normal self, but later I was to learn how wrong I was.

We arrived at the old town of Lubeck. The centre was completely surrounded by canals with countless bridges connecting the main streets to the areas outside the encircled town centre. In olden days there would have been perhaps only two or three bridges making it like an island and easy to protect.

Aunt Geraldine told the driver to take us to a posh hotel which was called the Berlin Hotel. This was where we were to meet for lunch. She gave Hugh a handful of notes and told him to buy us some ice cream or cakes. Aunt Pamela told me to look after Hugh and Mary as she wanted to go shopping with her sister-in-law.

So here we were, the three of us, in a strange town in a foreign country.

First of all I wanted to go to a bank so that I could change my five pound notes into marks. We soon found a bank and I got an awful lot of marks for my five pounds. Inflation was still very bad, but not like it was a few years back. If nothing else, Hitler had improved the financial state of the country.

I told my friends that I wanted to buy a map of the town so we set off in search of a book shop. Eventually I was able to buy one. I thought that if we went into a cafe for a snack, I could try to find the street called Kapitel. In between Mary's chat and Hugh's questions about what we had seen on our way into Lubeck, I managed to find what I was looking for on the map. When I paid the bill for Hugh I asked the waiter where Fegefeuer was. This was very adjacent to where I wanted to go and it was not far from where we were.

I confided in Hugh that I had to try and find a certain house for Mrs Jenkins. It was however, not to be mentioned and he must not tell Mary because girls cannot keep a secret for more than five minutes.

At last I found Kapitel Strasse. It was deserted, windows were boarded up and the whole street looked a mess. There were painted signs of the Star of David and the word 'Jew' daubed in red paint all over the place. There was no sign of any of the houses being occupied so my news for Mrs Jenkins will have to be bad. This must have been part of the Jewish quarter and I thought that we should move on as quickly as possible.

There were several cars parked in the street with two men in the front seats of each car. They just sat there and watched what was going on. Their presence prevented me from taking a photograph of this awful Strasse.

We continued our exploration and I bought some postcards to send home. One was for Polly, not that I told Mary about that one. We found a spot by one of the canals and sat on a seat to write our cards.

As I sat there I could visualise Mum, Dad and John at the farm and dear little Polly. I was getting myself into an awful mess with my two girlfriends. The trouble was that I found myself becoming more and more fond of them both. I think that Mary will be the real problem. She keeps linking arms and holding my hand and looking at me with those big brown eyes of hers, which I find most disturbing. I will have to watch my step otherwise she will lead me astray in more ways than one!

We heard a band playing in the distance which was becoming louder. Then it came into view followed by a large number of boys all in uniform. They marched very smartly and in perfect step. What struck me most forcibly was how similar they looked. Their hair was fair and closely cut, but not a smile could be seen on any of their faces. I asked a lady standing near us if they were boy scouts. She replied that they were members of the Hitler Youth Movement, which had replaced the boy scouts and girl guides in Germany. They were in fact the cream of Germany's youth and they will make Germany great again.

We found a post office and posted our cards. I expect that we will get home before them. As we walked back to the Hotel Berlin we decided not to mention our visit to the Jewish quarter as it might be embarrassing to Aunt Geraldine. We were early when we reached the hotel so we sat on a seat outside and watched the world go by. There were quite a few servicemen in uniform. There must be an airfield in the area as there had been quite a few planes flying over the town. I found it difficult to tell the difference between the army, air force and police uniforms. The SS wore black uniforms and strode around as if they owned the place.

It had been very interesting to watch Hugh during our morning in Lubeck. Whenever he had the chance he got out his small sketch pad and put on paper his impression of what he saw. I must remember to ask him to show me what he had drawn about Kapitel Strasse.

The two aunts finally arrived and we went into the hotel. We were told to wash our hands and were then shown to our table by a waiter. I had to explain to my friends what was on the menu and the three of us decided to have pork cutlets, red cabbage and mashed potatoes 'mit' dumplings. It was a smashing meal and we all seemed to be in a friendly mood. I then made the mistake of asking about the Hitler Youth Movement and could see that this had upset Aunt Geraldine.

She went into great detail about how she used to be the chief of the local girl guides and it was a great success. Likewise the boy scouts who visited England for a world jamboree to meet the chief scout, Lord Baden Powell, were also very successful. However, Hitler made the scout and guide movements illegal and formed the Hitler Youth, which of course was a completely different movement. As she spoke to us she looked around to see if anyone could hear what she was saying. I could see that she was upset and I soon changed the subject. I started to pull Mary's leg about what a huge lunch she had eaten and how fat she would get.

This caused a lot of laughter and eased the strain. Mary got her own back by squeezing my leg under the table and I had hell of a job to hide how I felt from her mother because it made me jump. Mary looked at me and gave one of her wicked little smiles and looked as though butter wouldn't melt in her mouth.

Aunt Geraldine told us that at the weekend there would be a Nazi Party rally and some high ranking Party members would be staying at the Castle for the night, so would we mind keeping out of the way and have our meals on our own, this would help no end as some of them were apparently a funny lot. As she said this she realised she had gone too far, but as she was with friends she was safe. She then told us that we could go back to Pansdorf in a round about way so that we could see some of the countryside.

We travelled back via an area to the North East of Lubeck passing Hemmelsdorfer, which was a very large lake connected to the sea by two rivers which became one by the time it reached the Baltic Sea.

We had some tea at a seaside town called Timmendorfer. It was a hot day and we were very envious of the people we saw bathing in the cool sea. Mary asked her aunt if we could swim in the river near the Castle as the water in the swimming pool looked a bit off. She replied that there was a very nice place which she will show us tomorrow. Mary's reaction to this news was a sharp dig in my ribs.

I managed to take a lot of snaps of my friends and the two aunts, but always with something interesting in the background which might be of interest to Jake and his friends. It would be quite a bonus if I could take a photograph of the big-wigs of the Nazi Party that were to visit the Castle at the weekend. Who knows? I might be lucky.

After dinner that evening my friends and I had a walk around a small part of the estate adjacent to the Castle. We decided to ask Uncle Willy if we could have the three ponies for the day and perhaps we could take a packed lunch with us so that we could really explore the estate.

The three of us all got on so well together and Mary had the habit of linking arms with Hugh and me. As we walked on that warm summer evening I started to think about the future and how it might all end.

Here I was, living in a fool's paradise, with people way out of my class. I was in a foreign country which may soon be at war with my own in a year or so and I have the job of surreptitiously taking photographs of bridges and other items which might be of interest to the Army Intelligence people.

I know that I am only fifteen years of age, but in my simple and innocent way I began to realise that I was falling in love with Mary. Being of tender years I presumed that this was what was happening to me. I wanted to be with her all of the time and when we had any physical contact it had a very strange effect on me. She was such a lovely girl, with a figure that was beginning to bloom and she was so full of confidence and fun, but at times she could be a vixen. I know that she has feelings towards me and I was not sure that perhaps it was not all part of a game to her.

When Hugh and I were together we felt so at ease with each other that at times we didn't have to talk. We seemed to be on the same mental plain. As we walked we were each having our own private thoughts. Hugh broke the silence by saying that he had been wondering why the three of us had been brought together, because of a bully called Joe. He said that the three of us had all benefitted from the incident in many ways. "I am not going to list them Henry, because in our hearts we know how we have all changed. Mary was a spoilt, bad-tempered little brat and I was afraid of my own shadow. You changed all that Henry. I also think that you had something to do with changing Papa's views of my drawing and painting." He continued to say that he and Mary had showed me how to behave in a higher society, which had changed me no end. "Luckily you are still the same Henry that we have always known and we must always remain friends."

I was quite moved by Henry's short speech. It was so unlike him to be so sentimental. He always seemed such a down to earth sort of chap, mind you he did appear to be in another world at times, but then artists are often a little odd.

Mary had remained very quiet but now she stopped in her tracks and told us that she loved us both. She then put her arms around my neck and said, "Dear Henry doesn't know it yet, but someday I am going to marry him!" With that remark she gave me a kiss that took my breath away.

We all burst out laughing and I told Mary that when she was older she would find a rich and handsome young man in her own class to marry. She would have lots of children and live happily ever after. She looked at me and told me not to be so silly. "Just you wait Henry my boy!"

Ever since I was very small I have had the most strange feelings about the future and some have been proved correct. As I was walking on that evening in Germany, for a brief second, a sort of dark cloud seemed to close my mind and I felt a panic for our future. This feeling soon passed but left me with an apprehension that was difficult to explain. To comfort myself I put my arm around Mary's waist and gave her a loving squeeze.

We had been walking for some time away from the Castle and towards a clump of trees and bushes. By now we were in a happy frame of mind and chatted away, but when we came closer to the trees we heard a moan coming from the undergrowth.

Mary was a bit frightened so Hugh and I went to investigate. Neither of us were prepared for the sight that was to meet us. We had never thought that we would see a human being in such distress. There was a young man, about twenty years of age. His head was shaved and he was so thin that the rags he wore as clothing seemed several sizes too large. He was in a filthy state and his poor face looked more like a mask. It was his eyes that really upset me. I had seen the same look in a rabbit's eye just before a fox or dog got it.

On the front of his torn coat was the word 'Jude'. I spoke to him in German and told him not to be afraid as we thought he must be one of the prisoners that were being hunted by the soldiers.

I had been warned by Jake and Major Davis not to get involved with the Jewish problem. But how could we not help this poor creature who was being hunted like an animal?

We didn't know what to do. I told Mary and Hugh the warning Jake had given me about helping Jews. If we were caught we would be in very serious trouble so we would have to think this out very carefully. On the other hand we couldn't just walk away.

We had to obtain some food and clothing from somewhere. The clothing would have to be German otherwise it could be traced to us if this poor soul was ever caught. Hugh remembered seeing some of the servants' clothing hanging on a line by the stables. Also some old coats were hanging just inside the stables.

We decided to return to the Castle and see what we could find. Mary said that she would go into the kitchen and scrounge some food. Hugh and I would try to get the clothes.

After explaining what we were going to do, we left the poor chap and went back to the Castle. I was not very happy about our plan, it was too much of a gamble. We could be found out. The Jew might be forced to tell his captors who had helped him.

With a great deal of luck, or perhaps with help from the Good Lord looking down on us, we must try to help him get away. After gathering the things we needed we returned to the undergrowth. Mary had been very thoughtful and had brought a wet cloth so that the Jew could wash his face and hands. He told us he was called Joseph and was very grateful to us for helping him. Hugh and I helped him into his new clothes while Mary kept watch.

I told Joseph to head north, keeping as close as possible to the railway line. A freight train may slow down or even stop and he may be able to get on board. That is if the poor chap had the strength to get that far. He may be lucky enough to stow away on a ship sailing into the Baltic.

When Joseph saw the food that Mary had brought for him, he ate as though he had never eaten before. As he ate he started to tell me some ghastly news about the things he had seen at the camps where he had been held prisoner.

I made up my mind to store this information away in my mind until I was safely at home in Devonshire. Even to think of it made me feel sick. I will spare my two dear friends this anguish.

We gave Joseph what little money we had on us and said our goodbyes. I asked him to take his old clothing with him and to dump them in the river, which would kill any scent the dogs may have.

We were in a very sad and subdued mood on our way back to the Castle. We would have to cheer up before we met the aunts for lunch or they might start asking questions.

We joined them in the main living room and asked Uncle Willy if we could have the three ponies for the day tomorrow together with a packed lunch so that we could explore the countryside. Uncle Willy suggested that we follow the river to the south until we came to a village called Rohisdorfer, but we were to keep out of the Reinfeld Forest because there was a large prison camp there and strangers were not welcome.

We talked for quite a while. I had to help Uncle Willy with his English and at times it was much easier to do a straight translation which pleased the old so and so.

Our conversation was interrupted by the entrance of the German equivalent of a butler. He was not a friendly sort of man and he looked very angry. He told his master that he had been robbed. Food had been taken from the kitchen and some clothes from the line. Should he report it to the local police? Aunt Geraldine said that as it was such a small loss and if the police came, they would be all over the place during the night. "Let us leave it at that," she said. As she said this she looked at my friends and I in an odd way. She may have seen us taking the clothes from the line. One thing is certain, we will never know. The episode was never mentioned again.

As Mary, Hugh and I went upstairs to our rooms we decided to go to Hugh's room and talk about the events of the day to try and calm ourselves down a bit. Mary seemed very upset and she kept talking about Joseph and how dreadful he looked. We decided that we would have to try to forget what had happened and not to mention it to anyone.

Of course, this was easier said, than done. I kept seeing Joseph's tortured face and the look of hopelessness in his eyes. I thought that his chances of escaping were nil. Who would help him? The German people as a whole hated the Jews and the punishment for any help given would be very severe.

At last we went to our separate rooms and eventually I fell asleep. However, my sleep was short-lived when I had the shock of my life. Standing next to my bed was Mary, quietly sobbing. Before I could do or say anything she was in my bed beside me. Instinctively I put my arm around her and tried to comfort her. She stopped crying and told me that she could not sleep, thinking about poor Joseph.

Mary only had on a thin nightgown and to feel her soft, warm body so close to mine was very disturbing. We started to kiss and I could taste her salty tears. Our kisses became more passionate. We were both very innocent about sex, I knew how the final sexual act was done, but that was something not even to be thought about. I also knew that some boys and girls experimented with each other.

What was happening to Mary and I was so natural and based on the fondness we felt for each other, without any thoughts of self-gratification. She took my hand and placed it on her young breasts and then she started to press her whole body against mine. I tried to hold back the course of nature, but in no time my seeds were sown on the front of Mary's nightie.

I really felt embarrassed and started to say how sorry I was. Mary shut me up with a kiss and told me how she loved me and to demonstrate how she felt she pulled up her nightie to that our bare bodies were close to each other. We lay like this for some time and what a wonderful feeling it was.

Suddenly I realised what we were doing and what the consequences would be if we were found out. I would be sent home in disgrace and Mary would be in big trouble. I explained all this to Mary and told her that she would have to go back to her room. We must tell no one about our wonderful experience.

I had quite a struggle to get her out of my room. The trouble was that we both would have liked to stay together for the rest of the night as we were both becoming sexually aroused again. I knew that we must part before anything else happened. At last I got Mary on her way and I returned to my bed that still had the sweet smell of Mary between the sheets.

As I lay there I thought about the mess I have got myself into. I will have to have a long talk to Mary tomorrow to see how we can hide our feelings for each other from Aunt Pamela. As I went to sleep that night I must admit I was so very happy.

When I awoke the next morning the sun was shining into my room and I felt quite happy at the prospect of riding around the estate with Mary and Hugh. It was more to my liking that walking around towns and shops.

I then remembered last night and my happiness turned to guilt.

136

However would I be able to face Mary? This problem was soon solved when Mary came into my room, this time in her dressing gown. She had a shy look on her face, but she soon got on to the bed and started to kiss me. How could I resist this lovely girl?

I began to give her a good talking to and told her how we would have to behave in the future. She laughed and with one of her wicked little smiles she said, "We will have to see about that won't we Henry dear?" After that remark I managed to push her off just before Hugh entered the room.

We started to talk about Joseph and wondered how he was getting on. We soon changed the subject because we had decided that we should try and forget this very disturbing episode. We had done all we could to help him under difficult circumstances.

Hugh and Mary went back to their rooms to get dressed and later we met downstairs for breakfast. Uncle Willy told us that he had three ponies for us and they would have saddle bags for our picnic and anything else that we wanted to take with us.

Aunt Geraldine suggested that we take our swimsuits with us as we would be passing the only place where we could swim in the river. Mary's reaction to the suggestion about having a swim was predictable. This time however she squeezed my leg much higher up and I got my own back by doing the same to her. This made her jump and lose her look of innocence. I was relieved to see that the grown-ups were deep in conversation and no notice was taken of our antics.

After a hearty breakfast we got our goods together. Of course, I concealed the camera in my haversack and we went to be introduced to our mounts for the day.

Uncle Willy was shouting at the stable hands and eventually three smashing ponies came into view. They had saddle bags with food neatly packed inside. We put our odds and ends in the bags and mounted the ponies. Soon we were on our way. It was really quite exciting to be riding forth in a strange country, not knowing where we would finish up.

It was a lovely morning and the sun was now high in the sky. It would be a very warm day and no doubt we will be glad of a swim to cool us down.

The countryside was divided by low hedges and ditches for drainage. On the slightly higher ground grew an abundance of trees of all sorts. There were oaks, elms, beech and I was surprised to see some walnut trees, which were becoming a rarity in our country.

We followed the river as best we could. There were parts that were so overgrown that the river just disappeared from view and we had to find where it came out again.

We came to the first bridge and I got my friends to pose on the bridge so that I could take a photograph. While I was at it I included a large part of the area.

Crossing the river and following the road, it was my plan to get as close as I could to the railway line. The map of Lubeck I had bought included a map of the adjoining areas. I calculated that we were not very far from the main line to Kiel.

The narrow road we followed took us through the forest and eventually we came to the railway line. At this point the river was not a great distance from the line so we followed it in a southerly direction. Several trains passed and there were quite a few bridges, so my camera was kept very busy.

We had just decided to get back to the river so that we could cool down in the water and had started to turn into the forest, when we heard a train coming down the track in the distance. We were just out of view of the train, but we could see it clearly as it passed by.

This train was very different to the others we had seen. There were army personnel on guard with guns and in the cattle trucks behind the engine it was just possible to see people huddled together inside. I managed to take several photographs as it passed by. I told Hugh and Mary that the poor people inside were going to the prison camp in the Reinfeld Forest. To keep the peace I asked them not to mention it to Aunt Geraldine or Uncle Willy, otherwise our wanderings may be curtailed.

At last we came to the point in the river which was suitable for swimming, described by Aunt Geraldine. By now we were very hot and the thought of a swim was just the job.

We gave the ponies a good long drink, loosened their saddles and tied them up in the shade where there was plenty of grass for them to eat.

It was a grand sight. There was a pool with a very low bank on one side and short grass growing down to the water's edge. The water was so clear that it was possible to see right down to the bottom. There was very little current because of the flatness of the terrain, but the water looked so clean and inviting. There were trees on the far bank and the river disappeared into a small wood as it went down stream. The river was quite wide at this point and pretty deep in parts.

We changed into our costumes and in no time were in the lovely cool water. I was trying to keep away from Mary, but she caught me by swimming under the water and coming up behind me. She wrapped herself around me and we both went under together. I broke away and swam to shallower water with Mary in hot pursuit. Hugh had swum down stream and was out of sight, so we were on our own.

We kissed and for the first time we fully explored each other's bodies which were so accessible in our swimming costumes. It was a lovely feeling, but very short-lived, as Hugh came into view. Mary went and lay on her towel and I joined her. The three of us sunbathed in the warm sunshine and just laid there, it was so peaceful and we didn't talk much. I think that we had our own thoughts and daydreams.

As I lay there my mind was occupied with thoughts of Mary as I lay next to her. I turned on my side so that I could look at her in her swimsuit. She not only had a lovely face, but her figure was perfection. To think that I had explored part of it was to me unbelievable. She must have sensed that I was looking at her because she slid one of her legs to rest against mine.

I will have a job getting used to not being with her all day and every day. Anyway, we have many more days left of our holiday, but even so, I must try to behave myself. Mary is making it so difficult with her tempting ways and her sexual inhibitions.

We roused ourselves and decided to eat. The cook had made us a smashing lunch complete with bottles of lemonade which we stood in the river to cool down. When we had finished eating we dressed and I fetched the horses to give them a drink.

The town map I had bought in Lubeck gave pretty good details of the surrounding countryside. According to my calculations there should be another bridge further down the river which would lead us to a village.

So far we had not seen anyone at close quarters. We had seen farmers working in distant fields so it would be a change to see what German country folk were like and perhaps we could buy an ice cream.

It must have been an unusual sight to see three young people on ponies, who were obviously not German. We were well stared at by the few people that were about. It looked a poor place. Of course, Germany had been through a very bad depression and that was how Hitler had come to power, by giving people work and hope for the future.

We stopped at what looked like a village store and our luck was in as they had some ice cream for sale. The shopkeeper was very friendly and asked where we had come from. I told him that we were staying with Graf Brecht and that we were English. This surprised him somewhat because of the way I was able to converse with him in German. I must remember not to show off so much!

We sat under a large tree in the centre of the village and ate our delicious ice cream. We thought that we ought to start our journey back to the Castle as during the day we had travelled quite a distance and it would take some time to get back.

We had a bit of a shock on the way back. We were stopped by an army patrol which seemed to come from nowhere. They were armed and had two very fierce-looking dogs with them, which I am glad to say were on a tight lead.

The officer in charge asked us for our papers so we gave him our British passports. I told him in very bad German that we were the guests of Graf Brecht and this changed his attitude completely. He asked us if we had seen a young escaped prisoner who seemed to have vanished. I asked him to describe what he looked like and of course he described Joseph.

One of the guards had taken his dog near to Mary's horse and it started to get scared. I shouted at the soldier in German to get out of the way and I must say that it made him jump. The officer apologised and we were once more on our way.

When we were well out of sight we had a good laugh, as it seemed that Joseph had made it out of the area. Mary told me that she felt proud of me for shouting at the soldier with the dog.

We were glad to get back to the Castle because by now we were very tired and in need of a hot bath. We met Aunt Pamela as we went into the hall and she told us that we smelt of horses so would we leave our clothes out to be washed. After I had my bath I felt refreshed and ready for a meal, so I went downstairs and sat in the garden until dinner time.

It was very peaceful until Uncle Willy joined me and I had to tell him what we had been doing all day. I told him about our swim down river and asked if there was a similar place up river, because our next trip would be in that direction. He told me that there were several nice places that we would find, but none were as nice as the one where we swam today.

Taking the bull by the horns, I asked him when his important friends were due to arrive. He told me that they were coming the next day at six o'clock. The big rally was being held at Lubeck in the big stadium on Saturday, the following day. They would be inspecting other places in the morning and would leave right after the rally.

I felt that I had to photograph the Nazi 'Top Brass'. I now had a time and all I have to do is find a place. I remembered that there was a cattle grid along the drive to the Castle. The cars would need to slow down going over this and if I could find some cover nearby I may be able to take some good photographs. I will suggest to my friends that we take a stroll in that direction after dinner.

Hugh and Mary joined us. Mary looked really lovely. She had washed her hair and her face was brown with the day's sunshine. As we walked in together to have dinner I whispered how smashing she looked and told her she was good enough to eat. She smiled and gave me a very old-fashioned look.

Of course, we had to tell everyone about our day, including the meeting with the soldiers. Uncle Willy told us that they were trying to catch a prisoner who was still missing before the 'Top Brass' arrived tomorrow. If they failed, someone would be in trouble.

We had a grand meal and really needed a walk. I told Hugh and Mary about my plan, which they thought was a bit odd, but they went along with it. There were some bushes by the cattle grid and I would be able to take my snaps without being seen. The sun would be at my back which would be a great help.

On the walk back to the Castle I asked Hugh if I could look at his sketch book to see his interpretations of what we had seen during the day. He said, "Of course, Henry. When I have finished them."

We thought it would be a good idea to have the horses again and to explore the North of the Castle. I told Hugh that Uncle Willy had said that there were other places to have a swim and we sat outside in the garden and talked until it was time for bed. The three of us felt pretty happy on that summer's evening. Sitting in a foreign country, miles away from home. I felt a bit guilty as I had not felt at all homesick in any way.

We went into the sitting room and asked if we could have the horses again tomorrow and this news seemed to please the aunts. We said goodnight and the three of us climbed the long staircase towards our rooms.

Hugh went into his room first, which left Mary and I alone on the landing. We both had the same thought at the same time and put our arms around each other for a kiss goodnight. I had a job to break up this embrace, but we heard someone coming up the stairs which quickly sent us both on our different ways.

It was a very warm night so I didn't bother to put on my pyjamas. I just lay there wondering how I will be able to settle down to my life at home. There will be no Mary, as she will be away at school and I will have to work like mad to get in to agricultural college. What will I say to dear little Polly? With these thoughts spinning around my head I finally fell asleep.

At first, I thought I was dreaming, but I soon woke up to the fact that Mary was in my bed and naked like me. Her hands were wandering all over my body and mine were all over hers. She took my hand and pressed it between her legs, inviting me to really explore her lovely body. Unfortunately, this lovely feeling was short-lived because I was unable to hold back the flow of nature, which went all over Mary.

When this happened she gave a cry of joy and pressed herself as close as she could to me and continued to rub herself against me. In no time at all she had me sexually roused again. This time it was not such a frantic affair and we enjoyed our lovemaking more than we thought possible. We were only playing at it because to take the ultimate plunge was something we could never think of doing. I thought that Mary would never stop kissing me.

Eventually she calmed down and we just lay there, whispering to each other about how we felt and we both knew that it was wrong. But it was such a natural and loving act that we consoled each other and felt that perhaps it was not such a sin after all. It bore no resemblance to the lurid tales I had been told by some of the boys at college about their sexual adventures.

I think that we must have dozed off laying in each other's arms. I opened my eyes to find that it was just beginning to get light. I looked at the sweet girl who I thought was asleep. She opened her eyes and said, "Please Henry darling, make love to me again." I told her that she had to return to her room otherwise we may be found out.

I had no choice, not that I really wanted one. She pulled me on top of her and wrapped her legs around me so that I was well and truly trapped. Each time seemed better than the time before, but at least Mary left me to ponder what had taken place in this bedroom in a Castle in Germany.

We must stop these nightly visits and we will have to try to hide our feelings for each other. I know what Mary will say. She will point out that we will not be sleeping under the same roof for a very long time, if ever again, so why not make the most of it? I know there is some logic in this thinking, but we are getting so very involved.

What we had just done was very dangerous. We could have slept until late in the morning and then we would have been well and truly in the soup. I never realised how two people could get so much pleasure from each other in such a natural way. I wonder why so many people look upon sex as a dirty word.

What has happened between Mary and I was not pre-arranged. It just happened and evolved into something that I will always remember with joy and as part of my education in life. I will never tell anyone about this. It is to me too sacred. Anyway, I have never liked people who kiss and tell.

I put on my pyjamas and managed to get some more sleep, until I was awakened by Mary looking very prim and proper in her dressing gown. Her hair was combed and she looked as fresh as a daisy. We just had time to kiss before Hugh came in.

Being with Mary made me feel embarrassed and to a certain extent I could see that Mary had a similar feeling. What had happened only a few hours ago was bound to have an affect on both of us. We have become more adult in such a short space of time.

Soon we were both more relaxed and back to being good friends as well as sweethearts.

The three of us sat on my bed and looked at the map. The river passed through forests and farm land. We decided to cross the river and follow it northwards to a village called Sarkwitz. With a bit of luck we would be able to find somewhere to swim.

As we were busy studying the map, Aunt Pamela came in to the room and had a good laugh at the three of us sitting cross-legged on the bed looking at the map. We told her we were making plans for the day.

She told us that there would be soldiers patrolling the grounds at night as Uncle Willy's guests were pretty high up in the German Government. We would have to keep out of the way as much as possible.

We would have our dinner in the breakfast room much later than usual. I was pleased to hear this as it would give me plenty of time to take some photographs. As she left Aunt Pamela told us that Uncle Willy had commented how well-behaved we all were. At this point Mary looked at me and we were both thinking if only they knew what we had been up to.

After a very hearty breakfast we loaded up and were on our way. We felt pleased and were looking forward to the day's prospects. The weather was fine and warm so we should have a good day.

For part of the way we had to ride single file. Hugh liked to lead, Mary was in the middle and I was at the rear. I liked this because I could look at Mary and relive what had happened to me since I arrived in Germany. At times I thought that it was all a dream and I would soon wake up in bed on the farm. I began to wish that I had never come to Germany and that I had retained the innocence that I had before I had come to Germany.

The path became wider and Mary dropped back to ride beside me leaving Hugh some way ahead. She asked me what I was thinking about and I told her that I was very worried about our relationship and how it had developed in such a short time. It would have to end when we went home. "You will be returning to school Mary, and not coming home until Christmas. What future is there for us?"

She reached over, took my hand and said, "Dear Henry, I have had the same thoughts and the only thing we can do is to enjoy each other while we are here and be very careful. Who knows what fate has in store for us? Always remember that I do love you, so very much." With that remark she galloped ahead to join Hugh.

We crossed the river and made for some higher ground that we

143

could see in the distance. The thought behind this move was that we would get a good view of the area. The ground was so flat that only a few feet above the average level would extend our vision a great deal.

When we reached the top of this small hill we dismounted and walked around to the far side. We were surprised to see a small airfield in the distance. This was only just visible because it was a long way away. I took a photograph of this but thought it was probably too far away.

We also spotted three different army units searching the ditches, hedgerows and bushes, presumably for poor Joseph. The sun was behind us and we could see the sun's reflection on the soldiers' field glasses pointing our way. It was strange because I had seen this happen in a film Polly and I had seen at the cinema.

As this came to mind I felt very guilty and looked at Mary. I thought about the mess I have got myself in.

Perhaps it was an unusual sight to see three young people on ponies. I must say that we had not seen anyone else on horseback. I expect we will during the weekend. By now the army units were spreading out and really searching the area.

The airfield was too far away and the rest of the countryside looked so very uninteresting, that we decided not to investigate further in that direction. Instead, we headed for the river as we were feeling very hot and hungry.

At last we found a suitable spot with a bank on one side that was shallow and the water fairly brisk in its flow. This will add to its freshness.

We gave the horses a good drink and tied them up in the shade. In no time at all we were in the water splashing about and having a great deal of fun.

After our meal we laid in the sun and Hugh started to sketch this beautiful spot. In spite of Hugh's presence, Mary snuggled up to me and we both fell asleep to make up for what we had lost last night.

We stayed by the river for quite a long time. Perhaps because it was so very peaceful, or we were just in a lazy mood. Hugh was quite happy to sketch and Mary and I had several swims and close encounters under the water. Not that it mattered much as Hugh became so engrossed in his work that I was sure that he was out of this world.

Mary and I teased each other and talked about all sorts of things. Somehow I could talk to her about some of the things I had dreams about and we seemed to be getting closer and closer to each other. I knew that our feelings for each other could only be of a short duration. We both decided to let nature take its course for the remainder of the holiday and worry about the consequences afterwards. We were both so very young and this was our first emotional adventure. We had no idea of what may happen in the future.

When we returned to the Castle we were surprised to see several army units on or near the road leading to the main entrance. It then dawned on us that they were keeping the area clear for the 'big white chief', whoever he may be.

We rode along the main drive to the Castle without seeing any more soldiers, but as Hugh said, they would be on the perimeter of the estate.

The Castle was a hive of activity. The servants were being shouted at by Uncle Willy, whose face was redder than ever. He looked as though he would go pop any minute!

We took the horses to the stables and made our way to our rooms to bath and change. There was no sign of the aunts, no doubt they were keeping out of the way as the Count was going around like a scalded cat.

Having a bath was a bit of a problem because there were two bathrooms for the whole landing and we usually let Mary have one while Hugh and I tossed a coin for the other one. I lost the toss so was last in line. Hugh gave me the all clear when he had finished and I went into the bathroom. I got a hell of a shock as Mary had hidden herself behind the door. She had her dressing gown on which was left open at the front so that I could see her lovely body.

What a tempting little vixen she is! I soon managed to push her out of the bathroom, but not before we had a passionate kiss. I told her that she would have to go as it was far too dangerous to take such a risk. As usual she told me not to be silly. I gave her bare bottom a good smack and with a laugh she was off.

When we were all ready we went downstairs and found Aunt Pamela. We told her that we were just going for a short walk before dinner. So with my camera hidden by a jumper over my arm we made our way down the main drive. When we came to the cattle grid I disappeared into the nearby bushes. Hugh and Mary sat on an old tree trunk.

We didn't have long to wait. It was just after six o'clock when we heard the sound of motor vehicles in the distance. We could see quite a cavalcade coming up the drive. There were two police motorcyclists in the lead, three large cars came next and then two motorbikes with side-cars were at the rear, which were manned by the army.

As expected, they were travelling at a fair old lick, but when they came to the cattle grid they slowed down quite considerably. They went over it at a crawl and I managed to take two photographs of the largest and most important-looking vehicle. When I saw who was inside, I realised what all the fuss was about.

When we were in Lubeck I had seen posters with large photographs of Herman Goering all over the place. I hadn't connected this with the visit that Uncle Willy had told us about.

Goering was the head of the German Air Force which was now called The Luftwaffe. Perhaps the airfield we had seen in the distance was of some importance. If my photographs come out they may be of interest to Major Davis and his chums. One thing is certain, no one at College will believe me when I tell them that I stayed in the same place as Herman Goering.

When the cavalcade had passed we made our way back to the Castle. By now we were all very hungry and hoped that dinner would not be long.

At last a maid told us that we could go into the breakfast room for our dinner. The two aunts were eating with the bigwigs so we had quite a bit of fun by ourselves. The food was smashing and I made a pig of myself, I'm glad to say that my friends were just as bad.

We took a long time to eat our dinner and we talked about the situation in Germany. In March, conscription was introduced. All the people with mental or physical imperfections were sterilised so that any children born in the future would be perfect specimens to carry on the German race.

We talked about these depressing subjects for some time, but we knew we had to face the facts. The Nazi Party were up to no good. Hugh and Mary were fairly ignorant about world affairs and I thought that their schools were trying to protect them from the real world. I made up my mind to let them know what was going on. I wanted to save them the shock of what might take place in the future.

We managed to move ourselves away from the comfort of the breakfast room and intended to go for a short walk to help our digestion. As we went out of the front door we saw Uncle Willy and his guests in small groups talking. He spotted us and to our dismay, called us over to be introduced to the honoured guest.

Mary was introduced first and she put on her shy young lady look. Then it was Hugh's turn and I could see his attitude was similar to how his father's would have been in these circumstances, very cool and aloof.

When it came to my turn I decided to break one of my rules and speak as near perfect German as I could. I was introduced as a friend of the family and when I spoke I could see that notice was being taken, not by Goering, but by an officer in a black uniform. He asked how I came to speak German so well and did many children of my age speak the language. I told him that I had a very good teacher and that German was not taught to a great extent as English seemed to be a universal language. After this remark he seemed to lose interest.

We managed to escape and walked down to the small river that ran through the estate before it joined the River Schwartau. There was a spot that was similar to my favourite place at Langley Hall.

I have no idea what came over me, but for the first time I felt homesick. I began to wonder how everyone was at the farm. I knew I was lucky to have this wonderful holiday, but somehow it all seemed so unreal. Especially my meeting with Herman Goering and his staff. Then of course there was my affair with Mary. That in itself was more like a fairy tale. I sat looking at her and she looked more lovely than ever. She must have sensed that I was looking at her because she turned and gave me such a sweet smile. She then came closer and sat beside me.

We talked about our plans for the next day and decided that we would explore the Castle and the grounds by foot, giving the horses a rest. Of course, this was subject to any plans the aunts may have.

I told Hugh and Mary that when we were in Lubeck I had seen that there were boat trips around the harbour and out into the estuary. Perhaps we could do that next week. I had spent very little money so far and this could be my treat.

There was method in my suggesting this. Lubeck was a busy port and a few photographs might be useful. Hugh was very enthusiastic because he loved to go on any type of boat and could do some good sketching.

Mary also approved of the idea. How she had changed over the few years that I have known her. At first she was a real bossy boots and rather spoiled, always wanting her own way. Now, she knew what she wanted, but her approach was very different.

It was getting very late so we made our way back to the Castle. In the distance we could see several army patrols with guns over their shoulders.

Mary had linked arms with me and Hugh was walking ahead as usual. I began to think that he knew that there was something cooking between Mary and I. She had the habit of putting her arm around my waist and then slipping her hand inside the back of my trousers. Needless to say I found this most disturbing in more ways than one.

She whispered, "Dear Henry, please may I come and visit you tonight?" I knew this would happen and had made up my mind to say no. But hell, how could I? I told her to come after her Mother had gone to sleep. I thought that Aunt Pamela would be late going to bed and by this time Mary would have fallen asleep.

When we entered the main hall we could hear laughter coming from the sitting room. We thought that we would steer clear of that and started to make our way up the high staircase. We met Aunt Pamela on the way and she said that she was going to bed soon. She was fed up with the arrogant Germans. She also told us that breakfast would be late, as the other guests would be served first. Aunt Pamela would let us know when we could surface in the morning.

Hugh told his mother that we were going to have a lazy day tomorrow and thought we would explore the Castle and grounds. She said that Aunt Geraldine had thought of taking us for a drive in the afternoon, but we would wait and see what happens. She wished us all goodnight and went downstairs to join the guests, not looking very happy at the prospect.

Hugh went into his room and Mary followed me into mine where I told her to buzz off. With one of her wicked little smiles she kissed me and said how strange it was that she had started to walk in her sleep since we had arrived in Germany. After that parting remark she went to her room.

I undressed and got into bed, but even with the window wide open it was very warm. I lay there with just a sheet over me and started to think about things in general.

I wanted Mary to visit me, but on the other hand I knew that we were pushing our luck and becoming too involved. I was beginning to think about nothing else and I wanted physical contact with her whenever possible. Somehow I will have to calm down, but it is all very difficult because she is a temptress in a very innocent way.

How would I settle down to the humdrum way of farm life after living in such luxury? My horizons have certainly been broadened. It seemed such a short time ago, that fateful day, when Mother asked me to deliver cream and butter to Langley Hall. My path may not have crossed that of Hugh and Mary if I had not made that journey. I would not be lying in a bed in a Castle in Germany, waiting for a sexual encounter with a gorgeous girl called The Honourable Miss Mary Howes. The more I lay and thought about this, the more I thought that it must all be a dream. No one at home would ever believe me when I tell them that I had been introduced to Herman Goering, so perhaps this is just a dream after all.

At this point I must have dropped off because the next thing I knew was that a young girl was lying next to me in her birthday suit, tenderly exploring my lower quarters. What a lovely feeling it was to have her next to me and to smell the female scent which was always present on her body.

We made love in the only way we knew how without Mary losing her virginity. We became more adventurous and somehow managed to satisfy each other more with each encounter. We both knew that complete satisfaction could only be obtained by breaking the rules, which we had both sworn not to do.

We lay there in each other's arms until nature took its course and once more we were making love. After this we blew caution to the wind and went to sleep in each other's arms. As I lay there before sleep took over me, I thought that this feeling of contentment must be something very few people have at our age.

To wake up with my dear Mary beside me was something that I will always remember with great joy. To see the sleepiness in her eyes and her dark hair spread over my pillow, the feel of her warm young body next to mine, is something I could never clear from my mind. I really think that she felt the same.

To get her to go back to her own room was a problem. I think that she would like to stay where she was all day. Come to think of it, so would I!

It was now becoming quite light and I had to push her out of bed before she made any effort to go back to her own room. We fooled around for a bit, then at last she left.

When I was eventually on my own I tried to sleep, but Mary was still very much on my mind and sleep was slow in coming. I could still smell her scent in the bed which didn't help matters.

It was much later than usual when I woke up, not that it mattered because we knew breakfast would be late this morning. However, I didn't have to wait too long before Mary and Hugh came in for our early morning conference.

Mary greeted me by saying "Good morning Henry dear. I hope that you slept well last night." She really is a little so and so. I had to turn away because I began to blush like mad. I would have liked to get my own back, but Hugh was in the room.

When I was washed and dressed I quietly opened Mary's door and went in. She was sitting at a dressing table doing her hair, wearing only her underwear and I could see where her swimsuit had been as it had left the rest of her body a warm cream colour in contrast to the sun-tanned parts.

I came up behind her, kissed the back of her neck and ruffled her freshly brushed hair. She tried to hit me with her hairbrush and chased me out of the room.

Breakfast went down really well. There was just the three of us and Aunt Pamela so it was a very relaxed meal. Mary gave me a rough time to repay me for ruffling her hair by tickling me where she shouldn't whenever I spoke to her mother. I found it very hard to keep a straight face and I hoped that Mary's mother didn't realise what was going on.

Young people to tend to think that their elders are a bit on the dim side. What they forget is the fact that when they were young they probably did the same sort of things. I do hope that Aunt Pamela has not twigged what was going on between Mary and I.

We had just finished breakfast when we heard the roar of several low flying aircraft. We rushed outside and were just in time to see a flight of fighter aircraft climbing high into the sky. The Nazi guests were standing in a group away from the main building. It then dawned on me that the planes were giving their Commander-in-Chief a salute.

We then heard a sound which was very disturbing. The planes came down in a vertical dive making a terrible screaming noise, which was enough to put the fear of God into you. It looked as though they were going to crash right in front of us, but they pulled out of the dive just in time. The Germans cheered and clapped their hands in joy at seeing this devilish display.

I walked up to one of the guards who stood nearby and asked him what the aircraft were that we had just seen. He very proudly told me that they were dive bombers called Stuka. I was not to know it then, but what havoc they were to cause in the future.

Hugh and I talked about what we had just seen and what a terrible weapon they would be. The sound would be very demoralising for anyone under attack.

We went back into the Castle and watched the departure of the Nazi mob. The staff were all lined up to give their show of respect. Herman Goering turned just before he got into his car and gave the Nazi salute and shouted "Heil Hitler." Uncle Willy and the whole staff returned the salute.

With a roar of engines the cavalcade was on its way down the drive to I know not where. I did however take the risk of taking more photographs of the whole company through the open window. Who knows, it might prove interesting to Major Davis.

We were just standing there trying to get over the frightening display we had just seen, when in came Aunt Geraldine to say that she would like to take us for a drive after lunch. If we felt in need of any refreshments during the morning we could visit cook in the kitchen. One thing is certain, we won't forget that advice.

We had been staying at the Castle for several days, but somehow had not really looked the place over. It really was a very large complex. The stables were very large indeed with many grooms and stable hands.

I tried to get into conversation with several of them but they all seemed unwilling to relax and talk freely. Most of them were older men and boys of my age. Conscription had taken the in between age group. I was to learn that they were not used to being treated as an equal. Once the barrier had been broken down they were a very friendly lot.

As we were looking at the horses there seemed to be one horse in a very unhappy state. Without thinking I went into the stall and spoke to the animal in English and at once he became quiet. I had not noticed that one of the older grooms was leaning over the gate with a broad grin on his face. He asked me how I knew that this horse had just been shipped in from England.

I explained that it was just luck because the only clue I had was the fact that the horse had an English bridle on. Anyway, it solved something that I had always wanted to find out, that animals had the same language problems as humans.

By now quite a number of the stable lads and grooms had gathered and before we knew it the atmosphere had changed. The man I had been talking to was the head groom and in charge of the stables. Hugh and Mary were bystanders while this was going on, but they got the gist of what was happening.

The head groom was called Kurt and he asked me to write down a few simple words of English which he could say to the horse until he became used to the German language. As we left he called after us, "Master, when you next want a horse I will give you the Englander." Thereafter the horse was always known as Englander.

By now we were feeling a bit peckish so we found our way to the kitchen. What I found so awful was the subservient attitude of the staff at the Castle. I could only compare this to the way things were at Langley Hall. I could look at this as an outsider and what I saw was very feudal, but to the extreme in Germany.

The kitchen was very similar to the one at Langley Hall, only much larger and with more servants busily preparing food. The cook was very friendly and gave us some very nice cakes and cups of coffee, which we took outside where we ate our feast sitting in the warm sunshine.

We then went to the back of the Castle and were surprised to see a very large kitchen garden.

In the distance we could see a small farm so we went to have a closer look. There were milking cows, masses of pigs and poultry running wild. I must say that I felt much more at home in this environment. We met the farmer and I was able to have a good chat with him. After having a good look around we made our way back to the Castle for lunch.

In the afternoon we went for a drive with Aunt Geraldine. This time we went on a westerly tack through some very dense forests and had tea in a very picturesque village near the Schwinkenrade Forest.

Mary, Hugh and I had a walk around the village and came to the conclusion that it was a bit of a bore. We decided that as it was Sunday tomorrow we would ask if we could have a day out on the horses. Next week we will see if we can have a trip on the river at Lubeck.

Dinner that evening was good fun. Uncle Willy was at the rally, shouting Sieg Heil and stabbing the air with Nazi salutes. Consequently, the atmosphere was more relaxed and as a special treat we all had wine with our meal.

Hugh mentioned our plans for the next two days and Aunt Geraldine thought that the trip in the harbour area was a good idea. She said she would arrange for us to be taken to Lubeck and fetched later in the day. On the other hand we might go into Lubeck for the day. She wanted to buy Mary a smart new dress and while they were buying this, Hugh and I could have our river trip.

This pleased Mary no end. The thought of a new dress and having drunk two glasses of wine made her very happy. She turned to me and asked what colour dress should she buy. I blushed like mad and said that I knew nothing of such matters, but I thought blue would suit her. She really put me on the spot and she knew it. The little monkey will pay for this later. Anyway, the aunts had a good laugh over my confusion.

We took our usual walk after dinner, but this time the aunts joined us and it was very pleasant. Aunt Geraldine kept asking me questions about my family and what my plans were for the future. I told her that sometimes I wanted to go to agricultural college and at other times I thought I would like to learn at least one other language.

When Mary heard this she offered to teach me French. Whilst saying this she linked my arm and kissed my cheek in front of the aunts, which I thought was much too friendly in front of them.

Aunt Pamela then said that she was so pleased that I had been able to come away with them, as somehow I was able to make Hugh and Mary happy and kept them out of trouble. (Oh boy, if only she knew what Mary and I had been up to!)

It was so difficult to know what people in such a high social class thought about things in general. Did Aunt Pamela take for granted my close friendship with Mary? In my class we were being very naughty. On the other hand I have never been told what was right or wrong where sex was concerned.

We were late going to bed that night. When we got back to the Castle Aunt Geraldine gave us another glass of wine and we talked about all sorts of things and generally enjoyed ourselves. At last we said goodnight and went to our rooms.

Mary had given no indication that she would be paying me a visit later in the night. Perhaps she would give it a miss tonight and catch up on her sleep. One half of me wanted her to come, but the other half told me that we should slow down our sexual activities.

I undressed and got into bed. I lay there for some time and decided to get some sleep when I heard my door open very quietly. I knew that Mary would soon be in my bed.

We were becoming more experienced in our lovemaking and gave each other so much more satisfaction. We had passed the adolescent frenzy of our early encounters and could now enjoy each other in a more leisurely way.

We had very little sleep that night and when we did sleep, we were in each other's arms. It was such a lovely feeling, the moistness of our bodies locked together.

It was almost daylight when Mary went back to her room. We were getting more and more daring with these nightly visits. We will be very lucky indeed if we are not found out before we return to England.

After breakfast we went to collect our horses. The head groom was at the stables and he led Englander for me to ride. He was a handsome horse and I was interested to know what he could do.

Our day out was very similar to previous outings with the horses. We had good fun and had an enjoyable day. We swam, once more in a different location, sunbathed and Hugh got busy with his sketch pad.

I photographed another section of the railway line and a few bridges, but nothing of great importance. What I was trying to do was to build up a picture of the area as a whole. It will then be up to Major Davis to use whatever is useful, if anything.

At dinner that night Uncle Willy kept raving on about how successful the rally had been. Aunt Geraldine tried to change the subject, but without success, so she let him ramble on in his very bad English.

Mary and I decided to behave ourselves that night. We were both very tired and needed a good night's sleep to make up for what had transpired last night. It may have been the wine, but we really let our hair down.

The next morning we were up early and right after breakfast we were on our way to Lubeck. Mary was excited at the prospect of having a new dress and Hugh and I were looking forward to our boat trip.

The females were dropped by the Hotel Berlin and then the chauffeur took us to the harbour. I had my camera, fully charged in case I saw any interesting subjects. We found a boat ready to leave which advertised a trip right around the town's perimeter canals, then around the harbour and on into the estuary.

It was very interesting to see this old town with houses right on the water's edge. There was the remains of a thick wall which ringed part of the town and would have been part of the town's early fortifications. Today there were nine bridges, but no doubt in olden days there would have been far less. I managed to get them all in the can, as they say in Yankee films!

The architecture was so very different to that of the British. For one thing the church spires were very tall and finished in a very sharp point. Overall, the buildings were much taller. They also looked as if they had been influenced by builders from the Middle East. Of course, Germany used to consist of different principalities and no doubt there were periods of war. Lubeck was quite a gem for an invader. It was an important trading port for the northern area.

Parts of the town had managed to grow trees close to the canals and this added to the beauty of the place. Hugh and I decided to have a closer look at the town centre if the opportunity arose.

The harbour was very busy and to our surprise we saw a British ship unloading clay. This must have come from Teignmouth because ball clay was only mined in Devon and it was sent all over the western world. I reminded Hugh of our holiday in Teignmouth a long time ago and how we had watched clay being loaded on to ships in the harbour.

In one part of the harbour we saw several small fast-looking Navy patrol boats. There were also other vessels painted in battleship grey. I took several photographs of this area. To remind me where it was on the map, I marked it with some dirt from one of the ship's rails. This would make it less obvious should anyone look at my map.

There were very few passengers on the boat so Hugh and I could move around quite freely. I could see from his expression that Hugh was really enjoying himself. How he loved to be on the water.

Looking at him I thought what a great friend he was and how well we got on together. I will miss him a great deal when he returns to school.

Sitting in the boat I began to daydream for a spell. Dad had said, on more than one occasion, that the only way to really get to know someone was to actually live with them for a week or two. That way you can see the different sides of their nature.

Where Hugh was concerned I think that I know him pretty well. He is not a complex person and his main passion in life is painting. Sometimes we talked and other times we were content just to be in each other's company with our own thoughts. He also had a great sense of humour and at times we pulled Mary's leg unmercifully.

Now, Mary was a very different cup of tea and in my young way I loved her dearly. We certainly had a very close sexual attraction and we seemed to be on the same wavelength. We were so at ease with each other and I think that I have seen most sides of her character. Of course, being female one never knows what is in her mind!

At the end of this holiday I will have been with her all day, every day and for that matter most of the nights. We should know each other by then. One thing is certain and that is that I am dreading not being able to see her every day when we go home.

How different it will all seem when I am back at the farm. It is such a different world with values bearing no resemblance to each other. However did I become involved in this complex situation? I was a visitor to a completely alien life, the sad part being that I liked it but could never be a part of it. It made me wish that I had not tasted the fruits of such a luxurious existence.

Perhaps it was the gentle rocking of the boat and the rhythm of the engine that made me have these thoughts. How would I be able to look Polly in the eye after my affair with Mary? This affair would have to end because we are so young and living a totally different way of life. We have been thrown together by fate and fate will no doubt decide our future, if there is to be one.

Hugh must have noticed how deep I was in my thoughts and he asked me if there was anything wrong. I told him about my fears and how unsettled I had become. I also told him of my feelings for Mary, but not about our nightly meetings. Much to my surprise he told me that he knew how Mary and I felt about each other and said that Mary could be a bit selfish and at times very bossy. However, he knew her well enough to know that she really cared for me.

He said, "Whatever you do, please do not hurt Mary. If the future frightens you let it take its course. I know that you are also very fond of Polly and you will have to make up your mind one way or the other. At the moment Mary is out of your reach because of the class barrier. She will no doubt get ideas from her friends at school. It is also very possible that she will meet someone else."

"I also know why you are with us," he continued. "I overheard Papa and Uncle Jake talking on the telephone. There will be a war. One only has to look around Germany to see that they are planning something. Now I am the only one that knows so please don't get worried."

"If there is a war you and I will be in it so stop thinking so much about the future and enjoy today. By the way Henry, I will have some very interesting things in my sketch book for you to show Major Davis."

Somehow I was pleased that Hugh knew about the reason for my visit to Germany. It will be great to be able to talk to someone about it.

We were now going towards the very large estuary. Parts of the shore were very bare. On one side there was a forest growing down to the water's edge. Looking on my map I could see that it was called the Schonberg Forest.

Some of the trees had recently been felled and I could see building activity going on. There were also two dredgers working near the shore. There were a lot of workmen visible on the site, so it had to be a large project.

I could just see the outline of the buildings under construction. They were very low, in fact they seemed to be partly underground. They were long, going inland, with narrow entrances at the water's edge. There were no windows and it looked as if they were being built of concrete.

One of the crew passed us at this point so I asked him what was being built. He told me that it was very hush-hush, but everyone knew that it was for submarines.

When he disappeared I took several photographs of Hugh with the shore in the background. Hugh pointed out that it would be a smashing place to have a submarine base as most of the trees were evergreen and it would have natural cover from the air.

We didn't go as far as the actual sea. We could see it and smell the fresh ozone on the inshore breeze. We turned around and made our way back to a point nearer to town. After we left the boat we managed to catch a bus to the Hotel Berlin where we were to meet the females.

We sat outside and watched the people go by. The Germans looked so similar to ourselves and yet they were so different in other ways. Perhaps it was the fact that, compared to our country, as a nation they were only just beginning their life. We have been a nation for many centuries, but Germany was only a couple of hundred years old as a united country. Perhaps feeling insecure has made them arrogant and so bellicose.

My daydreaming was brought to a close by a nudge from Hugh. He had spotted the females in the distance, loaded with parcels. Mary had her new dress on and she looked really lovely.

She ran up to me and gave a quick twirl. "Henry, do you like my new dress?" I told her that she looked really marvellous. Before I knew what was happening, she dropped her parcels and gave me a kiss so I put my arms around her waist and swung her around so that the skirt of her new dress billowed out.

I felt most self-conscious about my actions, but luckily the aunts thought it was a great joke. I picked up Mary's parcels and with her on my arm we went into the hotel. Mary told me that she had two new dresses and she would show me the other one when we returned to the Castle.

Much to my surprise she added that Aunt Geraldine had bought me a smart shirt and a jumper for Hugh. "Mama has bought you a jumper as well. I chose it so I hope you like it Henry." This was good news indeed as I did look the poor relation at times.

When we were settled at our table for lunch I thanked them most profusely for the gifts they had bought me. Mary was making me wait until we returned to the Castle before I could see them.

Lunch was most enjoyable and afterwards the aunts said that they would like to do some more shopping. Mary, Hugh and I decided to walk around the town. Four o'clock was our deadline so we had quite some time before we had to meet the aunts.

When Hugh and I were on the boat we had seen a very interesting building on one of the main canal crossings. The map gave it the name of Hoistentor and it was a museum. After asking the way we eventually found it.

It was an amazing old building built in 1466. It acted as a fortified entrance with two large round towers on either side of the gateway, both with very pointed spires. The gateway was very narrow and only suitable for medieval traffic. Looking at it one could see that in its time it would have kept away any unwanted visitors.

We had a good look around and found it very interesting. I had to translate the information given about many of the items on display which became tedious after a while, so I suggested we moved on.

We found a cafe with tables outside so we had some of Lubeck's ice cream. We sat there for some time talking and watching the people go by. We watched a group of the Hitler Youth Movement and somehow they gave the impression that they thought that they were far superior to the other young people not it their stupid uniform. This of course is what they had been taught.

The aunts soon came into view when we reached the Hotel Berlin. They were loaded with parcels and the morning purchases had been safely stored in the hotel, so this was another lot. How females love to shop, usually for clothes. How different it is with nature. The male is the one that makes a display of colour and finery and humans are the other way around.

For several days now I have had the impression that Aunt Geraldine was not very happy and she would like to come back to England with us. Listening to parts of conversations I understood that she had not visited her own country for a long time. She had dual nationality so she could of course come and go as she pleased. This freedom was not available to all the German people.

I really felt sorry for Aunt Geraldine. She was such a nice person and had accepted me into her household. She treated me as one of the family. Her husband, the Baron, was such an old bore and of course his fondness for the Nazi Party made matters worse where his wife was concerned. The Nazi's attitude was so different to the British way of life.

The car arrived as arranged and we began the journey back to the Castle. It had been a very pleasant day out and we all seemed in a good mood. I was trying to persuade Mary to let me have my two presents, but she would not give in. She said that I could have them after I had seen her wearing her second dress. Girls are really most strange creatures.

It was quite a long drive from Lubeck and by the time we arrived at the Castle it was almost time for our baths before dinner, but first I had to see this new dress.

It was a very smart affair which made Mary look older. The style showed off her smashing figure and I told her she looked good enough to eat. We were in her bedroom and after a struggle I managed to get my new shirt and jumper.

Hugh had bagged one of the bathrooms so I had to wait my turn. I was trying on my new shirt when Mary came into my room. She was only wearing her dressing gown and was on her way to the bathroom. She wanted to see what my new shirt looked like on me so I had to strip off the shirt I was wearing, then she was at me.

She let her dressing gown fly open as she chased me until we both fell on the bed laughing like mad. I had to be strong-willed not to make love to her, but much to her annoyance, I managed to push her out of my room. As she left she told me she would see me later, which of course she did when it was safe and everyone else was asleep.

We were to start the marathon trip home tomorrow. It would take the same pattern, but in reverse. We would have to make an early start to board the overnight ferry to Harwich, with the help of the Thomas Cook agent of course.

On this last day in the late afternoon I was sitting by the lake by myself. Hugh was putting the finishing touches to a sketch of the Castle that he was giving to his aunt and uncle. Mary was with her mother busy packing.

The last few days had gone by without anything of great importance happening. My friends and I had enjoyed ourselves and rode all over the district. As the fine warm weather held we were able to swim everyday. I managed to take some more photographs and only had one film left which I had kept for the return journey.

Sitting on an old log by the lake was so peaceful and I had time to think about things in general. My friends and I were very surprised to hear that Aunt Geraldine would be returning to England with us, which didn't please the Count. In fact relationships were rather strained during the last few days, but the Count soon got over it.

I looked at the lovely setting and wondered if I would ever see this place again so I must be sure that this picture is firmly set in my mind. I will then be able to recapture the very happy time I had here. Without a shadow of a doubt, it had been very happy indeed.

In such a short time I have changed from being a callow youth into a young man. Should I feel ashamed or proud of my achievements? I wish I knew. I had read somewhere that when in doubt go for the better option.

I must have been miles away because I didn't hear Aunt Pamela come up behind me until she said, "Can I join you Henry?" I got up replied "Yes, of course" and dusted off part of the old log, so that she could sit down.

She started by saying that she had become very fond of me and she knew how her children felt, especially Mary. She said that she had never seen them so happy and contented as they have been while I was with them. "You have entertained each other, in one way or another, every day, which has helped me no end, Henry."

She turned to look at me and said, "I am not blind Henry. I can see how you and Mary look at each other and I can tell that you are more than just good friends. When we return to England you are going to miss each other dreadfully and I am going to have a very unhappy girl on my hands. Could you come over to the Hall as much as you can until Mary returns to school? This is her first little love affair, so please don't hurt her Henry."

She also asked me to continue calling her Aunt Pamela when we were back in England. Then she kissed my cheek and before I could say a word she was off.

What had transpired really shook me. I began to wonder what Aunt Pamela knew about my relationship with her daughter. What ever will Mother say when I call Lady Howes Aunt Pamela? Brother John will surely smell a rat when he sees Mary and I together because he is the expert in such matters.

I tried to get myself back to normal when I started to think about what had happened last night. For the last time Mary came into my bed and we decided that tonight we had to get as much sleep as possible in readiness for the journey home.

I had a difficult time with Mary. She started to cry at the thought of not being able to be with me again. I must admit that I didn't feel any better. She stayed with me until dawn and it was a night that neither of us will ever forget.

Mary came across the wide expanse of lawn to join me on the log.

As I watched her walk towards me I wondered how on earth I had managed to get a girlfriend like her. She sat down and we just enjoyed each other's company.

I told her part of what her mother had said, leaving out the part about my visiting the Hall when we got home. When I told her that Aunt Pamela knew that we cared for each other Mary gave me such a big hug and kiss that we nearly fell off the log! I said that no one must ever know our secret about our nights at the Castle. We had a final stroll around the park and then went in to change for dinner.

Everyone was up with the lark the next morning and we were soon on our way down the long drive through the Castle grounds. I remembered so well our feeling of apprehension when we saw the Castle on our arrival. It looked so creepy and uninviting that we wished that we were back in Devon.

How first impressions can be so wrong. Even Uncle Willy turned out to be not such a bad old stick. We had really had a smashing time. At first the food seemed strange, but we soon became used to it. Although we had not been very adventurous in our travels, we saw what was of interest in the locality.

From my own point of view my command of the German language had improved beyond belief, as I had spoken German when ever possible.

We were to board the Hamburg train at Lubeck so the two cars, loaded with luggage and people, had quite a trip.

The Thomas Cook chap was there to explain our journey to us and in due course we were shown into a very comfortable compartment. We all seemed a bit sad and even Uncle Willy was not his usual robust and noisy self. After all, his wife was going with us and there had been no mention of for how long she would be away.

At last the train drew out of Lubeck Station leaving a lonely Uncle Willy on the platform.

I had managed to bag a window seat and with Mary beside me we settled down for our long trip.

During my stay in Germany I had kept a rough journal of my adventures, mostly under headings as I never seemed to have had the time to actually write. I now got this very tattered exercise book out and began to fill in more details. Needless to say I left out my meetings with Mary.

It was very noticeable how many soldiers and police were visible on the stations we passed through. We also had a visit from the guard and, I presumed, an SS Officer, each time the trains stopped to take on fresh passengers. They were very thorough checking all papers and tickets.

I could see the logic of this as our train was going direct to the Channel ports. If anyone wanted to get out of Germany this would be a good exit. Going through the Hamburg area I used up quite a bit of my last film.

We had a comfortable crossing on the ferry and at last set foot on British soil. I must say that the English coast line looked most inviting in the early morning sunshine.

Once more Sir James' friend, Major Davis, met us and put us on the train for Exeter. I was able to have a brief word with him and told him that I would let Jake have the films as soon as possible. I would however like to have copies of the films if this was possible and he told me that he would see to it.

It was nice to eat English food once again and we had a very pleasant meal on the train. Afterwards Mary and I stood in the corridor and talked, making plans to see each other.

I told her that I would ride over to the Hall the day after tomorrow. If the weather was nice we could have a swim. Mary gave me a squeeze and said, "Wouldn't it be nice if we could lose Hugh for a bit?" I told her to behave herself, but the thought of having a swim with Mary, on our own, made my imagination run riot.

I asked Mary to get her parent's consent to ride over to the farm. After all, she had been allowed to ride all over the countryside in Germany, so why not in quite Devonshire?

When we were back in the compartment the aunts were having a snooze and Hugh was sketching. Using me as a pillow, Mary was soon fast asleep and this gave me the opportunity to try and solve a few of my problems.

My main problem was Polly. What options do I have? Should I see her until we go back to college or do I tell her that Mary is my girlfriend now and that I do not care for her any more? I could pretend that everything is as it was before. One thing is certain, I still care for Polly, but in a very different way to how I feel about Mary.

I turned and looked at Mary fast asleep beside me. I thought that if only she was not The Honourable Miss Mary Howes life would be so much easier. I will be sure to lose her in the near future when she mixes with the social circle of her class.

I made a decision then which in itself was a minor one, but I didn't know how it would affect my future. I took the coward's way out and decided to let fate take its course.

As the train approached Dawlish and began its long journey along the coast and through the four tunnels, we could see Teignmouth in the distance. My friends and I had similar thoughts about the happy and innocent time we had there so many summers ago.

Unfortunately the train did not stop at Teignmouth and went straight through to Newton Abbot where Wills was waiting to collect us. It was a very tight squeeze getting in an extra passenger and luggage into the car. Mary sat on my knee and wriggled on purpose which was very disturbing.

We were now getting nearer to the farm so I started to thank Aunt Geraldine once again for such a lovely holiday, and of course I also thanked Aunt Pamela for including me in her family. As we came to familiar countryside I felt glad to be home.

The car pulled into the yard and Mother came running out of the house. After a quick kiss from Mary I got out of the car and what a reception I received from Mother! Anyone would think that I had been away for years. Micky came bounding out of the barn and went mad when he saw me.

Mother had quite a chat with the two aunts so Mary got out of the car and started to play with Micky. Soon, she was called back and looking very fed up she got into the car. In fact I thought she was going to cry which would have been most embarrassing. Soon they were off into their world leaving me to become acclimatised to my own once again.

Mother and I were soon joined by Dad, John and Aunt Betty. I had to tell them all about my holiday. I must have talked non-stop even through the evening meal. They laughed when I described Uncle Willy and how he acted before his important guests arrived. They took some convincing that I had been introduced to Herman Goering. They also thought that I was pulling their legs when I told them that I now called Lady Howes Aunt Pamela.

At last I managed to escape the endless questions and was able to go out to see my two friends, Henry and Daisy. When I called their names I saw Henry's ears prick up and soon they were both trotting over to see me. It was nice to see them again and to get such a friendly welcome.

When I returned to the house I asked Mother if I could telephone Mrs Jenkins and Jake to see if I could visit them tomorrow. I arranged to see Mrs Jenkins in the morning and Jake in the afternoon.

When at last I was in my bedroom and getting into my own bed, I realised how lucky I was to have such a lovely family and to live in a country that was free of turmoil and hidden fear, for that was what it was like in Germany.

I would have to get back into my routine and close my mind to the other world that I had grown to like. It began to dawn on me that Mary was the link and I do not have the wish or the willpower to break that link.

There was no Mary to keep me awake tonight so I soon went to the land of nod.

CHAPTER 7

As it was my first morning home, Mother let me off my jobs, so I saddled up Henry and started my ride down the familiar lanes to the little bridge. Here I sat on the old seat letting Henry have a drink and I listened to the sound of the running water. It reminded me of the river sounds of Lubeck. I really must stop this looking back and remembering the highlights of the past few weeks.

I mounted up and had a grand time riding through the fields with Micky acting as an out rider and chasing imaginary rabbits. I have not been on my own for several weeks and I had forgotten how I loved my own company.

The countryside was beginning to look a bit blowsy. The summer growth was beginning to mature and in late August the seeds were forming for next year's continuation of the species. The greens will soon be changing to shades of copper, gold and brown.

Some people like the autumn but I never have. To me it is a sad time. Nature puts up the shutters and battens down the hatches to prepare for winter. Some animals go to sleep, but mankind is not that lucky.

As I rode towards Mrs Jenkins house I wondered how I would break the bad news to her about her relations in Lubeck. I will eventually have a photograph of the Kapitel Strasse, so perhaps it will be best to tell her the truth.

In the distance I could see Mrs Jenkins pottering in her olde worlde garden. As I came closer I gave her a shout and she started to walk out to meet me. Having seen so many German females over the past few weeks, Mrs Jenkins certainly looked her part. It was difficult to believe that she had Jewish blood in her veins, with her fair skin and long fair hair.

She greeted me in the way that so many Germans do, that is to kiss the air by the side of your face and at the same time touch your cheek with their cheek. Men and women do this, but of course not men with men. They are also great hand-shakers.

Well, having got the greetings out of the way we went inside and in no time at all I was drinking coffee. We spoke in German all of the time and I told her about our visit to kapitel Strasse where so many of the houses were boarded up and had the word 'Jude' painted all over them. I told her about Joseph and about the train in the forest taking people to the labour camp.

I could see that she was upset so I told her about Herman Goering and Uncle Willy. I think that she really knew in her heart that my news would be bad. She was soon back to her normal self so I rummaged in my haversack and brought out a box of Lubeck Marzipan which she thought was smashing. I told her that when I got my photographs I will show them to her.

My time was up so I had to leave. She gave me a motherly hug and told me to come and see her whenever I had the time. As I was mounting Henry she told me to bring Mary along as she would like to meet her. This made me blush and I think that she knew that it would. We waved goodbye and I started my journey home.

As I rode back towards the little bridge I wondered when I should see Polly. Perhaps I should let her seek me out. I found it so difficult wondering how I should greet her. Should I greet her and act on the cool side, to give her some indication that my feelings have changed?

I could now see the little bridge clearly and a small figure was sitting on the seat. As I came closer I realised it was Polly. She stood up and waved so I had no way of escape.

As I approached her I realised what a lovely girl she was growing into. It has only been a few weeks since I saw Polly, but somehow I saw her in a different light. Perhaps it had something to do with my close encounters with Mary. I would like to know what Polly was doing at the little bridge.

We greeted each other shyly and she told me that she had heard that the Howes family were home so she assumed I must be home as well. She then telephoned the farm and Mother had told her that I was visiting Mrs Jenkins. Polly decided that she would surprise me.

I told her that I would give her a lift back to Teigncoombe and started to help her on to Henry. When she turned around she started to kiss me. I had to respond and before I knew what was happening I was enjoying it. I pulled myself together and put her on Henry.

I told her about my holiday and mentioned Mary quite a few times hoping that Polly might go off me a bit, but no such luck. I dropped her at the vicarage and with a quick farewell I was off. I had made no arrangements to see her because I wanted to see Mary as much as possible before she went back to college. I felt a bit of a heel, but all's fair in love and war.

Lunch was ready when I returned home and as I sat down Mother told me that my two girlfriends had been after me. Polly had telephoned and then Mary. Mother told them both that I had gone to Mrs Jenkins and this afternoon I was going to see Mr Spencer. I didn't have a very peaceful lunch, the family kept pulling my leg. Dad looked a bit wistful and said that he never had such lovely girls after him at the same time. "Henry my boy, you don't know how lucky you are."

I persuaded Mother to let me use the telephone and rang the Hall. Aunt Pamela answered and said she would get Mary for me, but before she did she wanted to ask me to come to the Hall for the day tomorrow. I said that I would love to. She then added that there was one problem, Hugh had to go with his father to Exeter for the day. I said that I would be over pretty early on Henry, so perhaps Mary and I could go for a ride for the day, just like we did in Germany. We could have a picnic lunch. "That's smashing Henry," she said. "Geraldine and I can have a day to ourselves in Exeter. Tell your Mother that cook will provide the lunch."

Mary then came on the telephone, very excited about our day tomorrow. I will have to make sure that we keep out of Polly's way. Oh dear! Oh dear! What have I let myself in for. Anyway, to see and be with Mary for a whole day will be smashing. We had a short natter and I said that I had to go because I had to visit Jake.

I got my camera and films, the map and rough notes and once more climbed on to Henry's back. We trotted across the fields to my wood. I didn't use my tree very much now as I was getting much too large.

I reached Jake's house and the more I saw of it the more I liked it. He came to the door and we sat in the afternoon sunshine. I talked for ages because I had a great deal to report. When I told him about Goering, like everyone else, he had to be convinced that I was not pulling his leg. He became very interested when I told him that I had photographs of Goering's party, that is if they all come out, as the light was not very good.

Jake told me that Major Davis will want to see me when the films had been developed. I gave Jake the camera, films and map after explaining what the dirty marks indicated. He had a good laugh at my caution in not marking the map with a pencil.

I stayed with Jake for most of the afternoon. We talked about all sorts of things, but always in German. If anyone had seen and heard us, they would have thought it most strange to see two people sitting in the middle of a wood in Devonshire, chatting away in German!

Jake told me that he was going to London for a week starting the day after tomorrow. Would I do him a favour and visit his house while he was away and to make sure that everything was alright? He showed me where he would hide the key and I would be very welcome to make myself some coffee if I needed a drink.

Evidently, the female who cleaned the house for him would also be away for the week. She would however get some food in for his return. We said our farewells and I gave Micky a shout and was on my way. I enjoyed the ride back to the farm. The weather looked set for a nice spell. I must ask Charlie what the prospects were for tomorrow. I was looking forward to having the whole day with Mary.

After our evening meal I had a long chat with Dad. I told him all about our meeting with Joseph. I had kept to myself the terrible stories Joseph had told me. The labour camps were inhuman and people starved and were made to work until they died. Then a fresh batch would be brought in to do the same and so it went on.

The guards had a game they played. They would pick out two or three of the fittest men and would pretend to let them escape. They would then place bets on which dog would get one first. Needless to say, the dogs killed most of them. This is how Joseph had escaped. He never had the time to tell me how he did it, but he did escape and this was why there was such a panic when he couldn't be found. The guards had broken the rules and they would be in serious trouble if he was free for any length of time.

I could see that what I had told Dad upset him so I didn't tell him about the train we saw in the forest of Raeinfeld. Dad said that I should write a proper report for Major Davis including all my observations. I hadn't thought of this and thought it was a damn good idea. I asked Mother if I could use the front room as it was quiet. Dad answered for her and I made a start that night. In fact, I became so engrossed in it that I continued writing in my room until the early hours.

After doing my early morning chores I was off to Langley Hall on Henry, complete with a towel and swim trunks. Whenever I made this trip along the now so familiar route, I always remembered my very first journey as a very young boy loaded with cream and butter. Today I had cream and butter in my saddle bag, but this time it was a gift. Mum and Dad are now more relaxed in the company of Sir James and Lady Pamela and they are on very friendly terms.

As I rode up the long drive I saw Mary sitting on a seat in the garden. When I got closer I could see that she had her hair tied back, which showed off her handsome face. When she saw me she stood up and started to run across the lawn to meet me. Oh what a lovely girl she was on that late August morning! I would have her all to myself for the whole day.

She climbed on to Henry behind me and told me to ride around to the stables. She started to kiss the back of my neck and as she had her arms around my waist one of her hands started to wander. I gave it a hard smack and told her to behave herself.

We rode into the stable yard and Mr Jones the groom greeted us. He had Mary's horse ready, plus our lunch from Cook.

We decided that our first port of call would be the river as by now it was very warm and a swim was called for.

The place we swam was quite some distance from the Hall and very secluded because of the summer growth. It was not easy to find. Its beauty had been enhanced by the rich foliage around the area and by hearing the water singing as it made its way to the sea.

I made the horses comfortable and we found a suitable spot to sit and change into our swimwear. Mary said, "Last one in the water's an idiot!" She then started to strip off and I did likewise. Before I knew what was happening, she had taken off all her clothes and went into the water in her birthday suit.

She stood up with the sun making her wet skin shine and told me not to be so shy, so I did the same. We were not strangers to each other's bodies, but somehow this was different.

It was a lovely feeling to swim without trunks on and to press wet bodies together was a feeling to be remembered. We fooled around and chased each other, then Mary ran out of the water and lay on her back with her arms stretched out for me to join her. By now I needed to do this more than anything else.

Everything was so perfect that we had to fight the temptation to break our vow and lose our virginity. Luckily sense prevailed and we satisfied each other in other ways. We made the most of this lovely day because it could well be our last chance. We both wished it could last forever.

We stayed like this in the warm sunshine until it was lunch time when we had a quick dip in the river to cool down, then we dried each other, which caused a great deal of laughter.

To be on the safe side we dressed in case anyone came our way. We also made the swim wear wet so that we didn't give the game away.

Cook had provided a smashing lunch for us. We were both very hungry and decided that lovemaking gave one a hearty appetite. We also found that it was a tiring pastime.

After lunch we lay in the warm sunshine and went to sleep. We must have been dreaming because when we awoke we had our arms around each other and nature made us want each other again.

At last we pulled ourselves together and started our journey back to the Hall. I did so hope that our happiness would not be too obvious to other people. We did feel on top of the world and I knew that dear Mary felt the same as I did, because she kept telling me so.

Mary's parents had given her permission to ride over to the farm if she wanted to. I would like that because I could show her over the farm and take her to some of my favourite places. I told her that I had to visit Jake's cottage while he was away and also that Mrs Jenkins would like to meet her.

When we got back to the Hall the whole family had returned from their different trips. They were having tea on the lawn so we took the horses to the stables and after a wash we joined them.

I had not seen Sir James since my return from Germany and I was very surprised at the warm welcome I received. I dreaded to think of the sort of welcome I would have received if he had known what Mary and I were up to.

The two aunts seemed happy enough and Hugh had enjoyed his day with his father. He asked me to come to his room as he would like to show me his sketches of Germany.

When we got to his room he gave me several smashing sketches of different aspects of our holiday, some of which will be of great interest to Major Davis.

Hugh told me why he had been to Exeter with his father. An uncle had died last year and because of a very complex Will it had been difficult to find an heir. He didn't fully understand it, but their solicitor had told him that he would be the heir to quite a large estate, including a house in London which had been kept fully staffed.

As we went down the stairs Hugh said, "Henry my boy, you will be able to come and stay with me in London."

I soon had to make tracks home so I went around to the stable to fetch Henry. Of course, Mary came as well. When I was in the saddle Mary led Henry over to a bench. She stood on the bench and climbed on to Henry's back behind me before I had a chance to realise what she was doing. She put her arms firmly around my waist and I tried to push her off, but there she stayed. As we rode up to the family they all started to laugh at the sight of the two of us on Henry.

I said my goodbyes and Mary told her mother that she would ride down to the gate with me. I must say that it was a very nice feeling having Mary so close behind me.

After we told each other what a wonderful day we had both experienced and had several kisses, I made my way along the lane. I looked back and she was still there waving. Mary had told me that she would let me know when she and Hugh could come over to the farm.

After my evening meal I thought that with a bit of luck I might be able to finish my report for Major Davis. The only really quiet place was outside in the garden. John and the future Mrs Blake, mark 2, were in the house and Gertie could talk the hind legs off a donkey!

I stayed outside writing until it was too dark to see. I almost finished the report, about another hour tomorrow should do the trick.

I went into the house and the family were sitting in the front room.

John and Gertie were talking to Mum and Dad about their wedding. I must admit that I have been too occupied with my own affairs to think about John's great adventure into married life.

He had been working very hard on the cottage and it was almost finished. I had helped in a small way with my woodworking skills. I must have a look tomorrow as I expect a lot of work has been done while I was away.

The wedding was set for the end of September, or as country folk would say 'Michaelmass'. Polly's father would be marrying them in Teigncoombe.

Mother told me that I would need a new suit for the wedding and I told her I would rather have some new breeches for the winter as mine were too small. She looked at Dad and he said, "We will see." That was always a hopeful sign!

Aunt Betty and Charlie were sitting there and somehow I had a feeling that when John had moved out of the house, these two dear friends will get married and live in part of our large farmhouse.

Somehow or other I must find time to finish the wedding present I am making for John and Gertie. I am making a stool and a small table to match, with the advice given to me by Peter's dad. I must try and go down to see Peter tomorrow.

I have not heard from Mary to say if they will be over tomorrow, so perhaps I will be able to get on with my jobs and see Peter.

When I finally got into bed that night I had no time to think about the events of the day because I fell fast asleep in no time.

The next morning, after doing my jobs, I settled in the garden and got on with my writing. Dad had read the first part and he thought that it was OK, in fact, he thought it was pretty good.

I sat there in the morning sunshine, quite at peace with the world. As I wrote I began to relive my stay in that foreign land and I put on paper what was on my mind. I kept returning to Joseph and the people like him and it made me feel so sad.

At last the report was finished and I read it through. I suddenly felt two hands cover my eyes from behind and I smelled a familiar scent. It was of course Mary. She gave me one of her wicked little laughs and told me that she had telephoned Mother earlier that morning and asked her not to tell me she was coming so that she could surprise me. Mother had also asked her to stay for the day.

I hoped that no one was looking as she gave me a smashing kiss. She then did a twirl in front of me to show off her new jodhpurs and shirt. I asked her where they had come from and she said they were a gift from Aunt Geraldine. She looked really fantastic. Her new outfit showed her lovely figure and made her look really handsome.

When I see her like this I wonder why she likes me so much. Perhaps it is because there is no one else around. Over the last year I have met several young people in her class and they were all a bit on the wet side.

Evidently, Mary had ridden over to the farm and John was looking after her horse so we went to relieve him of this chore. John had a twinkle in his eye and when he asked what we were going to do all day he said he wished he were young again and taking out such a lovely young girl. Mary blushed a bit and laughed.

I asked John if we could look at his cottage and he told us we were very welcome, but be sure to lock up again afterwards.

We went into the kitchen and had a cup of tea with Mother and Aunt Betty. Mary always seemed very much at ease with Mother and she also got on well with Dad. He usually pulled her leg about something or other.

As we were about to leave, Dad came in and asked what we were going to do. I told him that first of all we were going to have a look at John's cottage and then ride over to see Peter and his father. He gave Mary a friendly pat on the back and told us to enjoy ourselves. I think that, like John, he was wishing he was a young man again.

I found the key to John's cottage under the same flower pot and we went inside. John must have worked like mad while I was away because the place now looked smashing. There were only a few odd pieces of furniture in some of the rooms, but even so it had a homely feeling.

We went upstairs and looked at the way John and Gertie had decorated it. We both thought it looked a treat. Mary and I looked at each other and the temptation was too great. We started to kiss and get passionate, but both knew that this was not the time or place to get involved and calmed ourselves down. Then we left John's future home and rode down the lane to Peter's.

I was to learn in the future that if you are very lucky there would be times when you felt really happy. Real happiness is a very illusive frame of mind and if it can be obtained it remains in your mind for ever.

As we rode along these familiar lanes I felt on top of the world. It was a grand day. 1935 would be remembered as a very hot summer. Mary and I talked most of the time. We tried not to think of the fact that in just over two weeks Mary will be returning to college.

We stopped for a while by a gateway that gave us a grand view of Dartmoor. I reminded Mary of our trip to Dartmeet when we were staying at Teignmouth. It now seemed so long ago and once more I tried to explain to her how she and Hugh had changed my life. I even talked as they did and I had become used to the good life.

Mary put her arms around me and said that Hugh and she often

170

talked about this and that to them I was still the same old Henry they have had as their best friend for a long time now. "Henry, one day, no matter what you say, I will marry you." I told her not to be so silly. We were only teenagers and she will meet someone more suitable than I would ever be. She kissed me and said, "You wait and see."

We rode into the farm where Peter lived and I warned Mary about the farmer, Mr Ware. She had met Peter several times, but not his dad, so I introduced her to him.

We were chatting away when in came Farmer Ware, all twenty stone of him. He must have seen our horses tied up outside. He looked at Mary and said, "And who is this?" So I told him that this was the daughter of Sir James Howe. That soon changed his attitude as he was a tenant of Sir James'. I asked if we could water the horses and he said that Peter would show me where to go. I am glad to say that he soon pushed off leaving us to continue our chat.

Peter and his dad were very busy so we didn't stay too long. It is difficult to do the skilful sort of work that Mr Walker was doing if there were people watching.

We made a detour on our journey back to the farm because Mary wanted to visit the village store in Teigncoombe. I was none too keen in case Polly was about and as I rode towards the village I made up my mind that I would not think of Polly as I really loved Mary and would hang on to her for as long as possible.

Anyway, it must be pretty obvious to all and sundry how we felt about each other. As I rode behind her she seemed to be part of her horse. She was now a very good rider and in some ways quite a tomboy.

We rode into the village and to see the two of us mounted on our magnificent horses, with Mary looking so radiant, this must have started the tongues wagging. "What ever was Farmer Blake's son doing, out riding with Sir James' daughter?"

We went into the village store and I felt a bit self-conscious as Mary went regally up to the counter and asked if they had any flowers. The shopkeeper brought out a lovely bunch of mixed flowers which Mary bought. On the way out she took my arm and whispered "This will cause a stir dear Henry." She certainly was a little monkey.

I asked her who the flowers were for and she said, "You are stupid Henry, they are for your Mother of course for having me for the day." As she said this I thought she was going to kiss me right in front of the shop. Will I ever get used to this other world that I have become a part of?

We got back to the farm just in time for lunch. I took the saddles off the horses before putting them in the paddock for a break. Mary had gone on into the house with the flowers for Mother and when I joined them I could see that Mother was very pleased with her unexpected gift.

Lunch time was very pleasant and relaxed. We had quite a bit of leg pulling from John and Dad. After lunch we sat and talked for quite a while about John's wedding next month. Unfortunately all the aunts, uncles and cousins would be coming. I told John that he ought to just go off and get married as it would save a lot of bother and Mary told me not to be so silly, which shut me up.

I told Mum and Dad that we were going to ride around the farm and Dad asked me to see if the sheep were alright. This would save him a lot of time later in the day.

After saddling the horses we mounted and waved goodbye. We reached the field where the sheep were and they all looked fine. In the corner of the field stood an old barn so we dismounted and went to have a look in it. I hadn't been in this old place for several years, so I had no idea what was inside.

The barn was empty apart from some straw and hay. It was quite cosy looking. I looked at Mary and we both burst out laughing. We had both decided to be well-behaved, but the temptation was too great. I always carry a waterproof cape in my saddle bag so in no time at all we had a very comfortable, but somewhat primitive bed.

We enjoyed ourselves to the full that afternoon and had a great deal of fun. When at last we dressed we made sure that there was no hay or straw on our clothing or in our hair, because that would have given the game away, especially if John was around!

We had been away longer than I had realised, so by the time we got back to the farm it was time for Mary to make tracks for home. Mother insisted that Mary had a wash and brush-up and combed her hair so off they went upstairs. When they came down Mary looked smashing. Her hair looked different. Mary said, "Look Henry, your Mother has changed my hair. Do you like it?" I told her that she looked lovely.

I told Mother that I would ride half way to the Hall with Mary and Mother put on one of her fierce expressions and told me to see Mary all the way home. Much to my surprise Mother gave Mary a big hug and kiss before we left.

We enjoyed the ride back to the Hall. We were both very happy in more ways than one. Surely it cannot last much longer. Tomorrow I have to go into Newton Abbot and be measured for a new suit and I hope, some breeches. I will not be able to see Mary until the day after.

When I told Mary this she looked most put out. I also told her that I have to see if Jake's house is alright while he is away so I will try to nip down there when I return from Newton Abbot.

"If I can do this I would be able to come over to the Hall the day after tomorrow, that is if your mother will invite me." Mary tried to hit me in fun and said, "Henry, you know that you are always welcome and you don't need an invitation."

When we reached the main gates Mary insisted I take her to the front door as instructed by Mother. The whole family were sitting on the front lawn having a drink before their evening meal, so of course I had to join them.

Sir James said, "Why don't you stay and have a meal with us?" This really shook me – an invitation from Sir James. I explained that I had been on a horse for most of the day and was not very clean, so Sir James told Mary to take me upstairs for a wash. Mary, in fun, took hold of my ear and led me through the door. Going up the stairs she whispered in my ear, "Don't tell stories Henry. You told Papa that you have been on a horse all day when you were on me for most of the afternoon!"

When we came downstairs and joined the family, Aunt Pamela explained that she had telephoned Mother to let her know where I was.

After a very nice meal, which took some time, I said that I should be going home and thanked Sir James for having me. He told me that I was always welcome.

Mary walked down to the main gate with me and we arranged to see each other on the day after tomorrow. With a lengthy goodbye I started for home. By now it was getting late and the light was failing so I made Henry get a move on.

It was very interesting to see the nocturnal creatures beginning to venture out. There were owls flying silently in front of me and the bats were getting their evening meal from the unsuspecting insects in flight.

I let Henry have his freedom in the paddock and watched him gallop away. How lucky I was to have such a magnificent horse. He was now almost fully grown and we understood each other. He always did as he was told and became more friendly to other people. I sometimes let Mary ride him, which he accepted.

Daisy was not well and I had begun to suspect that she would not be with us for much longer. What a dear old friend she has been. Charlie, being the horse expert, told me that when he thought she was in any pain or distress, he would call the vet to put her out of her misery.

When I went into the house Dad was in the kitchen. Mother, Gertie and Gertie's mother were in the front room going over the wedding arrangements so I sat in the kitchen with Dad and we talked.

After he had given me a glass of beer he said that he wanted to have a word with me about Mary. My stomach started to churn around. Had someone seen us in the old barn? He went on to say that anyone could see how fond of each other we were and he didn't want either of us to get hurt. Soon Mary will probably be entering her world and meeting young people of her own class, spending more and more time away from home. I told him that Mary and I had discussed this which surprised him somewhat. I said that we both knew the dangers, but decided to let fate take its course.

I said that there will certainly be a war in a few years time. One has only to look around Germany to see what is going on. Our Government is either blind or daft, or perhaps both. Only the Good Lord knows what will happen to us all.

I explained that Mary, Hugh and I get on so well together and I have learnt so much from them, which is bound to help me in the future. They in turn have come out of the cocoon they were living in when I met them, which was of course what Sir James wanted. Anyway, Mary will be returning to college at the end of next week so I won't be seeing her until Christmas.

I thought to myself, why not confide in Dad? He is a wise old bird. So I told him about my problem with Polly and he had a jolly good laugh. He said, "Henry, however did you manage to get two such lovely girlfriends at the same time?"

He went on to say "The only advice I can give you is to get to know Polly as well as you know Mary. I would guess that you know Mary pretty well in more ways than one. You young people forget that we old ones were young once." Then he said, very seriously, "Henry, there is no need for me to tell you, but please be careful not to disgrace your family or either of these two lovely girls."

This made me go really red in the face, which gave the game away to a certain extent. I assured Dad that I could never do anything to hurt Mary or Polly, or for that matter my family.

Dad said I ought to poke my head around the front room door and say hello to Gertie and her mum, so I went into the room and said hello as instructed. Mrs Norris, Gertie's mother was never one of my favourite people, but then it takes all sorts to make a world.

Mrs Norris said that she had seen me in the village with Mary Howes. I thought that I would give the old bat something to talk about and told her that I had been out riding with Mary all day and that she had lunched here at the farm and I had just returned from the Hall having had dinner with Sir James and his family.

Mother added to the story by saying that Mary had given her the lovely flowers that were standing in a vase in a corner of the room. "She really is a sweet girl and we are all very fond of her." Mother said. She can be a bit of a card at times and I think that the wedding arrangements were not going her way.

I made my excuses and left the room. I went out into the garden and sat on a seat beneath the old yew tree.

I had so much to think about that I had no idea where to start. The weather looked on the change so tomorrow it will be a new suit in the morning and if the afternoon was wet I will get on with John and Gertie's wedding present.

The following day, if it is fine and hot, I will go over to the Hall and have a swim with Mary and Hugh, or perhaps I should inspect Jake's cottage. I will consult with Mary. This is all rather like a military operation, to get the maximum enjoyment for Mary and I for the last few days of her holidays.

When I saw Polly last week she mentioned something about her father giving her a pony for her birthday. Now, I should remember when her birthday is, but I just can't remember. If she gets a pony before Mary goes back to college I will really be in the soup. After all, I did teach her to ride and this will be the first port of call.

Dad's advice was a bit cruel. Am I to be unfaithful the moment Mary goes away and then play Polly along until I see what she is made of? That is the real essence of his advice.

After having two such lovely days on the trot I decided to take each day as it came, but only after my dear Mary had gone. To hell with everything and everybody else. With these thoughts on my mind I went to bed.

My visit to Newton Abbot was a bit of a bore and after a lot of argument Mother ordered a new suit and bought me some breeches. This pleased me immensely.

Mother had some more shopping to do so I decided to catch an earlier bus home. I didn't fancy trailing around the shops with Mother, so with my new breeches tucked under my arm I had a wander around the town to kill a bit time until my bus was due to leave. I was looking in a shop window when I felt a dig in the back and a voice said, "Hello Henry." It was of course Polly, which really put me on the spot.

I was hoping not to see her until Mary had gone back to college, but this was not to be. We had a rather stilted conversation and Polly told me that her pony would be arriving next week. She looked me straight in the face and said, "I hear that you were out riding all day with Mary. I hope you can find time to take me out." I told her that of course I would.

I looked at my watch and trying to escape said that I must fly to catch my bus. She said that she was catching the same bus and would come with me. Things were becoming more complicated by the minute. Somehow my plans were not going my way.

On the way home in the old bus Polly sat next to me. I had always thought of her as a bit on the shy side. Our kissing was so different to what Mary and I got up to. Today she was pressing the side of her body as close as she could to mine and I could feel the warmth of her through my clothing, which was very nice indeed.

I was looking at Polly and thinking how different she was to Mary. She was very blond with fair skin that had a creamy look. She was smaller, but everything was in proportion. She had such a pretty face that seemed to light up when she smiled. She was no longer the little girl I sat next to at the village school.

Mary on the other hand was a bigger girl and more handsome. She had dark brown hair and her skin was more olive in colour. To me she always looked good enough to eat and somehow we seemed to be on the same wavelength. The girls were complete opposites to look at.

When we came to my dropping off point I told Polly that I would be in touch and she must let me know when her pony arrives. I then beat a hasty retreat. I felt a bit of a heel, but what else could I do?

After lunch the weather looked quite good so I decided to have a look at Jake's cottage. I always enjoyed this ride and it brought back so many happy memories of when I was much younger. I remembered my first meeting with Jake and watching the family of badgers. Then the lessons on living off the land and being able to walk like an Indian. Now it all seemed like kids' stuff, but who knows, it might be useful in the future. After all, this knowledge had saved Jake's life.

When I reached the clearing with the house all closed up, it seemed a bit spooky and unfriendly. Micky ran around expecting to see Jake and as soon as I opened the front door he rushed in and had a good look around. He seemed most upset that Jake was not there so he went outside and disappeared into the wood.

Being very nosy I had a good look around. I didn't touch anything because knowing Jake he would find out. His powers of detection were very good. I went over to his desk and looking at some of his letters it appeared that he had contacts all over Europe. I was getting interested in what I was reading when Micky rushed in and then out again.

I took no notice of this but then nearly jumped out of my skin as two arms went around my waist and a hand gave me a dig well below the belt. Before I knew what was happening I was turned around and being kissed most passionately by Mary. When I got my breath back I asked what she was doing here and how had she found the cottage.

She had telephoned the farm and was told where I was so she decided to try and find it. Of course, she had been here before, but that was with me showing her the way. At one time she thought that she was lost, but Micky found her and she followed him to the cottage.

As usual she looked lovely. Her face was flushed with the excitement of her adventure and her shirt was open with the warmth, showing the valley of her breasts. She kicked off her boots and flopped full length on Jake's large settee. I joined her and we had a most enjoyable afternoon.

It was so lovely and peaceful and we were both so contented, but reluctantly we made ourselves presentable, straightened the settee and left the cottage. Outside we were back in the realms of respectability. We were both full of fun and happiness as we rode back through the wood and it was a good job that we didn't see anyone as it was so obvious from our expressions that we had experienced a furtive but happy time.

I accompanied Mary most of the way back to the Hall and told her how nice it was of her to seek me out so unexpectedly that afternoon. She made me promise to come over to the Hall for the day tomorrow.

I enjoyed the following day at the Hall. It was poor weather so unfortunately we had to miss our swim. Hugh told us all about his inheritance from an uncle he had never seen. Evidently he would have a large allowance until he is twenty-one when the trustees would pass everything over to him. There was a house in London which was still fully staffed. In this way the uncle could be sure that his faithful servants would have a home, which the three of us thought was jolly decent of the old boy.

Hugh went on to say that he and his Father were going up to London tomorrow to see the house and to settle his affairs. Hugh grinned and said, "Mary could come if she wanted to, but she would rather stay with you Henry."

He said that perhaps we could all go and stay in London during the Christmas holidays and I thought this would be smashing, but where on earth would I get the money from? Mary gave me one of her little smiles as if to say, that's something to look forward to Henry my boy.

The last few days have flown and what a wonderful time I have had. I have been with Mary as many times as possible and we visited Jake's cottage several times. I had to make sure the place was safe, anyway that's my story and I'm sticking to it!

On my friends' last day I had lunch at the Hall. Aunt Geraldine would be returning to Germany in a day or so and it was quite a farewell do.

Sir James told me to please come over and ride around the estate whenever I wanted to. "Don't bother to ask, just come over. We would both like to see you and sometimes I will join you for a ride, like we used to before Henry was yours."

Mary and Hugh would be off early in the morning and I have just had a very tearful farewell. I rode back to the farm feeling as if the end of the world had come.

177

I have been dreading this day. I knew it would be awful, but it has been much worse than I had expected. We agreed to keep in touch by writing to each other during the next term.

Riding home on this early evening I wondered how many times I have made this journey. Henry must know every pothole and turning to be negotiated. I now give him his head and he finds his own way. It made me sad to think that these journeys will be few and far between for the next few months.

Hugh's mention of a holiday in London set my mind working. I will have to try and make some more furniture to sell. Somehow or other I will have to make some money. Well, I will worry about that tomorrow.

It was not late so I went home via the little bridge. I felt that I needed to be in my favourite place. I sat on the old worn seat and began to contemplate what the next few months held in store for me. The past few months have been hectic in so many ways. The day after tomorrow I return to college and I will have to work very hard to win a scholarship to the agricultural college. Soon the dark evenings would be here which will restrict my activities.

As I rode up the hill to the farm I wondered how Mary was getting on and would she be the same when I saw her again.

Is this an end to a beginning or the beginning of the end? I do so hope that it is the former. With these sombre thoughts I went home feeling very sorry for myself.

CHAPTER 8

I was back at college and beginning to settle into the routine. It was nice to meet Bernie again and we had a lot to talk about after my trip to Germany. I told him about poor Joseph, my encounter with Herman Goering and the trains taking people to the labour camps to be worked to death.

John and Gertie were married and I was glad when the wedding was all over. The relations were pretty ghastly as usual, but of course it was a happy day for my family. Jenny came home and it is always nice to see her.

Polly and I were friends again. I took her out riding as promised on her new pony, but we remained just friends. I miss Mary so much and look forward to receiving her letters. I also miss the close contact with a female and I know that one day I will weaken and take Polly into my arms and try to comfort myself.

I had been back at college for about four weeks when I was told to report to the Headmaster's study. This of course put the wind up me so I nervously knocked on the door and went in.

To my surprise, Major Davis was sitting there and as I went in he got up and shook my hand and said, "Hello Henry." He went on to say how pleased he was with the way I had carried out the task he had given me.

The Head said that Major Davis wanted a few private words with me so he would leave us for a while. What it all boiled down to was the clarification of some of the photographs and my report. I was able to clear up these problems and then he sprung a real surprise on me.

"Henry, this may all seem very strange to you, but my Department is preparing for a war in a few years time. You have been over there and know what the score is. You speak German like a native and now we want you to speak French and would like you to pass your Certificate 'A' in the OTC," he said.

This really put me out. I told him that I had to win a scholarship to agricultural college and also had to make some items of furniture to keep me in pocket money. How the hell was I going to do it all?

He then told me that in the Country they had about ten young men like me who were being trained for the events of the future. His funds were unlimited so that they could get the right results, but finding the right candidates was a problem.

"I am not asking you to do anything now, except try to pass your Certificate 'A'. According to your Headmaster you are already learning basic French, which is a help with your gift for languages. A French version of Mrs Jenkins' German would be the answer."

He handed me a parcel containing the prints of my films and the camera which he said I could keep. He also handed me an envelope containing a small financial 'reward' for my services. "One day Henry, you might know how useful some of the information that you obtained for us will be," Major Davis told me. He asked me to thank Hugh for his sketches. We then talked about Germany and many other subjects until the Head came back. I said goodbye to the Major and he said I would not see him for quite a while. However, Jake would be my contact. Before I left the Head asked me to come and see him after prayers tomorrow.

On my way back to class I had a look into the envelope and to my surprise I found five crisp new five pound notes. This was indeed a fortune to me and will go a very long way towards a possible holiday in London.

I was glad that Polly was not on the bus going home because it gave me the chance to think about the events of the day. I didn't look at the photographs because I knew they would make me feel sad. I really must try to forget Mary for a bit and decided to renew my friendship with Polly. Anyway, that was the intention. Whether it will work out that way remains to be seen.

When I arrived home there was a letter from Mary waiting for me, which I kept to read in my room. I managed to find Dad and told him about the visit from Major Davis and the money he had given me. I asked his advice and he told me that it was up to me, but if he had been given such a chance he would have jumped at it.

Apparently Jake had told Dad some time ago that the Major would be putting such a proposition to me, but he was told not to tell me so that I could make up my own mind. Dad told me not to tell anyone about it, especially Mother.

I went up to my room early that evening. Mary's letter was quite cheerful and she kept on about how she missed me. She reminded me of some of our illicit encounters. I will write to her tomorrow and send some of the photographs. I must get some of the negatives printed and show them to all the family and Mary's parents.

That night I had difficulty getting to sleep. I had so much on my mind and wondered why I had been selected to have these problems.

After prayers next morning I knocked on the Head's door and went in to find him and the French teacher deep in conversation.

The Head was very complimentary and said that he was proud of my activities. He believes that he may have the answer to my French problem. After Christmas Mr Jarvis the French teacher, would be having a young girl to stay for several months to learn the English language. "She comes from Brittany and is about your age. Perhaps something could be fixed up which would be helpful to both of you," he said.

I didn't answer for a moment or two because I could foresee great female problems, then I told him "Providing this French girl is plain and fat it's a good idea. I have enough hassle with females at the moment without another one on the scene."

Mr Jarvis and the Head laughed at this and Mr Jarvis said that she was a distant relative of his wife's and he had never met her. "Anyway Henry, you will have to wait and see." With that remark and still grinning he told me to push off and as I closed the door I heard the two of them having a good laugh.

It's alright for them to laugh, but for some unknown reason girls seem to like me. I often see a sort of hungry look appear on their faces when I am on a bus or passing a bunch of them in the street. There is Mary and Polly both after me and a hot bit of stuff from France could make life very difficult indeed.

Just for fun I will tell Mary and Polly about this French girl to see their reactions.

Polly was on the bus that Friday evening which was unusual. She normally caught the early bus on a Friday. I told her that I had some holiday photographs and will let her see them some time. Then I told her about the French girl who would be helping me to learn her language properly.

Polly was very quiet for a while then she put her arm through mine and told me that she would like to ride over to the farm and could I show her around. I didn't know what had got into her as it was so unlike her to invite herself. She had always been a bit backward in coming forward.

I think that I was beginning to see a different side to Polly. It had been very strange since Mary went away. She kept turning up at the same places I visited. Being on the late bus tonight was a typical example. Perhaps she was going to reap the benefit of Mary's absence.

When the bus stopped Polly kissed me on the cheek and said, "Henry dear, I will see you tomorrow."

That evening I spread all the photographs out on the kitchen table and all the family plus Aunt Betty and Charlie, sat around the large table and talked about Germany for ages. They couldn't get over the

181

luxury I had got used to or the size of the estate. John of course had to comment on the number of photographs that I had taken of Mary.

I had cleared the possibility of telling my close family what I was really doing in Germany. Major Davis had told me that it would be OK, but I was not to say anything about the future.

I thought Mother would have a fit, but Dad calmed her down after I explained what I was expected to do. I made them all promise not to say a word to anyone about this and I looked at Gertie and told her not to tell her mother, otherwise the whole village would know. She laughed and told me not to worry.

John laughed when I told him about the extra French lessons and the French girl who was coming to stay with Mr Jarvis. He said, "Henry, you will be in big trouble with your two girlfriends. The French girls are hot stuff." Mother told him to behave himself.

I said that I had told Polly on the way home that evening and that she was coming over tomorrow to have a ride around the farm. It was now very late and to stop any teasing I said goodnight and went up to bed.

Somehow I had an uneasy feeling about Polly's visit tomorrow. I am not a complete twit and know that she is after me. Unfortunately she is such a lovely creature and I like her very much, but I do love Mary. I know that tomorrow will play a part in my future and I do wish that I didn't have this intuition about the future. I also knew that without the shadow of a doubt, the French question would also somehow play a very important role in my life. But just what, I had no idea.

As I lay in bed I felt that I had come to a crossroads. It would be up to me which turning I would take in the months and years to come.

I wished that Mary was here with me tonight. I do miss her so much. It is not just the sexual side of our relationship, I just missed having her near me. I must try to get over these feelings, but how?

When I awoke the next morning I felt a bit more cheerful. The sun was shining but it was a bit on the cool side, after all it was October.

After breakfast I had to feed Mother's ever-increasing collection of poultry which have now spread to another field. She must be making quite a packet with her side line. In fact, it can hardly be called a side line any longer. Nevertheless, she is still a bit stingy.

When I got back to the farmhouse Polly's pony was tied up outside. I went into the kitchen to find her sitting down having a cup of tea and a slice of bread and cream with Mother. I told her not to hurry as I had to saddle up Henry.

As I led Henry to the kitchen door I could see Polly standing there with the early sunshine showing off the different tints in her long blond hair.

She really looked a smasher. She had a new riding jacket and very close fitting jodhpurs which showed off her shapely figure. Mother came out to say goodbye and then told me that Polly was staying for lunch so we must not be late. This was news to me. Mother could have asked me first. She had no idea what I had planned for the afternoon. Anyway, looking at Polly it seemed a good idea.

Charlie had told me that there would be some heavy showers so I asked Polly if she had any waterproofs with her. She patted her saddle bag and said that she was prepared for any eventuality.

We were having a nice ride and good fun. In fact, we were getting on like a house on fire. We seemed much more relaxed in each other's company.

I noticed that it was clouding over and looked like rain. I told Polly that we must look for cover. There was a small wood in the corner of the field and we should make for that. She took out her cape in case it was needed.

Polly had spotted the old barn in the next field which I remembered so well and before I could stop her she was galloping off towards it. I had decided to keep away from the barn with its temptations and memories. Fate has decided otherwise and we reached it just in time. It poured down and it was a relief to be under cover. I made the horses comfortable and took my jacket off to give it a shake so that it would dry off a little bit. I had just hung it up on a convenient hook when I was attacked from behind by a very pretty young girl.

She had a handful of hay which she was trying to put down my shirt. I chased her trying to do the same. Out of the corner of my eye I noticed that there was a cape laid out on top of the hay which must have been Polly's handiwork. Then the inevitable happened, we both fell full length onto the bed of hay.

Of course, this was fatal. We started to kiss in a very passionate way and Polly put my hand inside her shirt to feel her firm young breasts. She started to explore my body all the time pressing herself closer and closer to me. This was all too much for me and I tried to break away. She held me and said, "Henry darling, please let nature take its course." Then she kissed me which added to my feeling of joy.

We lay there with our arms around each other and Polly started to talk. What she said, really took the wind out of my sails and I realised that she was no longer the shy Polly of the past.

"Darling Henry, I have watched you with Mary and I know that you both think that you love each other. You have not seen me but I have seen how the two of you treat each other since you returned from your trip to Germany. It is more than obvious that you have had a close sexual relationship with Mary. The villagers look upon you as Mary's boyfriend."

I was absolutely flabbergasted by what I was hearing. I was about to say something but Polly told me to be quiet until she had finished. "Henry, I love you dearly and have done since those early schooldays and I know that you care for me. However, you do have the problem of loving two girls at the same time, so why don't we share you? Mary can have you in the holidays and I can have you when she is away. One thing is certain, I'll make sure that no French girl gets her hooks into you my boy!"

I hadn't heard anything so crazy in all my life and it made me feel like Dad's bull. On the other hand, if it can make the three of us happy, even for a short time, surely that is something achieved. Why not flow with the tide and see what happens? It still made me feel guilty where Mary was concerned, but perhaps I will get over it.

It was still pouring with rain and Polly looked so lovely with her long blond hair spread out on our makeshift straw bed. I simply had to get involved again and started to kiss her. She pulled away and took off her jodhpurs and then bent down and undid my breeches, pulling them down. She laid down and pulled me on top of her.

"Dear Henry, do whatever you like, but please do not take my virginity." It seemed so strange that this was so similar to my lovemaking with Mary. Perhaps it is the same all the world over. How would I know? I am only a beginner.

Polly was a very passionate and sexy young lady and I had a hell of a job to get her to dress and get ready to go home for lunch. I would never have thought that she would be so lacking in inhibitions. She was most definitely not the usual vicar's daughter.

We were quiet on the first part of our journey home and then we both started to talk at the same time. However, I managed to speak first. I said that I felt awful about this morning and we shouldn't have done what we did. I said that it was not fair on her or Mary. It could only lead to trouble and unhappiness. Perhaps we should just remain good friends.

Polly looked rather cross and said that after this morning we could never be 'just friends' again. She stopped her horse and looking at me said she promised never to tell Mary what we got up to, "Let's enjoy each other while we can Henry, please think of me as well as Mary, because I do love you so much."

I didn't know what to say and I knew it would be very difficult to stay away from Polly. On the other hand the opportunities to be as we have been this morning would be very limited during the winter season. I also had a lot of work to do which would keep me out of mischief.

Before we went into lunch we put the horses in the barn and gave them some food. Checking that we had removed all traces of hay from ourselves, we had a very loving kiss as a sort of seal to our bargain.

Mother greeted us by asking us if we were alright. She thought we would be soaked and was worried about Polly. When I told her that we were lucky and sheltered in the old barn Dad looked up, but I managed not to look guilty.

To see Polly eating her lunch she looked as if butter wouldn't melt in her mouth. She had this quiet innocent air about her. What a different girl she was only a few hours ago! Looking across the table at her I seemed to be seeing her in a different light. She was no longer the little Polly that I had grown up with. She was now a beautiful and most desirable female who keeps telling me how much she loves me.

After lunch Polly asked if she could see the photographs and Mother suggested that we spread them out on the table in the front room. I had no qualms about Polly seeing so many snaps of Mary, because now we had this strange understanding.

We spent ages looking at the photographs and I had to explain so many of the details of the Castle and Lubeck and our various trips. Polly pinched one of the snaps of me and I pretended not to notice.

The weather had cleared up and Polly said that she ought to go home and would I please take her. Of course I said yes and she went off to find Mother to say goodbye.

I got the horses ready and as I brought them into the yard I saw Mother kiss Polly and tell her that she could come over whenever she wanted to, which I thought could be a bit dodgy. We then started our ride to Teigncoombe. I hope that I don't see the Vicar as I am sure that I would never be able to look him in the eye.

I had not been asked to the vicarage very often, but today I was asked in and given a cup of tea. The atmosphere seemed different, could it be my friendship with the Howes? People have some strange ideas.

Polly's parents were very pleasant people, very reserved, but at times they could be good fun. Her mother was small like Polly, but her father was tall and very fair, hence Polly's blond hair.

Once more I had to recall details of my trip to Germany and just to be bloody minded I referred to Lady Howes as Aunt Pamela. At last I managed to escape and offered to accompany Polly to where she kept her pony, who was called a very stupid name, Clive, after one of her favourite film stars.

Some way out of the village a farmer, one of the vicar's flock, gave Polly the use of a field and a small barn. It was a bit out of the way, but stabling a horse is always a problem.

We rode up to the stable which was in a corner of the field

amongst a clump of trees and hardly visible. Polly fed Clive and set him free. It is funny to see some horses when they are set free. They gallop off and kick their hind legs in the air as if to say I am free at last.

I was at fault this time. I collared Polly from behind and started to kiss her neck. She turned around and pressed her body against mine saying "Dear Henry, could we not finish our day the same way we started it? Please let's make love. We may not get the chance for a long time." So we did and it was a wonderful experience for both of us.

Unfortunately we could not linger as before. We were so happy and comfortable laying in that old barn. After all we were only supposed to be stabling Clive and Polly's parents may come looking for her.

Very reluctantly I lifted Polly onto Henry's back and we rode back to the vicarage. I said goodbye and told her that I would see her on the bus on Monday.

I tried not to let my mind wander as I rode home. So much had happened during the day. I still had the scent of Polly on me and I could see her so clearly in my mind and feel the softness of her lovely little body.

My situation seems to be getting worse instead of better. I suppose that some young chaps would think how lucky I was. Perhaps I have a conscience or a guilt complex. Anyway, I gave myself a good talking to and decided to enjoy life while I can. If Polly keeps her word Mary need never know.

When I got back to the farm, Mother told me that Sir James wanted to speak to me so I telephoned the Hall and Aunt Pamela answered. She asked me to come over to the Hall the following evening and could I please bring the photographs and negatives with me. That is if I had nothing else arranged. I said that I would be pleased to. I liked Mary's parents and they were so easy to talk to. The old man had such a dry sense of humour.

After lunch on the Sunday I went over to the Hall. Hooper, the butler, showed me into the sitting room and Aunt Pamela greeted me with the usual kiss on the cheek and said how nice it was to see me again.

Once more I explained the photographs and Sir James was very interested indeed in the harbour and countryside. Aunt Pamela wanted to see how she looked, but I don't know why as she always looked smashing.

After a while Sir James stood up and in his gruff way told me that he would have some prints taken off the negatives and send some copies to his brats. He looked at me and said that he was going for a ride and would I like to join him and meet his new gamekeeper. Of course I said yes.

I said goodbye to Aunt Pamela and we went to the stables to collect the horses. As we rode we chatted away and I told Sir James about my having to learn French. Evidently his friend, Major Davis had already told him all about it. However he had a good laugh when I told him about the French girl coming to stay with Mr Jarvis and he said that he wouldn't like to be around when Mary heard about it, especially if she was a pretty young thing.

He had a wistful look on his face and told me that many years ago he had a French girlfriend. He was quiet for some time after that and I thought that it must have brought back memories which he was reliving in his mind.

We found the gamekeeper in his domain in the middle of a large wood. This was new ground to me because the previous gamekeeper was a very grumpy old chap whom we used to avoid.

I was introduced and he seemed a very pleasant sort of chap. He was called Palmer and I was to be known as Master Henry. He told Palmer that I had the run of the whole estate. Sir James was like that, so very formal.

I told Palmer that one day I would like him to tell me all about pheasants and how he looked after them. This seemed to please him no end, to find someone who was interested.

While we were riding back to the Hall, Sir James asked me if I was still keen to go to college and learn all about farming and the management of estates. I told him that I had to win a scholarship first because Dad could not afford it. But I told him that this was my plan, unless there was a war in the meantime.

Sir James then told me about Hugh's inheritance. I knew all about it of course, but I pretended not to. "Hugh is not very interested in the land so when I am old Henry you will have to manage it for me." He continued "I know that there will be a war, but not for several years. All I hope is that the Government starts to prepare for it now. Anyway Henry, let's not be so morbid. There's plenty of life in the old dog yet!"

He was in a very talkative mood and told me to try and come over for a ride next Sunday afternoon. "I have an idea," he said. "I would like to talk to you about something and two heads are better than one and a young one at that. One day I will take you around to see my many tenants so that you can ride over their farms if you want to."

We had a most enjoyable ride and parted company at the main gate. I told Sir James that I would see him the following Sunday, unless it was wet. He told me that he would be able to return the negatives by then.

I rode back to the farm fairly quickly as by now it was getting quite dark. I had at the back of my mind the remark that Sir James had said about a manager for his estate in the distant future. I wonder what the old boy has on his mind for next Sunday. Anyway, time will tell and a lot of water will flow under the little bridge before I get any qualifications, if any at all.

I will write to Mary tonight and tell her about my visit to see her parents. I know that I will feel a bit of a heel writing to her after being with Polly. Needless to say, I think that I love Mary best of all.

Some of Mary's letters have been too detailed about our sexual activities so I have had to destroy those, but I have kept most of her letters. I do hope that the college doesn't censor pupils' letters otherwise she would be in big trouble.

Waiting for the bus the next morning, I felt a bit self-conscious about seeing Polly after having been so intimate with her in just one day. When the bus arrived she waved and kept a seat for me next to her.

She looked so innocent in her school uniform, but so very pretty. She sat as close to me as she could and it gave me a nice feeling to start a Monday morning with. Strange as it may seem, we both acted as if nothing had happened two days before.

The week went by which was most uneventful, except that at last Charlie and Aunt Betty told us that they were getting married and would live in part of the farmhouse. This was expected, but they certainly have taken their time about it!

They had decided to marry in the registry office in Newton Abbot because they didn't want a lot of fuss and bother. I was so glad to hear this as the thought of another wedding like John's filled me with horror.

Polly and I have only seen each other on the bus each day and we have had no opportunity to get together. We both catch the bus at different stops a long way apart, so it looks as if our meetings will have to be restricted to weekends only.

Friday came and it looked as if it would be a fine weekend. We decided to go for a ride on Saturday after lunch. I would call for Polly and then we would explore the far side of Teigncombe.

On Saturday morning I worked like mad in my workshop, making small pieces of furniture which I sold to a small shop in Newton Abbot. Peter's dad, Mr Walker, told me that I should charge more for my work so if they continue to sell I will put my prices up. Anyway, my bank balance is beginning to look quite healthy. I was a bit crafty because I never let on to Mum and Dad how much I had!

Life was becoming all hard work. I had a lot of homework to do each evening and after I finished that I went into my workshop. Mind you, the winter evenings can be very boring so I really only had the weekends to feel free. Now Sir James will be expecting me to visit on some Sunday afternoons, then of course there is Polly. She really is my only bit of pleasure during the dark evenings. How I hate the winter when I am confined to the farmhouse.

Dad came into my workshop, sat down and started to chat. I had told him about what Sir James had said and how he wanted me to see him every now and then to talk about the estate. We both wondered what he wanted to talk about when I saw him tomorrow, anyway I will soon find out.

After lunch I set off to see Polly. I decided to be on good behaviour as I was, so to speak, on home ground and she is the vicar's daughter. Not that she acted like one should. I think that some of these girls at college pass on what they learn about sex. Polly has already taught me a thing or two.

As I got to the vicarage Polly's parents were just about to leave in their car. Mrs Brown told me that they had to go to Exeter to see the Bishop. "After you have had your ride Polly will give you some tea. Would you mind keeping her company Henry until we return from Exeter?" she asked. What a lovely thought, being a 'baby-sitter' for Polly! Her parents must be mad. I asked how late they might be and they said that they would be home at around 6 o'clock and with a wave they were off.

Polly gave me one of her sweet little smiles and told me to take Henry around to the back of the house and put him in one of the sheds until we were ready to go. "While you do that I will put my jodhpurs and riding clothes on. I wondered why she was wearing a dress and not dressed for riding.

When I came back into the house Polly was still in her dress. She closed and locked the front door, ran upstairs and told me to come and see her room. I was very hesitant so she came down, took my hand and led me up the stairs. I knew what was in her mind and I started to protest by saying that it was too risky. I felt like a fly caught in a spider's web, I just had to follow her.

As soon as we were in her room she started to kiss me and began to take my clothes off. I found that she was well prepared and was wearing nothing under her dress. She was having difficulty with my clothing so I helped her. I lifted her dress up over her head and we stood there in our birthday suits. She looked down at me and with a giggle said, "What a big boy you are Henry!"

I picked her up and gently laid her on the bed and began to kiss her all over. I don't know what made me do this, it must have been natural instinct, but it had a terrific effect on Polly. She became so worked up and passionate that she wanted to stay the whole afternoon.

It was lucky that I was strong-willed otherwise the dear girl would no longer have been a virgin, because that is what she really wanted.

After a lot of persuasion I managed to get Polly ready to go for a ride. We made sure the room was presentable and I fetched poor Henry from the shed. With Polly sitting behind me, her arms tightly around my waist, we went to fetch her pony.

I caught and saddled up Clive and we started our very belated ride. We didn't go very far, for one reason we were both tired and another reason was that we were running out of time.

After giving Henry a good drink and some hay we put Clive out to graze, Polly became frisky again. But enough was enough, we just didn't have the time. I put her on Henry's back and we rode back to the vicarage where she gave me a very nice tea.

Polly's parents arrived home well before we thought they would, so it was a good thing that we were behaving ourselves. When I heard their car pull up outside I looked at Polly and noticed she looked so calm and innocent, really lovely. How different she had been only a few hours ago. When her parents came in they seemed full of beans and very happy. I got up to leave as I felt guilty and didn't want to show it.

I said goodbye and as Polly was showing me out Mrs Brown told me that they had heard some good news from the Bishop and Polly would no doubt tell me about it on Monday.

Polly accompanied me to the front gate and I asked her if she knew what the good news would be. She looked a bit sad and said that perhaps her father would have to move to a larger parish. She said that she hoped that this wasn't so because she didn't want to leave me. We kissed goodbye and I started my ride home to the farm.

Everything was quiet riding home in the half-light. Naturally I could think of nothing else but my afternoon spent in Polly's bedroom. I must be mad, anyone could have called at the vicarage. To me it had been pure heaven, but we had been too close to the breaking of our good resolutions.

After my lovemaking with Polly I realised how different it was when Mary and I got together in Germany. That was so natural. Perhaps it was because we were two innocents finding out what life was all about. One thing is certain, I must somehow cool my relationship with dear Polly. If I don't, we will do something that we will be very sorry for. She is such a tempting female and what makes it all so difficult is the way she looks at me.

I arrived home just in time for supper. There was quite a family gathering. John and Gertie, Charlie and Aunt Betty and of course Mum and Dad. It was nice for us all to be together, what a pity Jenny was not with us.

Of course, I was asked what I had been doing, so I said that I had been for a ride with Polly and then had to keep her company until her parents arrived back from Exeter. There was some good news afoot for them from the Bishop, but I had no idea what it was. Mother joined in and said that Mrs Brown wanted her husband to have a bigger and better parish so perhaps they will be moving.

Riding over to see Sir James after Sunday lunch, I wondered what he wanted to talk to me about. He was already in the stable yard talking to Mr Jones the head groom.. They both greeted me in a very friendly way. Sir James mounted up and said that we had quite a way to go so let's be off.

As we rode he explained that on the very far side of the estate there was some very rough land which didn't seem much use to anyone. When at last we reached the area in question I saw what he meant. It was scrubland, small wood and grass areas all mixed up and I could see that this covered quite a large area.

I had seen places like this in Germany and they had deer living quite happily in this sort of environment. I told Sir James about this, but there was a snag, the area would have to be fenced otherwise the deer would eat the crops of nearby farms. The other problem was water. I could see a stream in the distance and if this remained flowing in the summer it could be cleared to give water all year round.

I said that I knew nothing about deer, but thought they should be able to look after themselves and of course there would be a good supply of venison to sell, that is if there is a market in this part of the country.

Sir James looked at me and said that he had thought of deer and will make some enquiries. The fences are pretty good and perhaps while I was on one of my rides I could look at the perimeter.

He said that he had always wanted deer on his estate and to start a herd would make him very happy. He went on to say that making money out of them was no great concern, but on the other hand if venison could be sold it would be a bonus.

When we returned to the Hall. Sir James gave me the prints and negatives and after I had a brief chat with Lady Pamela I got ready to go home. I told the old man that I would try to ride around that piece of land next weekend.

Once more I was on this well-trodden path back to the farm. I was by myself and could have a chance to think. It was going to be very difficult to try and cool my relationship with Polly. To begin with a part of me would like to be with her as much as possible and how am I going to put her off without hurting her feelings? I will have to do something otherwise I will be in the soup. To put my problem in a nutshell, I love Polly, but I am also in love with Mary.

When I got on the bus on Monday I could see that there was something wrong with Polly. After a few tears she told me that her Father was to move to a much larger parish on the other side of Exeter. It would be a much larger living and he was very pleased.

She went on to say that she would have to change colleges or become a boarder at Newton Abbot, which she didn't fancy one little bit. It was all such a rush because the current vicar in the parish of Broadclyst had died suddenly leaving a full calendar and they had to move before next weekend. Then she burst out crying again and I had hell of a job to comfort her.

I know that I was going to try to see less of Polly, but not to see her at all was something I thought would never happen. Ever since I had started school I have seen Polly nearly every day, except in the holidays. Now we have become so close we have to part. Catching the bus will not be the same, in fact it will change my life.

When I got off the bus I watched this lovely girl walk so sadly away to her college. I tried to forget the news I had heard this morning by working as hard as I could, but somehow that didn't help.

When I met Polly by the bus stop that evening I could see that she had cheered up a bit and we agreed to catch the early bus tomorrow night, both get off at my stop and Polly could then catch the later bus home. This was the only way we could have an hour together.

This was the last time that we managed to have a close encounter before she went away. I told her that I would catch a train to Exeter and meet her in a week or two, but somehow I never did. I thought that Polly had gone from my life for ever. I was not to know then how wrong one can be.

CHAPTER 9

It was the Sunday before Christmas and I was sitting on the seat by the Little Bridge. I was going over in my mind the events of the past weeks and term. What a miserable term it had been. I had no idea that I would miss Polly so much as I have done.

I could hear the young girlish laughter when Peter and I used to play so many pranks on her on the way home from the village school. That was such a long time ago and so much has changed since then.

Our last meeting was for such a short time, but very hectic. We no longer had the comfort of the old barn, just a gateway in a lonely country lane to say our farewells. Polly got on her bus in tears and with a sad little wave she was gone.

We have written several letters to each other, but this somehow only prolongs the agony. To keep my mind off my problems I have been working like mad on my school work. Whenever the French master, Mr Jarvis, sees me he speaks to me in French and one day when my mind was elsewhere I replied in German.

When the weather was good I went to the Hall to ride around the estate. I completed a survey of the land set aside for deer and found a book in the college library which was full of information on deer in this country. I also made friends with the gamekeeper, Fred Palmer. He also knew how to rear deer which he had learnt from his previous employer. So the die is cast, there will be deer roaming the lands of Langley Hall.

I have had several rides with Sir James, visiting some of his farms and being introduced to his tenants. Some I knew by sight and of course they all knew Dad. They were surprised to see me riding around with Sir James who treated me in such a friendly way. Sir James told them that I may wish to ride on their land on his behalf in the future. He was treated with great respect and I found out that he was a very good and popular landlord who had been more than helpful in difficult times.

When the weather was bad I went into my workshop and busied myself with the orders I had in hand. I could also work in there on some evenings after I had finished my homework, Micky being my only company.

Charlie and Aunt Betty were married and now live in their part of the farmhouse, but we still seem to all mix in with each other, which is a good thing as we all get on so well together.

I suddenly remembered the old friend that I had lost. Poor old Daisy had to be put down as we couldn't see her suffer any longer. Charlie fixed it all up with the vet. What a dear old friend she had been to me and she was the one who started me on the road to being an accomplished rider. I taught Polly to ride on her when she was younger. Here I go again, thinking of Polly.

I am so looking forward to the day after tomorrow because my two friends Mary and Hugh come home tomorrow and with a bit of luck I will see them then. I began to wonder if Mary had changed. I hope she still feels the same way about me as I do about her. I have decided to keep very quiet about my affair with Polly. I don't know why but I am feeling a bit shy or perhaps apprehensive about meeting Mary again. Anyway, I will soon know. I certainly need some female company to make up for the loss of Polly.

The next day right after lunch, college broke up for Christmas. I said goodbye to my good friend Bernie and I was just about to leave when Mr Jarvis collared me. Speaking in French he told me that the girl from Brittany would be arriving during the holidays and he will telephone me so that a meeting can be arranged. "By the way Blake," he said, "she is fat and plain!" He then laughed and wished me a happy Christmas and I went on my way.

I wondered what time Mary would arrive home. Usually it was in the early afternoon, but I won't see her until tomorrow anyway. Perhaps she might give me a ring tonight.

When I got home I decided to spend some time in my workshop as I had some presents to finish off. I was making Mary a very nice little box with a fancy engraved top. A small tray was inside and there was a lock and key. I had made Hugh a new pallet as his was old and tatty.

I had just settled myself in the workshop with my permanent companion Micky, who was curled up on his bed in the corner having a snooze, when I noticed out of the corner of my eye as I was bending over a piece of wood, that Micky had gone out of the door. He then came bounding in and out again and I thought he must be having one of his odd spells again and thought no more of it.

Then I heard a voice that I knew so well say "Hello Henry darling," and two arms went around my waist from behind. I felt a warm body being pressed against my back and felt a kiss on the back of my neck. I turned around and there was Mary.

She was a sight for sore eyes. She had grown a little and her figure looked even more curvaceous and her face looked so lovely. Before we knew what was happening we were in each other's arms and were kissing each other as though there was no tomorrow. We were both becoming sexually aroused so we parted so that we could calm down in

194

case anyone came in.

We just sat on my seat holding hands and talked and laughed and felt at peace with the world. Micky got up so I knew that someone was coming. Much to my surprise Mother came in with a tray of cakes and two cups of tea. I thought that this was so kind of her because she must have known that we wanted to be alone.

Time was beginning to fly and Mary had to get back to the Hall. She had ridden over so I will have to ride back with her so we started to make a move. I went to change into my breeches and Mary went into the cowsheds to have a chat with Dad and John. When I came to collect her I could hear a lot of laughter, she always had fun with Dad and John.

Mary went into the house to say goodbye to Mother who kissed her and told her to come over to the farm when ever she wanted to. "There is never any need to be asked, just tell Henry and I can always find you some lunch my dear," Mother told her.

We started to ride back to the Hall and Mary said that her Papa had told her how helpful I had been on the estate and that I was no doubt in his good books.

It was grand riding back to the Hall with Mary, the light was beginning to fade and it was getting colder. I could clearly see the horses' breath condensing in the cold air.

Before we arrived at the main entrance to the Hall Mary suggested that we get off the horses and I was only too willing to agree. We managed to work off our built up passions. How nice it was to be near her again. It was such a relief to know by her actions that she still felt the same way about me.

As we rode up to the front door Hugh came out to greet us. Our friendship was such that although we hadn't seen each other for many weeks, he always acted as if our last meeting was yesterday. After a greeting he said that I must stay for dinner, that was an order from his mama who had telephoned the farm to let them know where I was.

"Come upstairs and have a wash Henry," said Hugh and we both chased Mary up the long staircase where she disappeared into her room.

Hugh had gone downstairs and I was on the landing when Mary came out of the bathroom wearing her dressing gown. As she passed me she opened her gown and ran off laughing. I managed to catch her and gave her a good slap on the bottom. It was then my turn to run for shelter. When I got downstairs and went into the living room, Sir James asked me what all the noise and laughter was about so I told him that his daughter was misbehaving herself and I had given her a hefty pat on the bottom. He laughed and told me that she needed more of that as she was just like her mother was when she was a young girl.

We all had a very pleasant time during dinner and I felt a bit out of place sitting down in breeches. The others all looked smart and Mary looked a smasher in what looked like a new dress. We all said what we thought we might have for Christmas and I told them I wanted some new clothes as I was growing out of so many things. Mary wanted new jodhpurs and Hugh wanted a camera.

It was a really strange feeling that I had during dinner that night at the end of 1935. We were all so naturally relaxed and completely at ease sitting around the very large dining table, being waited on by servants in starched uniforms.

I will never know why this happened to me. Sitting having dinner and being treated as part of the family and yet we were poles apart in so many ways. I know now that I am very much in love with Mary and I think that the family know that there is something going on between us. In a very simple and innocent affair, not the sexual encounters that are actually taking place without their knowledge. There must be a reason, but only time will tell.

Aunt Pamela then said that they were all going to London to stay in Hugh's house for a few days. "Would you like to come Henry?" she asked. "Hugh and his father have a lot of business to see to so you could keep Mary company."

Mary gave me such a kick on the shins that I had difficulty in hiding my reactions. I thanked Aunt Pamela for her kind invitation, but I would have to ask my parents first. Sir James interrupted by saying "I have already done that and you are coming with us my boy!"

Mary gave me one of her knowing little smiles as if to say Look out Henry, I will be after you.

Sir James then asked if we could all help him tomorrow as he had a herd of twelve deer arriving which would have to be driven to their new home across several fields. "The more people I have on horseback the easier it will be. They are wild and very difficult to control," he told us. I said that it would be great. Not a cattle drive, but a deer drive. Anyway, there would be no indians to worry about!

We seemed to take a long time over dinner and eventually I had to make tracks home. I thanked Aunt Pamela for the smashing food and went to get Henry from the stable. I was followed by Mary of course, and after I had saddled Henry and got my torch out of the saddle bag we started to kiss goodnight. She said that she wished that I was staying the night. I mounted Henry and saw Mary to the front door then off I started on my ride home.

It was a nice ride home, very cold, but quite bright with the moon being nearly full. I gave Henry a good rub down, some supper and bedded him down for the night in his warm barn.

I talked to Mum and Dad about my visit to London and asked Dad why he hadn't told me about it. He said that the Howes wanted it to be a surprise. Hugh had hinted at it during the summer, but I had never thought that it would come off. I had been saving my cash however, just in case I was lucky.

I went to bed early that night because I had to get up early so that I could do all my jobs and get over to the Hall in time for the arrival of the deer.

The next morning it was very cold and the ground was covered with frost and the water in the drinking troughs was solid ice. I liked these cold mornings. I liked to hear the crunch of my feet as I walked over the frozen ground. I completed all my jobs and was about to go when Mother came after me. She gave me some cream and butter for Aunt Pamela and a flask of hot coffee to put in my saddle bag.

She really was a proper old fusspot. She made me go back to the house and put on another sweater. At last I got away and started on my ride to the Hall. Henry was very frisky and I had a job to hold him back until we came to a short cut across a field. I let him have his head and we had a very good gallop which we both enjoyed very much.

I was on the last leg of my journey when to my surprise I saw Mary riding towards me. What a pleasant sight she was. The early morning sun was shining on her long dark hair and she greeted me with such a lovely smile. She brought her horse close to Henry, leant over and kissed me. What more can one ask for on a cold but sunny winter's morning?

As we rode she nattered, like females do. She said that her Papa was very excited about the deer and he thought a great deal of me for helping him organise this project. She went on to say that she thought he knew how we felt for each other.

She looked at me and said, "You do only love me Henry don't you? Now that Polly has gone out of your life." I was flabbergasted. However did she know? I stopped Henry and told her that of course I did. My worry was how long would she love me? Her answer to that was "Oh Henry! You silly boy. You ought to know by now!"

I told her that I was very fond of Polly and she had been a dear friend since my first day at the village school. I didn't go into the matter any further and this seemed to satisfy Mary.

When we reached the Hall I could see Sir James had mustered quite a team to help with the deer. There was Mr Jones, two grooms and the three of us plus Sir James, all on horseback. There were also several other members of the staff on foot. Fred Palmer the gamekeeper would be meeting us where the deer were to be unloaded.

It was quite a cavalcade that set off to meet the cattle vans delivering the deer. We didn't have long to wait at the delivery area and the chap in charge of the delivery told Sir James that it would be easier to get the stag going in the right direction as the rest would follow him. We found that this was easier said, than done.

When the deer were all let loose in the first field they scattered all over the place and it took us ages to round them up into a group. They were so nervous and timid that we had to drive them like sheep, very slowly and carefully.

We eventually got the hang of it and the deer seemed to be settling down. The stag was a magnificent creature with his large spread of antlers. I wouldn't like to get tangled in them. I could see that there were two very young bucks in the herd so the old boy will have a smashing time with the does for several seasons yet.

How strange nature is. These antlers will be discarded in February and another set will grow.

Several times the deer shot away from the herd and it was one hell of a job to get them back. They had a terrific turn of speed and it took the three of us to get them back into the herd. It was great fun. My friends and I acted as a team on one flank so there was a lot of shouting and laughter between us.

At last we got the deer into their new home. I think they were very relieved and we certainly were, as it had not been an easy drive. Hugh, Mary and I found somewhere to sit and I got out my flask of coffee. We only had the one cup but we didn't bother about things like that. I must say, the coffee put new life into us. Sir James, Mr Jones and Fred Palmer were having a swig from the old man's whisky flask.

I told Mary and Hugh to watch the stag. He was walking around the area where the herd was gathered and every now and then he urinated thus leaving his scent to warn any hopeful young buck to keep away from his territory.

Fred Palmer had scattered some food and hay to make the deer feel at home. Even so Mary said that she wondered if they would feel homesick. I told her that I thought they probably would for a few days. On the other hand if there was plenty to eat and drink they would soon be happy.

We rode back to the Hall with Sir James and Mr Jones and the grooms. Mr Jones told me to leave Henry with him for a day and he would give him a good clean up for Christmas. I thanked him and said that I would try to arrange it. The trouble was that I rode Henry nearly every day.

We had a late lunch at the Hall and Hugh wanted to do some painting, so Mary and I decided to ride down to the village. To be more precise, Mary wanted to go to the village shop so she suggested it.

We had a very pleasant afternoon. The village store had what Mary wanted and there were quite a few people about. The shop had holly and mistletoe on sale and before I could stop her, Mary picked up a bunch, held it over my head and gave me a smacking kiss. This caused quite a stir in the shop and I felt most embarrassed. As we went out Mary laughed and said, "That will give the old dears something to talk about, Farmer Blake's son out riding with Mary Howes again!"

To add insult to injury she put her arm around my waist as we walked to our horses. As we rode out of the village I asked her why she had put on that little show. She was quiet for a short spell and then said that we were both nearly sixteen and looked far older, so why shouldn't we go out together? The fact that she was the daughter of a titled family and I was the son of a local farmer made no difference whatsoever. "Anyway Henry, you seem to be part of the family already," she added.

We chatted away on the way back to the Hall. I said that Hugh wanted to go and see Mrs Jenkins so what would we do tomorrow. It was Market Day in Newton Abbot so why don't we catch a bus into town and have a look around. We could call in and see Mother in the market and if Mary was a good girl I said I would treat her to lunch. "Nothing posh mind you, because I'm saving for the trip to London," I told her.

Mary thought this was a smashing idea. She said that there was a bus stop near the Hall. On the other hand perhaps Wills could drive us in the car. I immediately said no to that suggestion and said, "Let's be ordinary people. I will ride over in my best breeches and jacket, as being Market Day that sort of dress is normal. Anyway, Polly always said how handsome I looked." I expected a reaction from Mary and she looked really fierce so I galloped off. When I stopped we got off the horses and she tried to hit me so I put my arms around her and we laughed and kissed each other in such a tender way.

When we arrived at the Hall we went to find Aunt Pamela. I explained our plans for tomorrow and she said It would be OK. She was quiet for a moment and then asked me to sit down saying that she wanted to talk to me about the trip to London.

"We have been invited to some parties and you will have to dress in the correct way. Sir James has arranged with your father for you to visit a tailor in Newton Abbot to have a dress suit made in time to take to London. Can we say that this will be your Christmas present from us all?" Aunt Pamela asked.

I didn't know what to say. Mary gave her mother a great hug and said thank you. By this time it had sunk in and I also said a very hearty thank you. Aunt Pamela said that tomorrow we must go to see the tailor and with a smile she added that she would put me in Mary's charge. I told her that in that case I would have to look out for trouble and Mary tried to hit me and we both fell on to the sofa laughing, which Aunt Pamela thought was a great joke.

I said that I should be going home and got up to leave. Aunt Pamela said that when we came back from Newton Abbot she wanted me to stay for dinner so that we could talk about our London adventure, so I should tell my mother where I would be.

When I got home I told Mum and Dad about the proposed visit to the tailors in Newton Abbot. I thought it a bit odd for the Howes to spend quite a bit of money on a dress suit for me to wear only once or twice.

Dad said that they were most insistent about it. "It seems that they are very fond of you Henry so don't worry about it. Just be grateful for the opportunities you are getting." I told them that I felt a bit worried about meeting people in London who were in Mary's social class and Dad's advice was very simple, "Just be your normal self Henry. If they don't like you they can lump it."

John came in and he was very interested to hear how the 'deer drive' had gone. I told him all about it and made him laugh by saying that the redskins gave us no trouble.

I told Mother that I had been asked to stay for dinner at the Hall tomorrow night and this pleased her. She would have one less mouth to feed and tomorrow she would be very busy with her poultry.

The Christmas panic was not as it used to be. Mother now had some women in from the village to help her and Betty prepare the poultry orders. She had expanded this side line a lot over the years, but nevertheless tomorrow would be Mother's big day. The car would be loaded up to the roof with turkeys and geese for the Christmas Market Day. Most of her birds now went to local butchers which made life easier for her.

I spent the evening working on the odd pieces to be finished off. It was a bit cold in my workshop, but so peaceful and it gave me a chance to think about things in general.

I still had this visit to London on my mind and the new clothing. I had the holiday in Germany and never really found out who actually paid for it. Was it Major Davis, Sir James, or Jake? It would have been very rude of me to ask but even so, I would like to know.

Hugh and Mary probably had something to do with it, but it just does not add up. Who am I to reason why?

When I woke up the next morning I was glad to see that the weather was fine for our day out. I did my jobs and made myself look reasonably smart. I said goodbye to Mother and told her that Mary and I will call in and see her at her stall.

As I was leaving Dad called me and gave me a pound note which he said I could use to pay for our lunch and bus fares. He said that if you took out a young lady like Mary for the day you must do the job in the right way. I was so surprised that I nearly forgot to thank him. A pound note was worth a lot of money to me, so I will make sure that we have a nice lunch.

When I got to the Hall I took Henry to the stable yard and asked Mr Jones if he would mind looking after him until after dinner that night. He seemed pleased and said that would give him plenty of time to give Henry his Christmas treat. I thanked him and made my way to the house.

I met Mr Hooper in the hallway and he told me that everyone had gone out, but Miss Mary wanted me to go up to her room. He gave me a friendly little smile and said, "I think you know the way Master Henry." He then went off in the direction of the kitchen.

As I walked up the staircase I thought that Mary would have been ready by now and I knocked on her door. She called "Come in," and as I entered I could see no sign of Mary. Then the penny dropped, she was behind the open door. So I closed the door and grabbed her. She was wearing a dressing gown and I picked her up and laid her on the bed. I turned her over and started to smack her bottom which was now quite bare. In no time at all we were making love in our own simple way.

Unfortunately we couldn't linger for long. We would have liked to have stayed there all day, it was a lovely start for our first day out together other than a day in the country. As we walked down the long drive hand in hand to the bus stop we both felt invigorated after out brief encounter.

Mary looked smashing in a very smart winter coat. Underneath she wore a nice dress. Looking at her I felt so proud. Before we had left the Hall Mr Hooper had said, "I hope you have a pleasant day, and may I take the liberty of saying what a handsome couple of young people you look." We both wondered what the old boy was thinking. He was probably wishing that he was young again.

We reached the bus stop just in time to see the bus coming around the corner. There were only two seats left so we were in luck. I never asked, but I had the feeling that Mary had never been on a local bus before. As it was Market Day the locals were making their weekly visit to Newton Abbot.

How stupid it all was. When we got on the bus there seemed to be surprise that Miss Mary from the Hall was actually riding on the bus and what was young Blake doing taking her to town?

It was a very bumpy ride in the bus. I had always left the bus at my stop before it continued past the Hall and then went into Teigncombe.

I explained to Mary that I had to call into the furniture shop to see if they had any cash for me. We then had to visit the tailors and would she like to see Mother in the market? She put her arm through mine and said that she would go wherever I wanted to.

The town was very busy. There were people everywhere and there seemed to be a continual background noise of chit-chat. We decided to go to the tailor's first. Aunt Pamela had given the necessary instructions by telephone.

The tailor measured me and then said that I might be lucky. Mary and I looked at each other not knowing what he was talking about. It would seem that to make a suit in the time required would be very difficult, but he had a top quality suit that he had made for a client that had never been collected and with a bit of luck it might fit.

I tried it on and it fitted perfectly, except for the length of the trousers and sleeves which would have to be altered. The tailor fixed me up with a shirt, tie and shiny black shoes. This would all be delivered to the farm before Christmas.

While this was going on Mary was having a good look around. She had spotted a super top coat which she made me try on. I soon took it off because no way could I have a coat like that.

Our next visit was to the furniture shop and I was so pleased that they had sold all of my pieces, so I collected quite a handful of cash.

I had to buy presents for the females of my family and with Mary's help this was much easier than I had anticipated. The plan was for me to be able to dump my parcels with Mother so that she could take them home in the car.

The Market Day just before Christmas was a real event for the farming community. The men met in different hotels and pubs and the womenfolk wore their best clothes and did their Christmas shopping having a good chat with each other.

I saw a few people I knew and also some of my college pals. I felt so proud to be walking alongside such a lovely girl as Mary. I kept looking at her as we talked and I could see that she was enjoying herself. I also noticed the looks of envy on the faces of some of the young men as we passed.

We went into the Butter Market as it was called. The place was packed with people buying and selling all sorts of goods. Stall holders were selling their goods and farmers' wives were selling poultry and dairy goods. This was their big day to harvest the fruits of their labours over the past few months.

Mother was pleased to see us and introduced Mary to the next two stall holders. The three of them had been on the same stalls for more years than I could remember so they greeted me as an old friend. Mother had sold all of her poultry and her stall looked very bare. I could see Mary and Mother deep in conversation and I wondered what they were cooking up between them.

I managed to steer Mary away from Mother and we made our way out of the Butter Market into the cattle market. This was really a man's world, but I thought it would be nice to find Dad. I saw him in the distance and when he saw us he made his way through the crowd towards us.

He looked very smart and handsome and when he came up to us he took Mary's hands and held her in front of him at arm's length and said, "How lovely you look Mary. I wish that I was Henry's age!" Mary then put her arms around his waist and gave him a big hug. We all had a good laugh, then he took us to see what was going on.

Mary had never been in a cattle market before and she kept asking Dad lots of questions. She was very intrigued by what she was being shown. There was a mixture of country folk. Wealthy farmers, and small holders who were only just managing to make a living. Dad and Mary were talking away like mad and after a complete tour of the market I managed to get Mary to leave so that we could have some lunch.

Dad recommended a restaurant in the main street where we managed to get a table and had a nice lunch. As I sat there giving the waiter our order, I thought that only a short time ago I would not have known what to do, or have the confidence to even go into such a place. How my friendship with Hugh and Mary had educated me in so many ways.

Mary was in great spirits. She put both of her hands across the table and clasped mine and said that she was having a wonderful day and how much she loved me. It made her feel grown-up to be out with such a handsome young man. It was my turn now to tell her not to be so silly.

I thought that now would be a good time to tell her about my French connection, so without going into great detail I told her that I had to learn how to speak French like a native. I then mentioned in a casual way that Mr Jarvis had a French girl coming to stay for a few months to learn English and we would be able to help each other.

Mary said that she hoped that the girl was plain and awful looking. "If she comes after you Henry she could start an Anglo-French war!" I told her that there was no need to worry about that and I gave her knee a squeeze under the table.

She then started to remind me about her French girlfriend, Martine, at school and how she used to have lessons before she went away to college. She continued in very good French, "Henry, if you need any French lessons, I will give them to you, not some French floozie."

We had a walk in the afternoon and I showed Mary where my college was and pointed out the different buildings and explained what they were used for. I explained that the house by the gate belonged to the Head, Mr Butler.

I was just about to say that the Head was not such a bad old so and so when a head appeared over the hedge and it was none other than the old man himself. "Hello Blake, what are you doing here?" I replied by saying that I was showing my friend my place of torture.

He asked me to introduce him to the very smart young lady I had with me and as we walked up the drive Mrs Butler came out of the house and I introduced Mary to them both as Mary Howes. The Head said that he had met Sir James on several occasions and asked if I wanted to show Mary any part of the college in particular. I replied that I just wanted to show her my college.

I had always got on alright with the Head ever since the help I gave him with Bernie. Today he seemed more human and not the austere person he appeared during term time. Mary was chatting to Mrs Butler, but then Mary chats to everyone!

We finally said our goodbyes to the Butlers and exchanged seasonal greetings. As we were leaving the Head said In German, "You have good taste in girlfriends my boy. I now understand your worry about the French girl coming to stay with Mr Jarvis." With a friendly wave he went into the house.

Of course, Mary wanted to know what that was all about, so I told her that he was just practising his German.

Time was getting on so we made our way towards the bus station. We were about to pass a second hand book shop when I noticed a book in the window about deer. We went in and I asked Mary if she thought her father would like it for a Christmas present. She thought it was very sweet of me to even think of it and I then asked her what sort of chocolates her mother liked. We found a sweet shop and I bought Aunt Pamela's present.

As luck would have it our bus was in so we got on board. Of course the driver on duty was the regular one and he asked how Polly was. I told him that she had gone to live near Exeter. He then gave Mary a puzzled look, as if to say and who is this? When we sat down Mary said that she was glad that Polly had left because I may have got too fond of her.

In no time at all we were walking up the drive to the Hall. Mary took my arm and said that she hadn't enjoyed herself so much for a long time and said how lovely it would be if the family were still all away. I told her to behave herself, but of course she only laughed, put her arms around me and gave me a great big kiss.

We made for the stables before we went into the house as I wanted to see Henry. Mr Jones was there and he had been working on Henry who looked so smart with a new pair of shoes as well. I had bought a packet of the foul smelling tobacco that Mr Jones smoked in his pipe which he always seemed to have in his mouth. When I gave it to him he seemed more than grateful. I think it was the thought and not the gift that pleased him.

All the family were back and Mary started to tell them about our day out and how she had enjoyed herself. In fact, she was talking to her parents non-stop for ages.

Hugh and I left her and went upstairs to have a wash before dinner. He had spent the day with Mrs Jenkins and told me that she wanted to see me before Christmas. I told him that I hoped to visit her and then Jake tomorrow.

I asked him what his plans were and he said that if I didn't mind he would like to stay at home and finish two paintings which he had done as presents. I decided that I would ask Mary if she wanted to come over to the farm for the day.

We all went into dinner and Aunt Pamela told us what the plans were for the London trip. We would be away for five nights including New Year's Eve. We would go on three days after Boxing Day and had been invited to several parties. She mentioned some names and Hugh and Mary gave the thumbs down on all but two. One was on New Year's Eve and another two days later. Evidently they were not keen on some of the party givers.

"We will probably go to a show as well," said aunt Pamela. She looked at me and asked "Henry, can you dance?" My immediate answer was no so she turned to Mary and told her that she must teach me using the gramophone in the library and we should start after dinner.

Sir James now took over and said that now the bad news. "Your grandmother has decided to come for a few days at Christmas." There were some loud groans from Mary and Hugh and Aunt Pamela added that her stay would be short because we would be off to London, so it shouldn't be too bad.

After dinner I asked about Grandmama and it seemed that she was a bit of an old dragon and thinks that Mary and Hugh are still young children. "She is Papa's mother so he will keep out of the way as much as possible because she tries to boss him about," said Mary.

Much to my disgust I was led to the library to have my first lesson in dancing. To begin with it was bit disastrous because when we had our arms around each other, dancing was the last thing we wanted to do. Luckily Hugh came in and Mary had the difficult job of teaching me not to tread on her feet.

It proved to be great fun and it was pleasant to hold Mary. We were making quite a lot of noise, so much so that Aunt Pamela looked in to see what was going on.

It was soon time for me to go home and I arranged for Mary to come over to the farm tomorrow. We would visit Jake and Mrs Jenkins. It was so cold that I said goodnight to Mary in the hall entrance and once again she whispered how she wished I was staying the night.

I fetched Henry from the stables and made my way home after having a really wonderful day.

When I got in I asked Charlie what he thought of the weather. He said that tomorrow would be dry, but there would be snow about in a day or two. We might even have a white Christmas.

When I got up the following morning I could see that Charlie was right. It was a cold bright morning and dry. Mary came over pretty early, well wrapped up with a cute woollen hat on.

We called on Jake first and exchanged Christmas presents and had a nice hot cup of coffee. Micky settled himself in front of the fire, but not for too long because we had quite a ride to see Mrs Jenkins. It was good to see Jake, he had proved to be such a good friend and he always made me feel so welcome.

Jake told Mary that he would see her over the Christmas as he would be staying at the Hall. She then warned him that her grandmama would be there, but this information didn't put him off and with a cheerful wave we were on our way.

We stopped at the Little Bridge to give the horses a rest and a drink and also gave each other a kiss or two to keep us going. As I sat on the old bench I had to remember another girl who had kept me company here so many times over such a long period of time. I wondered if they still had the Christmas party at the village school. I still had a very old and crumpled bar of chocolate tucked away in my private box.

Somehow I am unable to understand how I can love Mary so much and yet miss Polly. I wrote to Polly last week to wish her a Happy Christmas, but so far had not received a reply. Mary brought me back to the world by saying we should make a move.

Mrs Jenkins gave us a very warm welcome and we had a lengthy chat. I had brought her some cream and butter which she always appreciated. I liked to talk to Mrs Jenkins but eventually we had to leave. I told her that I would call and see her after Christmas so that we could have another chinwag.

On our way back Mary wanted to call into the village shop to buy Mother some flowers. It was a nice thought, but a waste of time. She did however buy her a box of chocolates because the shop didn't have any flowers at this time of year.

I had decided not to tell the family about the dancing lessons because I thought it was a bit on the cissy side. Mary of course soon changed that, which made everyone laugh.

After lunch we pottered around the farm for a bit, but after a while it became colder so we decided to go back to the Hall and continue the dancing lessons. Really it was only an excuse to have a little close proximity in the warm.

When we reached the Hall Hugh was busy painting so we went into the library and put the gramophone on and started to dance, or try to dance would be a better description. As before, our minds were on other things. Eventually we really got on and my dancing began to improve. It was very cosy, but not satisfying.

Aunt Pamela came in to tell us that it had been snowing really hard for some time and she thought that I should start for home. The curtains had been drawn so we had no idea what was happening outside. We looked out and the ground was white and it was snowing like mad.

I said goodbye to everyone and Hugh found me a large cape to give me a bit of cover until I got my waterproofs out of my saddle bag. I ran to the stables, hastily saddled up Henry, put on my waterproofs and went out into the wintry blast, or the blasted winter.

It was a very unpleasant ride home. The snow was beating into my face and the visibility was down to a few yards. Poor Henry didn't like it at all, but luckily he knew the way home and was very surefooted. In fact, by the time I got home I was very proud of him.

After I got Henry to the barn I gave him a good rub down and an extra helping of oats as a reward. When at last I went into the kitchen Mum and Dad were relieved to see me. Mother told me to telephone Mary to say that I had arrived home safely. I did this and Mary said that her father was very cross that I was not invited to stay the night because of the bad conditions outside. She said what a pity it was that her father was not around earlier and I knew what she was thinking.

Mary said that if I could get over tomorrow we could go tobogganing. "Come over as early as you can," then she whispered, "Love you," and hung up.

The next morning was bright and sunny and there had been no further snow overnight so I decided to go over to see Mary. It was so interesting to see the different tracks left by the animals in the snow. There were plenty of rabbit prints and the prints of a fox could be seen looking for any unwary rabbits. If I had the time I would like to follow the fox's prints so that I would know where he lived. It was rather sad to see where the snow had been disturbed after the fox had caught his supper.

When I joined the lane from the fields the trees and hedges were a picture with their covering of pure white snow. Fresh snow is always so white and after a few days it turns to an off-white shade and if it hangs about too long it becomes dirty from the air.

I rode along the lane and heard a commotion going on around the next bend. I could hear a car engine revving up and a female voice shouting instructions. When I came around the bend I saw a very old Daimler car with its rear wheel stuck in a ditch which was frozen over. A late middle-aged chauffeur was looking at the rear of the car and trying to work out what to do. All the time he was being shouted at by an invisible female in the back of the car.

As I got closer to the car a very autocratic voice told me to give the car a push, which I did, but it was well and truly stuck. The only way to get it out would be to fix a rope to the car and then to poor Henry. I always carried a length of rope in my saddle bag, perhaps I had seen too many westerns. Anyway it had proved its worth many a time in the past.

I looked into the back of the car and ask the old lady if she could get out. She said that of course she could, but she was not going to as it was too cold. I explained what I wanted to do and told her that I had to lessen the weight in the back of the car, otherwise it would be too much for my horse. She started to shout at me so I looked through the window and told her that she would have to stay there until the ice had melted. I raised my cap and said, good day madam and started to mount Henry.

She shouted that she would get out so I connected the rope and after a struggle Henry managed to pull the car out of the ditch and into the lane. The old lady thanked me, but not very enthusiastically, and then got into the car. She called me over and asked what she owed me for my trouble. I replied "It is one's duty to help a fellow traveller in trouble." With that remark I raised my cap once more to the old trout and went on my way.

I was getting nearer to the Hall when the car passed me. The chauffeur gave me a friendly salute and I suddenly realised that the old trout might be Mary's grandmother. If it is I will be in the soup, but somehow I didn't care because she needed to be put in her place.

I rode up the drive and Mary came running out to meet me. What a lovely sight she was. She climbed onto the back of Henry and we rode into the stable yard. With her arms around my waist and her head resting on my back, I thought how nice it was to be with this girl again.

As we turned the corner I saw the old Daimler so I told Mary about my meeting with her grandmother. I really thought she would never stop laughing. "Henry, she told us that a nice young man had helped her. If you can get one over on Grandmama you'll have a friend for life," she continued, "providing you don't give in to her without a struggle." She gave me a kiss and said how she loved me. What brought that on I have no idea.

Mary thought that I should go into the house and be formally introduced to her grandmother, so we went into the house and Mary led me by the hand into the living room. All the family were sitting around a very large fire, including the old trout. Mary said, "This is Henry Grandma," and turning to me she said, "This is my grandma, Lady Howes."

"So this is Mary's Henry that I have heard so much about," she said. "This is the young man who bossed me about, but in the end rescued me. I will forgive you this time young man, but don't try to boss me around again!" I replied that the moral is for you not to be stuck in a ditch again. She laughed at this and held out her hand to be shaken.

Hugh got up and said that we were going tobogganing, so the three of us left the room. As we were going out Aunt Pamela told me that I was staying for lunch and we were not to be late.

Hugh wanted to know in detail all about my meeting with Grandma Howes. It made him laugh and he said that he wished he had been there to see the old so and so stuck in the ditch. I told him that people like her were really verbal bullies and the only way to get back at them is to ignore them or answer them back. "You may find that underneath the old lady there may be quite a nice old stick. Perhaps she is lonely and unhappy," I said.

We collected the two toboggans from a barn in the stable yard and then made our way into the kitchen. Cook greeted me in broad Devonshire, "Hello Master Henry, how are you today my dear?" I went over and put my arm around her ample waist and said, "I'll be fine if I had some of your fantastic cakes and a hot cup of coffee inside me." She pushed me away and in no time at all we were sitting down to some cakes and a nice warm drink.

When we got outside Mary asked me how I got on so well with everyone. There was Grandmother for example. "Hugh and I are scared of her. Then there is Cook, she always makes a fuss over you." I had to think for a while and then I said that Dad had always told me to just be myself and to treat people how they treated you. But always try being friendly first of all. Some people cannot help being awkward because it is their nature.

We had to walk across two field to a suitable slope. We had several snowball fights on the way and a lot of fun. When we reached the slope, Mary and Hugh had a go and it looked grand. Then Mary had the bright idea of me lying on the toboggan and then she could sit on my back. Now this was great fun and we could have a crafty cuddle when Hugh was not looking.

It was really enjoyable, so much so that we had to hurry back to be in time for lunch. On the way back Mary and I started to talk to each other in French, which Hugh got a bit fed up with until we told him the reason why. He surprised us both by saying that he would take the French girl off my hands. Poor Hugh never saw any females. When Polly was around there was no interest either way. So we decided that when the French girl arrived in Newton Abbot we would invite her up to the Hall or the farm.

Lunch was quite pleasant. Aunt Pamela had placed me between Mary and Lady Howes, who started to ask me so many questions that I found it difficult to eat my meal. Then she asked me if I had known my grandfather on my father's side of the family. I replied that I had not been that lucky and she told me that she had met him so many years ago. Her face suddenly softened for a minute or two and she said, "What a handsome man he was. Not unlike you my dear. One day I might tell you about him." Then she quickly changed the subject.

Mary asked her father if we could ride over and see the deer after lunch and he agreed saying it would save him the trip. Hugh said that he had some work to do so it would just be Mary and I. Lady Howes said to her son, "James, do you think that is wise with all the snow about?" He told her that Henry looked after her this morning so he knew that I would look after Mary and that we both had good horses.

Riding on the snow-covered ground was a very pleasant experience. The lazy sunshine made the ice crystals shine as the horses' hooves kicked up the snow. The sun had set in a slight thaw and there was the sound of small lumps of snow falling on the ground from the trees and high bushes.

Otherwise there seemed to be a complete and ghostly silence. The only sounds were of distant crows and the raucous call of the cock pheasants. The snow even muffled the regular beat of the horses' hooves.

We didn't talk much, we were just happy to be in each other's company. When we reached the entrance of what we now called the Deer Park, we dismounted and of course this gave us an excuse to embrace each other, which was very pleasant, but not like the summer.

We were so bundled up in clothing that we kissed and I made Mary laugh by rubbing noses like the Eskimos do.

We saw the deer in the distance and it was interesting to watch them clearing away the snow with a front hoof so that they could find some grass to munch. As we rode closer to the herd the stag positioned himself between them and us. Consequently, we kept our distance.

I could see clouds building up and the wind was freshening so I told Mary that I thought we should make our way back to the house. We just managed to make it to the stables before it started to snow like mad.

Mr Jones told us that one of the lads would see to the horses so we went into the house by the back entrance to keep out of the snow. We had a chat with Cook, who was making a huge batch of mince pies and we pinched two of them. They were smashing!

Aunt Pamela was glad to see us back safely, but if the snow continued I must stay the night. Mary looked at me and gave me a wicked little grin.

We went into the library and continued our dancing lessons, but for most of the time it was just the gramophone playing because we made the most of being alone in a warm room with a very comfortable sofa. Much to Mary's disgust it stopped snowing and I had to leave her.

Tomorrow it would be Christmas Eve so I would be over fairly early in the morning. Jenny would be home during the afternoon and I wanted to be there to greet her. I said goodbye to Aunt Pamela and the old trout, who much to my surprise gave me a very sweet smile. Mary saw me off and I soon got home. Henry was extremely pleased to be in his warm stable.

My suit had arrived from the tailors and of course I had to try it on for the family to inspect. I felt a bit of a twit, but nevertheless it all looked very smart.

I told Dad about my encounter with Lady Howes which amused him a great deal. He had met her and her husband a long time ago. He remembered hearing that she came from a family that owned a very big farm next to the estate and that she and Grandfather were very friendly, but she married the Lord of the Manor.

"How strange it is that you and Mary are so friendly. I wonder what your grandfather would have said. If I were you I wouldn't mention this to Mary," Dad said.

I spent the evening wrapping up my Christmas presents. I will take my small gifts over to the Hall tomorrow morning. I will not be able to see Mary until after Christmas. The annual party that the Howes give every year is the day after Boxing Day. This is a tradition. My whole family are invited every year. John is not very keen, but Gertie is going to make him go this year.

There was a letter from Polly waiting for me when I got home that evening. I had not yet opened it because I thought that I would look at it in the privacy of my room. I still thought of her sweet little face, framed in her blond hair. She turned out to be such a passionate girl that it was perhaps just as well that she had to move away.

Her letter was quite cheerful, but underneath I thought that she was not the happy Polly I used to know. She was getting on so very well at her new college that she may be able to go to a university to finish her education. I always thought that she was a very bright girl, but had not realised she was that bright.

I still feel guilty about my affair with Polly and feel that I have let Mary down. On the other hand Polly and I should not have become so very involved. I think that perhaps I will go to Exeter to see her after Christmas.

As I fell asleep that night my mind was in a bit of a turmoil, Polly's letter had really upset me, especially at the end when she made the remark that she still loved me very much indeed. I would hate it so much if she was very unhappy because of me.

When I awoke and looked out of the window I was glad to see that the snow had nearly all gone except by the hedgerows. I could tell that it was much milder.

I got my goods together and with some cream from Mother loaded in my haversack I managed to get everything to the Hall in one piece. I think that Mary must keep watch from her window, because she never seemed to fail to come out to greet me.

She climbed onto Henry's back behind me and her hand always seemed able to find its way beneath the waist band of my breeches, which was very teasing. There was no one about in the stables so we gave each other a proper greeting.

She helped me carry in my few parcels to the library and I gave her the walnut jewellery box which I had made. She was really thrilled with it and gave me a big hug. Mary then brought forth a lovely riding crop with a silver handle and on a small shield it had a fancy HB engraved on it.

We then found Hugh and I gave him the pallet I had made for him and he gave me a smashing painting of my favourite place on the estate. It was a scene of the spot where we swam, which held such happy memories for me.

When we found Aunt Pamela and Sir James I thanked them most profusely for the dress suit and other items they had given me. I then gave them their small presents, which Mary told me afterwards they had not been expecting anything. Apparently Sir James was most intrigued with the book about deer.

Old lady Howes came in to the room followed by the butler, Mr Hooper, and a servant carrying a tray of coffee and some of Cook's cakes. Mr Hooper asked Lady Pamela if I would be staying for lunch, but I explained that I had to get home to see my sister.

We all chatted for quite some time and old lady Howes was very pleasant indeed, which seemed to be a surprise to everyone. I then had to wish everyone a happy Christmas and Aunt Pamela gave me a kiss and a hug and said that no doubt they would see me on Boxing Day. I grinned and said that I expect Mary will see to that and she gave me a playful clip under the ear, which I managed to dodge.

I went over to where old lady Howes was sitting to say goodbye. She said, "I have not been able to get you a Christmas present Henry so here is something for you to buy what you want." She then pressed a pound note into my hand and said, "Am I too old to have a Christmas kiss?" So I put my arm around her and gave her a kiss on the cheek.

Mary and I then left and when we got outside Mary turned to me and said, "What have you been saying to Grandma Henry? You have certainly made a friend there." She continued to say "Do you know Henry, the more I see of you, the more I love you." Then in front of Hooper who was standing in the hallway, she gave me such a kiss. She smiled at Hooper and said that she thought the mistletoe was in the hall. He laughed and said that believe it or not, he was young once. I walked over to him, shook his hand and wished him a very happy Christmas.

I hated the idea of not seeing Mary for a couple of days and yet only last night I was thinking of Polly. We said goodbye and I began my ride home. One thing I do know is that when my dear Mary returns to college I will be like a lost soul on a mountain. Anyway, I will worry about that when the time comes.

Jenny came home mid-afternoon the next day. She had been very extravagant and hired a taxi from the station. She looked so elegant in her city clothes and was so attractive. She seemed happy and full of beans, so life must be treating her kindly.

I left the females to natter to their heart's content and went into the cowshed to watch the milking. I had a chat with John and Charlie and then I thought that I should give Henry a good grooming for Christmas.

As I groomed Henry I thought of past Christmases, especially the one when I had Micky and dear old Daisy, that was really very special indeed. As one gets older the excitement goes and presents become more mundane and just useful. I am not expecting anything great tomorrow. Of course the Howes have given me an expensive outfit, but there are so many other things that I would rather have received which could have been bought with the money spent.

These days Mary occupies a great deal of my thoughts. It was getting a bit of an obsession of wanting to be with her all day and with a lot of wishful thinking at night. I am becoming more worried about how I would fit in with her friends in London. Would I be out of my depth? Or would I have the character to put myself above such feelings? There is no backing out now. I will have help from Hugh and Mary who will give me moral support. Only time will tell and after all, it could well be a part of my education.

We had a lovely Christmas Eve. John, Gertie, Betty and Charlie joined us for the evening and Dad was very generous with his beer.

Christmas morning held a big surprise for me. The family had all joined together and purchased the top coat that Mary had made me try on at the tailors. I was so pleased because my old coat was now too small and it would have been too shabby to take to London. How kind they all are to have planned this, with Mary's help.

CHAPTER 10

It was raining cats and dogs and I was sitting on my own in front of the fire in the kitchen. Christmas had been and gone and tomorrow I am off to London. We are catching the early train from Newton Abbot and then going to Hugh's house in Bruton Place in Mayfair, not far from Hyde Park. Jenny had told me that this was a very posh part of London.

Looking back on the last few days, they had all been very pleasant and having the whole family together was really smashing. I saw Hugh and Mary on Boxing Day and the day after they came to the farm for lunch as the Hall was being prepared for the party. It was very pleasing to see how well Jenny and Mary got on together. Hugh and I left them to natter and went our own way.

After Hugh and Mary went home I began to make myself look as smart as possible. I put on my new suit which I had for John's wedding and my new coat. Looking at myself in the mirror I thought that I looked quite presentable. So off we went. Even John and Gertie had decided to come.

My family were now used to the familiar routine of being introduced to the Howes family. I kissed Mary's hand and she curtsied, which added a bit of humour to the proceedings.

I knew most of the people there and it was interesting to mingle and have a chat. Mary always seemed to be at my side or not very far away. She clung to my arm part of the time.

Mary looked a real picture and I could see the looks of envy that some of the young men were making. It was strange how we had taken on this attitude of acting as a couple. It had become so natural and much to my surprise, Mary's parents appeared to accept it. Sir James made it quite obvious that he thought that our friendship was to his liking. On the other hand if he found out what we had been up to I would be banished from the Hall for ever and it would be the end of my friendship with Hugh and Mary.

Much to our surprise Hugh was talking to a pretty girl for most the evening, she being the daughter of a nearby farmer. Mary and I decided to keep away otherwise we might put him off. It was about time Hugh had some female company.

Dad had been collared by old lady Howes and they were in deep conversation about something or other. Then Sir James joined them and eventually Aunt Pamela. Mother on the other hand was busy nattering to her female cronies, no doubt learning all the local gossip.

Much to my surprise, John looked as if he was enjoying himself. Perhaps it was such a change for him because his social life seemed to revolve around the village pub. Jenny spent most of the evening talking to Jake. I had no idea that she knew him, but they seemed to be getting on well together.

At last the big day arrived. I got up early, made myself as smart as possible, had some breakfast and waited for the car to arrive from the Hall.

I had quite a bit of cash saved up because I expected to pay my way in some respects.

The car came into the yard and Mum and Dad came out to see me off. Mary jumped out and told me that she would have to sit on my knee because the car was a bit crowded. By her expression this seemed to please her. We all greeted each other and I said goodbye to Mum and Dad.

We had some fun on the way to the station. Mary kept fidgeting around on my knees. It was grand to feel the warmth of her soft little bottom on my knees. It was obvious that the little monkey was trying to excite me. When we arrived at the station, Wills organised porters to see to our luggage and while we waited for the train to arrive from Plymouth Mary, Hugh and I walked along the platform. Mary took my arm and told me how she was looking forward to the next few days. I told her in no uncertain terms that we would have to behave ourselves this time because her father was with us and it would not be like it was in Germany. Mary pouted and said, "We will have to see Henry dear."

We had a comfortable compartment and a very nice lunch in the restaurant car and it seemed that in no time we were on the outskirts of the big city. When we pulled into Paddington Station Sir James arranged for some porters to get us a taxi to take us to Bruton Place.

It was exciting driving through the busy London streets and being able to see the fine buildings and the large stores. We passed through some magnificent squares with very elegant private dwellings lived in by rich Londoners.

When we came to Bruton Place I had a shock. The square was flanked by terraces of tall buildings, some with very expensive-looking cars parked outside.

I expected a special sort of house but nothing as grand as this. Hugh's second uncle must have been very well off to have owned such a house.

As the taxi drove up outside the door opened and out trooped what looked like a butler and two footmen. All were very correctly dressed. We were led in by the butler and the footmen saw to the luggage.

We then followed the butler into the house and were greeted by the staff that were all lined up in the very large hallway, which was the same procedure as in the Castle in Germany. This must be the custom. Sir James told the staff who we all were and he referred to me as Master Henry, a friend of Master Hugh who was of course their employer.

Poor Hugh looked very embarrassed about all the fuss. After all, it is his house and staff. It has to be kept in being until Hugh is twenty-one and the trustees will pay all the bills. All of this was set out in the Will. Hugh was going to see the trustees while we were in London and he told Mary and I that he would let us know all about it.

It looked most palatial inside with a large hall and a wide staircase winding up to three landings. There were large oil paintings on the walls and the furniture shone like new pins. Even the ornate stair-rods were highly polished and the carpets had a very thick pile. My first impression of the house was that it was very old-fashioned, but expensively furnished.

The butler who was called Harris, showed us to our rooms. Sir James and Lady Pamela had a suite of rooms on the first floor at the front of the house which consisted of a bedroom, bathroom and a sitting room. We were told that this was the Master's quarters.

We were led up to the next landing. Hugh had a large room with his own bathroom situated at the end of the landing. Mary and I had rooms next to each other further along the landing.

My room was very nice and the bed was large and looked very comfortable. There was a fire burning in a small highly polished black grate. The furniture was made of mahogany, heavy in design and probably Victorian. In fact, the whole house had an atmosphere and seemed to be in a time warp, which I found quite pleasant. Perhaps it had been a happy home for a family in the past.

I have always been very conscious of atmosphere in houses. I hoped that it would prove a happy place for my good friend Hugh. I unpacked my bag and had a wash in the basin in the corner of the room. It was all very convenient having hot and cold water in one's room.

My peaceful reflections were shattered by the opening of a second door in my room. I had noticed this when I came in, but had taken little notice of it. The door burst open and in rushed a lovely young girl, with dark brown hair and flashing brown eyes. Mary had arrived. She told me that the key of her room fitted the other door which led to my room.

Mary was so excited at the prospect of such easy access to my room that I had difficulty in calming her down. I told her to go and lock the door immediately and come back via the landing. She did this and not before time, as Hugh came in to see how we were settling in. We told him that everything was smashing and what a lucky chap he was to have a house like this at his age. He put his arms around us both and said, "The three of us will share it."

Hugh suggested that we go for a walk while it was still daylight so we put on our coats and told Aunt Pamela what we were going to do. She said that would we mind if the aged parents joined us, so we all stepped out of a Victorian house into the modern world.

After we left the seclusion of Bruton Place, it was indeed a different world. The number of cars and taxis were unbelievable. There seemed to be a steady stream of red buses, all with different numbers, coming and going to other parts of this huge city.

Sir James knew his way around London and in no time at all we were in New Bond Street, which was such an eye-opener to my friends and I. We were really country folk in our different ways. Our shops in Newton Abbot and Exeter were really more like village stores in comparison to what I was seeing today.

Mary and Aunt Pamela went into a females' shop so Sir James, Hugh and I had to wait outside. Without thinking I said to Sir James, "Can you imagine what would happen in London if it was bombed like some of the towns in Spain?" It was a stupid thing to say, but I was really thinking out loud. He replied by saying that he had the same thoughts when he was in London several weeks ago. "By the way Henry, Major Davis is coming to dinner tomorrow evening and he will want to have a talk with you," he told me.

When the females joined us we made our way towards Regent Street. The light was now fading and Sir James wanted us to see the Christmas lights. By the time we came into Regent Street via Conduit Street, the lights were all on. What a sight they were! There must have been thousands of coloured electric light bulbs. I just could not get over this wonderful display. Some of the lights were going on and off at regular intervals which I thought was very clever.

Walking down Regent Street towards Piccadilly Circus, apart from looking at the goods on display in the shop windows, I looked at the people we were passing and began to wonder what their lives were like living in this vast city. It was similar in some ways to a bee hive or an ant hill, with them all being in such close proximity to each other. What a ghastly thought.

I managed to buy a street map of London from a small shop in Piccadilly, as I expect my friends and I will want to have a good look around. We will have to work out what we want to see. Jenny had told me that the best way to see a town is from the top of a double decker bus.

We had a smashing dinner that evening. The food was more fancy than the fare at Langley Hall and this made a nice change. After dinner Hugh said that he would show us around the rest of the house. It was decided to start at the top and work downwards.

Right at the very top the servants had their quarters in the attic with a staircase going up the back of the building. On the next floor the rooms were smaller and all the furniture was covered with dust sheets.

We then came to our landing and went into the other rooms not being occupied. They were very similar, but these rooms also had the furniture covered in dust sheets.

The first floor was very posh. All of the rooms had wash basins and expensive-looking furniture. I was so interested that I forgot to count the number of bedrooms. It was however a fair old number.

When we reached the hall, Harris the butler asked Hugh if he could be of any assistance. Hugh said that he was showing the house to his friend and sister and Harris said that he would be only too pleased to give us a guided tour. Some of the rooms were locked but he had the keys.

Of course, we had seen the dining room and the huge sitting room. Then there was a library. We came to a locked door and Harris said that this was the Master's private room where he kept all his papers and books. Inside it was like an office with files neatly kept in shelves on one wall. There were maps on one wall, but without looking closely it was impossible to see what they were.

Harris looked very sad when he told us that the Master would be missed. "Not that we saw a lot of him. In fact he had been away for over two years before he died. But he was like that, he would be away for ages and then would just turn up as though he had only been away for a few days." Harris turned to Hugh and said, "Perhaps Master Hugh you would like me to tell you more about your late uncle." Hugh said that he would like that very much indeed.

There were several cloakrooms and then we came to another room which turned out to be a sort of games room. There was a billiard table, a dart board on the wall and a gramophone. This was just what we were looking for. We thanked Harris and said that we would stay here for a while.

Hugh could play billiards so he tried to teach Mary and I. Mary was hopeless at it and I took a long time to get the hang of it. In between the billiard lessons Mary and I had a few dances which were rather nice. Eventually we went to join Aunt Pamela and Sir James.

When we were settled in the sitting room, Hugh told his parents about the office and the rest of the house. He asked his father if the two of them could spend some time tomorrow morning to really investigate the contents. "We might then know more about what the trustees are going to talk to us about when we meet them in the afternoon," Hugh said. Sir James thought this would be a good idea.

Aunt Pamela turned to Mary and said that perhaps she and I could explore London, because she wanted to look around the shops. I said that I might be able to put up with Mary for a whole day. Mary immediately tried to hit me but missed.

We were then told that tomorrow evening Major Davis and his wife were coming to dinner so we would have to wear our evening dress wear, which I thought was a bit daft. On the other hand it will get me used to it before the party on New Year's Eve.

The following night would be New Year's Eve and the party was being held at the house of a friend of the family. The daughter went to the same school as Mary so no doubt there will be other young females there.

Mary told her mother that she would like to go to a West End show, preferably something to make us laugh, or perhaps a musical. Aunt Pamela said that she would see what she could do.

After a very pleasant evening we all went to our rooms. Sir James stayed downstairs in the sitting room, probably to have another scotch. Saying goodnight Hugh went to his room. As I said goodnight to Mary I told her that we must behave ourselves. She looked a bit deflated, gave me a kiss and said, "I will be a good girl Henry."

It was nice in my room. The fire had now gone down and only the embers were left. The room was warm and inviting. I took my time washing and getting into bed. I thought that the visit to London had so far been fine. I lay in the comfortable bed and soon fell asleep.

It didn't seem long since I had fallen asleep before I felt the bed-clothes being lifted on one side and a young girl crept very slowly and quietly into my bed.

By now I was wide awake but I pretended to be asleep just to see what she would get up to. First of all she wriggled down beside me then undid my pyjama jacket and then my trousers. Her hands began to wander all over me and I could keep it up no longer. I burst out laughing, pulled her nightie off and we made love in our simple way.

We stayed like this, sleeping on and off, until the early hours of the morning. At last I persuaded Mary to go back to her own room.

At breakfast the next morning Aunt Pamela asked us how we all had slept and were we comfortable. I felt Mary's hand creep over my knee and we all said that we had slept well. I gave her hand a smack to make her behave herself.

I said that I thought that we could walk up Regent Street and along

Oxford Street to Marble Arch and then have a snack lunch somewhere. Little did I know how our plans would be altered.

Mary and I were the first to set off for the day. Walking up Regent Street with this lovely girl by my side, who seemed to be talking endlessly and looked so happy, I thought to myself how ever did I get here and surely I will wake up and find that it is all a dream. We were halfway up Oxford Street when I heard a male voice shouting, "Henry!" several times. A car pulled up by the pavement and leaning out of the back window was my good friend Bernie.

He started to talk in German and what he said was that he would like to buy us coffee so would we get in. I asked Mary if she would like that and she said she would. We drove into the forecourt of a large hotel overlooking Hyde Park and we went in. Bernie seemed very much at ease. It was a lovely hotel, very expensive looking and the coffee was very welcome.

Bernie told us that he had been on an errand for his mother and that is why he had the use of the car. He said that he should telephone her to let her know where he was. When he came back he had a broad grin on his face and said that his mother told him to use the car all day and to take my friends out to lunch and show them around.

This was smashing news for Mary and I because we really didn't have a clue where to go and see the best parts of London. Bernie told us that he would take us into the City of London area, that is where the money is made and sometimes lost he told us.

He would be able to show us where his father worked and we may be able to see him. "I know that he would like to see you again Henry. He wants to ask you something," Bernie said.

Bernie told the driver where to go and we began a real tour of the sights of London. We saw Buckingham Palace, the Houses of Parliament and we passed so many places of interest that in the end we became a bit overwhelmed.

When we reached the City we stopped outside a very important-looking building which was a merchant bank. Bernie got out of the car and ran inside. He soon came out and told the driver to park the car and we were to join him and see his father.

Going through the door I noticed a brass plate with several names engraved on it and one of the names was Bernstein. A very smartly dressed doorman opened the door for us and Bernie led us inside. It was all marble and brass with a rich red carpet on the floor. We got into a lift which was operated by a young man in uniform.

The lift took us silently up into the bowels of the building. When it stopped we found ourselves in a hive of industry. There seemed to be clerks and office staff rushing all over the place like mad things. Bernie led us through the throng and went into an office. A lady was sitting at the desk and when she saw us she lifted a telephone, said a few words and told Bernie to go in and see his father.

It was quite some time since I had seen the old man, but he was easily recognisable. Sitting at a huge desk he got up to greet us and Bernie introduced Mary. In turn he shook our hands and told Bernie to bring up some chairs. We chatted for a while about our visit and he then asked Mary and I if we could help him.

He asked us if we could remember what the Jew, Joseph, whom we helped in Germany, looked like. Did he have any distinguishable features of any sort? The old man sitting there looked so imposing that I didn't have the nerve to ask him what he wanted this information for.

Mary and I tried to remember as much as we could, bearing in mind that it was dusk and we never saw him in broad daylight. We remembered only too well the tales of horror he told us and I told Mr Bernstein that I would recognise his voice as he had a strange accent.

Mr Bernstein told us that he eventually reached this country and that he had been interviewed by a special committee that tries to help Jews escape from the Nazis. He went on to tell us that he sits on this committee and they have to be very careful only to help genuine refugees and not those people 'planted' by the Nazis. These were known as 'sleepers'. "They are inactive unless they are needed for action in the future. Also they might find out how we get some of these poor people out of Germany," he said.

He continued, "This fellow has described you and your friends very well indeed. In fact, too well considering the state he said he was in and your very short encounter. Also, no one has ever escaped from any of the prisons or camps in that area. The ground is so flat and devoid of any real cover."

"My committee thinks that if he is genuine you will hear nothing from him because he will not know who you were or where you came from. On the other hand if he is not genuine, he could have been given information about you and your friends and they may think that such a contact may be useful in the future.

It is quite possible that the Joseph we have is not the same man that you helped. He may have been captured and tortured into telling them who had helped him and we may have a very clever 'look a like'," he said. "What we cannot understand is how he got out of Germany so easily. If he should try to make contact with you or your two friends, please let me know."

He turned to Bernie and told him to take his good friend Henry and his beautiful girlfriend out to lunch. "You know where to go. All you have to do is sign the bill."

We said goodbye and I shook Mr Bernstein's hand. I said, "By the way sir, the other Henry sends his kind regards." It was nice to see the old boy have a good laugh.

We found the car and by now it was lunch time. We went back to the same hotel near Hyde Park and the head waiter told us that a table had been reserved by Mr Bernstein. So we settled down to a great lunch, complete with a glass of wine each.

As I sat there in this very luxurious and expensive hotel with my dear Mary and my great friend Bernie, having a lunch which must have cost a lot of money, it made me think how money can open so many doors and how our lives are geared to pounds, shillings and pence. The cost of this lunch would be much more than the monthly wages of a farm labourer in Devonshire, or one of the footmen in Hugh's house. It really is very unfair, but that is how things are.

After lunch we had a stroll around the park and fed the ducks in the Serpentine. Then we sat on a seat and talked. After a while we found the car and went back to Hugh's house. We took Bernie in and made him feel at home. He had told us that he found the school holidays lonely so we said that he should join us tomorrow. He thought that was a smashing idea, but could he telephone his mother to see if that would be alright.

He came back into the room looking very happy and told us that he could have the use of the car again for the day. Of course, that would be smashing for Mary and I and I did hope that Hugh would feel the same.

Just as Bernie stood up to leave, Sir James and Hugh came in and Hugh was more than pleased about the proposed arrangements for tomorrow. It was therefore agreed that Bernie would collect us at ten o'clock.

We had to dress for dinner because it was a formal affair. Major Davis and his wife were guests and Hugh told me that there would be other guests as well. My friends and I had our baths and put on our posh clothes. Of course, I had no idea how to tie a dress bow tie so Mary came to my rescue after taking full advantage of me. I saw myself in the mirror and I thought that I would pass. Mary really looked quite lovely in yet another new dress. One thing is certain and that is that I would never be able to marry Mary because I could never afford it. Anyway, what a stupid thought, I would never get the chance.

When I was ready I went downstairs to the sitting room. Sir James was there sipping a sherry. He passed one to me and asked me to sit down as he wanted to have a few quick words before the others joined us.

He said, "Henry, we are all very fond of you and Mary is more than fond of you, so we want you to listen very carefully to what Major Davis will be telling you after dinner. He will be giving you several options as to what you want to do over the next few years. I know what I would like you to do and that is to become qualified in how to run an estate, then come to run Langley Hall for me."

What Sir James said took the wind right out of my sails. I knew that the old boy liked me because somehow or other we got on well together. Sometimes he could be a very awkward sort of chap, but the best way to deal with that was to take no notice.

Sir James continued "The Major would like you to join the Regular Army and become part of his Department. My advice to you is not to do that, but act as if you will be hard to get. He might suggest that you try to get a course which may fit in with what you want to do at the University of Exeter and also to take an alternative subject." My reaction to this was the question of cost which would be impossible for Dad to finance. Anyway, everything rests with the results of my exams that I have to take in the forthcoming new year.

Our conversation was interrupted by the arrival of Hugh and Mary, both looking very smart. Then Aunt Pamela came in, or perhaps I should say, swept in. She looked very handsome and elegant.

The next to arrive were Major Davis and his wife who were accompanied by a tall foreign-looking chap. He was introduced as Monsieur Malraux. I greeted him in French and not to be outdone, so did Mary.

Everyone had a sherry and the usual pre-dinner talk was underway. Harris came to announce dinner was being served. It was a very pleasant dinner and when we had finished the ladies left the room, which I had learned was the custom. The port was then handed round and those that smoked lit up.

Sir James started the ball rolling by saying that whatever was said this evening had to be kept within these four walls. Major Davis turned to Hugh and told him that he had brought Monsieur Malraux so that he could meet me. "My Department have plans for your friend Henry in the future. We would like him to join the RAF or the Army, but I know that this life would not suit him. We would therefore like him to consider going to the University of Exeter. I know that cost comes into this, but there might be a way around this. Will you and Henry talk about this over the next few months Hugh?"

Monsieur Malraux started to ask me all sorts of questions, all in French, which I managed to answer reasonably well. The Major kept interrupting in German and then the odd word or two in English. I could see that this was a test of some sort. Perhaps to see how my mind reacted to the mixing of three languages. I was getting a bit fed up with this so I tried to get my own back by telling them about Joseph the Jew, but in three languages.

I explained how I had broken the rules given to me by Major Davis by helping a Jew who was in trouble with the Nazis. I then went on to tell them the whole story and what Bernie's father had told me this morning.

I could see that this information really put the cat among the pigeons. The questions kept coming left, right and centre. The Major told me to try to get a message to Bernie's father asking him if he would mind if I passed this information on to a friend I knew in the Intelligence Service. I told him I was spending the day with his son tomorrow and I will get him to ask his father.

"If this Joseph fellow does contact you or Hugh, please let Jake Spencer know. He would probably try to get in touch with Hugh as he is directly involved with Herr Brecht," said, Major Davis.

I then asked the Major if I could telephone Mr Bernstein now and talk to him. It would be quicker than sending messages. I looked at Sir James and he nodded his head and the Major agreed.

I had Bernie's telephone number in my shabby little book which I always had with me. One day I will have to renew it, but I had so much information in it that it would take ages to transfer it all.

I spoke to Mr Bernstein on the telephone and fully explained the situation. He was very pleased because it lifted quite a responsibility from the shoulders of the committee. He went on to tell me that he would like a chat one day. "I will arrange with Mr Butler for you and Klaus to come up to London for the weekend during next term. On the other hand my wife and I might be able to come down to Devon," Mr Bernstein said.

I returned to the dining room and reported my conversation. The Major said that Mr Bernstein was a very wealthy and powerful man and how did I get to know the family. So once more I had to tell the tale of helping Bernie and the gift of my horse, Henry. "Bernie has been my best friend at college and I hope he will continue to be so," I told them. Looking at the Major and Monsieur Malraux I said that I would never ever take part in anything to harm that family.

Hugh and I were then excused from the dining room and we joined the ladies. Mary was quite put out because we had been so long. She got up and gave me a hug which I thought was a bit public in front of her mother and Mrs Davis. Aunt Pamela only laughed and told us to go and have a dance in the games room. As we left Hugh asked her if we could invite Bernie back for lunch tomorrow and Aunt Pamela told him that it was his house and all he had to do was tell Harris what he wanted. "Don't forget that Bernie is a Jew and they are very fussy about

225

what they eat." She warned him.

I told Hugh that Bernie ate anything other than pork. His family were not very strict Orthodox Jews. Bernie had told me that he has a sister about a year younger than he was. "I have never met her so why not invite her to come over tomorrow." So once more I telephoned the Bernsteins and this time I spoke to Bernie. I asked him if his sister would like to come out with us tomorrow and then stay for lunch and he told me to hang on while he asked her. He said that Ruth would love to be included and thank you.

It was now getting quite late and the guests had all gone home. When I said goodbye to Monsieur Malraux he said, "I am glad that I have met you Henry. I am sure that we will meet again in the future."

I undressed and was sitting in my pyjamas in front of the remains of the fire. I had so much to think about and began to wish that I had never seen Major Davis. He has now sown the seeds of the idea of me going to Exeter University to study just farm management and not a full course on agriculture which was my original plan. Then there would be time for me to study another subject. But what, I asked myself, would that be? I will have to think about that problem tomorrow.

I had just got into bed and my light was still on when Mary came in. She pulled the bedclothes back and proceeded to take my pyjamas off. She then took off her dressing gown to reveal her lovely young body. She switched off the light and we were soon in each other's arms.

Later as we lay there she said, "No matter what you say my dear Henry, I am going to stay here with you all night. The party will be very late tomorrow night and we will be too tired, so let's make the most of tonight." I told her that I could think of nothing better, provided we woke up in time.

We made love again and then went to sleep, with Mary being the first to go into dreamland. I lay there with her head pillowed against my chest. I could feel her gently breathing and could smell the scent of her hair. What a wonderful feeling it was.

It was now getting light and I managed to get Mary back to her own room. We were both naked and for the fun of it I lifted the dear girl and carried her, laying her on her bed. She gave me a wicked little laugh and pulled me down on her. When at last I returned to my room I was glad to see that there would be a few more hours sleep.

As we all sat around the breakfast table it was difficult to imagine that Mary was the same girl who was in my bed only a few hours ago. She looked so serene and innocent.

Bernie arrived fairly early. His plan was to take us to his home, meet his mother and sister and have some coffee with them before he started his tour of London town. He lived in a part of London called Kensington and this drive in itself was very interesting. What wonderful planning it was to have so much parkland in such a crowded city.

Bernie's house was in a square. Most of the posh and expensive houses were in quiet squares or cul-de-sacs. Bernie led us in and we were greeted by his mother. As soon as she saw me she started to talk in German and said how nice it was to see me again. With that she put her arms around me and gave me a kiss on the cheek and a real hug. She then came to Mary and shook her hand, saying in broken English, "You are Henry's girlfriend so mind you look after him because we are all very fond of him."

The Bernstein home was very grand. I thought that the old boy must have been very clever to get his money out of Germany and invested in England. I was not to know then that he had a financial base in the City before Hitler became a real threat. We went into the spacious sitting room to have coffee.

As yet there was no sign of Bernie's sister, Ruth. I asked him about this and he told me that she was a bit shy. He said that he would go and find her. Mrs Bernstein was telling Mary and Hugh how kind I had been to her son Klaus when he was a new boy at College. I found this most embarrassing and I was glad when Bernie appeared with Ruth.

I wasn't quite sure what I expected Ruth to look like. I knew that she would be dark and small like her mother, but she was indeed very attractive in a foreign sort of way. I nearly burst out laughing when I looked at Hugh. He was just standing there looking in amazement at this lovely vision that had just come in with Bernie. She was introduced to everyone and I was last for this honour.

She stood and looked at me for a moment or two, although it seemed like an age before she started to talk to me in German. She said, "Klaus has told me so much about you and your family that I feel I have known you for a long time. I only wish that you could have helped me like you did Klaus." She then started to speak in English in a very soft and cultured voice. Turning to Mary she said, "Mary, I hope that you realise how lucky you are."

This was all becoming too much for me and I took Ruth's hand and took her over to where Hugh was standing. I told her that Hugh was the artist amongst us and I understood that she was also that way inclined. I could see that Hugh was a bit tongue-tied, but after a while they were chatting away like mad. I has the feeling that Mrs Bernstein didn't want us to leave. It was very interesting to see how she was getting on with Mary. They seemed to be able to understand each other quite well considering the language barrier.

Bernie took us all over London. We went to the Tower to see the famous jewels then on to the busy port area. To see the large ships loading and unloading their cargo from all over the world was a sight that I would not have missed for anything. We are such a small country and yet we export our goods and knowledge everywhere.

Our next port of call was Selfridges in Oxford Street. I was amazed at the size of the store and the variety of goods that they sold. Some of the Departments had sales on with greatly reduced prices. We quickly steered the girls away from the clothing Departments otherwise we would have been in there all day.

Above the din created by the vast number of people, we heard a female voice shouting "Mary!" A tall blond female rushed up and gave Mary a kiss and started asking all sorts of questions. Mary calmed her down and we were introduced to her school friend, Jennifer. When she came to me Jennifer said, "So you are Henry. We hear so much about you at school! When you come to my party tonight, please ask me for a dance." I warned her that she would be sorry as my dancing is not too hot.

She kept looking me up and down, rather like one would a horse before you bought it. It was a wonder that she didn't look at my teeth! Mary butted in and told me to take no notice of Jennifer as she was a terrible flirt. Jennifer then started to take notice of poor Bernie and asked him and Ruth if they would like to come to the party as well. Jennifer said that Mary would arrange it all and before we could say another word she was off. As she walked away she turned and said to Mary, "Keep a tight hold of your Henry, because I will be after him Mary!"

By now it was lunch time so we returned to Bruton Place. The cook had excelled herself and we had a very nice lunch. Aunt Pamela and Sir James left us to ourselves and Mary acted as hostess and sat at the top of the table.

As soon as we came in, Mary told her mother about the invitation given to Ruth and Bernie by Jennifer. Knowing how hair-brained she was Aunt Pamela telephoned Jennifer's mother to see if it was alright. It was therefore arranged for Bernie's car to pick us up and Mary's parents would go under their own steam.

We took ages over lunch and had a lot of fun. Ruth blossomed and we found that she had a good sense of humour. After pottering around the house and games room for a while it was soon time for Bernie and Ruth to go home. It was a bit on the early side, but Aunt Pamela said that we should all have a rest before the party as it would be a very late night because it was New Year's Eve.

After our two friends had gone we retired to our rooms to rest. I kicked off my shoes and flopped onto the bed. By now I was feeling pretty tired as I didn't have a lot of sleep the night before. I began to think of Mary who was such a short distance away, when I must have drifted into sleep.

When I awoke it was quite dark and looking at my watch I realised that I should be having a bath and putting my gladrags on. I took off my clothes and put my dressing gown on. Mary came in and of course we had a brief cuddle before she told me that we should be getting ready. So we went our different ways to make ourselves look smart.

Mary helped me with my bow tie and I left her to go downstairs. Meeting Hugh on the way, I asked him if he liked Ruth. He blushed and said that he thought she was smashing. The thought of her going to the party had cheered him up no end as apparently these parties are usually a bit of a bore and some of the boys were rather dim. I told him that I had never been to a proper party before, except for the ones at the Hall. His reply was brief, "Well Henry, believe me you haven't missed much."

We joined his parents in the living room. Perhaps it was a bit presumptuous of me, but I looked at Aunt Pamela and told her how lovely she looked and what a smashing dress she was wearing. Sir James gave me a grin and said, "It ought to look alright, it cost enough!" In fun she curtsied and said, "Thank you kind Sir." This made us all laugh.

Mary entered the room looking really marvellous and I just had to tell her how lovely she looked. Mary came up to me and straightened my tie giving me a light kiss. She said I looked very handsome. I felt most embarrassed in front of her parents but they appeared to take the event as quite normal. Hugh made us laugh by saying, "No one has said how smart I look." So we all said in chorus, "Hugh looks smart." This banter helped us all to get in a party mood. Bernie arrived and we were on our way.

Ruth and Bernie were a bit nervous, as they didn't know anyone who was coming to the party. I said that I had no idea who was having the party, or where it was being held. "Don't worry Bernie," I told him, "we will all stick together."

Hugh told us that the party was being held at a large house owned by Lord and Lady Betchley who were old school friends of his father's. Their daughter, Jennifer, went to Mary's school.

Mary had found my hand to hold and told me to keep clear of Jennifer. I let the others chat away while I had a brief daydream. Here I am once more going up the social ladder. I am now the guest of a Lord and Lady. However will it end? When I think of my humble background, how on earth will I be able to mix with the other guests at tonight's do? Well, all I can do is to take Dad's advice and just be plain old Henry Blake of Long Meadow Farm, Devonshire.

We eventually arrived and joined a line of cars waiting to unload their passengers. Bernie had arranged with his driver to telephone when we wanted to go home.

Soon it was our turn and we entered this magnificent house. The hall was like a large room and servants took our coats. Sir James came into view and led us into another room where I could see Jennifer standing in line and being introduced to people waiting to enter. Standing by her side were her parents.

Sir James went through the formalities of introducing all of us, which was a bit stupid because they all knew each other. Bernie, Ruth and I were the only strangers. When it was my turn I found our hosts very pleasant people and he seemed to know a great deal about me. My gift for languages being one of the things he knew. When I came to Jennifer, who had been giving me the eye ever since I entered the room, I thought that I would pull her leg. I quickly asked Mary if Jennifer spoke French. The answer was no.

When I was in front of Jennifer I said a few words in French and kissed her hand. She burst out laughing and gave me such a shove that I nearly fell over. She was a very handsome girl, but a bit angular and very tall like her father. This sort of broke the ice. I saw that Bernie was having quite a chat with Lord Betchley and I found out later that he knew Mr Bernstein well.

We went into the ballroom where a small band was playing. Tables were arranged around the dancing area and most of these were occupied. There were a lot of people in the room, both young and old. A member of staff led us to a table where a waiter served us from a large jug of punch.

I felt quite comfortable sitting there watching everyone, but Mary dragged me to my feet to dance. As we danced around the room Mary kept talking and waving to people she knew. I noticed that Hugh and Ruth were having a go at dancing as well.

When the music stopped Mary took my hand and led me over to a group of girls. "Henry, I want to show you off to some of my friends." I stopped in my tracks, but it was no good. I had to do as I was told. Some of her friends were attractive, others were rather plain. However, one stood out and this was the first one I was introduced to.

Mary said, "Henry, this is Martine." Then the penny dropped. I spoke to Martine in my very best French and I could tell from her expression that she was so pleased to be able to talk in her own language. The other girls were all a bit on the silly side, except one who was very shy and looked a bit like Ruth. Mary took her by the arm and marched her over to our table and introduced her to Bernie. In no time at all they were on the floor dancing.

While Mary was taking her friend, Faith, over to meet Bernie I was collard by Jennifer. I was standing talking to Martine when I felt a hand go around my waist and a voice said, "Henry, will you dance with me?" I had no option, after all she was our hostess. As we danced she pressed herself closer and closer to me and rested her cheek on mine. We talked a bit but I could tell that she was not the talking sort. Her interests were below my belt and not above it. I was glad when the music stopped as she was getting me all het up.

She kissed me on the cheek and whispered "That was nice Henry, we will do it again." I must admit that she was a most attractive girl and being older, I bet she could teach me a thing or two.

Mary was rather put out but I explained that dancing with Jennifer was not my choice. Just to tease her I said that it was very nice and Mary trod on my feet to pay me back. On the other hand she also started this more than friendly form of dancing which was very sexy, but very nice.

Strange how it may seem, I was beginning to enjoy myself. Somehow I didn't feel out of place. The young men that were there were very friendly but I thought a bit on the dim side. Some of the girls were real beauties and Mary's school friends kept looking at me. I began to wonder what Mary had been telling them about me.

Bernie was getting on fine with the girl Mary had introduced him to. Hugh was well away with Ruth. I had no idea what Sir James would say when he saw how interested Hugh was in Ruth. Even in this country there is a prejudice against Jews and being a German won't help.

Halfway through the evening, refreshments were served in another room from a marvellous buffet. We helped ourselves and took our overloaded plates back to our table and had a good tuck in. By now the grown-ups had got together at one end of the room and we were left to enjoy ourselves.

As the evening came closer to midnight, we were all served with a glass of champagne to toast in the new year. Just before the stroke of midnight, we all had to link arms and sing a song called Auld Lang Syne. A radio set was turned up to its maximum volume and, when we heard Big Ben, everyone went mad and started to kiss everyone else. Mary and I had a long and lingering kiss to wish each other a happy new year. She was then collared by various young chaps, and I made the most of this unique opportunity. Then Jennifer grabbed me and we had a very sexy session. Mary was on the look out and she came and broke it up.

I was just standing getting my breath back when Ruth came up to me and wished me a happy new year and thanked me for being such a good friend to her brother, Klaus. She then very shyly gave me a very loving kiss. She seemed such a gentle creature and, whilst the fun and celebrations were going on, my mind went back to Germany and I thought that so many young girls like Ruth would be in fear for their lives; not for what they had done, but for who and what they were.

With these thoughts in my mind I put my arms around Ruth and, kissing her on the forehead, I said, "God Bless you and your friends that you have left behind in Germany." Mary had witnessed this episode and she put her arms around my neck and, looking into my eyes, she said, "Darling Henry, I do love you so much."

By now the champagne was having its effect and everyone was full of fun and good humour. I told Mary that we should try to find her mother and father so that we could wish them a happy new year. We found them in yet another room and we wished them all the best for 1936. Sir James shook my hand and said, "I am so pleased we brought you to London with us and we now seem to feel that you are part of the family. You certainly know how to make my two brats happy." Aunt Pamela put her arms around me and, giving me a kiss, she said In a whisper, "Mary seems so happy when she is with you Henry and it looks as if Hugh has at last come out of his shell," and, with that remark, she gave me a hug and another kiss.

Mary and I went back to our friends hand in hand. I cannot help feeling so proud with Mary as my girlfriend. In my eyes she was the most beautiful girl there.

The party was now over and we were on our way home to Bruton Place. We thought that we should all meet tomorrow and Bernie said that he would get in touch with his new girlfriend, Faith, to see if she could join us.

New Year's Eve is always a peculiar time. One tends to be a bit sentimental about the past and things in general and, in a way, apprehensive about the new year; will it be better or will disaster strike?

When we got back to Bruton Place we were all tired and we soon made our way wearily up the stairs. Aunt Pam told us that breakfast would be later in the morning so that we could catch up on our sleep. I kissed Mary goodnight and I was soon in my bed and, as Mother used to say when I was very young, I would soon be in the Land of Nod.

As I lay in bed, my thoughts turned to the farm and I wondered how my family were, this being the first New Year's Eve that I had been away from them all and, with these thoughts I went to sleep.

When I awoke it was almost daylight and, much to my surprise, I was not alone in my large bed. Mary was fast asleep, curled up by my side. She must have crept in without waking me at some time during the night. I must have been tired not to have been disturbed.

It was light enough for me to study her while she was asleep. She was on her side facing me. Her hair partly covered her face. She looked so peaceful and somehow happy and so pretty. I just had to bend over her and kiss her cheek, trying not to wake her. She became half awake and, in no time, we were loving each other for the first time in 1936. What a wonderful way to start a new year.

After our passions were spent, we just lay there and talked. Mary told me that she had been in my bed the whole night. When she came into my room not long after we had gone to bed, I was fast asleep, so she didn't disturb me and she soon went to sleep. She knew that she had to go back to her room but she kept asking me if I loved her. I think that perhaps the interest shown by her friends in her Henry made her feel a bit jealous. I told her that she was the best thing that could ever happen to me.

My main worry was the fact that we were so very different and could I keep up with her way of life? I think that sometimes I am just having a very long dream and does my darling Mary really exist? Perhaps I am living in a fool's paradise and one day the paradise will just melt away.

She got out of the bed, bent over and kissed me and said, "One day soon I will show you how much I do love you Henry," and, with that parting remark she ran into her room, leaving me to ponder on what she was talking about.

The next two days were pretty hectic. There now seemed to be six of us. We went on a boat trip, in the rain down river to see the sights and, to please the girls, we wandered around the stores and shops. Hugh would insist on treating us to lunch. It was so nice to see how happy he seemed in the company of Ruth. Bernie's father had a financial interest in a West End show, so we all had smashing seats in a box, overlooking the stage. We all enjoyed it and, at times, we laughed ourselves silly.

The party we went on to on one of the nights was a very tame affair. Bernie, Ruth and Faith were not there. I had to fend off Jennifer but I managed to have a dance with Martine while Mary was having a dance with the son of the family giving the party. I must admit that I found Martine very attractive and, at times, her English was very amusing. She kept getting her nouns mixed up with her verbs.

On that last night of our holiday in London, we all felt a bit sad, because we had a really smashing time. Sir James and Aunt Pam left us to our own devices and were able to meet their friends without offspring hanging on. Mary and I had decided to throw caution to the wind and spend the whole night together, because we had no idea when we would spend a night under the same roof again. I will look back on that last night in London as one of my happiest times with Mary during our tender years.

When we were about to leave for the station, Hugh took me to where Harris, the butler, was standing and told me that if, at any time, I should need to stay at Bruton Place, I must be given the same treatment that he would be given. I thanked Hugh but thought it very unlikely that I would be in London for a very long time. He gave me one of his looks, which I had got to know so well, and said, "You never know Henry what may come up."

CHAPTER 11

I am back to sleepy Devon once more after the hectic few days in London, and how different it all is. I have been home for a few days but this is the first time that I have been able to saddle up Henry and go for a ride by myself.

Mary wanted to be with me all of the time but today she had to go to Exeter with her mother to get some new school clothing. She was now a big girl in many ways and she needed larger sizes, so I had a day to myself.

As usual when I wanted to have a think and be at peace with the world, I would sit by the Little Bridge or by the river at the Hall. Today I chose the Little Bridge.

Being mid-winter the stream was very full with the endless repetitive noise of running water. I always found this most restful and to me it was one of nature's symphonies, with the odd cry from nearby wood pigeons and other country sounds.

I had a lot to think about and decisions to make, my first hurdle being the big exam to be held during the summer term. I had to get very high marks if I wanted to or, for that matter, be able to go to Exeter University, so I will have to work like mad over the next few months.

I also have the O.T.C. exam to pass, if only to keep Major Davis happy. I have to meet the French girl that has arrived to stay with Mr Jarvis. I will have to meet her before Mary goes back to college so I might as well get it over with tomorrow. Mary will probably create, but orders are orders. I will try to fix it up when I get back to the farm and then ring her to tell her the bad news.

I will also have to find time to make a few pieces of furniture because my trip to London cost me a bob or two, so I will have to build up my bank balance again.

As usual, when I sit and have a think, my thoughts always go back to Mary. She will be going back to College next week and so will I for that matter. I will miss her like hell. We have been inseparable for the best part of three weeks and we won't see each other again until Easter. To make matters worse, Easter will be late this year. This is how it has to be so there is no point in feeling sorry for myself.

We have been more than lucky to have had the opportunity to get to know each other so well at our age and in such a natural way. The more I think of it, the more I realise how much I am going to miss her.

I haven't had the courage to think about this French girl situation. It all sounds so simple but as far as I can see there are two sides of the coin; one is that she will be plain and not very pleasant and to be with her will be an awful bore. She could, on the other hand, be attractive and good fun to be with. Perhaps it might be a good idea to let her meet Mary then all of the cards will be on the table. One thing is certain is that I must not get myself involved as I did with dear little Polly.

I still think of Polly with great affection and I often wonder how she is getting on. I would like to be invisible and to see how she is. She has probably forgotten all about me, although her last letter didn't tell that story.

When I got back to the farm, I rang Mr Jarvis and arranged to meet the French girl for coffee tomorrow morning. When Mary rang me, I told her about my trip to Newton Abbot. She was a bit peeved so I told her that I would ride over to the Hall after lunch, which pleased her.

I made myself look respectable and caught the bus into the town. It was with some trepidation that I rang the doorbell of Mr Jarvis' house. I had no idea what to expect, would she be fat, thin, pretty, short or tall? The door opened and the female standing there bore no resemblance to what I expected. We both stood there looking at each other and sizing each other up. She was small, her hair was short and more like a boy's. She had very large dark brown eyes, a very unusual face with a cute little nose, very white teeth that protruded slightly, a slim but very shapely figure. When all of this was added up, the end result was a very attractive female.

She stood there, smiled and said in a husky voice "You must be 'Enry," and then Mr Jarvis appeared and introduced me to this attractive creature called Celeste Prideaux.

I went inside to a very comfortable-looking house. Mrs Jarvis gave us a cup of coffee each and we were left to get to know each other.

It was very awkward at first. Celeste was very shy. I must say that I didn't feel much better. She talked in French and had a definite accent which, I found out, was characteristic of the Normandy area. I talked in French and, in no time, we were having quite a lively conversation.

I started to tell Celeste about my visit to Germany and I found that she was very knowledgeable about what was going on. Evidently her family were very anti-German, which dated back to the Great War. We talked about our families and she also lived on a farm, so we immediately had something in common.

As we talked, at times in English and, other times, in French. I had a chance to study this girl from Normandy. What I saw at this early

236

stage I liked. Of course one can never tell in such a short time but my mind was more at ease now that I had met the girl that will help me with my French.

I explained why she would have to put up with me for a bit and that if she got fed up with the idea she shouldn't hesitate to let me know. I also told her to correct me with my French pronunciation and I would do the same with her English.

She then surprised me by asking me if I could teach her a few phrases in German but this would be just between the two of us. I was to find this a very difficult task because she wanted to learn so much in the short time that we had.

It was quite amusing to watch her when she talked. She used her hands so much to express her words. In fact, her hands were never still when she was talking. I was to learn that so many French people were the same and some were most excitable and showed their emotions so easily.

I told her about my girlfriend, Mary, and Celeste said that she would like to meet her. I thought that this might be a good idea, so I suggested that, as it would be Market Day tomorrow, we could all have a walk around the town. It would also give us something interesting to look at. I would ask Mary what she thought of the idea and then telephone Mr Jarvis and let him know.

We seemed to have been talking non-stop and, looking at my watch, I said that I had to go to catch my bus. Celeste said that she would like to walk with me to the bus station if I didn't mind. She left to put on a coat and, whilst she was out of the room, Mr Jarvis came in and asked how we had got on. I told him that all was well, except that she was too attractive, which made him laugh.

She looked nice in her warm coat, complete with a scarf to match. Walking beside me, she looked so small. Perhaps a better description would be petite. I was so used to walking with Mary, who was a tall girl, and this, perhaps, made Celeste seem so small.

We walked to the bus station and I just managed to catch my bus and I left a lonely figure, standing in a strange town in a strange country.

During lunch at the farm I had to tell the family all about my meeting with this stranger from France. I also mentioned my tentative arrangement for a visit to the market tomorrow, that is, if Mary wanted to. I thought that Hugh might even want to come; anyway, I will know when I see them this afternoon.

Riding over to the hall after lunch, I began to wonder if it had been wise to think about letting Mary meet Celeste; anyway, Mary might not want to. When I had got to the drive, Mary had walked half way down to the gate. I helped her onto Henry, behind me, and she nestled into my back, which gave me a nice feeling. I told her about Celeste and that she wanted to meet her. Mary quickly said that she would like to do likewise and I added that perhaps Hugh might like to come as well.

Mary gave me a big squeeze and told me that her mother and father had taken Hugh to Exeter and "So, my dear, we are all on our own until well after teatime," she said. I put Henry into the stables and, as there seemed to be no staff around, like a shot we were up the stairs and concealed in Mary's room.

There was a log fire burning in the grate so we settled ourselves on the hearth-rug, slowly taking each other's clothes off and kissing each other all over as we did so. It was so nice to be able to study each other's bodies in daylight. We had done this before but not in such detail.

We were by now very worked up and nature soon took its course. We lay in each other's arms until we could make love again in a more leisurely way. We both realised that this would probably be our last chance to be really together until Easter so we made the most of it. We were loath to leave the comfort of the bedroom, but we had to.

Mary put on her jodhpurs and we went for a short ride around the estate. As we rode together, Mary kept asking me questions about Celeste; what she looked like, how old she was, an endless stream of questions. It seemed as if she was trying to get a mental picture in her mind before she actually met her.

By now it was getting dark so we went back to the Hall. We could see that the family were back from Exeter. A groom had appeared and he led Mary's pony back to the stables. I tied Henry up and went in, to be polite, and to say hello.

I got a very warm welcome and Sir James said that I had to stay to dinner so, as that was an order, I went out and took Henry round to the stables. When I got back, Hugh took me upstairs so that I could have a wash and brush up. I told him about our proposed trip the next day and asked if he would like to come and meet Celeste. He agreed to on one condition, that being he could treat us all to lunch. He told me that he had been to see the family solicitor and he had been told that he was a very wealthy young man. Therefore, who better to spend some of it on but his friends.

During dinner I told them all about Celeste and Sir James was interested when he knew that she came from (as the French say) Normandy. He asked me to ask her where she came from because he had some very old friends in that part of France. We had a pleasant dinner and the more I see of the family from, shall I say, the 'Top

Drawer', the more I liked them. I think that they must like me because I am always made so welcome. I am now to call Mary's mother Aunt Pam if I wish.

Sir James told Hugh that he could have Wills and a car tomorrow. Hugh refused because he wanted to go by bus. I asked Aunt Pam if I could ring Mr Jarvis about tomorrow. I got through to him and said that I was ringing from Langley Hall and told him what we wanted to do tomorrow. He said that it was OK by him so he would put Celeste on the phone. To make it easy for her, I spoke in French and told her to meet us at the bus station at ten thirty. I thought to myself how attractive the French accent sounded.

I had arranged to meet Hugh and Mary on the bus, so I made myself respectable and caught the bus at the end of our lane. It is a very round about trip to pass the Hall but at last the bus chugged its way to where Hugh and Mary were waiting.

Looking out of the window I had to have a laugh to myself when I saw how smart Mary had made herself look to meet Celeste. Girls are indeed very strange creatures.

I had saved a seat next to me for Mary and, when she sat down, she gave me a kiss on the cheek. She did this on purpose, knowing that the bus would be full of local people and it would make me feel embarrassed.

As we drove into the bus stop, I spotted Celeste waiting for us, looking very smart and pretty. I went through the formalities of introducing everyone. It really was so amusing to watch the two girls looking each other up and down. I also noticed that Hugh was giving Celeste a looking-over as well.

We made our way towards the market and I explained that we were going to see my mother at her stall. Hugh had not been to the Butter Market before and he was very interested in what was being sold. Celeste told me that there was a market in the town near to her farm but not under cover. The market was outside and, at times, it was wet and cold.

We wended our way through the crowds until we got to Mother's stall. She always gave Mary a hearty kiss whenever they met. I introduced Celeste to her and I saw the look of surprise on mother's face, as much as if to say that she didn't expect such a smart young thing as this.

After we had a good look around, we went into the cattle market and found Dad and John. Once more I introduced Celeste and I could see John's eyes light up when he saw the French girl. John was always pulling Mary's leg and I could see that he was saying something to her with a grin on his face. She gave him a good shove and came over to me and took my arm. She said, "That brother of yours has told me to watch out, otherwise you might run off with the French girl." I told her not to worry because I would never do that and she should know why. We said goodbye to Dad and John and went to find somewhere to have lunch.

We found a nice cafe and Celeste wanted to sample our fish and chips, which she had heard were our speciality, so, to keep her company, we all had the same.

By now Mary and Celeste were talking away, sometimes in French and then in English. It was quite funny to listen to them so, to make them laugh, I added a few sentences in German.

It was interesting to see that Hugh was trying to converse with Celeste and, in their way, they seemed to be making some headway. He asked her if she could ride and she looked most hurt when she said, "Of course I can."

Hugh then said that he would like us all to come to the Hall tomorrow for the day and he would fix Celeste up with a pony. Celeste said that she would like that very much but she had no clothes suitable to ride in. Mary butted in by saying that she had several pairs of jodhpurs which were too small for her and she was sure that she could fit Celeste out. I then joined in by saying that we could ride down to see the deer or over to the farm.

I thought that it was a good idea because if we could get Hugh involved with Celeste, it would give Mary and I the chance to be by ourselves.

We walked through the park to Mr Jarvis's house and Mary and I were arm in arm and, much to our surprise, I saw Celeste catch hold of Hugh's arm. Overall it had been a lovely day. Several hurdles had been jumped and the prospects for tomorrow looked good.

We got to Mr Jarvis' house and we were all invited in and made to feel very welcome. I explained our plans for tomorrow and, if he was in agreement, would he make sure that Celeste was on the early bus, which I will get on when it stops by the farm. He thought that it was a good idea and his wife thanked us for giving Celeste a nice day.

We said goodbye to Celeste and caught the bus back to the peace of the countryside. Mary tried to persuade me to come back to the Hall for dinner and offered Wills to drive me back later. I said that I thought her parents must be sick of having me around so much. Mary turned to me and said, "Henry you are a very silly boy, you should know by now how fond they are of you." I was persuaded so I paid the extra fare and went to Langley Hall for dinner.

Mary's parents were very interested to hear about Celeste and what we had done during our day in Newton Abbot. Somehow I felt a bit as if I was overstepping the mark, by spending so much time at the Hall and accepting their hospitality so often. These thoughts were soon forgotten because of the friendly reception I received from Sir James.

While we were having dinner, it suddenly dawned on me that there was a flaw in our arrangements for tomorrow. I had told Celeste that I would meet her on the bus but, of course, I would have to ride over to the Hall on Henry, otherwise I would be without a horse. Hugh had the bright idea that perhaps his father could send a car for Celeste. Sir James gave one of his snorts, which meant yes; anyway that was a problem sorted out.

After another very enjoyable dinner and a very pleasant evening, Wills got the car out and drove me back to the farm, after a sad goodbye from Mary.

When I woke up the next morning I was glad to see that the weather was dry and sunny and, if it stayed that way, we would have s smashing ride. I hoped that Celeste was a good rider, because by now my friends and I are very experienced. Anyway we will soon find out.

When I went up to bed the previous evening, I had a good look at my atlas and also a very useful book Jake had given me about Germany, which included a great deal of information about France.

In the northern part of Normandy, the farms are small with narrow lanes and small fields. The farms are similar to those in Devonshire, producing dairy produce and most important of all, apples for cider and a very strong drink called Calvados. The cider was much more refined than our Devonshire rough cider. I had learned a long time ago that if one has to get to know anyone, it helps to do a bit of homework on that person's way of life and I now have something to talk to Celeste about.

When I got to the Hall, Celeste had just been delivered into Mary's capable hands and, after she had given me a big hug and a kiss, she took Celeste up the stairs to her room.

Celeste, I could see was overwhelmed by the grandeur of the Hall and the way of life with so many servants around the place. Hugh seemed quite excited at the prospect of having a whole day in the company of this girl from across the water.

After a while, with a lot of girlish laughter, Mary brought Celeste down the stairs. She really was a sight for sore eyes. Mary had fitted her out with an outfit which showed up a smashing little figure and the two of them looked so lovely but so very different.

I took Mary's hand and led the way to the stables. I made the suggestion that we call and see how cook was getting on, in other words – did she have any cakes to give away. By now I had got to know Cook very well. When I got into the kitchen, I went up to Cook, putting my arms around her more than ample frame, and giving her a kiss on the cheek, I asked her if she had any cakes to spare. She said, "Master Henry you know how to get around people don't you. My dear, of course you can have some."

She brought forth cakes and a nice hot cup of coffee so we all sat around the large kitchen table and soon ate the cakes. Aunt Pam had not met Celeste so when she came into the kitchen, Hugh did the introducing. I could tell that she liked what she saw. She didn't stay long but, on leaving, she told us not to be late for lunch.

We decided to go and see the river where we used to swim in the summer. Hugh was getting on fine with Celeste, so Mary and I let them ride on ahead, leaving us to be able to have a crafty kiss, although it is very difficult on horseback.

As Mary and I rode side by side towards the river, we talked about the times we had during those warm summer days, which now seemed such a long time ago. We were feeling a bit fed up at the prospects of being parted for such a long time and we wondered if next summer would be so good to us.

We had to ride in single file going through the wood, and I noticed how well Celeste handled the strange horse she was riding. Hugh led the way and I came up in the rear. I liked to do this, then I could feast my eyes on Mary.

Whenever I visited this part of the river where we bathed, I felt that I was in another world. Even in the winter it was so beautiful and restful. There was a lot of water flowing, so the noise of the river could be heard well before it came into view. The trees and bushes looked bare without their canopy of leaves but, even now, there were signs of new life beginning once more. In a few months the area will be lush with the new growth of different shades of green.

Celeste and Hugh seemed to be getting on all right but every time I looked at them, Celeste was looking at me, which I found most disturbing. Mary had noticed the way that Celeste was looking at me. She said, "Henry, you look out, she has her eye on you, so mind that you behave yourself while I am away." We were standing by the river and Mary put her arms around my neck and we had a very passionate kiss. This would surely send a message to Celeste.

After a very nice lunch of Cook's famous meat pie, we decided to ride over to the farm via the Little Bridge. When we got to the bridge, we gave the horses a rest and let them have a good drink. The four of us sat on the old seat and, looking up the valley, we could see smoke coming from Mrs Jenkins' cottage and I told Celeste how I became so interested in learning other languages. She said that by the time she had finished with me, she would have me speaking like a Frenchman. I said that I hoped so because this is what I had to do.

We rode onto the farm and we gave Celeste a tour of Mother's poultry Department and we watched the cows being milked. John was in a very playful mood and he let Mary try to milk a cow, which caused a great deal of amusement. Not knowing that Celeste came from a farming family, he let her have a go and, of course, she did the job properly and so it was then our turn to laugh at John. We had a good look around and Celeste was very interested. She kept asking questions about all sorts of things to do with the farm. When Mother gave us some tea, Celeste got into a long conversation with her, about her poultry. I had to help out with some of the words but overall they conversed quite well.

I rode back to the Hall with them. Celeste changed her clothes and Mary insisted that she should keep the riding gear. Much to my surprise she told her that she could exercise her pony at any time – just to let Henry know and he will fix it up. I could see that this was to be a sort of test for me while she was away.

We all saw Celeste onto the bus and Hugh left Mary and I to say a passionate goodbye. We arranged to meet the following day and so I set off on my lonely ride back to the farm. I will be having a lot of lonely rides over the next few months and I will just have to get used to it. I will be seeing quite a bit of Celeste but I will have to be careful not to get involved, because I loved Mary so much and I would hate to hurt her in any way.

Mary goes away in three days time so I will be with her as much as I can and, on one of those days, we will visit the old barn and say goodbye properly.

CHAPTER 12

It was a fine summer's evening in July 1937 and I was feeling on top of the world. I had passed my exams with flying colours and have been accepted for the University in Exeter. I had won a scholarship but someone would be paying the balance and allowing me a reasonable allowance. I could not find out who this was and I was not to know for several years nor the reason why.

I was finding it very difficult to relax. I had had to work very hard indeed to pass my exams and I have enjoyed just sitting by the bridge and reliving the past twelve months or so. I had been so used to using my brain studying that, even when I was just sitting, it was still going around, so I let my mind go back over the past months; it was rather like getting into a time machine.

My life had been on a sort of seesaw of loneliness and then happiness, depending on when Mary was home. Last summer was a bit of a disaster – Mary and Hugh went on a world cruise with their parents, leaving me at the mercy of Celeste. When I think of this part of my life, I sometimes feel ashamed and yet the memories fill me with great joy.

What little spare time I had while Mary was away, I spent with Celeste. We went to the pictures which, of course, led to kissing and what went with it. This, in itself was quite innocent but one thing let to another and we were getting very involved. I had to cool this down, which I did by just not seeing her so often. This was alright for a while but fate and the weather had other ideas.

I had taken her home to the farm for quite a few visits and Mother told me that she had met Celeste in the market and had asked her to come up to the farm the following Saturday. I remember that Saturday in January of this year. It was very cold and grey and it looked like snow was on the way. I met Celeste at the bus stop and she had filled out in the right places during the twelve months she had been in this country. As we walked along the deserted lane to the farm she stopped and, putting her arms around my neck, she started to kiss me. She was such a lovely little thing that I could not resist the temptation.

We were having a pleasant day together. She had on the riding gear that Mary had given so I let her ride Henry and I rode John's horse. We couldn't go far because it started to snow. We took the horses into the barn and made them comfortable. By now the snow was very heavy and beginning to drift. Dad came into the warm kitchen and told us that the bus had got stuck and there would be no service for the rest of the day.

Mother looked at Celeste and told her that she would have to stay the night, because if the bus was unable to get through, our car would get stuck. She said, "You can sleep in Jenny's room, so come up with me, my dear and help me make the bed up." Jenny's room was at the top of the house, next door to mine, which might cause a few problems. Anyway I telephoned Mr Jarvis and told him what the situation was and that we would get Celeste back as soon as possible.

We had a very pleasant evening. Betty and Charlie came and joined us and, of course, the talk was all about farming in France and in Devon. Eventually we all made our ways to our bedrooms. Celeste had a nightie of Jenny's which she will find miles too big for her and I told her that I thought that she might get lost in it.

I kissed her goodnight and I went into my room and I was soon in bed. I lay there wondering how Celeste was getting on and I must have gone to sleep. I was awakened by feeling someone getting into bed beside me. That someone had no clothes on and, of course, it was the lovely girl from Normandy.

I will always remember that night in January because I lost my virginity. The temptation was too great and Celeste was so insistent. After all, there is only so much that a chap can stand. We were however very careful indeed and we made love several times. She left me just before daybreak, very tired and satisfied but feeling very guilty.

Celeste went home just before Easter and she did not see Mary again, which was just as well. In one way I was very sorry to see her go. I had become very fond of her but my feelings were not the same as those I had for Mary or, for that matter, dear little Polly. I only hope that no one else turns up to tempt me.

Another milestone in my life occurred on my seventeenth birthday in the early spring of this year.

John had bought an old car because his wife, Gertie, had got very fed up getting wet on the back of John's bike. He had been teaching me how to ride his old Norton and he cleaned it up and said that he was going to sell it. John was never one for cleaning things but eventually he did manage to make his bike look different all together.

Anyway, my birthday came and, much to my surprise, the family had all got together and bought John's bike for me. It was taxed, insured and petrol in the tank and they even bought me some goggles. I was over the moon, at last I had some transport and I wouldn't be tied to a bus timetable.

Celeste and I went all over the place on this bike. I was able to show her more of our countryside. We went to Exeter and down to the coast to the port of Teignmouth. We had to laugh when we saw a ship unloading a cargo of apple juice from Cherbourg. She wondered if there were any of her apples used to make the juice. I often lay in bed at night thinking of the tales that bike could tell about Celeste and I. No doubt the same could apply to John and Gertie. It was all so easy to find a quiet spot to enjoy each other.

I have had several meetings with Major Davis and, of course, many with Jake. They were not official, he just happened to be at Jake's cottage when I called. He did, however, seem to know about things even before they happened. He knew that I could go to Exeter University. He told me that I could take whatever courses I liked but he wanted me to take a new venture at the university called Radio Communications.

When he had said this, my first reaction was who the hell does he think he is to tell me what to do. And then the penny dropped, perhaps the government are paying for my future education, so I went along with it, not knowing how wrong I was.

He also asked me at another meeting, if I had the time it would be a good idea to join the University R.A.F. Volunteer Reserve, to learn how to fly. This really shook me. How did the old so and so know that this was what I wanted to do anyway.

Over the last twelve months I have been over to ride with Sir James many times and we were now great friends. Some evenings they made me stay to dinner and we talked about so many things. We rode down to see how his deer were getting on and it was proving to be a great success. When he spoke to me about them, he often referred to them as "our deer". This pleased me because it was, after all, my idea.

The media were playing down the German factor. There were some politicians that thought we should become friendly with Hitler. Peace at any price was their aim. The German bombers were helping the Fascists in the Spanish Civil War. Many thought that this was one way of teaching the pilots how to use their deadly weapons of war. At last this country had started to build modern aircraft and train aircrew.

Mary had told me in one of her many letters that Hugh would be away for a lot of the summer holidays. He was going on a painting trip to Africa with other artists, which was a course and a holiday all in one. When we heard that Bernie's sister, Ruth, was going as well, we both had the same thoughts.

As it was getting late, I got myself to the present time and I remembered that Sir James and Aunt Pamela wanted to see me tomorrow evening. I had no idea what for. I was just asked if I could come and have dinner with them.

Tomorrow was my last day at college. I had been very happy there and I had made some good friends. I will miss Bernie but he will still be able to come up to the farm for Mother's Sunday lunches. I went to see the Head and thanked him for giving me a good report, which helped me to get a place at Exeter.

On the way out of the grounds, Mr Bernstein and his wife drove up in a huge Bentley. The car stopped and I had a chat with these nice people. The old man said, "Henry don't forget what I told you a long time ago. If ever you want a job, the door is always open." He added that should I ever go to Germany again, would I let him know. They both wished me luck and they went to fetch Bernie.

As it was a nice evening, I rode Henry over to the Hall. By now I could make myself look very presentable in riding gear. I know that the Howes' would be in casual dress. They would not object to me not wearing a suit.

When I arrived, they were sitting on the lawn having a drink so I joined them and we talked. I told them that I felt quite sad leaving college. It was the end of a chapter and the unknown lay ahead.

Aunt Pamela started the ball rolling by saying that they wanted me to do them a favour. Sir James butted in by saying that his sister Geraldine was leaving her husband and wanted to return to England. The problem was that he was unable to go because of important meetings and Hugh would be in Africa, so could I go and look after his wife and Mary. There would be no Thomas Cook's fellow but they were sure that I would know what to do and, of course, they would pay for all of my expenses. "So what do you say Henry?"

I was really shaken by this proposal. Of course, I had no option. I had to say yes, they'd done so much for me over the past few years and I would be glad to repay some of the good turns. Nevertheless it sounded a bit too easy and there had to be a catch in it somewhere.

After a while I told them both that I would be only too pleased to help in any way I could but there were a few questions I would like to ask.

First of all, would the Count let his Countess leave him and return to England. Secondly, would Aunt Geraldine be able to take out of Germany her goods and her money and, most important of all, is it legal in that strange land?

Sir James then talked at great length in answering my questions. Geraldine had moved her investments to this country. She is, in any case, a very wealthy person. She has also been sending parcels and valuables back to her mother, Lady Howes. Most important of all, Count Brecht would be in Berlin for two weeks. "This is the excuse for asking my wife, Mary and you during this period. You must leave before her husband comes back from Berlin. He is such a funny fellow that he may try to use force to keep his wife in Germany. You will have to stay for only one week and I will send a telegram to say that my mother, Lady Howes, is very ill. It will, however, be up to you to sort out any problems in Germany. Major Davis thinks that you are quite capable. He does, however, want you to do a little job for him while you are in Lubeck."

I had to laugh about this last remark. I said, "Knowing the Major I bet that the little job is not so little." I then thought of Mary and asked if she knew about this plan of action. Aunt Pam laughed and said that she is more than pleased.

There were many things to talk about but Sir James said that there was also another problem. His mother, Lady Howes, had said that she wanted to see me and Mary before the German trip, "So Wills will have to drive you both up to North Devon for a weekend. You need only stay for two nights, but when she makes her mind up, that's it." He went on to say that it would be a bit of a bore and he had no idea why she wanted to see me but if it was all right with me he would fix it up.

I said that I would be quite happy to go. I quite liked the old lady. I have always liked people who say what they think. I don't think that she will ever forgive me for telling her off when her car got stuck. Aunt Pamela said that she had been dying to tick her off for years. She is such a bossy old so and so.

I then asked when this would take place. Mary would be home in two days time, which would be Friday. Aunt Pam thought that the following weekend would be about right. We had to go to Germany during the second week in August. The Count would be in Berlin from the 10th to the 23rd, so if we travelled on Monday the 11th, he would have gone and the coast would be clear. Sir James said that he would organise this tomorrow.

I found this all very exciting and, of course, I will be having a holiday with Mary and, I hope, some swims in the river. One thing is certain, we will have to behave ourselves when we visit old lady Howes. Whatever does she want to see us about? I have a feeling that it is something to do with my grandfather. I must have a chat with Dad.

After an enjoyable dinner I started my ride home. I had plenty to think about and it all sounded so easy but the more I thought about it, the difficulties seemed to multiply. To me the big problem will be to prevent any of the servants from knowing that Aunt Geraldine would be going for good. Some of them were very loyal to the Baron because their parents had also been servants before them. Anyway, I have a few ideas and I will think about this tomorrow.

When I got home I told the family the news and they were as surprised as I was to hear the part I was to play in this family drama. John, as usual, looked on the bright side and said that it will be another holiday and with Mary to keep me company. I tried to hit him but he ducked.

After everyone else had gone to bed, Dad and I sat and talked. I asked him about Grandfather. I knew that he had fallen in love with a girl from the next farm and that this girl married the attractive young son of the 'Lord of the Manor' which was Langley Hall. Dad then went on to say that there was a great deal of talk because a baby was born just over seven months after the wedding. Some people said that Grandfather was the father. The baby was a boy who died soon after it was born. Later Sir James and his sister were born.

Dad went on to say that the marriage was not a great success. The squire made a lot of money and built up the estate but he died at a young age leaving his widow very well off and the owner of two estates, one in North Devon and Langley Hall, which she made over to Sir James and his family. For some reason she was not a frequent visitor to this part of Devon. She got on well enough with her son Sir James but she became very eccentric and bad-tempered.

Dad thought for a while and then he told me that when he met the old lady Howes at the Christmas party, she kept asking questions about me and my friendship with Mary and Hugh and how it all came about.

He said, "She was also very interested in what I could remember about my father. You were unlucky not to have know him because he was a grand chap and a very good farmer. Henry, I have no idea what she wants to see you and Mary about, it could be that she is just lonely. On the other hand why just you and Mary and not Hugh. "Anyway, you will have to wait and see."

On Friday morning I got up full of anticipation. Mary was coming home today and the thought of seeing her again filled me with bags of joy. I always felt a bit apprehensive when Mary came home, after being away for several months. Today was no exception. I always had this fear that she may have changed her mind about how she felt towards me.

I did my odd jobs and, as I seemed to be getting in everyone's way, I saddled up Henry and had a good gallop which pleased him. He loved to be given his head and to stride out across the fields. It was a grand morning and we both enjoyed our trip. I gave Henry a good grooming and put him in the paddock.

I went into the kitchen and I was surprised to see Jake having coffee and scoffing Mother's cakes. He had come to see me so Mother made herself scarce and he told me that he had a message from Major

Davis.

Jake told me that the Major wanted to know what was going on at the airfield we had seen to the west of the Schwartau River. He told me "He doesn't think that you will be able to find out much but, on the other hand, you may be lucky especially as you will be guests of Graf Brecht. Anyway, do what you can, but we are not expecting any results."

We talked as we always did about all sorts of things. He told me to bring Mary over to see him before we went to Germany and he would have a much better camera for me to take with me.

Mother had persuaded Jake to stay to lunch and when Dad came on the scene, the three of us sat outside and had a glass of beer, which went down very well indeed.

Soon after lunch the telephone rang and it was Mary. It was super to hear her voice again. I told her that I would be on my way in two shakes of a dog's tail. I saddled up Henry and I was off, following the route that I knew so well. I could have gone on my bike but as Henry doesn't use any petrol, I use the dear old chap whenever I can.

There was a part of the route to the Hall which was very quiet and always deserted. Henry was trotting along when a figure appeared out of a gateway. It was a lovely young girl in a check shirt, well open at the neck, tight fitting jodhpurs and a very broad smile on her beautiful face. Of course it was my Mary. Gone were my worries about how she thought of me. I slid off Henry and we were in each other's arms.

Mary caught hold of Henry's reins and led him through the gate into the field where her horse was tethered. We lay down behind a convenient hayrick and made love, just using the warm grass as our bed.

Every time I see Mary after an absence of several months, she looks even prettier and more attractive. Looking at her lying on the grass with her hair all tousled and her cheeks flushed, she really was a lovely creature.

We lay and talked for a while but the talking was interrupted by Mary's passionate love-play. She was making up for the time she had been away. Eventually we made ourselves presentable, making sure that we had no telltale pieces of grass on our clothing, we got on our horses and rode back to the Hall.

Mary was excited about our trip to Germany. She was however not so keen on the visit to her grandmother's estate. I asked her if she had been there before. She said that she had but it had been a long time ago and she could only remember that it was a very big house and very old-fashioned. The estate was near Dulverton and close to Exmoor. I said that we should take our riding gear just in case there were any horses available. It would be nice to have a ride on Exmoor.

It was good to see Hugh again, I pulled his leg about going to Africa with Ruth. He retaliated by telling me how lucky I was to have Mary living just next door. He also asked if I had heard from Celeste. He gave me a dig in the ribs and said, "I bet she taught you a thing or two Henry." I saw Mary walking across the lawn towards us so I changed the subject, much to Hugh's amusement. Mary had changed into a dress, which improved her looks even more and, taking my hand, we went into the Hall for tea.

Aunt Pamela started to talk about the German venture. I said that I had been giving it a bit of thought. To me the most important problem would be getting Aunt Geraldine down to the station and on to the train without any of the staff getting to know what was going on.

One way would be for all of us to take more luggage than we required. We could make it heavy with a few well-placed bags of sand. We would then get rid of the sand and Aunt Geraldine could pack her goods in our suitcases and trunks. She could tell the household that she would be staying in Lubeck for the day and arrange for a car to pick her up in the late afternoon, by which time she would be in Holland.

When I had finished spouting forth and, in a way showing off, Sir James came in and I had to start all over again. He thought that it was brilliant idea. He said, "Now I know, Henry, why Major Davis has his eye on you."

Of course I stayed for dinner that evening and Mary asked her father if he could get in touch with his mother to see if there would be two horses for us to use when we went to stay with her. He said that he was sure that there would be and he would telephone her tomorrow.

After dinner we all sat in the garden and talked about all sorts of things. Hugh had his future all fixed up. He would be going to an Art College in London. Mary, on the other hand, didn't quite know what she wanted to do. She took my hand and said that she only wanted to be with me. This made everyone laugh.

One thing was for certain, she had no intention of going to one of those stupid Finishing Schools in Switzerland and learn how to be a Lady. She added that perhaps she could learn how to type and that sort of thing and then she could help Papa. Much to her surprise Sir James thought it was quite a good idea. I could tell by the expression on Aunt Pam's face that she thought the opposite.

The next week soon went by and by tomorrow Mary and I will be off to North Devon to see the old lady. It had been a smashing week. We had several swims in the river and my bike was so useful. We went all over the place, enjoying ourselves to the full. We both thought that the next few days would be a bit of a dead loss but we had to go and that was that.

Wills came and collected me and, as we drove over to the Hall, I could tell that he thought that it would be a bit of a bore. His only hope was that there would be a village pub nearby. He told me that he thought that the servants would all be old family retainers, like Lady Howes' chauffeur.

When we got to the Hall, Mary was waiting, looking as gorgeous as ever. We went to Exeter and then to Tiverton and followed the River Exe until we came to Dulverton. We could see Exmoor in the distance and the countryside was quite beautiful. We had to ask the way to Lady Howes' home which was called Wimble Manor. Of course we had passed the turning we should have taken. The Manor was about half-way between Exbrige and Dulverton. After asking several times, we managed to find it.

When we came to the imposing entrance, Mary and I had quite a shock. We never expected such a grand place. As we drove up the long drive to the house, we could see that everything was well looked after. The manicured lawns were broken up by masses of flower beds with not a weed in sight. Langley Hall was large but this building was huge.

There were several gardeners working on the estate that we could see but as we got nearer to the house, it was possible to see that the grounds stretched for a great distance, mostly parkland with some magnificent trees having been grouped together to form a sort of overall pattern.

I was taken by surprise because, for some reason, I thought that the estate would be run down. I had been led to believe that the old lady was very tight-fisted. To keep this place going would cost a great deal of money. I wondered what the inside would be like.

In front of the house there was a large round patch of lawn, with a drive around it. Consequently the car had to go around the circumference of this lawn to pull up in front of the steps leading up to the front door.

As we came to the entrance, the door opened and Lady Howes came into view. She had two lovely Retrievers standing obediently by her side. Wills opened the car door and Mary and I got out.

Without thinking I got down on my haunches and beckoned the two dogs to come to me. Like a shot they bounded down the steps and were soon all over me. I have always had this affinity with animals; somehow they look upon me as a friend.

Mary had gone up the steps to greet her grandmother. I managed to calm the dogs down and I nervously climbed up the steps to meet the old lady once again. She looked younger than when I saw her first of all. I could even see a bit of Mary in her. I had no idea how old she was but she had to be in her seventies and she looked very fit. I thought that it must be the North Devon air.

I shook her hand and she said, "It is nice to see you again Henry. You might give a poor old lady a kiss because it is not every day that I see such a handsome young man." So I did as I was told and, for luck, I gave the old dear a hug. I think that for some reason I felt sorry for her.

She took Mary's arm and we went into the hallway. She told two footmen who were hovering by the entrance, to bring in the luggage and to show the driver to his quarters. We were introduced to the butler, who looked older than Lady Howes and then to the housekeeper, Mrs Bell. Now she was much younger and seemed a very cheerful sort of person. Whenever I saw her she always had this large bunch of keys hanging by a chain from her waist.

When I went into the hall I expected it to be dark and dingy, but it was light and very inviting. Everywhere was spotless and well cared for. The paint-work was light in colour and not the dark brown which was the fashion. Even the many paintings on the wall seemed to show up their colours and were mostly of views and not grim-faced ancestors.

Lady Howes sensed that I was interested in the decor of the hall and she laughingly asked if what I saw met with my approval. I told her that it was nice to have so much natural light in such a large hallway. I added that to go into her daughter's home in Germany was like going into a cave. She gave a lady-like snort, similar to her son's and said, "My daughter, Geraldine, should never have married that awful German."

Mrs Bell then showed us to our rooms, which were very pleasant indeed and, once again, I was surprised that the furniture was of the very best quality but modern in design.

Mary's room was next door and we both inspected each other's rooms. After we had washed and made ourselves presentable, we went down the grand staircase to be greeted by Salter, the butler, who led us into a sitting room where the old lady was sitting flanked by her two dogs, which were called Peter and Paul.

Salter asked Mary and I if we would like a glass of sherry. We both said yes, really to be polite. I was not very keen on the stuff but this was much lighter in colour and I found that I liked it. It bore no resemblance to what Mother served up at Christmas.

It wasn't long before Salter came in to say that luncheon was served. I have no idea why I did it but I offered my arm to the old lady and we went in to the dining room for a smashing lunch.

The atmosphere had become most relaxed. We talked about different things but Lady Howes seemed to be pumping me for information about my family and myself and what I was going to do after the university. She must have done her homework on me pretty well because she seemed to know all about my prospects. She also knew all about my connections with Major Davis.

Mary was also being questioned in a similar way but, at times, this included me, which I thought very odd. To me it seemed that there was a plan formulating in her mind and I had no idea what it could be.

We finished lunch and Lady Howes said that there were two very nice horses at our disposal if we wanted to ride over the Estate. She told us she always had a good nap after lunch and that she would see us before dinner. Salter was to take us to meet Jack, the head groom and he would advise us where to go for a ride.

As she started to climb the stairs, she turned and said to Mary, "I wish I was your age and about to spend an afternoon with a young chap like Henry."

We followed the old lady up the stairs because we wanted to change into our riding gear. She disappeared right at the end of the landing into her quarters, which were a long way from where Mary and I were to sleep. I said to myself, "Don't weaken Henry. You know what we agreed about being on our best behaviour."

We changed and went to meet Salter, who took us to the stables where we met Jack. He was fairly old but such a nice fellow. He had picked out two smashing horses for us to ride while we were staying at the Manor. He advised us where to ride, so off we went to explore this lovely estate.

Part of the Estate was cultivated and there were fields of wheat and barley ready to be harvested. There were sheep and bullocks in other parts and I could see parkland and woodland in the distance. The main part of the Estate seemed to be in a very wide valley and, with the moors in the distance, the setting was perfect. At the far end of the valley I could see a very dense forest. I wondered if there were any pheasants reared there.

As we were in a valley I thought that there had to be a large stream or river, so I told Mary and we set out to see what we could find. We were skirting a small wood when all of a sudden we were confronted by a man on a huge horse, who very politely asked us who we were and asked what we were doing on the Estate.

Mary immediately said that she was Lady Howes' granddaughter and I was her friend, Mr Blake. Putting on her haughty voice she asked "And who are you?" He told us that he was the gamekeeper and explained that there had been a lot of trouble on the estate with uninvited guests riding all over the place, leaving gates open, which caused a lot of problems.

The gamekeeper's name was Jackson and he rode with us for a

while, all the time explaining the layout of the estate. I was right in my assumption that there were pheasants in the large wood at the far end of the estate. He asked us to visit his domain where he and his wife lived in a cottage and he would be only too pleased to show us around. Before he left us he told me how to get to the river and, with a very polite farewell, he went on his way.

At last we found the small but beautiful river and we dismounted and let the horses have a good drink. We tied the horses up, kissed for a while and then we started to walk along the river bank talking and holding hands. We were just happy to be with each other. We were by now feeling very warm, so we lay on the river bank and, using our hands, we doused our faces in the cool water.

In spite of our good intentions, the temptation was too great and we made love slowly taking our clothes off, until we had very little on. It was, indeed, a lovely afternoon.

While we were putting our clothes on we were trying to solve the problem of why were both invited to stay in North Devon. It would have been understandable if Hugh had been included in the invitation. I had this feeling that the old lady wanted to get something sorted out before her daughter came home from Germany. Mary was usually very good at sorting these sort of problems out but, like me, she was clueless. Anyway, perhaps time will tell.

We rode back to the Manor feeling content in more ways than one. We gave the horses back to Jack and went into the house. We were greeted by Lady Howes who said that by the look of us, we had had a pleasant afternoon. She told us to go and have a bath and get ready for dinner, and she would see us when we didn't smell of horses!

When I was ready to go down to dinner, I knocked on Mary's door and went in to find that she had yet another dress on which made her look even more gorgeous. We went down the stairs and we were met by Salter who showed us into the very spacious living room.

Lady Howes was there plus, of course, Peter and Paul. Salter gave us a glass of sherry each and, when we had settled down, she asked us how we had spent the afternoon. I did most of the talking and explained where we had been and what we had done, of course leaving out our enjoyable moments by the river.

I told her that Mary and I had fallen in love with her Estate. It was so beautiful in a wild sort of way. Mary butted in by saying that we had met Jackson the gamekeeper and that he had invited us to see his pheasants and his cottage. I could see by the old lady's expression that she was so pleased that we liked her home.

I asked her who helped her to run and look after the Estate. She very proudly said that she did, with the help of Jack and Jackson, and also Mrs Jackson, who was a fully trained secretary and who saw that the books were in order. These were fully checked by a firm of accountants from Tiverton. She said she would talk more of this later but we should now go in for dinner. She said, "Come Henry and take my arm."

I always thought that the food at Langley Hall was very good but the dinner we had was out of this world. I had great difficulty in not making a pig of myself. It was a very friendly atmosphere and Mary was telling her grandmother all about the cruise she had been on the previous year. Lady Howes asked me what I had been doing while Mary was away. I looked at Mary and, with a laugh, I said that I had had to entertain a very pretty French girl from Normandy, who had been helping me to perfect my French. Mary tried to lean over the table to hit me but, with luck, she missed. This caused the old lady to have a good laugh.

When we had finished dinner, Lady Howes said that coffee would be served in her favourite spot, which was on the western side of the Manor where French windows opened on to a very sheltered patio. One could then see the sun setting over the distant hills.

It was a very warm evening and, sitting there, I thought that, given the chance, this would also be a favourite place of mine to be. I told the old lady this and, for some reason, it pleased her no end.

When the coffee had been served and there were just the three of us. Lady Howes said, "I expect you are both wondering why I asked you both to come up to stay a few days with me." She sat looking into the distance and then she said that she would like to tell us a story.

Many years ago, she lived on a farm which joined the grounds of Langley Hall. On the other side of the Estate there was a farm owned by the Estate but rented to a Farmer Blake. He had a son called Henry Blake. This was, of course, my grandfather, and she informed me that I had been called after him.

She had gone to the village school with Henry and as they grew up they began to fall in love. "We had permission to swim in the river just as Mary and you have done and I would hazard a guess that this is one of your favourite places," she said. We both went a bit red and told her that it was.

Henry and I were a bit older than you two, but one day we were joined by a very handsome young man who we recognised as the only son of the Howes. We both felt very ill at ease in his company, because, in those days, the social gap was so much wider than it is today.

She paused to drink her coffee and I was sorry to see a look of sadness come over her face.

She then went on to say that growing old is very difficult. "One does tend to look back and think of the mistakes and what life could have been like if a different course had been taken. My life has not been unhappy, on the other hand it has not been very happy. I became bad-tempered and eccentric, I was left on my own as my husband died when James and Geraldine were only teenagers. I could have sold this lovely place and lived in London or somewhere gay.

I put a manager into Langley Hall and made it over to James, which became his when he was twenty-one. Geraldine met and married that stupid German. When one gets to my age there is very little point of thinking of the future, so one looks back and relives the past.

I have not been a regular visitor to Langley because it always made me feel sad. I decided to invite myself for Christmas because I felt sorry for myself and lonely. I had no idea that I would have such a shock, when this young man 'pointing a finger at me' offered to pull my car out of the snow. You see my dears it could have been the Henry I knew and loved so many years ago. It was uncanny to see someone who looked the same riding in the lane which we both knew so well.

Then I got to the Hall and you both came in together, and I discovered that you were the grandchild of my Henry and it was not very long before I discovered how you both felt about each other. So here we had the opposite situation of the farmer's son falling in love with the Lady of the Hall. How strange fate is. William, my late husband, really chased me and introduced me to the sort of life that I thought I could never have. I became very fond of him and I left poor Henry in the lurch. Anyway William and I got married. She paused and was silent for a few moments. Perhaps one day I will tell you about that. I have talked too much and you must be bored."

Mary got up and went over and put her arms round the old lady and told her that it was lovely, but sad, to hear this family history, so please tell us whatever you think we should know. I said that Dad had told me part of the story and all I can add is that if you had not married Sir William, Mary and I would not be here. My Father is always telling me that our lives are all planned for us and I am at last beginning to believe him.

The old lady rang a bell and in came Salter. She told him to bring in that very nice wine she had the other night. When we each had a large glass of wine in our hands and Salter had retired, she lifted her glass and said, "Here is a toast to the Howes and the Blakes." She looked at me and told me that I must call her Aunt Sally. She turned to Mary and said, "to you I am still Grandmother."

"Now you two, would you like to ride with me tomorrow, when I do my rounds of the Estate? I will soon be going to bed. I have to take a sleeping pill which puts me out like a light. So you two can please yourselves what you do as long as you tell whoever is on duty in the hall when you go to bed, so that he can lock up."

I am sure that it was my imagination, but I thought that the old dear gave me a wink when she mentioned her sleeping pills. She wished us a good night plus a kiss on the cheek and went to her room, with her memories which had been rekindled by the evening conversation about the past.

Salter came out onto the patio with half a bottle of wine and two glasses. He said that her Ladyship had told him to say that we might as well finish up the wine. That is, of course, if we wished to. He turned to me and said, "When you go upstairs perhaps you would be so good as to ring the bell so that we can lock up. It is also so nice to have young people about the house. It has made her Ladyship happy. On behalf of the staff we hope that you will visit us more often and we wish you good night."

Mary and I sat there on a warm summer's night, enjoying the wine and talking about our first day in North Devon. We could both understand why Mary was invited, but surely Hugh should have been with her and not me. I had only met the old lady very briefly at Christmas and then I thought that I had offended her. We came to the conclusion that it was all to do with my grandfather.

We both had this strange feeling that this weekend would play a vital part in our lives. It seemed yet another part of the jigsaw, which would, in time, tell a story. We both felt that we needed each other to clear a sort of cloud that was beginning to form over us. Maybe fate made us feel this way but perhaps it was the magic of the wine or just our needs, but we both knew that all of our good resolutions would go by the board, when we walked up the staircase to our rooms.

When we came down for breakfast, Aunt Sally, as I now have to call her, was dressed in old-fashioned riding clothes. I had wondered what form of transport she would be using to go around her estate.

After Mary and I had consumed a huge breakfast, we all walked around to the stables. Jack was waiting for us. We had the same smashing horses that we had yesterday. Jack had a big Hunter and Aunt Sally's steed looked nearly as old as she did. Jack helped her up and she rode sidesaddle. I could see that she was in complete control of her mount.

I was instructed to ride by her side and she gave me a running commentary of the different areas that we were riding through. In fact, she never stopped talking. It was as if the floodgates of her mind had become open.

Evidently she had several tenant farmers, whose lands were on the outskirts of the main estate. We were to visit the largest of these farms

258

today. She explained that she liked to keep in touch, but she also wanted some of their delicious cream.

We rode through some rough country and I told her what her son, Sir James, had done with his useless land. She knew all about the deer at Langley and her son had told that I had been instrumental in its conception. She thought for a while and said that she would contact James for more information.

When we got to the farm, we were greeted by the farmer and his wife. They were both in their late forties and were a very pleasant couple. We all went into their large kitchen and had cups of coffee and a plate of cakes to chose from.

On the way out the old lady told the farmer that he might see these young people riding over his land. The farmer said that we would be very welcome and he would be only too pleased to show us over the farm. With a friendly wave we were on our way.

On the way back to the Manor the old lady was very quiet and seemed to be deep in thought. Or perhaps she may have just run out of steam. She stopped her horse and turned to me and said, "Henry, would you and Mary stay until Tuesday and would you both come to church with me tomorrow morning, as I want to show you both off to some of my neighbours?"

This took me a bit by surprise and, to cover my confusion, I said that I must ask Mary what she would like to do and, with the same, I moved up to ride beside Mary. I put the question to her and she said, Yes without any hesitation and turned in her saddle to give her grandmother a friendly smile and a wave.

I dropped back to join Aunt Sally and told her that we would be very glad to stay the extra days. She then went on to say that she was very grateful to me for going to Germany to bring back her daughter Geraldine. "Now Henry, I insist in giving you a nice present for doing this very tedious chore. You can huff and puff as much as you like, but my mind is made up. I have even made up my mind what I am going to buy you. I want your chauffeur fellow to drive you and Mary into Minehead and fix yourself up with a smart new suit because yours is getting a bit small for you. I will telephone the Men's shop there and all you will have to do is to select what you and Mary like. I will have a word with Mary and I will give her full instructions."

I was about to say that she had no need to do this but she shut me up by saying that the subject was closed. "I want to do this Henry so that's that. I will telephone James to tell him that you will be coming back on Tuesday and I will ask him to let your parents know."

So, right after lunch, Wills drove up to the front door and we were off to the seaside resort of Minehead. I asked Wills how he was getting on and he said that he was enjoying his stay at the Manor and he had become very friendly with one of the footmen and they had had several visits to the local pub. After a lot of fussing around by Mary, I had a new suit, shirt and tie. It was very expensive but Mary had her instructions from the old lady and they were carried out to the letter.

We told Wills to drive us onto the seafront and we had a walk along the beach. It was a bit crowded but the air was so very refreshing. We had an ice cream each and we really enjoyed our afternoon. We were sorry that we didn't have our swimming costumes because the sea looked so inviting but we both thought that there might be another day.

On the way back to the Manor I confided in Mary that I felt a bit guilty in accepting such a handsome gift from her grandmother. Mary, using her favourite expression, told me not to be a silly boy. She went on to say that the family were very grateful indeed for the help I would be able to give when we all went to Germany. "Anyway," she said, "anyone can see that the old girl likes you. I don't blame her," and, with that, she put her arms around my neck and gave me such a lovely kiss. I could see Wills having a good grin as he watched us in his mirror.

When we got back to the Manor, Salter told us that her Ladyship was in the sitting room and would like to see us. We went in complete with our parcels. I had to try on the jacket for her inspection and she told Mary that she had good taste in suits and, with a very broad smile she added, "and young men."

At this point I thanked her very much for her generous gift and how I thought it was unnecessary because I would enjoy going to Germany. Besides it would help me to keep in touch with the language and, anyway, I would be with Mary which always made me happy.

I had let the cat out of the bag by telling the old lady how I felt about her granddaughter, which I had had no intention of doing, although it must be very obvious.

Dinner that night was once again a happy event. Aunt Sally seemed to have blossomed since we arrived and, after dinner, we settled ourselves on the patio and she said that she was going to continue her history lesson on the Howes and the Blakes.

"In those days, which were a long time ago, sex was never talked about and no information was ever given to the young people. Henry, your grandfather and I were very careless and without any real knowledge, so I became pregnant. This was a real disaster and a hopeless situation. I never told my Henry or William. I just married William as soon as I could. Henry was only a tenant farmer's son and his income at the age that he was, could not have kept a wife and family. I would have been a disgrace to my family and an outcast in my social life, so I took the coward's way out. A baby boy was born seven months after William and I were married but unfortunately the baby died just a few days after being born.

Now you two must promise me not to tell anyone what I have told you tonight. Henry I think that your father knows, but we will never mention it again. Perhaps you can now understand what a shock I had when I saw this young Henry on his horse at Christmas and this is why I want to get to know the two of you because it is like living one's life over again. If you will humour an old lady, perhaps you will come up to stay with me every now and again. I know that it is a bit boring for young people, being right in the middle of nowhere but you will have each other and I would be so very grateful."

Mary and I were at a loss for words but I managed to say that we would love to visit Wimble and explore the area. If there was anything we could do to help, we would, after all it was not all that far away. I told her "We want you to visit South Devon more often and I would like you to visit Long Meadow Farm once more, which will bring back some happy memories and I know that Mum and Dad would love to see you."

Mary then went over to her grandmother and sat on the arm of her chair and gave her a big cuddle and a kiss. I could see that the poor girl was very moved and was close to tears after hearing such a sad story.

The poor old dear then said that we must not feel sorry for her because she was now much happier but it must remain a secret. She paused for a while as if she was trying to put her thoughts into words.

She then said, "Now my dears, I don't want you to be offended by what I am going to say. I know that the young have far more knowledge today about life, so there may not be any need for me to interfere but I do ask you to be so very careful not to get yourselves into the situation that my Henry and I found ourselves in so many years ago."

Mary and I went a bit red in the face and Aunt Sally burst out laughing and told us that she could remember when she was our age. Young people always forget that their elders were, at one stage in their lives, exploring what life was all about and were not always old fuddy-duddies.

It was by now getting late and she said that she was off to bed. As she got up she rang the bell and in came Salter. She told him to give Master Henry and Miss Mary some of that special wine. We both instinctively got up and gave the old lady a goodnight kiss and a good hug. As she went out of the door, she turned and said, "Don't forget, church parade is at 10.30 and God bless you both."

After Salter had poured our wine and said goodnight to us, we both sat there with our thoughts. What we had heard that night had given us plenty to think about. We both started to talk at once, so I gave way for Mary. She started to open her heart to me. She told me how much she loved me and she was only happy when we were together. Looking a bit shy she said that we could sometimes make love properly. She had been told at college about certain times in each month when it was safer for girls to have sex. Also it was perfectly safe if the male knows what he is doing, "which I am sure you do, Henry, darling." She went on to say that she was sure that her grandmother knew what was going on between us, so we should make the best of our opportunities whilst we were there. She also said that she felt so sorry for the old lady and that we should try and give up the odd day or two to come to North Devon to visit her when, no doubt, she would provide transport.

So, we decided to become true lovers and we finished our wine and went up to our separate rooms. Mary wanted me to visit her room that night and I thought that it would be nice to smell her scent and to remain with her for the whole night. I was very gentle with the dear girl and it was a wonderful experience for both of us. It was a night that I would never forget and it all seemed so natural and made us feel so happy. We had at last taken the plunge and without any regrets. Mary was no longer a virgin and she lay in my arms fast asleep. We made love again during the night and I left her when it was dawn to creep back to my room.

When I was in my own bed I compared my lovemaking with Celeste and then with Mary and it was so different. I thought that it was the fact that I loved Mary so much and was not self-indulgent on my part. I was soon asleep again and I was awakened by a kiss on my forehead. Mary had come in to wake me up as I had overslept. She was already dressed in a smart dress, all ready for church.

I got my skates on and soon we were on our way down the stairs for breakfast. The night's activities must have agreed with Mary because she looked radiant. When I told her this she said that she felt on top of the world but she wished that it was time to go to bed again. With this remark she put on her innocent look and went into the breakfast room to give her grandmother a good morning kiss. I had to let the old lady have a good look at my new suit and she told me how smart I was. I bent down and gave the old girl a kiss on the cheek and thanked her once again for the smashing present.

After breakfast Mary and I walked around the rose garden, which was in front of the patio. It was nice and cool, being in the shadow of the large house. We both knew that we were reliving what had happened last night, consequently we had very little to say to each other. We were just content to be in each other's company. We were interrupted by Salter, who told us that her Ladyship would soon be ready to go to church. Mary put on a cheeky little hat and I made myself look presentable.

Aunt Sally looked very elegant and we got into the old Rolls, driven by Martin, the chauffeur, who looked very smart in his uniform. This was the first time I had seen him on his home ground. He gave me a smile and a crafty wink and said, "It is nice to see you again Master Henry. There is no snow about so we will be alright." Aunt Sally shouted at him to get on with it. These two always seemed to be at war with each other but in a friendly sort of way.

We were going to the church in Dulverton. It was a lovely morning and it was a very enjoyable drive. I could see the Brendon Hills in the distance, they dominated the area similar to the way that Dartmoor was always visible from my part of South Devon. The Brendon Hills were different to Dartmoor, they looked like an extended roller coaster of green landscape. Exmoor had a much softer look to that of Dartmoor. We were now in Somerset and, of course, so was Dulverton. Wimble Manor was only just in Devon and in some places the accent was a bit of a mixture, which I found most attractive.

Looking out of the car I thought that I could get to like this part of the country. The people I had met were so very friendly. That, of course, was a stupid thought to have, because I had only met members of the staff on the Estate. Perhaps today I would meet some of Aunt Sally's friends, which may change my mind.

The three of us were sitting next to each other with Mary in the middle. I had no idea what the two females were talking about. I was brought back to earth by Mary taking my arm and saying "We would love to wouldn't we Henry darling?" I said, Yes but what would I love to do?

Mary scolded me and told me that I had been daydreaming again, which made Aunt Sally laugh. Mary went on to say that we would love to come up to the Manor after we returned from Germany, so I endorsed this sentiment and thanked her for the kind invitation.

When we got to church, we got out of the car and, as we were about to go in, the vicar met us and Mary and I were introduced to this very jolly chap. I could tell by his attitude that the old lady was well thought of in this parish. He led us to our pew, which had the Howes' coat of arms carved on the end seat.

The church was well attended and, as we came in, many inquisitive eyes were looking our way. As we walked down the aisle, I walked behind Mary and Lady Howes and I thought how beautiful Mary looked. I could see a resemblance to her grandmother. When we were settled in our seats and, having said our prayers, I had a crafty look around and there were quite a number of boys and girls of a similar age to Mary and myself. Everyone had on their Sunday best clothing, which gave a distinct smell of moth balls.

I had been to church quite a lot with mother when I was much younger and I used to go with Polly on the odd occasion. My thoughts made me think of Polly and I wondered how she was getting on. I still knew in my subconscious mind that our paths would cross in the future.

During the sermon I thought of what Mary and I had done last night. Many would say that we had both committed a sin but how could a God that I had prayed to all my life and believed that was a God of Love, object to two people like Mary and I getting together because we loved each other. There must be a difference between lust and our union.

Before the very boring sermon finished I started to think about my position in this community. What on earth was I doing here, sitting in the pew reserved for the Lord of the Manor? I was holding the hand of a young titled girl, who was so beautiful and loving. I was a very welcome guest at the Manor and was about to start a course at a University with an allowance, paid for by someone unknown. I kept asking myself why? Mary gave me a big nudge to bring me back to this Sunday morning in Dulverton.

I was to learn that leaving Sunday morning church service could be a lengthy job. Aunt Sally kept introducing Mary and I to all and sundry. I could see that some of the young men were looking at Mary with a great deal of envy. Strange how it may seem, some of the females were giving me very friendly looks. Mary must have noticed this because she took my arm and gave the impression that I was not available.

When eventually we got into the car and were on our way back to the Manor, Aunt Sally said that she would like to give a party once again so that we could meet more of her friends. "I am going to invite myself to visit Langley for Christmas and perhaps you would come up and stay for a few days in the new year," she said. Mary gave her grandmother a hug and said that we would love to come and see her, especially if there would be a party. I added that perhaps Hugh could come as well.

After a smashing Sunday lunch, we found Wills and told him that we would like to have a drive onto Exmoor. He surprised us by saying that he knew Exmoor pretty well so, after Aunt Sally had retired for her afternoon nap, we were on our way. We had both taken off our finery and were now dressed in a more casual way, which put us in a real holiday mood.

I must say that Wills excelled himself because we had a most interesting drive. We stopped at a cafe which advertised cream teas and we both had a good feed.

After dinner that night we both wanted the time to fly so that we could get together again. Aunt Sally had other ideas. She wanted to talk and she kept including the two of us in so many thoughts she had about the future of the Estate. I found this very strange and Mary and I were to talk about it in the future.

Tomorrow was our last day and I asked the old lady if we could go and see Jackson, the gamekeeper and, as it looked as if it would be a fine, warm day, perhaps Cook could give us a packed lunch. She said that it was a good idea because she had to go into Minehead on business during the morning and that she would meet us for tea at about four thirty.

At last we went up the stairs to our rooms. We would have liked to run up the stairs but that would have been too obvious. We both had this urgency to get together. Mary had assured me that she was still in the safe part of her monthly cycle and I would be more than careful. Then we made love as nature had designed it. I went into Mary's bed and laying there was pure heaven. We may be doing what was wrong but somehow I felt that it was meant to be. We went to sleep in each other's arms, feeling contented and very happy. By now I was so close mentally to Mary that I could tell when she felt happy or unhappy and there was no doubt that this was what she wanted.

She woke me up in the night by laying on top of me and we made love in a way that I found most rewarding. I returned to my bedroom a little weary but so very happy. Somehow tomorrow we must try to hide how we felt from the rest of the world.

We both over-slept and when we came downstairs, Aunt Sally had finished her breakfast, so we had ours together, talking in whispers about our night together and how we only had one more night to enjoy each other.

Our last day was most enjoyable. We both had a lot to be happy about. We talked as we rode towards the wooded part of the Estate. Next Monday we would be on our way to Germany, which could be a bit tricky and not the relaxed atmosphere of the Manor.

Mary kept talking about how her grandmother had changed. Gone was the very grumpy old soul who was always bossing everyone about. Mary confessed to me that she had been dreading this visit and how Hugh had said that he was glad that he had not been invited. She was sure that the memory of her real love for Grandfather Henry Blake had softened her and brought a bit of happiness back into her life. One thing was certain and that was that Mary and I were in her good books. Strange how it may seem but I had grown quite fond of the old lady in a very short space of time.

When we got closer to the large forest, we could hear the raucous calls of the cock pheasants. They are very handsome birds so why they have such an awful call, God only knows.

Jack, the head groom, had told me how to find the gamekeeper so we started to venture into the very dense wood and it was not long before Jackson, the gamekeeper, appeared as if from nowhere.

He said that he would show us where the pheasants were reared and then perhaps we would like to see his cottage and have a cup of coffee with his wife.

We dismounted and walked in single file, deeper into the forest, until we came to a large clearing which had small hutches, set at regular intervals around the area. As it was only a matter of weeks before the pheasant season started, the hutches were deserted because the birds were now fully grown.

As Jackson entered the clearing, pheasants appeared from the undergrowth expecting to be fed. They were quite tame and it did seem a shame that by Christmas many of them would have been shot. Jackson got some corn from his shed and gave them a treat which I think was for our benefit.

After a while we walked to a nearby clearing and saw a picturesque cottage built of a grey stone, with white paint-work. It had a well-tended garden and a mass of colour from the countless shrubs around the house. Mrs Jackson came out to greet us and somehow she bore no resemblance to what I thought she would look like. She looked about thirty, very pretty and when she spoke it was obvious that she had been well educated. She asked us to come into the house and have some refreshments. When we were sitting down in a well-furnished front room, she started to talk about the estate. She said that her Ladyship had been on the telephone to her and she had been told to answer any questions that I might ask.

Mary butted in by thanking Mrs Jackson for the help she gave to her grandmother by looking after the books and correspondence. She added that she wanted to be trained so that she could help her father run his estate. She explained, "Henry and I are visiting the Manor more often in the future and perhaps you could show me some of the ropes?"

I only had one question and that was a very simple one. I asked if the Estate was self-supporting. Mrs Jackson thought for a while and said that it was but only just. She thought that it could be made very profitable but her Ladyship hated any change. The prospects of having a herd of deer on the rough land was a good idea. There were plenty of wild deer on Exmoor but there is a growing demand for venison.

After quite a chinwag, we left the Jackson's and made our way back into the open countryside. We found a comfortable spot and had our lunch. We then lay and sunbathed and had quite a snooze. This was understandable after the hectic time we had had the previous night.

When we got back to the Manor we were hot and dusty with our ride so we both had a bath and changed into clean clothing and went down the stairs to see if the old lady was about. Salter met us in the hall and said that Martin had something to show us on her Ladyship's instructions. He led us through the house until we came to the back, near to the stables. There was Martin, leaning against an open doorway and he seemed pleased to see us.

Martin looked at me and said, "Master Henry, you must be very privileged because no one except her Ladyship and members of the staff have been through these doors for more years than I can remember. It has been my job to look after what you will see and I have enjoyed every minute." Mary and I wondered what on earth was stored behind these doors. Going in out of the bright sunlight, everything seemed so dark and then Martin switched on the lights and what we saw took our breath away.

There were ten motor cars starting from the year dot and models which were more modern. In fact it was a study of the motor car from the very beginning to about twenty years ago. There were also two motor bikes, not so very old but of a world famous make. The cars and the bikes were in perfect order and shone like new pins. Martin stood there looking so proud of his charges. He then said something that shook me. "Master Henry, I had been told that you have to ride one of these bikes around the front of the Manor, so that her Ladyship can see you."

I picked the bike with the side-car and we wheeled it outside. Mary got in and it started at the first kick-start. It was very different to my old crock. There was so much more power. On the other hand I loved my old bike just like I loved my first horse, dear old Daisy.

We drove around the drives on the Estate and then we went to the front of the house. We could see the old lady looking out of her bedroom window and, even at that distance, I could see tears streaming down her face. Mary had also seen this. It made us wonder what memories this bike and side-car held to make her feel so sad.

We took the bike back to Martin and he told us that it was Sir William's favourite means of transport and he was riding it on the same day that he died of a heart attack. It had not been used properly since then. Martin added that he was only allowed to make sure that it was in working order.

When Mary and I walked back to the house, there was no sign of Aunt Sally. We could see that tea was set on the lawn so we sat down to await her arrival.

When she did appear there were no signs of tears or sadness. She asked many questions about our day around the Estate and asked if we liked what we saw. I told her how lucky she was to own such a beautiful place but that I thought a lot more could be made of it. I thought that introducing deer to the rough area was a good start. I paused and then I suggested that the river was a wasted asset and it should be cleaned out and dredged in some parts to put in a few trout for breeding.

Then I stopped talking and felt most embarrassed. I quickly said that I had no right to make such suggestions as it was none of my business. I was very sorry to have interfered in this way. Aunt Sally looked at me and said, "Don't be a silly boy. I would like you to help me in the future with these young ideas. You should get on well with Mrs Jackson because she is trying to get me out of my old-fashioned ways."

I looked at Mary and I could see that, like me, she was surprised at what we had just heard. I had another surprise coming. Aunt Sally put out her hand and took mine and said that she wanted me to have the other motor bike, which was more modern. "Mary tells me that you have a very old bike and you will need transport when you go to university. You can also bring Mary up to see me from time to time."

I told her that I couldn't accept such a handsome gift. Her manner changed and she turned to Mary and said, "My dear, do talk some sense into this young man, otherwise I will get cross." Mary told me that it was no good arguing with her grandmother because once she had made up her mind, that was the end of it. I picked up the old lady's hand and gave it a kiss and thanked her for being so kind. She took my hand and said, "Henry, I think that we will be great friends." She looked at Mary and said, "If I was younger you, young lady, wouldn't stand a chance." At that remark we all had a good laugh.

When we finished our tea the three of us walked around the walled garden. This was quite a place. There were greenhouses with peaches and grapes hanging and waiting to be picked. Aunt Sally picked Mary and I a peach each and she said that she would get the gardener to pick some for me to take home to my mother and father.

It was a grand sight to see the rows of vegetables growing, without a weed in sight. There were apples beginning to ripen. What a harvest there would be in the autumn. I wondered what became of all this produce and dare I ask the old lady? Anyway, I did and was told that a firm from Exeter purchased any produce that was surplus to the Estate's requirements.

Our routine that evening was the same as the others we had enjoyed during our stay. We sat with Aunt Sally on the patio and talked about our visit to Germany. I explained the many problems that could arise if the Baron found out that his wife was leaving him. It was a help that Aunt Geraldine had kept her British nationality because that would give her some protection.

Aunt Sally told us that the question of her nationality had tipped the scales. As her husband was a member of the Nazi party, his wife would have to become a German and forgo her dual nationality. She had been unhappy for a long time and felt very home-sick. "Mind you, she will soon be bored with life in these parts," the old lady continued, as if she was thinking aloud. "She seems to have plenty of money, perhaps she had a large allowance from her husband. On the other hand, when William's sister died, she left some money to Geraldine and I never did quite know how much the legacy was worth. Anyway, with a bit of luck, Henry, you will be able to rescue her."

After a while and a few glasses of wine, Aunt Sally got up to go up to her room. All of a sudden she looked very sad. She said, "My dears, I will miss these talks we have had. Tomorrow you will be on your way home. Please come up and visit me soon, because you have no idea how I have enjoyed your company. It seems to have put new life into me." She then gave Mary a big hug and kissed me on the cheek and made her way into the house.

When we were left on our own we both agreed that we had become very fond of the old lady and how very much we had enjoyed our few days in North Devon. We told Salter that we were going to bed and we walked up the large staircase for the last time.

I have no idea why we both felt at peace with the world and when we were in bed together our lovemaking seemed even better than it had been before. Mary was fast asleep and I lay there, looking at the moonbeams coming in through the window and I wondered who else had been in this room over the many years of its existence. Were there happy or sad spirits lurking in the dark corners? How can I be sure that fate has arranged for me to have dear Mary for my partner or it is to be someone else? With these sombre thoughts, I went to sleep.

After our breakfast we were getting ready to leave when Aunt Sally told Mary that she wanted to have a few words with her in private so I had to push off for a short spell. After a while we said our goodbyes and were driving down the long drive to the road to South Devon. Looking back we could see Aunt Sally, a forlorn, lonely figure standing on the spacious steps in front of Wimble Manor.

I thought that I would have to ask Mary what the private talk was about but this was not necessary. She told me that her grandmother had given her quite a lot of money to cover what we would need to enjoy ourselves in Germany. She also told me that we would be staying two nights in Hugh's house in London when we came back. This was news to both of us and good news at that. We knew that we would enjoy a day in London. No doubt we would be able to see Bernie and Ruth; that was, indeed, a light on the horizon.

It was a very pleasant drive back, we were quiet with our thoughts. I think that Mary was a bit tired, after all we didn't get much sleep during the last night at the Manor She had rested her head on my shoulder and, in no time, she was fast asleep.

Mary came to in time to tell Wills that we would go to the Hall as Master Henry would be staying to lunch. This was the first that I had heard of these arrangements but there was no point in not agreeing because it would suit me down to the ground.

We drove up to the grand entrance to Langley Hall and Aunt Pamela came out of the front door to greet us. We were both greeted as if we had been away for ages and, taking us both by the arm, we were led into the Hall.

The first question Aunt Pamela asked was "What have you both done to the old lady? She has been on the phone several times and at last she seems to be civilised and happy. She thinks that you two are the cat's whiskers."

Mary said that we had enjoyed our visit and we were going to see her more often because we both thought that she was a dear old thing who is so very lonely. Mary said, "It really is a lovely Estate and Henry and I have fallen in love with the place. So, Mama, when we come back from Germany, we will be leaving you again for a few days."

This news seemed to please Aunt Pam. She squeezed both of our arms and we went into the sitting room. Of course Mary had to tell her mother what we did and what her mother-in-law had talked about. Mary kept quiet about some of the things that we had heard, as instructed by her grandmother. Then Sir James came in and poor Mary had to start all over again for his benefit. We talked all through lunch, which was a bit difficult in between mouthfuls of Cook's smashing food.

After lunch I told Mary that I really had to go back to the farm to see my parents and asked if Wills could take me home. Mary said that she didn't want me to go but she knew that I had to.

As I was getting into the car she whispered into my ear, "Henry darling, I will be thinking of you when I am in bed tonight and wishing that you were with me." She closed the door and said that she would ride over to the farm the next morning at the crack of dawn so I was to get up early. I waved to the Howes, who were standing by the front door and soon I was well on my way to Long Meadow Farm.

It was smashing to see my family again. I know that it was only a few days that I had been away but it seemed ages. Mum and Dad were amazed when I told them about my two smashing presents. Mother looked at Dad in an old-fashioned way and asked him if I should accept them. Dad's reply was as expected – "why ever not? The old lady must like our young Henry," he said.

It took ages to answer all of their questions and it seemed that I had been talking non-stop until I went up into my lonely bed.

It was Sunday the 10th of August and I had not seen Mary all day. She was busy packing ready for our trip to Germany the following morning. It had been a very enjoyable week. Mary and I had been to Teignmouth for a swim in the sea. My bike had behaved very well indeed. I had visited Jake for the new camera and instructions from the Major. These were not as simple as they seemed but anyway I will worry about them tomorrow.

Bernie had asked me that if I went to Germany again, would I do something for his father? Of course I had no option, so I rang the old boy and asked him what he wanted me to do.

These instructions had to be carried out to the letter. I had to visit a certain bank in Lubeck, show my passport and collect an envelope. I then had to conceal it in my luggage and take it out of the country. It all sounded a bit fishy to me, but he did assure me that I would not be breaking any laws in this country.

I was thinking about these problems and having a nice daydream, sitting down by the Little Bridge and listening to the background music of the water gurgling on its way down to the River Teign. Mrs Jenkins' cottage looked so peaceful in the distance and this brought back such memories. What a dear friend she has been to me and how sad she must feel at the loss of her family in Germany.

I then remembered Polly. We no longer wrote to each other. It was difficult to know what to write about because my life seemed to be so tied up with Mary and her family. I still thought about her with her lovely blond hair and her sense of humour and most of all, her friendship in those early school days.

It was very strange how one's mind can sometimes play tricks on the way your thoughts go. Here am I having had a very loving relationship with Mary for the past few days and I am thinking of Polly. In an ideal world I would always like to be with Mary but I would like to see Polly as a friend. This, of course, is impossible because of our nature. She could never be just a friend and I could not be unfaithful to Mary. How sex complicates the course of life.

I suddenly realised that I was not looking forward to my trip to Germany. The more I saw of big towns, the more I loved the country. I also thought that I would have to be careful carrying out the two tasks set by Major Davis. I knew that one would be very difficult and he did not expect any results.

Sometimes I wish that I had never seen the Major. He seems to be running my life. I had to learn French with the help of Celeste. He wants me to learn all about communications and radio at the University when I go in September. I have to somehow try to get into the Luftwaffe base that we saw in the distance because they are testing a strange sort of aircraft that is without a pilot. I have an idea about this but I will need the help of Mary. Anyway, I will worry about this when we get to Germany.

Micky was having one of his many snoozes, stretched out in the sun. He opened, at first, one eye and then like a shot he was on his feet, looking towards the lane from the village.

Micky started to wag his tail so I knew that it had to be someone we both were familiar with. It was, of course, Mary. She always knew where to find me and I was so pleased to see her. The way she greeted me told me that she felt the same.

She told me that she had telephoned the farm and Mother told her that I had gone for a ride, so she decided to look for me in my favourite place. Mary and I just sat there for ages, just talking and being happy to be together. She had persuaded her parents to let her go to a college in London to study how to be a secretary, so that she could help her father and, for that matter, her grandmother.

I said that perhaps I could come and visit her when she was in London and stay at Hugh's place. He had given me permission to do so whenever I wanted to. This was good news for me because the thought of Mary going to a posh Finishing School was a danger signal.

Eventually we made a move and I rode part of the way back to the Hall. I didn't want to go all the way otherwise I would be asked to stay and I wanted to be with my family on the night before I set sail for enemy territory across the water.

Our journey to Germany was really a repeat performance of our first visit. I had more to do and organise but, overall, it was a very pleasant trip and indeed very comfortable. The family had taken my idea seriously and there were empty bags with disposable items such as sand bags so that we could bring home Aunt Geraldine's clothing and personal items without the staff knowing and, I hope, keeping the Baron off our tail.

I made a note of the large number of troops that were evident on most of the stations we passed through. We did not see the pleasant S.S. Officer on the train that we met on our last visit. We had our papers inspected many times during our journey, in a very arrogant sort of way. Some of them spoke in very poor English so I answered them in near perfect German. This made them change their attitude completely.

When we came to our journey's end we were met by Aunt Geraldine and in no time we were on our way to the Castle. It was not a very happy drive. The two grown-ups were deep in conversation and Mary and I felt a bit apprehensive. This was a duty and not a holiday as before but we did hope to enjoy part of our stay in the bleak Castle.

Aunt Geraldine had lost weight and looked quite poorly. I thought that a bit of North Devonshire air would soon put her back on her feet. We would have to try and cheer her up a bit. As long as the old Baron stayed in Berlin we would be all right. We got a good laugh out of Aunt Geraldine when we told her about my idea for her luggage and the sand bags.

When we arrived at the Castle, we had to go through the palaver of being introduced to the staff. Mary and I were then taken up the stairs and shown into the same rooms that we had before. This time, however, we were the only people sleeping in bedrooms on this landing and we had the luxury of a bathroom each.

Mary came into my room and gave me a very loving kiss and said, "Well Henry, we will be able to enjoy the nights, even if the days may seem a bit tense." I playfully smacked her cute little bottom and told her to behave herself.

After dinner, when the servants had all left the room, Aunt Geraldine let her hair down and told us a few disturbing facts about the iron rule of the Nazi government. Families were being spied upon by their young children who were members of the Hitler Youth Movement, having been brain-washed to such an extent that they would report them if they said, or did anything against the government. There were Gestapo agents everywhere and the trouble was that no one really knew who was who. She said that she was certain that one of the staff, probably one of the footmen, would be a minor agent, especially as William was an active member of the party, "So do be careful what you say," she told us.

People that dared to criticise Hitler or the Party would just disappear into a labour camp, never to be seen again. On the other hand, Hitler was a God-send to the majority of the German people because he gave them back their pride, gave them work and greatly improved their living standards. They had suffered greatly in the depression and their money became worthless. Hitler had put them to work building roads and arming at an incredible speed and getting ready for a war, that the experts had said could never happen again. Dictators have to be always in the nation's eye and in the news, so Hitler will have to expand his area of influence and try to get back parts of the old Germany that was in being before the war.

Aunt Geraldine said that her husband, the Baron, was fanatical about this and she could not stand it any longer. She no longer loved him and all she wanted was to get back to the English way of life, while it lasted.

Mary told her aunt that Grandmother was looking forward to seeing her and how the old lady had enjoyed having us both to stay. "We are both going up to Wimble in a week or two, so we will see you as well," Mary told her.

I asked Aunt Geraldine if we could have two horses for the day tomorrow. She laughed and said that Kurt, the head groom had a horse called Englander all ready for me. Cook would give us a lunch to take with us so we should have a pleasant day.

After a lovely night together, I eventually went to my own room and managed to snatch a bit of sleep. When I woke up it was bright and the sun was well and truly up. The prospects for our day looked very promising. I put on my dressing gown and went to see if Mary was in the land of the living. I crept into her room and there she was, fast asleep. I stood and looked down on this beautiful creature, with her hair spread out on the pillow and such an innocent expression on her face. It was difficult to realise that we had been together so passionately just a few hours ago. Seeing her curled up in her bed made me want to join her yet again, but I knew that it would be too dangerous. I just gave her a light kiss to wake her up and then I went back to my room before she had the chance to tempt me.

We joined the two grown-ups for breakfast, which, of course, was of the continental type and I had a hearty meal. I had grown to like these breakfasts when I was here before.

We got our gear together and walked around to the stable yard. There was Kurt, grinning from ear to ear as he came to greet us. He was a strange looking little man and, at times, he looked like a gnome. He had been so friendly during our last visit, once we had broken the ice and one could tell that he was glad to see us again.

He told us that he had the Englander all ready and the same horse that the young lady had before. I spoke a few words to my horse in English and it was so funny to see how his ears came up and he seemed to be pleased to hear his native tongue. When I gave him a sugar lump he crunched it up and then put his magnificent head back and neighed. This, of course, made Kurt and his staff have a good laugh.

Our lunch was already in our saddle bags, so we loaded up our gear and we were on our way. Kurt ran after us and, in a furtive sort of way, he warned us not to go into the forest as there were a lot of patrols about with some very nasty dogs. "There is something going on in the forest but no one knows. Please remember that I have not mentioned anything of this to you," he said.

I had brought my map with me and I was able to find the part of the River Schwartau which held such happy memories from our last visit. We rode as close to the river back as we could until we came to the small inlet where we could swim.

We had been riding for the best part of an hour and by now the sun was very warm and the thought of a cool swim made us hurry along. When we came to the inlet, the memory if its beauty came back to me. Somehow the area seemed even more secluded and the trees and bushes were now closer to the water. How inviting it looked as we got off our horses. I gave them a drink and made them fast, in the shade.

I went to put on my trunks and found that Mary was already in the water and her costume was on the river bank, so I just stripped off and joined her. We were soon in each other's arms and she lay down in a very shallow part and, with one of her wicked little laughs, she pulled me down on top of her and we made love in the River Schwartau, which was, indeed, a wonderful experience and very difficult to explain.

We dried ourselves and each other, which caused a great deal of laughter and we put on our swimwear in case any army patrols came our way. We lay in the sun and, with Mary's head on my chest, we both went to sleep.

I was awaked by the horses, which were restless. I could hear men's voices in the distance but coming closer, so I awakened Mary and we made ourselves look respectable. I went to keep the horses quiet and brought our lunch back, plus a bottle of wine which I put in the river to keep cool.

Eventually a young officer and six soldiers came into view. By now Mary and I were having a glass of cool wine. I greeted the officer in my best German and said that if he had a cup in his field pack he was welcome to join us for some cool wine. He sat down and I told him who we were and that we were the guests of Baron Von Brecht and we were staying at the Castle.

When the officer first came into view he looked bad-tempered and very officious but now he was friendly. His men were cooling themselves by the river and were glad of a rest.

I thought to myself that here was a chance to get to know an officer, low in rank but one never knows what may come of this encounter. I tested him to see if he understood any English by calling him a stupid twit. He showed no reaction so I could talk to Mary with safety. I asked her to bare with me for a bit and to smile most sweetly every now and again.

I asked this officer whatever he was doing on a hot day patrolling this area. He laughed and said that he was not quite sure himself, except that he had to inspect everyone's papers found in the area. With a smile he asked if he could see our passports. I got them from my saddle bag and he wrote down our names and where we were staying.

He got up to go and I said, "Perhaps it would be a good idea to tell your commanding officer about meeting us. The Baron is Mary's uncle and I believe that he is a member of the Party and is, at present in Berlin on Party business. We will be riding a lot in this area for the next week or so and we will keep out of the way of your patrols." With a laugh, I added "But we will not be keeping out of your lovely river."

We shook hands and, with a friendly wave, he was on his way with his very fed up patrol. Mary gave me quite a punch and said, "What was all that about and why were you so friendly?" I gave her a kiss and said that it was all part of a plan. I went on to tell her that I had two jobs to do whilst I was there and would need her help. "I have to try and get into an air base we saw in the distance when were last here and I have to collect a letter from a bank for Bernie's father. What I want you to do is to pretend to feel ill so that they will let us into this air base for treatment for sun-stroke, so this we will have to practice over the next few days. I will then know what sort of an actress you are."

We were both sitting down having finished our lunch and all of a sudden Mary jumped on top of me and told me how she loved me and how proud she was of how I thought things out. She said that of course she would help me to fool the Germans, "But Henry, my darling, you have got to make love to me again before we leave this heavenly place," she told me.

We got back to the Castle in the late afternoon to find the two aunts having tea on the lawn. We had a quick wash and joined them and of course we had to tell them where we had been all day. I said that we had had several swims and then I explained the meeting with the army patrol and how friendly the young officer had been. Mary butted in to say that I had given him a mug of wine which put him in a good mood, also the fact that we were guests at the home of Graf Brecht seemed to work wonders.

Aunt Geraldine said that something was going on deep in the forest which had to remain a secret, so the patrols were keeping everyone away. She told us "When we get to England, that is if we do, I will tell you what I think is being built there."

We sat and talked for quite a while and the conversation turned to our plans for leaving Germany. By now I had it all worked out to the last detail. It was very simple, so I tried to explain it.

During dinner, or when there were several staff members present, Aunt Geraldine would tell us that she was going to take German Nationality, as her husband wanted her to and to really please him she was going to have her hair changed into a Germanic blond colour. As this will be a long job she must let it be know that it will be done on the day that we leave.

276

She would come with us to the station and then send the car back to the Castle with the instructions to collect her from her hairdressers later in the day. In fact, much later, so that we will, by then, be over the border into Holland.

I seemed to have been talking for a long time but I could see that my plan was very acceptable. There was one further safeguard and that involved Aunt Pamela. She must go to the station and tell them that she had lost her return ticket to England and she would have to buy another one. This, of course, she would pass on to her sister-in-law.

It was also essential for Aunt Geraldine to leave instructions about what food she wanted the cook to provide for the evening meal on that day and also to make plans with the staff for future events.

By now I was feeling a bit embarrassed because the three females were looking at me in amazement when they heard that everything was organised. I told them that Sir James had asked me to get his sister out of Germany and I was just trying to do that. Aunt Geraldine turned to Mary and said, "Wherever did you find this boyfriend of yours?" Mary took my hand and said, "We found each other didn't we, darling Henry." We all had a good laugh and I blushed like hell.

Mary said to her aunt that we would like to spend the following day in Lubeck. She explained, "Grandmother gave us some money so we are going to have a boat trip and lunch out." Her aunt said that she and Pamela were going into town so we could have a lift with them.

The next morning, after we had our breakfast, we set off for the drive into Lubeck. It was quite an interesting drive because the autobahn was finished and it was a sight to see such a fine road going as straight as an arrow across the flat meadow-land. Needless to say I managed to get a photograph of this engineering feat. I wondered what had happened to some of the people that had built it. Since my last visit I had learned that political prisoners and not Jews were used as labourers for some of these projects. Many died because of the harsh treatment and the life expectancy was very low.

Mary and I left the aunts at the Berlin Hotel and if we wanted to have lunch with them we were to meet them at 12.30. If, on the other hand we wanted to have lunch elsewhere, the car would be going back to the Castle at four o'clock.

My first job was to find the bank that held the letter that I had to collect for Mr. Bernstein. It was in Fleischhauer Strasse and I had no idea where that may be, so we had a taxi, which was extravagant but it was the easy way out.

When we got to the bank, I went in and, feeling a bit scared, I said that my name was Henry Blake and that I had an envelope to collect. I had to show my passport and the Clerk was away quite some time, which made me feel even more nervous. Then Mary came in, looking very attractive. This somehow made my presence look more normal and it made me less nervous. At last the Clerk returned and I had to sign for a small envelope. I put it in my pocket and we slowly walked out.

I had no idea what was in the envelope and why it could not be sent through the post. Anyway, I had to help Mr Bernstein so perhaps one day he may tell me what I was to smuggle out of Germany for him. Mary thought that it was all a bit exciting but I told her not to say a word to her mother or her aunt.

It was a grand feeling to be walking down the quaint German streets with my lovely Mary, who always wanted to hold my hand or link arms when we were walking together.

The memories of my first visit to Lubeck were soon brought back to my mind and it really is a most attractive town. I would like to spend more time in exploring its small side streets but time is not on our side. I have a job to do for the Major so let us get that chore done.

We made our way towards the canal and after a time we found a boat that was offering trips out into the estuary. We went aboard and, as luck would have it, there were very few passengers so we were able to more around quite freely.

I had told Mary what I wanted to do and we started to go through the motions that would disguise the fact that I would be taking photographs of the submarine base. She posed by the side of the boat, sometimes fooling around and I took snaps of her. We did this several times and what we were doing was noticed by the skipper.

It took quite some time to reach the area that I was interested in so Mary and I sat in the sun and enjoyed the views and the unique situation of this lovely town of Lubeck. It was completely surrounded by water and it was difficult to tell if it was a man-made situation or whether it was nature's handiwork. Perhaps it was a bit of each.

As we chugged along towards the estuary I had one of my horrible mental trips into the future. Here I was taking photographs of a U boat base on the assumption that there would a war with Germany. If this were to be the case, this lovely area would be bombed by our aircraft and the fine old buildings, which have stood for generations, could be destroyed in only a few minutes.

I talked to Mary about this and her reply helped to put things in their right perspective. She said, "If the Germans start a war and their U boats kill our sailors, what is the value of a few old buildings in comparison." She took my arm and told me not to be so serious and to stop worrying about the future.

By now we were getting close to where I had seen the base being built two years ago. What I saw gave me quite a shock. It was difficult

278

to see clearly what had been built, but it extended over a much larger area and it was painted to camouflage the buildings and trees and bushes had been planted to hide its existence.

I now had to position Mary so that in the background the base would be visible. I told her to go to the opposite side of the boat and to act the fool a bit, which I photographed. Then she went to stand on the other side, with the base behind her and I could then take several snaps of the base which would be in the distance; the Major's experts could blow up the negatives and no doubt get the information required.

We continued into the estuary and then turned back for the return trip to the town of Lubeck. On our way back I could have photographed the base again but I thought that this would be pushing my luck too far.

I had very little real experience with females and looking at Mary sitting there I wondered what was in her mind. Mentally we seemed as one and now we have passed the last barrier in our sexual relationship, which was not of a selfish nature. We never seem to fall out, we argue but in a constructive way. I only seem to be happy when I am with her. She must feel the same because she is always wanting to be with me. In fact sometimes she even comes to find me. Will this mutual feeling last the tests of time? One thing is certain, and that is that only the good Lord knows.

When we got back to the quay and were on dry land, we had a walk and tried to make up our minds what we were going to do about lunch. Mary solved the problem by saying that we would leave the aunts to have their lunch and we would treat ourselves to a lunch on our own.

We found a nice cafe and we had a most enjoyable lunch, sitting outside in the shade of a huge beech tree. We both felt complete in each other's company and we talked about all sorts of things and were able to confide in each other our fears that we may find someone we might get to love more than we did each other. Mary put her hand out and tweaked my ear and said that as far as she was concerned, no one else was going to get me so I should stop being a silly boy.

I said that my main worry is what may happen to her when she is in London. She might meet a very handsome chap in her own class who will sweep her off her feet. Mary was beginning to get quite cross and told me to stop this sort of talk so I changed the subject.

After lunch I suggested that we have a look at Kapitel Strasse, where the Jews used to live. We made our way there, taking in the signs on the way, which we found so very interesting. It was so different to our towns of a similar size. There were no very large shops and they looked as if they were owned by shop-keepers, specialising in so many skills. Some of the merchandise for sale was being made there and then in the actual shop.

I noticed that trades were grouped together in various streets so you would be able to chose what meat you would buy, after seeing what was on offer in the other two or three shops. I had an awful job dragging Mary away from the shops selling female gear. She seemed to like everything she saw and I had to go into one of the shops to see how she looked in a dress. I found this most embarrassing and I made a rule there and then to fight shy of this activity in future. I had no option because no one in the shop could speak English and I had to help out.

At last we came to Kapitel Strasse and it bore no resemblance to the street we saw two years ago. The properties had all been repaired and painted, gone were the Stars of David and the name Jude, painted on so many of the doors. Of course there was not a Jew in sight. They had, no doubt, been moved to a ghetto in the town or to camps in the middle of nowhere.

We didn't linger long. I took a couple of snaps for Mrs Jenkins and then we sat on the bank of one of the canals until it was time to meet the two aunts.

We didn't have long to wait outside of the Berlin Hotel before the aunts came out of the hotel and the car pulled up outside. Of course the aunts had been shopping which could be seen by the parcels they were carrying.

On the journey back to the Castle, Mary gave a detailed report of our activities. I let the females prattle on and I had one of my daydreams. I had been trying to work out a plan to get into the air base. The more I thought about it the more I realised that my first idea of using Mary as a sort of decoy would be the best. It was so simple that even if it failed, it could not cause any suspicion to fall on us.

The more I thought about it, it made me decide to have a go the following day. The weather looked settled as it was essential that it had to be a hot, sunny day, because Mary had to be overcome with the heat and the sun.

Jake had always told me during our many talks that one should always have an alternative plan but so far I have had no inspiration. Anyway I would have to play it by ear.

When we got back to the Castle, the aunts said that they were going to have a rest before dinner and Aunt Geraldine said that we should do likewise.

We went up to our rooms and I took off most of my clothes and had a cold wash. It wasn't until I stretched out on my bed that I realised how tired I felt and in no time I was fast asleep.

I was awakened by a hand that was feeling me all over and I opened my eyes to see this lovely sun-tanned body hovering over me. It was a most beautiful sight. Everything about Mary's body was in the correct proportions, in fact at times I would like to eat her. We both knew that her safe time was almost over and we would have to make love in our simple way. This would be very difficult after having the real thing but we were resolved and very firm in this decision.

Anyway, this time had not come so we made the most of it and our satisfaction was marvellous. We would have liked to stay there for the rest of the evening but we got up and had our baths and dressed for dinner.

We went down to dinner, hand in hand. We seemed to be doing this most of the time now. Our two families seemed to have accepted that we were very fond of each other and we were more than just friends.

After dinner we agreed that Aunt Pamela would telephone Sir James and get him to Thomas Cook to book seats etc., for the next Monday. Also to send the telegraph about Aunt Sally being very ill. In the next day or so Aunt Pamela must go to the station to get another ticket saying that she had lost hers. Aunt Geraldine must also make an appointment for her hair to be done next Monday morning, about an hour after the train leaves Lubeck.

I sat for a while thinking while the females talked over my plan. Somehow I had missed an important item in my plan and then it came to me. Aunt Geraldine must telephone the Castle as soon as we were out of Germany and tell the housekeeper that she was on her way to England with her sister-in-law. This was most important as the staff at the Castle may report their employer as being missing and that would put the police on the alert and the press might even pick it up. I could see the headlines, "English wife of Nazi Party Chief flees to Great Briton, with the help of titled sister-in-law."

I came out of my daydream and told the females about this final stage in my plan and, as luck would have it, we were all in favour. Also, it would be a good idea for Aunt Geraldine to pretend to give some of the clothes to her sister-in-law, in front of her maid. Then some of the cases could be packed. I undertook to get rid of the ballast from the empty luggage we brought with us for this purpose.

Mary and I told the aunts that we would like to have a packed lunch tomorrow as we would like to explore some more of the countryside. We then went out into the cool evening air and had a walk in the grounds. It was good to be alone with Mary once more. We sat down by the lake and I explained our plan of campaign for the next day.

My plan was quite simple. We would ride near to the base and Mary would feel ill. We would then ride up to the entrance and ask for a drink of water and perhaps some help; anyway time would tell.

We sat there until the light began to fade and it was fun to watch the bats flying low over the water to catch their supper. We walked slowly back to the Castle. It was such a warm evening that the two aunts were sitting outside, drinking some wine. We joined them and had our share of the smashing German wine, which was grown and made in the area.

We were up fairly early the next morning as we had a long ride in front of us. We had finished our breakfast before the aunts came into the breakfast room and Mary went upstairs to say goodbye to her mother.

We had to follow the River Schwartau down stream towards Lubeck then cross the river and head westward towards the open countryside. The idea would be to be in view as much as possible of anyone watching from the base. We would not go anywhere near the base until after a swim and our lunch.

At last we found a nice place to swim and have our lunch. Mary had to keep her hair dry so she very craftily tied her hair up. She did this and we both shed our clothes and had a swim. This temporary hair style suited her; it showed off the fine features of her face.

We lay on the grass and let the sun dry our bodies which by now we knew so well. We had decided to behave ourselves today but the temptation was too great. Both of us felt the need so we made love. It was pretty marvellous with the sun shining down on us and we had the music of the river rushing by to harmonise our complete satisfaction.

After we had our lunch we started our ride into the open country towards the base. There was a small hill that overlooked the plain, so we climbed this and made ourselves very visible. The sun was behind us and we could see the reflection on binoculars looking at us from the base.

I told Mary to start her act. First of all she had to slouch in the saddle, then to stop and start with me looking as if I was giving her comfort. We continued this act and, at the same time, getting closer to the base.

There were now several binoculars trained on us and I quickened my pace and we were now only two or three hundred yards from the front gate. This now swung open and a small car drove out towards us. So far so good. I could hear the roar of a machine of some sort coming from inside the base. Mary was making herself look most distressed and putting on a smashing act.

The car came up to us and there was an officer in the front and two soldiers with guns sitting in the back. Before he could say anything, I went in at the deep end and said that my girlfriend, who was the niece of Graf Brecht, had been taken ill, no doubt with a touch of the sun, so could she have a drink of cold water.

I had spoken in my best German and explained that we were staying at the Castle on holiday. Before I was asked for them I pulled out our passports and handed them to the officer. So far I had not let the officer say a word. I had taken Jake's advice by taking control of the situation by going on the offensive. What a wise old bird he is.

The officer was very pleasant and told us to come into the base and visit the sick bay. As we went through the gates we were met by the young officer we had met two days previously and had given him some of our wine. Perhaps the wine will pay some dividends.

He gave us a very friendly greeting and he was told by the officer in the car, who was senior in rank, to take the two of us to the sick bay. He ordered one of the soldiers to take the horses and tie them up in the shade.

After coming through the main entrance we came out onto a very large open area or square. There were troops being drilled in one corner and there seemed plenty of activity one would expect on a Luftwaffe air base.

The noise of the engine was by now very loud so I innocently asked the young lieutenant what was making this most unusual noise. I think that the question being asked in good German put him off his guard and made him forget that I was English, because without hesitating he said the engine was an experimental type without a propeller to be fitted to a small plane without a pilot. He laughed and said what a waste of time because the so-called experts could not made it work properly.

By now we had crossed the square and were taken into a first aid room where a service doctor examined Mary and confirmed that she had been in the sun for too long. He gave her what looked like Aspirin and several glasses of cold water and told her to sit quietly for a while.

The room that we were in overlooked the actual airfield. I could see what looked like a slope with railway lines on it. It pointed towards the sky and parked at one end was a strange looking object. To describe it as a cigar with short stubby wings would be as near as I could get to a description. Near the tail there was a sort of cylinder, raised above the main body and in line with it. I could see that the noise was in fact coming from this strange-looking thing.

The doctor said to the Lieutenant, "They are going to try to make that stupid thing fly in a moment or two so let us have a look." He looked at Mary and said, "Not you, young lady, you just sit and rest." We then heard a warning siren and everybody moved away from the front of the launching contraption.

The noise got louder and smoke and flames belched out of the rear of the cylinder. Then, all of a sudden, the thing became airborne. It shot up into the air, levelled out and flew parallel to the earth's surface right across to the other side of the airfield. The engine began to splutter and it crashed to the ground and blew up.

The two Germans thought it a great joke and said that it was a great improvement but the boffins were unable to get it to land and what a terrible waste of money it was. They both looked at me and said that it would help if I had not heard their last remarks. I quickly reassured them that my hearing wasn't too good and we all had a laugh.

I went over to Mary and asked her how she felt and asked if she felt well enough to make the ride back to the Castle. She now gave me a wink and said that she felt fine and that we ought to be going soon as otherwise her mother may get worried.

We both shook hands with the doctor and we accompanied the Lieutenant out into the square. I wanted to get out of this place as quickly as possible without it looking too obvious. So far we had been very lucky indeed to have actually seen the experiments that were going on in the base. I would have to keep the picture in my mind as I dare not put it on paper.

Our horses were brought out for us and, with a very friendly farewell, we were out of the base and on our way back to the Castle. I was so pleased to have achieved what the Major thought was impossible.

As soon as we were out of sight of the base, we got off our horses and I thanked Mary for helping me. I gave her a big hug and a kiss and said that it would have been impossible to have got anywhere near the base without her help. She put her arms around me and said that she would do anything she could to help me and thought that it was most exciting. I made her promise not to tell anyone why we made a visit to the base and what we actually saw.

We would tell the aunts that she felt ill and say how kind the doctor was and how fine she now felt.

We started our journey back to the Castle and I rode side by side with Mary so that we could talk. I told her that when we got to London I would have to see Mr Bernstein and Major Davis so I would have to leave her to go on these two errands.

Mary stopped her horse and very forcibly said, "Henry my dear. I will have none of that nonsense. We have been a team, working together to carry out these two chores. So where you go, I will go as well and if your Major chap doesn't like it he will have to lump it." I told her that she was getting just like her grandmother. She tried to hit me but I ducked and rode off with this smashing female in hot pursuit.

We had a great deal of fun on that ride back. I think that it was the reaction of our afternoon's work. The more I thought about it the more I realised how lucky we had been.

When we got back to the Castle we had a quick cup of tea with the aunts and then asked to be excused so that we could have a bath and a rest before dinner.

The events of the day were still on our minds so we behaved ourselves and dozed in our own rooms. I had to impregnate on my mind what I had seen at the base so that I would be able to explain it to the Major. While I was at the base I had heard some of the soldiers talking about what they thought was being built in the forest. They seemed to think that a concentration camp was being built by political prisoners because a railway siding had been laid down for some time. Anyway, Aunt Geraldine said that she would tell us when we were out of Germany.

Mary and I came down the staircase together, both looking smart. I thought how daft, on a hot evening, we had to dress up for dinner but it was the system and it is best not to buck the system. This is what a public school had taught me and, unfortunately, it is the best way to survive and get on in this unfair world.

I was having a bit of trouble with Mary. She kept showing her feelings for me in public and in front of the aunts. She seemed to be always holding my hand or my arm and she had a habit of putting her hand down the back of my trousers when she thought the coast was clear. Of course I couldn't say anything to the dear girl but at times it was a bit embarrassing because it got me sexually excited.

As we came down the stairs, Mary got up to her tricks, which caused a lot of laughter. I think that the rest and a bath had made her a bit frisky. Anyway, I managed to calm her down and we walked sedately into the dining room to meet the two aunts.

I let Mary tell the aunts what had happened during the day. She enjoyed telling tales, usually in a very dramatic way, so I let her get on with it. I watched and had a few laughs to myself because she used her hands to accentuate important points. I started to copy her movements behind her back which made her mother laugh and, when Mary saw what I was doing, she gave me a good punch and told me that she would get even with me later.

Aunt Geraldine told us that she had met several of the officers from the base and some of them were very pleasant fellows. Some however were fanatical in their Nazi beliefs and were a real pain in the neck. She said that we must have been lucky but that we should keep away from the area in future.

After dinner we all had several glasses of wine and when Mary and I went up the now familiar staircase, we both felt full of the joys of spring. In no time at all we were in bed together and enjoying each other to the full.

Mary was becoming more and more passionate which, of course, was infectious and I think that we were now so relaxed with each other that perhaps this was how it should be.

Eventually Mary went to sleep and I just lay there by her side. I just couldn't stop thinking about the day's events. The more I thought about what I had seen at the base, the more it puzzled me. I could understand the advantages of having an aircraft without a pilot, but how could it be steered when out of view from the ground? It would be like a torpedo in flight, which could be seen and shot down.

To launch, it would require fixed launching pads and bunkers to hide them in and a stationary target. How could the wind direction be compensated and they would be disposable? This, in itself, makes it a very costly project.

If these things could be designed to go a long distance and carry a heavy load of explosives, the distance could be worked out by the amount of fuel it would take to reach a given point. There would be logic in its design, otherwise it is only a German scientist's pipe dream. With these thoughts still in my brain, I snuggled up to my darling Mary and went into a fitful sleep.

I woke with a start, having had a sort of nightmare. I was in a large town, it was somewhere that I didn't know. In fact everything was strange but very real. I was walking down a street and there were other people about, when I heard this noise of an engine coming from the sky. Everybody stopped to listen, so I did likewise. The sound was the same as I had heard that afternoon at the base. It got louder and then, with a sort of cough, it stopped.

Everyone started to run like mad for the cover of the nearest shop or building, so I joined in. As I was about to go into a doorway I saw a flash and heard a terrific explosion and the far end of the street just disappeared. An unknown force pushed me into the doorway and I fell flat on my face. I then work up feeling very disturbed. I had to write this down because dreams have a habit of fading from one's memory. Somehow I knew that this information was important and there had to be a reason why I had this dream.

I had to get out of bed without waking Mary. Luckily, I was in my room and I found some paper and a pencil and, by the light of the early dawn, I wrote down an account of my dream.

The last few days seemed to have flown by. Tomorrow we start our journey home; all our plans have been put into operation. It had been a mental upheaval for Aunt Geraldine but she was playing her part very well.

Mary and I have had a smashing time. Wherever I went she was sure to follow. One evening she followed me into the bath. This was only because the aunts were in Lubeck but we had great fun. I have missed being by myself so that I can think about this and that. I had managed to slip off and sit down by the lake until Mary found me.

As I sat there in the late afternoon in August, I wondered if I would ever see this place again. In spite of its connections with Hitler and a future conflict, it was a lovely area and the Germans that I had met were very pleasant people. I had got to know some of the staff and Kurt, the head groom, was a real old friend. I gave him some of the foul tobacco which he smoked in his pipe.

There was, however, one of the footmen who I could not get on with. I found him in my room, which he was supposed to be cleaning. This was just an excuse, as it was not his job. This made me think that he was the resident Gestapo agent as suspected by Aunt Geraldine. What I had to hide, he would never find, so he was unlucky.

When I found him in my room I gave him a real ticking off in my very best German and told him that if I found him in my room again I would tell the Baron. This really upset the poor fellow and I would have no more trouble from him.

Sitting there by the lake and watching how nature played its part and how beautiful God had made some of the plants and creatures which we have to keep us company during our lifespan, I was glad that my Mary found me because I was getting into one of my morbid moods.

She was running across the freshly cut lawn and what a picture she made with the sun shining on her hair, which was dancing as she ran down to the lake. I stood up to greet her and she put her arms around my neck and kissed me, saying that she had looked everywhere for me. Then she said, "Dear Henry, please don't ever leave me." I was pretty strong so I picked her up and swung her around and told her that I never would leave such a lovely creature as Mary Howes, or should I have said the Honourable Mary Howes.

We sat down together on the bench by the lake and talked about our visit and how we had both enjoyed being together in more ways than one and we felt a little sad leaving this place. We had made a sort of little world of our own in an oasis in the centre of a hostile land.

I told Mary that this second visit had confirmed what Major Davis had said when I saw him last. Hitler was preparing for a war with someone and whoever it was, we would be drawn into the conflict. This was not the way to end a happy holiday but one had to be realistic in one's thinking.

Mary and I had become so involved with each other that I had to tell her how involved I had become with the Major and his Government Department. In the next two years I had to pass the exams at the University and well within that period I had to learn to fly with the RAF Reserve at Exeter. I had also got to improve my French and the only way to do that was to spend a while in France. Mary interrupted, saying "But not with Celeste?" I told her of course not. Anyway, there may be some French students at University.

This kept her quiet but I knew that at some time in the future, I would see Celeste again but I had no idea under what circumstances that would be.

Everything had gone to plan. We were on the train and we were settled in our compartment, having joined the train from Berlin to the Hook of Holland. Our passports and tickets had been well looked at by the guard and two men in grey suits, who always seemed to be present. They were, of course, members of the Gestapo. Perhaps they were always there to check on the guard as well as the passengers.

We had changed trains at Hanover and, as we waited for the train to come in from Berlin, I made a mental note of the large number of troops there were waiting on the platform for various trains and this I would mention to the Major.

Mary and I were talking but standing away from the aunts, when we heard the clicking of heels and a German voice say "Guten Morgen Fraulien." We both turned around to see the young Lieutenant that had taken us into the base and who we had shared our wine with. We had a bit of a shock but we were soon having a pleasant conversation with him. This was cut short because our train came in. I was very sorry that we were unable to carry on our friendly chat as I found him such a nice fellow. It also gave me a chance to practise my German.

We were now getting close to the German border, which was near Enschede, when the train came to a stop. I looked out of the window to see several men in grey suits get onto the train. They then started to check all of the many passengers.

When it was our turn, I spoke for the females. Before they had the chance to ask Aunt Geraldine why she was going to England, I explained that her mother, Grafin Howes, was very ill and I asked her to show the officer the telegram sent by Sir James, her brother.

I then put into practice an attitude when dealing with Germans. This Jake had told me, time and time again, was often a way to bluff one's way out of a situation that could be difficult. It was quite simple, one had to try to seem superior to the person giving trouble.

I started to complain that the train was being held up and we had to catch the ferry to England, so what was the problem. I asked "Are you looking for a criminal on the run or are you just being bloody-minded?" The German went a bit red in the face. He bowed to the females and left our compartment.

As the train was pulling out of the station I saw the Gestapo chap coming out of a telephone booth and running to catch the train. As luck would have it he was too late. I somehow knew that he thought it strange that the wife of a party member as important as Uncle Willy was on the train out of Germany without her name being on his list. It was a gamble I had taken and it had paid off. Five minutes later we were in Holland and Aunt Geraldine was on her way to a new life.

It was quite a bumpy crossing on the ferry but none of us was seasick. Nevertheless, we were all glad to see Parkstone Quay at Harwich. We got to London and, with the help of several porters, we went by taxis to Hugh's house in Bruton Place.

We were greeted by Hugh's butler, Harris, and he seemed so pleased to see us. It struck me how lonely it must be in that house with only staff living in it, and an occasional visitor must surely be the highlight for the place.

The housekeeper, Mrs Gibbs, showed us to our rooms. The aunts were on the first floor and Mary and I were on the next floor. We were given the same rooms as before and Mrs Gibbs said that Mr Hugh had left instructions that these two rooms were to be kept for his sister and his best friend, Mr Henry. Also we must make sure that we both felt at home whenever either of us went to stay there.

I had started to unpack my bag when the adjoining door opened and Mary came in looking at the large bed and said, "Henry, I will be in that bed tonight so look out my boy." She then said that she was going to find her mother to see what time dinner was being served. I replied that I wanted to telephone Bernie so that we could meet tomorrow. I would also like to telephone Mum and Dad to let them know I was back in England.

I had a quick bath, while Mary was out of the way, made myself look presentable and went down the magnificent staircase, marvelling at the craftsmanship of the mahogany woodwork. In fact, I stopped several times to study different parts of the work that had been carried out so many years ago.

I didn't know that I was being watched by Harris, the butler and, when I eventually got down to the hall, he met me and said that it was nice to see someone who appreciated real craftsmanship and lovely wood. We talked on this subject for some time and I discovered that he knew what he was talking about.

By now I found that I was sitting on the bottom step of the staircase and having a fine chat with Harris. I then asked him where I could use the phone. He told me to follow him and he took out his large bunch of keys and we went into Hugh's late uncle's office. Harris fished around in his pocket and gave me a key and told me to feel free to use this office whenever I needed to use a telephone.

I telephoned Bernie first of all and had a good chinwag with him. I told him that I had a letter to deliver to his dad. He told me to hang on while he went to see his dad. When he came back he said that Mary and I were to go out to lunch with him and Faith and he would pick us up about ten thirty.

I then rang Mum and Dad and it was grand to hear their voices again. All was well at the farm and they were looking forward to seeing me. Dad came on the phone and said that Jake had been to see him and asked him to tell me to ring Major Davis. He then gave me a number, which I wrote down. As I was talking, I could see that Mary had come in. She had one of her mischievous expressions on her face. Before I could stop her, she took the phone away from me and started to tell Dad what I had done to help them get Aunt Geraldine out of Germany. They talked for ages until I could get the phone away from Mary.

I said goodbye to Mum and Dad and then I collared Mary and tried to get out of her what she and Dad were talking about. All I could literally get out of her was that there was a pleasant surprise for me when I got home.

I then rang Major Davis and his wife answered the phone, asking who was calling. I said, "Tell the Major that it is the young man from Lubeck." When the Major came on the line, I told him that I had a lot of information for him but there was a problem. Without Mary's help, none of it would be available and she insisted that she came to meet him when I did. There was a lengthy pause and then he said that he would take us both out to dinner that night when we could have a nice chat. I explained that we had just come back from Germany and we did not have any dresswear. I then said, "Why don't you come here for dinner, which will be very peaceful?" Mary looked pleased at this second suggestion and, when the Major agreed, she came over and kissed me in my ear.

Neither of us wanted to dress up tonight and go out. For one thing it would be a bit of a bore spending the evening with the Major and we both wanted to go to bed, not necessarily to sleep.

When we told Aunt Pam, she said that we should have asked the Major's wife as she was an old friend of Geraldine's. I asked her if she would care to telephone and ask her, which she did from the phone in the hall. The answer from the Major was yes, so I asked Harris if Cook could provide two extra dinners at such short notice. Here again the answer was yes.

The Major and his wife arrived and we had a pleasant dinner. It was very relaxed and the Major was in good form. Harris, the butler, was very liberal with Hugh's wine which helped us to forget the long journey we had only just finished.

When we had finished the meal, the ladies left and just Mary, the Major and I remained. I tried to keep my report as brief as possible but, even so, it took a long time. Aunt Geraldine had confirmed that a concentration camp was being built in the forest as suspected and I gave him the film of the submarine base to be developed.

His eyes really lit up when I told him about the contraption they were testing at the Luftwaffe base. Mary then put in her spoke by saying that I had this wonderful idea of seeking help from the base because she felt ill. I then told the Major what a good little actress she had been and it was because of her that I managed to get into the base.

I fished in my pocket and brought out the drawing I had made of this aircraft without a propeller or a pilot. The Major became most excited and he seemed to be mentally jumping up and down with joy. I then added fuel to the fire and told him about my dream. He asked when we were going back to Devon because he would like me to meet some of his colleagues. I looked at Mary and she said that we were free on Thursday. I added that any meetings on this information must include Mary. He gave me an old-fashioned look, but agreed.

He asked me if he could use our telephone so I took him into the office and left him to it. When he came out he was all smiles and said that a car would pick Mary and I up at ten o'clock on Thursday morning, to take us to the War Office.

He became very serious and said that I would have no idea how important my discovery was but on Thursday I should be prepared to be cross-examined very closely by some high ranking officers. "Will you pass this on to your most beautiful girlfriend. Henry you are a very lucky chap. Look after her well," he said. He laughed and told me to keep my trousers on when I met Celeste again, or someone like her in Normandy. I tried to get out of him what he meant about Normandy but he just laughed and joined the ladies.

Mary joined me in the hall and took my arm and whispered in my ear that she was so proud of me. She thanked me for insisting on having her included in this visit to the War Office.

The next morning we were picked up by Bernie and Faith. It was good to see my old friend and his girlfriend Faith, who had grown into a very lovely girl. She was very dark and there was no mistaking her nationality.

When we met Bernie in London he was always full of instructions from his mother or father. His first order to the driver of a very smashing car, was to take us to his father's bank. His old man wanted to see me forthwith, so this was our first stop.

Bernie took me into the bank and through the same bustling crowd of workers, until we reached the peace of Mr Bernstein's outer office. We were shown in and there he was, looking just the same, behind his huge desk. He shook my hand most warmly and told Bernie to wait in the outer office.

He told me to sit down and I put my hand into my inner pocket and handed him the small envelope. He picked up a very ornate paper-knife and slit it open. He looked at the contents and a smile of satisfaction came over his face. He said, "Thank you Henry. One day I will be able to tell you what was in that small envelope and you will know how important it is for me."

Mr Bernstein took out a bunch of keys from his pocket and unlocked a drawer in his desk. He took out an envelope and gave it to me. The old boy said In his quaint accent, "Henry, here is something for you. Buy Mary a nice present and treat yourself. Believe me, you have earned it." I tried to refuse this gift by telling him that his previous gift of Henry, my horse, would leave me in his debt for ever. Anyway, I had to accept it and he wished me luck and I started to leave the room.

As I reached the door, he called me back and told me that his committee had been unable to confirm that Joseph, the Jew, was a genuine refugee. In fact they had completely lost track of him. If he should try to get in touch with Hugh or I, would I please let him know. This made me think as I met Bernie in the outer office. I would tell Jake and he could pass this on to the Major.

When we were in the car, I told Mary about Mr Bernstein's gift and she made me open the envelope. Much to our surprise there were two crisp five pound notes, which to me seemed like a fortune. Even Bernie was surprised at his father's generosity and said that I must have pleased the old boy because we were to go out to lunch at his expense and there were very strict instructions that I must not pay for anything that day.

We really had a smashing day. The four of us got on so well together and, as we all had a good sense of humour, we had a lot of fun. Unfortunately our day was over and Bernie seemed quite sad that he would not see me at college, so I told him that I would be in touch and he would be able to come up to the farm for some of Mother's Sunday lunches.

When we went into the house in Bruton Place, it all seemed very quiet. We saw Harris and he told us that the two ladies were out shopping. I told him that we were tired and that we were going to have a rest before dinner. We both went up the staircase to our separate rooms.

It had been a warm day and I just lay on my bed in my underpants and I was almost in another world when my peace was shattered by the arrival of a beautiful girl with dark brown hair, brown eyes, a more than friendly smile and nothing on. A lot of her skin was a golden colour with sunburn and it looked strange to see the pale parts not touched by the sun.

I am glad to say that we no longer rushed at each other for our sex. We both like to savour the pleasure it gave us both and we got great pleasure in building up to the event.

We made love in our simple way which, of course, was not as satisfying as the real thing but the closeness of each other and being able to explore each other's bodies, made it all a wonderful experience. I am sure that we both love each other because there never seemed to be any self-gratification in our lovemaking.

Eventually we had our baths, dressed and went down to dinner. We all seemed to be tired that evening. Perhaps it was the reaction of our exit from Germany. Anyway, we had an early night. Mary and I kept to our own rooms for a change and we both had a full night's sleep.

The next morning at 10 o'clock sharp, a car drew up outside the house and a young Captain came to the door. Harris showed him into the hall just as Mary and I were coming down the staircase. When he saw Mary, he beamed and I detected a hungry look in his eyes. I thought to myself that this is going to be the trouble in the future. Mary did look ravishing, perhaps I would feel safe if she was not so attractive.

When we got to the War Office we were led into this magnificent building by the Captain and, after quite a walk up the stairs and along corridors, we were ushered into a room and told to make ourselves comfortable.

By now Mary and I were feeling apprehensive. This was likely to be quite an ordeal. After a while, Major Davis came in and, after asking us how we both were, he led us along a corridor and finally we were ushered into a room to be confronted by an array of top-brass officers from all three services, sitting on one side of a long table. There were three chairs facing them and the chairman of this meeting got up and thanked us for coming, asking us to sit down.

The Major introduced us and this included Mary's title. He gave a brief résumé of our adventure. He now referred to us by our Christian names, which made things less formal. He mentioned my visit to Lubeck two years earlier and how useful the information had proved to be.

The Major went on to say that we would have the photographs of the U boat base very shortly. He then turned to Mary and I and said that there were a lot of questions to be asked about the flying bomb, which was a new name for what I had seen.

While the Major had been talking, I had been able to have a good look at the people in the room. There were five service personnel, two male civilians, who looked very studious types and, on a separate table, sat a female taking notes and what looked like a Civil Servant.

I was questioned for about an hour and, with Mary's help, we were able, between us, to clarify some of the questions. Then, much to my surprise, one of the civilians started to talk to me in German. Without thinking I answered in German, as an automatic reaction. I was just getting over this change of events when I had a question asked in French. I answered in French and began to wonder what was going on.

The civilian had a broad grin on his face and said, "Well done Henry. You have a well-bred German accent but your French is very much from Normandy or the northern part of France. I must congratulate you on your quick reactions."

By now, Mary and I were getting a bit fed up with this long meeting, when there was a knock on the door and a messenger came in with my photographs. They caused a break because they were very funny in parts with Mary's actions.

We were asked a few other questions and then the chairman thanked us for our help and he then told us that they had been trying to find out exactly what was going on in Lubeck. Now, thanks to us, we now knew. He hoped we would join them for coffee and, as if by magic, the door opened and in came two waiters with lovely smelling hot coffee.

Everyone got up and started to stretch their legs. I was collared by the civilian who tried to catch me out with my two languages. He congratulated me on the way that I had reacted and he told me that I spoke like a German, but my French needed more practice.

He seemed a very nice fellow and we talked for some time, of course, in German.

I could see that Mary was deep in conversation with some of the top brass. I didn't blame them for having a chat with such a lovely girl. I expect it made them feel young again or made them wish that they were young again.

Major Davis came over to me with one of the Army Officers and introduced him as Brigadier Eastham and explained that he was his Commanding Officer. The Brig, as he would always be referred to, shook my hand and said that Davis gave him good reports on my activities and that I might be able to serve my country in one way or another, if the balloon went up. He said, "You have been over there and it looks very bad indeed." He thanked me again and wandered off. I was to learn in the future that he was always like that. He seemed to be in another world but what a brilliant mind he had. He always seemed to be one step ahead of everyone else.

When we had finished our coffee, Major Davis came up to us and said that he would show us to the car. The chairman came over and shook our hands and thanked us, once more, for what we had done and for giving up our time to come to the meeting. The Major escorted us to the car and told the driver to take us wherever we wanted to go and, with a friendly wave, he went back into the building.

On the way back to the house, we both admitted that we felt a bit drained after such a lengthy interrogation and, to cheer Mary up, I suggested that we asked to be dropped off in Oxford Street and I could buy her a present, as instructed by Mr Bernstein.

I thought that this could be a long job but madam knew exactly what she wanted. I gave her five pounds, which was her share and left her to it. I was very surprised what she managed to buy in such a short time.

We found a nice place to have lunch and then we ambled up Oxford Street past Marble Arch and into Hyde Park where we sat and enjoyed the afternoon sunshine.

We sat and talked for ages and watched the couples walking by. I explained to Mary that I could never understand what drew different boys and girls together. In some cases one of the pairs would be quite plain or ugly, very fat or very thin but they looked very much in love with each other. Could it be that their minds were on the same wave-length and that they were friends with the same interests, or could it be that the chemistry in their bodies formed a natural attraction for each other? This has to be yet another of nature's mysteries.

I had just finished holding forth when a young man, who was very short and fat, passed by with his arms around a very tall good-looking girl. Mary and I looked at each other and burst out laughing, because here was an example of what I had just been trying to explain.

Mary took my hand and said that she had fallen in love with a handsome young man. I replied that my girlfriends had all been smashers. She gave me a punch and said, "Henry don't you dare start thinking about Polly." I said that I was only pulling her leg and there was no need to ask who I loved.

Eventually we made our way back to Bruton Place, which was not a great distance from the part of Hyde Park that we had been sitting in.

We met Harris in the hall and asked him if he we could have some tea in the sitting room. Be both sank into the comfortable chairs and, in no time, in came a tray with tea and cream cakes. The two aunts were out somewhere and we were on our own.

After we had finished our tea we went up to our rooms and I had to see some of Mary's purchases and see how she looked in yet another dress. She then called me into her room and there she was laying on her bed with nothing on and the sight was most inviting. We made love and had a snooze before getting ready for dinner.

We both knew that our lovemaking would be very restricted for a week or two as we were going back to Devon tomorrow. We would make the most of our last night together so I hope that the aunts go to bed early tonight.

The next morning we caught the train from Paddington which went straight through to Newton Abbot. I was not sorry to be going back to peaceful Devon. I think that we all felt the same because our moods were most cheerful. It was a pleasant sight to see Sir James and Wills waiting for us on the platform.

We managed to get into the large car, which Sir James drove and the luggage was crammed into the smaller car driven by Wills. On the drive home Sir James gave us a running commentary on what had been going on in our absence.

His mother, old lady Howes had made a flying visit, which was unannounced and she had been lucky to find him in. She wanted to know all about the purchase and how to look after deer, which she was going to introduce to her Estate.

He went on to say that he had no idea why she had changed so much in such a short time. It was something to do with Henry and Mary. "She is more like the mother I knew when I was younger. She even visited your farm Henry as she wanted to see your father. She also would like the two of you to visit her for a few days before your holidays are over."

I looked at Mary and we both said that we had told her that we would like to visit her at the end of the summer. We had both enjoyed our stay with her and we had fallen in love with Wimble Manor and the countryside.

We went direct to the Hall and, much to Mary's disgust, I said that I had to go back to the farm as soon as possible because I wanted to see my family. I said my goodbyes to everyone and Mary saw me out into the hall where we kissed each other and I said that I would be in touch tomorrow.

By now I was really looking forward to seeing Mum and Dad and to be in my own surroundings for a change. Hopefully it will bring me back to earth and I will be able to be just Henry Blake for a while.

When Wills drove me into the yard it was grand to see Mother come out of the house to greet me and then Dad appeared followed by John. It seemed that they were as pleased to see me as I was to see them.

I had bought Mother and Betty some of Lubeck's famous marzipan and a German beer mug for Dad, John and Charlie. These were very fancy and they had a lid which opens up by means of a lever. I never found out why they all had these lids. As soon as I got into the friendly old kitchen, I got these presents out and handed them around, which pleased my family.

Dad said, "Before your mother starts to ask you hundreds of questions, I have a present to show you Henry, so come with me my lad," so we all filed out of the kitchen and then into the part of the barn that I used as a workshop. Needless to say, Micky was going mad at seeing me again so, of course, he joined us.

Dad opened the barn door, switched on the lights and there I saw a motor bike and side-car, looking as if it had never been used. At a glance I knew that it was old lady Howes'. Aunt Sally's chauffeur must have put in hours of work to get it in this wonderful condition.

I went and sat on it and then Dad told me how it came to be in my workshop. Mother had quite a shock because, three days ago, first of all a lorry came into the yard, followed by a large Rolls Royce. A chauffeur got out and opened a door and Old lady Howes stepped out. She turned to mother and said, "You are Mrs Blake, we met at the Hall at Christmas." By this time Dad had come into the yard and he took Lady Howes' hand and said how pleased he was to see her. Mother invited her into the house and started to walk towards the front door. The old lady said that she wanted to go into the kitchen because, when she was a girl, that was where she used to spend her time.

She took Dad's arm and asked him to take her in. She said to him "Could I call you Samuel and will you call me Sally. I seem to know you all so well from your charming son Henry. Talking of Henry, I have brought him a present which is in the lorry. You see, he and I are great friends and he will be able to bring Mary up to see me on this bike and side-car. It will also be useful as a means of transport to Exeter every day."

I was over the moon on seeing the bike. It was not the one I had ridden around the grounds and when the old lady said that she was going to give me the other bike, I had thought no more of it and I had never had a good look at it. Somehow, I thought that it was a pipe-dream on my part and I had no idea what a beauty it would be.

That evening I telephoned Aunt Sally and thanked her for her wonderful gift and I told her that Mary and I would be coming up to see her in the near future. Perhaps she could let us know when it would be convenient. She told me not to be silly because anytime would be convenient but asked me to be careful riding a strange bike.

By the time I went to bed that night I had talked so much that I felt quite hoarse. I had so much to tell the family and they kept asking questions about Germany and then London and my visit to the War Office. I tried to keep it as short as possible but it was very difficult.

At last I got up to my own room and it was only then that I felt really at home. There was no Mary to keep me company but at least I had a good night's sleep.

I woke up the next morning to hear the familiar farmyard sounds and I got up bright and early. I was dying to try out my new motor bike and I also wanted to see if Henry was all right.

I telephoned Mary and told her all about my bike which I found she already knew about. Her father had let the cat out of the bag as soon as I had left the Hall to come home.

She wanted me to come over right away to give her a ride but I told her that I would be over later in the day as I had several things to do. This didn't please the young lady but she made me promise to come over for lunch. This I agreed to because, being Market Day there would be very little for lunch. Anyway, one has to say no sometimes, even to girls like Mary.

The bike was taxed, insured and full of petrol, so I put Micky in the side-car and away we went. Being a bit of a show-off I rode through the village and my posh-looking bike caused a bit of a stir. I then decided to see if my good friend Mrs Jenkins was in her lovely cottage.

As I drove up the very narrow lane leading to Mrs Jenkins' home, I remembered so well my meeting with her in the woods so many years ago. She really started the change in the pattern of my life. Without knowing my capabilities in the learning of languages, I would not be going to Exeter University in a few weeks time and my visits to Germany would be non-existent.

I parked my bike and Micky as usual was my advance guard and announced my arrival. Mrs Jenkins came out to greet me and, by her expression, I could tell that she was glad to see me. She was not one to show much affection so it came as a surprise that she took my arm and led me into her living room.

In no time she had two cups of her famous coffee and I told her all about my visit to Germany. I showed the pictures of Kapitel Strasse and, as I expected, they upset her. On the other hand, the street may have looked as it used to when she was a young girl. We talked for quite some time, of course in German and, soon, it was time to go. As I left I felt sorry for her. She looked so lonely standing by her front door, perhaps she liked the solitude of living in such a quiet spot.

I drove past the little bridge but unfortunately I had no time to linger and have one of my daydreams. I would like to have done so, because I have so much on my mind which needs to be sorted out.

However, I had to take Micky back to the farm and then get over to the Hall in time for lunch.

Having taken Micky back to the farm and cleaned myself up a bit I made for Langley Hall. Driving through the lanes reminded me of how I used to ride dear old Daisy over to the Hall to meet my friends, Mary and Hugh. This seemed a long time ago, when I was young and so very innocent.

Now I see very little of Hugh and a lot of Mary in more ways than one and my circumstances had changed so dramatically. Sometimes I begin to wonder where I am and am I taking the right course?

I am only coming up to eighteen years of age. Am I putting all my eggs in one basket? Should I be playing the field as brother John did, or am I extremely lucky to have found Mary at such a young age?

Then, of course, there is Polly. She may have several boyfriends by now and never even thinks about me, so I may be kidding myself where she is concerned.

Anyway all of these thoughts left me as I rode up to the front door and I saw Mary standing on the front step. She ran down the steps and gave me a great hug and we stood back and admired our posh new means of transport.

Sir James came out and was most interested and asked if he could have a ride. Without even knowing if he could ride a motor bike I said, Yes and, before I knew what was happening, he was astride the bike and speeding around the front drive.

He certainly knew how to ride and then he disappeared down the drive to the main entrance and we heard the sound of the engine fading away in the distance.

The two aunts came out and started to pull my leg by saying that I have now lost my new bike. Aunt Pamela then said, "Henry you are now too old to have aunts, so Geraldine and I would like you to call us by our Christian names." This was quite a pleasant surprise for me and I knew that it would take some time for me to get used to this familiarity. No doubt I would get used to it. I seem to be able to adapt to most situations.

Mary took my arm and held it so tightly as if she had read my thoughts on my ride over to the Hall. We went in and waited for Sir James to return. When he came in he said how he had enjoyed the ride. It had made him feel young again. Quite naturally, I said that he was more than welcome to have a ride whenever he wanted to. He said that a motor bike would be so useful on the estate so he might look out for an old one.

I then had one of my few brainwaves. I had an old, but serviceable, bike that John had given me. I offered it to Sir James, with two conditions. The first being that John did not object and the second, that he would accept it as a gift. I could see that the idea pleased him greatly and I said that I would see John tonight and I would get it organised.

People are very strange. Sir James could go out tomorrow and buy a new bike but the thought of someone actually giving him one would give him so much more pleasure. I suppose that it was like giving him a sort of toy, which was very unexpected. The old boy was not mean in any way, in fact he had been more than generous to me.

After lunch I had to take Mary for a ride so she decided that she would like to go over and see Mum and Dad and, with a bit of luck, have some cream for tea. I warned her that it was Market Day and that my parents might not be back yet. Anyway, we set off with Mary sitting in comfort in the side-car.

When we got to the farm we found it very deserted. We eventually found John working in one of the barns. He always liked to see Mary because he still had an eye for a pretty girl. He always teased her and today was no exception and, in the end, she was chasing him around the barn trying to hit him. This caused a lot of fun and laughter and it was nice to see how well Mary got on with my family.

I explained the motor bike situation. John readily said that, as far as he was concerned, I could do whatever I liked with the bike. He had given it to me as a present but if I did not want two, it would be a good idea to give it to Sir James.

John told us that we could help him get the cows in for milking as Charlie was busy and had not come back yet. We had to walk across two fields to get to the cows. They were so used to the routine that, as soon as they saw John, they all started to make a move towards the gateway. Soon we were driving a herd of forty cows at a leisurely pace back to the yard to be milked.

Before milking, cows walked with a strange swing sideways. Their udders were full and heavy with milk and acted like a pendulum, swinging from side to side and to see them running was quite hilarious.

As we drove the cows into the yard, Mum and Dad arrived back from market. Dad shouted to Mary, "We will make a milkmaid of you yet Mary." Mary went and joined my parents while I helped John get the cows in their pens.

Mary seemed happy enough chatting to Mother in the kitchen so I started to give my old bike a good clean. After a while, Mary appeared in one of Mother's overalls and helped me finish the job. We had just finished when Mother came out to tell us that there was some tea going if we wanted some. We didn't have to be asked twice, so, after a wash, we scoffed some of her bread and cream.

Mary and I took our time driving back to the Hall. We stopped by the Little Bridge and talked. We decided that we would go up to North Devon to stay with Mary's grandmother next week, by which time Geraldine would have settled in. Mary put her arm around my waist and said that she hoped we would be given the same bedrooms. She said that she would telephone Grandmother and fix it up.

There was great excitement at the Hall when we got back. Hugh had arrived home without letting anyone know that he was even in the country. This was so much like him, he was in a dream most of the time.

It was grand to see him again and I went up to his room and helped him to unpack. I asked him how he got on with Ruth and he said that they were so very fond of each other and perhaps we could have a good chat about it. There was no need to ask me how I was getting on with Mary because it was obvious to anyone half-blind that we were both more than just fond of each other.

Because of Hugh's return, I was asked to stay for dinner, which was most interesting. Hugh told us lurid tales of life in Africa. Most of his stories included Ruth, so much so that I noticed a look that his mother gave to Sir James. I had this fear that there could be trouble in this quarter because Ruth was a Jewess and the Howes' were an old English family. Perhaps this was what Hugh wanted to talk to me about.

Mary asked Hugh if he would like to come up to North Devon to visit his grandmother but he said that he would rather stay at home and finish some of his paintings of Africa, so that he could take them to his new college as examples of his work.

It was strange that the three of us were about to start at new colleges at the same time, two in London and one in Devon. I am the odd one out in Devon and, in some ways, I am pleased. It will give me the chance to really concentrate on the two entirely different courses and I have to join the R.A.F. Volunteer Reserves.

On the other hand it is a long way to London to see Mary and a costly rail fare. Hugh had told me again that I could stay at his house at any time and perhaps Mary could get a weekend off and we could both enjoy Hugh's hospitality.

After dinner Mary telephoned her grandmother and a date was fixed for us to drive up to Wimble Manor, which would be in three days time, on Monday of next week. This seemed to please Mary no end and she came over to me and put her arms around my neck and said, "How exciting, to go all that way on a motor bike. Now you won't get lost will you Henry?" This made everyone laugh but it did remind me to have a word with Wills about the route. He would be taking Geraldine on the same trip tomorrow and it would be fresh in his mind.

It had been a very interesting evening. I was sitting on a seat in the front garden of the farm. Sir James had just left on my old bike. He was like a dog with two tails. I had brought him over on my bike earlier in the evening and we spent a long time on this seat together with Dad.

It was strange that a chap of his standing was, in a way, asking for our advice. His big worry was the fact that Hugh, the heir to the title and the estate, was infatuated with a Jewish girl. It was none of our business and Dad told him so, but he wanted to talk about it and I don't think he had anyone else with an unbiased view.

This put me in a very difficult position. Hugh and Bernie were my best friends and I had never thought about the fact that Bernie and Ruth were German Jews. My contribution to the discussion was a suggestion that Ruth and Bernie be invited down to the Hall for a day or so and then one could see how they fitted into a country way of life.

After a while, Sir James said that he thought that my idea may be an answer, "But it would help if you, Henry, came and stayed a night or two, so that we could make it a bit of a party. Please don't say a word to anyone about this idea until I have had a word with my wife. This includes Mary. I know what you two are like, you tell each other everything."

The next few days soon went by. I paid my good friend Jake a visit and gave him all the news from Germany. He is such a nice fellow and always seems glad to see me. He had heard from the Major and he was more than pleased with my report and they may send another chap down to see me about the flying bomb and pick my brains in case I had left anything out.

Jake went to his desk and brought out an envelope and handed it to me, saying "You must be on the payroll now Henry, because here is some cash from the Department." On the way back to the farm I opened the envelope and there was a cheque for twenty pounds which, to me, was a fortune.

The next morning was fine and, after loading Mary's clothes in the limited space available, we set off on our first long trip on my new bike. It was a straightforward route and we enjoyed it. To feel the fresh air in our faces and pass through some lovely countryside was indeed a great pleasure.

We saw a sign advertising coffee so we stopped and went into a very quaint old cafe and had some home-made cakes and hot coffee. This must have put us in a real holiday mood because as we drove on our way we started to sing at the top of our voices. As we passed through hamlets and small villages, the inhabitants must have thought us mad. I was to learn in the future that happiness is a very rare commodity. That morning in August 1937 was a very happy morning

302

for the two of us who were very much in love and one must savour every moment of such times.

When we arrived at the Manor, I sounded my horn several times as we drove up the long drive to the imposing front door. The front door was opened by Salter, the butler, and out came the old lady herself to greet us and what a friendly greeting it was. She took us both by the arm and led us into the hall. Salter and a maid took over the job of seeing to our luggage.

Aunt Sally told us that we were to have the same rooms, in fact we had to look upon them as our own bedrooms. I stopped and said, "Before we go any further I must thank you properly for the wonderful gift you brought down to the farm for me." I then gave her a proper kiss on her cheek and gave her a big hug.

She gave me a friendly clip under the ear and told me that it gave her great pleasure and not to be so forward in future. My actions must have pleased the old girl because her face became alive with smiles.

She told us to go up to our rooms and have a wash and she would see us in the living room and then we could have a good chat.

Mary and I went up to our rooms and unpacked our clothes. I wasn't alone for long. Mary came in and we enjoyed a passionate embrace. She whispered in my ear that we would be able to make love tonight because nature had finished its monthly brake on our sexual activities.

When we went downstairs we joined Aunt Sally and Geraldine in the sitting room. I had to, once more, relate our exploits in Germany. I left out our visit to the War Office. I tried to keep it short because Geraldine had heard it all before and, of course, she had been part of it.

Aunt Sally really took me by surprise by asking me how I came to know Brigadier Eastham. I took a long sip of the sherry I was drinking, which gave me time to think. To give me further time to think, I asked her why she asked this question.

She told me that the Easthams lived just a few miles from Wimble Lake and they came to dinner sometimes. The Brigadier had been a Lieutenant in her husband's regiment during that awful war. "Anyway, he thought that Mary was a lovely girl and he was most impressed with you, Henry, when you both went to the War Office," she told me. I said that I would like to tell her all about it but I was unable to because it was all to do with Hitler. She laughed and said that the Brig told her that she would get nothing out of Henry.

Mary asked her grandmother if we could have a couple of horses after lunch. She told us that Jack had it all organised. I said that we would like to have a ride around the Estate and, if it was alright with her, I would like to have a chat with Jackson, the gamekeeper.

The old lady said that she would like me to get to know Jackson better. She then surprised me by asking me to sit in and listen to her meeting with her book-keeper, Mrs Jackson, which would be tomorrow morning. She looked at Mary and told her that she could go into Barnstaple with Geraldine. Mary was about to object but she changed her mind. Lady Howes was a very forceful woman and it would have been a waste of time to argue with her.

After a very pleasant lunch, Mary and I changed into our riding gear and walked around to the stables. Jack was there already saddling up the same two horses we had on our last visit. It was nice to see the old boy again and we had a nice chat, mostly about horses. I could see that Mary was getting a bit restless, so we went on our way.

It was obvious that Mary was in a bit of a mood about the arrangements for the following morning but I told her not to be so silly. Who knows what Geraldine might treat her to something in Barnstaple, such as a nice 'dolly'. I galloped off before she could hit me with her crop.

Much to my surprise, we found Jackson's cottage and Mrs Jackson invited us in to her spotless home. She asked us to call her Peggy as 'Mrs Jackson' was such a mouthful. After a while she suggested that I go and find her husband, "And Miss Mary and I can have a nice chat." So I took the hint and was off.

I came across Jackson sitting on a bench watching some of his pheasants pecking away at the earth to find the last morsel of the last distribution of food. He got up and we shook hands and he said that it was nice to see me again. We talked about the deer and, without thinking, I said that our deer were doing very well. The rut takes place in October and because, as yet, we only have a small herd this could be a bit dodgy.

Jackson said that her Ladyship had ordered quite a large herd for delivery after Christmas. "I know that she will be asking you to be present when they arrive, so I am warning you, Mr Blake," he told me.

I then said to him "When we are talking like this, please call me Henry and I believe that you are called George," so henceforth this was how we addressed each other when we were on our own. I knew that I could learn a great deal from George both now and in the future.

We talked about my trip to Germany and he said that if there was a war, it would be the death knell for some Estates like this. It was, therefore, so important to make them self-sufficient now.

He went on to say that we had made a start with the deer but we should have more sheep and there could be a charge for some of the pheasant shoots. Also, some of the farms pay such low rents that the amounts were laughable. He stopped talking and said that, whatever I did, I must not let his wife know what we had been talking about. Her Ladyship was very tolerant but she might object to my ideas.

When I got back to the cottage, Peggy made us have a cup of tea and then we made our excuses and continued our ride. It really was a very large Estate, excluding the tenant farms and we both thought that so much space was wasted. Perhaps this was what gave it its charm and natural beauty.

We found our way back to the Manor by an entirely different route and it was getting late. We had a quick bath and just managed to present ourselves for dinner by the correct time.

The late evenings were now too cool for Aunt Sally so we were unable to sit outside as we had done earlier in the summer. We sat in the sitting room and talked until it was time to go to bed. Salter had kept our glasses well filled during the evening, so we went upstairs in a merry mood.

We were glad to see that we still had the landing to ourselves. Nevertheless, we did not join each other until the household seemed very quiet. I found this waiting very difficult but soon I heard my door open and Mary was in bed with me and we had a wonderful night together.

The next morning, Mary went off with Geraldine to Barnstaple and, when Peggy Jackson arrived, together with Aunt Sally, we went into her office. Peggy immediately set her books out on the table.

I soon gathered that this had become a regular routine, so I sat back and just listened. I had made up my mind that I would only speak if spoken to.

Peggy had a very simple system for her book-keeping and I soon understood what was going on. To me it seemed that the Estate was just paying its way, which was pretty good considering the different trading conditions for agriculture in the country. The slump was almost over but it had left a great sadness on some farming communities.

During a break for coffee, Aunt Sally asked me if I had any views on what they had been talking about. Should I be honest and tell her what I really thought or should I pretend that it was none of my business?

Rightly or wrongly I decided to be honest and held forth. I told her that I had several suggestions.

"Some you may like, others you will dislike.

"First of all a lot of your land is wasted, so you rear more sheep. Secondly the river could be dredged and a lake formed to breed trout. This has been one of the driest summers in living memory and yet there is still plenty of water in the river. The deer will become a great asset in time.

"Now here are some ideas that you may not like. There will be a war in a year or so and farmland will be at a premium. My father has told me how scarce food was in the last war so, with the modern weapons now available, this country would be very hungry.

"So one of my suggestions would be that when the leases come up for renewal the rents should be in line with other parts of the country.

"And, lastly, when I saw so many pheasants yesterday it made me think that some of your shoots could be paid for by those enjoying the sport. Some large companies entertain their clients in this way.

"I do hope that I have not been too forward. Some of my ideas may not be feasible. But you did ask for my views and to be really morbid I think that you should plan now for another war. As you know I have just come back from Germany and they are going to have a go at someone."

Much to my surprise Peggy spoke in support of my suggestions, some of which came from her husband. That, of course, was between the two of us. Then Aunt Sally said that she would go into the ideas with her solicitor. But, fundamentally, she thought that the ideas were very constructive.

The old lady was quiet for a very short time. Then she got up and went to the telephone and we heard her tell her solicitor that she wanted to see him tomorrow morning at ten o'clock and would he bring all the leases that belong to the estate. When she sat down there was a wicked smile on her face and she said that it was about time Mr. Baker earned his money.

She turned to me and asked me if I could meet the old chap when he comes over tomorrow morning. I said, "Of course I will, but you will have to keep Mary quiet."

Aunt Sally laughed and said that she knew how to do that.

We sat and talked about the Estate for quite some time and the old girl became most enthusiastic about some of the ideas. I think that the thought of entertaining perhaps interesting people for pheasant shoots gave her quite a kick. She made me smile when she said that she wondered what Jackson the gamekeeper would say. Little did she know that it was his idea.

Peggy then went home and soon Mary and Geraldine came back from their trip to Barnstaple. Mary had a parcel under her arm and looked very pleased with herself. She was now very open in showing her affection for me in front of her family. She came over and put her arms around my neck and gave me a good kiss.

She said that they had discovered a shop that sold hand-made sweaters, so she brought one for me and one for herself, which, of course, I had to try on there and now. It was smashing and it was just what I wanted. I told her what a clever girl she was, to get the right size.

At lunch Aunt Sally was full of what we had been talking about that morning and I was glad to hear that Geraldine was in favour. She was, after all, living on the spot and could help the old lady with some of the projects, such as pheasant shoots.

As expected Mary was fed up that she would not have my company tomorrow morning. Aunt Sally told her in no uncertain terms that she saw enough of me, so one morning will not hurt her.

After lunch Mary and I went to explore Exmoor and the Quantock Hills and came back via Minehead. It was lovely to see and hear the sea again and what a pleasure it was to ride my smashing new bike.

We had tea in a cafe on the sea front at Minehead and Mary told me how difficult Geraldine was finding life. "Her husband, the Baron, keeps telephoning her and verbally bullying her to return to Germany. His pride has been hurt, he has lost face. She is, however, going to divorce him as soon as possible and try to make a new life for herself. In a week or two she intends to move to London as she has several old friends there."

When one is driving a motor bike it is impossible to have much of a conversation with someone in the side-car. This does give you a chance to think things through. I could not tell Mary what I had been thinking about.

I told Mary that I could not understand I am very worried about how her grandmother gets me so involved in her private business. "I am not a relative and I have not known her for very long and I have very little experience in such matters."

Mary thought it was a bit strange but her father did not. He said that the old girl was lonely and she wanted a purpose in life. Also the views of the younger generation would be most helpful and, "Most important of all, she likes you Henry and her first love was Grandfather."

We talked about this for some time and we came to the conclusion that the best thing was to let things take their course.

We drove back across parts of Exmoor and it was so enjoyable that we were loath to leave it. We drove though a heavily wooded area and the late summer sunshine was casting shadows across the roadway in front of my bike. The trees were beginning to change from green to the wonderful autumn colours and I thought how lucky I am to be here with lovely Mary enjoying the same things that I do. Because she likes me she loved the country and everything to do with it.

Consequently we were a bit late for dinner, but we were forgiven and after a quick change we joined Aunt Sally and Geraldine. The moorland air must have given us both a good appetite because we both tucked in, much to the amusement of the old lady.

That evening, over coffee and then several glasses of wine, Geraldine told us about Germany over the past few years. In some parts the poverty was so bad that people were dying of starvation and disease. Unemployment was at its highest level, with no prospects of any improvement. This, of course, was food and drink for the Communists and the far right party led by Hitler and his Brown Shirts, the basis for the Nazi party of today.

All this started this awful resentment against the Jews. Someone had to be blamed and they were an easy target. In one respect they were to blame because they never tried to integrate with the population of the country they chose to live in. They were good at business and they prospered, consequently people were jealous.

There were these two main political parties, the Communists and the Brown Shirts, struggling for power. Hitler won and became Chancellor and he took control over the whole country.

He had got rid of all forms of opposition in one way or another, mostly by the use of labour and concentration camps. Most of the poor people sent to these camps were never seen again.

Geraldine paused for a while and said that she had tried to shut her mind to the state of the country, but it was a terrible strain living under a government and not being able to say anything against it.

We were to have several of these conversations and it taught me a great deal about dictators. There were now three in Europe; Russia, Italy and Germany, and Spain was going that way. I only hope that we will not be weak enough to let it happen to us.

Next morning Mr. Baker, the solicitor, came for the meeting. He was a very stiff old bird, complete with bowler hat and a wing collar. He didn't look the type that could be enthusiastic about anything. But, after a time, he had to admit that the schemes had merit.

The leases could be altered on the Michaelmas Quarter day, so there was very little time. However Mr. Baker said that he would seek advice about the market value of the rents and report back to Lady Howes.

Overall it was quite a successful meeting and it certainly pleased the old girl. She then told me to go and find Mary as she wanted to have a chat with Mr. Baker. Which was a polite way of telling me to push off.

Over the next two days Mary and I explored the area, either on my bike or on horseback. We were also able to enjoy each other every night in the comfort of a large bed. In fact we had a lovely short holiday staying with Aunt Sally.

When it was time to go back to Teignford I loaded my side-car with the wonderful preserved fruit that Aunt Sally told me to take back to Mother. I managed to get our luggage in but Mary had to ride on my bike. The dear old lady looked so sad and when she gave us both a kiss I could see a sign of a tear in her faded blue eyes and she made us promise to come up to see her during our Christmas holidays.

It was strange how Mary and I had become attached to Aunt Sally in such a short time. We both felt sad to leave her in this very large house with just her memories to keep her company. She would have Geraldine for a short time, but it was pretty obvious that the two of them had very little in common.

It was difficult for me to understand the different feelings I had for my parents and Aunt Sally's children for her. Then it dawned on me that the upper classes farmed their children out to a governess and then they were sent away to school. Consequently they never really got to know each other and there was not a closeness like most families in the lower levels of our class system.

I think that this had been the case with Sir James and Geraldine, but not with Mary and Hugh. They were close to their parents just like I was to mine.

When we got back to Teignford we had to report all of the news to our separate families. This was bit of a bore but it was best to get it over with, otherwise the questions would have gone on for ever.

One day while I was sitting down by the lake, waiting for Mary, Sir James collared me and thanked me for helping his mother and making her a human being again. He said that they had grown apart over the last few years and she had become a very unhappy person.

"It is definitely something to do with you and Mary. She started to change when she came down for Christmas and met you and your family for the first time. Whatever it is we are all very grateful."

He told me to forget the conversation we had about Hugh and Ruth because he wanted to let things take their course.

"Who knows what will happen by next year this time and sometimes it is better to keep quiet about a problem rather than highlighting it."

He paused for a while then he said that he hoped I would have time during the term to come over and have the odd ride with him around the estate. I replied that I would like to. Sir James said that he could see a shadow coming across the lawn. I looked up and of course he was referring to Mary who was looking as gorgeous as ever.

The awful day had come and Mary and Hugh had gone. Pamela had gone with them to see Mary settled into her new college. I was left on my own with just my memories to keep me company. In fact I felt very sorry for myself.

It would be my turn tomorrow to start at my new place of education, which will seem very strange indeed. What is even stranger was the financial arrangements to pay for my education at Exeter University, which had been made in the spring, by someone unknown.

I now had more details enclosed in a letter from a firm of solicitors based in London. They would pay all the bills directly to the University, and a bank account had been opened at Lloyds bank at Newton Abbot in my name and a suitable sum would be deposited there on the first day of each month to cover personal expenses. I had no idea who was doing this or why. I wondered if I will ever know.

I was sitting on my bench in the garden at the farm in the early autumn of 1937. I had been talking to Dad for ages but now I was on my own and I suddenly felt cold and a sort of shadow clouded my mind. It was a very strange feeling or warning of disaster. I had no idea what it was all about but I had these feelings in the past, which have turned out to have meant something. This, however, was of a greater intensity than before.

I knew that tomorrow would change my life. It would be like a crossroads and, for once, I might be able to choose which road I took. So far I have had very little choice because fate has made the decisions.

This was like the end of a beginning and the starting of a new and completely different chapter in my life.

CHAPTER 13

It was a lovely, early evening in July, 1938. Once more I was sitting by myself on a seat by the Little Bridge. For the best part of twelve months, my life had not been my own. For once I had the evening free and I could just sit here and ponder over what had been happening to me. I had no lectures or work to do and no one to meet.

Thinking back over the last months, I enjoyed life at the University and I am still thinking how lucky I am to be there. I have made some good friends and still managed to keep out of trouble. The Farm management course was a piece of cake and apart from the accountancy parts, it was really just common sense.

The other course was a different cup of tea. It was called communications, but really it was all about radio and radar and Morse Code thrown in for good luck. We were taught the theory of electricity and radio and we are to learn how to make and to experiment in this very complicated field. This would be in my last year.

All had been well at the farm. Sister Jenny had popped off and married her boss, who was a grand sort of chap. I was so pleased that there was no boring wedding to go to. Most important of all John would be a father at any time now and I would be an Uncle. Poor chap was getting himself into quite a state.

I have been spending a lot of time with Sir James and we have become very good friends. I have also seen Jake on many occasions, and somehow or other, I came away having learned something new about his war time work. I wish that I had known how this would help me in the future.

I often think about Jake and he has been a wonderful friend to me. On the other hand, he is now very normal and comes to the farm whenever he feels like it. So perhaps our meeting so long ago, when we watched the badgers could have some bearing on his return to the world away from his wood. For some reason, even now when I am older I feel so at ease in his company.

My love life with Mary was just as smashing. We could only see each other during college holidays. I only went to London once and stayed at Hugh's house. I just could not afford such expensive trips.

We made up for lost time when we went up to North Devon. Aunt Sally was getting me more and more involved with the Estate and Mary and I had to keep going up to see the Old Girl. Not that we objected, it not only gave us the chance to really get together, but we also liked it up there.

I heard what could be disastrous news last week. I was walking around Exeter when I heard a female voice behind me say, "Hello Henry." I turned around and there was Polly. She had grown into a really smashing female. When I looked at her it brought back such memories and for a moment or two I was lost for words and then we instinctively put our arms around each other and had a good hug. After which we both felt a bit self-conscious at this reaction.

We found a cafe and had some coffee and told each other what we had been doing since we last met. She had won a place at Oxford and had passed the first part of her studies with honours. She was however going to Exeter University so that she could study something special for one term, starting in September.

She had put her hand across the table and held mine, and with a very naughty smile she said, "Henry will you be able to give me a lift in your side-car?"

This could be a very difficult situation so I will have to be very careful that I don't get involved.

As I sat there, an aircraft flew over and seeing it made me feel a little nervous. Soon I will be making my first flight at the controls of an aircraft. The instructor will be at the main controls, but for a short time I will be flying the plane.

Major Davis must have a lot of influence because I was told by the Squadron Leader that he had been ordered to make sure that I could fly a light plane by the end of the summer term in 1939, I also had to swot up on the navigation side of it. Strange how it may seem, navigation was included in my communications course at Exeter so this was not a problem.

I had to make some excuses to my pals in the University Squadron, as to why I was getting this extra tuition. So I made up a yarn about having the chance of a Government job, because of my being able to speak German. Anyway they believed my tale.

The situation with Germany was getting more dangerous and orders came from the Air Ministry that training in the RAF, VR had to be stepped up and we had to have more lectures and parades.

I was now free for eight weeks, except for these extra flying lessons at Exeter Airport. I am not grumbling because I did enjoy them. I have spent so many hours of my life watching and studying birds in flight and with a bit of luck I will be able to copy them. Not with their grace and ease, but in principle the same.

Mary will be home in three days time and I am so looking forward to seeing her. I do hope that she feels the same way towards me. I have been without any real female company since Easter. Anyway, I just didn't have the time for any females.

It was now getting quite dark, so I gave Henry and Micky a shout and I made my way home. As I got into the yard there seemed to be lights on everywhere and John had a son. John was beside himself and I joined in the celebrations and had too many beers.

Gertie had been taken to the Hospital in Newton Abbot earlier in the day, and it was thought to be a false alarm, but evidently it was the real thing. I was glad that I had been out of the way while this was going on, otherwise I would have got myself into a state.

When I got up to my room that night, I thought that we now have another Blake in this world and as they write in the Bible, "He will be called Samuel and he will be able to sow the seed to make sure that the Blakes' continue to cultivate the land like his ancestors." By this time the beer must have had its effect and the next thing I knew was that I woke up with a bad head. So I turned over and went to sleep again. After all, I was on holiday.

What got me up was the smell of a cooked breakfast wafting up the stairs. That I could not ignore.

During the next two days I took things a bit easier. I had a flying lesson and that was very successful. The chap that had the awful job of teaching me was such a pleasant fellow. He was a Canadian by the name of Hank. I never found out what a Canadian was doing in Devon, teaching chaps like me to fly.

His surname was French, and I never got the hang of it. So like everyone else I called him Hank. After my lesson he asked me into the small canteen for a coffee and he told me that by the end of the summer I would have my first solo flight. This was indeed good news, although the thought made me a bit nervous.

Things at home were a bit tense. Gertie was still in hospital because she had a pretty rough time having little Sam. Anyway all seems to be well so I expect that she will be home soon. John's sleepless nights will then start.

Today was the day. Mary comes home after lunch and she will telephone me as soon as she gets home and I will go over to the Hall to see her. It was such a lovely day so I thought that I would ride Henry over to the Hall when I get the call. I changed into my riding gear and had my lunch and then I sat in the garden so that I could hear the phone when it rang.

I must have nodded off because the next thing I knew was the smell of the scent that I knew so well and feeling someone kissing my cheek from behind. Mary had arrived.

313

I stood up and we had such a loving embrace. I stood back and looked at this lovely creature. Her hair was a bit longer and tied back to show the fine features of her face. She had grown in some important places, which I am dying to explore.

We sat there for a while just holding hands and telling each other how we had missed each other and how much we loved each other. We went into the house and Mary gave Mother a hug and this was returned. I told her that we were going for a ride. Mother grinned and said that when we came back she would give us some tea.

We just walked our horses for a short while. Neither of us had mentioned where we were going, but we both knew. We were a respectable distance from the farmhouse, we put the horses into a fast trot. When we saw the old barn in the distance we put our steeds into top gear and laughed as we rode. We were soon hidden from the outside world, inside the old barn.

We had not been together for a long time and at first our lovemaking was frantic and selfish. After a while we had both calmed down and we made love, thinking of each other and how satisfying it was.

Riding back to the farmhouse we both felt so very happy. We had made sure that the straw had been brushed off our clothing and we had to look as if we had just been for a ride. As we dismounted, Dad came on the scene and he put his arm around her and she gave him a kiss. It always made me happy to see how well Mary got on with my family.

While we were having tea, Mary told me that I was invited to have dinner that night and we were going to fix up when we were to visit Grandma again. She wanted us to stay for at least a week. I explained about my flying lessons but 'Madam' said that she thought that the week after next would be a good time. As she said this she put her hand under the table and gave me a light pinch where she shouldn't have. This told me how her brain was working.

On our ride over to the Hall, we never stopped talking. We had so much to tell each other. Mary was getting on quite well at her college, but she just didn't like living in London and she missed me. She shared a room with two other girls and they had become friends.

When we got to the Hall, we were greeted by Pamela who said that it was nice to see two young people looking so happy. This made me feel embarrassed, which I tried not to show. Somehow I think that she knows what we get up to.

Dinner that night was more like a celebration for the return of Mary into the fold. Hugh will be home tomorrow and the whole family will be together again.

In the course of our conversation I said that Major Davis wanted me to spend a week or two in Normandy, staying with Celeste at her farm in Falaise so that I can improve my French. This caused one hell of an outburst from Mary. She said, "Don't you dare, Henry, you can stay with someone else but not Celeste. I know what these French girls are like, especially Celeste because she told me how she fancied you." This outburst made Mary's parents have a good laugh.

I put Mary's mind at rest by telling her that I hoped to have my first solo flight by the end of the summer, so I will have to go to France some other time. Anyway, I don't want to as I can only just manage an English girl, a French girl as well would be too much.

While the others were talking I remembered the times I had with Celeste when she was staying with Mr Jarvis. Anyway I expect she will have forgotten the inexperienced young chap in Devon who she led astray during a snow storm, when she had to stay the night at the farm. I lost my virginity that night and she was so sweet that it would be very difficult not to remember her with affection.

I had not thought of Celeste for some time. But in spite of the chatter I had one of my odd feelings and somehow I knew that I would see Celeste again but in very different circumstances.

This sense of doom and gloom soon passed and I was back in this world, looking at Mary and thinking how beautiful she looked. The two glasses of wine had added more colour to her cheeks and she was so vivacious.

We always sat next to each other and she took my hand and putting it to her lips she gave it a kiss and said how happy she was to be home again with the people she loved. I tried to pass this remark off by saying that I bet she had plenty of boyfriends in London. Mary's parents smiled and seemed to accept the way she felt.

Over our coffee we made definite arrangements for our visit to see Aunt Sally and it was decided by Mary that towards the end of next week would be quite a good time. My lessons at the airport were on Wednesdays so we would be off next Thursday. Mary got up and went to the phone and rang her grandmother to see it this would be alright. When she came back she was laughing because the Old Dear had said that Geraldine will have gone back to London, so we will have the place to ourselves. She had sent her love and was looking forward to seeing us both.

After we finished our coffee we all went for a stroll down to the lake and every time I looked at this beautiful parkland with its huge trees placed all in the correct places to give this wonderful vision. The grass was always cut so that it was always green. Mary and I were arm in arm and we were about to pass a very old tree. So for fun we spread our arms around the tree and we were just able to touch each other's fingers. Sir James saw what we were doing and he told us that this particular tree was several hundred years old.

He said that there is a treasure hidden beneath one of the trees in the park, no one knows which tree. This was hidden from the Roundheads, so the tale goes and it will only be found after a great explosion of unnatural forces made by man. "Henry my boy, sort that out because that is how the legend goes."

It was understandable why the treasure had never been found. I started to count the number of very old and large trees in the park, but I soon lost count. Some of these old legends are strange. I wonder what was meant by, "A great explosion of unnatural forces made by man." It was probably an old maid's tale of long ago.

The four of us sat by the lake until it was time for me to go. I said goodbye to Sir James and Pamela and Mary walked down the long drive to the main gates to say her goodbyes, which took quite some time.

Hugh came home and it was good to have him around again. The three of us went swimming and riding and it was just like old times. Hugh kept us very amused with his tales about some of the very weird students at his Art College. It seemed to be the thing to act and look strange if you wanted to be an artist.

I took Mary into see John's wife, Gertie, and little Sam. Mary had picked a bunch of flowers and some peaches from her garden, so we were well loaded up when we went into the hospital. We both thought that Sam was a grand little chap and while we were there he was well-behaved. Gertie's mother, Mrs Norris arrived so we pushed off. She really is a unlikeable person. I could see that Gertie was a bit fed up because she and Mary were having a fine old chat.

As we walked down the steps of the Hospital, Mary whispered in my ear, "Don't worry Henry, you won't be a father this month," and went off in shrieks of laughter. I took her by the arm and told her that it was no laughing matter and we will have to be very careful, this was of course why she wanted to go up to North Devon next week.

On the Wednesday before we were to go up to see Aunt Sally, I took Mary over to the airfield to meet Hank. It was really to show her off to some of the chaps that would be there. I think that the little monkey knew what I was up to and she made herself look even more glamorous. Consequently she caused quite a stir. Hank's wife was in the canteen and she looked after Mary while I was in the air.

We had decided to make an early start so the next morning we were all loaded up and away we went. We had asked Hugh if he wanted to come, because he could have ridden on my pillion seat, but he was not very keen. I think he had other ideas. He had met a girl at his college who lived near Exeter and I had a feeling that his friendship with Ruth had cooled off somewhat.

Our journey was uneventful and soon we were driving through the main gates and over a freshly laid cattle grid. The entrance end of the park had been fenced off and there were sheep grazing on the lush grass. When we came to the fence there was another grid.

I thought to myself that the Old Girl had this done since I was up here last and never mentioned it during our many phone conversations. I had been on to her about having sheep, and of course it was logical to let them keep the grass under control in the park.

I sounded my horn and in the distance I could see the old lady and her faithful retainer Salter come out of the front door to greet us. Every time I saw her she seemed to look better and so much more alive. After the usual kiss and hug, she took us both by the arm and we went inside.

Whenever I went to Wimble Manor, the hall and staircase never failed to impress me. The layout and design plus the fine furnishing, took one's breath away.

Salter was directing the unloading of our luggage and two maids took our things up the stairs to the rooms which we looked upon as our own. After a wash and clean up, we went down to have a chat with Sally before lunch.

Out came the sherry and we had to hear what she had been doing since our last visit. We had seen the sheep. I had helped to put the deer in their new home after last Christmas. A firm of engineers were dredging the river, starting down stream and working up to the far boundary of the Estate. In fact most of the ideas are now becoming fact and not fiction.

She said that she was still thinking about the pheasant shoots. Anyway it was too late for this year so perhaps next year. She then started to ask us countless questions about what we were doing and how our families were. Was Hugh still friendly with the Jewish girl? Mary said that she thought that it was cooling off a bit. The Old Girl poked me in the ribs and said, "Henry, I hope that your feelings are not cooling off Mary."

I laughed and said that there was no chance of that happening. On the other hand she might find a good-looking chap in London with plenty of money and forsake a poor farmer's son. Mary got up and came and sat on my lap and gave me a kiss, which said everything, much to Sally's amusement.

While we were having lunch, Sally asked us what we were going to do that afternoon. I said that we would like to borrow a couple of horses and have a ride around the Estate. She looked quite cross and said that, " No, you can't borrow the horses. How many times do I have

317

to tell you that the two horses you ride are yours and all you have to do is to tell Salter what time you require them."

I looked at Mary and she said that she would like to have a bit of a rest until it got a bit cooler and she felt tired after the trip up, plus the sherry. "Henry," she said, "Tell Salter about three thirty," which I did. I can read Mary's mind like a book. I only hope that Sally is unable to.

For an old lady, Sally was great company and we had a most enjoyable cold lunch. Somehow the three of us are completely relaxed in each other's company. I have been up to the Manor on two occasions without Mary and it had been the same. We have both tried to tell Sir James and Pamela about this and I don't think they believe us.

We arranged to meet Sally for a drink before dinner and we then made our way up to our rooms. It was very warm so I stripped off and just lay on my bed. As I lay there I wondered if Sally knew about our relationship and if she did, did she remember and relive the romantic side of her life? Perhaps at this very minute she would be resting on her bed, in a time warp and thinking of those youthful days.

I was miles away so I didn't hear my door open. I came to when I felt my underwear being taken off and a lovely girl started to kiss me all over. We had a wonderful afternoon and I thought to myself, how lucky I was to be where I was and with such a lovely and amorous girl. As I made love to Mary I was thinking of her. I think that this is the secret of being in love with someone. After quite a while we thought that we should show willing and make a move. So we dressed and went around to see Jack and our horses.

As we rode around the Estate on that fine summer's afternoon, we talked about what we would do during our stay at the Manor. We decided to go to the coast and have a swim. That is of course if the weather is suitable. We could also explore more of Exmoor. I told Mary that I thought that we would have the afternoons to ourselves, but the mornings we might have to fall in with the old lady's plans. Anyway the nights are our own if you behave yourself.

Mary tried to hit me but I was ready for the outburst and she missed. By now we were near George, the gamekeeper's domain. We decided to see if his wife, Peggy was in because with a bit of luck she might give us a cup of tea.

George was a bit like Jake, he had this habit of creeping up on you without you knowing that he was about. The next thing we knew was that he was riding with us and he asked us to come over to his cottage and see his wife.

She was very, genuinely pleased to see us and she made us very welcome. She gave us a cup of tea and we had a very pleasant hour with them and we would have liked to have stayed longer, but it was our first evening at the Manor and Sally would be expecting us to have a drink with her before dinner. As we left Peggy made us promise that we would call and see her in a day or so.

We managed to get back to the Manor in time to have a well-needed bath and in spite of a great deal of fooling about, we walked down the stairs in good time and looking as innocent as possible.

After a very enjoyable dinner, which was very light-hearted, it was warm enough to sit in Sally's favourite spot. She then told us that she would like us to accompany her tomorrow morning to see some of her tenants. She looked at me and said that there are quite a few that you have not yet met, Henry.

We sat outside until it was too dark. We had watched the sun setting behind the Quantock Hills. It was so peaceful that one could think that one was in another world. Gone were the worries of exams, flying lessons and Hitler never existed. Here I was with Mary who had become part of me and an old lady, who somehow or other had become part of my life and I had become very fond of her.

Sally got up to go to bed and told us that she would be making an early start tomorrow morning, so breakfast would be at eight thirty. I walked Sally to the bottom of the stairs, having left Mary in the garden. I had to kiss the old lady goodnight and I went to join Mary. We had another glass of wine each and we also went up the old staircase to our rooms.

This would be the first time that we were able to be together for the whole night since our last visit at Easter. We made the most of it and having been completely satisfied we went to sleep in each other's arms.

It was very difficult to leave Mary's bed, but I had to make my bed look as if it had been slept in. Walking down the stairs to breakfast, I looked at Mary and she looked as fresh as a daisy. Sex certainly agreed with her. She took my arm and we boldly walked into the breakfast room. Sally asked us if we had slept well. Of course, we said yes. I was sure she had a bit of a twinkle in her eye, when she asked this question.

Aunt Sally looked very elegant in her riding gear. Old-fashioned but very suitable for her position as the owner of a very large Estate. Martin, the ageing chauffeur seemed to be her companion on these trips. She was always shouting at him about something or other. He never seemed to take much notice and at times gave me a wink.

Mary and I were riding together at a fast walking pace, when Sally came up to join us. She said that we were going to the far side of the Estate which I had never seen. There is a small hamlet and a public house there which my husband bought lock, stock and barrel just before he died. She looked a bit sad and said that she had hardly visited it

319

since. I feel a bit different about it now that I have you two as my friends. She dropped back to shout at Martin about some minor thing.

We visited two farms and were warmly welcomed. The rent increases had not upset any of the tenants. Partly because farming was picking up in the country and of course the rents were so very low before.

We came to the hamlet called Wimble. It was a very charming place with such neat and well kept cottages and the front gardens were full of flowers. Sally told me that some of the workers from the Estate lived here. she added that the public house was very popular for people living in the area.

I asked her which came first: the Manor or the hamlet? For once she didn't know the answer. Martin however had the answer, evidently the Manor was built in the sixteenth century and the hamlet followed.

We came to the pub called the Wimble Arms. Our arrival had caused quite a stir. We all dismounted and tied our horses up to a rail. I noticed that there were three other horses already tied up and I wondered who they belonged to.

A very jovial-looking chap came out of the pub and shook hands with Sally, who introduced him as Mr Banks, the tenant of the Wimble Arms. Mr Banks said that his wife would be most upset if her Ladyship would not accept their hospitality, so we all trooped into the main bar.

After being in the sunlight for the whole morning, it took a little while for our eyes to get accustomed to the dark interior. I saw a young couple and an older man standing by the bar. He came to greet Sally with a big kiss and it was non other than Brigadier Eastham.

Sally said, "There is no need for me to introduce my granddaughter, Mary and her friend, Henry Blake, because I understand that you have met them before." The Brigadier then introduced his son, Tim and his girlfriend, Fiona.

Mr Banks, the landlord and his wife had a few words with Sally and then he asked us to have a drink on the house; as it was such a long time since her Ladyship had visited the Wimble Arms, which I thought was jolly nice of him.

Sally and the Brig were having a good chat, so we joined Tim and Fiona. It is always very difficult to start a conversation with complete strangers. One way of breaking the ice is to ask simple questions. I asked Tim what he was doing for a daily crust. This raised a bit of a laugh and he told me that he was at Sandhurst, following in his Old Man's footsteps. I told him what I was doing, and how I had to take my first solo flight in a week or two, and in no time, we were getting on fine.

I think that females can talk to strangers so much easier than men.

Mary and Fiona were nattering like mad. No doubt talking about their respective boyfriends.

This turned out to be a very pleasant interlude. It found the Brig lived in a fine, old country house on the way to Dulverton and it was not very far from the outskirts of the Estate.

Just to be polite, I asked Tim and Fiona if they would like to have a ride around the Estate, not thinking that they would be interested. Much to my surprise, they were very keen and asked when could this be fixed up.

Mary then took over and she went over to Sally and asked her if Tim and Fiona could come to lunch the following day. The old girl seemed delighted with the idea and in no time it was arranged that they ride over the next day, in time for a drink before lunch and then we could go for our ride during the afternoon. So after another drink, bought by the Brig, we all left the pub to go our different ways.

Riding back to the Manor, Sally told us how pleased she was that we had made some friends, almost in our own age group, to give us a bit of company while we were up here. Mary and I thought that they seemed nice people and it could be a bit of fun. Anyway, time will tell.

After lunch we made a quick get away and drove to Minehead for a swim in the lovely sea. We both liked to swim in sea water rather than fresh water. Somehow it was entirely different. We sunbathed in between our swims and we had a smashing time together.

Looking at Mary I could that she was catching up on her lost sleep. This gave me a little time to think about the happenings of the day. I had met Brigadier Eastham, only briefly last year and now on the edge of Exmoor, I met his son and I am going to spend the following afternoon with him. This strikes me as a very strange coincidence. The Brigadier must meet hundreds of people, how did he so readily remember our names? Was this meeting in the pub prearranged or was it fate playing its funny tricks again?

When Mary came back to life again, I mentioned this to her and much to my surprise she thought it very odd that her grandmother visited the pub. She added that by the look on Martin's face, this was a very unusual thing for her to do. However he thought it was a very good idea and he hoped that it would be on her future itinerary. I said that I would try to get some information out of Tim when we met tomorrow. All I wanted to know was if they often used the Wimble Arms or was today a one-off visit?

The next morning Tim and Fiona arrived in good time for a drink and a good chat before lunch. This was the first time that I was able to have a good look at Tim. He was tall, well-built and looked very much like his father. He had a pleasant face, but it was a soldier's face, complete with a small moustache, which seemed to be the fashion for Army chaps. I watched him ride up to our front steps and he certainly knew how to handle a horse.

Fiona was fairly tall like Mary, but she was not as pretty. She had an aristocratic-looking face, quite handsome but very attractive with long, fair hair tied back. As a couple looked very suitable for each other. I had no idea if they were mentally on the same wavelength.

Tim was very interested in what conditions were like in Germany when we were last there. A lot had happened since then. Hitler now had Austria and he had his beady little eye on Czechoslovakia; Parts of which were taken from Germany after the war. This is called Sudetenland and inhabited by Germans, so of course he will have a good excuse for occupying this area.

Tim told us that there was a lot of panic at Sandhurst. The course had to be shortened and intensified so that a larger number of Cadets could be trained in a shorter time.

The course was getting more and more complicated because of the new weapons that the Arms people kept coming up with. He seemed a bit fed up with it all but he said that he had to survive the next three months and with a bit of luck he would get his commission.

We then heard Salter having a bash at the gong to let us know that lunch was to be served. We had been sitting by the lake having our drinks, so when we went into lunch, we were all very surprised to see the Brig sitting at the table with Sally. This was unexpected and he must have gone into the house by the back entrance. As soon as I saw him I knew that something was brewing.

We had a very pleasant lunch which was very light hearted and we were about to go out of the room when Sally said to me, "Henry, would you mind having a word with the Brigadier as he wants to ask you to do him a favour?"

"Of course," I said. I sat down to await events.

When everyone had left the room the Brig said, "Blake, I have a problem, I have an acquaintance, who is a high ranking officer in the German Army. In fact I have known him for many years and he wants to have a very unofficial chat with me about the situation in Germany. This is to be an exploratory talk which has to be kept completely confidential and as far as you are concerned, all I want you to do is act as interpreter. My German is as bad as his English. You might think that I could get someone from my Department. If I did, it would mean it would have to become official and that would defeat the object of this meeting."

I asked when and where the meeting would take place and much to my surprise he told me that it would be the day after tomorrow at ten

322

o' clock, at the Manor. I looked up at the old boy and said that I thought he was taking me for granted and not leaving much time to spare.

He replied by saying that he was told that he would be able to count on my help, but not to forget that I was to help him get a business deal organised and what I heard must never be repeated. "Do I make myself clear?" he said. "Yes Sir," I replied.

We now joined the others and I could see that Mary and our friends were getting impatient. The Brig turned on the charm and said that it was his fault that we had kept them waiting for so long.

As we left to get our horses from the stables, the Brig said that he would see me as arranged. Mary's ears pricked up at this remark and demanded to know what I had let myself in for and when. I told her that I had to meet the Brigadier at ten o'clock the day after tomorrow, and no matter what she says I couldn't get out of it. She looked a bit surprised at my firmness but accepted it. For some unknown reason she took my arm and told me that she loved me.

The four of us had a most enjoyable ride and we even went as far as the park where the deer were kept. As we rode around the Estate I was explaining the different features as if I was showing off my Estate. I came to my senses and I explained that I helped Lady Howes when ever I could and I had fallen in love with the place, but it would take me a long time to get to know all of its changing moods.

When we got back to the Manor, Tim suggested that Mary could come with Fiona in their old car into Barnstaple, when I have the meeting with the Brig. This offer she gladly accepted which pleased me as I could imagine Mary kicking her heels waiting for me to finish with the meeting. Anyway this was one problem solved.

When our new friends were about to leave, Fiona asked if we would like to join them after the meeting and to go to Minehead in Tim's old car for a swim. We both thought it a grand idea.

The next morning after riding with Sally on her tour of inspection, which I am glad to say included another visit to the Wimble Arms, we met other friends of Sally's and of course several beers were consumed. This was a good excuse to have a restful afternoon, which we had, although it was not all that restful but more enjoyable.

At dinner that evening we told Sally what was planned for the next day. She was very pleased because she had some shopping for Mary to do for her in Barnstaple. During the evening she tried to get out of me what this meeting was all about. I managed to fob her off with a story about business. She snorted and said that the Brigadier knew nothing of business. His wife looked after their financial affairs. I kept her quiet by saying that I was sworn to secrecy, and that was all I could say.

We were a bit crafty, one night I would spend in Mary's bed and the next night, Mary would join me in my bed. This would make it look as if were behaving ourselves. The next morning it was my turn to leave Mary and go back to my room. I tried to go to sleep but my mind was occupied with the thoughts of the meeting with the German Officer. It all sounded very strange and very suspicious, and I wondered what I had got myself into. Anyway I would soon know.

When it was time to get up, I went into the bathroom to wash and shave and when I returned to my room, Mary was looking in my wardrobe, when I asked her what she was doing, she said she was looking for a spare hanger. I tried to grab her but she dodged me and ran laughing out of the room. It was a good job that I didn't catch her, because she only had a dressing gown and we would have been late for breakfast.

Tim and Fiona called for Mary in a very old-looking car and they went off to Barnstaple. I wished like hell that I could have gone with them, because I was not looking forward to my morning. Just before ten o' clock the Brig arrived and shortly afterwards the German stepped out of a very posh car; the driver of which remained in the car.

The German wore a well-cut civilian suit, but he still looked like a Prussian Officer of the old school as portrayed in films I had seen. The Brig and he shook hands and went into the house. I followed at a discreet distance. We went into the breakfast room and sat around the table.

The Brig started the ball rolling by introducing me as Henry, a close friend who could be trusted completely. At no time was the name of the officer mentioned. I had seen him before, but for the life of me I just could not remember where.

The conversation to begin with was polite, small talk. It would seem that they had met several times before when they were both younger. I was kept busy translating. They were both trying to speak in each other's language which made it more difficult for me. At last they got down to the reasons for this meeting and what I was about to hear would come as quite a shock.

To put it all in a nutshell, Hitler was dead scared of the Bolsheviks, that is why he helped Franco in Spain. He had a great respect for Great Britain and the way we ruled such a vast area of the world's surface. He did not want a war with Britain and would we unite with Germany against Russia?

I think that the Brig expected something like this and he listened very carefully to what was being said. The German went on to say that Hitler wanted to regain control of the Sudetenland and if Britain agreed to this he would have no further territorial ambitions in Europe.

It was now the Brig's turn and he said that the British people would never agree to the way that the Jews and other minorities were being treated. On the other hand they did not want a war with Germany or anyone else. There were some members of the Government who also thought this way and may be willing to trust Hitler to keep his word.

The Brig said that he would sound out some people he knew and he would be in touch. They then talked about their younger days as old friends.

The German started to talk to me and asked how I had learned to speak such good German. I told him my story about Mrs Jenkins and my visits to Lubeck. As I said Lubeck, it came to me where I had seen this Officer before. Of course he was in the party that stayed at the Castle with Herr Goering.

The Brig got up and that was a signal that the meeting was over. Hands were shaken all around and the German was on his way. When he had gone, the Brig and I had a brief walk down to the lake and back and during this time he thanked me for helping him out. Again he made me swear not to tell a living soul about the meeting and what we had heard.

As we got near to the house he said, "Blake, you mark my words, what we have heard today is only bluff and by the end of the year, Hitler will have marched into Czechoslovakia and not just the Sudetenland but the whole country and we will be at war by the end of next year."

We sat on a seat on the lawn and we were soon joined by Sally, followed by Salter with a tray of drinks. The Brig had a very large Scotch and I asked Salter if he could find me a beer. I had been talking for most of the morning and my throat was very dry. When Salter gave me a large glass of cold beer it went down a treat.

The Brig thanked Sally for the use of the Manor and once more thanked me for my services. Soon we heard Tim's noisy card and Sally walked with the Brig around to the back of the Manor to see him off. I think that the old man didn't want to get involved with the younger generation.

Tim dropped off Mary plus some parcels and said that he would pick us up at about three o'clock. Mary took me by the arm and look me inside the house and told me that she had some presents for me from Grandma. Laughing, she said that Grandma told her that I should look very smart to be her granddaughter's boyfriend. So before lunch I had to try them on. Mary chased me up the stairs saying that she would help.

She opened the parcels to reveal a smart Hacking jacket and flannel trousers. Mary had my trousers off and I put on the new ones and they fitted a treat. Then the jacket was put on and that was smashing. As I looked at myself in the mirror, I asked her how she managed to the get the sizes right? She told me that she had measured my clothes in the wardrobe. That was what she was doing this morning when I caught her in my room. What a crafty, little so and so she is.

We then went down to show Sally the coat and trousers she had bought for me. I thanked her for being so kind and generous and I tried to tell her not to do these things. She walked over to me and said that she had plenty of money and if she wanted to give her friends presents, she would. Anyway it gave her great pleasure. With that remark she took my arm and we went into lunch.

Tim and Fiona called for us and we were on our way to Minehead for a swim and a lazy afternoon on the beach. We had great fun that afternoon and for once the tide was in. When the tide was out at Minehead there was one hell of a walk to get to the sea.

On the way back we called at a country pub and we only just made it in time for dinner. When we got to the Manor, Sally was waiting for us and said that our friends must stay to dinner and she wouldn't take no for an answer. In fact she had telephoned the Brig to tell him that his son was staying to dinner. So that was the end of that conversation.

Our friends were shown where they could have a wash and brush up. Tim and I knew that the girls would be ages, so we went downstairs and had a chat with Sally.

She really was quite a nosy parker. She was always asking people questions about themselves. In no time, she had found out that Tim was only in the Army to please his Father, but as the situation was going we would all have to be in one of the Services. This made him think that perhaps he had made the right choice after all.

After dinner, we had a stroll in the park, but now it was getting dark much earlier and eventually after a lot of chit-chat and fooling around, Tim and Fiona went home.

Our holiday was nearly over and we would be driving back to South Devon tomorrow. We really had had a smashing time. It had been great fun going out with Tim and Fiona. Tim knew his way around Exmoor and he took Mary and I to some very beautiful places.

Sally seems to be getting me more and more involved with the business of the Estate and keeps asking me for advice about small problems. I also had to attend her meetings with Peggy Jackson, her book-keeper and secretary.

At times I find this embarrassing because I lack experience in this field. I am learning the theory at university, but I have a long way to go. Also I am not related to the old girl, although she treats me as one of the family, which of course I am not except with my close ties with Mary.

Anyway I have to go along with this, because I would hate to hurt the dear old thing. I have become very fond of her and she has been so very kind to me. I have mentioned this to Mary and she laughed and said, "Henry, darling, you are very clever at some things, but you are unable to understand how some females think. I know that you understand me but Grandma is a very different cup of tea. I know what is in her mind and one day you will know, but I have no intention of telling you, except that it will please you."

Mary and I made the most of our last night together and it was a very depressing thought that we will not have the comfort of these lovely, old beds until our next visit at Christmas.

At breakfast the next morning, Sally seemed sad at the thought of us leaving her and she made us promise to come again during the Christmas holidays. As we left I could see that her eyes were becoming moist with the odd tear.

Riding down the drive lined with the magnificent trees, which were just beginning to get their autumn tints. When I see them again the leaves will have gone and they will be dormant until they start to come to life in the spring.

Passing through the large gateway, I had the feeling of leaving the safety of one world and joining the harsh realities of the world outside.

CHAPTER 14

Mary and Hugh had gone back to college. I had started my last year at Exeter. Hitler had marched into the Sudetenland, without any great outcry from Britain or France, and tomorrow was to be my big day. I have to take my solo test and I feel very nervous indeed.

Flying a plane with a pilot as an insurance with the dual controls, is so very different to being up there all by one's self. I have practised so many times the different manoeuvres and I can land and take off quite well. I think that I am more scared of making a fool of myself than the physical dangers.

I have been working very hard and I was feeling sorry for myself so I missed a lecture that afternoon and I came home in time for lunch. I then saddled up Henry and I went where I usually went when I wanted to cheer myself up. Of course, I sat by the little bridge.

I was missing Mary like hell and it will be a long time until the Christmas holidays. Perhaps I would be able to afford a trip to London for a weekend.

Just before Mary had left for London, we had been in Exeter and unfortunately we had bumped into Polly, who had looked a real smasher. I tried to steer Mary in another direction, but it didn't work. Well we started to talk and of course Polly mentioned that she would be going to university until Christmas. While we talked Mary was holding my arm in a possessive way and I imagined that there were female signals flashing between these two lovely girls.

As Polly left us she said that she was looking forward to having a lift in my side-car. This really made Mary mad and we nearly had our first real row. I managed to calm her down and she told me that she could tell that Polly had her eyes on me. "So Henry," she said, "you had better watch your step otherwise I will cut your balls off."

We didn't mention Polly again, but after this encounter Mary seemed to be even more loving than before. How strange females are. I saw Polly out with a good-looking chap on several occasions, but she had the knack of turning up where ever I happened to be, but I will think about Polly the day after tomorrow.

I had just got back to the farm when Mary telephoned to wish me luck for my big day. I thought that it was jolly nice of her, because there was only one public telephone in the college and to use it, one had to wait ages. We were unable to talk for long, but it was smashing to hear her voice again.

The next morning seemed to be never-ending and I was unable to concentrate on the lectures. At last the time had come to drive out to Exeter Airport. I was lucky in one respect, the weather was fine and dry, with only a light wind and coming in from the east, which meant that I would be using the main runway.

I met Hank and after putting on the flying gear plus a parachute, I got into the biplane and after final instructions I was on my own. I had to taxi to the westward end of the runway so that I would be taking off into the wind. I tested my radio and after getting into position I awaited instructions from the control tower.

Now that I was all set to have a go, I felt excited and the nervousness left me. I was told to get cracking and I started to gather speed up the runway. As my speed increased I could feel the plane getting lighter and at the right time I gently pulled back the joystick and I was airborne.

Hank set me a course over the radio and this took me in the direction of the River Exe estuary and inland towards the farm and Teignford, over the farm and then back towards Exeter. I flew over the farm at a much lower level than I should have done and I could see Dad and John so I waved out of the cockpit and they waved back. Anyway, Hank wouldn't know.

Flying by one's self is a very strange experience. You are relying on the engine to keep you airborne, but you are master of your own destiny. You become part of kind of in-between world. From the ground clouds look solid and unfriendly, in an aircraft, clouds form a barrier and there is an excitement to see what is on the other side. There is also a feeling of peace perhaps it is because you are one step nearer to Heaven.

I was enjoying my daydreaming but Hank brought me back to this world and he told me to come into land. Landing is always the most difficult part of flying and it can be very dangerous. Hank had always told me to be very gentle and to cut the speed down as much as possible: always to keep the head up and the tail down.

Like all the other things I had been taught by Hank, with him in the plane there was always that sense of security. I also knew that all the staff watched the first landing made by a Solo. I didn't want to let Hank down and I didn't want to make a fool of myself. So I said to myself, "Here goes Henry, see what you can do."

The wind had freshened and as I put my flaps down I could feel the plane still wanting to be airborne. The design of the wings caused the feeling and there always seemed to be a battle as who would win.

I came in and I managed to keep in the centre of the runway, which was a good start. I touched down on both wheels and my tail soon followed. In fact I did a near perfect three point landing.

I taxied up to the front of the Clubhouse and as I got out of the cockpit there was a cheer from the few spectators. How I wished that my family and Mary had been there on this big day of my life.

It was a bit of a custom for the pupil that had passed his Solo to be bought a few pints by his friends. It was not until then that I knew how many friends I had in the flying fraternity. My ride home that evening was to put it mildly, very unsteady.

After an evening meal I was back to my normal self and Dad and I were sitting in the garden. I had several telephone calls. Sir James and Jake were the first to congratulate me. Then of course, my darling Mary rang which made my day.

After the upheaval of my flying test my life settled down to a rather boring routine of hard work and V.R. parades which were two evenings a week. The parade finished quite early for a change and a few of us went for a drink in a pub, which was a popular haunt for the students. I was just on my first pint and we were having a very lively conversation and I was getting relaxed and enjoying myself. I was sitting with my back to the bar and we were in a corner, so I was oblivious as to what was going on the rest of the bar. I had an unexpected finger poked in my back and a female voice said, "Hello Henry, aren't you going to buy and old friend a drink?" I knew at once that it was Polly's voice.

I walked with Polly up to the bar and she told me that she had been to an evening lecture and a girlfriend had asked her to come and have a drink before she caught the bus home to Broadclyst.

As I was waiting to be served I began to get worried. Polly was such a lovely girl so I must watch my step. We both talked about what we were doing at the University. It was difficult to get out of her exactly what she was doing. She said that some of the work was to do with decoding and ciphers. It was very hush-hush and very interesting. Of course I told her about my first solo flight and how I have to fly a certain number of hours to get my license.

We talked for ages and I had no reason to look at the time. However Polly should have done because she looked at the clock and then at me, with those big, blue eyes that I knew so well and said, "Henry, will you do me a favour and give me a lift back to Broadclyst?" I had no choice, but I knew that it was a trap as soon as she had seen me in the bar.

By now, the several drinks that we had consumed, began to break

330

down a few barriers and as we walked to my bike, Polly started to talk about our rides and she casually asked if the old barn was still standing. I quickly changed the subject.

I went to open the side-car but Polly said that she would rather sit on the pillion seat. I certainly knew why that was her choice. Anyway I got the bike started and Polly climbed up behind me and put her arms around my waist.

At first her arms were around my waist so that she would not fall off, but they began to get tighter and she started to snuggle her body up to mine. I was glad when we arrived at the vicarage because she had got me all het up, which of course she was fully aware of. She got off the bike and gave me a smashing kiss and whispered, "Not to worry Henry, I won't tell Mary," and then with a wave she ran into the house.

Broadclyst was quite a lot out of my way from Exeter. It was a fine night but the cold air began to clear my head and I was enjoying my ride home across the Haldon Moors and then down the narrow lanes to the farm. I stopped feeling guilty because I had only given an old friend a lift home and I had not been tempted by that gorgeous little vixen. Mary had told me not so long ago that I did not understand females. There was one female apart from Mary that I did understand and that was Polly.

Driving back through the lanes I wished that I could put into words the feeling of being so close to nature. The lanes seemed to be alive with God's creatures. There were rabbits, small creatures and I even saw a fox jump out of my way. It can give one a bit of a fright when a Grey owl swoops down in front of you to snatch a mouse or a vole for his supper.

It is a strange sensation to see your headlights reflected in the eyes of some wild creature in the hedge as you pass. It looks so ghostly. Sometimes one can tell what the animal is, by the distance between the eyes.

When I got home, only Dad was up and we had a brief chat before going to bed. He asked me where I had been and I told him that I had been to a pub with some friends. I didn't mention Polly because Dad was very fond of Mary and he would have given me one of his disapproving looks.

When I got into my bed I began to get very worried about how would I be able to keep out of Polly's way. Human nature being what it is, I knew that I might weaken and I would be very sorry indeed and I could not hurt Mary in any way.

Winter had now set in and it was early November. This was not my favourite time of the year. Everything seems to go to sleep until well into the new year. On one of my many visits to the Hall, which on this occasion was to have dinner with Sir James and Pamela. She had telephoned and said that she felt lonely and James wanted to talk to me about something. So, that evening I was to get quite a pleasant shock.

As I had no idea what it was all about, I made myself presentable and arrived in time for the usual drinks before dinner. I was always made to feel at home even by the staff and Hooper, the butler always made a point of greeting me when I arrived. I was now Mr Henry, having grown out of the title of Master Henry. I often think of the first visit through the front door and the disdainful looks the staff gave to that scruffy, little farmer's boy.

Hooper escorted me into the sitting room. There was this custom of shaking hands with Sir James and a kiss on the cheek for Pamela. I sat down and Hooper gave me a large sherry. They wanted to know how I was getting on and I told them that I was having two solo flights a week and I regularly flew over the Estate. I told them that it was quite a sight to fly in, fairly low over the deer and to see them run around their park, always being led by the current chief stag.

Hooper told us that dinner was being served and I took Pam's arm and we went into dinner. As we sat down Pam started to laugh and said that Cook had insisted that we have one of her famous pies as I was coming to dinner. We had a grand dinner and it was quite good fun. We retired to the sitting room for coffee and the business of the evening started.

Sir James said that the ladies must be first, so Pam started the ball rolling by saying, "Henry, we both know how fond you and Mary are of each other and I must say that we are more than pleased, so we would like you to visit her for the weekend in London and stay at Hugh's house. Now we don't want to offend you but we know it is an expensive trip, so would you do this if we paid all the expense? Mary has been on the phone to us and she is very unhappy and she would love to see you. She has until Christmas and then she can come home and finish her training in Exeter."

I nearly jumped for joy, and I think Mary's parents could see how pleased I was. I felt guilty about the funding of this visit, but that will pass. I said that I would be more than pleased. In fact I thought it was smashing. I asked when could this take place and Pam said next weekend if I was free from parades and lectures.

This was Thursday, so in a week's time I would be seeing Mary. I never thought that I would be so lucky, and for her to want to see me was indeed gratifying. Pam interrupted my thoughts by saying that Mary would be trying to telephone that evening and I would be able to chat.

Sir James was a very correct and sedate character. We got on like a house of fire. I rode with him at least once a week and we talked about all sorts of things. He had this gruff way of talking, and small talk was a foreign language to him. He looked at Pam and asked if she had finished, which was as much as to have said, "Shut up!, it's my turn now."

The Old Boy looked at me and said that according to Jake I was a fair shot with a twelve bore shot gun. He wanted me to go as his guest to his pheasant shoot on Saturday, which of course, would be the day after tomorrow. For a moment or two, I was speechless. I managed to say that I would love to and I will bag as many Pheasants as possible. To be invited to shoot with Sir James on one of his Pheasant shoots, was something unheard of, for a local person. These special occasions were reserved for his important friends from London and the 'County Set.'

In the past Mary and Hugh came over to the farm to keep out of the way of these 'Big-Wigs'. There was always bags of panic with the staff for these events. Everything had to be just so, and men from the village were employed as Beaters to drive the Pheasants towards the guns. There I was being asked as guest, not a helper. The news would probably give Dad a heart attack.

While I had been sitting there in a bit of a daze, Sir James had got up and poured out a couple of whiskies. He handed one to me, which was also very unusual, because he was very stingy with his favourite Scotch.

So then he started to hold forth in his abrupt way, "Henry, Pam and I have had a good talk about you, and my Mother in North Devon thinks that you are a fine fellow and she is very fond of you. We both look on you as part of our family. I get on very well with your Father and we have had lengthy talks about you, Henry. I am sure that you know that you are being trained in a very crafty way for special work if war breaks out. Pam and I are also looking to the future. When you have finished at University are trained in Estate and Farm management, and there will always be a job here for you." Here he paused and had one of his characteristic snorts, and said, "That is if I can keep my Mother from taking you up to North Devon." All of a sudden he looked sad and said that if there was a war then all of our lives would change for ever.

I had always liked Sir James and Pam, but it was not until now that I really felt a real affection for them both. We were so different in our up bringing and yet there seemed to be a bond of some sort. Perhaps it was my love for their daughter, Mary, or perhaps it was just one of those things. I now have to call Mary's mother Pam if I want to which adds to the affection.

I started to thank them both for what they had just told me, when

Hooper knocked on the door and came in to say that Miss Mary was on the telephone and wanted to talk to Mr Henry. So I was out the door like a shot and into the library and in no time at all, I was talking to Mary.

We soon made our arrangements for our weekend. I would find out the times of the trains and I would meet her at Hugh's house. Mary had asked Hugh if it was convenient and his reply was so typical, "What the hell do you ask me for? I keep telling you and Henry, that there are two rooms there which are yours, and will not be used by anyone else." We both had a good laugh at this.

When I told Mary about the Pheasant shoot, she was more than surprised and told me that to be invited as a guest to shoot at Langley Hall was a great honour in the district. She was silent for a moment or two and then she said, "Henry, my darling, you have no idea what Papa has done in asking you to join one of his special events." She went on to say that she would tell me more about it when we saw each other. We finished our telephone call by the both of us wishing that we could be together.

When I returned to the sitting room I told Mary's parents how pleased she was at the news. I asked Sir James to explain the procedure and the correct etiquette for a Pheasant shoot. What I should wear and countless other questions. The most important of all, what did I use for a gun?

This really made the Old Boy laugh. He started by telling me that Mr Jones, the head groom, who I was very friendly with, would be my loader and that I could borrow a pair of his guns. He talked for ages and by the time he had finished, I knew what the drill would be. It was now getting late so I thanked them both and made my way home, to another world.

Mother and Dad were still up and when I told them the news, they could hardly believe it. Then I told them about an offer of a job. This was too much for Dad, so he got out the whisky and we both had two large measures to celebrate my good fortune. I then told them about my visit to London to see Mary and it would be Sir James's treat. Mother gave Dad and I one of her old-fashioned looks and asked if it would be just me and Mary. To put her mind at rest, I told her that Hugh would be there and of course the housekeeper, Mrs Gibbs. I had no idea where Hugh would be, I just expected him to be there.

Mother went on to bed, but Dad and I were late that night. I was too revved up mentally to think about sleep; the thought of spending the weekend with Mary. The Pheasant shoot and then the job offers put my mind into orbit.

Dad kept talking about my job prospects, either with Sir James or

Lady Howes in North Devon. He asked me which I would like to become, fact and not just fiction. I told him that I had become very fond of Sally Howes in North Devon and for some reason I have fallen in love with the Estate. I would love for my father to come up and see it one day, I know that Aunt Sally would make him very welcome.

I gave Dad's question great thought and at last I said that Wimble Manor would be my choice, that was if Mary still remained to be my girlfriend and perhaps when we were much older, she might live up there. After I had said this, I knew that it was the whisky talking, because this was something that I thought could never happen. No doubt Sir James and his wife had great plans for Mary's future, which didn't include a farmer's son from Teignford.

When I went upstairs to my bedroom my mind was still very active and I began to remember what Sir James had told me about the shoot. I thought it would be quite a challenge. I had always been able to bring down woodpigeons in flight with Dad's twelve bore, which was not easy. Perhaps Pheasants would be an easier target. Anyway that part was not worrying me, it was the social side and the thought of meeting the important friends of Sir James, really giving me the willies.

Saturday morning came and I had on my best breeches and my new Hacking Jacket and I had given my riding boots an extra shine. Mother inspected me and she actually told me how smart and handsome I looked. I told her that she was looking through rose-coloured glasses.

I thought I would show off a bit and ride my grand-looking horse, Henry. It would perhaps be more dignified than a motorbike. I went in good time so that I could see Mr Jones and pump him for more information.

It was a nice, sunny morning and Charlie had said that it would be fine all day. I enjoyed the ride over to the Hall and when I rode up the tree-lined drive, I could see that some of the guests had already arrived and were standing in front of the house, having cups of coffee.

Sir James gave me a wave and he beckoned to Evans, who was standing nearby and said something to him. He came out to meet me and taking Henry's bridle and giving me a friendly smile, he told me that he had to take Henry to the stables, which of course upset my plans to see Mr Jones.

Sir James came over to welcome me. He took me by the arm and said that he wanted to introduce me to some of his friends and guests. Most of them were in the same age group as Sir James and there were a few females talking to Pam in a separate group to the men. I also noticed two younger men, probably feeling as out of place as I was.

I wondered how the old boy would introduce me and I must say that I was very surprised at what he said. I was introduced as, "A close friend of my daughter, Mary and an old friend of the family, Henry Blake."

I met the local Member of Parliament, a couple of titled bodies, and the others could have come from outer space because they were so different to my social standing.

What I found most strange was how I managed to talk to these people, without looking or feeling out of my depth. I found myself chatting to one of the younger men and his Father about the situation in Germany. I found this most interesting because they both worked in the Foreign Office.

We had all finished our coffee and Sir James got the transport organised and we made for the shooting area. This was in a large field near the edge of the forest, which concealed Fred Palmer, the game-keeper's cottage. This of course would be his big day. I wondered how he felt, seeing his precious Pheasants being killed? He had tended and protected them since their birth for a day such as this.

There were posts set out at intervals, each with a number fixed onto it. I was met by Mr Jones with a gun under his arm. We walked to number four and he very kindly told me what the score was.

Rule one, being that I should not fire at any birds that were in either of my neighbours' field of fire, and only at birds flying over my area. This gave us all bags of scope because the posts were wide apart. As soon as I had fired both barrels I had to hand the gun back to him and he would hand me a loaded gun to blaze away with. This would then give me a rapid rate of fire.

"Most important of all, Mr Henry, never shoot at a low level, always into the air." Mr Jones said with a laugh, "Let the battle begin." I had noticed that just behind the line of guns there stood chaps with dogs. Our dog was looked after by one of the grooms.

I could hear the noise that the beaters were making in the forest. Then the birds began to fly and I began to blaze away. I was knocking them down for a past time and the dog was kept very busy indeed. During a brief quiet spell Mr Jones looked at me and said, "Sir James told me that you had never been to a Pheasant shoot before and I would have to advise you where to aim when the birds were in flight. Mr Henry, do you realise that so far we have shot more than anyone else?" I asked him if I should ease off a bit because I had no idea what was correct in these circumstances. "No, Sir, the idea is to shoot as many birds as you can."

The noise was pretty horrendous and even with the breeze that had sprung up the air was full of the sickly smell of gun powder. I suddenly felt ashamed of myself for enjoying the killing of these poor birds. I consoled myself by what Dad had said a long time ago that the birds would not have been born if there were no Pheasant shoots."

The Flag went up and it was all over. Time had gone so quickly and I had enjoyed it so much. I thanked Mr Jones and gave him a large packet of his awful tobacco. He thanked me and told me that it had been a pleasure and that he had volunteered to be my loader. This really pleased me because I had become very fond of the old chap. I remembered how he had cleaned up dear old Daisy, now so many years ago.

My kills were all lined up in braces, and I must say that the number was very impressive. Sir James and some of the other guests came by and Sir James boomed, "Henry, have you had a bloody machine gun there today?" I replied, "Yes Sir, the new Browning and all of the birds had Swastikas on their wings."

This off the cuff remark caused a great deal of laughter and I could see that Sir James was more than pleased. I asked Mr Jones what happened to the Pheasants and he said that they belonged to the person that had shot them. So I told him to help himself to a couple of brace and give the groom a brace as well. They were so pleased that I began to wonder if I had done the right thing in giving staff Pheasants. Anyway I didn't care.

When we got back to the Hall, arrangements had been made for the guests to have a wash before having a buffet lunch. We then went into the large dining room and on a long table there was set a feast of cold meats and poultry. We all had drinks of different sorts according to our taste. I asked Hooper if he could find me a large beer and I started to tuck in.

By now there were a lot of females on the scene. Wives and daughters, plus the odd girlfriend. I was just about to visit the table again when Pam collared me and started to introduce me to her friends, as Mary's friend. There were some very snooty females there and there were several very attractive young girls. The two younger members of the shoot and myself were chatting away to these females and we were enjoying ourselves.

One of these girls had been looking at me as soon as I had come into the room and she was now transmitting very dangerous signals and to my horror I found that I was on the same wavelength. She was called Lady Vera something or other and I was glad to see her go. As she left she said, "Henry, no doubt we will meet again." I thought that if we do my dear I will put a padlock on my trousers.

All of the guests had now gone and I was about to leave, when Pam said, "Don't go yet Henry. James and I get to feel lonely after a do like we have had today. Anyway, James wants to talk to you."

Sir James came in and looked very pleased with himself. He sat down beside Pamela and taking her hand he said, "That was a great success and our Henry topped off the number of birds brought down." He looked at me and said that Jake had told him that I was a good shot, but not that good. I made the excuse that it was more by luck than skill. He replied that I was a damn good shot and it was very likely that I would be asked to shoot at other shoots in the area.

I got up to go and I asked if I could have a brace of Pheasants to take home to my parents. The Old Boy laughed and said that what I had shot was all mine and he would bring them all over to the farm tomorrow on his way into town.

I started to protest by saying that the cost of the cartridges could be covered by the sale of some of the birds. I knew that it was a waste of time to argue with the Old Boy. I went over and shook his hand and thanked him for a wonderful day. As I kissed Pam goodbye, she said that I would have to come over to see her before I went to London and to give her a ring to let her know which evening I could come over to dinner.

I walked around to the stables and met Mr Jones. He had got one of his staff to give Henry a good grooming and said that Mrs Jones had been grateful for the birds, which would be a treat for them both.

He was holding the bridle and he said, "Mr Henry, it was a real pleasure to act as loader for you today, but I would like to know where you were taught to shoot." I told him that it was a long story and one day I would tell him. Of course it was Jake, but it would be very difficult to explain.

By now it was late afternoon and I made up my mind that I would give Hank a Brace and of course, Jake. Perhaps Mother could dispose of what was left. I had been very greedy and I had shot about sixty birds. I doubt if I would ever do that again.

As I rode into the yard, Dad came out to greet me with such a grin on his dear old face. I got off the horse and Dad gave a bear hug and told me how proud he was of me. He said that Sir James had telephoned earlier and told him that I had out-gunned everyone else. "Henry, you never told me that you could shoot like that." I gave him a grin and said, "I don't tell you everything I do."

I had a busy time during the next week. I had lectures, parades, flying lessons and preparations for my trip to London. I had dinner at the Hall and Sir James presented me with a First class return ticket to London and the princely sum of twenty pounds. I told him that this was far too much and his reply was so typical of him. He said that I was to give Mary a good time, because it would keep his wife quiet, and anyway London was too damn expensive.

This visit to London was to see and be with Mary, so I would not meet anyone else. Major Davis and Mr Bernstein would not take any of my valuable time, as they have done on previous occasions.

Dad asked John to take me down to the station on Friday morning. I was going to take my bike but Mother put her foot down and said that she thought it was ridiculous for me to ride my bike to Newton Abbot, all dressed up in my best clothes. When Mother put her foot down, that was that.

John pulled my leg about my trip to see Mary. I am sure that he knew what was going on between us, after all he had been an expert before he got married and became a father. I told him about Polly and his advice was for me to keep my distance. "Watch out my lad," he said, "these females are a crafty lot."

John dropped me off at the station and I had a bit of time so I bought a paper to read on the train. When the train came in, I managed to get a seat by the window and for the time being, I would be the only occupant, so I settled down to read my paper.

What I read in the paper was very depressing. There was a night of violence against the Jews that were left in the various towns. They were treated as dirt and some had been taken away to labour camps. This night was called Kristallnacht (Crystal Night), because the windows of homes and shops were smashed by Storm Troopers, but that night and into the next day they were joined by middle class folk, who cheered as the 'Sub Humans' were beaten and killed. The streets were covered by broken glass and the final insult was that the Jews had to clear it up. Hence the name, Crystal Night, because of the glass.

I always enjoyed the train journey from Newton Abbot to Exeter. The line ran parallel to the River Teign and then into Teignmouth. This was indeed a lovely spot. The beauty of the natural estuary would take some beating, with the sun, now low in the sky, casting a shadow over Shaldon, the village below.

There were barges transporting clay down river to be loaded on to the ships in the harbour. I wondered where they were going. Perhaps to Lubeck. Somehow I thought that I would like to be on one of those ships and to feel free of the worries I seem to be collecting on my shoulders. Anyway that was a stupid idea because I would be without Mary.

When the train stopped at Exeter, two men came into my compartment. Their ages were about thirty to forty and after they sat down they started to talk to each other in German. One looked at me and said In very good English, "Good morning," and somehow I knew I had to answer in English. He then looked at his friend and said they ought to see if this fellow in the corner understands German. He then said that I looked like a pig of a Jew and several other unflattering remarks. I took no notice and continued to read my newspaper.

I now began to get very interested. I could see that they had small maps and they were making notes of any airfield or military establishments. There were not many for them to see from the train, nevertheless they seemed very busy.

Now what should I do? So I left my compartment and I managed to find the Guard. I told him a tale about having to make a phone call and which station would there be time to make this urgent phone call? He told me that there would be a wait at Westbury.

I had no idea if these men were going as far as London. Would Major Davis be interested in their activities? It would be a waste of time to telephone the Major in the war office, because I would have to be put through to different people before I would be allowed to speak to him. So I took the gamble that Jake would be in, so I rang him and told him what was going on. I gave him the number of the carriage and my seat number. It was a one-way conversation and I only just made it back to the train.

What I had done would probably be thought to be stupid, because we were not at war with Germany, on the other hand I did the same sort of thing when I went to Lubeck. Anyway time will tell.

Reading would be our last stop before London and I wondered if the two Germans would get off there, but I was glad to see that they were to carry on to the big city.

The train was just pulling out of the station, when the door of my compartment opened and two young men came in and settled down. They started to talk about general subjects and then one said that he might go down to Exeter and meet an old friend called Henry. As he said this he looked over towards me and as our eyes met, we both knew that contact had been made.

Perhaps I was not such a twit as I thought. After I had phoned Jake I was afraid that my reaction to the German's activities were a bit extreme. Now that these two chaps had been sent by the Department, I felt much better about it all.

When we pulled into Paddington and we all filed out of the train, one of the men from the Department hung back and said three words, "Thank you Henry." To me that made it all worthwhile.

I saw the two Germans well down the platform and they now had a young couple following them. The two chaps from the train seemed to have disappeared into thin air. I now closed my mind on the subject and devoted my thoughts to the prospects of being with Mary. I got a taxi and soon I was in Bruton Place and Harris opened the door and shook my hand, a lovely creature came flying down the stairs and ignoring Harris, she put her arms around my neck and we had a lovely kiss.

Harris gave my case to a footman and sent him upstairs to my room. Mary and I followed him up the stairs and informed Harris that we would be out until 5 o'clock and if there were any phone calls from the War Office to call back after then.

When we were in my room, I looked at Mary and she really is a very beautiful girl. I cannot see a single flaw in her features and her figure is out of this world. Her hair was a dark brown to match her eyes, that had a habit of flashing when she was about to lose her temper. It was a sort of early warning system. I know that love does tend to cloud one's eyes, but how I ever got Mary as a girlfriend is indeed a great mystery to me. It is so strange that we are so close on a mental plane and in other ways we seem to be as one.

We just stood and looked at each other and our thoughts were the same, because we both started to take our clothes off and in no time at all we were making love in a very tender way and not frantic as expected from a couple parted for several months. It was grand in my room, there was a coal fire in the grate and it was a place that we would have liked to stay in for the whole weekend, but we both knew that we had to appear to be more respectable. So we dressed and went down stairs into the hall.

Harris met us as we came down the stairs and told me that there had been a phone call for me and he had made a note of the number and that I should ring as soon as possible. He explained that there had been a very officious gentleman on the 'phone and that was his message. Harris led us into the office of Hugh's late uncle where there was a separate telephone.

I recognised the number which was a special number belonging to Major Davis. I had told Mary about my adventure on the train, so we were both interested to hear of the Major's reaction. Well he sounded more than pleased and said that Jake would tell me the whole story when I saw him next. We were very lucky that Jake was in, because he would never have got through in time. I was told that I did very well indeed, and the Brig sent his regards.

This really made my day. I had begun to think that I had made a fool of myself and my reactions were too dramatic. I will have to see Jake as soon as I get back to Devon.

Mary and I went into the sitting room and Harris organised some tea for us and we were able to have a good chat. Evidently, Hugh had something on at his college, but he will be able to join us on Sunday morning and the three of us will have a nice day together. It will be nice to see Hugh again, he is such a nice fellow.

We thought that we would go for a walk and look at the shops. Some were already preparing for Christmas and we tried on different pieces of clothing in some of the posh stores, with no intention of buying anything. But we both had great fun at the poor shop assistant's expense, which of course was very unkind. We were young, in love and so very selfish, but that is how things are in this unfair world.

I had thought of ringing Bernie but we both decided that all we wanted was just to be together and when at last we went to bed that night, we realised that this was what we wanted.

It was a wonderful weekend. We explored London by day and each other by night and the time seemed to fly. We had a great day out with Hugh on Sunday and when Monday morning came it was very difficult to say goodbye. We consoled each other by saying that Christmas was not a long way off and we would be going up to Wimble Manor for a least a week and we would be able to enjoy each other again.

I caught up with some of the lost sleep of the last few nights as the train sped back to Devonshire, I thought to myself. Back to the old routine of hard work and no play. Hank had told me that I would be in a position to take the exam for navigation in a week or two and if I passed that I would be able to try for my civilian flying certificate, before Christmas.

I had this strange feeling that someone was pulling wires so that I was getting more hours than the quota allowed for the V.R. Luckily this didn't cause any friction with my pals in the squadron. Not that I would be able to fly anything because the cost would be far too high. Anyway I am doing what the big white chief had planned for me. One day, I will know what it is all about.

When I had told Mary about the Pheasant shoot, she had said that she would tell me about her father's motives in asking me to be his guest. For once she seemed a bit shy and I had difficulty in getting any information out of her. What she told me, really shook me. She said, "Dear Henry, Papa is always way ahead of everyone else. In a way he is telling you and everyone else that you are acceptable as part of our family and when you are older you can marry me."

We were walking in Hyde Park when we had this conversation. When the dear girl said this she blushed and became most confused. She continued by telling me that I will probably fall in love with someone like Polly and I must forget what she had just said.

I stopped and putting my hands on her shoulders I said that I never thought that I would be acceptable and fate will determine if we are to be lucky enough to be together. She put her arms around my neck and kissed me and whispered in my ear how much she loved me.

She went on to say that, "in his way, Papa is very well thought of in Devon and he has some very powerful friends. If he takes you under his wing you will be surprised how it will help you."

I roused myself and decided to be very extravagant and have some lunch on the train. I walked, or to put it more correctly, staggered down the corridor to the dining car. I was just about to sit down, when a voice boomed out, "Blake, come and join me?" I looked around and there was the Brig.

I had no option so I joined the Old Boy. I sat down and he insisted on treating me. After we ordered and had a drink in our hands, he said how grateful his Department had been for the tip off with the two Germans on the train. By following those two, we cast our net and caught quite a bundle. They are now being questioned.

I asked how his son, Tim was getting on and his girlfriend, Fiona. He said, "You will no doubt see them at Christmas when I come up to the Manor with that lovely Howes girl. By the way, give Sir James my regards when you see him. He is a grand fellow, you are lucky to have him as a friend." He began to laugh. "Blake, I was so pleased that you out-shot everyone at James' last shoot. I thought Sally Howes in North Devon would never stop laughing when she heard about your efforts."

We finished our lunch and I was about to go when the Old Boy said that he understood that I would be finishing my flying lessons before Christmas. He said, "Blake, if you pass, I will agree for you to go to Cranwell on a month's course to get your RAF Wings. This is most irregular but we are in difficult times and you will be needed. This will then entitle you to a commission in the V.R." With that remark I could tell that the subject was closed and I had to make my exit. These were his ways which I would get to know so well in the future.

I found it very difficult to settle down after my weekend in London. I missed Mary like hell and being able to relax from my work and worries. I had to work so very hard to cover all that we were being taught about radio and the many uses it could have in the case of a war starting. I take my final exam next June and if I pass I will have some sort of letters after my name.

The Farm management course in comparison, is quite easy and I take my exams at the end of next term. I could of course pack it all in if I pass this exam because I have jobs available. Somehow I know that I will do my best to pass the real test.

I had no idea that on my return I would hear such bad news. Dear old Dad had been taken ill and the family had been told by the Doctor that he would have to take things very differently in the future. John will have to take over the running of the farm and Dad will have to be a back seat driver.

He had not been all that well for a week or two, but we all thought that it would pass. While I had been enjoying myself in London, the dear old chap had had a heart attack. Luckily, it was only a small one but it was a warning which could not be ignored.

This really upset me. I thought of Mum and Dad going on for ever and always being there to advise and help me, and the thought of life without either of them was unbearable.

I have had a chat with John and he seemed very confident about being able to run the farm, and of course, Charlie would always be his left hand. He had no thoughts of asking me to help, because he knew that my exams were so very important. Every difficulty has a silver lining and that would be John's exemption when the war starts. I have now resigned myself to thinking, not if there will be war, but when there will be. This is how I am going to plan my life for the next year or two.

I went to see Jake on the Saturday after my return from London and I had another shock. This was very minor compared with the news about dear old Dad. I rode Henry and it was grand to go over the very familiar route, which always reminded of the time, now so many years ago, when I plucked up courage to venture into the unknown forest.

Jake met me on the way through the wood and I dismounted and we walked to his cottage, through the trees which were now bare and ghost like. The woods are always so silent at this time of the year and our voices seemed to sound so much louder as if we were disturbing the nature's long winter sleep.

When we got settled in front of a nice log fire and a hot cup of coffee, Jake started to tell me how pleased he was with my episode on the train. I had almost forgotten it by now, it was just a natural reaction because I had done the same in Germany. He continued by saying that the Major wanted me to do another job in Europe. But this time in Normandy.

"You see, Henry, you have a friend there called Celeste, and her father served just like me in the last war and in his way he still does. So you are a natural candidate for the job. What we want you to do is to go to Normandy, stay at their farm and act like a long, lost cousin, or a friend of the family. You will have to try to be like a French man that has lived in England for most of his life. We will give you a proper background so that the very local population will know that you are connected in some way to the Prideaux family. Your job is quite simple. You are to spend every minute that you can by getting to know the countryside around the town of Falaise and up the channel coast. There are two main objects to this exercise, they are for you to be accepted as a friend of the Prideaux family and should you turn up in the future, you will be known. The second is for you to see if there are any flat areas, away from towns and villages, that a very light aircraft could land and take off again. Now Henry, I want you to think very carefully about this. Of course you can say no, on the other hand, you have been groomed for this sort of work. We all think that you can do it, and this includes your Father and Sir James. There will be a war so my boy you might as well get yourself organised. The Brig will see that you get a commission in the V.R. as soon as you pass your flying test. I also understand that have the choice of two jobs. I hope to God that you will be able to make this choice."

I sat there not knowing what to think. I know that I have to say yes, but there are several very important points that I have to raise with my mentor, Jake.

So I started to hold forth and I told Jake that Mary was one of my main worries. We both loved each other and she will go mad if I have to go anywhere near Celeste. I had quite an affair with this lovely French girl and I think that Mary really knew all about it, but she never let on. Of course, Celeste may be married or have a regular boyfriend. Somehow I don't think so because when ever I see Mr Jarvis in Newton Abbot, he always has a message to pass on to me.

The next question is how am I going to get there and what sort of transport will I have in France and most important of all, who is paying for this visit?

Jake said that he would answer the practical questions first of all, "We want you to ride your bike to Weymouth and take the Ferry to Cherbourg and then find your way to Falaise." This in itself will be a simple test for me to take.

"All of the costs will be paid for by the Department, plus a personal cash allowance for yourself and all the tickets will be obtained for you.

Your transport will of course be your bike plus the side-car. We want you to go after Christmas, before you go up to North Devon with Mary." He gave me a bit of a look and said. "You had better sort out the dates with her. There is another reason for you to go and that is to get to know the local accent. Henry, you will be busy because you will only have ten days in Brittany and I am sure that your Mary will not object. Anyway her father is going to give her a talking to about it." He started to laugh and said that all I will have to do is to be sure to keep my trousers on. He had one of his silent moods and after a while he said, "When I met you Henry, as a small boy, I never thought that I would be talking to you like this, and what a friend and a good pupil you have been. I am sure that you will never understand how you and your family helped to bring me back into this world, after my war experiences which had such a devastating effect on me."

We talked for a while and then Jake surprised me somewhat by telling me to be sure to give the impression that I am only visiting distant relations. I must under no circumstances, speak any German or to show any interest in the Nazis or the prospects of war against Germany. There are quite a number of French politicians that are willing to give in to Hitler's demands.

"Believe me Henry," he said, "there are some very queer people over the there. The Prideaux family can be trusted and you can talk freely to them." I then remembered that Celeste was always nattering on about the Germans and I used to pull her leg by talking to her in German.

I left Jake's cottage and rode Henry slowly through the wood which I had grown to love. I thought to myself how smashing it would be just being an ordinary sort of chap, without any connections with a Government Department, complicated courses about Radio and learning to fly in a very short space of time.

All I really wanted to do was to manage Langley Hall or Wimble Manor with Mary there to help me. At this point I thought of Celeste and what would be the reaction when I see her. I must be very careful indeed. I hope that she now has a regular boyfriend. She should have, because she is a smashing bit of French female and very sexy.

When I got back to the farm, I told Dad, but he was not surprised because Jake had confided in him several days ago. As usual I am the last person to hear about my future plans. I expect that Sir James knows all about it as well, I will have to tell Mary, but I will worry about that some other time.

It is now almost mid-winter, the longest day will soon be here and then of course Christmas will be with us once more. The plan that had been sketched out for me by other people, had started to take shape.

During the first week in December, I passed my flying test and the navigational side of it. There were two bods from the Air Ministry and much to Hank's surprise, a very crotchety RAF Squadron Leader turned up for my test, but not for the other two candidates. The three of us in turn had to take off and land several times, but always according to the wind direction.

When it was my turn, I had to take off and land with a cross wind, which can be very dodgy indeed. Anyway I managed to do it three times. When I came into the Club House, the Squadron Leader smiled for the first time and said, "Well done, Blake," and without another word, he pissed off, which we all thought was very rude indeed. Anyway I can now fly a light aircraft anywhere in this country and for that matter anywhere in the world. That night, we all had a bit of a party and as I got the worse for wear, Hank put me up for the night.

I was sitting by the lake at Langley Hall on this mid-December, Saturday afternoon. I now wandered all over the Estate whenever I felt like it and sometimes James, I now had to call the Old Boy, James, joined me, now Pam had taken up riding again, was often my companion. Today I was on my own and I loved to just sit here and daydream.

I had been called into see the C.O. of the V.R. and was told that I had been given a commission, and I had to get my uniform from a well-known tailor in Exeter. He was a bit put out by this, because it was very unusual. I had to tell him that it was all to do with my gift for languages. When I heard this news, I rang Jake and he confirmed that I had to be measured for a complete kit; all at the Department's expense. So now I am Pilot Officer Blake V.R. The V.R. is shown on my lapels.

It was so peaceful sitting by the lake and I was in another world, so I didn't notice that James had come to join me. We talked for some time and I asked his advice about telling Mary about my trip to France. He said that he would sort that out for me. He went a bit dreamy eyed and said that he still thinks about his French girlfriend during the war.

"So watch your step, Henry my boy, and don't leave any little Henrys behind," he said. With a good laugh he stood up and told me to come into the house and have a drink and Pam and he would be most offended if I didn't stay for dinner.

Over dinner that evening, we discussed plans for Christmas. Grandmother Sally, Geraldine and of course Mary and Hugh will all be descending on the Hall for the Christmas period. Pam then told me that there would be the usual tenants' party and she wanted my whole family to come. Then she said that they would like to have a party for New Year's Eve, which would include young people and their parents.

James wondered, "Do you think the Brig's son and girlfriend, Fiona could come, or for that matter, would want to come, so perhaps you could sound them out? We would like them to come because you and Mary get on well with them. They would have to stay the night and so would you Henry."

I always seem to be doing things for people, so I told James and Pam that we were having the University Christmas Ball, three days before Mary came home and I would love to take her.

"Is there any way that this could be fiddled?"

Pam looked at her husband, as much to say, Of course, you must get Mary home. James knew that he had to do as he was told so that was arranged.

Pam then said that she would get Wills to give us transport to and from the Ball, because a motor bike and side-car is not suitable. "It would also make it much easier if you and Mary stayed the night at the

Hall." I thought I will have to watch Mary's antics all night!" I asked if I would be in order in getting tickets for Mary and I.

"You might as well tell her that Polly will be there, so that will make up her mind," said Pam.

We all had a good laugh about this.

James wanted to know what Polly was studying. I said that I have been unable to find out, except that it was very hush-hush and something to do with the breaking of codes and that sort of thing.

It had been a very enjoyable evening and as it was such a dark night, James offered to take me home in his car and stable Henry at the Hall for the night. I refused his kind offer, as I would like to have a ride in the dark.

I said goodnight to my kind hosts and I rode into the darkness. When the light from the Hall had faded into the distance, I was enveloped by the darkness in the narrow lane so I took my torch out of my saddle bag to help me on my way. Not that there was much need because I gave Henry his head and he knew the way home.

I was so pleased that Mary could come to our Christmas Ball, and being asked to stay the night at the Hall was most unexpected. When I get back to the farm I will write to Mary and tell her the good news, and when I see Polly I will tell her the bad news, because she had been hinting that I might be able to take her to the Ball.

I have only seen Polly for the odd drink and I had behaved myself, which was becoming increasingly difficult because she looked at me with her bright, blue eyes, which were so inviting. I am glad that she goes back to Oxford after Christmas.

I like to ride in the night. It is quite an experience when the moon is full and there are some weird and strange shadows caused by the moonbeams through the trees. When I was younger I was quite scared but now it is a form of escape. I kid myself that I am in another world and I try to forget my problems. I think that this is perhaps why I love the country so much. The main ingredient of life is missing, and that is people and it is so peaceful, there is no stress.

Over the past few months I have had this feeling of impending disaster and it keeps coming over me. Dad's being ill didn't help matters and my mind is becoming more and more certain that a war is well on the way. Perhaps I have been working too hard. Anyway I will have to get over this feeling and my Mary will soon be home and I will have four weeks holiday and a week in France, and of course a visit to North Devon. I should feel so happy, but somehow I am fearful of the future.

When I at last reached the farm, bedded down Henry for the night, I joined Mum and Dad who were having a chat with Betty and Charlie. Dad gave me a glass of beer and I thought how friendly it all seemed.

But how different it was to where I had been only an hour ago. The atmosphere at the Hall is always very pleasant and happy and now it seems to be a second home. At times it is not easy to adjust to such changes.

Mary can mix in any sort of company. Perhaps it is because she is going down the social scale, whereas I always am going up the scale. It is not that I feel inferior, in fact sometimes I feel very superior mentally, it is just that perhaps I don't belong. Anyway fate had decreed that this was how it would be for Henry Blake.

Poor Mother had her usual pre-christmas panic on. Would she have enough turkey and poultry to satisfy her ever-increasing list of customers? We had this every year, to such an extent that we now ignore it. That is if it is possible. I went to bed that night and somehow it took me a long time to go to sleep.

When at last I got to sleep, my dreams were far from pleasant. They included people that I had never seen before and in a countryside that was so very strange to me. I was hiding in a wood with Celeste and other people. We all had guns and were ready to use them.

In a corner of the field next to the wood, stood a very dilapidated-looking aircraft. Somehow I knew that I had to get to the aircraft, together with an older man that was crouching by my side. Then the two of us started the engine and then all hell broke loose. My friends by the wood opened fire and this was returned by, I presume, Germans.

I had to try to take off with the wind, so I revved up the engine and saying a prayer I went across the field through the German field of fire and then I woke up. Over the next few months I would be having this dream several times, but I never found out if I made it. There was a final solution in my dreams many months ahead, which proved to be my saviour.

It was Christmas night and all the family were in the front room. John and Gertie had spent the day with us. Young Sam was asleep in another room, all cosy and warm in his portable cot. Jenny was not with us. It was her husband's turn to spend Christmas with his folks. They were going to visit us in the New Year.

I was having a bit of peace, sitting in front of the kitchen fire, listening to the ash burning in the grate, and I started to go over in my mind what had happened during the run up to Christmas.

My uniform had been delivered and I had to wear it to the next parade. I felt a bit of a twit and very much out of place. My friends pulled my leg but I was glad that I was still accepted by them. The other Officers also made me feel at home in the Squadron. Anyway I soon got use to the new situation.

The C.O. must have had information about me from 'up the line' because I was given the task of teaching the lads all that I knew about survival, woodcraft and simple unarmed combat.

Jake had been teaching me for years and I really failed to realise that I was being taught. Somehow it all registered and I could pass on this very useful information.

The University Ball was a great success. Mary looked radiant and I felt so proud to show her off to my chums. What I found to be so very amusing was to watch how Mary and Polly looked at each other up and down during their first encounter. They had not met for quite some time and they were both very beautiful females.

Polly was with one of the chaps from the Squadron, so we asked them if they would like to join us. It wasn't very long before we had quite a party at our table and we were having a very enjoyable evening. Mary as usual was full of fun and it was grand to see her so happy.

I had a dance with Polly and she got up to her old tricks of pressing herself as closely as she could to me. This of course started to rouse me sexually, which of course she could feel and much to her amusement I had to push her away. When the dance finished she whispered in my ear, "I will have you one day Henry, so watch out." Needless to say I didn't have any more dances with Polly that night.

When the Ball was over we went out into the Quad and there was Wills with the damn great Rolls. I had my leg pulled about this, but it was in a good humoured sort of way, and when Wills drove off there was a loud cheer. I could see in the mirror that Wills was having a good laugh. I thought he had brought the Rolls on purpose. I liked Wills, he had a good sense of humour, we have had many good laughs over the years.

I had never stayed the night at the Hall. I had been given a room next to Mary's, but we were on a different landing to James and Pamela. I remembered thinking that I may even see a family ghost.

When we got to the Hall, one of the maids let us in and asked us what time we would like breakfast. Mary quickly replied, not before ten o'clock. We slowly climbed the great staircase, hand in hand and feeling greatly in need of a close relationship. We kissed each other goodnight, as a sign of good behaviour and went into our separate rooms.

We were not alone for long. Mary came into my room and she was soon in my arms and to feel and smell her presence was pure heaven. We were no longer tired, just intent on enjoying each other. Sitting in front of the kitchen fire, I could remember every detail of that first night I spent in Langley Hall. Somehow it was very special.

We very nearly disgraced ourselves the next morning. We overslept and Mary had to make a run for it, before the house became alive with servants.

We washed and dressed and we both went down the staircase, to be met by Hooper who said he had a message from the cook to say that she had prepared a special breakfast for me and if I didn't eat it she would be offended. The three of us had a good laugh at this, because she had a habit of feeding me up whenever I came to the Hall. I think that she thought that I was still the skinny little chap of years ago.

I had a smashing breakfast and we decided to go for a ride. I could ride Hugh's horse and Mary sent a message to the stables that we needed the two horses in about half an hour.

I remembered that breakfast so well because I just couldn't keep my eyes off Mary. It has been said that beauty is only skin deep. Mary is the exception to this because she is to me a beauty in so many ways. Mary asked me why I was looking at her so much, so in my way I told her.

She got up and came over to me and putting her arms around my neck, she kissed me and told me how much she loved me. At that moment Pamela came in. I felt embarrassed but Mary said, "Mama, Henry had just told me that I am a beautiful girl and I have just told him how much I love him. Now how better could one start the day?"

Pamela looked at us both and said, "It is grand to see two young people looking so happy. It makes me wish I was a young girl again." She had sat down and we talked about the party she would be giving after we had been up to North Devon and before I went to France.

Every time France was mentioned, Mary gave me a kick or tried to hit me. She has however accepted that I have to go, but it would not be in the national interest for me to sleep with Celeste. This had become quite a joke between us. She kept thinking up the most ghastly things she would do to me if I strayed from the path of purity.

I had done very well for Christmas presents. I was glad that they were items to wear. Mary gave me some cuff links with my initials engraved on them, which were smashing. I gave her a necklace, the price of which made me very hard up, but she always wanted one like it, so she was more than pleased.

Mary had worked out that the best time for us to go to visit North Devon would be about the second week of January. This had been arranged with Aunt Sally when I saw her at the Hall on Christmas Eve. She told me that she would give me my Christmas present when I came up to the Manor. This intrigued me and I wondered what it could be. Anyway I will soon know.

My peace was shattered by Mother who said that I should join the family in the front room. This I did and I enjoyed the fun that always seemed to surround John wherever he went. For a moment I wondered where we would all be next year at this time. I managed to close my mind to these thoughts and I went to bed in a happy frame of mind.

If the weather is fine, Hugh, Mary and I will be having a ride. It will be grand to be with Hugh again. He doesn't come home much and Mary and I think that he has a girlfriend in London. We were however in for a big surprise when all will be revealed on Boxing Day.

Boxing Day was a cold, fine day and ideal for a nice long ride. I set off bright and early and as I rode up the long drive, I could see Hugh and Mary standing by their horses, but there was a third person, also with a horse, but talking to them. This person was a female and I recognised her as the pretty little thing that Hugh was talking to at one of the tenants Christmas parties. Her father farmed a large farm to the north of the Estate, that was all I knew about her.

I rode up to them and it gave me the time to have a good look at this new female. She was very pretty, slim, dark hair and large, brown eyes that gave me a good looking over. When I reached them I dismounted and Mary came over and gave me a real lover's kiss. She took my arm and introduced me to this stranger, "Henry this is Ann Hastings, Hugh's girlfriend, who is in college with Hugh. She lives a few miles beyond Teigncoombe." I told Hugh that he was a dark horse not to have let us into his secret. Hugh was by this time blushing like mad.

Mary said that I had to go in and see Grandmama, otherwise she would tick me off. I did like the Old Dear and I gave her a good kiss on the forehead and in return she gave my arm a tight squeeze. For some unknown reason James and Pam, always seemed pleased when Sally returned my sign of affection.

We all sat and had coffee. Quite naturally, Ann was shy, but we soon broke that down and soon she was more relaxed and sure of herself. James well and truly broke the ice.

He told me that I have been invited to a shoot with him at Lord Luscombe's estate later in January, after you come back from France. He had a twinkle in his eye when he continued by saying, "You remember Lady Vera, well Luscombe is her father and we will have to spend the night there. So you will have to lock your door that night!"

I could see Mary's eyes start to flash and she looked at me and then went over to her father and the two of them had a good humoured fight, and then she had a go at me. James then said that Mary was invited as well.

As we walked out into the hall, Pam told us that we were all expected to stay to lunch. James asked us where we thought of riding to and without thinking I said that perhaps the girls would like to visit Teignford and have a drink in the pub, after all it's Christmas. James looked at Pam and said that he might even join us, that is if we didn't

352

object to an old codger like him. Hugh took the bait and said that as long as you buy the round you will be very welcome.

It was a very pleasant ride down the country lanes. It was no longer the three of us. We were now four. I was riding beside Mary with Hugh and Ann in front of us. I watched how they acted towards each other and it was pretty obvious that Hugh was very fond of Ann. Somehow she didn't seem so demonstrative as he was. Perhaps she was shy and not so open as Mary, or for that matter Polly. Anyway for looks, Hugh had picked a stunner.

When we got to the pub I could see a large grey tethered outside. which told us that Sir James had beaten us by my going across the fields.

After being out in the bright, winter sunshine, the pub was very dark inside and it took me several seconds to see that the place was very busy. There was a grand smell of a wood fire and ale.

Over a pint or two, I collared Hugh and asked him about Ann and wondered why he had kept it a secret.

He confided in me that his mother still treated him as a young boy and he thought is wise to keep quiet about his feelings for Ann. I told him that I used to feel the same, but with a laugh I said that Mary soon changed that. He went on to tell me that they have been friends for quite a long time, but it had now sort of blossomed into an affair during the last term.

He said, "I met Ann's parents several times and I would see them at the tenants' party. Henry, will you put in a good word for my friendship with Ann? Papa always seems to listen to you. You are looked upon as one of the family. I do hope that one day in the future you will marry Mary as she loves you very much."

It was my turn to be surprised. Hugh had never had much to say about Mary and I. I am sure that he knew that we slept together. Who knows, perhaps he sleeps with Ann, he has his own house in London and he doesn't come home very often?

We heard a shriek from the other end of the bar. Brother John had come in and picked up Mary and carried her over to where the mistletoe was hung from the ceiling and he gave her a good kiss. She was laughing like mad and trying to hit John.

James shook John's hand and wished him a happy Christmas and bought him a pint of his favourite beer. John looked at Ann, but decided not to push his luck. He was always such a happy fellow and full of fun. I do hope that somehow I will be able to take after him. I doubt if I will be so lucky.

We really had a very enjoyable time on the Boxing Day of 1938. I will always remember it, with at times longing and other times a feeling of thankfulness.

The tenants' party was a great success. James made a point of introducing me to people that I didn't know, which I thought at the time a little strange. I was always referred to as, "Henry Blake, a friend of my daughter, Mary." I met Ann's parents and they asked me to bring Mary over to see them one day. I chatted to them for quite some time, or should I say we talked for some time, because Mary was always by my side.

Aunt Sally spent most of the evening talking to Dad. They got on like a house on fire. I never found out what they talked about.

Hugh, Ann, Mary and I slipped out and went into the games room and with the help of the Gramophone, we had a few dances. Polly was at the party with her mother and father, but I had managed to keep out of her way. When we all came into the Hall, there was Polly standing under the large bunch of Mistletoe. She pounced on me and before I knew what was happening, she had me under it and she gave me a smashing great kiss. She said, "Do you remember that we had our first kiss at Christmas so many years ago?" She looked at Mary and told her that she must hang on to Henry, otherwise she would be after him.

This really was the first open conflict between these two lovely girls, which I could see upset Mary. I gave her a hug and soon she was her usual cheerful self. She did however hang onto my arm for the rest of the evening. Polly was lovely and so very nice, but it was Mary that I loved, so she had nothing to fear. It made me think how lucky I am to have two such girls after my affections. I suppose that in a very different way I loved them both. It would be nice to be an Arab and have more than one wife.

There were great preparations going on at the Hall over the next few days to get things organised for Pam's New Year's Eve dinner party. Mary, Hugh and I spent most of the time at the farm. Mother said that she liked having us around because it made her feel young again.

It was quite a ride but Ann came over one day. Because of the position of her farm it was closer to Long Meadow than Langley Hall. She mixed in well with the family and Mother did us well, where food was concerned.

At last the big day arrived and I packed my evening clothes into my side-car and I was on my way to this posh dinner party. There were going to be a few younger people there, so Mary had got the games room cleared so that we could have a dance. Several of the guests were staying the night, so Mary and I decided to behave ourselves.

When I got to the Hall, Evans took my gear from the side-car and told me that he would take it up to my room. I drove my bike around to the stables and had a chat with Mr Jones. He looked at my bike and told me that it was a disgrace and he would get one of the lads to give it a good clean up. I made him laugh by telling him not to give it too many 'Oats'. He was such a grand chap and to me, such a good friend.

I was having a bit of a daydream as I walked from the stables to the front door of the Hall, when I was grabbed by my arm and pulled to a secluded part of the building by Mary, who proceeded to give me so many kisses. I asked her what caused this sexual outburst. She then told me that she would not be going anywhere else to be educated and she would be helping Papa with the Estate. This meant that she could see me whenever I could get away from my studies. The dear girl was so happy that I could even see it in her eyes.

She took my arm and we walked into the Hall. Extra decorations had been put up and it looked smashing. Geraldine had come home for the party and when she saw me she took my hand and guided me to the Mistletoe and gave me a very friendly kiss, in fact it seemed a bit more than friendly.

She said, "Dear Henry, I will never be able to thank you enough for helping me to run away from that beastly husband I had in Germany." After she said this it all flooded back into my mind, and how risky it had been. Pamela then came on the scene and told me that my room is the same as last time. "Mary take Henry up to his room and then come down and we will all have a cup of tea."

When we got into my room, after a very nice kiss, Mary gave me the run down on a dinner party of the type we were going to tonight.

She explained that it would be held in the large dining room. The table has been extended to form a massive eating area and capable of seating a large number of guests. The guests will be mostly older people from the County. There will however be a few younger couples and we will be able to have a dance after dinner. Tim Eastham and Fiona are invited, that is if his old car can get here, but they are unable to stay the night.

Mary put her arms around my neck and said that, "Papa insists that you are to stand with me as the guests arrive and you will be formally introduced to them. Henry, darling, you must understand that Papa thinks so much of you and he treats you as part of the family." She then took my arm and we went downstairs for tea in the sitting room.

As I went into the room, Aunt Sally told me that I had to come over and sit next to her because she wanted to have a good chat with me about our visit to the Manor next week. "James tells me that you can help me have a good Pheasant shoot while you are staying with me. It will also give you the chance to get to know some of the very boring people that live up here."

I looked at her and taking her hand I said, "You have been a bit

355

unfriendly for several years, because you have been unhappy. But you are a different person now. When I met you first of all I thought what a bad-tempered Lady you were, now you are still bossy, but we all love you. This will reflect on your neighbours." The Old Dear burst out laughing she said to Mary, "Henry tells me that I am bossy, is that right?" Everyone said as in one voice, "Yes you are!"

Mary came over and sat on my lap and started to talk to her grandmother about what she should wear that evening. She made herself quite comfortable, with one arm around my neck. It was strange that Mary's increasing signs of her affection for me are now taken for granted by the Howes' family. I have this feeling of friendliness from them all.

Our society was such that to be invited to a dinner party at Langley Hall, would be a highlight in some of the lives of local people. Here was I, having to stand with the family to greet the guests. Perhaps one day I will wake up and it is all a dream.

Eventually we got ready for the dinner party. Mary came into my room and tied my tie for me. She looked lovely. I told her that she looked so nice that I could eat her. She laughed and gave me a dig below the belt.

She then told me that Papa had a surprise for Hugh, but you must not say a word to him. Ann had been invited and Hugh knows nothing about it. Will has gone to fetch her and she will be staying the night. To see Hugh's face when she comes into the Hall will be worth watching. I was so pleased for Hugh's sake because the evening would be so boring for the poor chap.

I felt a real twit standing in the hallway waiting for the guests to arrive. When at last they started to be announced by Hooper, I found it quite interesting and it gave me a false feeling of importance. We had some good fun when Jake was announced. Mary started it off by giving him a curtsey, he returned by kissing her hand and telling her how beautiful she looked, which he said In French. When it was my turn, I clicked my heels and spoke in German.

We had a similar carry on when Tim Eastham and Fiona arrived. Mary told Fiona about Hugh's Ann and asked her to look after her while we were greeting the guests.

Mary gave me a nudge and we both watched Hugh's face, when he saw his Ann being escorted in by Hooper who, with a nervous smile on his face said, "Miss Ann Hastings." The poor girl looked so nervous and completely out of her depth. Mary gave her kiss and beckoned to Fiona, who came and took her under her wing. Well at last that ordeal was over. Hugh was like a dog with two tails and he thanked his parents for being so thoughtful.

Those of my generation gathered in one corner and had a few, quick drinks to get us in the right mood. While I was joining in the small talk I had a good look around at the guests. Some I recognised as local dignitaries and I saw Jake talking to a tall, military sort of chap. I had been introduced to him, but his name meant nothing to me, and then I remembered where I had seen him. He had been one of the bods that interviewed me at the War Office on my return from Germany. I would love to know what they were talking about.

Hooper came into the room and announced that dinner was being served. So we took our partners by the arm and walked into this magnificent room, with the table laid out with the family silver and centre pieces decorated with unusual flowers from the heated greenhouses in the walled garden.

It was a smashing meal of about six courses, with several different wines with each course. I think that the wine made me lose count of how many different sorts of food my stomach was forced to cope with.

We danced and had a very pleasant time and we were all sorry when the party had to break up. We had even been joined by some of the older couples, who had a dance or two. Who knows, perhaps they were trying to recapture their youth? Mary and I had joined the other guests in the sitting room and the hallway and acted as hosts, mixing and making small talk. I always liked to talk to strangers. I always seemed to learn something.

I joined Jake and his Military friend and I spoke to him in German, because he had tested me when I had the interview at the War Office. He laughed and we shook hands, now that I had recognised him. I told him that I had been told to visit France in a week or two, and as Mary had now joined us, I said that I knew a charming French girl in Normandy. Mary tried to hit me and this made the four of us laugh. I put my arm around her waist and said, "I dare not tell you what this young lady will do to me if I stray when I am in France."

When everyone had gone, we all sank into comfortable chairs and relaxed. We were all a bit worn out. James gave us a final drink and we once more wished each other a happy New Year.

It had been great fun at twelve o'clock. Hooper had given the gong a good bash, and the men shook hands and then we all kissed any kissable females that were the nearest. We then made a circle by joining hands and sang Auld Lang Syne. Everyone let their hair down and we were in 1939.

Eventually we made our way up the old staircase to our respective rooms. As I walked up the stairs I wondered what tales they could tell of past New Year celebrations? Looking at the portraits of Mary's ancestors hanging on the walls made me wish that I could go back in time and see how they enjoyed themselves.

Ann and Hugh disappeared to their rooms along the landing and Mary and I said our goodnights. She whispered in my ear that she would soon join me when it was all quiet. I told her that it would be a wonderful way to start the New Year.

I went into my room and took my clothes off and sitting in my dressing gown in front of the fire, which still had a bit of life left in it, I thought of the events of the last few hours and I had enjoyed myself. I had been a bit nervous and not really looking forward to it, but I was made to feel so welcome, which put me at my ease. I also found that I could talk to complete strangers, from a world well out of my country existence.

I thought of my dear Mary, who would soon be joining me. She kept by my side the whole evening, if not, she was only a few steps away. My bedroom door opened and she came in.

She ran over to me and her dressing gown flew open to reveal her lovely body which was soon pressed against mine. I lifted her up in my arms and carried her to the bed. I laid her down gently and kissed her all over and soon we were as one and enjoying what nature had provided for us. Over the last few months, we had become very adventurous in our lovemaking. But still more than careful not to go beyond the final limit.

Pam had told us that we could take it easy in the morning, as breakfast will not be served until after ten o'clock. Mary and I decided to risk it and spend the whole night together. How better to spend the New Year!

I woke up during the night and it was a wonderful feeling to have Mary curled up beside me. The moon had begun to wane, but there were still weak shafts of light coming through the windows.

Suddenly I had this feeling of warmth and well-being and then I saw a shadowy figure of a young girl at the end of my bed, and in a flash it was gone. Was I dreaming, or was it a ghost? The family ghost was a man and not a female so who was the young girl I thought I saw? Another thing was very strange, I had always understood that if one saw a ghost, the temperature became very cold. This was not so. In fact, seeing whatever I saw made me feel great.

Early the next morning I told Mary about this encounter. For a moment she was quiet and then she said that she had heard of this before. It was an omen of good luck and happiness. She gave a cry of delight and she was on top of me making love in a way that we had not experienced before. The news of the girl at the end of our bed, I had to explore because it had quite an effect on Mary. I had a very difficult job in getting her back to her room by a respectable hour.

Mary and I were the last to turn up for breakfast. Mary's parents were just finishing. Evidently, Hugh and Ann had an early breakfast and they had gone for a walk in the park, so soon we were all by ourselves and we discussed our program for the next few days before we went up to visit Sally.

Much to Mary's disgust I had a V.R. parade tomorrow evening and today I had to do some studying. In fact I had a lot to do before we went away and I would not be able to see much of the dear girl. Anyway I consoled her by saying that next week we will be with each other every day. With her wicked little grin she added, "And every night."

I found Sir James and thanked him for a smashing evening. He told me that some dinner parties can be a bit of a bore, so not to expect them all to be like that. He said that he has had to go some very boring ones and expected that I would too.

I said goodbye to the ladies and told Sally that I would see her next week. Martin was fetching her later in the day and he will have to put up with her back seat driving all of the way to North Devon.

Mary and I went around to the stables and Mr Jones asked me have a look at my bike. What a transformation. It looked like a new bike, the chrome shone in the weak sunlight and nowhere could one see a spot of dust or dirt. I thanked him most profusely, but he told me that he had enjoyed working on such a smashing bike.

I suddenly had an idea that the Old Boy could ride a motorbike, so I asked him and he told me that when he was younger he had a bike. "Mr Jones, when I come over again, I will insist that you have a ride on my bike, and I won't take no as an answer." He said that Sir James would not like that one little bit. Mary now butted in and said that she would fix her father.

He looked a bit self-conscious and said, "Mr Henry, may I wish you both a happy New Year and you will always be very welcome in my stables." We shook hands and then he hurried away.

Mary got the back of my bike and we drove it up to the front door. Evans had all my gear ready to put into my side-car. Mary had gone inside the Hall and when she came out she had her winter coat and hat on. She then got onto the bike behind me. I said, "Where do you think you are going, young lady?" She replied that she was going to the farm with me to see my family and to talk to them while I was working.

What a girl this was! Without me knowing she had telephoned Mother and invited herself. She liked John's wife Gertie and little Sam was the attraction who she liked to play with.

We were unable to talk on our way to the farm, but it was nice to feel the warmth of Mary's body next to mine. When we drove into the yard, Mother came out and she gave Mary such a friendly kiss and wished her a happy New Year.

We had arrived at a very opportune moment, because the family were gathered in the kitchen for mid-morning cups of tea. Mary and I had coffee, plus a slice of bread and cream. It was quite disgusting really, being able to eat this after one of Cook's special breakfasts.

Mother told us that Jenny had telephoned to say that she would be coming home tomorrow so you will be able to see her before you are off on your travels again. This was good news for me because I wanted to see Jenny. Her husband, Jim would be unable to come because of his business. I was not all that sorry, he was a nice chap but I had nothing in common with him, somehow he didn't fit in.

I explained to Mother that Mary was an uninvited guest and I had a lot of work to do. Mother scolded me for being so rude and Mary tried to hit me, so I pushed off in a hurry.

I managed to get through quite a bit of work during the day. Mary helped Mother and looked after little Sam, while Gertie worked around her cottage. She also spent some time talking to Dad and John. When I drove her home that evening, she said how she had enjoyed herself. It was a nice time in our lives, some days I spent at the Hall and others at the farm, but we were never very far apart.

I had packed my bag and stowed it away in the side-car. There seemed so much to take. We had strict instructions to take our evening wear, plus riding and everyday clothing, so God only knows what Mary will be taking.

I had taken the afternoon off, from work, from Mary and everyone. I had saddled up Henry and of course I was down by the little bridge and I was contemplating the many things that were to take place over the next few months.

My Lords and Masters wanted me to go to France before I went to North Devon, but this did not fit in with Mary's calculations, and as I was still only a volunteer, the date was changed. I had passed my exams and then I had to go to Cranwell for a month and most important of all I had to get a job because as soon as I leave University my allowance will stop (wherever it comes from).

At the back of my mind I had a feeling that Sally will be offering me a job as Manager of her Estate. This could be difficult because I would be away from Mary. On the other hand, Wimble Manor is only two hours away from Teignford and I could come home every weekend. Knowing Mary, she will find some excuse to stay with her grandmother every now and again. Anyway I will have to wait and see. One thing is certain and that is, it has all worked out for me no matter what I think.

I suppose that people that have had a happy childhood, at times long for the carefree early days. I would think that when one gets older the trials and troubles increase and one will be able to daydream about the past. To have a happy past must be a great blessing in old age. Or perhaps it makes the longing greater. I have a long way to go yet. But even now at my age, I long for the past. Sitting by this bridge brings it all back to me. I have sat here for too long. I must go home and back to this world.

I said goodbye to Mum and Dad and drove over to the Hall to pick up Mary. I hope that she had taken my advice and dressed up in warm clothing. I wore my breeches and if she is sensible she will have put on her Jodhpurs. I found out a long time ago that females will please themselves and only take advice when it suits them.

I rode up to the front door and Evans began to bring out some of Mary's luggage. He was being helped by a young girl, Mary now has a maid. She seemed a very pleasant person, by the name of Nora.

Mary soon came on the scene, together with her parents. After a great struggle, all the luggage was in the side-car. I was glad to see that Mary was well prepared for our cold journey. After a lot of kissing goodbye, we were on our way down the drive to join the outside world.

Mary snuggled into my back with her arms around my waist. She managed to tell me that Papa had given her some money to cover our expenses, which I thought was jolly nice of him. Above the noise of the engine, I told Mary that it would be a great help, but it made me feel a bit guilty not being able to pay my way. She used her favourite saying, "Don't be silly, Henry," and at the same time she got even closer to my back and her hands around my waist wandered a bit, which I had to stop so that I could concentrate on my driving.

We stopped at Tiverton to have a coffee and a quick look around. I wanted to buy Aunt Sally a small bunch of flowers, which we managed to pack into the side-car.

We were only a few miles from the Manor and driving through narrow country lanes which looked very bare and unfriendly. Then the sun came out and what a difference; the shadows danced on the road in front of my bike and all at once its natural beauty returned.

When we came to the main gates of the Manor and started to drive up the long drive, I seemed to feel glad that I was here again. I wondered why I liked this place so much. There must be a reason, perhaps one day I will find out.

As we got closer to the Manor, the front door opened and the rounded figure of Salter, the butler came out on to the front step. Behind him stood the friendly housekeeper, Mrs Bell. They both seemed so pleased to see us and Salter said, "May I welcome you both to Wimble Manor." He asked Mrs Bell to get the luggage up to our rooms. Out of nowhere, serving girls appeared and began to clear the side-car. I grabbed the bunch of flowers before they were taken up to our rooms by the very efficient Mrs Bell.

Salter led us into the warm sitting room to greet Sally. Of course we had only seen her last week, but she gave us a very enthusiastic welcome. When I gave her the flowers, she seemed so pleased and she told us that she was unable to remember when a handsome, young man had given her flowers. As she said this I could see that her eyes were becoming moist. I gave her a kiss on the cheek and said, "I bet you say that to all your men friends." This made her laugh and her mood changed.

After a while, I told Sally that I would like to take my bike around to the stables and find Martin, who would look after it for me. Sally said that I would probably find him asleep in the back of one of his cars that he was always playing with. Sally and her old retainer were always at each other, but fundamentally in their odd way they were old friends both living in the past. Sally was always shouting at him, but he never seemed to take any notice and it become a game.

I rode my bike around to the part of the stables that Martin used to garage Sally's cars, which her husband had collected. I found Martin under a very old Bentley that he was restoring. He came out, covered in oil and we greeted each other as old friends. We had a chat and then I found the head groom, Jack and he told me that our two horses would be ready if we wanted them after lunch.

I had no idea what Sally has said to her numerous members of her staff, but they were so very helpful and in their reserved sort of way, friendly.

The staff in these large country estates were unique. Sometimes two or three generations worked in some capacity on the estate. Some in Service in the house and others, outside. There was a sort of class distinction between them all. From the young kitchen maid to the butler. Below the butler was the housekeeper and so on down the line. Some employers were rotten, but good employers like Sally and James, had the complete loyalty of their staff.

Some were badly paid, but they did have some degree of protection from the outside world. In one respect it was like a very large family. Discipline was very strict and there was an element of fear of the next stage of the servants' hierarchy. To get into any real trouble and to be without a good reference, was a disaster. It was strange that some of the servants were at times more snobbish than their employers.

When at last I got back to the house, Mary said that she thought of sending out a search party to find me. I gave her a good slap on the bottom and chased her up the staircase to our rooms. We fell on her bed, laughing, and then I sat up with a start and said that the room was different.

The furniture had been changed around, the walls had been re-papered and it had been made to look more female. To me the most noticeable difference was the appearance of a door, where there had been a wardrobe. I got up and opened the door and I was in my room.

This room had also been changed. There was a proper man's wardrobe and a desk had been added. This now looked like a man's room. Mary had followed me in and we just looked at each other in amazement. Sally had told us that we were to look upon these rooms as our own, but the adjoining door came as quite a shock and it sort of gave us a license to join each other at night.

Mary and I sat and thought about this, because we will have to thank her for making the rooms so nice. But on the other hand, what do we say about the door? She must be accepting that we spend our nights together and perhaps in a way, condoning the fact. Otherwise why would she go to so much trouble?

We both thought that we would ignore the door situation, unless she said anything about it. What a grand old dear she is to have gone to all this trouble. Knowing that her efforts would make us happy.

I took Mary's hand and we walked around our private domain. There were fires in each room and they looked so inviting. We both would have liked to stay there, but we knew that we had to go down to see Sally.

We went down stairs and when we saw Sally, I felt a bit sheepish. We both thanked her for making our rooms so nice. She was silent for a second or two and then she said In a wistful sort of way. "Don't you two forget that I was young once, and in love like you are, but I didn't have the knowledge that young people have today." She quickly changed the subject and told me to look behind the chair that I was sitting on and I would find my Christmas present.

I looked behind my chair and I saw a long parcel. When I picked it up it was heavy and I had no idea what was in it. I soon had the paper off, and I saw a case and then I knew what it was. I opened the case to find a pair of 'Purdy' double-barrelled shot guns. I couldn't believe my eyes, they were magnificent and it was perfect. I looked at Sally and asked her how ever did she get my arm measurements. "Quite simple my boy, from your tailor."

I gave the old dear a hug and sat down again in a bit of a daze. Evidently Mary knew all about it, but kept it a secret. Sally said that she would like me to act as host to a shoot she had organised for the day after tomorrow. I would like you to see Jackson and you, Mary can help me on the social side.

I just couldn't believe what I was hearing. I have been asked to act

363

as host at a shoot in two days time. I would have no idea who was who and it could be very difficult. I told Sally about this and she said that Martin will be by my side because he knows everyone. That is if I can make him look a bit respectable. Jack can be your loader and he also knows most people.

I thought a while and said to Sally, "Have you mentioned this to Martin and Jack." She gave me one of her sweet smiles and said, "I thought that I could leave it to you Henry."

After lunch Sally retired for her usual rest and we arranged to meet for a drink before dinner. On the way around to the stables, Mary and I discussed what Sally wanted me to do over the next few days. I was a bit fed up with the prospects because it was one hell of a responsibility. Mary squeezed my arm and said, "Don't worry dear Henry, I know that you can do it."

When we got to the stables, I got Martin and Jack together and I told them what was expected of them. They took the news quite philosophically and told me that they knew what had to be done.

George Jackson, the gamekeeper thought that this was in the wind, so he had made plans to put into action at short notice. I told Jack to saddle up a horse and he could come over to see Jackson. For some reason this idea seemed to please him, and in no time the two of us were on our way to find the gamekeeper.

We called at his cottage and as luck would have it, he was there talking to his wife, Peggy. We were invited in and of course, a cup of tea was soon on the table.

The discussion was very formal. Jack, the head groom was a bit ill at ease, but I soon made him lose his stupid class complex. Jack was given the job of getting the beaters. George would mark out the area with the help of the gardening staff and of course the cartridges had to be collected from the nearest gun shop. I said that Martin could do that tomorrow. I looked at Peggy Jackson and asked her to telephone around and see who had the large quantity required. I knew that as she did the book-keeping for the Estate, she would have the necessary authority.

Peggy said that she had a meeting with Lady Howes tomorrow morning and she would see how many guests were coming and check that the food and drink would be forthcoming. She laughed and said that knowing her Ladyship, this would all be under control. She has left the difficult bits for you, Mr Henry.

I then went over it all again, different jobs were allocated to other members of the staff and following it through would be seen to by the gamekeeper and to a lesser extent, Jack the head groom.

Jackson said that there would be about seven or eight guns at the shoot, so to be on the safe side he said he would cater for eight.

I said that I knew very little about such events and Lady Howes has told me that I am to act as host. Would I be shooting? Jackson said that of course I would.

Mary and I then left Jack behind and continued our ride. What struck me most forcibly was the enthusiasm shown towards this project. Even Martin seemed to come alive at the prospect of being included.

I confessed to Mary that I had been quite scared of the job Sally had thrust on me, but now with such willing helpers the prospects didn't look so grim. She drew her horse in beside me and taking my hand she said, "My dear Henry, I knew that you can do what the Old Dear expects of you, so don't be silly."

We enjoyed the rest of our ride and we were back at the Manor in time for a bath and a very enjoyable spell on my bed. As we dressed we had the door open and we were able to talk while we were dressing and in fun we helped each other.

We went down the stairs and we were greeted by Salter, who asked me to enquire what drinks were needed for the shoot. I said that I would talk to her Ladyship and let him know.

We had our usual drinks and I said to Sally, "the shoot is being organised to your liking. Next time, play the game and give me warning." She laughed and said that she wanted to see my reaction.

It was strange that I could give her a mild ticking off, but she never seemed to mind.

I asked if there would be the usual eight guns. She said yes and started to reel off some very distinguished names. Tim and Fiona would be coming, the Brig will be bringing some French friends just to watch and to learn a bit about our way of life. I could tell that she didn't think much of this arrangement, as she was no great lover of the French.

I explained that I wanted Martin to get some cartridges, which is being organised by Peggy Jackson. Sally then told Mary that she could go as well and buy herself a new warm outfit to wear at the shoot. "While you are at it you can bring home some coats for Henry to try on. There was a twinkle in her eye when she said that you ought to know his size by now."

I started to protest, but it was a waste of time. Anyway Mary had told me that her Grandmother was a very wealthy lady.

I was informed that my services were required with Peggy concerning the accounts and I would no doubt have to see Jackson to finalise the arrangements for the next day.

I then passed on the message from Salter. "She said that he knows exactly what is required and all he wants you to do is to tell him to get on with it. She snorted and said that the silly, old fool is always doing this. He hates to do anything off his own bat."

We had a very enjoyable dinner with Sally, who was in good spirits. Cook was really first class. I bet that there will be bags of panic in the kitchen to prepare the food required for the shoot.

I must have a word with Salter one of these days, because I keep seeing different members of the staff and I would like to know how many there were.

After a few drinks and a good chat with Sally, Mary and I went up the large staircase to our rooms. How nice it was to close the doors on the outside world and to be in a sort of heaven. Our first day at the Manor had been full of surprises. Somehow I have the feeling that there would be more to come.

That first night at the Manor, we sat on the rug in front of the fire and talked well into the night. We were exploring each other's minds. I would think that it would take a lifetime to know everything about each other and even then there would be parts that would be sealed forever.

Eventually we went to bed, made love, and feeling at peace with the world, we slept in each other's arms until the new day dawned. I was the first to wake up and I propped myself up on one elbow and looked at Mary.

She lay there with her hair spread out over the pillow and she looked so natural and beautiful. She was breathing very gently and I wondered what she was dreaming about, because there seemed to be half a smile on her lovely face.

I had to wake her, so I kissed her and automatically her arms went around my neck and we became as one again.

After breakfast, Mary and I went our different ways. I found the meeting with Sally and Peggy, her book-keeper very interesting. My suggestions of two years ago were beginning to bear fruit. The deer and sheep had multiplied many times over and were very profitable. The stream had grown into a small river and a few trout were making it their home. The tenants were now paying a more up-to-date level of rents, in fact the situation looked very good.

I did however put the cat amongst the pigeons. The course I had just finished at Exeter made a point of staff on a large Estate being divided into units with someone being in charge of that unit and he would then be responsible to a Manager or Bailiff.

I enlarged on this by explaining that the house staff had the butler. The stables, the head groom. The garden staff, the head gardener, but what about the men who looked after the sheep and deer and the maintenance of the Estate and the fabric of the buildings? I could see Peggy nodding her head in agreement, so I carried on. There should also be a meeting perhaps every month with the heads of the Departments. These meetings have to be informal so that a free discussion can take place.

The results of these meetings then have to be taken to the owner and it will then be up to he or she to make any final decisions.

I looked at Sally and said that it was possible that there would be a war next year and some of the staff would have to join the forces. So if one can make things as efficient as possible now, you will be prepared for what I hope will never happen.

Sally reached over the table and took my hand and said, "Henry, please say whatever you think needs to be said while we have you here."

So in I went into the deep end. "I think that Mr Jackson would rather be a gamekeeper, but perhaps he could act as a Manager until you find someone that would be suitable. If you could find a man not of military age it would be a safe guard for the future."

When I had finished talking there was a long silent spell and I thought I had gone too far, but I could see by the Old Girl's face that she was very pleased.

Sally said that she would like to talk to me about my ideas later in the day and we can meet again after the shoot. She turned to Peggy and told her to ask her husband if he could attend. I also told her that Jack and I would be over to see him after lunch.

Mary didn't come back for lunch, she had telephoned to say that she had met Fiona and they were having lunch in Tiverton. I was very pleased because I had a lot to do.

I managed to get everything sorted out with the help of Jack and George, and I could safely say that the shoot was organised. The Gods may smile on me and give us a fine, clear day tomorrow.

It was nearly dark by the time I got back to the Manor and Mary greeted me as if I had returned from an expedition into the unknown. This really made Sally laugh and then of course I had to try on several coats. I had nothing to say in the matter. How can one argue with two females? Anyway I am glad that I let them get on with it, because I finished up with two smashing coats.

Mary then made me go up stairs to see what she had bought. Needless to say one thing led to another and we just made it in time for a drink before dinner.

While we were having our coffee in the sitting room after dinner. Sally told Mary about my ideas for the Estate and then she dropped a bit of a bomb shell. The Old Girl looked at me and said, "Henry would you be my Manager? You could live in the Manor and you could go down to South Devon for each weekend. I would be able to pay you a good salary and Mary could come up to see you when ever she wanted to."

Mary and I looked at each other. Mary told her grandmother that it

367

was a very kind offer, but it was up to Henry. I found this a fantastic turn of events and for once I was speechless. In fact there was complete silence all around for quite a spell. My mind was working on overdrive, then I started to talk but really I was thinking aloud.

What I have to do in the next few months is quite frightening, so I tried to explain this to these two dear females.

"In two weeks time I have to go to France for at least ten days." I looked at Sally and told her "For my sins, I am involved with a special section of the War Office, which is run by the Brig and Major Davis. It all started a long time ago, because I could speak German like a native and it seems to have taken over my life.

I received special lessons to learn to fly. I now hold a licence to fly civilian aircraft. I have to go to Cranwell on a special course to get my RAF wings, which in itself is most unusual. This is in about a month and I have to take my finals at the University. I have to swot up for these finals because I must pass the exams. Someone is paying for my education and I cannot let them down. I haven't the slightest idea who it is, but one day I might find out.

Also while I am doing this I have to attend the RAF V.R. parades each week and I haven't mentioned this to Mary, but I have been asked by the University to teach German twice a week. I will of course get paid quite well for this extra chore.

So my dear kind Sally, how can I take up your offer. I would love to work here, to me it's like another home. I already have the Farm, Langley Hall and now you are offering me the chance to live at Wimble Manor. The real blot on the landscape is of course that awful, little man called Hitler and it is impossible to plan anything with any certainty for the future. So Sally, how can I accept your offer? In the meantime you must get a Manager because it will be too much for you. If there is anything I can do please let me know."

Sally looked disappointed but I could tell that she understood my situation. She then said, "After tomorrow, would you have a chat with Jackson and in some way tell him how to get these units you talked about organised. Who knows, perhaps Jackson might be capable of acting a Manager for the time being, which of course would increase his salary. There is also no reason why he could not take on a young chap to help with the Pheasants and to keep the poachers at bay."

I told the Old Dear that of course I would do that for her, and when we have formulated a plan in more detail, we would report back to her for her approval. This seemed to have lifted a load off her mind and she made us have another drink to seal the bargain we had just made.

It was not long after this that Sally went off to bed, leaving Mary and I to talk about what had happened. We sat on the sofa and Mary curled up beside me, which was very nice. It seemed ages before either of us said a word. Then Mary started to hold forth.

She snuggled up as close to me as she could and told me how pleased she was that Grandmother had made this offer. She started to look a bit dreamy and said that she liked North Devon and like me she loved the Manor and it was not just because we had made love here so often. She looked at me with those dark, brown eyes and said, "Dear Henry, who knows perhaps one day we will both live here." She then put her arms around my neck and gave me such a sweet kiss.

For a brief moment, I was away into the future and somehow I knew that she could well be right, but only after a long spell of turmoil. Now was not the time to make plans that may not come to fruition because of circumstances beyond our control.

I looked at Mary and I said, "Mary, I could think of nothing better than living with you at the Manor, but a lot of water has to pass under the bridge before this can happen. Every day I seem to love you more and more and I know that I will never love anyone else in the same way. Somehow I think you feel the same."

Mary got up and said, "Let's go to bed and I will show you how much I love you, darling Henry." So we went to bed and making love, Mary lived up to her promise.

The next morning I managed to creep out of Mary's bed without waking her. It was very early and the sun was a large ball of red fire rising over Exmoor. It was fine and frosty, the Gods had been kind to me so far.

In my heart I was very nervous about today. Somehow Mary knew how I felt and she said that she will be with me as much as possible to give me moral support.

I had a quick, light breakfast, sitting at the kitchen table and talking to Cook. This of course was not the thing to do, but I could tell how this was appreciated by the staff. How odd life is that a gesture like this is even thought about. I asked one of the maids to go around to the stables and ask them to saddle up my horse.

Jack, the head groom was not in evidence, but my horse was ready for me. As I rode down the long drive, I felt a bit like the Lord of the Manor, which was very wrong of me. I was just standing in for Sally as host for the day.

I made my way towards where the shoot would take place. It was not very far, but far enough for me to enjoy the ride. The more I saw of this place, the more I liked it. I then knew that I would like to live here. I have no idea why, because I loved my home area and there was no little bridge in North Devon, and then I thought to myself, we have a small river, why not build a bridge. I then came back to earth as I reached the shooting area and I saw Jackson had got there before me.

He gave me such a friendly greeting that I knew that his wife, Peggy had told him about my plans for the Estate. We had no time to talk about this and all our thoughts were on the shoot, which will take place in a few hours time.

When I got back to the Manor, I changed and put on one of my new coats, which made me look quite reasonable. Mary came into my room with her new outfit on and she looked a real stunner. We both walked down the staircase to be greeted by Sally, who told us what a handsome couple we were. I told her how elegant she looked; a real Lady of the Manor. Martin was in his best suit and on hand to tell me who was who. We stood outside and Mary joined me. It was too cold for Sally so she waited in the hallway.

Soon the guests started to arrive. I introduced myself and Mary, and said that I was acting on behalf of Lady Howes, because it was too cold for her to stand outside.

Salter offered everyone a glass of Punch, which soon broke down any barriers. There were several bods with titles and snooty-looking females, the local Member of Parliament, who seemed a pleasant sort of chap. The Brig arrived with a Frenchman and his female. I greeted them in my best French, which caused a bit of a stir for the people in hearing distance. Tim and Fiona came up the drive in his noisy, old sports car and Mary and I were so glad to see them

I was trying to do my job of talking to the guests and with Mary's help and information from Martin, I didn't find it too difficult. I had this feeling of being watched by the Brig and that he was assessing my efforts. I made a point of talking to his French friends and trying to find out what they were doing in North Devon. I had no luck and all I could find out was that they came from Paris.

It was now time to get the guns and their loaders into position. Numbers had been drawn out of a hat, so everyone knew where to go.

As the host, I had to fire the two shots to let the beaters know when to start. In no time, the Pheasants started to come. My new guns were smashing, but today I wanted someone else to get the best bag. Jack knew his job and we were a good team.

George Jackson came out of the woods when it was all over and I could see that it had all been a great success by the broad grin on his face. There were a lot of Pheasants that had been shot so I told him to give some to the staff that had helped today. "Of course make sure that Cook has all that she needs, and that the guests have their share." He looked at me and said that it was not the usual thing to give staff Pheasants. I told him very firmly that times are changing and that is how it will be done in the future.

I then said to him "I would like you and your good lady to come over to the Manor tomorrow morning at about ten o'clock as there is a lot of work to be done in the next few days. If this is not convenient, will you let me know?" He looked at me as if I had just come from outer space.

"Mr Henry, if you want to see my wife and I tomorrow, of course we will be there."

We all went back to the Manor and Cook had prepared a wonderful spread of cold meats and pies. Salter was doing his stuff with serving the drinks that were needed.

What I found most interesting was the fact that Sally had taken a back seat all during the day. It seemed that it was all to do with Mary and I. We were mixing and talking to the guests and when I looked over to see Sally, she had a satisfied smile on her face. Everyone seemed to be enjoying themselves and it is always a good sign when guests are not in a hurry to go home.

At last they all went their different ways and it was all over and, oh boy, was I pleased? It had been a bit of an ordeal but very successful.

Over the next few days I had several meetings with Jackson and the ideas I had brought up at the meeting with Sally and Peggy, began to take shape. Jackson was now acting as Manager and he was on the look out for an assistant gamekeeper.

All good things come to an end and Mary and I just managed to get all of our things into the side-car. Taking Sally's advice we left some of our gear in our rooms as we would be visiting the Manor more often in the future.

We could see that Sally was sad to see us leave and in our way we were feeling the same, unfortunately she had loneliness to contend with and there was no answer to this problem. Our problem will be to find the time to do all that has to be done over the next few months.

When we got back to Teignford, it took us ages to tell our respective parents all that had taken place at Wimble Manor. Dad didn't seem all that surprised and I think that Sally had spoken to him when she met him at Christmas. He was very envious when he saw my two Purdy guns. He said In a very serious way, "Henry, you must try and take the job Lady Howes has offered you, I don't think you realise how lucky you are or what the future may hold for you in North Devon." I asked him what he meant by that remark, but he changed the subject, so I didn't press him for an answer.

The time had come for me to go to France and I was not looking forward to it one little bit. I had got all of my instructions and French Francs from Jake and I said a sad farewell to my Mary. Mother got herself all worked up at the thought of me going to France all by myself. She still thought of me as a boy and not a young man of nearly nineteen.

I went to bed that night in my own room and I wondered where I would be sleeping for the next ten nights, unfortunately not with Mary. I have to make a very early start in the morning to catch the ferry at Weymouth for Cherbourg.

For some unknown reason, the Major had given me Celeste's home town as Falaise, I knew that this was wrong, so I double-checked and it gave me great pleasure to tell the old, bossy boots that he had made a mistake. She lived near a small town called Crasville. With these thoughts, I eventually went to sleep.

CHAPTER 15

I was lucky with the weather for my trip to Weymouth and when I started, it was just getting light, with the sun beginning to rise its head above the distant hills, shrouded by mist. There was no one about, but as I looked along the lane to where I would have to turn off for Exeter, I saw a lonely figure sitting on a horse and then I realised that it was Mary, who had made the effort to get up early and wait for me to pass by the road junction.

How grand it was to see her and to say again, our fond farewells. When at last I had to go, I could see the signs of a tear or two forming in her lovely, brown eyes. I told her to go over to the farm and have some of Mother's cream for breakfast. She then galloped off in that direction and with a final wave she had gone. I think that her abrupt departure was to hide her feelings.

I bypassed Exeter and I found my way onto the Honiton Road. As I drove along I kept thinking how kind it was of Mary to come and see me off. She really was a dear girl.

Dorset is so very similar to Devon and as it was so early in the day, the traffic was very light so I could have a good look around as I rode on my way.

I found that I had plenty of time so I stopped at Dorchester and had some coffee and cakes in an old pub called the King's Arms. This put new life in me and I was on the short, last leg of my journey.

I made my way to the ferry terminal and boarded the ferry. My Lords and Masters had booked a small cabin for me, because we would not dock until the early hours of tomorrow.

It was a pleasant crossing and I am now on my bike heading towards Valognes on a very pleasant road. It took a bit of getting used to, riding on the opposite side of the road. To quote Sir James, "Trust the bloody French to ride on the wrong side of the road."

It was difficult to understand why the fields were so small and the lanes so narrow. The countryside seemed so very similar to the West Country, but on a smaller scale. One of the jobs given to me by the Major is to get to know the countryside and to make a note of remote fields large enough to be able to land and take off a small aircraft. Some of the fields I have seen were too small to swing a cat, leave alone, land a plane on. Anyway, as the good Lord said, "Seek and Ye shall find."

I branched off from Valognes across the country to Tyhaigne and then to Verbisson. This trip was very dodgy and I had to ask my way several times. The hedges were high and the lanes narrow and without a compass it would have been very difficult.

I had one of my thoughts into the future and for some unknown reason I started to look at this area from a military point of view. It was what I would call, Cowboy and Indian country. If one put one's head above a hedge, bang you are dead. This is how we used to play this game in Devon as children.

I was not to know then that this would prove to be a nightmare for troops in the future. I do wish that I could stop having these glimpses into the future because at times they are most disturbing.

At long last I found Crasville and I was directed to Celeste's farm. It sat in a valley and looked a large and well-kept place. I had noticed that the French never used much paint, their buildings were on the whole very shabby.

The countryside was on the whole very flat, but the Prideaux family had managed to find a valley to have their farmhouse.

Well here goes. I started up my motor and rode down to the farmhouse. From a distance I could see a female come out into the yard and even at this distance I could see that it was Celeste. As I got nearer we waved to each other and when I drove into the yard I could see that she was even more attractive than when I last saw her two years ago, or was it three?

I got off my bike and she ran up to me and putting her arms around my neck she kissed me and said in her broken English, "Oh! Enrie, it is so lovely to see you again. You have no idea how I have been looking forward to your visit." She had really taken the wind out of my sails, because I enjoyed seeing her again. I can foresee a very difficult week ahead.

I was led into the farmhouse to meet Celeste's parents. Monsieur Prideaux was a very large man, quite an athletic figure of a man. What I liked was his face, I could see a look of friendliness in his very dark, brown eyes. I knew at once that we could be friends. Madame Prideaux was small and pretty like her daughter, Celeste.

When Celeste introduced me to her parents, she said that it would be best for me to call them by their Christian names. So her father became Jacques and her Mother, Louise. Celeste brought forth a bottle of wine and we sat for ages talking about why I was staying with them.

I had to pretend that I am a distant relation, having lived in England most of my life. By trade I made and sold furniture. Strange how it may seem I could now compete with the best of them. This had been a skill passed on to me by Peter's dad. Many times I had thought that how I would like to do this for a living, but then in life, one cannot pick and choose one's destiny.

In a very short time I had to get to know the district and become known as a member of the Prideaux family. I had with me a passport to back up this story so for a week I am Henry Prideaux. I had to speak in French and never in German. If in the future should I ever have to come to this part of France, I will be known as a Prideaux.

I saw a tall handsome young chap come into the kitchen. I was introduced to Celeste's brother, Pierre. He seemed to size me up and down and then a broad smile spread over his weatherbeaten face. He shook my hand and then I knew that I had been accepted.

Celeste took me up to my room which was very basic, very clean and quite warm. I unpacked my bag and changed into clothes more suitable for a member of a farming family. I then joined my new family for my first real French meal, washed down with plenty of red wine.

I slept like a top that first night and woke up early in the morning to hear similar sounds to our own farm in England. I washed and dressed and putting on a warm coat, I went outside to explore the lay out of the farmyard.

Pierre and his father were milking a large herd of cows, with the help of several farm hands. We talked and I was trying all of the time to imitate the Normandy accent. In the next few days this would cause great amusement when I was with Celeste.

I looked upon this visit as a sort of education, and I couldn't have wished for a prettier teacher than Celeste. My first day was Market Day in Crasville and this proved to be a golden opportunity to meet friends of the Prideaux family.

I soon found out that I would have to drink a lot of local red wine and many cups of very strong black coffee, and what a noisy and excitable lot the French people are. I knew then that I would find it very difficult to copy their actions. Anyway I will have to try.

In France people gathered in cafes, not in pubs, they sat at tables, all talking at once. After our evening meal I joined Pierre for his nightly visits and this helped me a great deal to understand and learn about the locals.

The weather was very kind to me, and Celeste and I could motor around the countryside making it possible for me to photograph several sites suitable for a light aircraft to land and take off. These were made to look like holiday snaps by including Celeste and sometimes, she took a photograph of me.

After several days of exploring I had a terrible shock. We had stopped at a gateway and there before my eyes I could see the field that I have so many dreams about. It was exactly the same in every detail.

Celeste and I were leaning over the gate and she could tell that something had upset me. She asked what was wrong, so I told her and before I knew what was happening, she put her arms around my neck and we were kissing in a very passionate way, and we were both getting very sexually aroused.

I managed to stop things going any further by telling this lovely French girl that I was in love with Mary and one day I may be lucky enough to marry her. She looked at me and said, "What you mean Henry is that one day Mary may be lucky to marry you. Anyway whatever may happen between you and I, will always be a secret."

She continued by saying that she had a regular boyfriend called Fransour. He is training to be an Officer in the Army. "I think that I love him and one day we will be married. So let us both have our last fling before the knots are tied. She looked at me and told me that she will always love me and that it has to be Mary for me and never would she ever do anything to make me unhappy."

I thought that this visit could be very difficult, but never quite like this. Anyway nature will have to take its course. I felt that I was a bit in love with Celeste, but it was so different to how I felt towards dear Mary.

When I got on my bike, Celeste sat behind me and not in my side-car. She had her hands around my waist and I could feel the warmth of her body. This in itself was temptation and difficult to ignore.

On our way back we stopped at the cafe the family used. We were having a coffee when we were joined by a small, odd-looking man. I could see an instant dislike on Celeste's face. Anyway she froze him our and he pushed off. She told me that she thought that he was a German spy and planted in Crasville as a 'Sleeper'.

Celeste had to do a bit of shopping so I wandered off and had a look around the town. I found a smashing Florist's shop, so I bought a bunch of flowers for Madame Prideau and one rose which was well out of season, for my charming French companion.

The shopkeeper called me Monsieur Prideau, which proved that news gets around in small towns. He asked me about life in England. I had to be very careful to remember that I was now wearing a very different hat. While I am in France I am a cabinet maker and not a Pilot Officer in the RAF V.R. and a university student at Exeter.

I was told by Jake that I had to get myself known as semi-local, should I have to turn up in the future. The more I think about it, the more I realise that I have got myself tied up with a very special section of the security side of the War Office. I was having one of my daydreams, when a pretty French girl put her arm in mine and we walked back to my bike.

I gave Celeste the special rose and one would have thought that I had given her one hundred pounds. She looked so pleased and gave me a kiss in the cheek and said that she will try to keep its petals on until I leave.

I think that we both knew that we were snatching a few days together and being able to enjoy each other for this short time, which could never be repeated and it would always be our secret to be shared by no one.

We had a very pleasant evening meal and as usual Pierre and I went into the town for a drink. This was only my third evening but by now I was greeted as a friend and not a complete stranger. I had no idea who thought that my visit would be beneficial, perhaps it was Jake or even Major Davis. Anyway they certainly knew what they were doing, because their theory was beginning to work.

Pierre and I were talking to some chaps about our age and the subject of War came up. The comments about the Germans were not very flattering and I was asked if it was the general opinion in Great Britain, that there would be a war with Germany and were there signs of preparation.

Before I could answer these questions, the man Celeste disliked, in the cafe, joined us. He was known as Jouvin. This made me pile it on and I said the British were getting well-prepared, and that people as 'Sleepers' were being watched very closely. Jouvin asked me how I knew this and I told him that I had a friend in the Police force, who let this information slip out one night after having too many beers. For good measure, I added that no doubt the French police had similar knowledge.

Jouvin started to ask me quite a few questions, so I went on the attack and asked him some very personal questions, such as how long had he lived in the area, what did he do for a living, was he a German sympathiser and what were his views on the Jewish question? He soon got fed up with this barrage of questions and pushed off. No doubt he will poke his nose into other people's conversations, but somehow I don't think he will bother me again.

These evenings I spent with Pierre were very rewarding. Not only did I get to know many different locals, but I also got to know their way of life and most important, all the local habits. I must have been a bit of a bore because I asked Pierre and Jacques so many questions.

Of course we all had a common interest in farming and they in turn asked me about farming in the West Country, which turned out to be very similar.

That night when we got back to the farm, the females had gone to bed. Celeste had a bath and washed her hair. Her father said that she had left a message for me to say that if I wished, we could have a ride around the farm. This was good news, because I have missed my rides.

After a drink with Jacques, I made my way up to my bedroom, which was right at the back of the farmhouse and remote to anyone else. Someone had made up the fire, so there were a few flames flickering in the grate, which made the room look more inviting. I slowly got myself ready for bed and got in between the coarse linen sheets.

I lay there watching the shadows made by the few flames left in the fire and I thought of Mary back in England and what Celeste had said earlier in the day and the thoughts of our lovemaking two years ago in my bed on the farm, during a snow storm, which had prevented her going back to Newton Abbot. This had continued until the early summer when she went back to France and Mary came home from college.

Here I am again in similar circumstances. I was told that she loved me and wanted me to make love to her. If I make love to Celeste, will I be able to face Mary, when I return to England? I did before, so I will have to do it again. In our hearts we all know that soon there will be a war and anyone with any sense, must know this depressing fact. So perhaps there is an excuse to have a last fling, as Celeste called it.

I am lying in this bedroom in Normandy and all of a sudden I seem to go forward in time and I was looking out of the window at what looked like a giant fireworks display. Celeste was with me and the whole house was in darkness and there was a feeling of fear in the air. In a flash I was back in time, lying in a warm bed and wishing that I could stop these visions of the future. I am unable to understand them, because they are never complete.

I think that I was just about to go to sleep, when I heard the door of my room being opened very slowly. I could see that it was Celeste creeping into my room.

I pretended to be asleep, and I watched her come over to my bed and take off her dressing gown. By now she was standing close to my bed and I could smell her perfume. By now I had no choice but to throw caution to the wind. In one quick move I grabbed her around the waist and pulled her into the bed, and she fell on top of me squealing with laughter.

Celeste stayed with me for most of the night. Our lovemaking was very natural but very careful and we both derived such pleasure from each other during the several times we made love on the first night together in France.

When I woke up in the early hours of the next morning, my bed was empty. Celeste had gone back to her own room. At first I thought that I had been dreaming, but I soon smelled her perfume, and when I fully came to, the events of the night were remembered with great joy.

I should feel guilty and ashamed of myself, but I only felt very happy. I then decided that when I get back to England I will blot out my affair with dear Celeste. She said that she will do the same. she called it our last fling, but only time will tell if this is possible.

When I went down to a continental breakfast, Celeste looked so calm and innocent, but when I looked at her, I saw a different look in her eyes. It had a look of satisfaction and fulfilment together with affection for me.

One of the farm hands had saddled up two horses for us and we were riding side by side over the fields. Celeste started to ask me so many questions about my life and Mary, and as I was talking to her and answering her questions, I realised how my life was fully involved with Mary and the Howes' family.

I told her about Sally in North Devon and how she had offered me a job, which subject to there not being a war, I would love to have. I then started to ask her about her boyfriend and her life. Over the next few days, we both knew everything that there was to know about each other.

I asked Celeste if the field that I had seen so many times in my dreams, was a long way away. She said that it was only a few fields away. So we went to see it from another angle. I wanted to ride over it to see if I could get some more information out of it. One could see that it was very possible to land and take off a small aircraft in the space allowed, taking into consideration the trees and the large barn in one corner.

Without any ulterior motive, I asked Celeste if we could look into the barn because I would like to get the inside size. We went in and Celeste brought in the horses, I paced out the rough size and made a note in my little book.

I had not noticed what Celeste was up to until I found two hands around my waist from behind and one became very inquisitive. She led me over to a bed she had made out of straw and once more we made love.

Afterwards as we lay on the straw bed, Celeste said, "My darling Henry I have you for only three more days and nights and in that short time I am going to have you as many times as possible." I once more put my arms about her and told her nothing would please me more. In no time we were together again.

During the next few days, I gathered more information and made copious notes, which I intend to formulate into a report to Major Davis. I got on very well with Celeste's family. I even met Uncles and Cousins of the Prideaux clan. I loved being with Celeste, but I was missing

Mary. How strange life is and oh so difficult where females are concerned.

It was my last evening in Crasville and Celeste and her mother put on a special meal in my honour. After the meal we sat and talked about the future. Jacques told me that he and some of his friends have formed a sort of bond to hold them together, if the Germans ever came to Normandy. He went to a desk in the corner of the room and came back with a letter. "Henry, would you please give this to Major Davis? It is very important but I have been told that I can trust you." I put it safely in my pocket and told him that I will get it to him as soon as I get back to England.

I thanked the family for treating me so well and making me so welcome because after all I was a complete stranger. Celeste said, "Your family made me very welcome when I was in Devon." Jacques said, "We almost knew you Henry because Celeste was always talking about you and your friends, Mary and Hugh. I would like you to know that you will always be welcome here whenever you care to come. All I hope is that your visit will not be because of a war."

That last night in bed with Celeste was rather sad. After we made love, we lay and talked for ages, but eventually we went to sleep, knowing that we would never be able to repeat the lovely week we had together because fate would not be that kind.

I had said my goodbyes to everyone and to a very tearful Celeste. I sat on my bike at the top of the hill and looked down at the Prideaux farmhouse and I could see the small figure of Celeste standing by the door and giving me a last wave of farewell. I had one of my awful premonitions again, and I knew that I would see this valley again, but it would be far from peaceful.

My journey to Cherbourg was uneventful. I had some spare time in Cherbourg so I bought some French perfume for Mary. I felt a bit of a heel because it could be thought by some as a peace offering. In fact I had decided before I went on this journey, to bring back some perfume for her.

It was a very rough trip back, the sea was very rough and so many of the people on board were sick that I went into my cabin and at last I managed to get some sleep. It suddenly struck me that sleep was something I had very little of during my stay in France. I then made up my mind that I would try to forget the last seven days, or rather nights, because this was a sort of pact that Celeste and I had made.

When I got to Weymouth, I telephoned Mother to say that I was on my way home. How nice it was to hear her dear voice again. I decided to go home by the coastal route. First to Dorchester and then through Bridport and into Lyme Regis. I had lunch at a pub called the

Royal Lion and it was so nice to have some English food, free of garlic.

For some reason I was in no hurry to go home. I stopped at several places to have a look around and I began to wonder why I was in no hurry to get home. Then I realised why. I had been on holiday, away from all the worries of exams, the expected training at Cranwell and every day problems. In fact I was acting like a coward and trying to run away.

When I got to the very familiar lanes of South Devon, I began to feel better and I felt excited at the thought of seeing everyone again. I drove down the last, long lane to the farm, and there was Mary waiting for me, looking more beautiful than ever. I got off my bike and we ran towards each other. When her arms were around me, I felt at home and my fears had gone.

After much kissing and very loving embraces, Mary got on my bike behind me and I felt the familiar arms around my waist and we drove down the lane to my home and family.

It took me the rest of the day and part of the evening to tell everyone about my visit to France. Dad and John were very interested in the aspect of how the farming was carried out. I managed to answer most of the questions. Mother and Mary were more interested in the farmhouse and the females. I found this very difficult, especially the fact the Celeste was my guide every day.

Whenever I mentioned Celeste's name, Mary's eyes seemed to bore into me as if she was searching my mind for information that I had not talked about. I closed my mind and tried not to show any signs of guilt.

After supper, I drove Mary back to the Hall. As we walked to my bike, she said that she had had a long chat with Celeste this morning, when she telephoned her. She laughed and said, "Papa will get a shock when he gets the bill."

I could hardly believe my ears when I heard this news. My stomach nearly fell to the floor, as I thought all was lost.

Mary continued by saying that she wanted to know what time I would be home and she had got the telephone number from Jake. She took my hand and said, "I think Celeste is very fond of you, but you have been a good lad in Normandy, which I think disappointed Celeste quite a bit."

I managed to keep calm and how glad I was that it was dark. I gave a deep sigh of relief and in my mind I blessed Celeste for being so kind. This will have to be the end of the French connection. Little did I know then that it was far from over.

CHAPTER 16

At last, spring is on the way and it will soon be Easter egg time. When I was a small boy I loved Easter, because of the abundance of chocolate. Next week I will be taking my final exams. I now know more of the mysteries of Radio and Radar. I can now find my way around the world, without getting lost. I think that if I pass the exams it will be a miracle.

Since the New Year, Mary and I have been up to North Devon for several weekends which were business and a great deal of pleasure. Mary and I are getting on better than ever, and Celeste is never mentioned. I also never mention that we write to each other every now and again.

I still have a bit of a problem with Polly, she keeps turning up at the most odd places. But so far I have kept her at bay.

I have just been to see Mrs Jenkins, what a dear friend she has been to me. On the other hand, she started me on the road to being of use to the Government because of my gift for learning languages. How different my life would be without this connection.

I love this time of the year, during April the trees come to life and the bird and wild animals mate to carry on their species and the early morning chorus is in full swing. There seems to be some hope in the air. Unfortunately the news is very depressing and try as I may I am unable to clear my mind of its implications.

On March 14, Hitler marched into Bohemia and on the fifteenth, he entered Prague. I heard on the news before I came out for a ride, that Britain, France and Poland signed a mutual assistance pact. If all of this is not a receipt for war, what is?

I have taken my exams and I now await the results which will be published in June. I was told by the Bank Manager that my allowance will cease at the end of May. On the other hand, the V.R.C.O. told me that I will be paid the usual pay of a Pilot Officer, while I am at Cranwell. This cheered me up no end as I thought that I would be very hard up until I started to work for Sally.

It was a lovely early evening, sitting by the bridge. The only sounds were the Evensong from birds and the never-ending symphony played by the stream, swollen by the late winter's rain in its hurry to get to the sea.

I must have been far away in another world, because I didn't hear the sound of a horse coming down the lane. I came to and saw this lovely girl waking her horse towards me.

Mary had been helping her father to run the Estate since Christmas and the fresh air and outdoor life certainly suited her. She looked so well and her skin had become a lovely colour. In fact every time I saw her she looked more beautiful. We hadn't arranged to meet, but she was often doing this to me, she seemed to be always able to find me. We had become quite a joke with our two families. Wherever there was one, the other would soon follow.

I would be off to Cranwell, next week and she was getting very broody about it, so we had decided to visit the Manor for the weekend, so we can spend a couple of nights together and I have to sort out my job with Sally.

After a while we decided to ride into the village and have a drink at the local. We often did this because it was nice to meet some of the regulars. The motor car had changed the way of life. Some of the cottages were now lived in by people working in nearby towns, so socially it was quite a mix up. It was strange to hear cultured voices mixed in with the broad Devon accent.

I escorted Mary back to the Hall and of course I had to have a night cap with Sir James and Pamela. As usual Mary rode down to the gate on the back of Henry with her arms around my waist. We kissed each other goodnight and I started my lonely ride home.

I started to plan my next two days before I set sail for North Devon. Tomorrow I had some unofficial flights with Hank at Exeter Airport. Mary and I had become very friendly with Hank and his wife. We never really found out if she was his wife, anyway she was good fun. I also had to get my gear ready for the month I had to spend at Cranwell. The list received from the RAF was quite lengthy.

I had to wear my uniform and I had to take some civilian, casual clothing and P.E. shorts and shoes. This made me think that there would be more to this course than the flying of an aircraft. I asked Jake about this but he hadn't a clue. I also asked my V.R.C.O. and all he could tell me was that as far as he knew, this course was something very special and out of the ordinary. Anyway I will soon know, and as I have to go, there is no point in worrying about it.

We arrived at the Manor in time for lunch on the Friday and we would return to Teignford on Monday. That would give us three nights together, and according to Mary's calculations, it was a safe time.

Sally greeted us and it is so nice to see how her face lights up when she saw Mary and I. When we had settled in, Mary and Sally were deep in conversation so, after getting a pint of beer from Salter, I wandered down to the lake and I sat and had a bit of a daydream.

I still find it so very difficult to adjust to the position I find myself in. One day I hope to marry Mary, who is a titled female. I seem to have become part of Sir James and Lady Howes' family, and Mary's grandmother, Lady Howes treats me as an equal and has come to rely on me for the running of the Estate and after all, I am only twenty years of age. In fact, at times it is very embarrassing, because to her I am one of the family.

I mentioned this to Hugh and laughed and said that I was doing him a favour, because he hated North Devon and he had no interest in Wimble Manor. "Anyway Henry, I look upon you as the best friend I have, and you have no idea how you have helped me over the years. So shut up you clot and enjoy what you have."

I had a busy three days at the Manor, talking and planning with Jackson and his wife. Mary had by now become involved with the Estate and she proved to be a great help. It was interesting to watch Sally's expression when this was all going on. One could see that a great load had been lifted from her mind.

On our last evening at the Manor, Sally brought up the question of my future salary. She offered the princely sum of five hundred pounds a year plus living at the Manor. I told her that this was far too much. She gave me one of her looks and Mary gave me a kick in the shins, so I shut up.

Sally continued by suggesting that I bring up my horse, Henry. "James will lend you a horse to keep at the farm for when you are at home on some weekends. He told me that there is a grey in his stable that you would like to ride. There is a room that my husband had as a study. I will get that fixed up as a sitting room and office with a telephone." She smiled and said that I would be able to retreat in there, away from her nattering.

"So there you are Henry my dear. How does this all sound to you? Will you be able start as soon as you come back from Cranwell?" By now I was getting overwhelmed, and a bit lost for words, but I managed to say "That will be smashing and I am very lucky to have such an offer."

During the next two days, Mary and I rode all over the Estate and I tried to meet as many of the staff as possible. By now they all seemed to know that I would be their new boss. My plans were in operation and working well indeed. George Jackson, the acting Manager had made a good job of his task, but I knew that he wanted to return to his Pheasants.

Mary and I enjoyed our nights together, and we made the most of our opportunity because we would be parted for a month, which is no joke considering how we felt for each other.

Once more it is time for us to leave the Manor. This time Sally didn't look so sad. It could well be that she believed that she had at last got things organised to make her life easier. When we left, she gave me a big hug and said, "I do wish that your grandfather could see you Henry, and you look so much like him that I keep thinking that you are the other Henry."

I told Mary about this conversation, and she told me that I didn't realise how fond her grandmother was of me and how she has changed since she met me and my father. I didn't think much of this conversation, but I would remember it well in the future.

Well I was all packed and ready to go to Cranwell. I said goodbye to Mary and my family, and drove myself to Newton Abbot to catch the London train. I said goodbye to my dear Dad and went onto the platform. Then I saw Mary, the dear girl had come to see me off, which really made my day.

I got on the train and I felt very sad to see the lonely figure standing on the platform giving me a last wave.

I had been sent a travel voucher and all details of what trains to catch and a list of what I had to take with me. Much to my surprise my tickets were First Class, so I had a comfortable journey in front of me. After the Exeter stop I went along to the restaurant car for a coffee.

I started to read my newspaper, when I heard a very familiar voice say "Can I join you Henry?" Of course, it was Polly, looking very smart in a tweed suit and a very saucy, little hat. She sat down and we started to talk, I explained where I was off to and what I had been doing since Christmas. She gave me one of her sweet smiles and told me how handsome I looked in my uniform. I asked her what she was doing and where she was off to.

She told me that she was going to work in a Government Department, which was very hush-hush, and try as I may, I could not get any information out of her.

She thought that she would be working at the War Office to begin with, but out of London if there was a war. She seemed to know that I had something to do with a Government Department. I also kept my council on this matter.

I told her about my job in North Devon and of course she asked about Mary, and was I still in love with her. I told her that I seem to love her more and more. Polly put her hand across the table and held mine, saying very sadly, "I do wish that you had never met Mary, because I love you, Henry and I always have since that first day in school."

By now I was feeling quite upset and I had to tell her that I was very fond of her and I loved her in a different way to Mary. I asked her if we could continue to be very good friends.

She put my hand to her face and kissing it she said, "My dear Henry, I would never do anything to make you unhappy." She then put on one of her wicked little expressions, saying, "Henry, one day, by hook or by crook, I will have you in bed. There would be no strings attached, but I want that more than anything."

We had not realised it but we had been talking for so long, that we were getting near to Paddington Station. We parted with a very sweet kiss and went back to our compartments.

When the train pulled into the station, I looked out of the window and much to my surprise, I saw Major Davis' driver standing on the platform. Being nosy, I waited to see who he was meeting. When I saw that it was Polly, I thought that she must be mixed up with the same mob as I am working for. I sincerely hope not, because she is such a tempting beauty.

I took my taxi to Kings Cross Station and just caught the train to Peterborough. Much to my relief, I saw that there was a restaurant car, so I went to have some lunch. This time it was peaceful, but my mind was filled with the females in my life.

I had a letter from Celeste, which made me laugh. The post script said, "You can breath again, dear Henry, because there won't be any little Henrys in Normandy for you to worry about." Needless to say, I soon got rid of the last page.

I changed trains at Peterborough for a very slow train to Sleaford. When I got there, there were RAF bods everywhere. A Corporal made contact and I was led to a service van and in no time I was on my way to RAF Cranwell.

The Corporal introduced himself as Crocker and he said that he would be looking after me during my stay at the Station. He added that he would point me in the right directions at the right time. I would be on special courses together with five other officers.

When we got to the main entrance to the camp, my papers were inspected and with a smart salute, we were let in. The college looked a magnificent building, but I was not for there. We eventually came to a new low building near the airfield. I went into an outer office and then I was shown into another office, which was very comfortably appointed. Sitting at a desk sat a Wing Commander. I marched up to the desk, saluted and said, "Blake reporting as instructed, Sir."

He returned my salute and told me to sit down. He pulled out a file from one of the drawers in his desk. "According to your file, Blake, you are very talented and thought highly of by our Lords and Masters. I have to see that you earn your Wings and that you can fly anything that can land and take off in short distances. I also have to teach you the

RAF flying procedures and lastly how to behave as an officer in the RAF. My name is Hicks and you will use the permanent staff mess. There are five other chaps on this special course and I will introduce you to them in the Mess before dinner tonight."

Crocker showed me to my quarters, which were very nice indeed. He had taken my gear from the van and it was all put away. He handed me a paper with a list of what would happen for the first week. He told me where to find the Mess and said that he would see me in the morning at 0700 hours.

Looking at the paper, it seemed that every morning at seven o'clock there would be either P.E. or a cross-country run. After that, a shower and breakfast to follow. During the day there will be lectures and at some time during the day there would be flying. This is the program for the first week, after that, one will have to wait and see.

I had a good wash and then I had a walk around the adjacent area and eventually found the Mess. I was met by the Wing Commander, who introduced me to my fellow class mates. The six of us were then given a beer and left to our own devices.

Meeting these chaps turned out to be most interesting. They all came from different parts of the country from Land's End to the John O' Groats and they all had a command of a foreign language. Some could fly and others were qualified in radio or explosives. Three of us were in RAF uniform, two were in the Army and one in the Navy. I later found out that they were red hot in their own subject. The three not in the RAF were regulars.

We soon got to know each other and we had an enjoyable first evening. The other officers in the Mess, were mostly older but quite pleasant, but they soon made it very clear that it was their Mess and we had to behave ourselves.

The first week was a bit of a bore. The weather was fine so the early morning keep fit classes I enjoyed. Some of my class mates were city dwellers and they found them a bit too much. Anyway the Flight Sergeant in charge soon got them into shape.

We were lectured and shown how aircraft were controlled, from the control tower. To see some of the cadets from the college learning to land and take off, made us all have a good laugh. One of the Controllers told us that only a few of the cadets became pilots. Evidently you had to be first class to pass from Cranwell.

We also had a lecture of RAF etiquette and regulations and of course this only applied to the RAF V.R. chaps. During the first week I flew in three different sorts of aircraft and the Flight Lieutenant seemed very pleased with my efforts. He was a very dour Scotsman, but we took to each other and he was to be my mentor for the whole course in flying. Four of us could fly and the other two went off each day to expand their knowledge in aircraft radio and bombs.

I became very friendly with the Army chap from London. It is always very strange that out of a small crowd, or a large one for that matter, two people seem to make contact and become friends.

On the first Sunday, we went to Lincoln for the day, and explored this lovely, old town, with its magnificent Cathedral. We had lunch in a very old pub and overall we enjoyed ourselves. He was called Peter Tackell and he also had a girlfriend, so we were not 'Bird Hunting'.

We talked about ourselves and our problems. He was in the Army because his father had been, and he had very little choice. But so far, he was enjoying it and if only he can come away from Cranwell with his Wings, he will be so happy, because it will help for promotion. I said that we had to forget that as we had been chosen for something very different to the usual service life. I came right out with it. "We are going to be in the Secret Service, or something like that. If there is a war, we will have no choice in the matter."

On the Monday morning of my second week, I was introduced to an aircraft that I was to get to know so well. It was called a Lysander. It was a single wing aircraft but made to take off and land in restricted areas. In the future I was to love this plane, because it saved my life so many times and it helped me to save others.

As soon as I sat in this odd-looking aircraft, I knew that I could do whatever I liked with it. After going through the usual flying actions and passing them all, I asked my instructor if I could play around a bit. I made the plane do all sorts of things, not expected of it. When I landed and taxied in, the ground crew gave me a clap which really made my day.

During the second week, the course intensified. We had a full day, starting at 7 o'clock and finishing at 5:30pm. Flying took up most of the time, which included navigation and emergency repairs to the aircraft and the radios, which were pretty basic on the small planes. We also had survival tests.

These tests were great fun to me because I had so many years of Jake's tuition behind me, that I found them a piece of cake. We were taken out in a closed van and dumped in the middle of nowhere. We were all acting on our own, as if our plane had come down and we had to make our way back to the camp, avoiding RAF guards put on special alert.

We had a compass and a very rough map. Perhaps I had been lucky with where I was dumped, because I soon found the camp. Getting in was not as easy. Lincolnshire being so flat, cover was non-existent except on one side of the camp, which was wooded, well-fenced and plenty of guards. It was of course an exercise for these bods as well so they were well on their toes.

After a long wait I managed to slip under the wire, while a guard fell out to attend to nature's needs. I got through the woods with great ease and then I had a bit of luck. We were given old overalls to wear during this exercise and I saw that some builders were working on a new hut that they were putting up. I pinched a couple of planks and boldly walked through the camp to our unit's headquarters.

As I walked into the small compound in front of our unit, I saw the Wing Commander walking towards me. By now I was in a bit of a mess and I really looked like a workman. He passed me, but then stopped and said, "Where do you think you are going, my man?" I replied "After a shower, I am going into the Mess for a beer." He said, "Well I am damned, it's Blake isn't it, back from your survival test? Well done, I will buy you that beer."

So after a shower and a change into clean clothing, I went into the Mess and much to my surprise the Wing Co. was there and he bought me a beer. He asked me how I had managed to get back so quickly. So I told him about my friendship with Jake and how skilful he was in the art of woodcraft and survival and I had been his pupil since I was about ten years of age.

He asked me a lot of questions about myself and then he changed the subject, by saying that he had a message from his daughter, Jean. "It seems that she was a friend of your Mary Howes at college and she has been asked by this young lady to look after you while you are at Cranwell, so will you come and spend the weekend with us? By the way I know Sir James very well and he thinks a great deal of you."

I looked at him in utter amazement, and I could hardly believe my ears. I had to accept the invitation, but it will be strange spending the weekend with complete strangers. I thanked him and said that it was very nice of them to ask me. I pointed out that I only had very little clothing with me and would a jacket and trousers be acceptable? He laughed and said, "Wear what ever you like, but not your uniform, we are very informal at home."

He got up to go and told me that he would tell Crocker when and where to take me to after lunch on Saturday. I thanked him and said that I was looking forward to meeting his daughter.

After he left I sat and had a good think about this turn of events. This network of the upper classes was really quite amazing. It seems that if you are part of it, and your keep you nose clean, it is a sort of world-wide club. Trust my dear Mary to go to the bother of making contact with this female called Jean. One thing is certain and that is Jean will be fat or plain.

It was difficult to find a telephone kiosk that was not in use, or with chaps waiting to use the phone, so I caught the bus into Sleaford. I had seen a pleasant-looking hotel and I thought that they would be sure to have a pay phone. I went into the bar and ordered a pint and found a phone. I dialled Mary's number and as luck would have it, she answered my call.

How smashing it was to hear her voice. When I could get a word in, I asked her about Jean Hicks. I got the low down on the Hicks family and she said that Jean was a proper tom-boy, but very attractive and shy with men. With one of her laughs she said, "I think that you will be quite safe there, I am sure that she won't be creeping into your bed." She gave a deep sigh and added that she wished she could creep into my bed. I asked her to ring Mother and tell her that I am O.K. By now my money ran out so we had to say a quick goodbye.

After my phone call, I felt very homesick and fed up, so I went into the bar and ordered another pint. I started to read a paper that someone had left behind. Out of the corner of my eye I noticed a couple that had just come. It was Flight Lieutenant Maclean in civvies and a very petite female. Much to my surprise, they came over to where I was sitting. He introduced the female as his wife, Francois, but we all call her Fran for short.

I asked them if I may buy them a drink. As soon as Francois started to speak I knew that she was French, so I spoke to her in my best French, leaving out the Normandy accent. Her face lit up when she heard her own language, she seemed to come alive. Of course I had to tell her how I became fluent in French and that I had just returned from Normandy. We had several drinks and it turned out to be a very pleasant evening.

I had to leave so that I could catch the last bus. The Lieutenant walked with me to the door and said, "By the way when we are not on duty they call me Jock and having looked at your file, you are Henry. That is of course if you want to." I replied that nothing would please me more. I caught the bus and added Jock to my list of friends.

The course was becoming very hectic and I had to spend a lot of time in the evenings swotting up. I met Jock and his wife on the Friday evening and told them about my visit to the Hicks' home that weekend. Jock told me that I was indeed honoured. I quickly told them that it was all to do with females and I was not looking forward to it one little bit. Jock told me that the old man came from these parts and he had a smashing home near Grantham.

It was after lunch on Saturday and complete with my suitcase, Crocker picked me up in a RAF car. He had proved most helpful during my first two weeks at Cranwell and I must say that we got on very well.

It was very difficult to break down the class barrier. I did manage it to a certain degree, so we had an understanding.

The Hicks' home was in between Cranwell and Grantham. It was a grand-looking house in large grounds. I could see several horses grazing on the lush-looking grass. This was a sign of hope. Perhaps I might have a ride, then I remembered that I had no gear with me.

As we pulled up in front of the house, the Wing Co. appeared and gave me a very friendly welcome. Crocker took my case into the hallway and then went on his way. As I got used to the darkness of the hall compared with the sunshine outside, I saw a female come down the stairs. She was well-built, with short, blond hair and an exquisite face which looked shy but full of energy and fun. I found it so very difficult to analyse what I was looking at. I pulled myself together because I had been staring for so long.

She came down the stairs and said, "I am Jean and of course you must be Henry. I feel that I know you, because Mary talked about you so much." Her father told her to take me up to my room. As we walked up the stairs she asked if I would like to have a ride. I said that I could think of nothing better, but I had no clothes to wear. She looked at me and said that she could fix me up with some of her brother's. He is away, but she had asked him and he had said that it was O.K. by him.

I could tell that she was very nervous. She spoke too quickly and seemed to be all over the place. I decided to take drastic actions. I took her two hands and said, "I have talked to Mary about you and she is very fond of you and will you please get into that very pretty, little head that I won't eat you. So relax, and just be yourself, because I think that we could be great friends if we are just ourselves."

She gave a big sigh and I could see that I had taken the right tack. There seemed as if a great load had been lifted off her shoulders. She looked at me and she said, "I am beginning to understand why Mary loves you so much," and then she gave me a kiss on the cheek.

I managed to fix myself up in riding gear from the brother's wardrobe. I even found an old pair of boots which were a reasonable fit. Not that I would like to go on a route march with them.

Before we left the house, I asked Jean if she could find me a couple of lumps of sugar. She had her own horse in the stable. I had to catch mine in the paddock. Jean warned me that this may be difficult. Anyway I soon caught a fine-looking horse and after two lumps of sugar and a bit of a chat, he was as good as gold.

We had a smashing ride around the area, and I soon realised that Jean was a first class rider. She rode more like a man than a female. Perhaps this is why Mary said that she was a bit of a tomboy.

When we had the chance, we chatted away like mad, she now

seemed quite relaxed and I was enjoying her company. She asked me countless questions about Mary and I, and did I see much of her. After I told her that we were nearly always together, she was silent for a bit and then said that she didn't have a boyfriend, "I somehow scare them away."

I didn't answer her right away, but we stopped by an old log, and got off and sat down. I said, "I think that you are scared of young men and they may sense this in the way you behave. When we met first of all, you were all over the place and as nervous as a kitten. You really are a lovely girl and you should have a boyfriend." I took her hand and told her that I would try to give her a few tips over the weekend.

Jean got up and bending down, she gave me a smashing kiss. "There Henry, I am not scared of you. I wish that you were my boyfriend," then she blushed like mad and got on her horse and galloped down the lane. I had a good laugh and followed her.

When we got back to the house, I met Mrs Hicks, who really was an older version of her daughter, Jean. I had a bath and made myself presentable. I was shown into a sitting room and joined the Wing Co. and his wife for the usual glass of sherry before dinner. Conversation was very easy and interesting, mostly about life on RAF camps all over the world. By now I was wondering where Jean was, and then she came in.

What a transformation, she looked smashing and she had definitely put on her war paint. I turned to Mrs Hicks and said, "Would you please introduce me to this gorgeous, young lady." In fun, Jean curtseyed in front of me, so I got up, took her hand and kissed it, as they did in the old days. She then burst out laughing and gave me a hearty push so that I fell back into my chair. This made her parents laugh. I did however notice a look that Mrs Hicks gave her husband. As much to say This isn't our shy Jean, what has come over her in such a short time?

I was very sorry when Sunday evening came and Crocker came to take me back to the camp. Just before I was about to leave Jean asked me if I would do her a big favour. Without thinking I said, yes. There was going to be a special Ball at the college and she had to go with her parents, she looked at me and said, "Dear Henry, would you come as well, if Daddy can fix it? It would make me so happy if you would." I said that I would have to speak to her father about it and if he thinks that it is O.K., I would love to.

She then put her arms around my neck and gave me another kiss. This time I could not resist the temptation, so I returned it. Crocker then came and I escaped into the safety of the car.

I have survived over two weeks at Cranwell. I have been working very hard, learning all sorts of things. I met Jock and his wife several times, and Jock let the cat out of the bag by telling me that I had been recommended for my Wings. So I must keep my nose clean for the rest of the course.

I was in the Mess one evening looking out of the window at some Hurricanes parked nearby, I was in another world and I didn't hear the Wing Co. come up behind me. He said, "I bet that you would like to fly one of those, Blake." I told him that I would give my eye-teeth for a chance. He smiled and said, "My boy, if you will take me daughter to the 'do' at the College on Saturday, I will let you have a go." I replied "That's a deal Sir, not that I need to be bribed. There is however a problem. What do I wear?"

"Just your uniform, and of course you will spend the weekend with us."

I just couldn't believe my luck. Fancy being given the chance of flying a Hurricane. When I told Jock, he knew all about it and Friday was the big day. So roll on Friday. I was glad to hear that Jock and Fran were going to the Ball. They were however surprised that I was going, because it is a very sought after invitation.

I thought that Friday would never come. During the week Jock had been explaining the different controls and any likely pitfalls that might crop up. In fact I felt that I could fly the plane in theory. To do so in practice may be another story. On the other hand, the powers that be think that I am capable, otherwise I would not be allowed this trip.

As I walked out to the plane, I could sense that many eyes were watching to see if I make a balls of it. When I taxied to the end of the runway I could feel the immense power of the engine, which was waiting to released into the blue sky. I had the all clear from the Control Tower and I was off.

I lifted her gently off the ground and went into a steady climb. What a joy it was to fly such a powerful plane. I climbed to a good height and then went into a sharp dive, pulling out in time to fly fairly low over the Control Tower. I was only allowed a short time in the air, so I made the most of it. Much to my surprise I felt completely in control.

I felt on top of the world, like an eagle about to swoop down on its prey, and I imagined that I was shooting up a German convoy. I was brought back to earth by the Controller, telling me to come in now. I was lucky, I made a reasonable landing and taxied up to the hangers. The Flight Sergeant in charge of the ground crew looking after the Hurricanes said, "Well done Sir, that was a good show."

Jock was very pleased with my efforts and my class mates were very envious, but in a friendly way. It took some time for the feeling of elation to wear off. I was so lucky to have had the chance, and it was a miracle that I didn't balls it up, so I had a few beers in the Mess that night to celebrate.

After lunch on Saturday, Crocker picked me up and he delivered me to the Hicks' abode. He told me that his pals in the Ground Crew, had placed bets that I would make a mess of my flight in the Hurricane. He laughed and said that he had won a couple of quid. He added, "Well done Sir, I knew that you could do it." We arrived and Crocker said that he would see me on Sunday night to take me back to camp.

Jean came out to greet me. She looked rather nice, she must have had her hair done for the Ball. She had her Jodhpurs on so I took it that we were to have a ride. As she led the way up the stairs, I asked her where her parents were and she said that they had gone out shopping and we were all by ourselves in the house except for the odd servant. She left me and I unpacked my bag and as it was a warm day I kicked off my shoes and was just about to take my trousers off, when in she came to show me the dress she would be wearing that evening. She held against her and did a quick twirl.

She put the dress over a chair and came up to me and said, "Dear Henry, please kiss me, I am sure Mary won't mind if I have just a tiny bit of you for a day or two." By now she had her arms around my neck and I had no option but to oblige. Anyway one would have to be a saint to just walk away and it would have killed her confidence, which was beginning to build up.

I thought that this young lady was supposed to be shy. She pulled out my shirt and her hands were feeling my bare back. So I did the same to her. Except that I undid her bra from the back and found her firm, young breasts.

By now we were close to the bed. Jean gave me a mighty push and I fell on the bed and she fell on top of me, laughing like mad. By now we were both very sexually aroused. I suddenly realised what was happening and I knew that we had to stop this going any further, but how without hurting her feelings?

I sat up and putting my arms around her I said, "Jean darling, we must stop this going any further. I would love to make love to you, but it wouldn't be fair to you, and Mary would have a fit. Do you know that I think that you are a real smasher and any chap that has you as a girlfriend, would be more than lucky."

She looked at me and said, "Dear Henry, I think that I could fall in love with you, in fact I think that I half way there already. I know that you will be leaving in a couple of weeks, but could you not let our bodies get together without me losing my virginity. I have been told that it is a lovely feeling and no one need know and no harm will be done."

394

"Well Jean, your father would have me Court Marshalled and shot at dawn if he found me in bed with you and I would hate to do anything to make you feel unhappy. So let us get dressed and go for a ride and worry about this later."

We got our horses and we both acted as if nothing had happened in the bedroom such a short time ago. I felt very worried about the turn of events. Somehow or other, I had to nip this problem in the bud. No way could I get involved with yet another female, but how could I manage it without hurting Jean's feelings and without her losing the confidence she had gained since I met her?

I could make sure that we were not given the opportunity again. The odd kiss could do no harm, on the other hand this can lead to other things. So I will have to be very careful. We had a very pleasant ride and when we got back to the house, her parents had returned.

We had a light meal because there would be food available at the college. During the meal the Wing Co. told me that he had watched me handle the Hurricane and he said that he would like me to train me as a fighter pilot, but unfortunately I was for other duties. I replied that this was unfortunate because that is what I would like to do, when the war starts.

We all went up stairs to make ourselves look smart. As usual the ladies were the last to get ready. When Jean came down the stairs, she looked ravishing and good enough to eat. Her mother also looked very smart. The Wing Co. had on his dress uniform which made him look a bit out of it. But then I was only a Pilot Officer in the V.R.

I told Jean how lovely she looked and she took my arm as we walked outside to a large car plus a driver. I was on a bit of a cloud, because I had found out that to be invited to the end of a course Ball was indeed the ambition of many of the staff not connected directly to the college. To be a guest of a Wing Commander was indeed an honour.

I felt very small indeed going through the main doors of the college. Jean must have seen how I felt and she took my arm, and in we went into yet another world.

We had to be introduced to the Camp Commander, who was a Group Captain. As we were ushered up towards him and his wife, I saw an officer standing next to the Group Captain say something to the Old Boy. When it was my turn, he said, "You were the young chap that was throwing that Hurricane around yesterday. Well done young man. If I was your age, I would like to do the same. They tell me that you are here to earn your Wings for some special duty they have in mind for you. If that is the case, I will see you again when I present you with your Wings."

To begin with the evening was a bit on the stiff side, all the cadets were on their best behaviour. Their very difficult course was almost over and on no account did they want to blot their copy book. But as the evening wore on the drinks were making the bods more relaxed. Jean and I joined Jock and Fran. It was smashing practice for me to speak French for most of the evening.

Jean turned out to be a very good dancer and looking around she was one of the most attractive girls at the Ball. Like a clot, I told her so and this started her getting a bit sexy when we were on the dance floor. I told her to behave herself, and I am glad that she started to calm down.

After the smashing refreshments people began to let their hair down, and it became noticeable that couples were disappearing into the darkness of the spacious gardens outside.

After a rather energetic dance, Jean complained of feeling the heat and that she must have some air. She took my hand and I was led unwillingly into the garden, which of course proved to be fatal.

As soon as we were out of view, she became so very amorous. It was as if she had suddenly lost all of her inhibitions and was no longer the shy, young girl before I met her. I had to admit to myself that it was a very enjoyable interlude. Quite harmless but natural and she looked even more radiant when we returned to the Ballroom.

By now we joined Jean's parents and soon it was the last dance and we said goodbye to Jock and Fran. Right up to the last, we nattered away in French to each other, much to the amusement of the Hicks family.

It had been a very enjoyable evening and I thanked my hosts most heartily for inviting me. I had to have a night-cap with the Wing Co. and he then told me that I would be receiving my Wings, together with the Cadets. This would take place at the end of next week. With a laugh he said, "Make sure your buttons are clean that day my boy."

We then went to our rooms. I got into my bed and lay for a while thinking about the past few hours. It was good news that it now seemed certain that I would get my Wings, and at the end of next week I will be on my way back to Devon and Mary. Somehow I have to keep Jean at bay. Why do I have this trouble with females? I have no idea, they just seem to like me and I can't help that. I had kissed Jean goodnight after her parents had gone into their room. I then went up onto the next floor to my room.

With these thoughts in my mind I went to sleep. I thought at first that I was dreaming, but as I slowly came back into this world, I realised that I was not alone in my large bed. It was of course Jean. She must have been very quiet not to wake me or I must have been in a very deep sleep.

She saw that I was awake and she whispered "Dear Henry, don't think badly of me. I have never done anything like this before, but somehow you seem to be different. I know that I can trust you and I think that I am falling in love with you. I also know that you belong to Mary. So darling, will you love me tonight, if only in the safe way. I can then look back on my first real encounter with someone that is really sweet."

So what could I do? She is such a smashing girl and I found that I was getting fond of her, in such a short time. She started to explore my body and I could tell that this was her first sexual adventure. I then took her in my arms and gently made love to her. Leaving the final pleasure for her to enjoy in the future.

When her adventure was over, I thought that she would never stop kissing me. It seemed to make her so happy. I got very little sleep that night. I am however ashamed that I enjoyed it as much as I did.

The next morning, very early, I awoke and looking down on this sweet girl, who was still asleep. She had a look of contentment on her lovely face. It was a look I had seen on Mary's face so often. Anyway it was grand to know that I have made someone happy, before unhappiness begins.

I woke her up by kissing her and her reaction was to put her arms around my neck and bury my head in her young breasts. Eventually I persuaded her to go back to her own room. I then managed to get some sleep until it was time to get up.

When I went down to breakfast, apart from looking a bit tired, Jean looked so happy and when no one was looking she gave me a shy wink. Looking at her made me wish that it would help me to get mixed up with females that are fat and plain. Perhaps it's my fate to be tempted. There is Polly, Mary, Celeste, and now Jean. Every one of them real smashers, but Mary is the jewel in the crown.

After breakfast, the Old Man said that he wanted to have a chat with me so we had a walk around the grounds. Naturally he called me Blake and I called him Sir. Anyway what he wanted to talk about was Germany. He said, "Blake, you have been to Germany on two occasions, can you tell me what it is really like? I know some of the information you have is very hush-hush, but what is your general impression?"

I then held forth for some time. He was very impressed that I had met Herr Goering and I managed to give him a picture of what I had seen. Some things I couldn't mention, because I had been told not to. The Old Man seemed very pleased and then shook me a bit by saying "Blake, how have you managed to get my daughter to become so confident and happy in such a short time? She seems a different girl. All I hope is that it will last after you leave next week. By the way, I have arranged for a bit of a party after the Wings parade, so you will come and stay with us on your last couple of days at Cranwell?"

I didn't know how to react to this news, because I had to travel back to Devon on the Saturday this is what I had told Mary and this is what I wanted to do.

I told the Old Man that it was very kind of his family to go to the trouble and they had made my stay at Cranwell most enjoyable. The Wings parade is on the Thursday of next week, so perhaps I could come over after the parade and return to camp on Friday. I would then get ready to leave first thing on Saturday morning.

The Old Man thought this was a good idea. He looked at me with a bit of a twinkle in his eye and said that I would have to sort it out with Jean. He told me that he usually went down to the local for a pint on Sunday mornings, so perhaps Jean and I would care to join him. I said that I would love to.

Jean and I had a lazy morning, we just sat around and talked. I told her all about my trips to foreign parts, and my plans for the future. She looked at me and said, "I wish that your plans included me. Anyway if there is a war I will join the WAAF and who knows, we might meet again."

I told her not to be silly, because she will soon meet a handsome, young man and fall in love with him. "You will need to play hard to get because there are some rotters about, and don't go into too many strange beds."

She gave me a good clout and with a laugh, she had her arms around me and it was with difficulty that I broke away from her clinch.

We had a very pleasant drink in the local and the Old Man was quite human, like his daughter he had a sense of humour and we joined up with some of his friends.

After lunch Jean and I caught the horses and went for a ride. I had told her that if I wanted to think, I would go and sit by the Little Bridge. She told me that she would take me to her secret place.

We rode into a wood, which was very overgrown, but we went along a well worn path, which eventually led into one of the most beautiful glades I have ever seen.

The leaves were very young and the different colours of green were a wonderful sight. There were birds everywhere and it was so peaceful. It was as if one was in another world, away from all the many problems. We dismounted and Jean took out a rug from her saddle bag and, taking my hand she led me to a green patch under a huge beech tree.

She spread out the rug and we both sat down and just enjoyed where we were. By now the sun was quite warm and we stretched out and sunbathed for a while. She turned to me and with her face being supported by her bent arm, she looked right into my face and began to tell me how she had been so fearful of young men and not having a regular boyfriend at nineteen was very odd. "Dear Henry, I think that you have cured me of my phobia."

I looked at her and I thought that it seemed impossible that such a lovely girl had not been captured by some bright, young man. He had to be bright because Jean is very intelligent and someone a bit dim would not be very compatible.

The more I saw of this female, the more I realised how beautiful she was, and that Sunday afternoon I began to realise how I felt about her, which was most disturbing.

I started to get up but I didn't stand a chance. She was on me like a shot and said, "If you won't make love to me I will make love to you." And so it was that we made love in her secret glade, with the sunshine glistening on our hot, young bodies. Seeing everything in daylight increased her desire and we were there for most of the afternoon.

As we were making ourselves presentable, I decided to take the bull by the horns and put a stop to this affair. So I tried to tell the dear girl that it had to end, otherwise several people would hurt. She came up to me and put her arms around my waist and said, "I quite understand, but it won't stop me from loving you, and remembering my first love for the rest of my life."

She went on to say that we would meet next week for my big day and after that, her parents were giving a dinner party and perhaps my friend, Jock could come with his nice wife. I would be staying the night, but she would be a good girl.

"This is why I love you Henry, I can talk to you as a friend and yet we can be lovers, perhaps this is the secret. No doubt I will find out and learn from my mistakes."

We mounted up and made our way back through the wood. On my way I cut a small twig and put it in my pocket. This will remind me of a lovely girl and a beautiful place in Lincolnshire. Jean saw what I had done and pretended not to have noticed.

When we rode into the grounds of Jean's house, her parents were sitting in the garden having a pre-dinner drink. So after a wash and a change of clothing, we joined them.

After dinner, the Old Man said that he would drive me back to the camp as Crocker had the week off. Anyway he wanted to collect some work from his office and he would be ready in about half and hour.

I went up to my room and packed my bag. Jean said that she would help, but as expected she was more of a hindrance. I think that given half a chance she would have had me on the bed again.

At last I managed to escape and laughing like mad, we ran down the stairs. I said goodbye to Mrs Hicks and Jean gave me a very polite kiss, but she whispered in my ear, "I wish that it was last night."

Sitting in the car, I also wished that it was last night. Somehow or other this girl had really got to me and I had enjoyed being with her and I will be sorry to leave Cranwell. On the other hand I think that it is just as well that I am off back to Devon next weekend.

When the Old Man dropped me off at my quarters, he said, "I will be in touch about the arrangements for next weekend, and my wife and I are sorry that you are leaving, because it has been a pleasure having you with us, and to see Jean come out of her shell has made us very happy." He looked into the distance and said that it made him feel young again.

I had got out of the car and he leaned out of the window and said, "By the way Blake, when I see Sir James, I won't mention the interlude with my daughter," and with a laugh, he drove off, putting his hand out of the window and giving me a friendly wave.

I went into the Mess that evening for a drink and I had my leg pulled most of the time about my friendship with the Old Man's daughter. How the hell did I manage to get an invitation to the Ball at the college? It took me a long time to convince these chaps that no one was more surprised than I was.

The next morning, we were told that the four of us that were trying to earn our Wings, had passed the tests, and we would get our Wings on Thursday and be free to go home on Saturday.

The passing out parade was very impressive in front of the college. The relations and girlfriends were there to give their loved one moral support. My classmates and I were not included in this very formal event. We were last on the agenda and I did feel so very proud when I had to march up to receive my Wings from the Group Captain I had met at the Ball.

I nearly had a fit, because after he gave me my Wings, he said In fluent German, "Well done Blake, I wish you luck, because I feel that you will need it. Davis told me about you." I replied also in German, "May God be with you Sir, we will all need some help in the future." I saluted and marched smartly away.

Jean and her mother were at the ceremony, so I went and joined them. Jean put her arms around my neck and gave me a kiss to congratulate me. She looked so very lovely on that afternoon in the late Spring of 1939.

I have no idea why it meant so much to me to have Wings on my uniform. Perhaps it was pride of an achievement for a farmer's son from the sticks of Devon. My great regret was that Dad was not there to share my joy.

Later I went back to Jean's home and the first thing she did was to take my jacket off and very carefully sewed on my Wings. She said, "Darling Henry, where ever you are, you will be wearing something to remind you of me."

The dinner party was grand fun. Jock and Fran were there, together with some young friends of Jean's. After dinner we all trooped down to the local pub and had a real booze up. In fact it was a really smashing party.

During my last night in Jean's home, we both behaved ourselves. She came into my room early in the morning and we said our sad farewells in the privacy of my room.

After breakfast the Old Man took me back to camp, and I tried to put into suitable words a thank you for being so hospitable to a complete stranger. The Old Boy laughed and said, "Don't forget Henry, if you are ever in these parts again, we would love to see you. Please give my regards to Sir James and Pamela." He delivered me to my quarters and I shook his hand and I gave him a salute, which of course he returned.

He had driven off about a few yards, when he reversed and called me over. He pulled down his window and said, "Blake, will you do me favour? Do you think that you could write to Jean every now and again, because I know that it would make her very happy? I know that it is a bit of a cheek, but I would be most grateful." I told him that I was going to in any case. He gave me a wave and he was on his way.

My last night at Cranwell is a bit hazy. I managed to bag a telephone and I rang Mary to tell her when I would be back to Newton Abbot. She immediately said that Wills would meet me at the station. It was grand to speak to her again and I told her that I was longing to see her. She told me that it had been a long four weeks. My money ran out and this cut us off.

The six of us met in the Mess and we all had far too much to drink, but after all we had a very good excuse. We were all very different, but we had Major Davis in common and in our hearts we knew that we would meet again.

I only just caught my train in the morning and I settled down to sleep my way to London. When I got to Peterborough, the London train had a restaurant car aboard and after a meal I felt my usual self.

When the train pulled into King's Cross, I got my gear together and got onto the platform. I then had a wonderful surprise. I saw Mary waving like mad by the gate, together with Hugh grinning like a Cheshire cat.

Mary ran up to me and she started to kiss me like mad. It was grand to have her in my arms and to smell her natural perfume. She managed to tell me that Hugh had invited us to stay in London for the weekend. He only had this bright idea after I had telephoned last night, so she couldn't let me know. She said that she even got in contact with Jean Hicks who had said that she would try and get a message to me. I thought that I bet Jean didn't very try very hard, if at all.

Hugh had his car, so we were on our way to his house in Bruton Place. Mary was hanging on to me as if I might disappear into thin air. We didn't sop talking until we arrived at Bruton Place.

It was nice to see Hugh's butler, Harris, because by now we were old friends likewise, Mrs Gibbs, the housekeeper.

Hugh didn't come in with us. He said that he had a few errands to do, and Ann Hastings would be joining us for dinner. Harris had my luggage taken up the now familiar staircase. As I walked up with Mary on my arm I remembered the first time. It now seemed so long ago.

Needless to say Mary and I were a long time before we came down the wide staircase again. I realised that there was only one girl that I really loved and one day I hope that she will be my wife.

After we had made love for the second time, we lay on the bed and talked. I told her all that had taken place over the last four weeks. She then interrupted me by telling me that she thought that Jean had fallen in love with me. I then explained Jean's problem with boyfriends, and if nothing else I had cured her of that.

I told her that Jean was a very sweet girl, with very kind parents and they looked after me so well, during my stay at Cranwell. With my fingers crossed, I told her that I had not been unfaithful, just the odd kiss here and there. Mary pounced on me and started hitting me, but only in fun and she then said that she would let me into a secret.

She had asked Jean to look after me while I was at Cranwell, because she knew all about her problem and she knew that I would put her right. I got hold of Mary and I turned her over and smacked her bare bottom, telling her not to put temptation my way again. Anyway it is more than anyone can hope for, is to make someone happy every now and again.

I went on to explain how kind her parents were to me and what a lovely girl Jean is. We became good friends and that was all. Her father asked me to write to her every now and again, which I intend to do. This is the only way I can repay their hospitality.

We dressed and went downstairs. My first job had to be the telephoning of Mother. I told her that I had been met at the station in London and I am staying the weekend with Hugh and Mary. She already knew because Mary had told her before she left for London.

I told that I was looking forward to seeing them all and I would give her all of the news on Monday. I made her laugh by saying that I was looking forward to some of her home cooking and a ride on Henry.

It turned out to be a smashing idea of Mary's to meet me in London, because we had a grand weekend. Hugh and his girlfriend Ann seemed to be very much in love. Ann stayed the night at Bruton Place, and like Mary and I, she and Hugh were sleeping together.

Unfortunately, Monday morning came and we were once more on the train home to Devon. I only had a week at home before I started my new job at Wimble Manor.

Mary soon fell asleep on the train, catching up on what she had lost during the last two nights. This enabled me to have a good think about the past month and the next few weeks.

Jean's father had told me that there was a RAF air station at Chivenor, which is near Barnstaple and perhaps they have a VR flight nearby. This could be good news to me if I am able to fly a plane every now and again. I must get in touch with the Major to see what he can wrangle. Anyway I have well and truly got the flying bug, and after my very brief love affair with the Hurricane, I would love to have another go.

My mind drifted back to Jean and I wondered how she was getting on. In such a short time I had become very fond of her. Apart from physical attraction, we were on the same wavelength in so many ways. My feelings for her bore no resemblance to how I felt about dear Mary. Nevertheless, I do not want to be tempted like that again. Little did I know then that there were three females in my life and this number had grown to four.

Mary brought me back to earth and we went along to the restaurant car for lunch. I have always enjoyed talking and, at times, arguing with Mary. Very few people can argue without getting over-heated. Mary and I were lucky in this respect.

We were having an argument about next week when I started my job with Sally. Mary said that she was coming up to North Devon with me for a least a month. I said that this would put me off and my concentration would suffer. I knew that I was on a losing wicket, when she told me that Sally had suggested it. She said, "Henry dear, I can type and organise your office and be your secretary and you know how naughty some bosses are with their secretaries." When she said this her hand wandered under the table and gave my knee a squeeze.

I told Mary that I must ask Martin to teach me how to drive a car. It seemed daft that I could fly a Hurricane but not drive a car. We really ought to have a car of some sort before next winter so, as soon as I get up to the Manor, I will put this plan into action. As I said this last sentence, I had one of my awful visits to the future.

I was on the train going to London. It was in the night and, looking out of the window, there were no lights to be seen. I was shouted at by a passenger to cover the window that I was looking out of. The train was packed with men in uniform, some with kitbags and others in full battle gear. Then it all vanished from my mind and the sun was shining through the window and making my Mary look even more beautiful.

When we got to Newton Abbot, Wills was there to meet us. As we were getting into the car he said how pleased he was that I had got my Wings. He said, "We are all very proud of you Mr Henry."

I had persuaded Mary to drop me off first of all at the farm, because I knew that if I went to the Hall, I would be there for ages and I so wanted to see my family. When we got to the farm, Mum and Dad gave me such a greeting that one would think I had been away for ages.

Mary had made me wear my uniform home and she put her arms around me and said, "What a handsome son you have Mrs Blake." Dad had a look at my wings and, for fun, I said that Jean had sewn them on very well for me. Mary then went for me but, of course, only in fun. She said, "Henry, I am going to take them off and sew them on myself," but she never did.

After a lot of leg pulling by John, who had, by now joined us and with a very loving kiss from Mary, I was at last home and along with my family.

That night we had a lovely family party with Charlie and Betty, John and Gertie and dear old Mum and Dad. I had so much to tell them all. What impressed John was the fact that I had flown a Hurricane. I told them about Jean and her family and how kind they had been to me. John's reaction was very much to the point. He thought that Mary was a clot to introduce me to such an attractive girl. In my mind I thought that, of course, he was right.

I was having a very busy week before I moved to North Devon. I had to report back to the VR C.O. and with the help of Major Davis I would be able to have a weekly flight at Chivenor. I said goodbye to my pals in the Flight. I was sorry to leave their good company. We had some good times together and our visits to the Local could be very hectic.

I had a long session with Jake and he told me that if there was a war, I might have to train with the Army for a week or two. On the other hand I might have to kick my heels at an air base until things got organised. He added that I would see the Brig in North Devon and he would put me in the picture if the balloon went up.

CHAPTER 17

It had been quite an upheaval moving to the Manor and, to help us, Sir James decided that he should visit his Mother, so he loaded all our gear into his car, which Wills drove. Mary could have gone in the comfort of the car but she wanted to ride on my bike.

I found it very strange at first actually working for Sally and having the responsibilities of managing such a large estate. I soon got the hang of it because after all I had been taught what to do at the University and I had set in motion a system which was proving to be very successful. The Acting Manager, Jackson, had done a damn good job but he was happy once more, looking after his pheasants and the ever-increasing herd of deer.

Mary had organised my office and she and Peggy Jackson got on so well together that they seemed to enjoy doing the paper-work involved. Sally just stood back with a satisfied grin on her face.

I had the gardeners to clear a spot next to the stream, which was now more like a young river. This they did and built a seat which I used as a place of peace. It doesn't come up to the little bridge, but who knows, one day I might build a bridge.

It will soon be the longest day and the evenings were so lovely, just watching the sun setting behind the distant hills. I went over in my mind what I had done during my first weeks at the Manor.

I have been writing to Jean as arranged and I had told her that I hoped to fly from Chivenor and other odd bits of news. Some of her letters were a bit sad in some respects but like her, very chatty.

I telephoned the Adjutant at Chivenor and he invited me over to see him. He knew all about me, no doubt from the Major. He then told me to hang on, and after a time he came back onto the phone and said that tomorrow after lunch would be fine.

Well I had just gone over to the camp, which was about an hour and a half to drive from the Manor. I met the Adjutant and we talked small talk to begin with. He then said that the camp C.O. wanted to see me, so I was taken in to see the Old Man, who got up and shook hands which in itself was unusual.

He said that his good friend Wing Commander Hicks had been in touch and asked him to look after me, with a postscript from his Godchild, Jean. "So Blake, welcome to RAF Chivenor."

We had a long conversation about what I had to do and he told me that I would be able to have the use of a plane at least once a week. With a smile he added that these were his orders from Group headquarters. "All you will have to do is arrange it all through Flight Lieutenant Biggs, the Adjutant. You will also be very welcome in our Mess."

Sitting by the stream, it made me realise that it is not what you know, but who you know. Because I was a friend of Sir James Howes, I got to know Wing Commander Hicks and now it seems that the C.O. at Chivenor is a friend of Hicks. So I now have a friend in high places at Chivenor. What a chain of events. I am not grumbling, but it does seem a bit unfair to have all of these advantages.

I had my first driving lesson today and Martin thinks that it won't take long before I can venture on to the open road. When Sally heard about these lessons, she got very interested and of course I asked her if I could borrow one of the cars in the garage. She said that Martin would know which one was the most suitable.

The cars in the very large garage were Martin's pride and joy. They reminded him of his Master, Sally's late husband. His hobby was the collecting of old and that matter, new cars. Martin had brought forth a sporty, medium-sized car. It was a real smasher. I told him that it was far too posh for me, so he put that away and brought out a much smaller sports car, called an M.G. Now this was more like it. We then decided that this was to be the car the I would learn to drive.

I told Sally about all of this and she said that she had forgotten that she had this particular car. Then with a laugh, she admitted that she really didn't know what she had. "Perhaps you could list them and let me know, Henry."

I soon discovered that now that the Estate was more organised, I had a very cushy job and Mary and I could spend a lot of time together. We went to the coast and swam quite often. We also got mixed up with some of the chaps at the camp and we had some very noisy parties in their Mess.

Mary and I went down to Teignford every other week and if the weather was nice we would swim in the river, where we had started our love affair.

Our two families seemed to accept that our relationship was now becoming a long-term affair. We talked about this in a very rational way, and decided to get engaged.

We had been together now for so long that we had become part of each other and we loved each other dearly. Neither of us wanted any fuss, or special party, so we first of all went to see James and Pamela, and they were delighted to hear the news and asked us why it had taken us so long. Mum and Dad and my family were also very pleased. Of course John had to say that it was about time that I made an honest woman of her.

Mary and I went into Exeter and I nearly broke the bank by buying her a lovely ring. She kept waving her hand in the air, so that the sun made the stones flash. I think that in my life this had to be my happiest day.

When we got back to the Hall, Pamela had a surprise for us. She had arranged a dinner party for the two families. Even John and Gertie were coming, which I found hard to believe.

It was such a happy event and so wonderful that the two families could mix in the strange system that was ruled by class distinction. We all had a good time and what pleased me a great deal, were the congratulations we received from the staff. After dinner, Hooper, the butler asked me if Miss Mary and I could spare a moment, could we pop in to see Cook?

Going into the kitchen reminded me of my first visit, when Mary filled my basket with fruit and cakes. Ever since then Cook and I had been great friends.

When we went into the kitchen, there she was now much older but still very round in figure. She came forward and put her arms around me and gave me a kiss. Saying in her broad Devon accent, "God bless you both, Mr Henry I am so happy that it will be you looking after Miss Mary. Somehow I always thought that it would be you." Mary then came over and put her arms around the dear old friend and I could see a tear or two in her eyes.

When we went inside again, Mary whispered in her Father's ear and he then gave Hooper some instructions. I asked Mary what was going on and she said that she had asked Papa to give the staff a drink from us.

We were all talking and enjoying ourselves. Mary had left the room for quite a while. When she came back, she had a smile on her face. So I asked her what she had been up to. She told me that she had telephoned her grandmother to tell her the good news. All she said was, "and about time."

Going back to the Manor after our hectic weekend, we both felt on top of the world and even more in love than ever. While we were driving up the long drive the front door of the Manor, we could see that there was a bit of a panic. The staff were trooping out under guidance of Hooper, the butler and lining up in front of the main door, and then Sally came out.

It then dawned on us that this was in our honour and they wanted to congratulate us on our engagement. So we had to shake hands with all of them. Some of the young maids were so very shy. They all looked spotless in their starched white aprons. There faces were red and shiny as if they had been scrubbed.

What pleased me was the look of pleasure that they showed on hearing the news and Salter said a few well chosen words on their behalf. As he shook my hand he whispered, "Well done Mr Henry, this makes me very happy."

We went into the Manor with Sally. She linked arms with both of us and she shouted to Salter to bring in the champagne. I now understand why she often shouted to Salter. The poor chap was going a bit deaf.

As he poured the champagne, Sally asked him what it was like. He smiled and replied, "However would I know your Ladyship?" Sally gave one of her snorts and we all laughed. Sally then told him to give the staff a suitable drink with their lunch.

When we had settled down with our special drink, Sally said that she had some news for us. She went on to say, "I would like to give you both that nice car that Henry is learning to drive. Somehow it seems to suit you. It is a GB or something like that?" I added that it is an M.G.

We were so very pleased that we both went over to her and gave her a hug and a kiss.

She raised her glass and wished us the very best of luck, and said that she could see it in the wind, but why ever did we take so long. We talked about our future and we had decided to get married next year. Mary joined in by adding that I had to save up first. Sally snorted and said, "Anyway, you can support the both of you."

I looked at Mary and I could see that she was annoyed. I had often wondered where Mary got her money from, and now it has come out that she has an income of her own. I could see that she was a bit upset, so I decided to pretend that I didn't hear.

Sally then really surprised the both of us. She said, "Now that you are engaged and you, Henry are almost part of the family, I have decided to go on a cruise. I am going to take Mrs Bell and we are off next week for one month. You, Henry will be in complete charge of the Estate, with the help of Mary. We will go to Barnstaple in a day or so and see Baker, the solicitor, to give you authority to sign cheques and other things while I am away." She laughed and said that there was no point in having a dog and barking yourself!

She looked at us both and said that we have no idea how happy she was to have someone like me to look after her affairs. It is as if the other Henry had come back to help her in her old age.

Perhaps it was the champagne talking, but there was no stopping her. She said that she often thought about how I had pulled her out of the snow, and gave her a good ticking off. When she first saw me, she thought that it was a ghost of her other Henry. "I often think that he would have loved Wimble like you do, Henry."

We were both flabbergasted by what we had just heard, and we got up as one and went over and gave the Old Dear a hug and a very big thank you.

Mary and I went up to our rooms to get ready for lunch. I was in my room and she came in and putting her arms around me, she said, "I know that you are going to ask me about my money, so I will beat you to it by explaining it all to you. Many years ago, I was left a lot of money by an Old Aunt, who I hardly knew. I came into it on my eighteenth birthday. I decided not to tell you because I thought that it might put you off me."

Mary looked scared at what my reaction would be. I took her lovely face in my hands and told he that she should know that nothing would ever put me off her. After that we went down the stairs hand in hand.

As we walked down, Mary held up her hand and the sun's rays coming through the window made her ring come alive, which gave it a look of magic. I may be a bit daft, but I thought this house had a presence or power not of this world.

Sally had departed to Southampton, with enough luggage for six people. As usual Martin grumbled like mad, having to pack it all into the large Rolls, leaving just enough room for Mrs Bell.

Mary and I felt a bit envious. A cruise to the West Indies and parts of America sounded just the job. We hoped that she would be alright, after all she was no chicken, but she had a very capable Mrs Bell to look after her.

At last I have heard from the University, and much to my surprise I got a reasonable pass. I will have to go down to Exeter to receive my degree. I will have to get a gown because I can put the letters B.A. after my name. I find it all a bit daft, because I have the sort of job I really want and I only took this second subject on the orders from my Lords and Masters at the War Office. Anyway who knows, it might be a help for me in the future.

It was strange at first, living at the Manor without Sally, but we soon began to like it. We were like the Lord and Lady of the Manor. We were waited on, and fed like fighting cocks, in fact the staff enjoyed the situation.

We tried to keep our sleeping arrangements a secret, but we both knew that it was common knowledge that we slept together and how enjoyable it was to make love in such comfort. So much so that our visits to Teignford became few and far between.

Thinking that they would never accept our invitation, we asked Mum and Dad up for a weekend. Wonders will never cease, they said that they would love to come, so it was arranged that Martin would fetch them next weekend.

Mary felt a bit nervous, having to act as host, but it proved to be a great success. I will never forget Mother's expression when she walked into the magnificent hallway. She knew that it would be grand, but it went well above her expectations. However Mary soon made her feel at home.

After lunch, I fixed Dad up with a horse and I took him around part of the Estate. We met the Jacksons and he was very impressed with what we were doing to make the Estate more productive because of the danger of war. Dad had always been a good mixer, and he had the knack of getting to know people. So in no time he was talking to Jackson like an old friend and he certainly hit it off with him.

On the Sunday morning I asked Dad if he would like to come up to our local for a drink, as expected he said that he would like to. Mary butted in by saying that the females of the family would also like to come. Mother looked quite shocked at the thought. Mary took her by the arm and marched her upstairs to put on her hat and coat. I told Salter to ask Martin to bring the car around to the front door in about an hour. I thought that we could have a drive, before going to the pub.

I left the driving to Martin and the running commentary on the different aspects of the countryside. Mother still looked a bit apprehensive when we got to the pub. Anyway we went in and a voice boomed out, "Hello Blake, let me buy you a drink." Of course, it was the Brig. I introduced him to my parents. He took Mother's hand and said, "This is never your Mother, Blake, she looks far too young!" Mother laughed, she always looked so pretty when she laughed.

We had a very enjoyable time and soon it was time to go. Before we left, the Brig said, "Henry, will you and Mary come over for dinner tomorrow evening, because I have something to talk to you about?" I looked at Mary and she said that we would love to. I thought that the old so-and-so must want something, because he called me Henry.

When Mary and I went to our rooms that night, we both thought Mum and Dad had really enjoyed the weekend. It had made me so happy to entertain them and to give them a bit of luxury, if only for a few days. Of course I had to give my dear Mary full marks for her contribution.

Every time I look at her, I am still unable to believe that next year, God will give her to me as my wife. We get on so well, of course we have the odd tiff but that is usual.

Waving goodbye to them both, made me feel sad. I have no idea why. I do so hope that this is not one of my walks into the future. Dad and I had a long talk, while the females were out of the way, while we were having a drink before dinner on the Sunday evening.

He was never one to heap on the praise about anything, but he told me that he was very proud of what I had done, and how lucky I was to have a girl like Mary. He then told me "This Brig chap thinks very highly of you, Henry. We had quite a chat in the pub, so play along with him and see what is forthcoming."

He went on to say that he never thought that a son of his would be an Officer in the RAF, and have a degree. "Whatever you do Henry, look after Mary because your life will revolve around her."

By now I could drive a car, not all that well mind you, but well enough to keep to the quiet roads of the area. Mary and I went in the M.G. to the Brig's for dinner. Mary loved to drive in the car with the hood down. She looked smashing with the wind blowing through her hair.

The Brig and his wife greeted us and much to Mary's pleasure, Fiona was also there. Her presence made the evening much easier and we had a fine time. That is until after dinner, when I had to listen to the Brig for over an hour.

He was the bearer of good news, to begin with. By the end of the week there would be a Lysander plane based at Chivenor for me to fly whenever I could. He went on to say that there is a field next to the airfield for me to practise taking off and landing in a confined space. "You might try with the help of some special glasses that will make it seem like a not very dark night." He fished a pair from his pocket.

He said that his Boffins had told him to tell his bods to wear them walking about during the day, so that they got used to them before they start to fly.

The Old Boy passed me another drink and continued. "When you are used to this plane I want you to fly over to Normandy and land in one of the fields that you selected, when you were over there. Anyway I will organise it all and let you know well in advance. Now Henry, if war should break out, I want you to report to Chivenor and act as Intelligence Officer, and you will remain there until I need you. Chivenor will become an operational training camp for very raw pilots and one of your jobs will be to teach them how to survive in Germany if they were shot down. You will be getting a load of 'bumph'. Most of it will be a load of old tripe, but you may find it useful."

The Old Boy looked at me and smiled, "I wish that I was younger, and not having to sit behind a desk all day, pulling strings as if the people in my Department were puppets. By the way I have seen the C.O. at Chivenor and fixed this all up and as from the first of August

411

you will become Flight Lieutenant Blake. This will enable you to take up these duties when the balloon goes up."

At last I could perhaps get a word in. I asked the Brig if I could tell Mary any of the news he had given me. His answer to this was yes, except about flying to France, that is until I actually go.

I then tried to get out of him what my role would be if there was a war. Try as I may, I couldn't get him to open up. He did say that should France fall to the Germans, I might be needed to ferry people in and out of occupied territory. He was then quiet for a second or two and said that I might even have to enter Germany as a spy. "Anyway Henry," he said, "let us join the ladies and I can feast my old eyes on your gorgeous Mary."

Driving back to the Manor, I was very quiet and Mary wanted to know what was wrong. So I told her, what I could about my chat with the Brig. She snuggled up to me and said, "I am so proud of you, but let us not worry before it happens. Who knows what will happen in the future, so let's live day by day and enjoy each other while we can."

Everything on the Estate was fine, in fact it seemed to run itself. During the few weeks that I have been in charge, I have created a system which would work during a war.

I divided the workforce into five Departments, with men above Military age to be in charge. They had a deputy in case of illness. We would have a meeting once a week, George Jackson would be there as my deputy. Jackson being within the Military age limit, but the poor chap had TB as a youth and it left him unfit for service. On the other hand he would be more than capable to be a gamekeeper or Manager. If war came, it would be impossible to rear Pheasants for people to shoot at.

This system had been started several months ago, on my suggestion, but in a loose sort of way. Now it was well organised with the Department heads, having more authority and delegation was complete. Mary and Peggy Jackson had the job of keeping the books in order. Sally's accountant checked the figures every month to make sure that no one was on the fiddle.

It was now mid-Summer and I was sitting on my seat by the stream. Mary was in the house doing some female chore, so I was on my own and I could sit and have a think about the previous week or two.

I started to think of my introduction to the Lysander aircraft now stationed at Chivenor. I had flown one at Cranwell. This one was a bang up-to-date model, which even had a very powerful machine gun. These planes first came into service as reconnaissance planes on the North West frontier of India. They can fly at low altitudes over difficult

412

terrain. They can also keep out of the way of high speed fighter planes.

On the camp a Corporal mechanic and an L.A.C. mate had the job of looking after this funny looking plane. They were however to get very attached to it and so would I. The plane was a two-seater and for reconnaissance duties a navigator would be a second member of the crew.

I had a long talk to the camp C.O. and he told me that he had been instructed to let me use the plane as much as possible. The camp was being enlarged and the runways were being extended, huts were springing up and he confirmed what the Brig had told me.

The C.O. Wing Commander Hughes asked me who was this Brigadier fellow, who came to see him, and who seemed to have so much power and authority? I laughed and told him that his bark was worse than his bite. He is however a big cheese in the Intelligence Service. I then thought that it would be more helpful if I told him of my involvement. I also told him that if war was declared, I had to report to his camp as Intelligence Officer. I was glad to hear that he knew all about this posting.

I have been flying all over the area, and I made a point of flying low over the Manor, if only to show off to Mary. When I flew over the area that the deer inhabited, it was quite a sight to see them running away from the path of the aircraft. I had seen familiar sights at the Cinema, when planes flew over the wide plains of Africa, driving the vast herds of wild animals in all directions.

As I sat there listening to the music of the stream, with the background chorus being provided by the countless birds that lived in the nearby trees, I looked into the distance and saw my friend Henry having a bit of a frolic with the other horses. It was grand having him up here with me, because I have not found another horse like him.

Mary came to join me, bringing a bottle of wine and two glasses with her. I watched her walking towards me. The sun was setting behind her and the dying rays of the sun seemed to enhance the colour of her hair and the beauty of her face.

She sat down beside me and told me to stop daydreaming because she had some news for me. She had decided to have a party at the Manor, while her grandmother was still away. She sat down and put her arm through mine and said, "Henry I know that you find parties a bit of a bore, but we could invite some of your friends from the camp. Also Tim Eastham and Fiona will be home so we can ask them." So of course I had to be enthusiastic. So a date was fixed and invitations were sent out.

There had been great activity in the kitchen and Mary was running around like a mad thing organising it all. I kept well out of the way.

When at last the time came for our guests to arrive, Mary was so excited as this will be her first own party. I therefore had to pull my weight.

It all proved very successful, everyone enjoyed themselves and we had a job to get our friends to go home. This is always a good sign, and plenty to drink made everyone let their hair down.

To be polite we had to ask the C.O. and his wife, thinking that they would refuse. They accepted and his wife turned out to be a great fun and even the Old Man got a bit sloshed.

When everyone had gone home Mary and I were really worn out. We had a last drink and staggered up stairs to bed, and we were asleep as soon as our heads touched the pillows.

I woke up in the night and I had one of my trips into the future. I got out of bed without waking Mary, I stood by the window, hoping that it would pass, but this made things clearer. The moon made the view from my window so very clear, I could see the nearby fields had crops growing in them, and the Park was full of sheep. I heard the drone of a heavy aircraft overhead, making its way towards the airfield. I could hear sirens in the distance and then I saw several large flashes and I heard some loud explosions in the distance.

I thought of my friends that had been to our party that evening and I was fearful for their safety. Then it all vanished and I was back in 1939. I went back to bed feeling very shaken and trying to get rid of the vision I had just had. I do wish that these, whatever one can call them would stop, because they were most disturbing and at times frightening.

When I got up the next morning I managed to get the events of the night out of my mind. A telephone call from Major Davis, gave me plenty to think about. He telephoned right after breakfast and told me that I had to make a trip to Normandy at the weekend. Wing Commander Hughes will give me all the details of when and where to refuel if necessary. "You will be a civilian and you are to land and take off, using a field of your choice. If you are asked why you landed, pretend that your engine failed. Before you leave let me know the map reference of the field and I will let Prideaux know." He added that I had to remember that I was flying an expensive aircraft, fitted with a lot of extra gadgets and these will be explained to me in due course. He wished me the best of luck and hung up.

I told Mary about this and she looked very worried. Then she started to look angry. "Henry, mind you keep away from that French girl or I will be very cross." I laughed and taking her in my arms, I told her that she had nothing to worry about.

Wanting to know what was in store for me, I telephoned the camp and made an appointment to see the C.O. As luck would have it, he could see me that afternoon. So after an early lunch I set off to hear what fate had in store for me. Mary had decided to come with me, so that she could visit one of the young wives of a member of the camp staff. These two females have become quite good friends and they loved to have a natter. The friend was called Joan Ashley and her Old Man was called Eric. He was quite a nice chap and in charge of the small control room.

I dropped Mary off and went into see the C.O. He was very pleasant and the orders were very straightforward. I would set off at first light on Friday morning, subject to a favourable weather report. My call sign would be Amber One, which I though was a bit odd. He told me to head for Guernsey, but only land there if there were any problems. There would be someone on the small airfield if I needed any help. I would then cut across the Cherbourg Peninsular to Crasville and I am to land and take off from any of the fields that I thought were suitable and had mentioned in my report.

There would be a member of the Prideaux family in each of the fields to greet me (written in the Major's spidery handwriting, if you dally with Celeste I will tell Mary). We both laughed at this comment in the margin of the order. I should try to get back before first light and there will be a small airfield, near Gonnerville and as in Guernsey there will be one of our boys there all day, should I get into any trouble.

Wing Commander Hughes will give me a letter of credit from a London bank and some Francs. If I spend any, I must get receipts.

"Remember that you are Henri Prideaux, with nothing to do with the RAF or the Government. You must stick to this story at all costs and you are on your own. If you get into any trouble, you will have to talk your way out of it. Your plane will have civilian markings and it is fitted with a long range tank under the fuselage, so you should be quite alright for petrol. If you run short you can refuel in France or Guernsey. By the end of August I want you to be able to find your way to this part of France, with your eyes closed. I regret to say that time is running out, and I must have a link with Normandy for the future. Henry, you are my only iron in the fire, so don't let me down."

The C.O. looked at me and said that he would get everything laid on for Friday. He would organise a flight path over parts of France. This would be easy because he had a pal in Civilian aviation at Exeter who could fix this up.

I thanked the C.O. and I was on my way out, when he told me that he would soon have some Hurricanes for the raw pilots to play with. "I know from my friend Hicks that you can fly one pretty well. When they come I will let you have a go." He added, "Best of luck on Friday."

When I left the C.O. I went to have a chat with Corporal Fred Rice about the Lysander. I went into the hangar and the first thing I noticed was that the RAF markings had been replaced by civilian numbers. I saw Fred standing back and looking at the plane. The first thing he said, when I joined him was that it was a special plane with several modifications, which he didn't understand. There would be a chap coming from Westlands next week to explain it all.

He knew all about my trip and he took me into his office where he had a set of Civilian flying gear, which he wanted me to try on. As luck would have it everything fitted. So I told Fred that I would see him on Friday morning, bright and early.

Friday morning came and I was on my way to the airfield, when I began to worry a bit about my trip. To begin with I was not Henry Blake, but Henri Prideaux with a passport to back it up. I had told Mary that should anyone telephone and ask about Henri Prideaux, she must say that he had been at the Manor giving advice about antique furniture and how it should be restored.

I have no idea why I thought up this cock and bull story. It must be this second sense, which I seem to be able to switch on sometimes. Of course Mary thought that I was daft, and I am beginning to think likewise.

As I got into the plane I thought to myself, that there will be hell of a lot of water to cross, so Henry keep your fingers crossed and say the odd prayer.

I had decided to fly to the east of Exeter, across Lyme Bay, then parallel to Chesil beach and leave land at Portland Bill. This was perhaps not the shortest route, but it cut down the expanse of water to be crossed.

It was a lovely morning and as I headed East, the sun was just rising, as a huge golden circle, forever getting bigger, as it forced its way over the horizon, until one could see its full beauty.

It really was beautiful sight to see the early sun rays dancing on the small waves. I felt very privileged to witness this display. Of course one could see the same from the shore, but to see it from the air is very different.

I had thought that I should try to fly as low as possible, because that is what I would have to do in case of war. I flew low over the Dorset coast and I was able to see fishing boats making their way into Lyme Bay to reap their harvest of mackerel, which are in abundance at this time of the year.

Portland Bill was now far behind me. I had set my course, allowing for the wind compensation for the Cherbourg peninsular. I now felt very much alone in the world and to a degree at risk to the quirks of fate. Anyway I pulled myself together and it was not long before I saw the French coastline in the distance.

As I got close to the French coast and near to the airfield at Gonnersville I received a radio call, which I returned with my call sign, and I was given permission to carry on my flight.

At first it was difficult to find the field that I wanted to land in, but at last I saw Celeste's farm and in no time, I saw the field. Somehow it looked so much smaller from the air. There was a bit of a cross wind, but I managed to land and then taxi into the far corner, in between the two clumps of trees, which made the plane invisible, except from one angle.

I could see no signs of any member of the Prideaux family, but I got out of the plane and in the distance I could see the figure of a female coming and running across the field towards me.

Then things started to happen at once. I saw two men running to cut off the approaching female, who I could now see as Celeste. At the same time I felt something hard being pressed into my back, and a French voice said, "Don't move, you are to come with us." I then felt a pain in my bottom, which I realised was a needle from a syringe, and then I must have passed out.

I had no idea how long I was unconscious, but when at last I came back into this world. I had a headache but apart from that my mind was quite clear. There was a very bright light set into the ceiling of a windowless room. I got up from a very uncomfortable bunk and stretched my legs.

It was impossible to understand what had happened to me. Then I heard the door being unlocked and two very large chaps came in and led me along a dark passage into another room and told me to sit down at the only table in the room. Another man came in and sat opposite me.

He sat for some time, which to me seemed like hours, before he started to talk. He spoke in a very cultured German voice. He asked my name and what was I doing in France, and why did I land in the field and then try to hide my plane.

I remembered one of Jake's golden rules, if questioned in any language other than what your identity card states, pretend that you have no idea what is being said. If possible butt in and start to create a fuss. You may get a bash or two but it may pay off.

Taking his advice I asked, "What the hell is going on?" and saying over and over again that, "I am Henri Prideaux and I am here to see some of my distant relations. I own a plane because I am a famous restorer of antique furniture and I have to visit places all over Great Britain. If you want to verify this, telephone Wimble Manor in North Devon, where I have been working." I gave them the telephone number and told them to ask for Miss Howes.

One of the heavies left the room so perhaps they had taken my bait. By now I was being questioned in French and English. The final test for my knowing German, was a stream of the most revolting insults fired at me and I was watched to see if I had any reaction. Somehow I managed to ignore them.

The questioner and one of the heavies started to get a bit nasty, but I stuck to my guns. By now I tried to work out who these people were and where was I. I asked many questions, which were ignored, so I decided not to say another word. I have no idea how long this questioning took, but at last I was led back to my cell and much to my surprise I was given a large mug of coffee.

As I drank the coffee I tried to understand what was going on. For some unknown reason 'they' were trying to make me say that I was Henry Blake and not Henri Prideaux and that I worked for a British Government Department. They kept on about the particular field that I had landed in. Of course my answer to this was that a fault had developed in my engine. I was told in no uncertain terms that, no fault could be found, in fact everything was in perfect order. I replied that the fault must have cleared itself.

I wondered what had happened to Celeste and for the first time I began to feel scared. I got up and looked around the room for some sort of weapon and any means of escaping, but it was a hopeless situation.

I decided to lay on the bunk and if anyone came in I would pretend to be asleep until they were close enough for me to grab them. I was pretty good at unarmed combat and I would have a go.

I heard the door open, so I kept as still as I could with my eyes closed. Who ever it was told me to get up. I didn't move so he bent over and started to shake me. Then I got him. I leapt up and hit him, with a chop behind the neck and he was out for the count. I took off his tie and tied his hands behind his back and stuffed a handkerchief in his mouth.

I made him comfortable as I had no idea who he was, and I didn't want to do him any real harm.

I went out and locked the door and started to creep down the passageway until I came to a half-open door. I could hear voices so I looked through the narrow space by the hinges of the door. What I saw shook me ridged and I couldn't believe my eyes. Sitting around the table, drinking wine, was the chap that had fired the questions at me, the other tough guy, Monsieur Prideaux, Celeste and Major Davis.

In a flash it dawned on me that this had all been a test of some sort. The rotten buggers, I was to get my own back on this lot. I looked around the room and saw that the only window of the building had bars on it. My luck was in and there was a key in the door.

I closed the door with a bang, locked it and in French, German and

English, I wished them all a good day. I made sure that they could hear me laughing as I walked out of the building. I then had another shock, because my prison was part of the Prideaux farm, which was well away from the farmhouse.

I went into the kitchen and I had such a greeting from Madame Prideaux. She put her arms around me and I did likewise. She then asked where her husband and Celeste were, so I told her that they were a bit tied up for the moment. She got out a bottle of her best wine and we both had a glass or two. I then said that I thought that I would try and find Celeste and her father.

My first job was to let the poor chap free, that I had tied up, so I returned to the room that had been my cell. I apologised most profusely before I undid his hands in case he decided to have a go at me. I told him that in future never to bend over a person that looked as if he was asleep.

I told him what I had done to his pals and I thought that he would never stop laughing. We shook hands to show that there were no hard feelings and we both went along the passage to release my prisoners.

I unlocked the door and the men looked very sheepish. Celeste ran over and putting her arms around my neck, she gave me a smashing kiss. Celeste's father, Jacques, shook my hand and kissed me on both cheeks, which is a ghastly French habit.

The Major, for once, had lost his composure. He also shook my hand and told me that I had passed the tests with flying colours. He said that the Brig will probably kick his arse for being caught out by one of his own pupils.

Walking to the farmhouse, the Major told me that my plane was under guard but it would be wise not to fly back until tomorrow. The drug may still be in my system and anyway it was now too late in the day.

He looked at me and laughed saying that he had telephoned Mary to tell her that the plane had developed a fault and I would be back after lunch tomorrow and I would phone her this evening from the Prideaux farm. Eventually a car came to collect the Major and his men leaving me with the Prideaux family.

I telephone Mary and explained as much as I could in a very short time telling her that I would be a good boy, as Celeste was now engaged to her Fransour and I said, "In any case, I love you too much to be led astray by a French girl. I will see you tomorrow and I will ring you as soon as I land."

I was collared by Celeste with a bottle of wine and two glasses in her hands and taken to a seat in her garden. We sat and talked for ages. She made me laugh explaining the surprised look on the Major's face when I made him a prisoner. "Anyway Enrie they were all more than pleased with your efforts and because of this we will see more of you in the future."

Suddenly she put her arms around me and started to kiss me and I returned her very passionate embrace. With difficulty I broke away and told her that we must behave ourselves. I added that I was finding it very hard as she looked so lovely and so desirable but I had to be faithful to Mary.

Celeste got up and taking my hand, she said, "It is such a pity that you Englishmen are so faithful." We then went into the house and had a really smashing meal, with a great deal of wine.

Celeste's father and her brother, Pierre, kept on returning the conversation back to what had happened during the day, which they thought was a great joke.

The conversation became very serious and Jacques told me in confidence that it had been decided that if war was declared I would be their link with GB in more ways than one. "We feel that we can trust you, which is more than can be said of the several idiots the Major has brought over in the past few weeks. He has been keeping you up his sleeve for something else so only time will tell what will actually happen. Do not forget my friend that I have not spoken to you on this subject."

We all sat in the garden until it was almost dark. Sometimes we talked and sometimes we were quiet with our own thoughts. The Prideaux family were realists and they had this fear of a war with the Germans, and I think that these thoughts were never very far from their minds.

As I watched the bats flying in between the farm buildings, they reminded me of my farmyard at home and this, in turn, made me think of the Manor and, of course, Mary. I thought that here I was, in another world, sitting so close to a truly lovely French girl that I could feel the warmth of her body through my clothes and I had to stop myself from thinking unfaithful thoughts about her.

At last it was decided that we should all go to bed. Celeste led me up the stairs to the same room that I had had on my previous visit. It looked the same with the coarse linen sheets, neatly turned back on the very old-fashioned bed. I kissed Celeste goodnight and she departed to her own room. As I got into bed, I thought, so far so good. Temptation has not come my way. I lay down and instantly went to sleep.

The next morning I began to come round and I saw the early rays of sunshine creeping through the window. I then felt a hand shaking me and trying to get me back into this world. I looked up to see Celeste bending over me. She had a dressing gown on but, as she bent over me, the top of her gown opened to reveal her lovely young breasts. Of course we kissed but that was all that we did because we were both very strong in our convictions to behave ourselves.

She told me that I could borrow Pierre's razor and breakfast would be ready in half an hour, "So my boy get your skates on." She slid off the bed and, to make sure that I got up, she pulled the bedclothes back to reveal a naked young man very ready to make love. She looked down at me and her parting words were, "Oh, Enrie, what a waste." She then ran off back to her room.

After a good tuck-in for breakfast, Jacques drove me back to the field. Celeste was very quiet and I sensed that she didn't want me to leave.

When we got to the field, I went aboard and started the engine. I didn't have to let it run for a while but, to be on the safe side, I got out of the plane and had a few final words with my two friends. We said our goodbyes and I clambered into the cockpit. When Celeste kissed me goodbye, she pressed a small box in my hand to bring me luck.

I revved up my engine and, gathering speed, I took off with plenty of room to spare. I went into a steep bank and flew over Celeste and her father, tipping my wings in salute. I turned to the north, got clearance from nearby airfield and I started to cross the Channel. It was such a smashing plane to fly that one could imagine what it would be like to be a bird.

I opened the small box that Celeste had given to me and found a small silver cross on a chain with her name engraved on the back. I found a spot for it to hang and it would stay there as my good luck token.

I found the journey a bit tedious because, for quite a spell, I had the sun in my eyes. I then remembered the special glasses given to me to teach me how to fly at night, so I put these on and the scene turned into a moonlit night.

Before I got to Chivenor I flew over the Hall and I could see Mary rushing out of the front door; I tipped my wings and then made for the base.

When I landed I was greeted by a very indignant Fred Rice wanting to know what was wrong with this plane. When I told him that it was only an excuse he calmed down. He gave me an old-fashioned look and said that French girls were hot stuff. I gave him a friendly kick in the pants and told him to mind his own business.

The Control Tower had told me to report to the C.O., so I made my way to his office. He seemed a bit cheesed off because a plane from his station had actually broken down in a foreign country. I told him that it was only an air lock in the fuel supply and it was not the fault of his mechanics.

The Wing Commander looked at me and, with a smile, he said that he thought that the tale told to him by the Major was just a load of flannel. Anyway, he had given the game away by telephoning from France. "I know that you are not allowed to tell me what really happened in France," he said, "so let us leave it at that."

He picked up a letter and said that he had received a signal from London authorising me to fly at least once a week until further notice. He went on "Also Henry my boy, as from now you have been promoted to a Flight Lieutenant." He got up and congratulated me and shook my hand.

He then said, "One golden rule you must stick to, you must take the route given to you by the Controller, otherwise you will be in big trouble. The French are very edgy at the moment so watch your step."

As I got up to go I said, "By the way Sir, I am sorry that I am unable to tell you what sort of game I am playing at but I fear that you will know sooner rather than later." I saluted and left his office.

On my way out of the office block I met Biggs the Adjutant, who congratulated me on my promotion and he said that he had a buckshee set of rings I could have. He fetched them from his office and said that perhaps Mary would sew them on for me.

I drove back to the Manor as quickly as I could and, as I got towards the end of the long drive, Mary rushed out and greeted me as if I had been away for weeks and not just two days.

By now I was very hungry and, as I tucked into a huge meal, I told Mary what had happened. She then caught me on the hop by saying that she knew all about it because Celeste had telephoned her. "She told me that you had been a good boy but if ever I decide to leave you, dear Henry, I have to let her know. So I told her that there was no chance of that happening."

That evening would be the last dinner we would have on our own because Sally would be coming home tomorrow. I would be glad to see the dear old girl. She would always be part of the Manor and she added to its charm.

On the other hand, Mary and I had been able to live like a married couple and it had been a marvellous experience not given to many young people. We had known each other for so many years that we understood the odd change of moods and we seemed to be able to read each other's minds.

After dinner we sat outside in the garden and I thought that this would be as good a time as any to get a few things off my chest. I told her about my promotion and asked if she would sew on my new rings. I then told her that I had to fly to Normandy at least once a week and eventually on several night trips. Also that Jean Hicks would be calling to see us in a day or so.

Mary came and sat on my lap and said that she knew all about my future trips to France. Papa had told her what to expect in the future and, she went on, "As for Jean, I have invited her to stay next weekend." She laughed when she saw my expression and said, "Henry, my darling, don't worry, I will be looking after my interests when you meet these girls that have fallen in love with you. All we want is for Polly to turn up but they won't stand a chance."

In fun I put her across my knee and spanked her lovely little bottom. We then went to bed.

Sally returned with far more luggage than when she went away. She had taken the opportunity of buying new clothes in America and, much to Mary's delight, she had been included in this shopping spree. Sally had also not forgotten me. I was presented with some very posh-looking shirts and pullovers. They were a bit colourful for this part of the world but I would have to wear them otherwise Sally would be offended.

She talked for about three days, telling us about her holiday. She was more than pleased with our efforts on the Estate. It was difficult to get a word in edgeways but when I explained about my weekly flights to France she quite understood and, with a laugh, she said that she and Mary were quite capable of holding the fort.

My flights were now very different. They were RAF flights authorised by the French Government, so I had to wear my uniform and the plane was painted and camouflaged so that it would blend in with the countryside. In fact it was now all very official. I could, however, say when I wanted to go and the frequency of my trips was not limited in any way. If anything they were encouraged.

The airfield was a hive of activity. There was a smell of conflict in the air. The Establishment had grown considerably over the last few months and, most important of all, the Hurricanes arrived.

The C.O. kept his promise and he let me take one up. Oh! Boy! what a dream it was to fly. I seemed to be able to do whatever I wanted to do with it and I must admit that I showed off to the large audience on the ground.

What I didn't know was that the Group Commander had arrived without any warning. When I landed, the C.O. was deep in conversation with this Group Captain. When I got out of the plane he called me over and I expected quite a wigging because of my antics in the air.

I was introduced to the Group Captain and the first thing he said was "How often have you flown Hurricanes?" When I told him that this was my second flight, he told me that it was a terrible waste for me to have to fly a Lysander. I replied that I would like to fly Hurricanes but I had no choice in the matter so I would have to accept it. The Group Captain grunted and said, "Damn shame," and marched off with the C.O.

My flights to Normandy had become very frequent. I used four different fields which were well separated and I had been using the special night glasses to give the impression of flying in the dark. I had to give the map reference of the field that I was going to land in, well in advance to the controller who, in turn, would tell the people in France.

Somehow or other Celeste managed to turn up for a chat. To keep the peace, I kept this from Mary. As I drove to the airfield on a fine summer's evening, I was feeling very apprehensive. Tonight I had to make my first night landing. There would be very low-powered lights laid out to give me the line for the approach but I would have to take off without the lights. I also had to find my own way there. All I hoped was that the moon shone that night.

I got my final orders from the Control Tower and, having been wished good luck by my friends in the Mess, I was on my way for my first trip to France in the dark. Little did I know that it would be the beginning of so many trips in the future and not always to Normandy.

Once I was airborne my confidence returned and I enjoyed the flight. It was like flying into the unknown but when I saw the lights of the French coast I tried to imagine what it would be like, if there was a war on and all lights were put out. Without a moon it would be very difficult indeed and, with enemy aircraft around, plus anti-aircraft guns, life would be very unhealthy indeed.

For my first adventure in the dark I had chosen the first field I landed in and the one which I kept dreaming about. I could see no light as I flew into the area. I knew exactly where I was. Then, to my amazement, torches were lit and flames started to spring up in two parallel lines, marking my approach.

I landed and I was greeted by a French Airforce Officer who saluted and said, "Well done, Monsieur, but would you please take off and land again so that we complete the exercise." The lights were put out and I took off without any difficulty. I then circled and waited for the torches to be lit and I landed again.

When I landed the second time I got out of the plane and I soon had a pair of arms around my neck and Celeste gave me a very welcoming kiss. Her father and brother were also there and to see them again was indeed a great pleasure.

Jacques gave me four bottles of his lovely wine and, of course, a good swig from another bottle. How I would have like to have stayed with the Prideaux family but I had to leave because orders were orders and I knew that the rules had to be kept in the game that I was part of.

The whole pattern of my flights to France changed dramatically as the calendar changed to August. I could no longer make the flights when I wanted to. I was given short notice and, at times, the weather could be very dodgy. In fact bad weather conditions were picked on purpose.

It was very obvious that war would be declared in a matter of weeks, rather than months. Germany had become an armed camp and no one in their right mind would go there unless they had to. We were all pleased that Geraldine had got out when she did because it would be very difficult now.

Mary and I spent every weekend in South Devon. I wanted to be with my family as much as I could and I am glad to say that Sally understood my situation. Dad, being a wise old bird, bought as much live-stock as he could afford in the anticipation of a shortage in the future. My brother John would be in a reserved occupation. I knew that I would be in the first lot to be called up, so Mary and I made the most of the first few weeks of August.

We both enjoyed Jean's visit. Mary pulled my leg because Jean followed me around wherever I went on the Estate. She was good fun and we took her into the Mess at Chivenor. This upset some of the wives because their husbands got a hungry look in their eyes when they saw Jean.

Wing Commander Hughes invited Mary and I for dinner one evening while the Hicks were there. There were two generations there but we had a smashing evening and we were both sorry to leave such good company.

During dinner I had asked Jean if she thought of joining the WAAFs. She said that she might but she was unable to make up her mind which Department to try for. To pull her leg I suggested that the kitchen staff might suit her. She managed to find my leg under the table and gave it a hefty kick. She then got her own back by saying that if the Intelligence Department would have a dimwit like Henry Blake, she would stand a good chance. She went on "In fact Henry, you have made up my mind for me. Intelligence it will be and, who knows, I might even be posted to the same station as you." She turned to Mary and said that she would make sure that I behaved myself.

Towards the middle of August war clouds were gathering at a frightening speed. The Government began to prepare the country for war. People were advised how to blackout windows. There was talk about food, petrol and clothing being rationed. Bomb shelters were being built in some of the larger towns. Men above military age were asked to join a Civil Defence force called the A.R.P. They would be responsible for enforcing the black-out and helping people to find shelter in case of an air raid.

These precautions were taken in a casual but official way so as to give the impression that we were just playing it the safe way and not really preparing for war. The true facts had not really sunk in to a large percentage of the population. They were taking their summer holidays by the seaside and having a last fling.

It was a very different cup of tea in the Services. They had at last awakened from their deep slumber. A frightening new word had been added to the British language. (It means lightning war). The days of trench warfare were gone for ever. This new type of warfare is called Blitzkrieg and implemented by planes.

I could sense this different attitude at Chivenor. Security had been greatly improved. A strong force of the RAF regiment was drafted in to patrol the airfield at night. Gone were the carefree days of entering the base. A uniform was not a pass to enter, we all had to show our identity cards. Air raid shelters were being built. New planes were being delivered fully camouflaged and the training of the new pilots was stepped up.

I was very envious of the pilots being taught to use the Hurricane as a fighter. I watched some of them and I thought that they would have to go a long way before they came up against the experienced Luftwaffe pilots.

My plane had been fitted with a short ladder to enable passengers to get in and out of the rear cockpit quickly. The radio had been up-dated and, with a gunnery officer as a passenger, I was taught how to use the machine guns in the wheel cowlings.

This was great fun shooting at a boat pulling a target and then a plane towing an elongated cloth target. I was very surprised how quickly I got the hang of it and so was the instructor so, unfortunately, I only had a few lessons.

I was having a drink with the C.O. in the Mess and he told me that he had been told to find me an office and that I would be the Intelligence Officer for the station. This would only happen if the balloon went up. He said, "One of your jobs will be to see that the security of the base is O.K. Also you will have to give some lectures on survival to the pilots. You will have to take your turn as duty officer but you will be able to live out at the Manor. All of this will be temporary until you are needed. It does seem that this will be your base for some time."

This, of course, was good news for me but, knowing the Brig and the Major, I knew that this all sounded too good to be true. Mary and I were going down to Teignford at the weekend so I would try to see Jake and I may be able to pick his brains.

Jake had become very illusive. He was spending more and more time away from his cottage. I did manage to catch him and he was able to tell me more about my role in a war. It seemed that part of my job would be to take people behind the German lines and then bring people out. He said that it would be a very dangerous job. There might even be the need to impersonate German Officers as a cover for whatever I had to do. In time I would have to go to a special school to be taught how to kill quickly and silently.

He continued "Henry my boy, you still have a lot to learn, I have passed on many of my skills which will help you no end. One thing is certain, because of the perfect German you can speak and the way you can fly that plane of yours, you will be only used on important missions. Now please do not say a word to anyone about our conversation."

It took me quite some time to accept the news that Jake had given to me in his peaceful cottage, during the lovely afternoon on August the 23rd. When I got back to the farm, Dad gave me the news that Hitler and Stalin had signed an unholy alliance which set a seal on a future war and making Poland Hitler's next victim.

On the six o'clock news, we were told that Poland was being mobilised. The French were to call up their Reserves and we were doing likewise. In fact it was all very depressing. I telephoned Mary at the Hall and told her that we should return to the Manor after dinner because I had a lot to do in the next few days.

We had dinner with James and Pamela and all we could talk about was what would happen in the next few weeks or even days. We didn't linger after dinner and we were soon on our way back to what we now considered our home. We had both decided to get married next year as planned. Mary knew what sort of job I had and she wanted me to be free from any worries until I had got into the run of things. We were, for all intents and purposes, living as a married couple and our two families did not seem to mind.

During the last week in August I completed the blacking out of the Manor. I had persuaded Sally to install a petrol tank in one of the many barns, well away from the house and I got this filled up without the world knowing and paying cash for same. Not perhaps the correct thing to do but I had to try to keep the Manor as it always had been.

The airfield was in quite a panic. Every day fresh orders came from Group HQ and although I didn't have to, I helped out. I made my first taxi trip to France.

This was at night. I landed at Exeter and picked up a man in his middle years and delivered him to Normandy. This was a very military operation, there were Army bods to meet the plane and this chap was rushed away at top speed. On my way back I wondered who he was and what was so special about him.

I was not quite used to making this trip by night. No doubt it would be very different in the complete dark. I would have to fly very low over the water to avoid detection if I was to go anywhere near the German lines.

I suddenly felt very cold and depressed. I knew then that this would be my last flight across the Channel in peace time. I could also foresee a life full of danger and sadness. I would look back in envy at my first nineteen years on this earth and thank the Good Lord for giving me those good years.

Flying by night had its advantages, it gave one time to think. As long as the compass bearing was correct and a weather eye was kept on the instrument panel, there was nothing much else to do.

Suddenly, I had this most remarkable insight into the future. As usual it is disconnected, and at times I am looking down on myself. Tonight I am flying the plane, but another part of me is sitting by the Little Bridge, and I have two lovely females with me.

One is Mary, whose hand I am holding, and the other one is Polly in the uniform of a WAAF Squadron Leader. I could see my reflection in the water and this is what I find so strange. I am wearing an Army Uniform and I have the rank of Colonel, complete with a full row of ribbons below my RAF wings. My other arm is around Polly's waist.

The scene then moved to Wimple Manor. The Park had Army type huts on its perimeter and there were Service Personnel going about their business. I also saw three Lysanders, partly hidden under camouflaged netting.

I then saw Mary and Polly sitting by the bridge I had built as a replica of my favourite place in South Devon. There were two small boys playing with a red setter, and watching over them, I saw a female holding a small baby. Whoever she may be, I have no idea.

The vision began to fade, but before doing so, the horrors of war began to flash through my mind, which I tried to cut out, so I was glad to hear the RT come to life, telling me that an escort is in my area and I felt so glad to be back to the present time.

I still had quite a few miles to cover before I was home and dry, so this gave me the opportunity to try to understand my visits into the future. How could I transfer from the RAF to the Army and obtain such a high rank?

The prospect of The Manor being turned into an Army camp filled me with horror, and the Park could be changed for ever. All I hope is that what I have just seen will turn out to be fiction and not fact. Anyway, only time will tell.

I saw the coast of Dorset in the distance and I looked at my watch and saw that the time was one thirty on the first of September. When I landed I was told by the Duty Officer that "The bloody Germans had invaded Poland at 0100 hours." These poor people were being bombed and killed while we were talking in the early hours on an airfield in peaceful Devonshire.

I drove back to the Manor and I prayed for the poor Polish people. We would be at war in a day or so and suddenly I wanted to feel the comfort of Mary's arms around me. I wished that I did not have these brief glances into the future. Perhaps it was an early warning system given to me for some special purpose in the years to come.